Ghosts:
Recent Hauntings

OTHER BOOKS EDITED BY
PAULA GURAN

Embraces
Best New Paranormal Romance
Best New Romantic Fantasy
Zombies: The Recent Dead
The Year's Best Dark Fantasy & Horror: 2010
Vampires: The Recent Undead
The Year's Best Dark Fantasy & Horror: 2011
Halloween
New Cthulhu: The Recent Weird
Brave New Love
Witches: Wicked, Wild & Wonderful
Obsession: Tales of Irresistible Desire
The Year's Best Dark Fantasy & Horror: 2012
Extreme Zombies

Ghosts:
Recent Hauntings

Edited by Paula Guran

PRIME BOOKS

For my daughter Karis—
who has always believed in ghosts
and loves stories about them.

Contents

Introduction: Questionable Shapes
Paula Guran

> Angels, and ministers of grace, defend us!
> Be thou a spirit of health, or goblin damn'd.
> Bring with thee airs from heaven, or blasts from hell.
> Be thy intents wicked or charitable.
> Thou com'st in such a questionable shape,
> That I will speak to thee.
> —William Shakespeare, *Hamlet,* Act I, Scene 4

Have we ever *not* told ghost stories?

Ghosts remind us of our mortality even while, paradoxically, offering hope there is some form of immortality. If such entities exist, then surely they are evidence that although the death of our physical bodies is inevitable, our essential selves must continue to survive beyond death, that we may somehow be connected to something beyond the tribulations of our own world.

And, evidently, we do believe in ghosts. In 2009, CBS News pollsters discovered forty-eight percent of Americans claim to "believe in ghosts, or that the dead can return in certain places and situations . . . More than one in five Americans says they have seen a ghost themselves, or have felt themselves to be in the presence of one."

But whether we think there are spirits among us or not, ghosts have been the inspiration for fiction (and the other creative arts) for as long as we've been human and ghost tales are part of almost every culture.

Our concept of the ghost is based on the idea that one's soul or spirit—the essence of the individual—continues to survive after the physical body dies. Rituals to ease a spirit's passage to an afterlife and to ensure it would not return to negatively interfere with the living are the earliest indications of such a belief. *Homo sapiens* began burying their dead with grave goods at least one hundred thousand years ago, and surely there were stories of encounters with the departed even before.

Our most ancient records from Mesopotamia and Egypt make references to ghosts. Ghosts appear in the *Iliad* and the *Odyssey*. The Romans believed in several types of shades of the dead. Virgil, Ovid, Pliny, and others related tales of haunted houses, vengeful specters, and phantoms of the ill-fated dead.

According to the New Testament, Jesus had to convince his followers he was not a ghost when he walked on water and again after his resurrection. (Evidently a belief in spooks was easier to accept than miracles, even for disciples.)

Early Christian theologians tangled with the concept of apparitions; any form of worshipping the dead was to be avoided, so contact between the living and the deceased posed a theological problem. By the Middle Ages, the church taught ghosts might be either manifestations of God, saints, and angels or the Devil and demons—often disguised as a dead person—so ghostly tales tended to be accounted for one way or the other. Hallucination was another possibility. The Roman Catholic Church allowed for ghosts who returned to Earth from Purgatory in order to warn the living they must repent, but Protestants believed specters were angels or devils disguised as the familiar dead. Angels brought divine messages and devils might try to tempt still-living relatives into damnation.

The Renaissance awakened an interest in all things supernatural. Fictional ghosts began to appear not only in oral folktales and ballads, but in written poetry and plays. Ghosts appear in five of Shakespeare's known plays, and are mentioned or reported in seven more. In *Hamlet* and *Macbeth* they were figures of great dramatic impact.

In the eighteenth century, ghosts became a staple of Gothic fiction. According the Ghost Story Society:

> The classic English ghost story was born in the 1820s, and was popularized later that century by Charles Dickens, who promoted the idea of ghost stories at Christmas-time. For many people, the heyday of the ghost story was in the years between the turn of the last century and the Second World War: a time when book and magazine publishers provided a ready market for authors of supernatural fiction.

Perhaps there is no longer such a "ready market," but fictional ghost stories are still flourishing.

Intents Wicked or Charitable

The presence of dead spirits where the living dwell is considered unnatural and anything outside what is accepted as "normal" tends to be seen as frightening. As Confucius said, "Respect ghosts and gods, but keep away from them." Scary ghost tales abound, but so do those showing more fascination than fear. As chilling as many ghost stories may be, ghosts are not always seen as inherently evil or even scary. The souls of departed ancestors are worshipped in some societies. Communicating with the dead is considered desirable in some contexts in most cultures. Ghosts are sometimes considered benevolent or helpful; they occasionally even act as protectors of or guides for the living.

There's also considerable diversity in spectral intent. The unquiet dead can be seeking revenge or justice, they may want closure or need assistance with personal issues in order to find lasting peace. Phantoms sometimes have important information to convey to the living. They may simply be attached to people or places they did not want to leave behind. Some just endlessly repeat events in their lives or reenact their deaths. Other apparitions seem to be merely mischievous. One of the most ancient ghost story motifs is the reunification of those who are deeply in love—love never dies—as in the myth of Orpheus and Eurydice. Ghosts can be whimsical, humorous, and endearing.

Still, even benign ghosts disturb us: Casper the Friendly Ghost inadvertently scares almost everyone when he first meets them. Contact with the dead is always an uncanny experience.

Twenty-first Century Ghosts

In the twenty-first century we seem to be no less fascinated with ghosts than our ancestors. If this anthology of short stories first published from 2000-2012 is not enough to convince readers that the literary ghost is livelier than ever, specters have inspired notable novels in this century as well. *The Lovely Bones* by Alice Seybold (2002), is narrated by the angelic ghost of a murdered teenage girl. Peter Straub, author of the iconic *Ghost Story*, has published two twenty-first century novels—*lost boy lost girl* (2003) and *In the Night Room* (2007)—that are superbly told ghost tales. John Harwood's *The Ghost Writer* (2004) and *The Séance* (2009) both harken back to Victorian ghost stories. Hilary Mantel's brilliant *Beyond Black* (2005) portrays communicating with the dead as both funny and frightful. In *Joplin's Ghost* by Tananarive Due (2005), an up-and-coming female singer is haunted by the ghost of the famous ragtime composer. The characters and house in *The Little Stranger* by Sarah Waters (2009) are haunted by more than the supernatural. An aging rock star encounters a vengeful ghost in Joe Hill's *Heart-Shaped Box* (2007). Diane Setterfield's *The Thirteenth Tale* (2007) is filled with family secrets, lies, and ghosts. Michael Marshall Smith's short novel, *The Servants* (2007), is a unique, completely captivating contemporary ghost story. *The Girl Who*

Stopped Swimming by Joshilyn Jackson (2008), the ghost of a fourteen-year-old leads the protagonist to her body; psychic journalist Paul Seaton confronts a demonic specter in *The House of Lost Souls* (2009); and a haunted yacht is featured in *Dark Echo* (2010), both by F.G. Cottam. Michael Koryta leads readers to the small-town ghosts of Baden, Indiana in *So Cold the River* (2010). A ghost haunts an English school in *The White Devil* (2011) by Justin Evans. *The Haunting of Maddy Clare* by Simone St. James (2012) combines ghost hunting and romance. Gin Phillips's *Come In and Cover Me* (2012) features a heroine with a connection to her long-dead brother. Although Caitlín Kiernan's *The Drowning Girl: A Memoir* (2012) is not a novel of ghosts per se, it is a story about the fundamental nature of hauntings, how they begin and perpetuate.

Ghosts and ghost hunters have also made frequent appearances in numerous paranormal and urban fantasy novels. Many recent books for younger readers—most notably *Coraline* (2002) and *The Graveyard Book* (2008) by Neil Gaiman—feature the ghostly.

Twenty-first century (so far) anthologies with ghostly or haunted themes include *The Dark: New Ghost Stories,* edited by Ellen Datlow (2003); *Haunted Legends*, edited by Ellen Datlow and Nick Mamatas (2010); *Ghosts by Gaslight: Stories of Steampunk and Supernatural Suspense* (2011), edited by Jack Dann and Nick Givers; *House of Fear: An Anthology of Haunted House Stories*, edited by Jonathan Oliver (2011); and *Haunts: Reliquaries of the Dead*, edited by Stephen Jones (2011).

Books, of course, are (unfortunately) not as accurate a measure of popular culture as film and television. Films since 2000 that were haunted by ghosts include *The Others* (2001), *Thir13en Ghosts* (2001), *Dragonfly* (2002), *The Ring* (2002), *Ghost Ship* (2002), *Pirates of the Caribbean: The Curse of the Black Pearl* (2003) and *Pirates of the Caribbean: At World's End* (2007), *Gothika* (2003), *The Corpse Bride* (2005), *Dark Water* (2005), game-based *Silent Hill* (2006), *Ghost Town* (2008), the comic-based *Ghost Rider* (2007) and its 2012 sequel *Ghost Rider: Spirit of Vengeance*, *Shutter* (2008), *Paranormal Activity* (2007) and its 2020 and 2011 prequels, *Coraline* (2009), *The Haunting in Connecticut* (2009), *Ghosts of Girlfriends Past* (2009), and *The Woman in Black* (2012). Ghosts also appear in all eight Harry Potter films.

As for television, the popular series *Ghost Whisperer* (2005-2010) featured a woman with the ability to communicate with still-earthbound spirits of the recently deceased. *Medium* (2005-2011) focused on a woman who could talk to dead people and, with their guidance, assisted the police in solving crimes. A ghost lives with a werewolf and a vampire on the BBC's comedy-drama *Being Human* (2008-). The short-lived series *Haunted* (2002) and

Dead Gorgeous (2010) were ghost-themed. More recently, the specter-filled *American Horror Story* (2011-) found millions of fans. Current medical drama *A Gifted Man* (2011-) centers on a surgeon who communicates with his dead ex-wife. The storyline for the recently premiered (7 June 2012) *Saving Hope* evidently pivots on a ghost doctor.

Although not specifically about phantoms, spooks played key roles in the series *Angel* (1999-2004), *Six Feet Under* (2001-2005), *Carnivàle* (2003-2005), and *Supernatural* (2005-), as well as the miniseries *The Dresden Files* (2007). Anthology series *Masters of Horror* (2005-2007) and the 2002 revival of *The Twilight Zone* both included episodes with ghosts.

Even more abundant on the twenty-first century small screen are "reality-based" television series about bogies. These shows are far too numerous to list, but the most notable are: *Most Haunted* (2002-2010), a British "documentary" series; SyFy's *Ghost Hunters* (2004-) and its spin-offs, *Ghost Hunters International* (2008-) and *Ghost Hunters Academy* (2008-); Discovery Channel's docudrama series *A Haunting* (2005-2007), the A&E Network's *Paranormal State* (2007-), the Travel Channel's *Ghost Adventures* (2008-), and *Ghost Lab* (2009-), another Discovery Channel series.

I Will Speak to Thee

In literary terms, a "ghost story" need not always have a specter in it. Supernatural elements are central to plot, theme, and character development; a certain atmosphere is evoked—but true phantoms need not be present.

For this anthology of stories published in the twenty-first century, however, I sought tales with ghosts in them—or at least in which the reader or the characters (or both) assume there is a ghost or the possibility of such, even if such assumptions are eventually shown not to be entirely correct. Admittedly, some stories are open to interpretation, but to *me* they said "ghost."

As for a definition of "ghost," in the context of this volume, it is a person or animal that was once alive but is no longer, yet still has some form of contact with the living. Traditionally, ghosts manifest themselves in some way to the living: they can be seen, or heard, or their presence can be felt. Such apparitions are still, of course, common in many stories. But this is the twenty-first century, and these are twenty-first century ghost stories. We are constantly communicating with other live folks without ever seeing, hearing, or feeling their presence. Why confine the dead?

Many great ghost stories are effective because one does not realize, at first, they are about phantoms at all. The atmosphere may evoke apprehension or the feeling of dread as we slowly realize it is ghostly. Conversely one may think they are reading non-supernatural "slice of life" fiction, and only gradually does the reader realize something ghostly is afoot or, perhaps at the end, discovers the spectral is involved or that the dead have been in discourse with the living. Ghosts sometimes don't realize they are ghosts; the living may have no idea they are communicating with the dead.

Unfortunately, devising a theme and slapping a title on a compilation like this takes away much of the element of revelation in such stories. Since one is expecting specters, our suspicions are already aroused and we are far less likely to be surprised when the spooks show up. Lessening the impact of any story is a disservice to both author and reader. Nevertheless, the fine writing and immensity of imagination at work in these tales from the last twelve years still manage to chill, astonish, and entertain.

It is a privilege to introduce (or re-introduce) you to them.

> GHOST:
> But that I am forbid
> To tell the secrets of my prison-house,
> I could a tale unfold whose lightest word
> Would harrow up thy soul, freeze thy young blood,
> Make thy two eyes, like stars, start from their spheres,
> Thy knotted and combined locks to part
> And each particular hair to stand on end,
> Like quills upon the fretful porpentine:
> But this eternal blazon must not be
> To ears of flesh and blood. List, list, O, list!
> —William Shakespeare, *Hamlet,* Act I, Scene 5

List!
Paula Guran
June 2012

New York City is full of ghosts. Mags believes a hole got blown in the city on 9/11 and the ghosts came back, looking for their homes . . .

There's a Hole in the City
Richard Bowes

Wednesday 9/12

On the evening of the day after the towers fell, I was waiting by the barricades on Houston Street and LaGuardia Place for my friend Mags to come up from Soho and have dinner with me. On the skyline, not two miles to the south, the pillars of smoke wavered slightly. But the creepily beautiful weather of September 11 still held, and the wind blew in from the northeast. In Greenwich Village the air was crisp and clean, with just a touch of fall about it.

I'd spent the last day and a half looking at pictures of burning towers. One of the frustrations of that time was that there was so little most of us could do about anything or for anyone.

Downtown streets were empty of all traffic except emergency vehicles. The West and East Villages from Fourteenth Street to Houston were their own separate zone. Pedestrians needed identification proving they lived or worked there in order to enter.

The barricades consisted of blue wooden police horses and a couple of unmarked vans thrown across LaGuardia Place. Behind them were a couple of cops, a few auxiliary police and one or two guys in civilian clothes with ID's of some kind pinned to their shirts. All of them looked tired, subdued by events.

At the barricades was a small crowd: ones like me waiting for friends from neighborhoods to the south; ones without proper identification waiting for confirmation so that they could continue on into Soho; people who just wanted to be outside near other people in those days of sunshine and shock. Once in a while, each of us would look up at the columns of smoke that hung in the downtown sky then look away again.

A family approached a middle-aged cop behind the barricade. The group consisted of a man, a woman, a little girl being led by the hand, a child being carried. All were blondish and wore shorts and casual tops. The parents seemed pleasant but serious people in their early thirties, professionals. They could have been tourists. But that day the city was empty of tourists.

The man said something, and I heard the cop say loudly, "You want to go where?"

"Down there," the man gestured at the columns. He indicated the children. "We want them to see." It sounded as if he couldn't imagine this appeal not working.

Everyone stared at the family. "No ID, no passage," said the cop and turned his back on them. The pleasant expressions on the parents' faces faded. They looked indignant, like a maitre d' had lost their reservations. She led one kid, he carried the other as they turned west, probably headed for another checkpoint.

"They wanted those little kids to see Ground Zero!" a woman who knew the cop said. "Are they out of their minds?"

"Looters," he replied. "That's my guess." He picked up his walkie-talkie to call the checkpoints ahead of them.

Mags appeared just then, looking a bit frayed. When you've known someone for as long as I've known her, the tendency is not to see the changes, to think you both look about the same as when you were kids.

But kids don't have gray hair, and their bodies aren't thick the way bodies get in their late fifties. Their kisses aren't perfunctory. Their conversation doesn't include curt little nods that indicate something is understood.

We walked in the middle of the streets because we could. "Couldn't sleep much last night," I said.

"Because of the quiet," she said. "No planes. I kept listening for them. I haven't been sleeping anyway. I was supposed to be in housing court today. But the courts are shut until further notice."

I said, "Notice how with only the ones who live here allowed in, the South Village is all Italians and hippies?"

"Like 1965 all over again."

She and I had been in contact more in the past few months than we had in a while. Memories of love and indifference that we shared had made close friendship an on-and-off thing for the last thirty-something years.

Earlier in 2001, at the end of an affair, I'd surrendered a rent-stabilized apartment for a cash settlement and bought a tiny co-op in the South Village. Mags lived as she had for years in a run-down building on the fringes of Soho.

So we saw each other again. I write, obviously, but she never read anything I publish, which bothered me. On the other hand, she worked off and on for various activist leftist foundations, and I was mostly uninterested in that.

Mags was in the midst of classic New York work and housing trouble. Currently she was on unemployment and her landlord wanted to get her out of her apartment so he could co-op her building. The money offer he'd made wasn't bad, but she wanted things to stay as they were. It struck me that what was youthful about her was that she had never settled into her life, still stood on the edge.

Lots of the Village restaurants weren't opened. The owners couldn't or wouldn't come into the city. Angelina's on Thompson Street was, though, because Angelina lives just a couple of doors down from her place. She was busy serving tables herself since the waiters couldn't get in from where they lived.

Later, I had reason to try and remember. The place was full but very quiet. People murmured to each other as Mags and I did. Nobody I knew was there. In the background Resphigi's *Ancient Airs and Dances* played.

"Like the Blitz," someone said.

"Never the same again," said a person at another table.

"There isn't even anyplace to volunteer to help," a third person said.

I don't drink anymore. But Mags, as I remember, had a carafe of wine. Phone service had been spotty, but we had managed to exchange bits of what we had seen.

"Mrs. Pirelli," I said. "The Italian lady upstairs from me. I told you she had a heart attack watching the smoke and flames on television. Her son worked in the World Trade Center and she was sure he had burned to death.

"Getting an ambulance wasn't possible yesterday morning. But the guys at that little fire barn around the corner were there. Waiting to be called, I guess. They took her to St. Vincent's in the chief's car. Right about then, her son came up the street, his pinstripe suit with a hole burned in the shoulder, soot on his face, wild-eyed. But alive. Today they say she's doing fine."

I waited, spearing clams, twirling linguine. Mags had a deeper and darker story to tell; a dip into the subconscious. Before I'd known her and afterward, Mags had a few rough brushes with mental disturbance. Back in college, where we first met, I envied her that, wished I had something as dramatic to talk about.

"I've been thinking about what happened last night." She'd already told me some of this. "The downstairs bell rang, which scared me. But with phone service being bad, it could have been a friend, someone who needed to talk. I looked out the window. The street was empty, dead like I'd never seen it.

"Nothing but papers blowing down the street. You know how every time you see a scrap of paper now you think it's from the Trade Center? For a minute I thought I saw something move, but when I looked again there was nothing.

"I didn't ring the buzzer, but it seemed someone upstairs did because I heard this noise, a rustling in the hall.

"When I went to the door and lifted the spy hole, this figure stood there on the landing. Looking around like she was lost. She wore a dress, long and torn. And a blouse, what I realized was a shirtwaist. Turn-of-the-century clothes. When she turned toward my door, I saw her face. It was bloody, smashed. Like she had taken a big jump or fall. I gasped, and then she was gone."

"And you woke up?"

"No, I tried to call you. But the phones were all fucked up. She had fallen, but not from a hundred stories. Anyway, she wasn't from here and now."

Mags had emptied the carafe. I remember that she'd just ordered a salad and didn't eat that. But Angelina brought a fresh carafe. I told Mags about the family at the barricades.

"There's a hole in the city," said Mags.

That night, after we had parted, I lay in bed watching but not seeing some old movie on TV, avoiding any channel with any kind of news, when the buzzer sounded. I jumped up and went to the view screen. On the empty street downstairs a man, wild-eyed, disheveled, glared directly into the camera.

Phone service was not reliable. Cops were not in evidence in the neighborhood right then. I froze and didn't buzz him in. But, as in Mags's building, someone else did. I bolted my door, watched at the spy hole, listened to the footsteps, slow, uncertain. When he came into sight on the second floor landing he looked around and said in a hoarse voice, "Hello? Sorry, but I can't find my mom's front-door key."

Only then did I unlock the door, open it, and ask her exhausted son how Mrs. Pirelli was doing.

"Fine," he said. "Getting great treatment. St. Vincent was geared up for thousands of casualties. Instead." He shrugged. "Anyway, she thanks all of you. Me too."

In fact, I hadn't done much. We said good night, and he shuffled on upstairs to where he was crashing in his mother's place.

Thursday 9/13

By September of 2001 I had worked an information desk in the university library for almost thirty years. I live right around the corner from Washington Square, and just before 10 a.m. on Thursday, I set out for work. The Moslem-run souvlaki stand across the street was still closed, its owner and workers gone since Tuesday morning. All the little falafel shops in the South Village were shut and dark.

On my way to work I saw a three-legged rat running not too quickly down the middle of MacDougal Street. I decided not to think about portents and symbolism.

The big TVs set up in the library atrium still showed the towers falling again and again. But now they also showed workers digging in the flaming wreckage at Ground Zero.

Like the day before, I was the only one in my department who'd made it in. The librarians lived too far away. Even Marco, the student assistant, wasn't around.

Marco lived in a dorm downtown right near the World Trade Center. They'd been evacuated with nothing more than a few books and the clothes they were wearing. Tuesday, he'd been very upset. I'd given him Kleenex, made him take deep breaths, got him to call his mother back in California. I'd even walked him over to the gym, where the university was putting up the displaced students.

Thursday morning, all of the computer stations around the information desk were occupied. Students sat furiously typing e-mail and devouring incoming messages, but the intensity had slackened since 9/11. The girls no longer sniffed and dabbed at tears as they read. The boys didn't jump up and come back from the restrooms red-eyed and saying they had allergies.

I said good morning and sat down. The kids hadn't spoken much to me in the last few days, had no questions to ask. But all of them from time to time would turn and look to make sure I was still there. If I got up to leave the desk, they'd ask when I was coming back.

Some of the back windows had a downtown view. The pillar of smoke wavered. The wind was changing.

The phone rang. Reception had improved. Most calls went through. When I answered, a voice, tight and tense, blurted out, "Jennie Levine was who I saw. She was nineteen years old in 1911 when the Triangle Shirtwaist Factory burned. She lived in my building with her family ninety years ago. Her spirit found its way home. But the inside of my building has changed so much that she didn't recognize it."

"Hi, Mags," I said. "You want to come up here and have lunch?"

A couple of hours later, we were in a small dining hall normally used by faculty on the west side of the Square. The university, with food on hand and not enough people to eat it, had thrown open its cafeterias and dining halls to anybody with a university identification. We could even bring a friend if we cared to.

Now that I looked, Mags had tension lines around her eyes and hair that could have used some tending. But we were all of us a little ragged in those days of sun and horror. People kept glancing downtown, even if they were inside and not near a window.

The Indian lady who ran the facility greeted us, thanked us for coming. I had a really nice gumbo, fresh avocado salad, a soothing pudding. The place was half-empty, and conversations again were muted. I told Mags about Mrs. Pirelli's son the night before.

She looked up from her plate, unsmiling, said, "I did not imagine Jennie Levine," and closed that subject.

Afterward, she and I stood on Washington Place before the university building that had once housed the sweatshop called the Triangle Shirtwaist Factory. At the end of the block, a long convoy of olive green army trucks rolled silently down Broadway.

Mags said, "On the afternoon of March 25, 1911, one hundred and forty-six young women burned to death on this site. Fire broke out in a pile of rags. The door to the roof was locked. The fire ladders couldn't reach the eighth floor. The girls burned."

Her voice tightened as she said, "They jumped and were smashed on the sidewalk. Many of them, most of them, lived right around here. In the renovated tenements we live in now. It's like those planes blew a hole in the city and Jennie Levine returned through it."

"Easy, honey. The university has grief counseling available. I think I'm going. You want me to see if I can get you in?" It sounded idiotic even as I said it. We had walked back to the library.

"There are others," she said. "Kids all blackened and bloated and wearing old-fashioned clothes. I woke up early this morning and couldn't go back to sleep. I got up and walked around here and over in the East Village."

"Jesus!" I said.

"Geoffrey has come back too. I know it."

"Mags! Don't!" This was something we hadn't talked about in a long time. Once we were three, and Geoffrey was the third. He was younger than either of us by a couple of years at a time of life when that still seemed a major difference.

We called him Lord Geoff because he said we were all a bit better than the world around us. We joked that he was our child. A little family cemented by desire and drugs.

The three of us were all so young, just out of school and in the city. Then jealousy and the hard realities of addiction began to tear us apart. Each had to find his or her own survival. Mags and I made it. As it turned out, Geoff wasn't built for the long haul. He was twenty-one. We were all just kids, ignorant and reckless.

As I made excuses in my mind, Mags gripped my arm. "He'll want to find us," she said. Chilled, I watched her walk away and wondered how long she had been coming apart and why I hadn't noticed.

Back at work, Marco waited for me. He was part Filipino, a bit of a little wiseass who dressed in downtown black. But that was the week before. Today, he was a woebegone refugee in oversized flip-flops, wearing a magenta sweatshirt and gym shorts, both of which had been made for someone bigger and more buff.

"How's it going?"

"It sucks! My stuff is all downtown where I don't know if I can ever get it. They have these crates in the gym, toothbrushes, bras, Bic razors, but never what you need, everything from boxer shorts on out, and nothing is ever the right size. I gave my clothes in to be cleaned, and they didn't bring them back. Now I look like a clown.

"They have us all sleeping on cots on the basketball courts. I lay there all last night staring up at the ceiling, with a hundred other guys. Some of them snore. One was yelling in his sleep. And I don't want to take a shower with a bunch of guys staring at me."

He told me all this while not looking my way, but I understood what he was asking. I expected this was going to be a pain. But, given that I couldn't seem to do much for Mags, I thought maybe it would be a distraction to do what I could for someone else.

"You want to take a shower at my place, crash on my couch?"

"Could I, please?"

So I took a break, brought him around the corner to my apartment, put sheets on the daybed. He was in the shower when I went back to work.

That evening when I got home, he woke up. When I went out to take a walk, he tagged along. We stood at the police barricades at Houston Street and Sixth Avenue and watched the traffic coming up from the World Trade Center site. An ambulance with one side smashed and a squad car with its roof crushed were hauled up Sixth Avenue on the back of a huge flatbed truck. NYPD buses were full of guys returning from Ground Zero, hollow-eyed, filthy.

Crowds of Greenwich Villagers gathered on the sidewalks clapped and cheered, yelled, "We love our firemen! We love our cops!"

The firehouse on Sixth Avenue had taken a lot of casualties when the towers fell. The place was locked and empty. We looked at the flowers and the wreaths on the doors, the signs with faces of the firefighters who hadn't returned, and the messages, "To the brave men of these companies who gave their lives defending us."

The plume of smoke downtown rolled in the twilight, buffeted about by shifting winds. The breeze brought with it for the first time the acrid smoke that would be with us for weeks afterward.

Officials said it was the stench of burning concrete. I believed, as did everyone else, that part of what we breathed was the ashes of the ones who had burned to death that Tuesday.

It started to drizzle. Marco stuck close to me as we walked back. Hip twenty-year-olds do not normally hang out with guys almost three times their age. This kid was very scared.

Bleecker Street looked semiabandoned, with lots of the stores and restaurants still closed. The ones that were open were mostly empty at nine in the evening.

"If I buy you a six-pack, you promise to drink all of it?" He indicated he would.

At home, Marco asked to use the phone. He called people he knew on campus, looking for a spare dorm room, and spoke in whispers to a girl named Eloise. In between calls, he worked the computer.

I played a little Lady Day, some Ray Charles, a bit of Haydn, stared at the TV screen. The president had pulled out of his funk and was coming to New York the next day.

In the next room, the phone rang. "No. My name's Marco," I heard him say. "He's letting me stay here." I knew who it was before he came in and whispered, "She asked if I was Lord Geoff."

"Hi, Mags," I said. She was calling from somewhere with walkie-talkies and sirens in the background.

"Those kids I saw in Astor Place?" she said, her voice clear and crazed. "The ones all burned and drowned? They were on the *General Slocum* when it caught fire."

"The kids you saw in Astor Place all burned and drowned?" I asked. Then I remembered our conversation earlier.

"On June 15, 1904. The biggest disaster in New York City history. Until now. The East Village was once called Little Germany. Tens of thousands of Germans with their own meeting halls, churches, beer gardens.

"They had a Sunday excursion, mainly for the kids, on a steamship, the *General Slocum,* a floating firetrap. When it burst into flames, there were no lifeboats. The crew and the captain panicked. By the time they got to a dock, over a thousand were dead. Burned, drowned. When a hole got blown in the city, they came back looking for their homes."

The connection started to dissolve into static.

"Where are you, Mags?"

"Ground Zero. It smells like burning sulfur. Have you seen Geoffrey yet?" she shouted into her phone.

"Geoffrey is dead, Mags. It's all the horror and tension that's doing this to you. There's no hole . . . "

"Cops and firemen and brokers all smashed and charred are walking around down here." At that point sirens screamed in the background. Men were yelling. The connection faded.

"Mags, give me your number. Call me back," I yelled. Then there was nothing but static, followed by a weak dial tone. I hung up and waited for the phone to ring again.

After a while, I realized Marco was standing looking at me, slugging down beer. "She saw those kids? I saw them too. Tuesday night I was too jumpy to even lie down on the fucking cot. I snuck out with my friend Terry. We walked around. The kids were there. In old, historical clothes. Covered with mud and seaweed and their faces all black and gone. It's why I couldn't sleep last night."

"You talk to the counselors?" I asked.

He drained the bottle. "Yeah, but they don't want to hear what I wanted to talk about."

"But with me . . . "

"You're crazy. You understand."

The silence outside was broken by a jet engine. We both flinched. No planes had flown over Manhattan since the ones that had smashed the towers on Tuesday morning.

Then I realized what it was. "The Air Force," I said. "Making sure it's safe for Mr. Bush's visit."

"Who's Mags? Who's Lord Geoff?"

So I told him a bit of what had gone on in that strange lost country, the 1960's, the naïveté that led to meth and junk. I described the wonder of that unknown land, the three-way union. "Our problem, I guess, was that instead of a real ménage, each member was obsessed with only one of the others."

"Okay," he said. "You're alive. Mags is alive. What happened to Geoff?

"When things were breaking up, Geoff got caught in a drug sweep and was being hauled downtown in the back of a police van. He cut his wrists and bled to death in the dark before anyone noticed."

This did for me what speaking about the dead kids had maybe done for him. Each of us got to talk about what bothered him without having to think much about what the other said.

• • •

Friday 9/14

Friday morning two queens walked by with their little dogs as Marco and I came out the door of my building. One said, "There isn't a fresh croissant in the entire Village. It's like the Siege of Paris. We'll all be reduced to eating rats."

I murmured, "He's getting a little ahead of the story. Maybe first he should think about having an English muffin."

"Or eating his yappy dog," said Marco.

At that moment, the authorities opened the East and West Villages, between Fourteenth and Houston Streets, to outside traffic. All the people whose cars had been stranded since Tuesday began to come into the neighborhood and drive them away. Delivery trucks started to appear on the narrow streets.

In the library, the huge TV screens showed the activity at Ground Zero, the preparations for the president's visit. An elevator door opened and revealed a couple of refugee kids in their surplus gym clothes clasped in a passion clinch.

The computers around my information desk were still fully occupied, but the tension level had fallen. There was even a question or two about books and databases. I tried repeatedly to call Mags. All I got was the chilling message on her answering machine.

In a staccato voice, it said, "This is Mags McConnell. There's a hole in the city, and I've turned this into a center for information about the victims Jennie Levine and Geoffrey Holbrun. Anyone with information concerning the whereabouts of these two young people, please speak after the beep."

I left a message asking her to call. Then I called every half hour or so, hoping she'd pick up. I phoned mutual friends. Some were absent or unavailable. A couple were nursing grief of their own. No one had seen her recently.

That evening in the growing dark, lights flickered in Washington Square. Candles were given out; candles were lighted with matches and Bics and wick to wick. Various priests, ministers, rabbis, and shamans led flower-bearing, candlelit congregations down the streets and into the park, where they joined the gathering vigil crowd.

Marco had come by with his friend Terry, a kind of elfin kid who'd also had to stay at the gym. We went to this 9/11 vigil together. People addressed the crowd, gave impromptu elegies. There were prayers and a few songs. Then by instinct or some plan I hadn't heard about, everyone started to move out of the park and flow in groups through the streets.

We paused at streetlamps that bore signs with pictures of pajama-clad families in suburban rec rooms on Christmas mornings. One face would be circled in red, and there would be a message like, "This is James Bolton, husband of Susan, father of Jimmy, Anna, and Sue, last seen leaving his home in Far Rockaway at 7:30 a.m. on 9/11." This was followed by the name of the company, the floor of the Trade Center tower where he worked, phone and fax numbers, the e-mail address, and the words, "If you have any information about where he is, please contact us."

At each sign someone would leave a lighted candle on a tin plate. Someone else would leave flowers.

The door of the little neighborhood Fire Rescue station was open; the truck and command car were gone. The place was manned by retired firefighters with faces like old Irish and Italian character actors. A big picture of a fireman who had died was hung up beside the door. He was young, maybe thirty. He and his wife, or maybe his girlfriend, smiled in front of a ski lodge. The picture was framed with children's drawings of firemen and fire trucks and fires, with condolences and novena cards.

As we walked and the night progressed, the crowd got stretched out. We'd see clumps of candles ahead of us on the streets. It was on Great Jones Street and the Bowery that suddenly there was just the three of us and no traffic to speak of. When I turned to say maybe we should go home, I saw for a moment a tall guy staggering down the street with his face purple and his eyes bulging out.

Then he was gone. Either Marco or Terry whispered, "Shit, he killed himself." And none of us said anything more.

At some point in the evening, I had said Terry could spend the night in my apartment. He couldn't take his eyes off Marco, though Marco seemed not to notice. On our way home, way east on Bleecker Street, outside a bar that had been old even when I'd hung out there as a kid, I saw the poster.

It was like a dozen others I'd seen that night. Except it was in old-time black and white and showed three kids with lots of hair and bad attitude: Mags and Geoffrey and me.

Geoff's face was circled and under it was written, "This is Geoffrey Holbrun, if you have seen him since Tuesday 9/11 please contact." And Mags had left her name and numbers.

Even in the photo, I looked toward Geoffrey, who looked toward Mags, who looked toward me. I stared for just a moment before going on, but I knew that Marco had noticed.

Saturday 9/15

My tiny apartment was a crowded mess Saturday morning. Every towel I owned was wet, every glass and mug was dirty. It smelled like a zoo. There were pizza crusts in the sink and a bag of beer cans at the front door. The night before, none of us had talked about the ghosts. Marco and Terry had seriously discussed whether they would be drafted or would enlist. The idea of them in the army did not make me feel any safer.

Saturday is a work day for me. Getting ready, I reminded myself that this would soon be over. The university had found all the refugee kids dorm rooms on campus.

Then the bell rang and a young lady with a nose ring and bright red ringlets of hair appeared. Eloise was another refugee, though a much better-organized one. She had brought bagels and my guests' laundry. Marco seemed delighted to see her.

That morning all the restaurants and bars, the tattoo shops and massage parlors, were opening up. Even the Arab falafel shop owners had risked insults and death threats to ride the subways in from Queens and open their doors for business.

At the library, the huge screens in the lobby were being taken down. A couple of students were borrowing books. One or two even had in-depth reference questions for me. When I finally worked up the courage to call Mags, all I got was the same message as before.

Marco appeared dressed in his own clothes and clearly feeling better. He hugged me. "You were great to take me in."

"It helped me even more," I told him.

He paused then asked, "That was you on that poster last night, wasn't it? You and Mags and Geoffrey?" The kid was a bit uncanny.

When I nodded, he said. "Thanks for talking about that."

I was in a hurry when I went off duty Saturday evening. A friend had called and invited me to an impromptu "Survivors' Party." In the days of the French Revolution, The Terror, that's what they called the soirees at which people danced and drank all night then went out at dawn to see which of their names were on the list of those to be guillotined.

On Sixth Avenue a bakery that had very special cupcakes with devastating frosting was open again. The avenue was clogged with honking, creeping traffic. A huge chunk of Lower Manhattan had been declared open that afternoon, and people were able to get the cars that had been stranded down there.

The bakery was across the street from a Catholic church. And that afternoon in that place, a wedding was being held. As I came out with my cupcakes, the bride and groom, not real young, not very glamorous, but obviously happy, came out the door and posed on the steps for pictures.

Traffic was at a standstill. People beeped "Here Comes the Bride," leaned out their windows, applauded and cheered, all of us relieved to find this ordinary, normal thing taking place.

Then I saw her on the other side of Sixth Avenue. Mags was tramping along, staring straight ahead, a poster with a black and white photo hanging from a string around her neck. The crowd in front of the church parted for her. Mourners were sacred at that moment.

I yelled her name and started to cross the street. But the tie-up had eased; traffic started to flow. I tried to keep pace with her on my side of the street. I wanted to invite her to the party. The hosts knew her from way back. But the sidewalks on both sides were crowded. When I did get across Sixth, she was gone.

Aftermath

That night I came home from the party and found the place completely cleaned up, with a thank-you note on the fridge signed by all three kids. And I felt relieved but also lost.

The Survivors' Party was on the Lower East Side. On my way back, I had gone by the East Village, walked up to Tenth Street between B and C. People were out and about. Bars were doing business. But there was still almost no vehicle traffic, and the block was very quiet.

The building where we three had lived in increasing squalor and tension thirty-five years before was refinished, gentrified. I stood across the street looking. Maybe I willed his appearance.

Geoff was there in the corner of my eye, his face dead white, staring up, unblinking, at the light in what had been our windows. I turned toward him and he disappeared. I looked aside and he was there again, so lost and alone, the arms of his jacket soaked in blood.

And I remembered us sitting around with the syringes and all of us making a pledge in blood to stick together as long as we lived. To which Geoff added, "And even after." And I remembered how I had looked at him staring at Mags and knew she was looking at me. Three sides of a triangle.

The next day, Sunday, I went down to Mags's building, wanting very badly to talk to her. I rang the bell again and again. There was no response. I rang the super's apartment.

She was a neighborhood lady, a lesbian around my age. I asked her about Mags.

"She disappeared. Last time anybody saw her was Sunday, 9/9. People in the building checked to make sure everyone was okay. No sign of her. I put a tape across her keyhole Wednesday. It's still there."

"I saw her just yesterday."

"Yeah?" She looked skeptical. "Well, there's a World Trade Center list of potentially missing persons, and her name's on it. You need to talk to them."

This sounded to me like the landlord trying to get rid of her. For the next week, I called Mags a couple of times a day. At some point, the answering machine stopped coming on. I checked out her building regularly. No sign of her. I asked Angelina if she remembered the two of us having dinner in her place on Wednesday, 9/12.

"I was too busy, staying busy so I wouldn't scream. I remember you, and I guess you were with somebody. But no, honey, I don't remember."

Then I asked Marco if he remembered the phone call. And he did but was much too involved by then with Terry and Eloise to be really interested.

Around that time, I saw the couple who had wanted to take their kids down to Ground Zero. They were walking up Sixth Avenue, the kids cranky and tired, the parents looking disappointed. Like the amusement park had turned out to be a rip-off.

Life closed in around me. A short-story collection of mine was being published at that very inopportune moment, and I needed to do some publicity work. I began seeing an old lover when he came back to New York as a consultant for a company that had lost its offices and a big chunk of its staff when the north tower fell.

Mrs. Pirelli did not come home from the hospital but went to live with her son in Connecticut. I made it a point to go by each of the Arab shops and listen to the owners say how awful they felt about what had happened and smile when they showed me pictures of their kids in Yankee caps and shirts.

It was the next weekend that I saw Mags again. The university had gotten permission for the students to go back to the downtown dorms and get their stuff out. Marco, Terry, and Eloise came by the library and asked me to go with them. So I went over to University Transportation and volunteered my services.

Around noon on Sunday, 9/23, a couple of dozen kids and I piled into a university bus driven by Roger, a Jamaican guy who has worked for the university for as long as I have.

"The day before 9/11 these kids didn't much want old farts keeping them company," Roger had said to me. "Then they all wanted their daddy." He led a convoy of jitneys and vans down the FDR Drive, then through quiet Sunday streets, and then past trucks and construction vehicles.

We stopped at a police checkpoint. A cop looked inside and waved us through.

At the dorm, another cop told the kids they had an hour to get what they could and get out. "Be ready to leave at a moment's notice if we tell you to," he said.

Roger and I as the senior members stayed with the vehicles. The air was filthy. Our eyes watered. A few hundred feet up the street, a cloud of smoke still hovered over the ruins of the World Trade Center. Piles of rubble smoldered. Between the pit and us was a line of fire trucks and police cars with cherry tops flashing. Behind us the kids hurried out of the dorm carrying boxes. I made them write their names on their boxes and noted in which van the boxes got stowed. I was surprised, touched even, at the number of stuffed animals that were being rescued.

"Over the years we've done some weird things to earn our pensions," I said to Roger.

"Like volunteering to come to the gates of hell?"

As he said that, flames sprouted from the rubble. Police and firefighters shouted and began to fall back. A fire department chemical tanker turned around, and the crew began unwinding hoses.

Among the uniforms, I saw a civilian, a middle-aged woman in a sweater and jeans and carrying a sign. Mags walked toward the flames. I wanted to run to her. I wanted to shout, "Stop her." Then I realized that none of the cops and firefighters seemed aware of her even as she walked right past them.

As she did, I saw another figure, thin, pale, in a suede jacket and bell-bottom pants. He held out his bloody hands, and together they walked through the smoke and flames into the hole in the city.

"Was that them?" Marco had been standing beside me.

I turned to him. Terry was back by the bus watching Marco's every move. Eloise was gazing at Terry.

"Be smarter than we were," I said.

And Marco said, "Sure," with all the confidence in the world.

• • • •

The ocean, the bay, the waters of the world are God's imagination. The sea is a place where seemingly wild stories can turn out to be frighteningly true . . .

The Trentino Kid
Jeffrey Ford

When I was six, my father took me to Fire Island and taught me how to swim. That day he put me on his back and swam out past the buoy. My fingers dug into his shoulders as he dove, and somehow I just knew when to hold my breath. I remember being immersed in the cold, murky darkness and that down there the sound of the ocean seemed to be inside of me, as if I were a shell the water had put to its ear. Later, beneath the striped umbrella, the breeze blowing, we ate peanut-butter-and-jelly sandwiches, grains of sand sparking off my teeth. Then he explained how to foil the undertow, how to slip like a porpoise beneath giant breakers, how to body surf. We practiced all afternoon. As the sun was going down, we stood in the backwash of the receding tide, and he held my hand in his big callused mitt, like a rock with fingers. Looking out at the horizon where the waves were being born, he summed up the day's lesson by saying, "There are really only two things you need to know about the water. The first is you always have to respect it. The second, you must never panic, but always try to be sure of yourself."

Years later, after my father left us, after I barely graduated high school, smoked and drank my way out of my first semester at college, and bought a boat and took to clamming for a living, I still remembered his two rules. Whatever degree of respect for the water I was still wanting, by the time I finished my first year working the Great South Bay, the brine had shrunk it, the sun had charred it, and the wind had blown it away, or so I thought. Granted, the bay was not the ocean, for it was usually more serene, its changes less obviously dramatic. There wasn't the constant crash of waves near the shore, or the powerful undulation of swells farther out, but the bay did have its perils. Its serenity could lull you, rock you gently in your boat of a sunny day, like a baby in a cradle, and then, with the afternoon wind, a storm could build in minutes, a dark, lowering sky quietly gathering behind your back while you were busy working.

When the bay was angry enough, it could make waves to rival the ocean's and they wouldn't always come in a line toward shore but from as many directions as one could conceive. The smooth twenty-minute ride out from the docks to the flats could, in the midst of a storm, become an hour-long struggle back. When you worked alone, as I did, there was more of a danger of being swamped. With only one set of hands, you could not steer into the swells to keep from rolling over and pump the rising bilge at the same time. Even if you weren't shipping that much water and were able to cut into the choppy waves, an old wooden flat-bottom could literally be slapped apart by the repeated impact of the prow dropping off each peak and hitting the water with a thud.

At that point in my life, it was the second of my father's two rules that was giving me trouble. In general, and very often in a specific sense, I had no idea what I was doing. School had been a failure, and once I'd let it slip through my grasp, I realized how important it could have been to me moving forward in my life. Now I was stuck and could feel the tide of years subtly beginning to rise around me. The job of clamming was hard work, getting up early, pulling on a rake for eight to ten hours a day. There was thought involved but it didn't require imagination, and if anything, imagination was my strong suit. Being tied to the bay was a lonely life, save for the hour or so at the docks in the late afternoon when I would drink the free beer the buyers supplied and bullshit with the other clammers. It was a remarkable way to mark time, to be busy without accomplishing anything. The wind and sun, the salt water, the hard work, aged a body rapidly, and when I would look at the old men who clammed, I was too young to sense the wisdom their years on the water had bestowed upon them and saw only what I did not want to become.

This was back in the early seventies, when the bay still held a bounty of clams, a few years before the big companies came in and dredged it barren. There was money to be made. I remember certain weekends when a count bag, five hundred littleneck clams, went for two hundred dollars. I didn't know many people my age who were making two to three hundred dollars a day.

I had a little apartment on the second floor of an old stucco building that looked like a wing of the Alamo. There was a guy living above me, whom I never saw, and beneath me an ancient woman whose haggard face, half obscured by a lace curtain, peered from the window when I'd leave at daybreak. At night, she would intone the rosary, and the sound of her words would rise through the heating duct in my floor. Her prayers found their way into my monotonous dreams of culling seed clams and counting neck. I drove a three-door Buick Special with a light rust patina that I'd bought for fifty dollars. A big night out was getting plastered at The Copper Kettle, trying to pick up girls.

In my first summer working the bay, I did very well for a beginner, and even socked a little money away toward some hypothetical return to college. In my spare time, in the evenings and those days when the weather was bad, I read novels—science fiction and mysteries—and dreamed of one day writing them. Since I had no television, I would amuse myself by writing stories in those black-and-white-marbled notebooks I had despised the sight of back in high school. In the summer, when the apartment got too close, I'd wander the streets at night through the cricket heat breathing the scents of honeysuckle and wisteria, and dream up plots for my rickety fictions.

That winter the bay froze over. I'd never seen anything like it. The ice was so thick you could drive a car on it. The old-timers said it was a sign that the following summer would be a windfall of a harvest but that such a thing, when it happened, which was rare, was always accompanied by deaths. I first heard the prediction in January, standing on the ice one day when some of us had trudged out a few hundred yards and cut holes with a chain saw through which to clam. Walking on the water that day in the frigid cold, a light snow sweeping along the smooth surface and rising in tiny twisters, was like a scene out of a fairy tale.

"Why deaths?" I asked wrinkle-faced John Hunter as he unscrewed a bottle of schnapps and tipped it into his mouth.

He wiped his stubbled chin with a gloved hand and smiled, three teeth missing. "Because it can't be any other way," he said and laughed.

I nodded, remembering the time when I was new and I had, without securing it, thrown my anchor over the side in the deep water beneath the bridge. The engine was still going and my boat was moving, but I dove over the side, reaching for the end of the line. I managed to grab it, but when I came up, there I was in forty feet of water, my boat gone, holding onto a twenty-pound anchor. The next thing I saw was old Hunter, leaning over me from the side of his boat, reaching out that wiry arm of his. His hand was like a clamp, his bicep like coiled cable. He hauled me in and took me back to my drifting boat, the engine of which had sputtered out by then.

"I should've let you drown," he said, looking pissed off. "You're wasting my time."

"Thanks," I told him as I climbed sheepishly back into my boat.

"I only saved you because I had to," he told me.

"Why'd you have to?" I asked.

"That's the rule of the bay. You have to help anyone in trouble, as long as you've got the wherewithal to."

Since then, he had shown me how to seed a bed, where some of the choice spots were, how to avoid the conservation guys, who were hot to give tickets for just about anything. I was skeptical about what connection a frozen bay had to do with death in the summer, but by then I had learned to just nod.

Spring came and my old boat, an eighteen-foot, flat-bottom wooden job I'd bought for a hundred and fifty bucks and fiberglassed myself, was in bad shape. After putting it back in the water, I found I had to bail the thing out with a garbage can every morning before I could leave the dock. Sheets of fiberglass from my less-than-expert job were sloughing off like peeling skin from a sunburn. I got Pat Ryan, another clammer, to go out with me one day, and we beached the leaky tub on a spit of sand off Gardner's Park. Once we landed, he helped me flip it, and I shoved some new occum, a cottony material that expands when wet, into the seams and recaulked it.

"That's a half-assed job for sure," Pat told me, his warning vaguely reminding me of my father.

"It'll last for a while," I said and waved off his concern.

Just like the old-timers predicted, the clams were plentiful that spring. There were days I would have to put in only four or five hours and I could head back to the dock with a count and a half. It was a season to make you wonder if clamming might not be a worthy life's work. Then, at the end of May, the other part of their prediction came to pass. This kid, Jimmy Trentino, who was five years younger than me (I remembered having shot baskets with him a few times at the courts in the park when I was still in high school), walked in off the shore with a scratch rake and an inner tube and a basket, dreaming of easy money. A storm came up, the bay got crazy very fast, and either weighted down by the rake or having gotten his foot stuck in a sinkhole, he drowned.

The day it happened, I had gotten to the dock late and seen the clouds moving in and the water getting choppy. John Hunter had told me that when the wind kicked up and the bay changed from green to the color of iron, I should get off it as quickly as I could. The only thing more dangerous was standing out there holding an eight-foot metal clam rake during a lightning storm. I got back in my car and drove to the Copper Kettle. Pat Ryan came in at dinnertime and told everyone about the Trentino kid. They dredged for a few days afterward, but the body was never found. That wasn't so unusual, given what an immense, fickle giant the bay was with its myriad currents, some near the surface, some way down deep. As Earl, the bartender, put it, "He could be halfway to France or he might wind up on the beach in Brightwaters tomorrow."

A week later I was sitting on an overturned basket, drinking a beer at the dock after having just sold my haul. A couple of guys were gathered around and Downsy, a good clammer but kind of a high-strung, childish blowhard, was telling about how this woman had shown up at his boat one morning and begged him to take her out so she could release her husband's ashes.

"She was packing the fucking urn like it was a loaf of bread," he said, "holding it under her arm. She was around thirty but she was hot."

As Downsy droned on toward the inevitable bullshit ending of all of his stories, how he eventually boffed some woman over on Grass Island or in his boat, I noticed an old Pontiac pull up at the dock. A slightly bent, little old bald man got out of it. As he shuffled past the buyers' trucks and in our direction, I realized who it was. The Trentino kid's father was the shoemaker in town and had a shop next to the train tracks for as long as I could remember. I don't think I ever rode my bike past it when I was a kid that I didn't see him in the window, leaning over his work, a couple of tacks sticking out of his mouth.

"Hey," I said, and when the guys looked at me, I nodded in the old man's direction.

"Jeez," somebody whispered. Pat Ryan put out his cigarette and Downsy shut his mouth. As Mr. Trentino drew close to us, we all got up. When he spoke, his English was cut with an Italian accent.

He stood before us with his head down, his glasses at the end of his nose. "Fellas," he said.

We each mumbled or whispered how sorry we were about his son.

"Okay," he said, and I could see tears in his eyes. Then he looked up and spoke to us about the weather and the Mets and asked us how business was. We made small talk with him for a few minutes, asked him if he wanted a beer. He waved his hands in front of him and smiled, shaking his head.

"Fellas," he said, looking down again. "Please, remember my boy."

We knew what he was asking, and we all said, almost like a chorus, "We will." He turned around then, walked back to his car, got in and drove away.

We were a superstitious bunch. I think it had to do with the fact that we spent our days bobbing on the surface of a vast mystery. So much of what our livelihood depended on was hidden from view. It wasn't so great a leap of imagination to think that life also had its unseen, unfathomable depths. The bay was teeming with folklore and legend—man-eating sharks slipping through the inlet to roam the bay, a sea turtle known as Moola that was supposedly as big as a Cadillac, islands that vanished and then reappeared, sunken treasure, a rogue current that could take you by the foot and drag you through underground channels to leave your body bobbing in Lake Ronkonkoma on the North Shore of Long Island. I had, in fact, seen some very big sea turtles and walked on an island that had been born overnight. By mid-June, the Trentino kid's body had, through our psyches and the promise made to his old man, been swept into this realm of legend.

Almost daily, I heard reports from other guys who had seen it floating just below the surface only twenty yards or so from where they were clamming. They'd weigh anchor and start their engines, but by the time they maneuvered their boats to where they had seen it, it would be gone. Every time it was spotted, some mishap would follow—a lost rake head, a cracked transom, the twin-hole vampire bite from an eel. The kid was soon understood to be cursed. One night, after Pat Ryan got finished relating his own run-in with the errant corpse, Downsy, who was well drunk by then, swore that when he was passing the center of the bridge two days earlier, he'd seen the pale, decomposing figure of the kid swim under his boat.

"Get the fuck outta here," somebody said to him and we laughed.

He didn't laugh. "It was doing the god-damn breast stroke, I swear," he said. "It was swimming like you swim in good dreams, like flying underwater."

"Did you end up boffing it on Grass Island?" somebody asked.

Downsy was dead serious, though, and to prove it, took a swing at the joker, inciting a brawl that resulted in Earl banning him from the Kettle for a week.

I asked John Hunter the next day, as our boats bobbed side by side off the eastern edge of Grass Island, if it was possible the kid's body could still be around.

"Sure," he said, "anything's possible, except maybe you raking more neck than me in a day. My guess is that you wouldn't want to find it at this point—all bloated and half-eaten by eels and bottom feeders. Forget the eyes, the ears, the lips, the belly meat. The hair will still be there, though, and nothing's gonna eat the teeth."

"Could it be cursed?" I asked him.

He laughed. "You have to understand something," he said. "If I was talking to you on dry land, I'd think you were nuts, but this is the bay. The ocean, the bay, the waters of the world are God's imagination. I've known wilder things than that to be true out here."

The image of what was left of the kid when John Hunter finished his forensic menu haunted me. At night, while I was trying to read, it floated there in my thoughts, obscuring whatever story I was in the middle of. Then the words of the rosary threaded their way up from downstairs to weave an invisible web around it, fixing it fast, so that the current of forgetting couldn't whisk it away. One hot midnight at the end of June, I couldn't take thinking about it anymore, so I slipped on my sneakers and went out walking. I headed away from The Copper Kettle, to the quiet side of town. I'd been burnt badly by the sun that day and the breeze against my skin made me shiver. For an hour or more I wandered aimlessly until I finally took a seat on a park bench next to the basketball court.

I realized it was not chance that had brought me to that spot. They say that when you drown, your life passes before your eyes in quick cuts like a television commercial. I wondered if in that blur of events, the kid had noticed me passing him the ball, getting the older guys to let him play in a game, showing him how to shoot from the foul line. What before had been a vague memory now came back to me in vivid detail. I concentrated hard on my recollection of him in life, and this image slowly replaced the one of him drowned and ravaged by the bay.

He was a skinny kid, not too tall, not too short, with brown silky hair in a bowl cut. When I knew him, he was about ten or eleven, but he had long arms, good for stopping passes and stealing the ball. He was quick and unafraid of the older guys who were much bigger than him. What I saw most clearly were his eyes, big round ones, the color green of bottle glass tumbled smooth by the surf, that showed his disappointment at missing a shot or the thrill of playing in a game with high-school-aged guys. He was quiet and polite, not a show-off by any means, and I could tell he was really listening when I taught him how to put backspin on the ball. Finding him in my thoughts was not so very hard. What was nearly impossible was conceiving of him lifeless—no more, a blank spot in the world. I thought about all the things he would miss out on, all the things I had done between his age and mine. Later that night, after I had made my way home and gone to sleep, I dreamt I was on the basketball court with him. He was shooting foul shots, and I stepped up close and leaned over. "Remember, you must never panic," I said.

Come July, the bottom fell out of the market, and prices paid for counts went way down due to the abundance of that summer's harvest. Not even John Hunter could predict the market, and so although we'd all made a killing in May and June, we were now going to have to pay for it for the rest of the season. We'd all gone a little crazy with our money at the bar, not thinking ahead to the winter and those days it would be impossible to work.

I started staying out on the water longer, only getting back to the dock when the sun was nothing more than a red smudge on the horizon. Some of the buyers would be gone by then, but a couple of them stayed around and waited for us all to get in. I also started playing it a little fast and loose with the weather, going out on days that were blustery and the water was choppy. In May and June I'd have written them off and gone back to bed or read a book, but I wanted to hold on to what I had saved through the flush, early part of the season.

One afternoon, in the last week in July, while over in the flats due south of Babylon, I had stumbled upon a vein of neck, a bed like you wouldn't believe. I was bringing up loaded rake heads every fifteen minutes or so. After two straight hours of scratching away, the clams were still abundant. Around three o'clock, in the midst of my labor, I felt the wind rise, but paid it no mind since it invariably came on in the late afternoon. Only when I had to stop to rest my arms and catch my breath an hour later did I notice that the boat was really rocking. By my best estimation, I'd taken enough for two count bags of little-neck and a bag of top-neck. While I rested, I decided to cull some of my take and get rid of the useless seed clams and the chowders. That's when I happened to look over my shoulder and notice that the sun was gone and the water had grown very choppy.

I stood up quickly and turned to look back across the bay only to see whitecaps forming on the swells and that the color of the water was darkening toward that iron gray. In the distance, I could see clam boats heading back in toward the docks.

"Shit," I said, not wanting to leave the treasure trove that still lay beneath me, but just then a wave came along and smacked the side of the boat, sending me onto my ass between the seat slats and into the bilge. That was all the warning I needed. I brought in my rake, telescoped the handle down, and stowed the head. When I looked up this time, things had gotten a lot worse. The swells had already doubled in size, and the wind had become audible in its ferocity. By the time I dragged in the anchor, the boat was lurching wildly. The jostling I took made it hard for me to maneuver. I had to be careful not to get knocked overboard.

"Come on, baby," I said after pumping the engine. I pulled on the cord only once and it fired up and started running. I swung the handle to turn the boat around in order to head back across the bay to the dock. Off to my left, I noticed a decked-over boat with a small, red cabin, and knew it was Downsy. He was heading in the wrong direction. I followed his path with my sight and for the first time laid eyes on a guy who was scratch-raking about a hundred yards to my left. He was in up to his chest and although he could stand, the walk back to the shallows by the bridge was a good four hundred yards. He'd never make it. Without thinking, I turned in that direction to see if I could help.

As I chugged up close, I saw Downsy move quickly back into his cabin from where he had been leaning over the clammer on the side of the boat. His engine roared, and he turned the boat around and left the guy standing there in the water. His boat almost hit the front of mine as he took off. I called to him, but he never looked back. I pulled my boat up alongside the guy in the water and was about to yell, "How about a lift," when I saw why Downsy had split.

Bobbing in that iron-gray water, trying to keep his head above the swells, was the Trentino kid. He wasn't the decomposed horror show that John Hunter had described, but his skin was mottled a very pale white and bruise green. Around the lower portion of his throat he had that drowned man's blue necklace. His hair was plastered to his head by the water, and those big green eyes peered up at me, his gaze literally digging into mine. That look said, "Help me," as clearly as if he had spoken the words. He was shivering like mad, and he held his arms up, hands open, like a baby wanting to be carried.

I sat there in the wildly rocking boat, staring in disbelief, my heart racing. What good it was going to do me against the dead, I didn't know, but I drew my knife, a ten-inch serrated blade and just held it out in front of me. My other hand was on the throttle of the engine, keeping it at an idle. I wanted to open the engine up all the way and escape as fast as possible, but I was paralyzed somewhere between pity and fear. Then a big wave came swamping the kid and slamming the side of my boat. The whole craft almost rolled over, and the peak of the curl slapped me in the face with ice-cold water.

The dead kid came up spluttering, silently coughing water out of his mouth and nose. His eyes were brimming with terror.

"What the hell are you?" I yelled.

His arms, his fingers, reached for me more urgently.

"Deaths," the old-timers had said, as in the plural, and this thought wriggled through my frantic mind like an eel, followed by my realization that what Downsy had been fleeing was the "curse." I took another wave in the side and the boat tipped perilously, the water drenching me. Clams scattered across the deck as the baskets slid, and my cull box flew over the side. I felt, in my confusion and fright, a brief stab of regret at losing it. I looked back to the kid and could see that he seemed anchored in place, his foot no doubt in a sinkhole. Another minute and he would be out of sight beneath the surface. I thought I'd be released from my paralysis once his eyes were covered by the gray water. I dropped my knife and almost thrust my hand out to grab his, but the thought of taking Death into my boat stopped me in mid-reach.

I had to leave or I'd be swamped and sunk just lolling there in the swells. "No way," I said aloud, with every intention of opening the throttle, but just then the kid made one wild lunge, and the tips of the green-tinged fingers of his left hand landed on the side of the boat. I remembered John Hunter telling me it was the rule of the bay to help when you could. The boat got slammed, and I saw the kid's hand begin to slip off the gunwale. I couldn't let him die again, so I reached out. It was like grabbing a handful of snow, freezing cold and soft, and a chill shot up through my arm to my head and formed a vision of the moment of his true death. I felt his panic, heard his underwater cry for his father, the words coming clear through a torrent of bubbles that also released his life. Then I came to and was on my feet, using my season-and-a-half of rake-pulling muscle to drag that kid, dead or alive, up out of the bay. His body landed in my boat with a soggy thud, and as it did, I was thrown off balance and nearly took a dive over the side.

He was curled up like a fetus and unnaturally light when I lifted him into a sitting position on the plank bench at the center of the boat. A wave of revulsion passed through me as I touched his slick, spongy flesh. He'd come out of the water wearing nothing, and I had no clothes handy to protect him against the wind. He faced back at me where I sat near the throttle of the engine. There was a good four inches of water sloshing around in the bottom. I quickly lifted the baskets of clams and chucked them all over the side one at a time. I had to lighten the load and get the boat to ride higher through the storm. Then I sat down with those big green eyes staring into me, and opened the throttle all the way.

Lightning streaked through the sky, sizzling down and then exploding over our heads. The waves were massive, and now the storm scared me more than the living corpse. I headed toward the dock, aiming to overshoot it since I knew the wind would drive us eastward. If I was lucky, I could get to a cove I knew of on the southern tip of Gardner's Park. I had briefly thought of heading out toward Grass Island and beaching there, but in a storm like the one raging around us, there was no telling if the island would be there tomorrow.

I never tried harder at anything in my life than preventing myself from wondering how this dead kid was sitting in front of me, shivering cold. The only thought that squeaked through my defenses was, "Is this a miracle?" Then those defenses busted open, and I considered the fact that I might already be dead myself and we were sailing through hell, or to it. I steadied myself as best I could by concentrating on cutting into the swells. The boat was taking a brutal pounding, but we were making headway.

"We're going to make it," I said to Jimmy, and he didn't smile, but he looked less frightened. That subtle sign helped me stay my own confusion, and so I just started talking to him, saying anything that came to mind. By the time we reached the bridge and were passing under it, I realized I had been laying out my life story, and he was seeing it flash before his eyes. I did not want to die that afternoon with nothing to show but scenes of the bay and my hometown. What I wished I could have shared with him were my dreams for the future. Then I noticed a vague spark in his gaze, a subtle recognition of some possibility. That's when the full brunt of the storm hit—gale-force winds, lashing rain, hail the size of dice—and I heard above the shriek of the wind a distinct cracking sound when the prow slammed down off a huge roller. The boat was breaking up.

With every impact against the water came that cracking noise, and each time it sounded, I noticed the kid's skin begin to tear. A dark brown sludge seeped from these wounds. Tears formed in his big eyes, became his eyes, and then dripped in viscous streams down his face, leaving the sockets empty. The lightning cracked above and his chest split open down to his navel. He opened his mouth and a hermit crab scurried out across his blue lips and chin to his neck. I no longer could think to steer, no longer felt the cold, couldn't utter a sound. The sky was nearly dark as night. We fell off a wave into its trough like slamming into a moving truck, and then the wood came apart with a groan. I felt the water rising up around my ankles and calves. Then the transom split off the back of the boat as if it had been made of cardboard, and the engine dropped away out of my grasp, its noise silenced. One more streak of lightning walked the sky, and I saw before me the remains of the kid as John Hunter had described they would be. The next thing I knew, I was in the water, flailing to stay afloat amidst the storm.

I was a strong swimmer, but by this point I was completely exhausted. The waves came from everywhere, one after the other, and I had no idea where I was headed or how close I had managed to get to shore. I would be knocked under by a wave and then bob back up, and then down I'd go again. A huge wave, like a cold dark wing, swept over me, and I thought it might be death. It drove me below the surface, where I tumbled and spun so violently that when I again tried to struggle toward the sky, I instead found the sandy bottom. Then something moved beneath me, and I wasn't sure if I was dreaming, but I remembered my father riding me on his back through the ocean. I reached out and put my hands on a pair of shoulders. In my desperation, my fingers dug through the flesh and latched onto skeleton. We were flying, skimming along the surface, and I could breathe again. It was all so crazy, my mind broke down in the confusion and I must have passed out.

When next I was fully aware, I was stumbling through knee-deep water in the shallows off Gardner's Park. I made the beach and collapsed on the sand. An hour passed, maybe more, but when I awoke, the storm had abated and a steady rain was falling. I made my way, tired and weak, through the park to Sunrise Highway. There, I managed to hitch a ride back to the docks and my waiting car. It was late when I finally returned to the Alamo. I slipped off my wet clothes and got into bed. Curling up on my side, I quickly drifted off to sleep, the words of the old crone's rosary washing over me, submerging me.

The next day I called the police and reported the loss of my boat, so that those at the dock who found my slip empty wouldn't think I had drowned. Later on, when I was driving over to my mother's house, I heard on the radio that the storm had claimed a life. Downsy's boat was missing at the dock. Ironically enough, they found his body that morning washed up on the shore of Grass Island.

A few days later, it was also discovered that the storm had left some interesting debris on the beach at the south end of Gardner's Park, close to where I had come ashore. Two hikers came across pieces of my boat, identified by the plank that held its serial numbers, and a little farther up the beach, the remains of Jimmy Trentino.

I went to two funerals in one day—one for a kid who never got a chance to grow up, and one for a guy who didn't want to. Later that evening, sitting in a shadowed booth at the back of The Copper Kettle, John Hunter remarked about how a coffin is like a boat for the dead.

I wanted to tell him everything that happened the day of the storm, but in the end, felt he wouldn't approve. He had sternly warned me once against blabbing—even when drunk—about a bed I might be seeding for the coming season. "A good man knows when to keep a secret," he had said. Instead, I merely told him, "I'm not coming back to the bay."

He laughed. "Did you think you had to tell me?" he said. "I've seen you reading those books in your boat on your lunch break. I've seen you wandering around town late at night. You don't need a boat to get where it's deep."

I got up then and went to the bar to order another round. When I came back to the booth, he was gone.

I moved on with my life, went back to school, devoted more time to writing my stories, and through the changes that came, I tried to always be sure of myself. In those inevitable dark moments, though, when I thought I was about to panic, I'd remember John Hunter, his hand reaching down to pull me from the water. I always wished that I might see him again, but I never did, because it couldn't be any other way.

• • • •

"Are you always so nice to dead people?" she asked.

A Soul in a Bottle
Tim Powers

The forecourt of the Chinese Theater smelled of rain-wet stone and car exhaust, but a faint aroma like pears and cumin seemed to cling to his shirt-collar as he stepped around the clustered tourists, who all appeared to be blinking up at the copper towers above the forecourt wall or smiling into cameras as they knelt to press their hands into the puddled handprints in the cement paving blocks.

George Sydney gripped his shopping bag under his arm and dug three pennies from his pants pocket.

For the third or fourth time this morning he found himself glancing sharply over his left shoulder, but again there was no one within yards of him. The morning sun was bright on the Roosevelt Hotel across the boulevard, and the clouds were breaking up in the blue sky.

He crouched beside Jean Harlow's square and carefully laid one penny in each of the three round indentations below her incised signature, then wiped his wet fingers on his jacket. The coins wouldn't stay there long, but Sydney always put three fresh ones down whenever he walked past this block of Hollywood Boulevard.

He straightened up and again caught a whiff of pears and cumin, and when he glanced over his left shoulder there was a girl standing right behind him.

At first glance he thought she was a teenager—she was a head shorter than him, and her tangled red hair framed a narrow, freckled face with squinting eyes and a wide, amused mouth.

"*Three* pennies?" she asked, and her voice was deeper than he would have expected.

She was standing so close to him that his elbow had brushed her breasts when he'd turned around.

"That's right," said Sydney, stepping back from her, awkwardly so as not to scuff the coins loose.

"Why?"

"Uh . . . " He waved at the cement square and then barely caught his shopping bag. "People pried up the original three," he said. "For souvenirs. That she put there. Jean Harlow, when she put her handprints and shoe prints in the wet cement, in 1933."

The girl raised her faint eyebrows and blinked down at the stone. "I never knew that. How did you know that?"

"I looked her up one time. Uh, on Google."

The girl laughed quietly, and in that moment she seemed to be the only figure in the forecourt, including himself, that had color. He realized dizzily that the scent he'd been catching all morning was hers.

"Google?" she said. "Sounds like a Chinaman trying to say something. Are you always so nice to dead people?"

Her black linen jacket and skirt were visibly damp, as if she had slept outside, and seemed to be incongruously formal. He wondered if somebody had donated the suit to the Salvation Army place down the boulevard by Pep Boys, and if this girl was one of the young people he sometimes saw in sleeping bags under the marquee of a closed theater down there.

"Respectful, at least," he said, "I suppose."

She nodded. " 'Lo,' " she said, " 'some we loved, the loveliest and the best . . . ' "

Surprised by the quote, he mentally recited the next two lines of the Rubaiyat quatrain—*That Time and Fate of all their Vintage prest, / Have drunk their cup a round or two before*—and found himself saying the last line out loud: " 'And one by one crept silently to Rest.' "

She was looking at him intently, so he cleared his throat and said, "Are you local? You've been here before, I gather." Probably that odd scent was popular right now, he thought, the way patchouli oil had apparently been in the '60s. Probably he had brushed past someone who had been wearing it too, earlier in the day.

"I'm staying at the Heroic," she said, then went on quickly, "Do you live near here?"

He could see her bra through her damp white blouse, and he looked away—though he had noticed that it seemed to be embroidered with vines.

"I have an apartment up on Franklin," he said, belatedly.

She had noticed his glance, and arched her back for a moment before pulling her jacket closed and buttoning it. " 'And in a Windingsheet of Vineleaf wrapped,' " she said merrily, " 'So bury me by some sweet Gardenside.' "

Embarrassed, he muttered the first line of that quatrain: " 'Ah, with the grape my fading life provide . . . ' "

"Good idea!" she said—then she frowned, and her face was older. "No, dammit, I've got to go—but I'll see you again, right? I like you." She leaned forward and tipped her face up—and then she had briefly kissed him on the lips, and he did drop his shopping bag.

When he had crouched to pick it up and brushed the clinging drops of cold water off on his pants, and looked around, she was gone. He took a couple of steps toward the theater entrance, but the dozens of colorfully dressed strangers blocked his view, and he couldn't tell if she had hurried inside; and he didn't see her among the people by the photo booths or on the shiny black sidewalk.

Her lips had been hot—perhaps she had a fever.

He opened the plastic bag and peered inside, but the book didn't seem to have got wet or landed on a corner. A first edition of Colleen Moore's *Silent Star*, with a TLS, a typed letter, signed, tipped in on the front flyleaf. The Larry Edmunds Bookstore a few blocks east was going to give him fifty dollars for it.

And he thought he'd probably stop at Boardner's afterward and have a couple of beers before walking back to his apartment. Or maybe a shot of Wild Turkey, though it wasn't yet noon. He knew he'd be coming back here again, soon, frequently—peering around, lingering, almost certainly uselessly.

Still, *I'll see you again*, she had said. *I like you.*

Well, he thought with a nervous smile as he started east down the black sidewalk, stepping around the inset brass-rimmed pink stars with names on them, I like you too. Maybe, after all, it's a rain-damp street girl that I can fall in love with.

She wasn't at the Chinese Theater when he looked for her there during the next several days, but a week later he saw her again. He was driving across Fairfax on Santa Monica Boulevard, and he saw her standing on the sidewalk in front of the big Starbuck's, in the shadows below the aquamarine openwork dome.

He knew it was her, though she was wearing jeans and a sweatshirt now—her red hair and freckled face were unmistakable. He honked the horn as he drove through the intersection, and she looked up, but by the time he had turned left into a market parking lot and driven back west on Santa Monica, she was nowhere to be seen.

He drove around several blocks, squinting as the winter sunlight shifted back and forth across the streaked windshield of his ten-year-old Honda, but none of the people on the sidewalks was her.

A couple of blocks south of Santa Monica he passed a fenced-off motel with plywood over its windows and several shopping carts in its otherwise empty parking lot. The 1960s space-age sign over the building read RO IC MOTEL, and he could see faint outlines where a long-gone T and P had once made "tropic" of the first word.

"Eroic," he said softly to himself.

To his own wry embarrassment he parked a block past it and fed his only quarter into the parking meter, but at the end of his twenty minutes she hadn't appeared.

Of course she hadn't. "You're acting like a high-school kid," he whispered impatiently to himself as he put the Honda in gear and pulled away from the curb.

Six days later he was walking east toward Book City at Cherokee, and as was his habit lately he stepped into the Chinese Theater forecourt with three pennies in his hand, and he stood wearily beside the souvenir shop and scanned the crowd, shaking the pennies in his fist. The late afternoon crowd consisted of brightly-dressed tourists, and a portly, bearded man making hats out of balloons, and several young men dressed as Batman and Spiderman and Captain Jack Sparrow from the *Pirates of the Caribbean* movies.

Then he gripped the pennies tight. He saw her.

She was at the other end of the crowded square, on the far side of the theater entrance, and he noticed her red hair in the moment before she crouched out of sight.

He hurried through the crowd to where she was kneeling—the rains had passed and the pavement was dry—and he saw that she had laid three pennies into little round indentations in the Gregory Peck square.

She grinned up at him, squinting in the sunlight. "I love the idea," she said in the remembered husky voice, "but I didn't want to come between you and Jean Harlow." She reached up one narrow hand, and he took it gladly and pulled her to her feet. She could hardly weigh more than a hundred pounds. He realized that her hand was hot as he let go of it.

"And hello," she said.

She was wearing jeans and a gray sweatshirt again, or still. At least they were dry. Sydney caught again the scent of pears and cumin.

He was grinning too. Most of the books he sold he got from thrift stores and online used-book sellers, and these recent trips to Book City had been a self-respect excuse to keep looking for her here.

He groped for something to say. "I thought I found your 'Heroic' the other day," he told her.

She cocked her head, still smiling. The sweatshirt was baggy, but somehow she seemed to be flat-chested today. "You were looking for me?" she asked.

"I—guess I was. This was a closed-down motel, though, south of Santa Monica." He laughed self-consciously. "The sign says blank-R-O-blank-I-C. Eroic, see? It was originally Tropic, I gather."

Her green eyes had narrowed as he spoke, and it occurred to him that the condemned motel might actually be the place she'd referred to a couple of weeks earlier, and that she had not expected him to find it. "Probably it originally said 'erotic,' " she said lightly, taking his hand and stepping away from the Gregory Peck square. "Have you got a cigarette?"

"Yes." He pulled a pack of Camels and a lighter from his shirt pocket, and when she had tucked a cigarette between her lips—he noticed that she was not wearing lipstick today—he cupped his hand around the lighter and held the flame toward her. She held his hand to steady it as she puffed the cigarette alight.

"There couldn't be a motel called Erotic," he said.

"Sure there could, lover. To avoid complications."

"I'm George," he said. "What's your name?"

She shook her head, grinning up at him.

The bearded balloon man had shuffled across the pavement to them, deftly weaving a sort of bowler hat shape out of several long green balloons, and now he reached out and set it on her head.

"No, thank you," she said, taking it off and holding it toward the man, but he backed away, smiling through his beard and nodding. She stuck it onto the head of a little boy who was scampering past.

The balloon man stepped forward again and this time he snatched the cigarette from her mouth. "This is California, sister," he said, dropping it and stepping on it. "We don't smoke here."

"You should," she said, "it'd help you lose weight." She took Sydney's arm and started toward the sidewalk.

The balloon man called after them, "It's customary to give a gratuity for the balloons!"

"Get it from that kid," said Sydney over his shoulder.

The bearded man was pointing after them and saying loudly, "Tacky people, tacky people!"

"Could I have another cigarette?" she said as they stepped around the forecourt wall out of the shadows and started down the sunlit sidewalk toward the soft-drink and jewelry stands on the wider pavement in front of the Kodak Theater.

"Sure," said Sydney, pulling the pack and lighter out again. "Would you like a Coke or something?" he added, waving toward the nearest vendor. Their shadows stretched for yards ahead of them, but the day was still hot.

"I'd like a drink drink." She paused to take a cigarette, and again she put her hand over his as he lit it for her. "Drink, that knits up the raveled sleave of care," she said through smoke as they started forward again. "I bet you know where we could find a bar."

"I bet I do," he agreed. "Why don't you want to tell me your name?"

"I'm shy," she said. "What did the Michelin Man say, when we were leaving?"

"He said, 'tacky people.'"

She stopped and turned to look back, and for a moment Sydney was afraid she intended to march back and cause a scene; but a moment later she had grabbed his arm and resumed their eastward course.

He could feel that she was shaking, and he peered back over his shoulder.

Everyone on the pavement behind them seemed to be couples moving away or across his view, except for one silhouetted figure standing a hundred feet back—it was an elderly white-haired woman in a shapeless dress, and he couldn't see if she was looking after them or not.

The girl had released his arm and taken two steps ahead, and he started toward her—

—and she disappeared.

Sydney rocked to a halt.

He had been looking directly at her in the bright afternoon sunlight. She had not stepped into a store doorway or run on ahead or ducked behind him. She had been occupying volume four feet ahead of him, casting a shadow, and suddenly she was not.

A bus that had been grinding past on the far side of the parking meters to his left was still grinding past.

Her cigarette was rolling on the sidewalk, still lit.

She had not been a hallucination, and he had not experienced some kind of blackout.

Are you always so nice to dead people?

He was shivering in the sunlight, and he stepped back to half-sit against the rim of a black iron trash can by the curb. No sudden moves, he thought.

Was she a ghost? Probably, probably! What else?

Well then, you've seen a ghost, he told himself, that's all. People see ghosts. The balloon man saw her too—he told her not to smoke.

You fell in love with a ghost, that's all. People have probably done that.

He waited several minutes, gripping the iron rim of the trash can and glancing in all directions, but she didn't reappear.

At last he was able to push away from the trash can and walk on, unsteadily, toward Book City; that had been his plan before he had met her again today, and nothing else seemed appropriate. Breathing wasn't difficult, but for at least a little while it would be a conscious action, like putting one foot in front of the other.

He wondered if he would meet her again, knowing that she was a ghost. He wondered if he would be afraid of her now. He thought he probably would be, but he hoped he would see her again anyway.

The quiet aisles of the book store, with the almost-vanilla scent of old paper, distanced him from the event on the sidewalk. This was his familiar world, as if all used book stores were actually one enormous magical building that you could enter through different doorways in Long Beach or Portland or Albuquerque. Always, reliably, there were the books with no spines that you had to pull out and identify, and the dust jackets that had to be checked for the dismissive words *Book Club Edition*, and the poetry section to be scanned for possibly underpriced Nora May French or George Sterling.

The shaking of his hands, and the disorientation that was like a half-second delay in his comprehension, were no worse than a hangover, and he was familiar with hangovers—the cure was a couple of drinks, and he would take the cure as soon as he got back to his apartment. In the meantime he was gratefully able to concentrate on the books, and within half an hour he had found several P.G. Wodehouse novels that he'd be able to sell for more than the prices they were marked at, and a clean five-dollar hardcover copy of Sabatini's *Bellarion*.

My books, he thought, and my poetry.

In the poetry section he found several signed Don Blanding books, but in his experience *every* Don Blanding book was signed. Then he found a first edition copy of Cheyenne Fleming's 1968 *More Poems*, but it was priced at twenty dollars, which was about the most it would ever go for. He looked on the title page for an inscription, but there wasn't one, and then flipped through the pages—and glimpsed handwriting.

He found the page again, and saw the name *Cheyenne Fleming* scrawled below one of the sonnets; and beside it was a thumb-print in the same fountain-pen ink.

He paused.

If this was a genuine Fleming signature, the book was worth about two hundred dollars. He was familiar with her poetry, but he didn't think he'd ever seen her signature; certainly he didn't have any signed Flemings at home to compare this against. But Christine would probably be able to say whether it was real or not—Christine Dunn was a book dealer he'd sometimes gone in with on substantial buys.

He'd risk the twenty dollars and call her when he got back to his apartment. And just for today he would walk straight north to Franklin, not west on Hollywood Boulevard. Not quite yet, not this evening.

His apartment building was on Franklin just west of Highland, a jacaranda-shaded old two-story horseshoe around an overgrown central courtyard, and supposedly Marlon Brando had stayed there before he'd become successful. Sydney's apartment was upstairs, and he locked the door after he had let himself into the curtained, tobacco-scented living room.

He poured himself a glass of bourbon from the bottle on the top kitchen shelf, and pulled a Coors from the refrigerator to chase the warm liquor with, and then he took his shopping bag to the shabby brown-leather chair in the corner and switched on the lamp.

It was of course the Fleming that interested him. He flipped open the book to the page with Fleming's name inked on it.

He recognized the sonnet from the first line—it was the rude sonnet to her sister . . . the sister who, he recalled, had become Fleming's literary executor after Fleming's suicide. Ironic.

He read the first eight lines of the sonnet, his gaze only bouncing over the lines since he had read it many times before:

To My Sister

> Rebecca, if your mirror were to show
> My face to you instead of yours, I wonder
> If you would notice right away, or know
> The vain pretense you've chosen to live under.
> If ever phone or doorbell rang, and then
> I heard your voice conversing, what you'd say
> Would be what I have said, recalled again,
> And I might sit in silence through the day.

Then he frowned and took a careful sip of the bourbon. The last six lines weren't quite as he remembered them:

> But when the Resurrection Man shall bring
> The moon to free me from these yellowed pages,
> The gift is mine, there won't be anything
> For you—and you can rest through all the ages
> Under a stone that bears the cherished name
> You thought should make the two of us the same.

He picked up the telephone and punched in Christine's number.

After three rings he heard her say, briskly, "Dunn Books."

"Christine," he said, "George—uh—here." It was the first time he had spoken since seeing the girl disappear, and his voice had cracked. He cleared his throat and took a deep breath and let it out.

"Drunk again," said Christine.

"Again?" he said. "Still. Listen, I've got a first here of Fleming's *More Poems*, no dust jacket but it's got her name written below one of the poems. Do you have a signed Fleming I could compare it with?"

"You're in luck, an eBay customer backed out of a deal. It's a *More Poems*, too."

"Have you got it right there?"

"Yeah, but what, you want me to describe her signature over the phone? We should meet at the Biltmore tomorrow, bring our copies."

"Good idea, and if this is real I'll buy lunch. But could you flip to the sonnet 'To My Sister'?"

"One second." A few moments later she was back on the phone. "Okay, what about it?"

"How does the sestet go?"

"It says, *'But when the daylight of the future shows/ The forms freed by erosion from their cages,/ It will be mine that quickens, gladly grows,/ And lives; and you can rest through all the ages/ Under a stone that bears the cherished name/ You thought should make the two of us the same.'* Bitter poem!"

Those were the familiar lines—the way the poem was supposed to go.

"Why," asked Christine, "is yours missing the bottom of the page?"

"No—I've—my copy has a partly different sestet." He read to her the last six lines on the page of the book he held. "Printed just like every other poem in the book, same typeface and all."

"Wow. Otherwise a standard copy of the first edition?"

"To the best of my knowledge, I don't know," he said, quoting a treasured remark from a bookseller they both knew. He added, "We'll know tomorrow."

"Eleven, okay? And take care of it—it might be worth wholesaling to one of the big-ticket dealers."

"I wasn't going to use it for a coaster. See you at eleven."

He hung up the phone, and before putting the book aside he touched the ink thumb-print beside the signature on the page. The paper wasn't warm or cold, but he shivered—this was a touch across decades. When had Fleming killed herself?

He got up and crossed the old carpets to the computer and turned it on, and as the monitor screen showed the Hewlett Packard logo and then the

Windows background, he couldn't shake the mental image of trying to grab a woman to keep her from falling into some abyss and only managing to brush her outstretched hand with one finger.

He typed in the address for Google—*sounds like a Chinaman trying to say something*—and then typed "cheyenne fleming," and when a list of sites appeared he clicked on the top one. He had a dial-up AOL connection, so the text appeared first, flanking a square where a picture would soon appear.

Cheyenne Fleming, he read, had been born in Hollywood in 1934, and had lived there all her life with her younger sister Rebecca. Both had gone to UCLA, Cheyenne with more distinction than Rebecca, and both had published books of poetry, though Rebecca's had always been compared unfavorably with Cheyenne's. The sisters apparently both loved and resented each other, and the article quoted several lines from the "To My Sister" sonnet—the version Christine had read to him over the phone, not the version in his copy of *More Poems*. Cheyenne Fleming had shot herself in 1969, reportedly because Rebecca had stolen away her fiancé. Rebecca became her literary executor.

At last the picture appeared on the screen—it was black and white, but Sydney recognized the thin face with its narrow eyes and wide humorous mouth, and he knew that the disordered hair would be red in a color photograph.

The tip of his finger was numb where he had touched her thumb-print.

I'm Shy, she had said. He had thought she was evading giving him her name. Shy for Cheyenne, of course. Pronounced Shy-*Ann*.

He glanced fearfully at his front door—what if she was standing on the landing out there right now, in the dusk shadows? He realized, with a shudder that made him carry his glass back to the kitchen for a re-fill, that he would open the door if she was—yes, and invite her in, invite her across his threshold. I finally fall in love, he thought, and it's with a dead woman. A suicide.

A line of black ants had found the coffee cup he'd left unwashed this morning, but he couldn't kill them right now.

Once his glass was filled again, he went to the living room window instead of the door, and he pulled the curtains aside. A huge orange full moon hung in the darkening sky behind the old TV antennas on the opposite roof. He looked down, but didn't see her among the shadowed trees and vines.

And in a Windingsheet of Vineleaf wrapped,
So bury me by some sweet Gardenside.

He closed the curtain and fetched the bottle and the twelve-pack of Coors to set beside his chair, then settled down to lose himself in one of the P.G.

Wodehouse novels until he should be drunk enough to stumble to bed and fall instantly asleep.

As he trudged across Pershing Square from the parking structure on Hill Street toward the three imposing brown brick towers of the Biltmore Hotel, Sydney's squinting gaze kept being drawn in the direction of the new bright-yellow building on the south side of the square. His eyes were watering in the morning sun-glare anyway, and he wondered irritably why somebody would paint a new building in that idiotic kindergarten color.

He had awakened early, and his hangover seemed to be just a continuation of his disorientation from the day before. He had decided that he couldn't sell the Fleming book. Even though he had met her two weeks before finding the book, he was certain that the book was somehow his link to her.

Christine would be disappointed—part of the fun of bookselling was writing catalogue copy for extraordinary items, and she would have wanted to collaborate in the description of this item—but he couldn't help that.

His gaze was drawn again toward the yellow building, but now that he was closer to it he could see that it wasn't the building that his eyes had been drawn toward, but a stairway and pool just this side of it. Two six-foot brown stone spheres were mounted on the pool coping.

And he saw her sitting down there, on the shady side of one of the giant stone balls.

He was smiling and stepping across the pavement in that direction even before he was sure it was her, and the memory, only momentarily delayed, of who she must be didn't slow his pace.

She was wearing the jeans and sweatshirt again, and she stood up and waved at him when he was still a hundred feet away, and even at this distance he was sure he caught her pears-and-cumin scent.

He sprinted the last few yards, and her arms were wide so he hugged her when they met.

"George," she said breathily in his ear. The fruit-and-spice smell was strong.

"Shy," he said, and hugged her more tightly. He could feel her breastbone against his, and he wondered if she had been wearing a padded bra when he had first seen her. Then he held her by her shoulders at arm's length and smiled into her squinting, elfin eyes. "I've got to make a call," he said.

He pulled his cell phone out of his jacket pocket, flipped it open and tapped in Christine's well-remembered number. He was already ten minutes late for their meeting.

"Christine," he said, "I've got to beg off . . . no, I'm not going to be home. I'm going to be in Orange County—"

Cheyenne mouthed *Overnight*.

"—overnight," Sydney went on, "till tomorrow. No, I . . . I'll explain it later, and I owe you a lunch. No, I haven't sold it yet! I gotta run, I'm in traffic and I can't drive and talk at the same time. Right, right—'bye!"

He folded it and tucked it back into his pocket.

Cheyenne nodded. "To avoid complications," she said.

Sydney had stepped back from her, but he was holding her hand—possibly to keep her from disappearing again. "My New Year's resolution," he said with a rueful smile, "was not to tell any lies."

"My attitude toward New Year's resolutions is the same as Oscar Wilde's," she said, stepping around the pool coping and swinging his hand.

"What did he say about them?" asked Sydney, falling into step beside her.

"I don't know if he ever said anything about them," she said, "but if he did, I'm sure I agree with it."

She looked back at him, then glanced past him and lost her smile.

"Don't turn around," she said quickly, so he just stared at her face, which seemed bony and starved between the wings of tangled red hair. "Now look around, but scan the whole square, like you're calculating if they could land the Goodyear blimp here."

Sydney let his gaze swivel from Hill Street, across the trees and broad pavement of the square, to the pillared arch of the Biltmore entrance. Up there toward the east end of the square he had seen a gray-haired woman in a loose blue dress; she seemed to be the same woman he had seen behind them on Hollywood Boulevard yesterday.

He let his eyes come back around to focus on Cheyenne's face.

"You saw that woman?" she said to him. "The one that looks like . . . some kind of featherless monkey? Stay away from her, she'll tell you lies about me."

Looking at the Biltmore entrance had reminded him that Christine might have parked in the Hill Street lot too. "Let's sit behind one of these balls," he said. And when they had walked down the steps and sat on the cement coping, leaning back against the receding under-curve of the nearest stone sphere, he said, "I found your book. I hope you don't mind that I know who you are."

She was still holding his hand, and now she squeezed it. "Who am I, lover?"

"You're Cheyenne Fleming. You—you're—"

"Yes. How did I die?"

He took a deep breath. "You killed yourself."

"I did? Why?"

"Because your sister—I read—ran off with your fiancé."

She closed her eyes and twined her fingers through his. "Urbane legends. Can I come over to your place tonight? I want to copy one of my poems in the book, write it out again in the blank space around the printed version, and I need you to hold my hand, guide my hand while I write it."

"Okay," he said. His heart was thudding in his chest. Inviting her over my threshold, he thought. "I'd like that," he added with dizzy bravado.

"I've got the pen to use," she went on. "It's my special pen, they buried me with it."

"Okay." Buried her with it, he thought. Buried her with it.

"I love you," she said, her eyes still closed. "Do you love me? Tell me you love me."

He was sitting down, but his head was spinning with vertigo as if an infinite black gulf yawned at his feet. This was her inviting *him* over *her* threshold.

"Under," he said in a shaky voice, "normal circumstances, I'd certainly be in love with you."

"Nobody falls in love under *normal* circumstances," she said softly, rubbing his finger with her warm thumb. He restrained an impulse to look to see if there was still ink on it. "Love isn't in the category of normal things. Not any worthwhile kind of love, anyway." She opened her eyes and waved her free hand behind them toward the square. "Normal people. I hate them."

"Me too," said Sydney.

"Actually," she said, looking down at their linked hands, "I didn't kill myself." She paused for so long that he was about to ask her what had happened, when she went on quietly, "My sister Rebecca shot me, and made it look like a suicide. After that she apparently *did* go away with my fiancé. But she killed me because she had made herself into an imitation of me, and without me in the picture, *she'd* be the original." Through her hand he felt her shiver. "I've been alone in the dark for a long time," she said in a small voice.

Sydney freed his hand so that he could put his arm around her narrow shoulders, and he kissed her hair.

Cheyenne looked up with a grin that made slits of her eyes. "But I don't think she's prospered! Doesn't she look *terrible*?"

Sydney resisted the impulse to look around again. "Was that—?"

Cheyenne frowned. "I've got to go—I can't stay here for very long at a time, not until we copy that poem."

She kissed him, and their mouths opened, and for a moment his tongue touched hers. When their lips parted their foreheads were pressed together, and he whispered, "Let's get that poem copied, then."

She smiled, deepening the lines in her cheeks, and looked down. "Sit back now and look away from me," she said. "And I'll come to your place tonight."

He pressed his palms against the surface of the cement coping and pushed himself away from her, and looked toward Hill Street.

After a moment, "Shy?" he said; and when he looked around she was gone. "I love you," he said to the empty air.

"Everybody did," came a raspy voice from behind and above him.

For a moment he went on staring at the place where Cheyenne had sat; then he sighed deeply and looked around.

The old woman in the blue dress was standing at the top of the stairs, and now began stepping carefully down them in boxy old-lady shoes.

Her eyes were pouchy above round cheeks and not much of a chin, and Sydney imagined she'd been cute decades ago.

"Are," he said in a voice he made himself keep level, "you Rebecca?"

She stopped in front of him and nodded, frowning in the sun-glare. "Rebecca Fleming," she said. "The cherished name." The diesel-scented breeze was blowing her white hair around her face, and she pushed it back with one frail, spotted hand. "Did she say I killed her?"

After a moment's hesitation, "Yes," Sydney said.

She sat down, far enough away from him that he didn't feel called on to move further away. Why hadn't he brought a flask?

"True," she said, exhaling as if she'd been holding her breath. "True, I did." She looked across at him, and he reluctantly met her eyes. They were green, just like Cheyenne's.

"I bet," she said, "you bought a book of hers, signed." She barked two syllables of a laugh. "And I bet she's still got her fountain pen. We buried it with her."

"I don't think you and I have much to say to each other," said Sydney stiffly. He started to get to his feet.

"It was self-defense, if you're curious," she said, not stirring.

He paused, bracing himself on his hands.

"She came to my bed," said Rebecca, "with a revolver. I woke up when she touched the cold muzzle to my forehead. This is thirty-seven years ago, but I remember it as if it were last night—we were in a crummy motel south of Santa Monica Boulevard, on one of her low-life tours. I sat up and pushed the gun away, but she kept trying to get it aimed at me—she was laughing, irritated, cajoling, I wasn't playing along properly—and when I pushed it back toward her it went off. Under her chin. I wrote a suicide note for her."

The old woman's face was stony. Sydney sat back down.

"I loved her," she said. "If I'd known that resisting her would end up killing her, I swear, I wouldn't have resisted." She smiled at him belligerently. "Crush an ant sometime, and then smell your fingers. I wonder what became of the clothes we buried her in. Not a sweatshirt and jeans."

"A black linen suit," said Sydney, "with a white blouse. They were damp."

"Well, groundwater, you know, even with a cement grave-liner. And a padded bra, for the photographs. I fixed it up myself, crying so hard I could barely see the stitches—I filled the lining with bird-seed to flesh her out."

Sydney recalled the vines that had seemed to be embroidered on Cheyenne's bra, that first day. "It sprouted."

Rebecca laughed softly. " 'Quickens, gladly grows.' She wants something from you." Rebecca fumbled in a pocket of her skirt. "Bring the moon to free her from these yellowed pages."

Sydney squinted at her. "You've read that version of the sonnet?"

Rebecca was now holding out a two-inch clear plastic cylinder with metal bands on it. "I was there when she wrote it. She read it to me when the ink was still wet. It was printed that way in only one copy of the book, the copy you obviously found, God help us all. This is one of her ink cartridges. You stick this end in the ink bottle and twist the other end—that retracts the plunger. When she was writing poetry she used to use about nine parts Schaeffer's black ink and one part her own blood."

She was still holding it toward him, so he took it from her.

"The signature in your book certainly contains some of her blood," Rebecca said.

"A signature and a thumbprint," said Sydney absently, rolling the narrow cylinder in his palm. He twisted the back end, and saw the tiny red ring of the plunger move smoothly up the inside of the clear barrel.

"And you touched the thumbprint."

"Yes. I'm glad I did."

"You brought her to this cycle of the moon. She arrived on the new moon, though you probably didn't find the book and touch her thumb till further on in the cycle; she'd instantly stain the whole twenty-eight days, I'm sure, backward and forward. Do you know yet what she wants you to do?"

If I'd known, Rebecca had said, *that resisting her would end up killing her, I swear, I wouldn't have resisted.* Sydney realized, to his dismay, that he believed her.

"Hold her hand, guide it, I guess, while she copies a poem," he said.

"*That* poem, I have no doubt. She's a ghost—I suppose she imagines that writing it again will project her spirit back to the night when she originally wrote it—so she can make a better attempt at killing me three years later, in 1969. She was thirty-five, in '69. I was thirty-three."

"She looks younger."

"She always did. See little Shy riding horseback, you'd think she was twelve years old." Rebecca sat back. "She's pretty physical, right? I mean, she can hold things, touch things?"

Sydney remembered Cheyenne's fingers intertwined with his.

"Yes."

"I'd think she could hold a pen. I wonder why she needs help copying the poem."

"I—" Sydney began.

But Rebecca interrupted him. "If you do it for her," she said, "and it works, she won't have died. I'll be the one that died in '69. She'll be seventy-two now, and you won't have met her. Well, she'll probably look you up, if she remembers to be grateful, but you won't remember any of . . . this interlude with her." She smiled wryly. "And you certainly won't meet me. That's a plus, I imagine. Do you have any high-proof liquor, at your house?"

"You can't come over!" said Sydney, appalled.

"No, I wasn't thinking of that. Never mind. But you might ask her—"

She had paused, and Sydney raised his eyebrows.

"You might ask her not to kill me, when she gets back there. I know I'd have left, moved out, if she had told me she really needed that. I'd have stopped . . . trying to *be* her. I only did it because I loved her." She smiled, and for a moment as she stood up Sydney could see that she must once have been very pretty.

"Goodbye, Resurrection Man," she said, and turned and shuffled away up the cement steps.

Sydney didn't call after her. After a moment he realized that he was still holding the plastic ink-cartridge, and he put it in his pocket.

High-proof liquor, he thought unhappily.

Back in his apartment after making a couple of purchases, he poured himself a shot of bourbon from the kitchen bottle and sat down by the window with the Fleming book.

> But when the Resurrection Man shall bring
> The moon to free me from these yellowed pages,
> The gift is mine, there won't be anything
> For you.

The moon had been full last night. Or maybe just a hair short of full, and it would be full tonight.

You might ask her not to kill me, when she gets back there.

He opened the bags he had carried home from a liquor store and a stationer's, and he pulled the ink cartridge out of his pocket.

One bag contained a squat glass bottle of Schaeffer's black ink, and he unscrewed the lid; there was a little pool of ink in the well on the inside of the open bottle's rim, and he stuck the end of the cartridge into the ink and twisted the back. The plunger retracted, and the barrel ahead of it was black.

When it was a third filled, he stopped, and he opened the other bag. It contained a tiny plastic 50-milliliter bottle—what he thought of as breakfast-sized—of Bacardi 151-proof rum. He twisted off the cap and stuck the cartridge into the vapory liquor. He twisted the end of the cartridge until it stopped, filled, and even though the cylinder now contained two-thirds rum, it was still jet-black.

He had considered buying lighter-fluid, but decided that the 151-proof rum—seventy-five percent alcohol—would probably be more flammable. And he could drink what he didn't use.

He was dozing in the chair when he heard someone moving in the kitchen. He sat up, disoriented, and hoarsely called, "Who's there?"

He lurched to his feet, catching the book but missing the tiny empty rum bottle.

"Who were you expecting, lover?" came Cheyenne's husky voice. "Should I have knocked? You already invited me."

He stumbled across the dim living room into the kitchen. The overhead light was on in there, and through the little kitchen window he saw that it was dark outside.

Cheyenne was sweeping the last of the ants off the counter with her hand, and as he watched she rubbed them vigorously between her palms and wiped her open hands along her jaw and neck, then picked up the half-full bourbon bottle.

She was wearing the black linen skirt and jacket again—and, he could see, the birdseed-sprouting bra under the white blouse. The clothes were somehow still damp.

"I talked to Rebecca," he blurted, thinking about the ink cartridge in his pocket.

"I told you not to," she said absently. "Where do you keep glasses? Or do you expect me to drink right out of the bottle? Did she say she killed me in self-defense?"

"Yes."

"Glasses?"

He stepped past her and opened a cupboard and handed her an Old-Fashioned glass. "Yes," he said again.

She smiled up at him from beneath her dark eyelashes as she poured a couple of ounces of amber liquor into the glass, then put down the bottle and caressed his cheek. The fruit-and-spice smell of crushed ants was strong.

"It was my fault!" she said, laughing as she spoke. "I shouldn't have touched her with the barrel! And so it was little Shy that wound up getting killed, *miserabile dictu*! I was . . . *nonplussed* in eternity." She took a deep sip of the bourbon and then sang, " 'Take my hand, I'm nonplussed in eternity . . . ' "

He wasn't smiling, so she pushed out her thin red lips. "Oh, lover, don't pout. Am I my sister's keeper? Did you know she claimed I got my best poems by stealing her ideas? As if anybody couldn't tell from reading *her* poetry which of us was the original! At least I had already got that copy of my book out there, out in the world, like a message in a bottle, a soul in a bottle, for you to eventually—"

Sydney had held up his hand, and she stopped. "She said to tell you . . . not to kill her. She said she'd just move out if you asked her to. If she knew it was important to you."

She shrugged. "Maybe."

He frowned and took a breath, but she spoke again before he could.

"Are you still going to help me copy out my poem? I can't write it by myself, because the first word of it is the name of the person who killed me."

Her eyes were wide and her eyebrows were raised as she looked down at the book in his hand and then back up at him.

"I'd do it for you," she added softly, "because I love you. Do you love me?"

She couldn't be taller than five-foot one-inch, and with her long neck and thin arms, and her big eyes under the disordered hair, she looked young and frail.

"Yes," he said. I do, he thought. And I'm going to exorcise you. I'm going to spread that flammable ink-and-rum mix over the page and then touch it with a cigarette.

It was printed that way in only one copy of the book, Rebecca had said, *the copy you obviously found, God help us all.* A soul in a bottle.

There won't be another Resurrection Man.

He made himself smile. "You've got a pen, you said."

She reached thin fingers into the neck of her blouse and pulled out a long, tapering black pen. She shook it to dislodge a thin white tendril with a tiny green leaf on it.

"May I?" he asked, holding out his hand.

She hesitated, then laid the pen in his palm.

He handed her the book, then pulled off the pen's cap, exposing the gleaming, wedge-shaped nib. "Do you need to dip it in an ink bottle?" he asked.

"No, it's got a cartridge in it. Unscrew the end."

He twisted the barrel and the nib-end rotated away from the pen, and after a few more turns it came loose in his hand, exposing a duplicate of the ink cartridge he had in his pocket.

"Pull the cartridge off," she said suddenly, "and lick the end of it. Didn't she tell you about my ink?"

"No," he said, his voice unsteady. "Tell me about your ink."

"Well, it's got a little bit of my blood in it, though it's mostly ink." She was flipping through the pages of the book. "But some blood. Lick it, the punctured end of the cartridge." She looked up at him and grinned. "As a chaser for the rum I smell on your breath."

For ten seconds he stared into her deep green eyes, then he raised the cartridge and ran his tongue across the end of it. He didn't taste anything.

"That's my dear man," she said, taking his hand and stepping onto the living room carpet. "Let's sit in that chair you were napping in."

As they crossed the living room, Sydney slid his free hand into his pocket and clasped the rum-and-ink cartridge next to the blood-and-ink one. The one he had prepared this afternoon was up by his knuckles, the other at the base of his palm.

She let go of his hand to reach out and switch on the lamp, and Sydney pulled a pack of Camels out of his shirt pocket and shook one free.

"Sit down," she said, "I'll sit in your lap. I hardly weigh anything. Are there limits to what you'd do for someone you love?"

Sydney hooked a cigarette onto his lip and tossed the pack aside. "Limits?" he said as he sat down and clicked a lighter at the end of the cigarette. "I don't know," he said around a puff of smoke.

"I think you're not one of those normal people," she said.

"I hate 'em." He laid his cigarette in the smoking stand beside the chair.

"Me too," she said, and she slid onto his lap and curled her left arm around his shoulders. Her skirt and sleeve were damp, but not cold.

With her right hand she opened the book to the sonnet "To My Sister."

"Lots of margin space for us to write in," she said.

Her hot cheek was touching his, and when he turned to look at her he found that he was kissing her, gently at first and then passionately, for this moment not caring that her scent was the smell of crushed ants.

"Put the cartridge," she whispered into his mouth, "back into the pen and screw it closed."

He carefully fitted one of the cartridges into the pen and whirled the base until it was tight.

George Sydney stood up from crouching beside the shelf of cookbooks, holding a copy of James Beard's *On Food*. It was his favorite of Beard's books, and if he couldn't sell it at a profit he'd happily keep it.

He hadn't found any other likely books here today, and now it was nearly noon and time to walk across the boulevard to Boardner's for a couple of quick drinks.

"There he is," said the man behind the counter and the cash register. "George, this lady has been coming in every day for the last week, looking for you."

Sydney blinked toward the brightly sunlit store windows, and in front of the counter he saw the silhouette of a short elderly woman with a halo of back-lit white hair.

He smiled and shuffled forward. "Well, hi," he said.

"Hello, George," she said in a husky voice, holding out her hand.

He stepped across the remaining distance and shook her hand. "What—" he began.

"I was just on my way to the Chinese Theater," she said. She was smiling up at him almost sadly, and though her face was deeply etched with wrinkles, her green eyes were lively and young. "I'm going to lay three pennies in the indentations in Gregory Peck's square."

He laughed in surprise. "I do that with Jean Harlow!"

"That's where I got the idea." She leaned forward and tipped her face up and kissed him briefly on the lips, and he dropped the James Beard book.

He crouched to retrieve the book, and when he straightened up she had already stepped out the door. He saw her walking away west down Hollywood Boulevard, her white hair fluttering around her head in the wind.

The man behind the counter was middle-aged, with a graying moustache. "Do you know who your admirer is, George?" he asked with a kinked smile.

Sydney had taken a step toward the door, but some misgiving made him stop. He exhaled to clear his head of a sharp sweet, musty scent.

"Uh," he said distractedly, "no. Who is she?"

"That was Cheyenne Fleming. I got her to sign some copies of her books the other day, so I can double the prices."

"I thought she was dead by now." Sydney tried to remember what he'd read about Fleming. "When was it she got paroled?"

"I don't know. In the '80s? Some time after the death penalty was repealed in the '70s, anyway." He waved at a stack of half a dozen slim dark books on the desk behind him. "You want one of the signed ones? I'll let you have it for the original price, since she only came in here looking for you."

Sydney looked at the stack.

"Nah," he said, pushing the James Beard across the counter. "Just this."

A few moments later he was outside on the brass-starred sidewalk, squinting after Cheyenne Fleming. He could see her, a hundred feet away to the west now, striding away.

He rubbed his face, trying to get rid of the odd scent. And as he walked away, east, he wondered why that kiss should have left him feeling dirty, as if it had been a mortal sin for which he couldn't now phrase the need for absolution.

• • • •

She'd lived with the watcher for over two months, felt it in every room, felt its strength increase from hour to hour as the day waned. Whatever her rational mind said, she was afraid.

The Watcher in the Corners
Sarah Monette

Lilah Collier was washing the windows the first time the sheriff showed up.

It was April 9, 1930, a beautiful sunny Saturday in Hyperion, Mississippi, and Lilah was taking advantage of the weather. She had been the Starks' housekeeper for four months, ever since she and her husband Butch came into town, and since Butch drank more of his paycheck than he brought home, she was hanging onto this job like grim death, even if she didn't much like Cranmer Stark *or* his pale, nervous wife Sidonia. So she cooked for their fancy dinner parties and kept their house spotless, and if Mrs. Stark didn't want the help talking to her little boy, then all right the help would keep her goddamned mouth shut. She felt sorry for Jonathan, a pale, silent child who always did as he was told, but not sorry enough to risk her job.

She was in the guest bedroom when the doorbell rang, and came panting down the stairs, only to pull up short when she recognized a lawman's silhouette against the frosted glass. She wiped the sweat off her face, made a futile attempt at smoothing down her hair, braced herself for whatever disaster Butch had caused this time. Opened the door.

And the sheriff, a stocky, tired man with watchful blue eyes, said, "Mrs. Collier, I hate to trouble you, but is Jonathan in the house?"

"Jonathan? No, sir, he's out with his mama."

"You seen him today?"

"No, sir. Mrs. Stark, she left me a note. They was gone when I got here. What's the matter?"

"Mrs. Collier, may I come in?"

She stood aside, her heart banging against her ribs, and when he hesitated in the front hall, led him back to the kitchen.

He sat down when she did, sighed, and said, "Mrs. Collier, it seems like Jonathan Stark has gone missing."

"Missing?"

"Straight out of the middle of Humphreys Park, from what his mama says. Now, we got men searching, but we're also trying to figure out what might make him run off. If he *did* run off. So, when did you see him last?"

Lilah told the sheriff what she knew. She'd given Jonathan his dinner early the night before, since his parents were having company: tomato soup and a cheese sandwich in his room. An hour and a half later, when there was enough of a lull in the dinner preparations, she'd gone up to get the tray. He'd been sitting upright in bed with the lamp on. She'd said good night to him, and he'd said good night back, being a polite child, and she'd gone out, and that had been that. No, she hadn't seen him at all on Saturday. Saturdays were her half days, and she hadn't come in until noon, when Mrs. Stark and Jonathan had already left.

"You sure of that, Mrs. Collier?"

"Sure of which?"

"That you didn't see him today."

"I done told you twice, they were already gone when I got here."

"And what were you doing this morning?"

"My own cleaning. Do I need an alibi, sheriff?"

"Not 'cause I suspect you, Mrs. Collier, just so as I don't have to start."

"My husband was home. We left the house together—matter of fact, he drove me here."

"Anybody else see you?"

"I was washing windows, so you might ask the neighbors. And Maddie Hopper can probably tell you I arrived when I said I did."

"She already has."

"Said you didn't suspect me, sheriff."

He put his pencil down and rubbed his eyes. He looked like a man who didn't get enough sleep. "So far, Mrs. Collier, there ain't nothing to suspect nobody of. But little boys don't just vanish into thin air, and they don't have that generous variety of enemies that adults might do. We're asking these questions of any adult that knows Jonathan Stark, for the pure and simple reason that we ain't got nowhere else to start."

"His daddy's a powerful man," Lilah observed.

"Don't I know it. And, yes, I think it's a kidnapping, and, yes, I think we're gonna be hearing from somebody here in another hour or so saying what it is they want. But it bugs the shit out of me, begging your pardon, that they could grab him in broad daylight in the middle of Humphreys Park and not have nobody the wiser. So I'm covering all my bases." He looked her squarely in the eyes then. "Do you know anything that might help us?"

"Like what?"

"Damned if I know. Like anything that might explain where he went or why somebody took him or *anything*."

"I don't know nothing to explain that, sheriff. I'd tell you if I did."

"I hope you would, Mrs. Collier. I sincerely do. Thank you for your time."

He left her sitting there in her clean kitchen, gooseflesh crawling up and down her back.

No communications from kidnappers were received, not in the next hour, not in the next two weeks. No one was found who seemed to have any motive for harming Jonathan Stark; even his father's enemies were equipped one and all with unassailable alibis. No one was found who had seen him after his mother's last sighting of him at 12:30 p.m. in Humphreys Park. The park, which was not large, was searched with a fine-toothed comb, and the pond was dragged. No evidence of Jonathan Stark was discovered, although a remarkable assortment of other things came to light. As far as anybody could tell, Jonathan Stark *had* vanished into thin air.

Sidonia Stark took to her bed; Cranmer Stark took to drink. Lilah Collier took to cleaning the Stark house with a passion that surprised her. She had instructions to do nothing to Jonathan Stark's room—not even to dust—and she obeyed, but the rest of the house became antiseptically spotless.

She began to have the feeling, alone on the first floor of the Stark house, that she was being watched. She told herself she was being stupid and high-strung (her father's phrase for such airs was "being missish," and it was a good way to get a casual clout across the back of the head), but every day she talked herself out of it, and the next day by noon the feeling would be back again. Something watching, something small and white. She'd find herself glancing around, as if she could catch it in a corner, but she never saw anything, never anything that wasn't the curtains or a lace doily or her own dust rag left on a side-table. She sometimes got a feeling, towards dark, that there was something cloudy in her peripheral vision—sometimes on the left, sometimes on the right—but it was never something she was sure of. "Missish," she grumbled to herself, and was glad to leave the house for the dubious security of Butch's car.

And then, in the middle of June, the sheriff showed up again. Cranmer Stark had driven Sidonia to Memphis to consult a nerve-specialist; taking advantage of their absence—and desperate for something to keep herself occupied against the watchfulness filling the house—Lilah was washing the curtains, and she had to rinse soap suds off her hands before she could answer the door.

"Mrs. Collier," the sheriff said.

Lilah only realized after she'd done it that she'd glanced at the height of the sun in the sky, only realized it as she was thinking, We got another two hours before it really gets bad. "Sheriff Patterson," she said, controlling the impulse to weep with gratitude at the sight of another human face, the sound of another human voice. "They ai—Mr. and Mrs. Stark aren't home."

"I know that. I don't want to talk to them. May I come in?"

Oh, thank God, Lilah thought. Even being arrested for murder would be better than being alone in the Stark house any longer. "Come on back to the kitchen. You want some coffee?"

"You're a good woman, Mrs. Collier. I'd love some."

So Lilah made coffee, and the sheriff sat at the kitchen table, looking at the clean counters and the sultanas on the windowsill.

"What can I do for you, sheriff?" Lilah said when she'd given him the coffee and sat down herself.

"I ain't suspecting you, Mrs. Collier," he said, "but I want to ask you again about April eighth."

"You can ask, sheriff, but I can't give you no new answers."

"I just want to hear it again." He sipped the coffee. His eyebrows went up appreciatively, and he said, "I do wish you'd give lessons to my wife. Now. April eighth."

"There was a dinner party."

"Who?"

"High society folks," Lilah said and shrugged. "Three married couples, and a couple men on their own, and Mrs. Stark's cousin Renee from Oxford, and the lady who owns the gravel pit."

"Miss Baldwin, then. So what happened?"

"I did dinner. Or-derves and soup and salad and beef burgundy and a chocolate mousse. The party seemed pretty happy. Nobody fighting or nothing."

"When'd you leave?"

Lilah thought back. "Everybody was gone by ten, and I was doing the washing up—I can't abide to leave it overnight—when Mr. Stark comes in and says, 'You had a long day, Lilah. Why don't I run you home?'"

"Did he? Had he ever done that before?"

"No, sir."

"Done it since?"

"No, sir."

"Could you tell me about what time that was?"

"'Levenish, I'd guess. I'd got all the big stuff done, and I was just as happy not to have to walk. So I said, 'Them plates'll keep,' and he drove me home. Sheriff, what is it you're after?"

"Now, just bear with me. Tell me again when the last time you saw Jonathan Stark was?"

"I took up his dinner at five, I guess. His mama was in with him, showing him her pretty dress and letting him smell her perfume. So I put the tray on that big deal table they got in his room and went back down. Then, I guess it was six-thirty or so, I'd got the soup simmering and the beef in the oven, and the mousse to chill in the ice-box, and there wasn't nothing more I could do for another fifteen minutes at least, so I went back up for the tray."

"And he was there."

"Yes, sir. And alive. He was sitting up in bed and hanging on to that ratty toy bunny that drove Mr. Stark so wild."

"Did he say anything?"

"His mama was on him pretty sharp about not talking to me or Mr. Wilmot who comes about the lawns and such. He did say good night, but I think that was it."

"Are you sure?"

"Why? I mean . . . "

"Excepting his mama, you seem to be the last person who saw or spoke to Jonathan Stark. And, forgive me for saying it—and please don't repeat it—we ain't getting no manner of help out of his mama at all."

"She's a pretty nervous lady."

"She says she can't remember nothing about that Saturday morning. Not what he was wearing, not what they said to each other—and I *can't* believe that a boy and his mama could walk to Humphreys Park without a single word being passed between them."

"D'you think she's lying?"

"I don't know. Like you say, she's a nervous lady. But she ain't helping. And, Mrs. Collier, I got to say, I don't think this *is* a kidnapping."

"You think he's dead." Lilah's hands were ice-cold, and she was thinking of that feeling in the house, that feeling of being watched that got worse as the day darkened.

"I'm *afraid* he's dead. Did he say anything to you? Anything at all, even if it don't seem important." He held a hand up. "I know if it'd seemed important, you would've told me at the time. But *anything*."

"God, sheriff, let me think." Lilah forced her mind off the emptiness of the house and back to that Friday night. "I was in a hurry, and I wasn't paying much heed to Mr. Jonathan. Sometimes kids say things, you know, and you answer 'em, but you ain't rightly listening?"

"Yeah," the sheriff said heavily. "I know."

"I could smack myself for it now. But we both knew he wasn't supposed to talk to me, and he was a quiet little boy anyways. Never said much at all."

"Mrs. Collier—"

"I'm trying. Lemme think. I came in and said, 'You done, Mr. Jonathan?' And he said, 'Yes, Mrs. Collier.' The tray was on the table where I'd left it. He was in bed, with his rabbit."

"What was he wearing?"

"His pajamas, I think. Blue striped." She shut her eyes, to remember better. "I went over to pick up the tray . . . and he *did* say something. Christ Jesus, I can hear his voice in my mind, but I can't remember the words."

"Was it about the party? About his parents?"

"It was about his mama looking so pretty," Lilah said and opened her eyes. "That's what he said. He said, 'My mama's the prettiest lady in town.' "

She took a deep breath. "I said, 'Yes, Mr. Jonathan,' because, well, I wasn't giving her no competition. And he said, 'Do you think Daddy thinks so?' And I said, 'I'm sure he does, Mr. Jonathan.' And then I said good night and he said good night, and I went out the door. I'm sorry, sheriff. That don't help you much."

The sheriff said, "And you never saw him again?"

"No, sir, like I said. Saturdays I don't come in 'til noon, and they were already gone."

"Would Mrs. Stark have gotten the boy his lunch?"

"Lunch?" Lilah said blankly.

"You do the cooking, don't you, Mrs. Collier?"

"Well, yes, sir. 'Cept Saturday morning, but I think Mr. Stark mostly takes 'em out to the Magnolia Tree."

"Magnolia Tree," the sheriff said, making a note. "And for Saturday lunch?"

"Well, I do that. Baked eggs at one o'clock, regular as clockwork. That's how Mr. Stark is."

"Did they go out to the Magnolia Tree on the ninth?"

"I don't know, sheriff."

"Where was Mr. Stark that Saturday? Do you know?"

Lilah could feel her eyes widening, and her mouth was dry as cotton. "I don't know, sheriff. Cross my heart and hope to die, I don't got no idea."

"Thank you, Mrs. Collier. I got one other question, and you can say no, and that's just fine."

"What is it?"

"I'd like to see Jonathan's room. I don't got a warrant, and you're within your rights to refuse."

"This ain't my house. I can't tell you what you can and can't do. But ain't it illegal for you to go wandering around without Mr. Stark says it's okay?"

"Mr. Stark says he don't want his wife bothered, and he says since Jonathan was kidnapped out of Humphreys Park, there ain't no point in me mucking up his boy's room. Mr. Stark ain't gonna say it's okay until sometime after Hell freezes over. But I'd dearly like to look."

Although raised to distrust and dislike the police, Lilah Collier had been alone or almost alone in that house for over two months, and she was quick enough to see where the trend of the sheriff's questions was leading. She said, "Okay, but if he finds out, I was at the grocery store and you just walked in."

"That's fine, Mrs. Collier. You don't have to come with me."

"I think we might both be happier if I did. This way, sheriff."

They climbed the stairs together. The sheriff said, "Mrs. Collier, are you the only help the Starks have?"

"Me and Mr. Wilmot, who comes on Tuesdays to do the lawns and the flowerbeds. Why?"

"No reason." But he was looking around uneasily. "There ain't nobody else home?"

"No, sir." And she couldn't help asking, "Do you feel it, too? Like you're being watched?"

The look he gave her was answer enough.

"It gets worse toward evening," she said, almost babbling with relief. "And it's been *terrible* today, I think 'cause there's nobody else home. I ain't dared ask Mrs. Stark if she feels it, and . . . and I ain't dared ask Mr. Stark neither." They were at Jonathan's door, and she stopped with her hand on the knob.

"Has the house always been like this?" the sheriff asked. "'Cause you're right. I can feel it."

"Just since . . . since after he disappeared."

Lilah opened the door.

It was the first time she'd been in the room since the eighth of April. Dust was everywhere, and the room smelled musty and unpleasant. There was a tang to the air, so faint that Lilah almost thought it was her imagination, the smell of something rotting. The sensation of being watched was heavy and cold, like water deep enough to drown in. Lilah and the sheriff both glanced over their shoulders, and neither advanced so much as a step into the room.

"Did the boy always leave his room this neat?" the sheriff asked.

Lilah looked around carefully, looked twice at the bed. "He was tidy-minded, for a child so young. But he couldn't manage the sheets like that. He'd do his best, but the bed was always rumpled a little, even if it was just that you could see where his knees had been when he was getting the top straight."

The sheriff grunted. His eyes traveled around the room again. He said, "Mrs. Collier, you mentioned a toy rabbit. I don't see it."

"Ain't it on the bed? That's where he kept it." But she looked for herself, and the dingy, ragged bunny was nowhere to be seen.

"He wouldn't have taken it with him?"

She shook her head. "That bunny drove Mr. Stark wild. He couldn't stand it that a son of his would be carrying it around. Jonathan wasn't allowed to take it out of his bedroom, and he did what his daddy said. Always."

"Could it've fallen off the bed?"

They looked at each other. Lilah saw her own feelings mirrored in his face; he didn't want to go into that room either. She supposed it should have made her feel better—less missish—to know that a middle-aged sheriff had the creeping, crawling horrors the same way she did, but it didn't. It made her feel ten times worse.

Finally, she said, her tongue dry and dusty in her mouth, "I'll look."

She walked into the room slowly, her heart thudding wretchedly in her chest. The sheriff stood in the doorway. Step by step, she walked around the bed, to the side not visible from the door. "Nothing," she croaked.

"Jesus," the sheriff said and armed sweat off his forehead. "Mrs. Collier, I hate to say it, but will you check under the bed?"

"I think you oughta swear me in as a deputy first," she said, and they both yelped with laughter. Then Lilah, knowing she would have had to, even if the sheriff had said nothing, slowly bent and lifted the counterpane. She straightened up again in a hurry, all but gasping for breath. "Nothing," she said. "Just dust. It ain't here."

"Christ on a crutch," the sheriff said. "You come on out of there, Mrs. Collier. I ain't doing no more without I got a warrant."

"Yes, sir," Lilah said and left the room, gratefully and fast.

They went back down to the kitchen. The sheriff said abruptly, "How old are you?"

"Sixteen," Lilah said. She was past the point where she could lie to Sheriff Patterson. He'd felt the wrongness in Jonathan's room.

"Christ. I ain't leaving you here by yourself. This house ain't no place to be alone in. You write a note—tell 'em you took sick or something. I'll drive you home."

"And it ain't so far off the truth, neither," Lilah said, finding the pad of paper she used for shopping lists. "Sheriff, what do you reckon happened? What's the *matter* with this house?"

"That's a question for a preacher," the sheriff said. "But you want the honest truth, I reckon Jonathan Stark never left this house, and I further reckon he was dead a long time before Saturday noon."

"Me, too," she said, shivering.

Lilah left her note ("SORRY MRS. STARK. FEELIN BAD. GONE HOME. COME IN ALL DAY SATERDAY. L COLLIER"), and climbed into the front seat of the sheriff's car. "Never thought I'd be glad to be riding in one of these," she said, and he laughed.

"Where'm I taking you?"

Suddenly, Lilah could bear the thought of her own empty house no better than she could bear the Starks'. "Take me up to the pit office, if you'd be so kind. I'll just meet my husband."

"You're sure?" he said, giving her a sideways look.

"I can talk to Emmajean 'til he's done."

"Okay," the sheriff said, and she knew he understood.

He didn't leave her at the gate, as she'd expected, but drove up to let her out directly opposite the office door. She stopped halfway out of the car and said, "Sheriff, you got somebody you can go talk to or something? Or you can come in and Emmajean'll give you coffee. Ain't as good as mine."

He smiled. "Thanks, Mrs. Collier, but I got to go down to the station and figure out how I'm going to persuade any judge in this county to give me a warrant to take a look at Cranmer Stark's house. There's plenty of people around, though, don't you worry."

"All right. Thanks, Sheriff."

"Thank *you*, Mrs. Collier. You been a world of help." She got out, closed the door. He drove away. Lilah went in to talk to Emmajean, although later she could not remember one word Emmajean had said. She kept hearing Jonathan Stark, the words she hadn't heeded at the time, but that now wouldn't leave her alone. *My mama's the prettiest lady in town. Do you think my daddy thinks so?*

Butch's shift ended at six; Emmajean had passed the word that Butch Collier's wife was waiting for him, but it was six-thirty when Butch came sauntering into the office like he owned the world. "What's happening, Lil?"

Lilah hated it when Butch called her "Lil," just as she hated the way he would make her wait for him, purely because he could. Today, she didn't care, almost nauseated with gratitude only from knowing that she wouldn't have to be alone all night.

"Nothing much, Butch," she said. "Let's go home."

"Sure thing. Stay pretty, Emmajean."

"You, too, Butch," Emmajean said sweetly. Lilah bit the inside of her lower lip hard, and did not laugh. Butch almost never noticed jokes at his expense unless someone laughed at them.

In the car, heading out the gravel drive, Lilah made her mistake. When Butch asked, "What's the matter, Lil? Why'd you leave work?" she didn't answer, I came over funny, or even, There was nobody home and I got spooked. She told him the truth.

She told him because it was killing her to keep it all pent inside, not thinking about its effect on him. She had forgotten Butch's desire to see himself as a hero, a character out of the pulp magazines he read in the same habitual, thoughtless way he cracked his knuckles. He said, "Lilah! Are you serious?"

"What d'you mean?" she said, belatedly wary.

"Do you really think Mr. Stark killed his little boy and buried him in the cellar?"

" 'Course not," Lilah said. "Don't be silly." But, of course, it was what she thought, she and Sheriff Patterson both, and she couldn't entirely keep that out of her voice.

"They ain't back yet, are they? You said they was going to Memphis today."

"Butch, what are you thinking?"

He swung the Model T in a wide, looping turn. "You got a key, don't you? We can go look!"

"You're crazy!"

"Sheriff Patterson'll be grateful. Maybe he'll make me a deputy or something."

"Butch, we can't break into their house!"

"We ain't. You forgot your purse. And if the basement door ain't latched right, that ain't *our* fault."

"Butch, please!"

But Butch was more pig-headed than a pig, and Lilah knew from experience that no argument of hers would make him change his mind. She could only hope, noticing uneasily that the last of the sun was disappearing below the horizon, that the atmosphere of the house would do the job. And she hoped it would do it quickly.

Butch, however, noticed nothing spooky about the house at all. Lilah felt it the instant she opened the back door, moving out at them like a wall of ice; Butch walked in like it was his own house. "Nice things," he said, then looked back. But he was looking for Lilah, not for the watcher in the corners. "You coming?"

She wanted to say no. No, Butch, thanks, think I'll wait in the car. But she knew if he figured out she was too scared to come in, she would never hear the end of it, and Butch would never again pay the slightest attention to anything she said. And that would last a lot longer than the ten minutes it would take for Butch to look at the cellar and get bored. "Coming," she said, amazed at how clear and normal her voice sounded. She walked into the house.

The cellar door was in the back hall, under the stairs, a place (Lilah now realized) that she had been avoiding, completely unconsciously, for weeks. The house was full of twilight around them, and the thing in Lilah's peripheral vision was more than a cloud. When she turned her head, it wasn't entirely gone, although that might just have been the shadows.

"Butch," she said, and now her voice was trembling. "I really don't think this is a good idea."

"Don't be such a scaredy-cat. This the door?"

Before she could say yes, no, or maybe, he'd opened it. That smell of rotting that she had noticed in Jonathan's room was here as well, and, though still faint, it was distinctly stronger.

"*Something's* down there," Butch said with satisfaction. "They got lights?"

"Yeah, there's a bulb," Lilah said, "but, Butch, don't—"

Butch found the cord, yanked it. For Lilah, the light made everything worse. It was harder than the dark, uglier, and anything it showed her would be true beyond any possible hope of redemption. Butch, oblivious, started down the stairs. It was the last thing in the world she wanted to do, but Lilah moved into the doorway to watch his progress.

"It sure does stink," Butch called up. "I think he's really down here, Lilah. I ain't kidding."

Oh, I believe you, Butch, she thought. That cloudy thing that she couldn't quite see was down at the foot of the stairs now. She said, "Butch, come on up and we'll call Sheriff Patterson. I don't think he needs a warrant if we call him in."

"Just wait a minute, Lilah. It'll be better if I can find him first."

"Come on, Butch." Without wanting to, she started down the stairs, as slowly as she had walked across the floor in Jonathan's room. She did not love Butch Collier—didn't even like him much—but she knew her duty toward him, and her duty right now said she had to get him out of the cellar before something horrible happened. "Let's just go call the sheriff, huh?"

"My Christ, Lilah, what're you scared of? The boogeyman?"

"'Course not," Lilah said. Butch and that cloudy shape, small and white, were converging on the same patch of floor. "But I don't think it's safe. The Starks come back and find us in their cellar . . . *we* might disappear next, Butch. I ain't kidding."

Butch knelt, putting his face on a level with that small, white, cloudy presence; Lilah reached the bottom of the stairs and froze there. She told herself she was being silly, that Jonathan Stark had been a meek, mild, sweet-tempered little boy, and that even if his spirit was vengeful, those who had not killed him should have nothing to fear. But she'd lived with that watcher for over two months, felt it in every room, felt its strength increase from hour to hour as the day waned. Whatever her rational mind said, she was afraid. She clutched the banister, licked her lips, said, "Butch—?"

Butch said, "Holy Christ, he's right here!" She saw the dirt swept aside by his broad, grimy hand, saw, unmistakably, the shapes of small fingers being uncovered.

Then, several things happened at once; Lilah was never able, no matter how carefully she thought them through, to put the pieces together in order. She knew that the front door slammed open; she knew that Butch, looking up, seemed finally to see the small, white watcher. She did not know what he saw—she never, first to last, saw the watcher's face—but she saw Butch's face change, saw his death before he could have fully known it was on him.

Butch Collier screamed.

Lilah, watching helplessly, sagged sideways off the stairs, ending up on her knees, still clutching the banister as if it could save her. She heard footsteps along the hall, heard Cranmer Stark say, "Go *upstairs*, Sidonia! I'll deal with it." Then he appeared in the doorway.

"*What the hell is going on here?*" he demanded, in a roar like that of a beast, set his foot on the first step, and started down.

At the same moment that Lilah realized the white, watching presence was no longer beside Butch, she saw it, as clearly as she ever did, on the cellar stairs just below Cranmer Stark. Its back was to her, but she saw its child shape, saw the tilt of its head. It was looking at Cranmer Stark.

She didn't think he saw it fully. He saw *something*; he shouted wordlessly, tried (she thought) to dodge it, and pitched headfirst down the stairs. She was close enough to hear the crack when his neck broke.

Lilah, who only realized later that she was screaming, flung herself up the basement stairs, slammed and bolted the door behind her, and half-scrambled, half-fell into the kitchen to call Sheriff Patterson.

When they unearthed Jonathan Stark's body, they found his toy bunny clutched under one arm.

Lilah WAS in Sheriff Patterson's car again. He'd taken her statement, tried to talk to the hysterically weeping Sidonia Stark, got his deputies started on the basement. Then he'd come back to the kitchen and said, "Mrs. Collier, would you care to come with me?"

"Am I under arrest?" she asked when he opened the door for her.

"Nope." He got in the car, started it, said, "I believe you. I busted up enough fights with Butch Collier somewhere near the middle to know what he was like. And I was in that house today. I believe it happened just like you said." He turned left at the end of the Starks' street, away from the middle of town. "But, and I hate to say this, there's a bunch of folks in Hyperion who ain't gonna see it like I do. They're gonna see one woman and two men in a cellar, and only the woman comes out, and they're gonna say, we don't know nothing about who put that little boy down there, but we know what two men end up dead over when there's a woman in the room. They're gonna like it better than the truth. Now, those folks can't make me arrest you, but I can't keep them from lynching you, neither. You understand?"

"Oh, yeah," said Lilah. "I hear you, sheriff."

"So I was thinking—I got your testimony, and I think when Sidonia calms down some, she maybe is gonna tell us the truth. And the man who needed prosecuting is dead, besides. So if you was to just . . . vanish, people could think what they liked and nobody'd get hurt. And I can't believe you'll be sorry to see the last of this town."

"I'll be grateful," Lilah said. "I mean, it's a nice town and all, but . . . "

"I know," he said as they passed the city limits sign. "You'd always be thinking about whether you had to go past the Stark house on your way home."

"Yeah."

They drove in silence for a long time. He said at last, "Near as I can make Sidonia out, Cranmer was carrying on with Miss Baldwin. She says she knew it and didn't care, and whether that's true or not, I don't know. But the way I figure it, the little boy got out of bed and saw something he shouldn't've—or said something he shouldn't've, maybe—and his daddy . . . "

"Made him be quiet," Lilah said. "That's about all I ever heard the man say to the little boy. 'Be quiet.' "

"He might not've meant to," the sheriff offered after a cold moment.

"Maybe. But he still must've meant to hurt him."

"So," said the sheriff. "I hear you, Mrs. Collier. And the rest of it, he planned out like a snake. Buried the little boy in the basement, worked up that lie for his wife to tell, bullied her into telling it—I can tell you one thing, Sidonia was scared clean out of her mind by her husband. And it was a good lie. There wasn't nothing we could check, nothing to say it wasn't true. They didn't go to the Magnolia Tree—I got that nailed down this afternoon—but that ain't a crime, just like it ain't a crime for a woman to use her own kitchen or a man to go in and work on a Saturday morning. That's where he was. In his office, and the secretary he dragged in with him to testify to his whereabouts. He had it all worked out."

"Yeah." Lilah thought of Cranmer Stark on the cellar stairs, thought of the thing he maybe hadn't seen—but maybe had. She said, "If I was you, I'd tell Mrs. Stark to sell that house. Or burn it, maybe. If it was mine, I'd burn it."

"Me, too. Sidonia claimed she hadn't noticed anything funny . . . but she was looking over her shoulder the whole time. I was, too."

"I don't think it can hurt people 'cept in the cellar, and maybe only after dark. I mean, it had two months to get me or Mrs. Stark—or Mr. Stark—and it didn't." She shivered. "But it wanted to."

"I never saw the boy but twice. Was he . . . was he a mean little boy?"

"No. That's the worst thing. He wasn't mean at all." She gulped, feeling her eyes start to prickle with tears. "He just wanted his daddy to love him. And his daddy didn't love him, and his mama didn't love him, and I didn't love him, neither. Didn't nobody love him, and maybe that's enough to make anybody mad." She got a handkerchief out of her purse and cried. Sheriff Patterson drove and didn't say anything.

Finally, calm again, Lilah said, "Where're you taking me, sheriff? You planning to drive all night?"

"It's another fifteen minutes to the state line. That should give you as much head start as you need on any trouble I can't box up."

"Well," Lilah said with a sigh, "Arkansas can't be any worse'n Mississippi."

The state line was marked by a sign so weather-beaten that only the letters "ARKA" were legible. Sheriff Patterson pulled over. He said abruptly, "What do you think killed Butch? Do you think it was just fright?"

"I dunno," Lilah said. "I told you, he hadn't seen it, and he didn't feel it. I mean, you felt it—not right away maybe, but you felt it."

"Yeah," said the sheriff. "I felt it all right."

"Butch didn't. He didn't feel it at all until he looked up from . . . from the body. And if I got to guess, I think it was like it was too sudden. Like, my brothers knew a boy who died of jumping in a lake, because it was so cold and he went in all at once, and his heart just stopped. I think it was like that."

"You don't think . . . you don't think the little boy could have done it?"

"No," Lilah said.

"That's good," said the sheriff. "That's good to hear."

Lilah got out of the car, slung her purse on her shoulder. She started toward Arkansas, then suddenly turned and ran back to the car. The sheriff looked up at her.

"Burn the house," Lilah said. "Do it yourself. Do it tonight."

Sheriff Patterson looked at her a moment, silently; they both knew what had killed Butch Collier, and it hadn't been fright. Butch had seen the watcher's face.

The sheriff touched the brim of his hat, said, "Ma'am, you're a smart woman." He shifted into first, pulled the car in a long, slow loop just shy of the Arkansas state line, and started back for Hyperion.

Lilah watched until his tail-lights were no more than dim red sparks in the distance. Then she turned, squared her shoulders, and—sixteen years old and six hours a widow—walked out of Mississippi forever.

••••

All a ghost can really do is scare folks a bit. It's not like they can shoot you or attack you or anything, just kind of stand around and moan . . .

The Palace
Barbara Roden

I

"What does the night wind say?"

The voice came from what looked like a pile of rags, half-concealed in a recessed doorway behind him, and Mark almost dropped his cigarette. He had nipped out of the hotel for a quick smoke, and had thought he had the street outside The Palace Hotel to himself. It was past one o'clock, the pubs and hotel bars had disgorged their patrons a half-hour ago, and he had been enjoying the quiet Vancouver night, mild despite the fact that October had set in. He had walked fifty yards or so from the hotel's main entrance, leaving behind the gleaming stone and glass of the hotel's frontage, exchanging it for the dirty, shabby row of shops which occupied the rest of the block. That, Mark reflected, was downtown Vancouver for you; it didn't take long to go from splendour to squalor. All the world in a city block.

The figure in the doorway moved slightly, and Mark saw that it was Jane, one of the permanent residents of the downtown Vancouver streets. Her lined and weathered face gave no secrets away as to her age, or history, or the circumstances which had brought her here; she simply was, in the same way as the Woodwards building or the Ovaltine Café. He had seen her several times, shuffling along the sidewalk or hunched in a doorway, but it was the first time she had spoken to him, although Mark wondered if she actually was speaking to him, or merely talking to herself. But her eyes, incongruously bright in her dark face, were looking directly at him, as if in expectation of an answer, and she asked again, "What does the night wind say?"

"I don't know," Mark replied. He glanced at the trees planted along the sidewalk of Hastings Street, their leaves still green and, tonight, undisturbed by even a hint of breeze. "I don't think it's saying much of anything. Perfect Vancouver night."

"Perfect?" Jane moved forward so that she could look round the edge of the doorway, and her glance moved down the street to where the lights from The Palace's lobby gleamed softly onto the sidewalk. "No. Not perfect. Not here." She tapped the side of her head, near her eyes. "I see. Too much." She shook her head. "Beautiful place. I come here long ago because someone say this city so beautiful. But ugly, too. The night wind knows. Sees beautiful city, with ugly people, sometimes."

Mark had moved closer to her, to hear her words better. She was a Native woman—he could see that now—and her voice had a softness, a musicality to it which had not been ground out of her by the life she led, so far from where she must have grown up. He wondered for a moment where that place was, and if she could go back to it.

As if she had read his thoughts, she said, "No go back. Past is dead place; bad place. Ugly people there too. Ugly people everywhere." She looked at Mark sadly. "Everywhere," she emphasized. "Ugly people do ugly things, and cannot fix."

"Do they try?" She was like the Ancient Mariner, fixing him with her eye, and he found he wanted to stay and listen.

"Sometimes." Jane was silent then, and Mark thought the conversation, such as it was, had ended; but as he started to say he had to get back to work, she said, "Some bad things, cannot be fixed. Some things too bad, too hard. Night wind knows, says these things, but people not hear."

"I see." Mark did not know if he saw or not, but his answer satisfied Jane, who was still looking towards the front doors of The Palace. Mark looked that way too, and remembered that he had a job to be doing. "Well, I've got to go," he said somewhat awkwardly, and Jane looked at him for a moment, then nodded.

"Yes. You go. But watch for ugly people. You watch."

"Yes, yes I will." He hesitated for a moment, then pulled his wallet from his pocket and took out a two-dollar bill. "Here. Have this." He stretched out his arm, and her hand snaked out to take the money. For a moment her fingers brushed his, and then money and hand had disappeared within the folds of clothing around her, and Mark had turned and started towards the hotel. When he got to the door he looked back, but could see nothing of Jane. He glanced once more at the trees and sky, and shivered slightly as an errant breeze, harbinger of the coming winter, blew down the street. Then he was inside the warmth and radiance of The Palace, and the night wind was forgotten.

• • •

II

"Do you believe in ghosts?"

"What is this, quiz night?"

"What do you mean?"

"Nothing." Mark shook his head. "No, I don't."

"Do you believe in vampires?"

"No." Relieved at something that put his encounter with Jane out of his mind, he smiled. Sylvia, looking down, didn't notice.

"Do you believe in werewolves, mummies, or zombies?"

"No, no, and yes."

"Yes?" Sylvia looked up, startled. Mark's smile had broadened into a grin, and she grinned back. "Now you're being silly."

"Silly? Me? I'm not the one who started with the Twenty Questions. Anyway, I have seen zombies. So have you; in the morning, when the guests start to check out." He leaned over the front desk. "What is this, some sort of magazine quiz you're doing? 'Are you open to the paranormal,' that kind of thing? Don't you have work to do?"

"No, it's not a quiz, and I am working, actually, in case you hadn't noticed." Sylvia held up a stack of registration cards, then resumed sorting through them. "It's just something I saw on the news the other night; there was this special series they're doing before Halloween, and they were going around Vancouver and showing all these places that're supposed to be haunted, and there was this one place in Burnaby that's an art gallery now but the people who work there keep hearing things, like footsteps in the hallway when no one else is there, and one time this workman put down his hammer or something and walked away, and when he came back it had been moved to the other side of the workbench, but there he was all alone in the building, so no one else could have moved it, and I just thought, you know, I'm glad I work here, because wouldn't it be creepy to work somewhere like that?"

Sylvia finished off in a rush, the way she often did, like a car running out of gas. Mark laughed.

"Some people would say it was really creepy to work graveyard shift."

Sylvia frowned. "Well, yeah, I suppose it's not for everyone. But you like it, don't you, Raymond?"

This was directed down the length of the front desk towards where a tall, thin man in hotel uniform—standard male employee issue of light brown suit, white shirt, and cheap burgundy tie—stood, entering figures on a sheet of paper. He looked up and blinked at Mark and Sylvia. "What's that?"

"I said, you like working the graveyard shift, don't you?"

Raymond considered her thoughtfully for a moment, then shrugged. "It's a job," he said finally. "You get used to it after a while."

"Not me." Sylvia shook her head. "Soon as I get enough seniority, wham! I'm outta here, onto afternoons. No more graveyard shift, thanks very much. Let someone else have the fun. What about you, Mark?"

He shook his head. "I don't know. It's not too bad; like Raymond says, you get used to it after a while. I guess you can get used to anything, if you try. But it's not up to me. I'm just a Duty Manager; I don't have seniority like you union guys. I'm here until someone decides it's time for me to move on to bigger and better things."

"Aw, listen to this, 'I'm just a Duty Manager.' Poor guy." Sylvia shuffled the reg cards some more, made a note on one, continued shuffling. "I don't know how you do it, Raymond," she said in the night auditor's direction. "How long have you been doing this? Five years?" She shook her head. "No way I could work graveyard that long. No way."

Raymond gave a small polite smile which almost reached his eyes before flickering out. He shrugged again. "You get used to it," he repeated. "I have, anyway. It's quiet. Usually." He bent back down to his sheet of figures.

Where some people would have taken his final word as an insult, Sylvia picked up on the fact that it was just Raymond's way, and that no insult had been intended. She was quick, and bright; wasted, really, on the graveyard shift, Mark thought. If she'd started at the beginning of the summer she'd have soon moved on to better hours, but she had been hired after the busy season had ended, when several of the temporary summer staff—students, mostly—had left, and would now be stuck on graveyards until someone higher up the pecking order moved on. She would have most of her work done by the time update started at around 3:30, and would then settle in by the switchboard, reading, until early morning checkouts began. The job itself wasn't bad; just the hours. Unless you were a bat, or a vampire.

"So what was the verdict on this haunted art gallery? Any idea who's doing the haunting? Or is it just some story the news guys worked up to give people a scare?"

"Well, they're not sure; I mean, I don't think anyone's really seen anything, but then I guess that isn't surprising, 'cause if you could see ghosts—if they're real—then I guess they'd be all misty and everything and half the time you wouldn't even know you'd seen one, but they think it's the woman who used to own the place, who's angry because her husband didn't leave the house to the right people when she died, or something like that, and now she's not happy."

"So she moves hammers around?"

"I guess there's not much else she can do, when you think about it. I mean, if she wanted something, and her husband didn't do it for her after she died, then I guess she'd be kinda upset, but since he's dead it wouldn't really be fair to go after other people, innocent people, I mean, who didn't have anything to do with it; she'd want to get back at him, and so now all she can really do is scare folks a bit, remind them of what happened so she won't be forgotten. And isn't that all ghosts can do to you? Scare you? It's not like they can shoot you or attack you or anything, just kind of stand around and moan."

There was a muttered curse from the other end of the desk, and Mark and Sylvia both turned. Raymond was tearing a strip of paper from the adding machine he had been working on, and they watched him ball it up and throw it in the garbage can beside him. Mark could tell, from Raymond's posture, that he knew he had attracted their attention but was determined not to look at them, and when he glanced at Sylvia he saw that she realized it as well. She shrugged slightly, as if to say "Takes all kinds," but before she could say anything they heard the switchboard ring, and she went to answer the phone. The graveyard shift was a lean machine, as Danny, the night bellman, said: apart from him and the three behind the desk, the only other staff member was Bob, the elderly security guard who was probably out prowling the parking garage, making sure no drunks were bedding down in the stairwells.

Mark continued to watch Raymond, who was now punching—somewhat ostentatiously, Mark thought—the buttons on the adding machine, in an "I don't know about you but someone around here has got to work" kind of way. Raymond was a nice guy, and a hard worker, and certainly knew his job—five years doing the same thing in the same place tended to do that to you—but on the serious side, which was what five years of graveyard shift would certainly do to you. Their paychecks reminded them every two weeks that "Ours is a service industry," but Mark was sometimes thankful that night audit involved little direct contact with the guests.

The sound of heavy doors closing echoed through the lobby, and moments later Giovanni appeared round the corner from the direction of the hotel's lobby bar, a dark, wood-paneled space which looked out onto Hastings Street. It had been a fixture in the hotel for years, a place where people went to do some serious drinking; anyone who wanted drinks with mildly salacious names, or with paper umbrellas stuck in them, usually ended up in the lounge on the top floor, with its views over downtown, and live jazz on weekends. The King's Arms, with its doors onto the street, attracted a somewhat rougher clientele, but Giovanni—known to all as Joe—had presided over it for more than two decades, and was known to run a tight ship. More than one unruly drunk, mistaking Joe's affable manner for weakness, had found himself quickly, and effectively, disabused of this notion.

On this night Joe was all smiles as he tossed a packet of credit card slips and bills onto the counter in front of Raymond. "Here you go," he said. "All finished and closed up."

"Any trouble tonight?" Mark asked.

"No, everyone was pretty quiet. Slow night."

"So I can go clear the machine, then?" said Raymond.

"Go right ahead, my friend."

Mark passed Raymond the keys, and the auditor put down his pen and hurried out from behind the desk. Mark and Joe watched him as he crossed the lobby and went round the corner. Joe shook his head.

"Weird guy," he said. "Harmless, I guess, but weird."

Mark was about to ask what he meant when Sylvia came back out from the switchboard.

"Some people from England, asking about reserving a room for Expo," she said, shaking her head. "Second call like that I've had this week. And Expo's not until 1986!"

Mark smiled. "Some people like to plan ahead," he said. "Besides, two years'll go faster than you know it. They're probably smart to book this far ahead; I think a lot of people are going to want to come to Expo, and Vancouver's pretty short on hotel space for a big city."

Sylvia rolled her eyes. "Yeah, maybe. But if I plan a vacation two weeks ahead I think I'm taking a long-term view."

"Remind me not to plan any vacations with you."

Sylvia winked at him. "Ah, c'mon, could be fun."

"I'll think about it."

Joe, who had been listening to the conversation, nodded his head thoughtfully. "Lots of people will come for Expo. Vancouver is a beautiful place. All my family back in Italy wants to come over in two years, to see this beautiful place I tell them about."

Sylvia still looked doubtful. "Yeah, Vancouver's beautiful, in the right places. Not down here, though. There's too much . . . " She paused, looking for the right word.

"Ugliness?" Mark supplied, remembering Jane's words.

"Yeah. There's so much ugliness down here."

"Look." Joe gestured towards the main doors, where a group of well-dressed people had just alighted from a taxi. Laughing and chatting, they clattered towards the elevators, their voices echoing around the empty lobby. Outside, the taxi pulled away, and they watched as the flags hanging above the door stirred in the wind. They looked soft and golden in the light from the lobby, and it was hard to remember that only steps away there was desolation and suffering and the darkness of people ground down by life.

"You see?" said Joe. "Beautiful people in a beautiful city. In two years we will show the world what it is like here, and many more people will come after that."

The flags continued to flow gently in the night wind. Mark wondered what it was saying.

III

Mark stood on the sidewalk outside The King's Arms, watching as the woman made her way down the street. A few scattered curses could still be heard, growing fainter as the figure moved away. A cold breeze brought more leaves off the trees, and they skittered along the road, making dry, rasping noises. He shivered and turned to Bob. "Think we're okay now?"

"Yeah." The security guard nodded. "That should do it for the night. I'll keep an eye open and make sure she doesn't come back." He shook his head. "The drunks I can handle; what gets to me are the women. Maybe it's 'cause I have two daughters."

Mark watched as the retreating figure turned a corner and disappeared from sight. "I don't know how they can live like that."

Bob shrugged. "No place else to go, most of 'em. At least it's warmer here than in Toronto. That's what brings 'em to Vancouver. It's what brought me here when I retired."

"You were a cop, weren't you? Toronto City?"

"Yep. Thirty years. Saw some things, I can tell you. Still, it was a piece of cake in comparison, from what I can see. We had problems downtown, but nothing like you see here." He shook his head again. "More drugs here; port city and all that. Stuff goes down here that you just don't get in Toronto. The Sutton case—never had anything like that in Toronto."

"The Sutton case." Mark nodded. "Yeah, I remember that. Seven women?"

"Eight. Jeez, that was bad. Bring back the death penalty, I say. Fucker like that—excuse my French—doesn't deserve to be alive, even if he is rotting in a jail cell in Kingston. Waste of taxpayers' money. Never should have got to eight, either. Wouldn't have, if it had been in North Van or Kerrisdale or anywhere except down here, Skid Row. One woman disappears from some middle-class neighborhood, her body turns up in a dumpster a few miles away, people are going to be screaming for the police to do something about it, but women disappear from down here, and who cares? Who even notices?

Didn't look good for the Vancouver cops; black eye for the city. Especially when they found out they had the right guy after five murders, and let him go."

"Yeah, I'd forgotten that." Mark frowned, recalling. "Something about some other person making crank calls to the police, led them in the wrong direction."

"That's it. Police had Sutton in the frame, main suspect, and then they got calls from someone claiming to be the murderer, along with a letter from—where was it?—the interior somewhere, Kelowna or Vernon, same place as the calls, anyway. Seemed legit, police took it seriously, and since they knew Sutton hadn't been there they let him go. He killed three more women before he got caught. Figured the calls and letter were from some wannabe copycat, or someone's idea of a sick joke gone wrong." Bob shook his head. "Some twisted, sad people out there. You'd've thought something like that would keep women off the streets down here, but they're still around, worse than ever. Now the city's talking about trying to do something about them and the drunks and the drug dealers, get 'em outta sight before Expo comes along; looks bad for the tourists, seeing junkies and prostitutes all over the place. They'll just end up moving them along somewhere else, let someone else deal with them. Cosmetics, that's all it is; like putting a Band-Aid on a broken leg. And nothing's really changed since the Sutton case, that's the really sad thing. Whole fucking mess could happen all over again any time, and get to more than eight, for all the notice anyone'd take. There's a few people trying to help, but not many." He jerked his thumb over his shoulder in the direction of the lobby. "Raymond in there, for instance."

"Raymond?" Mark exclaimed. "What does he do?"

"Helps out at a shelter on Cambie, near the cenotaph. Didn't you know? Yeah, I've seen him there a couple of times. Asked him about it once, but he didn't want to talk about it."

"Yeah, he's not the talkative type, Raymond. Keeps to himself."

Bob laughed. "I noticed. Just goes to show, you never can tell about people." He looked at his watch. "Gotta go check the parking lot and back entrance; found a couple of winos behind the dumpster there two nights ago, want to make sure they haven't come back. It's getting colder now, they're looking for somewhere more sheltered. Page me if our friend comes back."

"Will do."

Mark watched the burly figure of the security guard walk away down the sidewalk and turn the corner towards the entrance to the hotel parking lot. He fumbled in his pocket and lit a cigarette, taking a deep drag. Further down the street a movement caught his eye, and he saw a figure stagger out of a doorway and turn away, weaving down the street. A car that was driving along Hastings slowed, then stopped as another figure moved out from the shadows close to the buildings and leaned in the open passenger window. Mark could see that it was a woman, dressed, despite the weather, in a short skirt and short-sleeved, clingy top. He wondered if it was the same woman Bob had seen off the premises a few minutes earlier. It could have been; it was hard to tell at that distance. The thought flitted through Mark's head that all the women down here looked the same anyway, and he shook himself angrily. Wasn't that part of the problem that Bob had been talking about?

He heard the sound of a door slamming, and realized that the woman had disappeared into the car which had stopped for her. It pulled away and drove off down Hastings. They don't call it the world's oldest profession for nothing, Mark thought. Nothing'll ever change.

There was a flare of light behind him, and he turned to see that someone had entered The King's Arms. Mark moved closer to one of the windows, peered through the glass, and saw that it was Raymond, obviously going to clear the cash register where the bartender and servers rang up the orders. He watched as the tall man disappeared behind the bar and walked to the machine at the far end. It was darker down there, and Mark wondered how he could see what he was doing. Five years he's been doing it, he thought. He could probably manage it blindfolded.

He watched as Raymond set the machine clearing, and then was surprised to see the auditor turn away from the register and look into the corner of the bar furthest from where Mark stood. He had his back to Mark, but it looked as if he was speaking with, or to, someone: his head bobbed up and down, and his hands moved in a gesture which made it look as if he were trying to explain something. Mark squinted through the glass, trying to see who he was talking to, but it was dark in the corner, and all he could make out were shadows. If there was someone else there, the person was keeping well out of view.

Mark was even more surprised when, a moment later, Raymond reached up and turned on the television set which was mounted in the corner over the bar. The glow from the screen illuminated that section of the room, but only faintly. The shadows were still thick, but . . . yes! There was someone there, he thought. There, in the corner, a figure, surely. . . .

He leaned closer to the window, and inadvertently struck it with his forehead. He pulled back in surprise, but not before he saw the auditor turn with a visible start. Mark thought that Raymond said something, but he could not hear it through the glass. He saw the man reach up and turn off the television set, and the corner retreated into shadows.

A moment later Mark was back inside the hotel, and had pulled open the doors leading into the bar. He reached to his right and flicked on the bank of switches there, and immediately the room was flooded with light. Raymond was behind the bar, his attention focused on the cash register as if his life depended on it. Mark scanned the room, but there was no sign of anyone else, and no way that anyone could have left without being seen. Unless that person was behind the bar with Raymond . . . but that was ridiculous. Mark cleared his throat.

"Uh, Raymond . . . sorry if I startled you. I was just . . . I thought that . . . hey, if you want the TV on when you're in here that's fine, not a problem . . . " He trailed off, aware that he was babbling and obscurely angry about the fact. He took a breath. "If there's something you want to talk about . . . " Why had he said that? "Okay. I'll just leave you to it." He turned and left the bar before Raymond could say anything.

IV

For the rest of the night Mark found himself thinking, at odd moments, about what he had seen in the bar. On the surface, there seemed little that was troubling. What had actually happened? Raymond had been talking to himself; well, that wasn't exactly uncommon. He had turned on the television in the bar; not a hanging offense. He had seemed startled when Mark banged the window; who wouldn't be, well after midnight, in a dark bar, alone?

But had he been alone? Mark realized that was the aspect of the whole business that was niggling at him. He could have sworn there had been someone else present, in the shadows in the corner. Thinking about it, he saw that the presence of another person made the whole scenario perfectly simple. Raymond had been talking to someone, had turned on the TV for that person, and had been startled when he had been spotted.

Only there hadn't been anyone else there. Raymond had come out almost immediately after Mark, and had locked the doors behind him. Later, feeling slightly embarrassed, Mark took advantage of the auditor's absence behind the desk to go and check the bar. Both sets of doors—the one into the lobby and the one that opened onto Hastings—were firmly locked, and there was no one in the room. Mark stood by the doorway for a few moments, shaking his head. With the lights on the room looked commonplace, resolutely ordinary, stools lined in orderly fashion against the bar, chairs and tables empty, waiting for the next day's custom. The brass footrail against the bar gleamed softly; glasses sparkled; bottles of liquor glowed dully, amber and red and gold, full of promise. Yet in spite of this, Mark shivered. The King's Arms was not, he thought, somewhere he would care to drink, or spend any more time in than he had to. If Raymond wanted to sneak in and put the television on to pass some time, he was welcome to the place.

Mark snapped the lights off and took one more almost involuntary glance backward. The movement in the shadowy corner furthest from him he put down to the reflections from the street light outside. He pulled the doors to, made sure they were securely locked, and headed into the brightly lit lobby.

Behind the desk Raymond had his head down, and seemed to be studiously avoiding catching Mark's eye. Sylvia was busy posting bar charges to guest accounts, and Mark didn't want to say anything in front of her. Besides, what was there to say? The graveyard shift was a funny place; the normal rules didn't apply. Everyone knew that. Probably Raymond had been caught doing the same thing by another Duty Manager, and been hauled over the coals for it, and now feared a repetition. Mark decided that the best thing to do was forget about it.

Later that night he was in the kitchen, rustling up a sandwich. Sylvia was already at one of the tables in the empty restaurant, eating a piece of pie and reading a thick paperback. Mark took his sandwich and a glass of milk over to the table and slid onto the bench opposite. He glanced at the title of the book.

"*Tales of Mystery and Imagination*, huh? What're you trying to do, impress someone?"

Sylvia grinned. "I like to surprise people. My mom actually got me onto Poe; read me 'A Cask of Amontillado' when I was about eight. Scared the crap out of me; I had nightmares about being bricked up alive for days afterward. I loved it, though. It's brilliant stuff. Listen to this." She opened the book and began to read aloud, rather self-consciously:

"During the whole of a dull, dark, and soundless day in the autumn of the year, when the clouds hung oppressively low in the heavens, I had been passing alone, on horseback, through a singularly dreary tract of country; and at length found myself, as the shades of the evening drew on, within view of the melancholy House of Usher."

She looked up. "Great stuff, isn't it? Here's another favorite." She flipped forward a few pages, cleared her throat, and read:

"And travellers now within that valley,
Through the red-litten windows, see
Vast forms that move fantastically

To a discordant melody;
While, like a ghastly rapid river,
Through the pale door
A hideous throng rush out forever
And laugh—but smile no more."

"That explains why you watch stuff about ghosts on TV."

Sylvia slid a bookmark between the pages and laid the book down on the table. "I guess. I've just always liked things like that: Bigfoot, Loch Ness Monster, Ogopogo. Bring it on, I say."

"I'm surprised you can work graveyard shift. Doesn't it spook you?"

Sylvia took a bite of pie and considered the question for a moment. "Nah, not really." She met Mark's gaze and added, "Well, sometimes." There was a pause. "Front desk isn't so bad. Night audit's kind of creepy sometimes, wandering around the hotel when it's dark, clearing the machines. Glad I only do it two nights a week. Don't know how Raymond stands it the rest of the time."

"Funny how he never joins us for some food. Doesn't the guy get hungry?"

Sylvia swallowed another mouthful of pie. "Yeah, 'course he does. He's not that weird."

Mark remembered Joe's words of a few weeks ago. "You think Raymond's weird, then?"

"Kind of. Not that there's anything wrong with him; I've worked with worse, believe me. It's just that . . . " She paused. "I guess I'm just not used to working with people I don't know much about. I mean, you work with someone, especially on graveyard shift, you talk, right? Like we do. Just stupid stuff, everyday stuff, not trying to solve all the problems in the world, just shooting the breeze. But Raymond—he never talks about himself. I asked him once where he was from, and he just said he was from the Interior, and I said "Gee, must be kind of different, living here in Vancouver, then", thinking maybe he'd open up a bit, but he just said yes, it was, and that was it. Every time I try to talk with him it's like that; not unfriendly, just . . . It's like trying to play tennis with someone who never hits the ball back to you, so I've pretty much given it up. Some people just don't like talking about themselves."

"He ever mention a family, anything like that?"

"Nope. I asked Kathie on the morning shift about him once—she's been here forever, knows everything about everyone—and she said he's never mentioned anyone else. Came here five years ago from another hotel in the chain—Victoria, I think—and been here ever since. They tried to get him to go up to the accounting department a couple of years back, she said—figured he'd had enough of the graveyard shift, and he's not the greatest person in the world with customers anyway—but he said no, he was fine where he was." Sylvia took another bite of pie. "Oh yeah, another thing she said was that there was some fuss a couple of years ago—kind of thing you wouldn't remember about anyone else, but Raymond's so . . . what's the word . . . "

"Weird?"

"Yeah, weird about sums it up. Anyway, Kathie said that they found out he hadn't taken any vacation in the three years he'd been here. I dunno how they missed it, but he just kept coming in to work, week in and week out, and no one noticed he hadn't taken any holidays. I guess it's easy in a hotel, everyone working shifts, not like in an office nine to five. There was a fuss about it, I guess, and they tried to make him take a big whack of holidays all at once, but he just said no way." Sylvia shook her head. "Crazy, huh? It's not like he would have lost pay or anything, but he just refused, said he didn't need a holiday, didn't want to go anywhere, he didn't care if he lost the time or the pay or anything."

"So what happened?"

Sylvia shrugged. "Kathie says they came to some kind of arrangement; he got back pay for the time he'd accrued, but he was told he had to take his holidays in future, it was in the contract and there'd be hell with the union otherwise. Apparently Raymond wasn't very happy. Guy never gets sick, either; Kathie figures he must have weeks of sick time stored up."

Mark thought this over. "Do you think . . . do you think he's got a problem of some kind?"

"What kind of problem?"

"I don't know." Mark paused, thinking of the scene in the bar earlier. "Could he . . . could he have a drink problem, maybe?"

"Drink problem? Raymond?" To Mark's surprise she looked thoughtful, almost concerned. "What makes you think that?"

Mark sighed. It all seemed so stupid, really, and yet he found he wanted to talk about it. So he told Sylvia about the scene in the bar earlier, expecting that she'd laugh and tell him he needed to get moved off the graveyard shift before he started seeing pink elephants in the elevator, but instead she just looked at him silently for a few moments and then said slowly, "That's weird."

"There's that word again."

"Yeah, it kind of comes up naturally where Raymond's concerned." She was silent, as if trying to decide what to say. "You know I do night audit two nights a week? Well, the three nights when Raymond's on audit and I'm on desk, I can't help noticing that he . . . well, he seems to spend a lot of time in

The King's Arms. Now hang on"—seeing the expression on Mark's face—"I don't say he's got a drink problem, but I kind of think that . . . well, that maybe he did, once."

The silence stretched out for what seemed a long time. Finally Sylvia continued, although now her eyes did not meet Mark's; instead, her fingers played over the edges of her book and her gaze was fixed on the bird on the cover. "My dad had a drinking problem," she said finally, in a low voice. "It got worse as the years went on, and when I was about—oh, eleven or twelve— things really got bad. I don't know what happened in the end—my mom's never talked about it—but she walked out and took my sister and me with her. We lived with my grandparents for a few weeks, and I remember my dad coming round to see my mom, and them talking for a long time while my grandma took us for a walk or something. I guess they finally reached an agreement, and Dad went on the wagon. He was out two or three nights a week; afterwards I realized it was AA meetings. It worked; I mean, things weren't brilliant, but it was okay. Better than it had been, at least." She took a deep breath. "Anyway, what I'm getting at is that I see the signs in Raymond. My dad hasn't taken a drink since then—far as I know—but sometimes we'll be at a restaurant or a family gathering or something, and there's some booze there, and Dad'll just get this look on his face, kind of half-scared, half-longing." Sylvia shrugged. "It's hard to describe; I guess you have to live through it. But I see that—or think I see it—in Raymond. When he was training me on audit I saw him standing there in The King's Arms, looking at the bar and all the bottles, and I saw that same look on his face that Dad has sometimes."

"I see." Mark was silent for a moment. "So you think Raymond spends too much time in the bar?"

"Yeah. No . . . I mean, what's 'too much'? All I know is that it takes me about five minutes, tops, to clear the machine in there, and he's in there for twenty at least. And if you're wondering why I've never said anything, it's 'cause it doesn't seem to matter. He gets the job done, right? So he likes to hang out in the bar; well, we hang out here, so what's the difference? Except I can't see why anyone'd want to hang out in there, especially after it's closed. Place gives me the creeps."

"Why?"

"I don't know. I just don't like it in there after it's closed. The cleaners don't, either."

"Don't they?"

"Nah. That's why they're always there soon as it closes, to give it the once over while Joe's still in there cashing out and getting things put away. I talked to Sunita about it one night."

"What did she say?"

Sylvia shrugged. "Just that they don't like it in there. Too many shadows."

"What on earth does that mean?"

"Just what she says. C'mon, you say you saw it yourself tonight. That corner, over in the back, near the machine. It's like there's someone there, just out of sight. Sometimes I think that if I look out of the corner of my eye I'll actually see whoever it is."

"Have you?"

"No. I've never tried."

There was silence then. Sylvia looked at her watch, sighed, and picked up her book.

"C'mon, Mr. Duty Manager, time to get back to work, or we're gonna be in trouble. Danny'll be sending out a search party. We've got us a hotel to run."

V

The truth was, the hotel pretty much ran itself at night, something that the graveyard shift workers never really admitted to anyone else. Yes, the hours were crap; but apart from that it was a great job, as Mark had to admit.

As November turned into December and the countdown to Christmas began, he found himself watching Raymond with—curiosity was too strong a word, more a mild interest. There was nothing in the man's demeanor or behavior to excite such curiosity; he seemed the same as always, quiet, hard-working, and competent. Still, Mark found himself mentally keeping tabs on what the auditor did during his shift, and realized quickly that Sylvia was right: he did seem to spend more time in The King's Arms than the work demanded. He refrained from saying anything, however. The man did his job, and gave no cause for complaint. Whatever he did in there wasn't hurting anyone.

Mark also tried to draw the other man out about himself, but quickly found that Raymond was not forthcoming. He answered questions politely, yet with a bare minimum of information that almost verged on curtness but stayed just the right side of the line. It was if he felt that any information he volunteered about himself came with a price, and that he had spent many years ensuring that he kept the books balanced.

One evening in mid-December they were in their usual places: Raymond at the far end of the desk working on the Sales and Labor report, Danny off collecting menu cards, Bob on his rounds, and Sylvia sorting keys from the drop box into the wooden slots in the drawers in the desk. It was nearly 3:00 am, and somewhere far off Mark could hear the dim buzz of a vacuum cleaner as the night cleaners went about their business. A car drove slowly past on Hastings, headlights causing shadows to skitter across the lobby floor. Mark watched it disappear from view.

"Wonder what they're doing here this time of night," he said, more to break the silence than anything else.

Sylvia looked up. "That's what they call a rhetorical question, isn't it?" Mark looked puzzled. "C'mon, you're not that innocent. There's only one thing people come down here for at this time of night. Well, two things, really."

"Oh, I know that." Mark looked back out at the now quiet street and shook his head. "You can't really imagine it, though, can you? That kind of life. It's like another world out there. You walk out there in the daytime, it's all—I don't know—normal people, shopping, catching buses, going to work, all that everyday stuff we all do. But when you go out there at night. . . . Jesus, you wonder where these people are all day. Hidden away, like vampires, waiting for the night."

"They're not that hidden in the day," Sylvia pointed out. "You just have to know where to look; or where not to. But yeah, it's a lot worse at night. On Thursday I got propositioned twice walking here from the bus stop. Never happens during the day. And if you even think about making a joke about that comment I'll throw a tray of keys at you."

Mark stared at her. "You get propositioned?"

Sylvia put on an air of mock anger. "Don't sound so surprised. And I did say it only happened at night. Seriously, yeah, happens all the time."

"What do you say?"

"Depends. If they ask how much I charge I tell them they can't afford it, and if they ask me if I'm available I tell them that I will be at 8:00, when my shift at the police station is over. Usually does the trick, no pun intended."

Mark shook his head. "I can't believe it." Seeing Sylvia's look, he added hastily, "I don't mean it that way, I mean that . . . you don't look like a prostitute, that's all."

"What's a prostitute look like?" Sylvia countered. "I mean, they're women, same as me. They don't all wear skirts up to here and tops down to here and fishnet stockings. Anyway, I get the feeling that the guys who proposition me don't even see me, if you get what I mean. They just see a woman, and figure if a woman's down here at this time of night, on her own, there's only one reason for that. Far as they're concerned, we're all interchangeable. I bet that five—no, two—minutes after a guy propositions me, he couldn't tell you what color my hair was, what I was wearing, or anything. I'm just a piece of meat to them. You're shopping for dinner, looking at steaks in a grocery store, they all look pretty much the same. That's why stuff can happen to these women and no one makes a fuss. They're interchangeable. One of them disappears, who knows? Who cares? There'll be another one to take her place. That's how that guy—what's-his-face, Sutton—could get away with it. No one cared."

"Bob said pretty much the same thing to me once."

Sylvia nodded. "Well, he's right. There's Sutton, killing all these women, and no one even noticed they were gone until some of the families began kicking up a fuss, wouldn't take no for an answer. Even then no one suspected there was a serial killer on the loose." She dropped a key into its slot, checked the inside of the key drop box, and closed the drawer. "Anyway, there's no reason you'd ever have to think about things like getting hit up on the street; you're a guy, you'll never have to worry about someone rolling down their car window and asking you how much you charge. Unless you're on the asking end," she added, "and I can't picture that, somehow, unless you were plastered. No telling what stupid things otherwise nice guys'll do when they're drunk."

There was a clatter and a muffled curse from the far end of the desk, and Sylvia and Mark turned to look. Raymond was scrabbling with a bottle of white-out which had dropped to the counter; as they watched, a small pool of milky white spread out across the half-completed report he had been working on. Sylvia grabbed a box of Kleenex from under the desk and hurried down, but Raymond almost pushed her away.

"It's fine. I'll clean it up. I don't need any help."

"Are you sure? Here's some Kleenex, let me . . . "

"No! Leave me alone!" This time he did push out, and Sylvia backed away, holding up the Kleenex box like a shield. It would almost have been funny in other circumstances, but there was not a trace of humor in the situation. Raymond drew himself upright with a hissed intake of breath and seemed about to say something; then he turned away from Sylvia, carefully picked up the report, and deposited it in the garbage can by his side before pulling a handkerchief out of his pocket and dabbing at the small puddle of white left on the counter. Then he began gathering together papers with hands which, Mark saw, trembled slightly.

"I'm going to take this into the back office," he said in a voice that sounded strained. Before Mark could say anything, Raymond had opened the door beside him and disappeared.

"Well." Sylvia watched the door swing back into place. "There's something you don't see every day." She moved back to her station and put the box of Kleenex back under the desk. "Was it something I said?"

"Maybe. You were talking about getting drunk."

"Yeah." She looked at Mark, eyes wide. "Jeez, I didn't even think, it just sort of came out."

"I don't think that's what got him upset. I was watching him while you were talking about Sutton; he was looking kind of . . . " Mark stopped, trying to think of the right word to describe the look on Raymond's face, and it came unbidden. "Haunted."

Sylvia stared, puzzled. "But why would that bother him? It's ancient history; the guy's in prison. Raymond couldn't possibly . . . "

"I don't know." A fragment of conversation came back to Mark. "Bob says that Raymond works—volunteers—at some shelter down on Cambie. Maybe—I don't know, it's a long shot, but maybe he knew one of the women who was killed."

"Jesus." Sylvia looked pale. "Maybe I should go and say something, apologize."

"For what? 'Sorry for making conversation'? Besides, he's the one who should be apologizing to you. Let it go."

It was easy advice to give, but Mark found it hard to take. For the rest of the night Raymond stayed in the back office, head down, working at his reports. To say he was ignoring the others would not have been accurate, as outwardly he seemed the same as always. Twice, however, when Mark went through the office, he saw the auditor sitting, staring at the desk, only resuming work when he realized that Mark was there. Raymond's hands, Mark noticed, were still shaking slightly.

"I think maybe Raymond's coming down with something," he said later to Sylvia, as the first of the morning team began coming on shift. "He doesn't look well. Thank God he's only got one night to go before the weekend; with luck he'll get it out of his system over the next few days. Even if he's not getting sick, it'll give him a chance to cool down, and things can go back to normal."

Mark was to remember those words, with something like regret, less than twenty-four hours later.

VI

Saturday was never Mark's favorite night of the week; the prospect of dealing with rowdy drunks coming out of The King's Arms always depressed him. But he had little time to think about that the next night, for within half an hour of arriving he received a phone call which put all other thoughts out of his mind.

"Just had a call from Air Canada at the airport," he informed the night shift. "They're shut down out there; bad fog. They had hoped it would clear, but no luck; nothing's taking off. All the hotels in Richmond are full, and they're sending a bunch of people our way. About a hundred, from what I gather, but it could be more. Too bad we didn't know about this half an hour ago, we could have kept some of the evening shift on." He thought for a moment. "Sylvia, I need you to set up a group name, start blocking off some rooms, get reg cards made up. Danny, keep an ear out for the switchboard and give Sylvia a hand with keys; I want them in envelopes with all the reg cards for when the guests get here. Raymond, I need you to start getting meal vouchers ready. They're too late for dinner, but they get $8.50 a person for breakfast. Here." Mark fished a couple of pads of vouchers out of a desk drawer. "Start writing. When you get finished you can help Sylvia with the reg cards."

Raymond stared at Mark as if he had started speaking in Greek. "But what about the night audit?"

Mark shook his head. "Forget night audit right now; we need to get as much sorted out as possible before the buses arrive. We're going to have a hundred tired and pissed-off people here inside of"—he looked at his watch—"twenty minutes. When they get here, they're going to want to get checked in and get to their rooms. The easier we make that process, the easier our lives will be. Get busy."

The first bus arrived at 12:30, with another hard on its heels, and a third one arrived soon after. The stream of people seemed never-ending, and although Mark, Sylvia, and Raymond worked as fast as they could, the line-ups didn't seem to get any less long, while tempers, in contrast, got shorter as the minutes ticked by. Sylvia kept a cheery smile on her face, but Raymond checked his watch every other minute, or so it seemed to Mark, until he wanted to shake him. Joe had long since closed up The King's Arms by the time the last of the guests were checked in, and Raymond had been ordered to go and sit by the switchboard to take the steady stream of wake-up call requests while Sylvia got the check-ins processed. This he did with a bad grace that pushed Mark's already frayed temper almost to the breaking point; when he emerged from the switchboard just after 2:00 and headed for the door, Mark snapped.

"Where do you think you're going?"

"The bar." Raymond nodded his head in the direction of the pub. "I have to go and clear the machine in there."

"No. There's still work to do here. We need to get all these charges posted so we can start update, otherwise there'll be hell to pay when people start checking out. You can help Sylvia."

"But . . . but we need to clear the machines!"

"Yes; after we get the charges posted."

"But you don't understand . . . "

"I understand, Raymond, that I've asked you to do something. Just do it. Sylvia, hand me those bar bills, I'll give you a hand."

Sylvia handed Mark a stack of bills, and he walked to a computer midway down the desk. For a time there was silence as the three of them worked, but it was a strained, uncomfortable silence, and Mark was relieved when the last of the charges had been posted. He stretched, looked at his watch, and turned to Raymond, who looked nervous and twitchy.

"Right. Machines. You can go and do the restaurant and the lounge. Sylvia can do the bar."

"What?" Raymond and Sylvia's words echoed each other; only whereas Sylvia looked puzzled, Raymond looked almost panicked.

"You heard me. Go and get those machines cleared; Sylvia, take the key and go clear the machine in The King's Arms. We're way behind; we don't need anyone lingering in the pub tonight."

Raymond's head jerked back as if he had been hit; then, without a word, he turned and headed out from behind the desk, in the direction of the restaurant. Sylvia started to say something, but took one look at Mark's face and thought better of it.

She was back quickly, trailing a roll of machine tape behind her. Mark thought she looked pale. Not surprising, he told himself, and thought no more of it.

The rest of the night—or what was left of it—went by in a blur. There was no time even to go and get a cup of coffee; Danny brought them sandwiches around 4:00, but they were left largely untouched. It was well past 8:00 by the time they had finished everything, and by then the morning shift and senior management had arrived, a steady stream of guests was checking out, The Palace had shrugged off its night-time air of darkness and silence, and become once more a bustling downtown hotel.

Mark and Sylvia went for a bite of breakfast in the hotel restaurant; one of the perks of the graveyard shift. They ate in silence for the most part; a not uncomfortable silence, thought Mark, who was happy enough to let his mind wander. He was brought back to his surroundings by a sudden question.

"Why did you make me go and clear the machine in the bar?"

"Why . . . what?" He shook his head. "I don't know, I just wanted it done fast. If Raymond'd disappeared in there we wouldn't have seen him for ages. And to be honest, he was pissing me off, looking at the time every few seconds, like we were keeping him from something important."

"I wish you'd sent him, though."

Mark remembered Sylvia's pale face. "Hey, is something wrong?" he asked in concern. "Did something happen?"

"I don't know." Mark waited. "Remember what I said about shadows in there? Maybe it's just me, maybe I was tired and stressed, but . . . it just seemed like there were an awful lot of them." She gave a weak laugh. "I could've sworn, though, there was someone in there, in that dark corner, moving around, like they were . . . I don't know . . . impatient? No, that's not it." She thought. "Angry," she said finally. "There was a real feeling of anger in there." She looked at Mark's face. "I know, I know, overactive imagination. Still, I didn't like it." Sylvia took a last gulp of coffee. "At least I don't have to go in there tonight, with the bar being closed on a Sunday. And you're right, I think Raymond is coming down with something. At least he gets a couple of days off now. As long as we don't get any more delayed flights, we'll be okay. Things couldn't really get any worse."

She was wrong, Mark realized later. Things could get much worse.

The calm before the storm, Mark thought, long after; two quiet nights, where the only untoward event was Sylvia's nervousness about going into The King's Arms on Monday to clear the machine. Mark noticed that she made sure to go in to the bar even before Joe had closed up, but he refrained from making any comments, even as a joke. Somehow it didn't seem a joking matter.

By unspoken common consent, neither Sylvia nor Mark spoke about what had happened on Saturday. When Mark came in on Tuesday he found himself hoping that Raymond had shaken off whatever was bothering him. The auditor still looked pale, but apart from that seemed more or less his usual self, and Mark hoped this signaled that normal service—normal for Raymond, anyway—was now being resumed.

The phone call came in not long after midnight, when the night shift had gone and Sylvia was responsible for answering the telephone. Mark only half-noticed as she went to answer, and when, a minute or so later, she came back behind the desk he didn't even look up until he heard her whisper "Mark."

He turned to her. "Yes, what is . . . " he started to say; but one look at her face cut the words off in mid-flow. "Jesus, what's wrong? Are you okay?"

Sylvia, wide-eyed, her face white, shook her head. "I'm fine; but Mark, that was a bomb threat."

"What!?"

Sylvia nodded. "Someone—a guy—just phoned, said there was a bomb in the hotel, in The King's Arms, and it was going to go off sometime tonight. What do we do?"

"Keep calm, that's what we do." Mark grabbed the walkie-talkie off the counter. "Bob, Mark here. Come to the front desk immediately; we have a security alert." He turned back to Sylvia. "Keep calm. Raymond, go and find Danny, tell him to come here right away. I'll phone the police."

By the time he was off the phone Bob had arrived. Mark was only too happy to let the older man take charge.

"Sylvia, don't answer the phone if it rings; let Mark do that. Go in the back office, get a piece of paper, and write down everything you can remember about the phone call: what the caller said, anything about his voice, if you could hear any sounds in the background. Do it now while it's fresh in your head. He said the bomb was in The King's Arms?"

"Yes."

"And did he say exactly when it would go off?"

"Just that it would be tonight."

"Should we go and evacuate the bar, tell everyone they have to leave?" asked Mark.

Bob shook his head. "You wanna be the one to go in and tell a bunch of serious drinkers they have to leave before closing time? Believe me, they won't care about a bomb threat, but they will care about being cut off before the bar shuts. The police'll be here any minute; let them take care of that."

Four police cars arrived within two minutes, and a no-nonsense sergeant took charge of the situation immediately. He listened to Sylvia's account of the phone call she had taken, and nodded in approval when Bob told him what he had advised.

"That's right; we need you"—he looked at Sylvia—"to write down all you can remember." He turned to Mark. "We're going to have to evacuate the hotel as well as the bar, sir. Bomb goes off in there"—he jerked his head in the direction of The King's Arms—"this whole building is compromised. How many rooms are occupied?"

"About fifty. We're nowhere near full."

"That's good. I'll need printouts showing all the occupied rooms. Two of my men will go and get everyone out of the bar; anywhere else open?"

"The lounge on the top floor."

"Right, we'll need to get them out too. I'll get some of my men knocking on room doors. It would be helpful if you and another staff member could come with us, reassure people."

"Couldn't we just ring the fire alarm?"

The sergeant shook his head decisively. "We don't want to panic people; the last thing we want is people stampeding out of here. And in my experience you always get people who ignore fire alarms. No; we need to go door to door, tell people they have to get dressed and leave immediately, and send them to a designated spot clear of the building. We'll need another staff member there with an occupancy list, so we can make sure everyone's accounted for. I'd suggest the parking lot down the block. We'll have some more men out there to make sure everyone gets clear of the hotel, and in the meantime the bomb squad will check out the bar. How many staff do you have on?"

Mark gestured down the length of the desk, where Sylvia, Raymond, Bob, and Danny were standing. "This is it, except for the cleaners, and the staff in the bar and lounge."

"Right." The sergeant eyed them up, then nodded at Bob. "You round up the cleaners and then go up to the lounge, get everyone out. I'll send someone with you. You and you"—he gestured to Mark and Raymond—"go with my men and start knocking on doors. You"—this to Danny—"can take a list and start checking people's names off when they get to the parking lot. And you can help him," he said to Sylvia, "as soon as you've written down everything about the call while it's fresh in your mind. Now let's go; we don't know how much time we have, if there is a bomb."

Mark went with the sergeant and another policeman, and began knocking on doors. Thank God this didn't happen last Saturday, with an almost full hotel he thought, as they knocked on yet another door, and politely but firmly told the startled occupant that there was a police matter under investigation, could you please get dressed as quickly as possible, leave your belongings, and proceed outside. There were no real difficulties—the presence of two policemen seemed to stifle any urge guests might have had to get angry or ask questions—and Mark was glad when they had finished and were outside.

A chill wind blew down the street, and Mark wished he'd put on his coat. The parking lot was full of anxious people, milling about in some confusion, and the police were dealing with two drunk bar customers who had objected to being cut off early. Looking around in between stints of reassuring anxious guests, Mark saw that they had attracted—not a crowd, for it was nothing that conspicuous, but certainly a group of interested onlookers, who were, however, keeping well back in the shadows: perhaps out of deference to the police presence, or perhaps, Mark thought, because their lives were naturally lived out of plain sight, and they were more comfortable seeing without being clearly seen. He shivered again.

"Cold?" Sylvia asked. She had finished writing down her statement and was standing beside Mark, stamping her feet up and down.

"Yes. Sort of. You okay?"

"Yeah." She shook her head in disbelief. "Just when you thought things couldn't get any worse. Everyone accounted for?"

"Yes, everyone's here. Plus a few extras. Could have sold tickets."

"Or coffee. Mmm, what I wouldn't give for a cup of coffee right now. This wind is freezing."

"'What does the night wind say?'" asked Mark.

"What?"

"It's something someone said to me a while back. An old street woman, Jane. You've probably seen her."

"Yeah, I know who you mean." Sylvia scanned the faces around the parking lot. "Isn't that her over there, near Raymond?"

Mark looked in the direction Sylvia was pointing. There was someone standing near Raymond, at the edge of the crowd, but before he could be certain the figure had slipped away into the shadows. He turned back to Sylvia. "Could have been; hard to tell."

"What did she say about the night wind?"

Mark tried to remember. "Something about it seeing a beautiful city with ugly people in it; people who look nice, but do bad things, and sometimes try to fix them, but can't."

Sylvia stared at him. "What a weird thing to say. What did she mean?"

Mark shrugged. "I have no idea; I didn't really want to get into a philosophical debate with her. But she's been around here a long time, seen some things herself, so I guess she knows what she's talking about."

Their conversation was interrupted by the sergeant, who came to report that the bomb squad had finished searching The King's Arms and found nothing suspicious. "A false alarm, sir; most of them are, but you can't be too safe. You can start moving the guests back in; we'll keep a couple of men here for the rest of the night, just in case."

"Thanks, sergeant. Okay, troops." He turned to Sylvia, Raymond, and Danny; the rest of the evening staff had been sent home long ago. "Let's get these good people back inside. Danny, head to the restaurant and get some coffee going for anyone who wants it. Raymond, you're really going to have to hustle on the audit so we can get into update. Sylvia, I'll give you a hand with the posting as soon as I get everyone settled. Let's go."

Back in the hotel, it did not take long for the lobby to empty, most guests preferring the warmth of their beds to a cup of hotel coffee. Raymond came to ask Mark for the key to the bar.

"Don't think you need it; the door's open. Couple of policemen still there."

Raymond stared at him. "What do you mean? What are they doing there? How long will they be?"

Mark frowned. "I have no idea; why don't you ask them? Anyway, what's it matter? I'd think you'd be glad of some company in there for a change."

They were idle words, meaning nothing, and Mark was unprepared for the alteration that came over Raymond's face. He went white—Mark thought he was going to faint—and when he spoke his voice was hoarse.

"Why did you say that?"

"I don't know. Hey, are you all right?"

"Yes, yes, I'm fine." He looked far from fine, however.

"Look, Raymond, I don't mean this to sound harsh, and I know we've all been through a lot, but we really do need to get a move on. We've got less than an hour to get ready for update. Do you want Sylvia to . . . "

"No." Raymond pulled himself together with a visible effort. "I'll go. I'll do it."

Mark watched him walk round the desk and head towards the bar, and the thought flashed through his mind that this was what someone walking to his own execution would look like. He shook his head. It had been a long night.

He and Sylvia worked at getting bills posted to guest accounts, and Mark barely noticed as Raymond walked past on his way to the restaurant. He only looked up when, a moment later, a policeman arrived at the desk.

"Excuse me, you Mr. Johnson, the night manager?"

"Yes."

"Found this in the parking lot." The policeman held up a man's wallet. "It might belong to someone here. There's a B.C. driver's license inside, name of Raymond Young. He a guest?"

"No, he's my night auditor. He'll be back in a few minutes."

"Perhaps you could give it to him then, sir. Must've fallen out of his pocket when he was outside. Ask him to check it; if there's anything missing he can report it to one of the officers."

"Yes, I'll do that." Mark watched as the policeman walked away across the lobby, then opened the wallet. A driver's license showed Raymond's unsmiling face; there was one credit card tucked in another slot, and some paper money. Apart from that the wallet appeared to be empty.

"His wallet's about as forthcoming as he is," said Mark.

"They say you can tell a lot about someone from something he carries around with him all the time. Guess it's true." Sylvia watched as Mark began investigating the various slots inside the wallet. "Hey, what're you doing?"

"Just looking," he said. "I want to see what else . . . ah, what's this?"

He had opened a small flap that was fastened with a snap, and pulled out a yellowed piece of paper. It was newsprint, and from the creases and wear on it had obviously been in the wallet for some time. Mark opened it carefully.

"Andrew Sutton, who was charged with the murder of eight prostitutes from Vancouver's Skid Row area, has been found guilty of eight counts of first degree murder.'" Mark looked up, frowning. "Why on earth has he got this?" He looked more closely at the piece of paper. "It's from the *Vancouver Sun*; June 1975." He scanned the article. "It's a summary of the case and a report on the verdict."

"I don't get it." Sylvia looked puzzled. "Why on earth does he carry that around with him? It's ancient history."

"I don't know." Mark carefully folded the piece of paper and returned it to its place inside the wallet. "But I know one thing: I don't want to be the person who asks him about it. Remember how he got last week, when you were talking about it? Once was enough. He's acting oddly enough as it is."

"Maybe he did know someone involved in the case. Maybe he carries it around to remember."

"Maybe. Most people'd carry a picture, though. Look out, here he comes. Hey, Raymond, you lost your wallet."

Raymond looked at Mark, eyes dull. Like an animal in a trap, thought Mark automatically.

"Did I?" He reached into his back pocket, and for a moment a flare of panic welled up in his eyes.

"Don't worry, here it is. Police found it in the parking lot. Said you should check it, make sure nothing's missing."

"Yes. Yes, I will." He took the wallet and placed it in his pocket; then, like an automaton, he took his place at the end of the desk without another word, and was silent for the rest of the night.

The next night should have been the start of Mark's weekend, but shortly after getting home he had a phone call from the hotel. Peter, who did graveyard Duty Manager shift two nights a week, was ill; it was a lot to ask, given what he'd gone through, but they were short on people who could do the job, and there was sure to be catching up to do, and would Mark mind . . .

Mark did mind, but he knew better than to say so. "Duty Manager," he muttered to himself, burying his head in the pillow to try to block out the wan December sunlight that found its way through the curtains. "Glorified dogsbody. Wonder what I'll get tonight?"

But all was blessedly quiet when he got to the hotel just after eleven. Sylvia was off, doubtless enjoying the first of her two days of freedom, her place taken by Shelley, a gum-chewing blonde Mark didn't care for. Raymond was down at the far end of the desk, and one glance showed that he was seriously unwell. At first Mark thought he had come down with the same bug that was currently laying other employees low, but a closer look disabused him of the notion.

He looked like a . . . like a whipped dog approaching its master, anticipating another blow and yet unable to stay away. Mark took a deep breath and was about to say something, but the look in the auditor's eye stopped him. There was nothing he could say in the face of such obvious despair.

He did a round of the hotel with Bob, then went back to the desk and retreated into the front desk manager's office near the switchboard, intent on catching up on the paperwork he hadn't got to the night before. He barely noticed when Raymond came in for the key to the bar shortly after 1:00; he found the man's presence disquieting, and was glad when he took the key silently, with a hand that was shaking, and left the office without a word.

Some time later Mark was roused by a tap on the door. Shelley poked her head round the edge.

"Hey, any idea what's happened to Raymond?"

"Why? Is he ill?"

"I dunno." Shelley shrugged. "He went off to clear the machines and I haven't seen him since."

"Jesus!" Mark looked at his watch. "That was forty minutes ago! And you've only just noticed?"

Shelley looked hurt. "Hey, I'm not his mother. I thought you might have had him doing something. And he's so quiet, most of the time you don't see him even when he's there."

"Shit. Okay, Shelly, I'll deal with it. Get back to the desk."

Mark went out the door that connected the office to the main lobby and headed for The King's Arms, sure that was where he would find the auditor. He swung round the corner and was confronted by the closed doors of the bar; when he tried the handles he found they were locked. Perhaps he was wrong—if so, where on earth could . . .

He heard a sound, small and stifled, from inside. He put his ear to the door. Silence. No, there it was again. Was it words? It was hard to tell. Then he heard what sounded like laughter, only it was a humorless, mirthless laughter that sent shivers down Mark's spine.

There was a spare set of keys in the manager's office, and Mark hurried back to the desk. Shelley looked up.

"Find him?"

"Yeah; yeah, everything's fine," Mark said. But he was lying, and he knew it. He did not know what lay behind the door, but whatever it was it was not fine, it was light years from being fine, and although he did not want to go in there he knew that he had no choice.

Back at the doors of the bar, Mark inserted the key and felt the heavy bolt slide back. He pulled one of the doors open as quietly as possible and slipped into the gloom inside. He was on the wrong side of the door for the lights, and had to cross to the other side of the entrance to reach them, and in that brief moment his eyes swept the bar and saw Raymond in the far corner, amongst the darkest shadows, huddled on the floor. He was turned away from the door, looking up, his arms reaching out as if in supplication, a stream of words Mark could not make out issuing from his lips. A moment later the room was flooded with light and Raymond screamed; but not before Mark saw what was surrounding him, the three figures with pale faces and burning eyes and an air of terrible anger mixed with profound sadness.

He hurried over to Raymond—it took all the courage he could summon to force his feet across the intervening distance—and knelt down beside him. The auditor turned to Mark and grasped at the lapels of his jacket.

"Did you see them? Did you?" he begged. His eyes were huge and staring, and looked over Mark's shoulder rather than directly at him. Mark moved so that his own back was against the wall, and there could be nothing behind him.

"What's going on, Raymond?" he asked, as quietly as he could. Raymond had twisted so he could look up into the corner. Mark refused to follow his gaze.

"You saw them, didn't you? Didn't you?" he demanded. Then, more quietly, as if exhausted, "I can tell that you did. I can see it in your eyes. And you only saw them for a moment. I used to see them all the time. Then I found a way for them to leave me, so I could have some peace. They like it here; it's dark and quiet, and near where they used to live. So now they stay here, but when I don't come and see them they . . . they get angry. So angry. I try to tell them if I won't be here . . . warn them . . . but I couldn't this time. . . . "

"Raymond, I . . . I don't know what I saw. I don't know if I saw anything."

"You did. I can tell." Raymond's head sank down on his chest, and Mark thought that he had fainted. Then he heard the auditor say, in a voice that was barely audible, "I was young and stupid . . . drunk . . . thought it was just a joke. I don't know why I . . . " Raymond stopped, and took a deep breath. "It was so long ago. I thought I could make them happy, but I can't. No matter what I do. And I try so hard." Then he began to cry, low, choked, rasping sobs, and Mark could think of nothing to say.

Mark was not surprised, when he returned to work two days later, to find that Raymond was off on sick leave for an indeterminate period. The doctor's note was vague, merely stating that Mr. Young would be unable to return to work for some weeks due to illness; at Mark's urging the matter was not pressed. Three weeks later Raymond sent in a letter of resignation; his two weeks' notice would be taken as sick leave. He asked that his final paycheck be mailed to his home address. It was highly irregular, but after Mark had a quiet word with the personnel manager, the matter was dropped.

While he was in the personnel office, he took the opportunity of looking through Raymond's file. He had worked at another hotel in the chain, in Victoria, and previous to that had worked at a hotel in Kelowna. Both gave good, although not glowing, references, commending him for his work habits but indicating that his inter-personal skills were, perhaps, lacking. A note on his application form, presumably scribbled by whoever had interviewed him for the job at The Palace, read, in a section titled COMMENTS ON APPLICANT: "Steady, quiet, polite, good with numbers. Has worked graveyard shift; says he likes the hours, wants to work in downtown Vancouver." Beside this, a small notation in the margin read "Drink problem (?)."

With Raymond gone, Sylvia took over as night auditor five nights a week. She reported to Mark that the shadows in The King's Arms were gone, a change which she attributed to new light fixtures. She still does not like going in there, however; she can't say why, precisely.

Mark has never tried to explain. Occasionally, though, when he goes outside to smoke a quiet cigarette in the middle of the night, he finds himself looking in through the window of The King's Arms, searching the far corner where the shadows are darkest. Sometimes he thinks, just for a moment, that he sees movement there, and hears laughter which does not contain the faintest trace of warmth or humor. He shivers then, and tells himself it is only the night wind, and hurries back inside The Palace, and tries not to think about what the wind is saying.

• • • •

The room's cold air curdled, hostile, its space become a little theatre where only
unpleasant things might play out. Then she rustled at him
out of the darkness . . .

The Proving of Smollett Standforth
Margo Lanagan

Always she sprang from the same dark corner. Smoll could never anticipate the moment she would appear, though night after night she came in the same way, and performed the same actions in the same order. He fixed his attention on the place, all terrified expectation, but each night her appearance startled him as greatly as it had the first time. She seemed to wait, indeed, before she leapt forth, for approaching sleep to lower his guard by a fraction, to loosen his joints and sinews, to slow his heartbeat to a pace no more urgent than would be expected of an organ going to its rest upon a day's gainful industry.

The corner from which she rushed was not the corner with the door. Or at least, not the door Smoll used himself—and Mrs. Gallon used it too, he supposed, for she swept and grumbled everywhere about the house, so it was likely she swept and grumbled here too—and which a casual observer would maintain was the only door to the attic room. No, there had once been a door in the other corner. By day, seams in the wall showed where boards had been used to seal it, and in Pinkney's room below, short, staggered lines in the wall boards showed where steps so steep as to be almost a ladder had once angled up. Not only was the night-lady a phantom herself, she also emerged from a phantom house. Eyeing the rectangle of the no-longer-existent doorway, Smoll wondered about the person—a grown man, stronger and more practical and authoritative than Smoll was—who had tried to shut her out, the tilting woman, her beads, her voice. And when all the sawing and hammering and painting-over had failed, the man, sensibly, had gathered up his household and left. Smoll wished heartily that he could pursue them. *Please, oh please!* he wished he could say. *Let me come with you, to whatever safe place you found!*

It was not that Mr. Beecham's house was not perfectly safe in the daytime, and full of distractions—even, on occasion, amusements, even for a boy so timid and easily mortified as Smoll. But night time always loomed again. Always the glad morning (the darkness easing, the clop of the passing milk-horse giving him heart) was followed—no, rushed upon, hurried out of mind, pounced on and briskly swept aside as of no account—by oncoming evening. However much Smoll lingered over the boots in the evening (*See your face in 'em yet?* Ridley would say, passing behind him with the last slop-pail from the kitchen), there would come a point where they were done, when they were placed each pair outside the doors: Mister's and Missus's, Miss Edwina's, Miss Pargeter's, Miss Annabelle's, Master Howard's, Mr. Pinkney's—and sometimes Mr. Rossiter the coachman's as well, those wonderful long boots with all their mud that Smoll was always so grateful for. And Smoll having placed them must proceed up his flight of tiny stairs, through the hole in his floor, through the door not much larger than a coalhole cover. He must shut himself away behind that door, shake off his clothes and shrug on his chilled nightshirt and leap abed, blow out the candle and wrap himself tightly in the clean patched sheet and the blanket—as if tonight of all nights that wrapping, that tightness, might be effective against her, when every previous night, since first Smoll had been elevated from country scamp to Beechams' boot boy, it had utterly failed to protect him.

"Smoll, are you well?"

"Quite well, thank you, Mr. Pinkney."

"It is only that you have . . . well, rather a *burdened* look about you."

Smoll felt it, and unrounded his shoulders. "Oh no, sir. I am nothing like so burdened as I was at home, carrying water and wood."

"That is better, Smoll. It behoves a young man to maintain a good posture, whether he be in the public gaze or no, do you not think?"

"Yes, sir."

She was neither old nor young, the dream-lady; she was neither beautiful nor monstrous to look upon. She was *difficult* to look upon; though her presence was so sudden and so strong in the sensations it produced, her actual shape was indistinct against the surrounding darkness, except in the middle, where it resembled an hourglass. Above and below the narrow waist, she was corseted into a shape that even Smoll, whose eyes were so often cast down in the presence of ladies, or indeed of anyone taller or more important than himself, recognised as old-fashioned. Below this shape she gave to skirts that faded to nothingness, although their rustlings pressed most forcefully upon his ear. Above it, her flat-bound bosom and hunched shoulders supported a head all the more terrible for being entirely without features, except for the impression of a wealth of hair, pulled and piled and pinned into place with the same energy of compression that had been exerted on the body below. Tightness, tightness was all, about this body and about the personage that was borne about in it—tightness and a little madness, which the tightness held in check.

She carried her faceless head with an intent tilt, and it was in this tiltedness that Smoll's fear formed, for she was intent on *him*; she tilted her head at *him*. He would scramble upright in the bed, his back pressed to the wall, the back of his head hard against the frame of the little uncurtained window, which, admitting as it might the fullest moonlight or the strongest effusions of a clear night's stars, never showed him what he needed to see of the woman, never illuminated her brightly enough to convince him that he had seen all the evil there was to see of her, that he now knew what she was, that he could begin to bring some measure of rationality to his encounters with her. Instead he only underwent yet again this deep abjection, this wholesale shrinking of body and being from whatever she was, whatever she wanted.

For she did want something; she made the same demand of him night after night. She rattled the beads in her hands and pushed them at Smoll, pushed them *into* him sometimes. Did her touch itself, her thrusting at his middle, produce those pond-ripples of horror up and down him, or was only the *idea* of her touch, in his appalled mind, sufficient to generate them?

The beads themselves were grotesque, bulbous; her handfuls of them reminded him of Arthur Cleal at Hobson's farm, gathering up innards after the butchering, the slippery tubes and organs overflowing the bowl of his hands.

Take it, she hissed, and shook the thing, and pushed it at him again. *Take it; I don't want it.* Her voice was muddied—from having crossed time to reach him, perhaps, or from the invisibility of her mouth. She was hurried, and guilty; she crouched at him. *'Tis not as if I can ever wear it. Take it!*

He might say *No.* He might say *I don't want it either.* He might ask her who she was, and why she plagued him. Whatever he said, fear crawled and shook in his voice. And she always answered the same, angrily: *Take it!* bobbing at him, bobbing into him a little, bobbing back. There might be the flash of an eye, fixing on him with horrible inexactitude, as if she were blind; there might be something of a mouth, a ghost of teeth, momentarily, against the hollow attic room behind her, which resounded with the muddied sounds of ghost-steps. *What would I do with it, for heaven's sake? Take it! Take it, before Mistress comes!*

At first he felt only faint pains, here and there about his neck, a slight heat in the skin of his chest where the locket lay. Sometimes these were itches and no more, and if he lifted the neck of his shirt to search for signs of them, he saw no mark—the first few times, the pains themselves eased utterly, he was so reassured by the sight of his clear skin.

Then a redness began to grow and to glow in the flesh there, visible in the light of a bright day outdoors but not by candlelight or lamp. The reddened skin was sensitive to the touch of a finger, or the rubbing of shirt cloth; if he scratched it absent-mindedly it would sting and burn, and the pain of that would linger.

There rose blisters, then, pepperings of them where each bead had lain in the night, and a flowering on his breast from the locket's weight. They burst and itched and wept, and the skin stayed raw; sometimes by nightfall it had healed dry, but the dream-lady's visit would inflame it again, when she forced the unnatural burden of the ghost-beads on him.

The wounds never quite bled; at worst they leaked a watery fluid that stained Smoll's shirt and nightshirt yellow. "What have you spilt on yourself?" Cook might scold him, but it was less a question than a lament at the general carelessness of boys, and she did not pursue him for an explanation.

The dream-lady would thrust the beads one last nervous time at Smoll, her shining, rattling handfuls of them. His own hands would turn palm-up to take them. He was an obedient boy, and before he had left to live here his mother had kissed him and instructed him to do exactly as he was told by all at Mr. Beecham's house. Also, he was afraid that the beads, if he did not catch them, would slither and crash to the floor. The noise they would make terrified him enough; the consequences of such a concussion, he could not begin to imagine.

And once she had poured the beads into his hands, their weight and coldness compelled him; he understood himself to have made some kind of pledge in accepting them. There was no handing the necklace back, however much it pained him to hold it, the weight like a load of polished river stones. They chilled his hands, and the dragging of the over-spilt ones made his whole arms shake. She had pushed them out of her time into his, and by taking them he had taken them *on*, somehow; he had become responsible for them. *That's right*—you *have* it! she now exulted, and she had an eye again, a jagged gleam on the darkness as she nodded. *It's beautiful, isn't it?*

He might say *Yes.* He might creak out the truth: *It is the ugliest thing I have ever seen.* He might gather the spills of beads or leave them depending from the fat gold locket for which the whole embarrassment of ivory, amber, and jet had been assembled. No matter what he chose to do—if choice, indeed, played any part in it—she would nod and gleam in the same way; the same impression of her tight smile would hang there in the night before him. *Put it on*, she now said; they were only partway through whatever bewitchment she was working. Her voice issued not from her tensed lips but from the fearful air all around; it rose at Smoll from inside him, from the marrow of his own small bones.

Always he put the necklace on, although it was cold, and painfully heavy. The sooner he put it on, the sooner this trial would end.

You see? The woman melted into relief. Her head tilted more. Her smile flickered, then became more distinct; for an appalling moment it was too large for her face, the next instant it shrank too small, then the mouth was extinguished altogether. *It suits you*, she said unctuously, mouthlessly. Then she leaned forward and hissed, *Hide it under your clothes, before Mistress comes and sees.*

He did as she bid him, covering the noose of beads and locket with his nightshirt. Each time, they made him gasp, the cold striking through his breastbone, the sudden weight straining at his neck.

Yes, that's right, the lady would say—she was not a lady, of course; she was a servant like himself. She leaned at him; she had eyes and teeth. Her words caught up with her mouth, and some nights he would feel not only the ice-burden of the beads but also feathers of her historical breath against his face and front. By now he was fixed and imprisoned, by the beads and by his fear, by her face tilted forward, her forehead white and broad, the eyes wide and drinking up the sight of the hidden necklace.

Then she would be gone. But the necklace would stay, coldly burning. And the horror of her presence stayed too, the boxed-in attic air crawling with it as a street-dog's coat crawls with vermin. All Smoll's skin crawled too, and his ears still heard her hisses, and his spine still jolted with the ghost noises behind her, the ghost-steps climbing the nonexistent stairs.

When the steps ceased, and the fear loosened its hold on him sufficiently, he lay back down, crushed to his little bed by the beads and locket, collared and chained down. To breathe, to lift the locket-weight on his chest and let in air underneath, he must summon some force and determination. He lay entirely imprisoned, hauling himself from breath to breath, and whether he failed in that effort for want of air, or the task of breathing exhausted him, eventually he would sleep.

"Why, look here! A letter has come for a Master Smollett Standforth."

Smoll looked up from his porridge. Mr. Pinkney placed the note before him. "Posture, boy!" Smoll straightened, and the raw skin of the sores crinkled and burned beneath his shirt.

"That's a nice hand," said Cook, passing behind him with her own bowl.

"The priest will have written it," he said, "for my Ma."

Cook sat all bustle across the table corner from him. "Shall I read it to you?"

"Please, if you would." He pushed it towards her. He did not want it near. It promised nothing but complications, and he had not the energy to accommodate them.

"I hope it is not bad news." Cook gave him a kind and serious look through her porridge-steam. She examined the glossy seal with approval before breaking it, then she laboured through some of the writing within. "She hopes you are well," she said, "and she sends you her love. They are all well there—no bad news, then." Cook patted Smoll's hand before toiling on. "Only Biss has been laid low with a fever. That has broken. All is well. She is coming good. Biss is your sister?"

"She is my cousin. But she lives with us, as good as a sister." And Smoll lost his good posture again, thinking of Biss waving him off in the carriage that day, a little weeping to lose him; of Biss how she laughed too much sometimes and had to be sat and calmed; of Biss ill and subdued, lying abed (unimaginable!), and how he had not been there to help Ma care for her, or to share in the worrying.

"Ah, here is the business. 'Your brother Dravitt has come into the good fortune of being apprenticed to Nape's uncle George Paste down at Caunterbury, and he will be coming through London on the twenty-ninth of January—' " Cook read on, frowning, crouched over the letter. If he had not known her, by her expression right now he would have thought her a most bad-tempered person.

"Your porridge will get cold," said Smoll. His own porridge was all spooned up and eaten, fast and nervously, he had been rendered so self-conscious by the letter, and by his home life being brought out around the breakfast table, here in his new life. It pained him, the thought of Ma relaying to the priest all she wanted Smoll to know, and the way the priest had corrected and embroidered her words with priest-language, putting himself and his education between Smoll and his Ma.

"She hopes Mr. Beecham will permit young Dravitt to stay here a night on his journey, is the sense of it, boiled down."

They both looked to Mr. Pinkney, at the far end of the table with his tea and thin toast, his braces and his white, white shirtfront on which never a drop was spilt, never a crumb was deposited.

Pinkney tipped his head, sipped his tea. "I am sure Mr. Beecham will have no objection. Dravitt, is it? Should be no trouble to us, sharing your little eyrie for a night." He took another sip and glanced along the table, a glint in his eye. "Unless he is of a much different make from yourself, Smoll. Is he a wild boy, your brother?"

"Oh no, sir. Drav would be timider than me, by far."

"Oh, Smoll." Cook laughed a little at Smoll's earnestness, and gave his hand a brisk rub where it lay there on the table.

He barely noticed, he was so occupied with the warring emotions inside him. He felt a stab of missing Dravitt and all the littlies, and Biss and Ma, and the house, and all around it, the village he knew, so humdrum, every stone and weed of it, every codger and kid. This keen distress was cut through by the relief it would be to see Drav again and show his new life to him—yet it would be pain, too, for it would agitate Smoll's homesickness, which until now had been thoroughly obscured by the novelty of his new duties and worries. And all these complexities were in turn flattened by the stark dread, the absolute impossibility of Drav's visiting, the intractable necessity for Mr. Pinkney and Mr. Beecham to forbid it. *Sharing your little eyrie for a night*— that must not happen. Drav must never endure a night with Smoll in the attic room! Clearly Cook and Pinkney knew nothing of what happened up there, once the household slept. Smoll gathered up his posture again, lifted his chin, and the necklace of raw patches stretched and twinged.

"I will ask Mr. Beecham this morning," said Pinkney, "but I dare say he will be entirely happy with the idea."

It was near a fortnight before Dravitt was to come. Smoll proceeded towards the day mazed with terror. Dravitt must not see the dream-lady, he knew that much. He *certainly* must not be forced to take her beads. But even if Smoll took them himself, as usual, how could he save Drav from being terrified by the whole transaction, by the mere sight of the woman, by her voice—now foggy, now sharp and clear—by her urgent attentions?

In a bid to be moved from the attic room he revealed his wounds one morning to Cook. "Gracious!" she cried, "How long have you gone about like this? Look at the boy, Pinkney! What are these? Have you seen anything like them?" And they turned Smoll about and exclaimed some more, the pair of them.

But all they did was smother the lesions with a strong-smelling grease that Cook mixed up, that everyone remarked on and made faces at when Smoll was near—everyone but the dream-lady, who only went at him with her customary combination of impatience and flattery. *It suits you*, she said just the same, as the beads burned on Smoll's slippery chest, and the attic room might have been suspended from a hot air balloon miles above the Beecham house, or might be a wind-whipped hut out on the Arctic ice, for all the help he could expect from beyond its walls.

The night before Dravitt was due, Cook made Smoll bathe, his own small personal bath so that he would not infect anyone with his disease, if infectious he was. He sank back disconsolate in the stinging, soothing water, behind the screen in the kitchen. *Don't rub at them; just soak*, Cook had said, and so he soaked, staring up at the ceiling and listening to Cook come and go, and others who must be explained to, about Smoll and his condition, and his coming brother. *We will bandage you up, the night he's here*, Cook had said, *and put clean sheets on your bed, so's he doesn't catch it. We don't want to send him down Caunterbury covered in bibulous plague, do we? Won't impress his new master.*

Soggy-warm from bathing and freshly anointed with the foul salve, Smoll tottered upward through the cold house, carrying his candle and the wrapped hot-brick for his bed. He would meet Dravitt at the coach tomorrow afternoon; Drav would be looking out for him, excited, perhaps a little frightened that Smoll would not be there; when he saw Smoll he would beam, all relief and pleasure at having a companion in his adventure. He would be looking to Smoll for advice, for explanation. He knew nothing of the world, Dravitt, and he was very small (though he would have grown some since Smoll last saw him in the summer); he was easily cowed.

Smoll stood on the steep wooden steps, halfway through the floor into his room, clutching his brick and candle there on the threshold of his exile. The very air felt different here; the top half of him was tainted with its solitude and horror, while his legs stood in a freer, kindlier atmosphere below. He summoned his energies and stepped up wholly into the attic, and went to the bed and put down the candle and tucked the hot-brick under the blankets. Then he came back and closed the door in the floor, shutting himself in, untethering himself from the safety of Beecham's household. He climbed into bed, the bed that Dravitt would be sharing tomorrow. He blew out the candle with a frosty breath and hugged the hot-brick to his stomach, and he wept a little for Dravitt, for Dravitt's innocence (which once he himself had shared), and for the distance he was from home and Biss and Ma, and for his own want of courage.

He was dozing when the attic announced the dream-lady's imminence, its cold air curdling, hostile, its space become a little theatre where only unpleasant things might play out. Then she rustled at him out of the darkness, the hourglass waist of her, the cocked featureless head. She thrust at him her handfuls of gleam: *Take it.* Smoll flattened to the wall as always, without deciding to; the fear never lessened, however well he knew her, however often she uttered the same words. There was something distressing, indeed, in their repetition, in the mechanical nature of her performance, the fact that she could be neither paused nor halted.

The necklace shone in the darkness. *What would I do with it, for heaven's sake?* hissed the rustling lady, and Smoll's flesh crept from her touch, and his salved wounds winced and pained. His hands unstuck themselves from the wall as they always did, because he was obedient, and because she would go away if he obeyed, and the most important thing in the world was that she go away.

He had thought he had no room, when the woman was there, for considering or scheming, for outwitting her. She took him over, he had thought, and his whole being underwent her visitation, was ground through it like meat through Cook's great dark mincing machine down in the kitchen.

But tonight he found that he did have an extra thought spare, a small pocket in his mind where ruled, unafraid because unaware, his younger brother—not Dravitt as he would be now, skinny and bright-faced and ready to start his new life apprenticing, but Dravitt when he was small and round and red-curled, a plaything for Smollett and his sisters; the sleep-sodden Dravitt whom Smollett had carried home after the midsummer bonfire; the Dravitt who had run stout and screaming with laughter, Biss and Clara pursuing him, towards Smollett, whose one hand was tip-fingered on the oak that was Home for this game, whose other reached out to Drav, so that he might reach safety sooner.

The beads began to rattle, from the lady's hands to Smoll's, and to weigh on his palms, fall over his fingers. In the cold light of the winter moon pouring through the attic window each bead was vaguely its own color, the ghostly ivory, the implacable jet, the flecked transparent warmth-that-was-not-warm of the amber. They piled and slid on Smoll's palms; the woman's white hands were emptying; her breath from the other time blew warm, sour and intent on his forehead. He had only these few moments while she poured, while she reached through from her time to his; once the last bead left her grasp, he would be helpless against her returning tomorrow, and including his brother in her terrors.

"No." Smoll's voice was small, ineffectual. No matter. The voice it was uttered in did not matter.

He grasped a bead and sprang with it up from his bed. He pushed his arms through from his time into hers, forced his head into the cold syrup of the past. "No," he said to the woman's clear, bright-eyed face, to her alarm, to the smell of the past, of an old, gone meal, part of it burnt. Against the force of her will and her magic, with all his small strength he pushed the loop of beads back through the thick air, and over her head.

He forced it down around her neck. Her face, aghast, almost touched his. "Mistress!" cried Smoll into the syrup, dropping to the bed again, dragging on the necklace, all but swinging from it. "Come quickly! She has your necklace, your lock—"

Her hand stopped his cry. It was not a soft lady's hand; it was worked to leather, cold and strong and real, and smelled of laundry soap. She took him by the mouth and by his nightshirted ribs, and hissing she began to push him out of her time, her eyes wild, her eyes *afraid* as he had never seen them. He saw the enormity of what he was doing, the disgrace and punishment it would entail for her, not a ghost-woman or a dream-woman at all but an ordinary servant like himself, whose good name in her household was the only wealth that she had in the world. Still he fought to stay, to make his voice heard in the house of her time, to make as much noise there as he could, whether words or no. He yammered behind her hand; he threw himself about to loosen her grip on his mouth, and let out more noise.

Slowly her strength succeeded against his—but he had not meant to conquer, only to delay her, only to keep her fighting and in possession of the necklace until the other person, the maker of the dream-footfalls, reached the top of the stairs and entered. He listened for the mistress through the strain and pain and noise of the struggle. His ears were right at the border between the two times now, and all sounds were warped there, the dream-lady's grunts compressed into quacks, her panting concertina'd to weirdly musical whistles. The knocking on the attic door he heard as thunder; the mistress's voice was a god's calling across a breadth of sky.

And then as the doorknob rumbled in its turning, the servant-woman pushed Smoll wholly through the divide, the magicked aperture between the times, back into his rightful night. As she and her era fell away, as she shrank, she tore the necklace off and flung it after him. Soundlessly it splashed against the intervening time as against a window between herself and Smoll. She watched in dismay as it fell, and the door opened behind her no bigger than a playing card now, and the dark opening swallowed up woman and beads and attic and all.

The two times snapped apart to their proper distances; Smoll felt the event of that, in his ears and in the punching of air into his throat and lungs. Somewhere between sprawled and sitting, he stared from his rumpled bed, out into a darkness utterly free of reverberations. No dread sang there, and no historical glee resounded. No weight sat bead-by-bead around his neck or ached against his breastbone. There was only Smoll in his eyrie, the odor of Cook's salve, warm from his exertions, clouding up from the neck of his nightshirt, the light of the moon pouring down on him from the window.

· · · ·

Visiting them, there had been times she'd been sure she could feel . . . she didn't know what. A something there in the house with them . . .

The Third Always Beside You
John Langan

That there had been another woman in their parents' marriage was an inference that for Weber and Gertrude Schenker had taken on all the trappings of fact. During the most recent of the late-night conversations that had become a Christmas-Eve tradition for them, Weber had christened the existence of this figure "The Keystone," for *her* and her intersection with their mother and father's marriage were what supported the shape into which that union had bent itself.

Over large-bowled glasses of white wine at the kitchen table, his back against the corner where the two window seats converged, Web met his eleven-months-younger sister's contention that, after all this time, the evidence in favor of *her* remained largely circumstantial by shaking his head vigorously and employing the image of the stone carved to brace an arch. Flailing his hands with the vigor of a conductor urging his orchestra to reach higher, which sent his wine climbing the sides of its glass, Web called to his aid a movie's worth of scenes that had led to their decision—during another Christmas Eve confab a decade earlier—that only the presence of another woman explained the prolonged silences that descended on the household without warning, the iciness that infused their mother's comments about their father's travels, the half-apologetic, half-resentful air that clung to their father after his trips like a faint, unpleasant smell. The other woman—*her*, the name custom had bestowed—was the stone that placed a quarryful of cryptic comments and half-sentences into recognizable arrangement.

As for why, ten years on, the two of them were no closer to learning *her* real name, much less any additional details concerning *her* appearance or the history of *her* involvement with their father, when you thought about it, that wasn't so surprising. While both their parents had insisted that there was nothing their children could not tell them, a declaration borne out over thirty-one and thirty years' discussion of topics including Web's fear that his college girlfriend was pregnant (which, as it turned out, she wasn't) and Gert's first inkling that she might be gay (which, as it turned out, she was), neither their mother nor their father had asked the same openness of their children. Just the opposite: their parents scrupulously refrained from discussing anything of significance to their interior lives. Met with a direct question, their father became vague, evasive, from which Web and Gert had arrived at their secret nickname for him, the Prince, as in, the Prince of Evasion. Their mother's response to the same question was simple blankness, from which her nickname, the Wall, as in, the Wall of Silence. With the Prince and the Wall for parents, was it any wonder the two of them knew as little as they did?

Web built his case deliberately, forcefully—not for the first time, Gert thought that he would have made a better attorney than documentary filmmaker. (They could have gone into practice together: Schenker and Schenker, Siblings In Law.) Or perhaps it was that he was right, from the necessity of the other woman's existence to their parents' closed-mouthedness. Yet if the other woman was the Keystone, her presence raised at least as many questions as it answered, chief among them, why were their mother and father still together? A majority of their parents' friends—hell, of their parents' siblings—were on their second, third, and in one case, fourth marriages. If their mother and father were concerned about standing out in the crowd, their continued union brought them more sustained attention than a divorce, however rancorous, could have. Both their parents were traversed by deep veins of self-righteousness that lent some weight to the idea of them remaining married to prove a point—especially to that assortment of siblings moving into the next of their serial monogamies. However, each parent's self-righteousness was alloyed by another tendency—self-consciousness in their mother's case, inconstancy in their father's—that, upon reflection, rendered it insufficient as an explanation. Indeed, it seemed far more likely that their mother's almost pathological concern for how she was perceived, combined with their father's proven inability to follow through on most of his grandiloquent pledges, had congealed into a torpor that caught them fast as flies in amber.

It was a sobering and even depressing note on which to conclude their annual conversation, but the clock's hands were nearing three a.m., the second bottle of wine was empty, and while there was no compulsion for them to rise with the crack of dawn to inspect Santa's bounty, neither of them judged it fair to leave their significant others alone with their parents for very long. They rinsed out their glasses and the emptied bottles, dried the glasses and returned them to the cupboard, left the bottles upended in the dishrack, and, before switching off the lights, went through their old ritual of checking all the locks on the downstairs windows and doors. Something of a joke between them when their family first had moved from Westchester to Ellenville, the process had assumed increased seriousness with an increase of home invasions over the last several years. When they were done, Web turned to Gert and, his face a mask of terror, repeated the line that concluded the process, cadged from some horror movie of his youth: "But what if they're already inside?" Gert, who had yet to arrive at a satisfactory response, this year chose, "Well, I guess it's too late, then."

The fatality of her answer appeared to please Web; he bent to kiss her cheek, then wound his way across the darkened living room to the hallway at whose end lay the guest room for which he and Sharon had opted—the location, Gert had reflected, the farthest possible distance from their parents' room but still in the house. This had left her and Dana the upstairs room, her old one, separated from her mother and father's bedroom by the upstairs bathroom. Gert could not decide whether Web's choice owed itself to a desire to maintain the maximum remove from their parents for his new wife and himself, or was due to an urge to force the closest proximity between her and Dana and her parents, who, seven years after Gert's coming out, and three years since she'd moved in with Dana, were still not as reconciled to their daughter's sexuality as they claimed to be. Of course, Web being Web, both explanations might have been true. Since some time in his mid-to-late teens, the closeness with which he had showered their mother and father, the hugs and kisses, had been replaced with an almost compulsive need for distance— if either parent drew too near for too long, tried to prolong an embrace, he practically vibrated with tension. At the same time, he had inherited their parents' self-righteousness, and given an opportunity to confront them with what he viewed as their shortcomings, was only too happy to do so. If Gert was uncomfortable, it wasn't in the plastic pleasantness that her mother and father put on whenever she and Dana visited, to which she'd more or less resigned herself as the lesser of many evils—it was in being fixed to the point of the spear with which Web wanted to jab their parents.

As she mounted the stairs to the second floor, she wondered if Web was anxious about his marriage going the way of their mother and father's, if his need for the downstairs room was rooted in anxiety about him and Sharon being contaminated by whatever had stricken their parents. It wasn't only their behavior that displayed the souring of their union. Physically, each appeared to be carrying an extra decade's weight. Their father's hair had fallen back to the tops of his ears, the back of his head, while their mother's had been a snow-white that she refused to dye for as long as either of their memories stretched. Their parents' faces had been scored across the forehead, to either side of the mouth, and though they kept in reasonable shape, their mother with jogging, their father racquetball, the flesh hung from their arms and legs in that loose way that comes with old age, the skin and muscle easing their grip on the bones that have supported them for so long, as if rehearsing their final relaxation. The formality with which their parents treated hers and Web's friends buttressed the impression that her brother and her were a pair of last-minute miracles, or accidents. Without exception, Gert's friends had been shocked to learn that her mother and father were, if not the same age as their parents, then younger. She thought Web had received the same response from his classmates and girlfriends.

Although she swung it open gently, the hinges of the door to her and Dana's room shrieked. *No sneaking around here.* In the pale wash of streetlight over the window, she saw Dana fast asleep on her side of the bed, cocooned in the quilt that had covered it. Leaving the door open behind her, Gert crossed to the hope chest at the foot of the bed and unlatched it. The odor of freshly-laundered cotton rose to meet her, and along with it came the groan of the floorboards outside the door.

"Mom?" She stood. "Dad?" The hall sounded with whichever of them it was hurrying to their room. Gert waited for the hinges on their door to scream, wondering why they hadn't when whoever it was had opened it. After ten years of promising to do so, had her father finally oiled them? She listened for the softer snick of their door unlatching. She could feel someone standing there, one hand over the doorknob, their eyes watching her doorway for movement. "For God's sake . . ." Five steps carried her out into the hall, her face composed in an expression of mock-exasperation.

The space in front of the door to her parents' bedroom was empty, as was the rest of the hallway. For a moment, Gert had the sensation that she was *not* seeing something, some figure in the darkness—the feeling was kin to that she had experienced looking directly at the keys for which she was tearing up the apartment and not registering them—and then the impression ceased. The skin along her arms, her neck, stood. *Don't be ridiculous,* she told herself; nonetheless, she made certain that the door to her room was shut tight. Later on, she did not hear footsteps passing up and down the hallway.

II

Gert's decision to pursue the question of the other woman, to ascertain her identity, was prompted not so much by that most recent Christmas-Eve conversation as it was by a chance meeting with an old family friend in the din of Grand Central the week after New Year's. While waiting in line to purchase a round-trip ticket to Rye (where lived an obscenely wealthy client of her firm's who insisted on conducting all her legal affairs in the comfort of her tennis-court of a living room), she felt a hand touch her elbow and a voice say, "Gertie?" Before she turned, she recognized the intonations of her Aunt Victoria—not one of her parents' sisters, or their brothers' wives, but an old friend, perhaps their oldest, at a dinner party at whose house their father first had met their mother. With something of the air of its presiding genius, Aunt Vicky, Auntie V, had floated in and out of their household, always happy to credit herself for its existence and therefore, by extension, for hers and Web's. During Gert's teenage years, Victoria had been a lifesaver, rescuing her from her parents' seemingly deliberate lack of understanding of everything to do with her life and treating her to shopping trips in Manhattan, weekends at the south Jersey shore, even a five-day vacation on Block Island her senior year of high school. In recent years, Victoria's presence in their lives had receded, the consequence of her promotion to Vice President of the advertising company for which she worked, but she was still liable to put in an appearance at the odd holiday.

Victoria's standing in the line was due to a speaking engagement with a sorority at Penrose College, in Poughkeepsie, to which she had decided it would be pleasant to ride the train up the east shore of the Hudson. She was dressed with typical elegance, in a black suit whose short skirt showed her legs fit as ever, and although her cheeks and jaw had lost some of their firmness of definition, her personality blazed forth, and Gert once more found herself talking with her as she would have one of her girlfriends. The result of their brief exchange was a decision to meet for lunch, which consultation with their respective Blackberries determined would occur a week from that Saturday; there was, Victoria said, a new place in NoHo she was dying to try, and this would provide the perfect opportunity. Gert left their meeting feeling as she always did after any time with Victoria, refreshed, recharged.

Not until the other side of her visit with Miss Bruce (ten minutes of business wrapped inside two hours of formalities), as she was watching the rough cut of Web's latest film on her laptop, did the thought bob to the surface of her mind: *Maybe Aunt Vicky was the other woman.*

The idea was beyond absurd: it was perverse; it was obscene. Victoria Godfrey had been a *de facto* member of their family, closer to the four of them than a few of their blood-relations. She had been present during the proverbial thick, and she had been there through the proverbial thin. To suggest that she and Gert's father had carried on, were carrying on, an affair, was too much, was over the top.

Try as she might, though, Gert could not banish the possibility from her thoughts. The same talents for analysis and narration that had placed her near the top of her class at NYU seized on the prospect of Auntie V being *her* and found that it made a good deal of sense. While both her parents had known Victoria, her father's friendship with her predated her mother's by several years. In fact, Victoria and her father had spoken freely of the marathon phone conversations with which they'd used to pass the nights, the restaurants they'd sought out together, the bands they'd seen in concert. Certainly, the connection between them had endured the decades. And during those years, her father's consulting job had required him to travel frequently and far, as had Aunt Vicky's work first in journalism and then in advertising. That Victoria, despite her declarations that all she wanted was a good man to settle down with, continued to live alone seemed one more piece of evidence thrown on top of what had suddenly become a sizable pile.

But her mother . . . Gert closed her laptop. In the abstract, at least, Gert long had admitted to herself the probability that her father had been unfaithful to her mother, perhaps for years. Restricting her consideration to her father and Aunt Vicky, she supposed she could appreciate how, given the right combination of circumstances, their friendship could have led to something else. (Wasn't that what had brought her and Dana together?) Factor her mother into the equation, however, and the sides failed to balance. Her father's relationship with Victoria might be longer, but her mother's was deeper; all you had to do was sit there quietly as they spoke to know that, while their conversation's focus might be narrow, it was anchored in each woman's core. Gert had no trouble believing her aunt might be involved with a married man if the situation suited her, but she could not credit Auntie V betraying one of her dearest friends.

Nonetheless, the possibility would not quit her mind; after all, how many divorces had she assisted or managed in which the immediate cause of the marriage's disintegration was a friend or even in-law who had gone from close to too-close? That the same story might have repeated itself in her parents' marriage nauseated her; without changing its appearance in the slightest, everything surrounding her looked wrong, as if all of it were manifesting the same fundamental flaw. She shook her head. *All right*, she told herself, *if this is the truth, I won't run from it. I'll meet it head on.* False bravado, perhaps, but what was her alternative?

A week and a half later, pulling open the heavy glass door to Lettuce Eat and stepping into its low roar of voices, Gert repeated to herself the advice that she gave the new lawyers: *Act as if you're in control, and you will be.* She had not been this nervous arguing her first case: her heart was thwacking against her chest; her palms were wet; her legs were trembling. In moments scattered across the last ten days, she had auditioned dozens of opening lines, from the innocuous (*Hi, Aunt Vic*) to the confrontational (*What do you say we talk about you and my father?*) and although she hadn't settled on one (she was leaning towards, *I'm so glad you came: there's something I'd like to talk to you about*), she was less concerned about the exact manner in which they would begin than she was with the substance of their talk. What she would do should Auntie V confirm the narrative whose principle points Gert had posited on a legal pad she hadn't shown anyone, she could not predict. Nor did it help matters any that Victoria, in addition to a black turtleneck and jeans, was wearing a pair of dark sunglasses, the necessity of which, she explained as she stood to kiss Gert, arose from an office party that had not ended until 5:00 a.m. "I'm not dead yet, by God," Victoria said as she resumed her seat and Gert took hers. "I can still give you kids a run for your money."

Gert answered her aunt's assertion with a polite smile that she maintained for the waitress who appeared at her side proffering a menu. In reply to the girl's offer to bring her something to drink, Gert requested a Long Island iced tea and focused her attention on the menu, whose lettuce leaf shape was printed with the names of eight lunch salads. After the waitress had left for her drink, Victoria said, "That's kind of heavy-duty for Saturday brunch, don't you think?"

"Oh?" Gert nodded at Victoria's Bloody Mary.

"Darling, this is practically medicinal. Really: if I thought my HMO would cover it, I'd have my doctor write a prescription."

Despite herself, Gert laughed.

"Now," Victoria continued, "you don't look as if you were sampling new cocktails till dawn, so that drink is for something else, isn't it? Everything okay with Dana? Work?"

"Fine," Gert said, "they're both fine. Couldn't be better."

"All right, then, how about your brother? Or—his wife, what's her name, again? Sharon?"

"Sharon's fine, too. Web is Web. He's working on a new film; it's about this painter, Belvedere, Thomas Belvedere. Actually," Gert continued, "there is something—in fact, it's something I need to talk to you about."

"Sweetie, of course. What is it?"

"It has to do with my parents."

"What is it? Is everything okay? Nobody's sick, are they?"

"Here you go," the waitress said, placing Gert's drink before her. "Do you know what you'd like to order?"

Gert chose the Vietnamese salad, which, Victoria said, sounded much more interesting than what she'd been thinking of, so she ordered one, as well, dressing on the side. Once the waitress had departed, Victoria said, "The last time I saw your mother, I told her she was too skinny."

"Nobody's sick," Gert said.

"You're sure?"

"Reasonably."

"Oh, well, thank God for that." Victoria sipped her Bloody Mary. "Okay, everybody's healthy, everybody's happy: what do you want to discuss."

The Long Island Iced tea bit her tongue; Gert coughed, lowered her glass, then raised it for a second, longer drink. The alcohol poured through her in a warm flood, floating the words up to her lips: "It's my Dad. I need to talk to you about the other woman—the one he had the affair with."

At NYU, the professor who had taught Gert and her classmates the finer points of cross-examination had employed a lexicon drawn from fencing to describe the interaction between attorney and witness. Of the dozen or so terms she had elaborated, Gert's favorite had been the *coup droit*, the direct attack. As she had seen and continued to see it, a witness under cross-examination was expecting you to attempt to trick them, trip them up on some minor inconsistency. If the opposing counsel were conscious, they would have prepped the witness for exactly such an effort; thus, in Gert's eyes, it was more effective (unexpected, even) to get right to the point. The strategy didn't always succeed—none did—but the times it worked, a certain look would come over the witness's face, the muscles around their eyes, their mouths responding to the words their higher faculties were not yet done processing, which Gert fancied was the same as the one you would have witnessed on the person whose chest your blade had just slid into. It was a look that mixed surprise, fear, and regret; when she saw it, Gert knew the witness, and probably the case, were hers.

It was this expression that had overcome Victoria's face. For an instant, she seemed as if she might try to force her way past it, pretend that Gert's question hadn't struck her as deeply as it had, but as quickly as it appeared to arise, the impulse faded. Her hands steady, she reached up to her sunglasses and removed them, uncovering eyes that were sunken, red-rimmed with the last night's extravagances. Trading her eyeglasses for her drink, Victoria drained the Bloody Mary and held up the empty glass to their waitress, passing near, who nodded to the gesture and veered towards the bar. With a sigh, Victoria replaced the glass on the table and considered Gert, who was helping herself to more of her drink, her mind reeling with triumph and horror. The thrill that sped through her whenever her *coup droit* succeeded carried with it a cargo of anguish so intense that she considered bolting from her chair and running out of the restaurant before the conversation could proceed any further. The next time she and Aunt Vicky saw one another, they could pretend this exchange had never happened.

But of course, it was already too late for that. Victoria was speaking: "How did you find out? Your father didn't tell you, did he? I can't imagine—was it your mother? Did she say something to you?"

"No one said anything," Gert said. "Web and I put it together one night—I guess it was ten years ago. We were up late talking, and the subject turned to Mom and Dad, the way it always does, and all their little . . . quirks. I said something along the lines of, *It's as if there's another woman involved*, and Web took that idea and ran with it. It was one of those things you wouldn't have dreamed could be true—well, I wouldn't have—but the more we discussed it, the more sense it made, the more questions it answered. Since then, it's something we've pretty much come to take for granted."

"Jesus," Victoria said. "Ten years?"

Gert nodded.

"And this is—why haven't you asked me about this before?"

"For a while, we were happy to let sleeping dogs lie. Web still is, actually; he doesn't know I'm talking to you. Recently, I've—I guess I'm at a point where I want to know, for sure, one way or the other. At least, I think I do."

"No, no," Victoria said, "you're right. You should know. I should've spoken to you—not ten years ago, maybe, but it's past time. You have to understand—"

Whatever was necessary for Gert's understanding was pre-empted by the return of their waitress with Victoria's drink and their salads. Gert stared at the pile of bean sprouts, mango, banana, rice noodles, and peanut in front of her and thought that never had she felt less like eating. With each breath she took, her internal weather shifted sharply, raw fury falling into deep sadness, from which arose bitter disappointment. That she managed an, "I'm fine, thanks," to the waitress's, "Can I bring you anything else?" was more reflex than actual response.

Before the waitress left, Victoria was sampling her next Bloody Mary. She did not appear any more interested in her salad than Gert was in hers. "All right," Victoria said once she had lowered her glass. "I want—you need to remember that your father loves your mother. She loves him, too—despite everything, they love each other as much as any couple I've ever known. Promise me you'll do that."

"I know they love one another," Gert said, although she could think of few facts in which she currently had less confidence.

"They do, honey; I swear they do. But your Dad . . . " As if she might find what she wanted to say written there, Victoria's eyes searched the ceiling. "Oh, your father."

"Yes," Gert said.

"Let me—when you were, you must have been two, your father spent about three days calling everyone he knew. Anyone he couldn't reach by phone, he wrote to. All those calls, those letters, said the same thing: for the past seven years, I have been having an affair. He had decided to end it, and the only way he was going to be able to follow through on that choice was if he came clean with all his family, all his friends, starting with your mother."

Gert tried to imagine her father being that decisive about anything. "How did you feel about this?"

"In a word, shocked. It's one of those times I can remember exactly where I was, what I was doing. I was in this sleazy motel outside D.C., prepping an interview with a guy who claimed he had dirt on the junior senator from New York. There was a single, coin-operated bed in the room that had the most hideous green and orange spread on it. The walls were covered in cheap paneling and were too thin: for about an hour, I'd been listening to a couple on one side of me having drunken sex, and a baby on the other side of me wailing. Very nice. It was a little after nine o'clock; I had the TV on in an attempt to drown out the circle of life around me and the theme from *Dallas* was playing. When the phone rang, I thought it was my editor, calling with yet another last-minute question. The senator already had a reputation as a vengeful son-of-a-bitch, and my editor was nervous about any story that wasn't ironclad.

"Anyway, I heard your father's voice, and at first, all I could think was, *How did he get this number?* Then I caught up to what he was saying," Victoria shook her head. "If you'd had a feather, you could have knocked me to the floor with it. I consider myself pretty perceptive. There isn't much that happens with my friends that I didn't see coming a mile away. But this . . . "

"What was it that surprised you?" Gert said.

"Are you kidding? Your father was cheating on your mother. He had been all through their relationship, their engagement, their marriage. Who does that? Okay, plenty of people, I know, but your father, he was—I guess you could say, he played the part of the devoted husband so convincingly . . . that isn't fair. He was devoted; it's just, he'd gotten himself into such a mess. I screamed at him: *What the fuck have you done, you asshole?* I mean, there was your mother with two little kids. What was she supposed to do?"

Was the alcohol slowing her comprehension? Gert said, "What about the other woman?"

"*Her.*" Victoria spat out the word as if it were a piece of spoiled meat. "I know," she said, holding up her hand to forestall the objection Gert wasn't about to make, "that isn't fair. It takes two and all, but . . . " Victoria slapped the table, drawing glances from the diners to either side of them. "She was already married, for Christ's sake! She had been for years."

"Did—did you know her?"

"No, which is funny, because she lived three doors down from me. This is back when I had the place on West 71st. Over the years, I must have seen her God knows how many times, but I'd never paid any attention to her. Why should I have? Little did I know she was—well, little did I know.

"That changed. Although it was after eleven when I finally hung up with your father, I was back on the phone right away. There was this guy, Phil DiMarco, a private investigator we used at the paper. He specialized in the cheating spouses of the rich and powerful; we turned to him whenever the rumor mill whispered that this politician or that movie star wasn't living up to their marriage vows. He was expensive as all hell, but he and I had this kind of thing, so he said he'd have a look around and get back to me."

"Why?" Gert said. "Why did you call a PI?"

"One of my oldest friends had just admitted that he'd been lying to me for years: not exactly a statement to inspire you with trust. Who knew if this was him coming clean, or some other lie? I was pissed off. I was afraid, the way you are for your friends when they're sliding down into something very bad. I felt sick. I kept thinking about your mom and you and your brother. This was when you were living in the house on Oat Street; I don't know if you remember it, but the front door was this gigantic thing you'd expect on a castle, not a modified Cape. It was ridiculous. Whenever I hauled it open, Web would shout, *Aunt Wicky!* and run at me on those chubby legs of his. You were much more reserved: you'd hide behind your Mom with that bear, Custard, clutched to your chest like a shield, until she stepped aside and urged you forward. And now . . . your father had fucked up your lives royally. The whole situation was so unfair—I figured I could at least find out if he was telling the truth; it seemed like one thing I could do for your mother, for you."

"What did this Phil guy find out?" Gert asked. "Was my father telling the truth?"

"As far as Phil DiMarco was able to determine—he did a more thorough job than I'd expected; although he said he could take things further if I wanted him to, which I decided I didn't—anyway, yes, your Dad had been honest with me, with us.

"Which was good," Victoria said. "I mean, it beat the alternative. But there was still the matter of what he'd been so honest about. There's no way you and Web could remember any of what followed, the next year. Not to sound melodramatic, but there are large portions of it I'd like to forget. There wasn't—it's difficult to see, to hear people you love in pain. And I did love both of them. Furious as I was with your father, he was still my friend who'd made a terrible mistake he was trying to set right. Your mother was—she'd been very happy with your father, with you and Web, with all of you as a family, and then, it was like . . . " Victoria waved her hand, a gesture for chaos, unraveling.

"How is everything?" Their waitress stood beside the table, nodding at their untouched salads.

"Wonderful," Victoria said.

"Are you sure?" the girl asked. "Because—"

"Wonderful," Victoria said. "Thank you."

While Victoria had been speaking, Gert had been aware of restraining her emotions; in the pause created by the waitress's interruption, a flood of feeling rushed through her. Gert could distinguish three currents in it: relief, regret, and dread. The relief, sweet and milky as chai, was that her Auntie V could remain her Auntie V, that Gert would not have to hate her for an error she had made decades prior. The regret, sour as a rotten lime, was that her father had in fact betrayed her mother, that her and Web's elegant theory had been incarnated into sordid fact. The dread, blank as water, was that she had not yet heard the worst of Victoria's story, a groundless anxiety which, the instant she recognized it, she knew was true.

Some of what she was feeling must have been visible on her face, set loose by the alcohol she'd dropped into her empty stomach; it prompted Victoria to say, "Oh honey, I'm so sorry. This is too much, isn't it? Maybe we should change the subject, talk about the rest later."

Gert shook her head. "It's all right. I mean, it is a lot, but—go on, keep going. Tell me about the woman, the one my Dad was with. What was her name?"

"Elsie Durant. Did I mention she was married? I did, didn't I? She was a few years older than he was; I can't remember exactly how much, six or seven, something like that. Coming and going from my apartment, I kept an eye out for her, and managed to walk past her a couple of times. She was nothing special to look at: pointy nose, freckles, mousy hair that she wore up. About my height, big in the hips, not much of a chest. When I saw her, she was dressed for work, dark pantsuits that looked as if she'd bought them off the rack at Macy's."

"How did they meet?"

"At a convention out west, in Phoenix, I'm pretty sure. Your Dad was looking to drum up clients for his business, which was only a thing on the side back then. She was a sales rep for one of the companies he was hoping to snag. When they met, it was as professionals, and that they both came from the same town was a coincidence to be exploited so he could continue his sales pitch. Their conversation led to drinks, which led to dinner, which led to more drinks, which led to her hotel room." Victoria shrugged. "You've attended these kinds of things, haven't you?"

Gert nodded.

"You know: a certain percentage of the attendees treat the event as an opportunity to hook-up. It's like, while the cat's away, she's gonna play. If I were a sociologist, I'd do a study of it, try to work out the exact numbers.

"So your Dad and Elsie started out as one more tacky statistic. They could've stayed that way if he hadn't called her the week after they returned from the convention—to follow up on the matters they'd discussed. Fair enough. He had a legitimate interest in securing this contract. It was just about enough to allow him to ditch his day job, and it was the kind of high-profile association that would put him on the map. Obviously, though . . . "

"His motives were ulterior."

Victoria smirked. "You might say that. I'm not sure if he knew that she was married, at first, but if he didn't, then he found out pretty soon. Her husband was a doctor, an endocrinologist at Mount Sinai. He was Polish, had immigrated when he was eighteen. In another instance of six-degrees-of-separation, one of my friends was under his care for her thyroid. She said he was a great physician, but had all the personality of a pizza box."

"Did he know? About them?"

"I don't know. Your father insisted he must have, and it's hard to believe he didn't suspect something. Although, apparently he was a workaholic, out early in the morning, home late at night, busy weekends, so maybe he wasn't paying attention. Or could be, he was carrying on his own affair.

"To be honest," Victoria said, "there's a lot of this part of the story I have only the faintest idea of. The night your father called me, I wasn't especially interested in hearing the detailed history of his relationship with this other woman. Later on—when, I admit it, I was curious—encouraging him to revisit the details of his and Elsie's affair seemed less than a good idea. I have the impression that things were pretty intense, at first, but aren't they always? If you're in the situation, it's . . . its own thing, fresh, new; if you're outside looking in, it's a movie you've seen one too many times. He wanted her to leave her husband. She promised she would, then changed her mind. He threatened to go to her husband. She swore she'd never speak to him again if he did. Eventually, they settled into an unhappy routine. A couple of pleasant weeks would be followed by one or the other of them promising to break things off because of her marriage.

"After your father met your mother, he and Elsie didn't see one another for a while. Apparently, she was pretty pissed at him for becoming involved with somebody else. Hypocritical, yes, but what's that line about contradicting yourself? I don't know why he returned to her, and I cannot understand how he continued the affair once he was engaged, and then married, to your mother. I gather their encounters had slipped from regular to occasional, but even so . . ."

"You must have asked him about it," Gert said.

"Oh, I did. He told me he'd been in love with two women. He had been, but he'd decided to make a choice, and that was your mother."

"Do you . . . "

"Do I what? Think he was still in love with Elsie?"

"Yes."

"Your mother asked the same question," Victoria said. "She was obsessed with it. Of course your father had told her that she was the only woman he loved but really, what else was he going to say and have any chance of her not leaving him? This left it to me to hash out with her whether he was telling the truth."

"You told her he was."

"What else was I going to do? I knew that he loved your mother—that he loved you and your brother. If he and your Mom could hang in there, gain some distance from what he'd done, I was sure they would work things out. Which they did," Victoria said, "more or less."

"You still haven't answered the question."

"You noticed that. Sweetie, I don't know what to tell you. I thought he was fixated on her, mostly because he'd been unable to have her . . . completely, I guess you could say. Because she'd remained with her husband. I tend to think that isn't love—it certainly isn't the same as what he felt towards your mother."

"But it could be as strong."

"It could."

"Obviously, Mom decided to stay with him," Gert said.

"She told me your father had chosen her, and that was enough. Maybe she believed it, too—maybe it would have been, if—"

"What? If what?"

Victoria answered by draining the remainder of her Bloody Mary. Her heart suddenly jumping in her throat, Gert brought her own glass to her lips. The alcohol eased her heart back into her chest, allowing her to repeat her, "What?"

"That first year was bad," Victoria said. "Your father spent months alternating between the couch—until your Mom couldn't stand having him around, and ordered him out of the house—and a motel room—until your Mom freaked out at the prospect of him there by himself and ordered him back to the house. There wasn't much I could do for him: when I phoned, your Mom wanted to speak with me, and it wouldn't have worked for me to take him out somewhere. He had done wrong; it was his duty to suffer. Once in a while, I would stop over and find your mother out; then I would have a chance to talk to him. Not that there was much to say. Mostly, I asked him how he was doing and told him to hang in there, your Mom still loved him.

"Which was the same thing I said to your Mom: *He loves you; he loves you so much; he's made a terrible mistake but he loves you.* Nights your Dad was home to watch you guys, I'd take her out. There was a little bar down the road from the house you were living in, Kennedy's—we'd go there and order girly drinks and she could say whatever she needed to. What didn't help matters any was that your father hadn't stopped traveling. In fact, he was gone more. He'd won that contract with Elsie's company, and their association had had exactly the effect he'd expected. By the time he met your Mom, he was worth a couple of million; by the time you arrived, that amount had tripled. But whatever the money his firm brought in, it wasn't enough. (I swear, how he found the *time* to carry on an affair, I'll never know.) For about a month after he came clean on Elsie Durant, your Dad put that part of his life on hold, turned the day-to-day running of the firm over to his number two guy. During that month, though, Number Two was on the phone to him at least three or four times a day, and in the end, he made the decision to return. I wanted him to sell the business, take the money and invest it, live off that, but that was a non-starter."

Their waitress passing near, Victoria held up her glass.

"So . . . what?" Gert asked. "Was my father meeting this woman on his trips?"

"Not as far as Phil DiMarco could tell. Your Dad went where he was supposed to, met with whom he was supposed to, and otherwise kept to himself. No clandestine meetings, phone calls, or postcards. His one indulgence was presents, mainly toys for you and your brother; although he brought back things for your Mom, sometimes. Most of it was jewelry, expensive but generic. Your Dad's never had much taste when it comes to stuff like that; all your Mom's nice jewelry is stuff I told him to buy for her. There was one thing he brought back for her, a little figure he found on a trip to, I think it was Utah of all places, that was kind of interesting. It was a copy of that statue, the Venus of Willendorf? It's this incredibly old carving of a woman, a goddess or fertility figure, or both, all boobs and hips. The copy had been done in this grainy stone, not sandstone but like it, coarser. It was just the right size to sit in your hand."

"Okay," Gert said, "I'm lost."

"Here you are." Their waitress placed a fresh Bloody Mary beside Victoria and removed the empty glass. "How is everything?"

"Wonderful," Victoria said. This time, the waitress did not pursue the matter, but smiled and departed. Looking over the rim of her drink, Victoria said, "By your third birthday, your parents were—I wouldn't say they were back to normal, but they were on the mend. Finally. And then, one afternoon, the phone rings. Your Mom picks it up, and there's a woman on the other end. Not just any woman: her, Elsie Durant."

"No."

"Yes. She said, *My name is Elsie Durant. I know you know who I am. I'm sorry to call you, but I need to speak to your husband.*"

"What did Mom say?"

"What do you think? *What the fuck are you doing calling here, you fucking bitch? Haven't you done enough?* She was so angry, she couldn't relax her grip on the phone enough to slam it down—which gave Elsie the time to say, *Please. I'm dying.*"

"No."

"Yes."

"What kind of . . . ?"

"I know," Victoria said. "Your mother said the same thing, *How stupid do you think I am?* But the woman was ready for her. She told your mother she'd sent a copy of her latest medical report to your parents' house, along with her most recent X-ray. Your mother would have it tomorrow, after which, she could decide what she wanted to do."

"Which was?"

"To start with, she called me and asked me what I thought. I said she should forget she'd ever spoken to the woman and find out what she'd have to do to have her blocked from phoning them. What about the report, the X-Ray? *Don't even open that envelope,* I said. *Take it out back to the barbecue and burn it.*"

"She didn't."

"She didn't. As I'm pretty sure Elsie Durant must have known, the lure of that plain brown envelope was too much. She tore it open, and learned that the woman who had been the source of so much pain in her marriage was suffering from *glioblastoma multiforme.* It's the most common type of brain cancer. It's aggressive, and there were fewer options for treating it then than I imagine there are now. The patient history included with the report revealed that Elsie hadn't sought out treatment for her headaches until the tumor was significantly advanced. As of this moment, she was down to somewhere between six weeks and three months; although three months was an extremely optimistic prognosis. When your mother held up the X-Ray to the light, she could see the thing, a dark tree sending its branches throughout the brain."

Gert said, "She told him."

"She did. How could she not? That was what she said to me. *How could I keep this from him? She's dying.* It was too much for her to keep to herself. I would lay money that bitch knew that was exactly how she'd feel."

"What happened? Did my father see her?"

"He spoke with her. Your mother told him everything, and when she was finished, he went to the phone and called her."

"What did he say?"

"I don't know. Your Mom walked away—"

"She what?"

"She couldn't be there—that was how she put it to me."

Gert found her drink at her lips. There was less left in it than she'd realized. When the glass was empty, she said, "You must have asked Dad what they talked about."

"He wouldn't tell me."

"Why not?"

Victoria shook her head. "He wouldn't say anything. He just looked away and kept silent until I changed the subject. At first, I thought it might be too soon for him to discuss it, but no matter how much time elapsed, he wouldn't speak about it."

"What about Mom? Did he ever tell her?"

"She refused to ask him. She said if he wanted her to know, he'd tell her. I may be wrong, but I think he was waiting for her to ask him, which he would have taken as a sign that she had truly forgiven him."

"While Mom was waiting for him to come to her as a sign that he had truly repented."

"Exactly."

"Jesus." Gert searched for the waitress, couldn't find her. "How long—after she and Dad spoke, how long did Elsie Durant last?"

"Two weeks."

"Not long at all."

"No."

"How did they find out?"

"The obituary page in the *Times*," Victoria said. "I saw it, too, and let me tell you, I breathed a sigh of relief. As long as Elsie Durant was alive—not to mention, local—she was . . . I wouldn't call her a threat, exactly, but she was certainly a distraction. They could have moved, someplace out of state, but your father traveled as much as he ever had. With Elsie permanently out of the picture, I assumed your parents would be able to go forward in a way they couldn't have before—free, I guess you might say, of her presence. I had half a mind to drop in her funeral, just to make sure she was gone.

"As it turned out, I got my wish."

"You were there?" As soon as the question had left her mouth, its answer was evident: "For my father: you went to find out if he went."

"Your mother was convinced he would attend. To be honest, so was I, especially after his silence about his and Elsie's final conversation. Of course, I didn't say this to your Mom; to her, I said there was no way he'd be at the funeral. I mean, if nothing else, the woman's husband would be there, and wouldn't that be awkward? She didn't buy it. It was all I could do to convince her not to go, herself. *For God's sake*, I said, *stay home. Hasn't this woman had enough of your life already? Why give her anything more?* That had more of an effect on her, but in the end, I had to promise her that I would attend. If anybody asked, I figured I could pass myself off as a sympathetic neighbor."

"Did my Dad—"

"Yes. Elsie Durant's funeral was held upstate, at St. Tristan's, this tiny church about ten minutes from the Connecticut state line. It was a pretty place, all rolling hills and broad plains. I don't know what her connection to it was. The church itself was small, much taller than it was deep, so that it seemed as if you were sitting at the bottom of a well. The windows—some of the stained glass windows were old, original to the church, but others were more recent—replacements, I guess. The newer ones had been done in an angular, almost abstract style, so that it was if they were less saints and more these strange assemblies of shapes.

"Your father and I sat on opposite sides at the back of the church, which still wasn't that far from the altar. The funeral was a much smaller affair than I'd expected: counting the priest and the altar boys, there were maybe ten or eleven people there. The rest of the mourners sat in the front pews. There was an older man with a broad back who appeared to be the husband, a cluster of skinny women who were either sisters or cousins of the deceased, and a couple of nondescript types who might have been family friends. Honestly, I was shocked at how empty the church was. I—it sounds silly, but Elsie Durant had been such a—she had loomed over your parents' lives, their marriage, over my life, too—she had been such a presence that I had imagined her at the center of all sorts of lives. I had pictured a church packed with mourners—maybe half of them her illicit lovers, but full, nonetheless. I was unprepared for the stillness of—you know how churches catch and amplify each sob, each cough, each creak of the pew as you shift to make yourself more comfortable. That was what her funeral was to me, an assortment of random sounds echoing in an almost-empty church.

"After the service was over, before they'd wheeled the coffin out, I snuck out and waited in my car. Not only did your Dad shake Elsie's husband's hand—and say I can't imagine what to him—he accompanied the rest of the mourners as they followed the hearse on foot across the parking lot and into the cemetery. He stayed through the graveside ceremony, and after that was over, the coffin lowered into the ground, everybody leaving, he remained in place. He watched the workmen use a backhoe to maneuver the lid of the vault into place. He watched them shovel the mound of earth that had been draped with a green cover into the hole. Once the grave was filled, and the workers had heaped the floral arrangements on top of it, he held his position. Finally, I had to go: I hadn't been to the bathroom in hours, not to mention, I was starving. I left with him still standing there."

"He'd seen you—I mean, in the church."

"Oh yes," Victoria said. "We'd made eye contact as soon as I sat down, glanced around, and realized he was directly across from me. I blushed, as if he were the one catching me doing something wrong, which irritated me to no end. I kept my eyes forward for the rest of my time there—when I left, I stared at the floor."

"What did he say to you about it?"

"Nothing. We never discussed it."

"What? Why not?"

"I assumed he would call me; it was what he'd done before. And I was— frankly, I was too pissed-off to pick up the phone, myself."

"Because he'd done what you thought he would."

"Yes. But—"

"You were afraid of what he might say if you did talk."

"All things considered, wouldn't you have been?"

"What did you tell Mom?"

"Pretty much what I said to you: that he'd been at the back of the church and I'd left before he did."

"Did you mention him standing at the grave?"

"She didn't need to hear that."

"I assume they never talked about it."

Victoria shook her head. "No. She knew, and he knew she knew, but neither wanted to make the first move. Your mother discussed it with me— for years. I would come over and we would sit at the dining room table—this was when you were in the house on Trevor Lane, the one with the tiny living room. However our conversation started, it always ended with her asking me what your father attending Elsie Durant's funeral meant. Needless to say, she was certain she knew what his presence in that back pew had implied. Well, that's not it, exactly: she was afraid she knew its significance. Who am I kidding? So was I. Not that I ever let on to your Mom. To her, I said that your father hadn't been doing anything more than paying his respects. If he'd loved Elsie Durant that much, he never would have ended things with her; he wouldn't have elected to stay with your Mom. All the while, I was thinking, *What, are you kidding me? Maybe he changed his mind after he called things off. Maybe he wasn't the one who ended the affair: maybe she did, and in a fit of pique, he made his confessions. Maybe—God help me—he was in love with two women at once.* The possibilities were—it would be an exaggeration to say that they were endless, or even that they were all that many, but they were enough.

"We would make our way through a bottle of red, repeating what had become a very familiar argument. Your Mom would have the little statue—the souvenir your Dad had brought her, the Venus of Willendorf—in one hand. While we talked, she's turn it over in her palm—by the end of the night, her skin would be raw from the stone scraping it. On more than one occasion, that statue's pores were dotted with blood.

"After one of those conversations, I had a nightmare—years later, and I can recite it as clearly as if I'd sat up in my bed this very minute. Your Mom and Dad were standing in a dim space. It was your house—it was all the houses you'd lived in—but it was also a cave, or a kind of cave. The walls were ribbed, the grey of beef past its sell-by date. Your parents were dressed casually, the way they were sitting around the house on a Sunday. They looked—the expressions on their faces were—I want to say they were expectant. As I watched, each held out an arm and raked the nails of their other hand down the skin with such force they tore it open. Blood spilled over their arms, streaming down onto the floor. When enough of it had puddle there, they knelt and mixed their blood with the material of the floor, which was this grey dirt. Once they had a thick mud, they started pressing it into a figure. It was the statue, the Venus, and the sight of it sopping with their blood shot me out of sleep.

"You don't need to be much of a psychiatrist to figure out what my dream was about; although, given how your parents have been looking these past few years, I sometimes wonder if it wasn't just a little bit predictive. But I think about them—I have thought about them; I imagine I'll keep thinking about them—alone in that big house with that space between them, that gap they've had all these years to fill with their resentments and recriminations. Visiting them, there have been times I've been sure I could feel . . . I don't know what. A something there in the house with us. Not a presence—a ghost, no, I don't think they're being haunted by the spirit of Elsie Durant, but something else."

Gert thought of standing in the hallway looking at the door to her parents' room and not seeing anything there. She said, "What? What do you mean?"

Victoria said, "I don't know."

Returned at last, the waitress took Gert's empty glass and her request for another with an, "Of course." Once she had left, Gert sat back in her chair. "So that's it," she said. "The outline, anyway. Jesus Christ. If anyone had bothered to talk to anyone else . . . Jesus."

Victoria remained silent until after the waitress had deposited Gert's second drink on the table and Gert had sampled it. Then she said, "I understand, Gertie. When I arrange everything into a story, it seems as if it would have been so easy for the situation to have been settled with a couple of well-timed, honest conversations. But when I remember how it felt at the time—it was like having been dumped in the middle of the ocean. You were trying to keep treading water, to keep your head above the swells. If all of us had been different people, maybe we could have avoided this . . . it's quite the clusterfuck, isn't it?"

"It's my life," Gert said, "mine and Web's. This . . . what happened . . . what's still happening . . . "

"I understand," Victoria said. "I'm sorry; I'm so, so sorry. I don't know what else to say. I tried—we all tried. But . . . "

"Sometimes that isn't enough," Gert said. "It's just—why? Why did they stay together?"

"I told you, sweetie: your Mom and Dad love one another. That's . . . I used to think the worst thing in the world was falling out of love with someone. Now, though, I think I was wrong. Sometimes, you can stay in love with them."

III

One week after her lunch with Aunt Veronica, well before she had come to terms with much if any of what they'd discussed—well before she'd shared the details of Elsie Durant with Dana—Gert found herself opening the front door to her parents' house. She had spent the day a few miles up the road, surrounded by the luxury of the Mohonk Mountain House, at which she'd been attending a symposium on estate law that seemed principally a tax-cover for passing the weekend at Mohonk. While Gert could have stayed at the hotel—which would have allowed her to continue talking to the attractive young law student with whom she'd shared dinner and then an extensive conversation at the hotel bar—she had arranged to stay at her parents', whom she'd felt a need to see in the flesh since Aunt Vicky's revelations. That need, together with a sudden spasm of guilt over having spent so long in the company of another woman so clearly available when Dana was at home, working, sped her to the hotel's front portico, where a valet fetched her Prius without remarking the lateness of the hour. Her reactions slowed by the pair of martinis she'd consumed, Gert had navigated the winding road down from the mountain with her palms sweaty on the wheel; with the exception of a pair of headlights that had followed her for several miles, while she worried that they were attached to a police car, the drive to her parents' had been less exciting.

Now she was pushing the door shut behind her, gently, with the tips of her fingers, as she had when she was a teenager sneaking home well after her curfew's expiration. She half-expected to find her mother sitting on the living room couch, her legs curled under her, the TV remote in one hand as she roamed the wasteland of late-night programming. Of course, the couch was empty, but the memory caused Gert to wonder if her mother hadn't been holding something in her other hand, that weird little statue that seemed to follow her around the house. She wasn't sure: at the time, she had been more concerned with avoiding her mother's wrath, either through copious apologizing or the occasional protest at the unfairness of her having to adhere to a curfew hours earlier than any of her friends'. Had her mother been rolling that small figure in her palm, or was this an image edited in as a consequence of Auntie V's disclosures?

The air inside the house was cool, evidence of her father's continuing obsession with saving money. His micro-management of the heating had been a continuing source of contention, albeit, of a humorous stripe, between him and the rest of the family. Shivering around the kitchen table, Web and she would say, *You know how much you're worth, right?* which would prompt their father to answer, *And how do you suppose that happened?* to which Web would reply, *You took all those pennies you saved on heating oil and used them to call the bank for a loan?* at which he, Gert, and Mom would snort with laughter, Dad shake his head. Gert decided she would keep her coat and gloves on until she was upstairs.

Halfway across the living room, she paused. The last time she had stood in this space, the Christmas tree had filled the far right corner, its branches raising three decades' worth of ornaments, its base bricked with presents. Together, she and Dana, Web and Sharon, Mom and Dad, had spent a late morning that had turned into early afternoon opening presents, exchanging Christmas anecdotes, and consuming generous amounts of Macallan-enhanced-eggnog. It had been a deeply pleasant day, dominated by no single event, but suffused with contentment. *Except*, Gert thought, *that all the time, she was here with us. Elsie Durant. She watched Dana tear the wrapping from the easel Mom and Dad bought her. She sat next to me as I held up the new Scott Turow Web had given me. She hovered behind Sharon at the eggnog.*

Nor was that all. Elsie Durant had been present at the breakfast table while she, Web, and their mother had teased their father about his stinginess. During the family trips they had taken, she had accompanied them, walking the streets of Rome, climbing the Eiffel Tower, staring up at the Great Pyramid of Giza. As Gert had walked down the aisle at her high school graduation, Elsie Durant had craned her neck for a better look; when Web's first film had played over at Upstate Films, she had stood at the front of the line, one of the special guests. Every house in which they had lived was a house in which Elsie Durant had resided, too, as if all their houses had possessed an extra room, a secret chamber for their family's secret member.

A sound broke Gert's reverie, a voice, raised in a moan. She crossed to the foot of the stairs, at which she heard a second, louder moan, this one in a different voice from the first—a man's, her father's. Her foot was on the first stair before she understood what she was listening to: the noises of her parents, making love. It was not a chorus to which she ever had been privy; although Web claimed to have eavesdropped on their mother and father's intimacy on numerous occasions, Gert had missed the performances (and not-so-secretly, thought Gert had, as well). Apparently freed of the inhibitions that had stifled them while their children were under their roof, her parents were uttering a series of groans that were almost scandalously expressive; as they continued, Gert felt her cheeks redden.

The situation was almost comic: she could not imagine remaining in place for the length of her Mom and Dad's session, which might take who knew how long (was her father using Viagra?), but neither could she see creeping up the stairs as a workable option, since at some point a stray creak would betray her presence, and then how would she explain that? After a moment's reflection, Gert decided her best course would be to play slightly drunker than she was, parade up the stairs and along the hall to her room as if she'd this minute breezed in and hadn't heard a thing. Whether her parents would accept her pretense was anyone's guess, but at least the act would offer them a way out of an otherwise embarrassing scenario.

To Gert's surprise and consternation, however, the clump of her boots on the stairs did not affect the moans emanating from the second floor in the slightest. Unsure if she were being loud enough, Gert stomped harder as she approached the upstairs landing, only to hear the groans joined by sharp cries. *Oh come on*, she thought as she tromped toward her room. Was this some odd prank her parents were playing on her? They couldn't possibly be this deaf, could they?

She supposed she should be grateful to learn that her mother and father had remained intimate with one another, despite everything, despite Elsie Durant. Yet a flurry of annoyance drove her feet past the door to her bedroom, past the door to the bathroom, to the door to her parents' room, open wide. She had raised her hands, ready to clap, when what she saw on the big bed made her pause, then drop her hands, then turn and run for the front door as fast as her legs would carry her. Later, after a frantic drive home, that she had not tripped down the stairs and broken her neck would strike her as some species of miracle.

Of course, Dana would awaken and ask Gert what she was doing home, wasn't she supposed to be staying at her parents'? The smile with which Gert greeted her, the explanation that she had missed her lover so much she had opted to return that night, were triumphs of acting that brought a sleepy smile to Dana's lips and sent her back to bed, satisfied. *I am my father's daughter.* On top of the tall bookcase in her office, dust clung to a bottle of tequila that had been a gift from a client whose divorce Gert's management had made an extremely profitable decision. She retrieved it, wiped the dust from it, and carried it through to the kitchen, where she poured a generous portion of its contents into a juice glass. She had no illusions about the alcohol's ability to cleanse her memory of what she'd seen: the image was seared into her mind in all its impossibility; however, if she were lucky, its potency would numb the horror that had crouched on her all the drive back. At her first taste of the liquor, she coughed, almost gagged, but the second sip went down more smoothly.

IV

The streetlight that poured through the tall windows in her parents' room reduced its contents to black and white. The king-sized bed at its center was a granite slab, the figures on it statues whose marble limbs enacted a position worthy of the Kama Sutra. Startled as Gert was by her mother and father's athletics, she was more shocked by their skin taut against their joints, their ribs, their spines, as if, in the few weeks since last she had seen them, each had shed even more weight. In the pale light, their eyes were blank as those of Greek sculptures.

There seemed to be too many arms and legs for the couple writhing on the bed. Her father stroked her mother's cheek with the back of his hand, and another hand lingered there, brushing her hair behind her ear. Her mother tilted her head to the right, and another head moved to the left. Her parents arched their backs, and in the space between them, a third figure slid out of her father and into her mother with the motion of a swimmer pushing through the water. While her mother braced her hands on the mattress, the figure leaned forward from her and drew its hands down her father's chest, then turned back and cupped her mother's breasts. Her parents responded to the figure's caresses with a quickening of the hips, with louder moans and cries that might have been mistaken for complaints. In the space between her mother and father, Elsie Durant drew herself out of their conjoined flesh, the wedge that braced their marriage, the stone at its heart.

• • • •

Life went on, as did Death. But she did so miss her feet . . .

The Plum Blossom Lantern
Richard Parks

Michiko's servant girl Mai carried the deep pink lantern to light their way through the dark city streets. Mai was dead. Since Michiko was, too, that didn't seem so strange. In fact, very little about the situation struck Michiko as odd or even very different from when she was alive. She did have one regret, however—her feet. Michiko missed having feet.

Specifically, *her* feet. They had been quite lovely feet, she thought. Once, in Michiko's honest estimation, her very best feature, and that in a young woman with many good features: long black hair, a lovely smile, fair and unblemished skin. Now where her feet should have been there was almost nothing; at best a slight vapor, like mist rising on a cold morning or the smoke from a dying fire. She glided along, not quite walking, not quite flying, with Mai leading the way with a paper lantern the color of plum blossoms in spring.

Michiko was going to see her lover. She would come to him in the night and be gone before first light. This was how such things were done. This was proper. A certain amount of discretion was expected from a lady, a delicacy of sensibility and appreciation for the finer points of dress and deportment. While Michiko could no longer change her blue and gold brocade kimono to match the seasons, in all matters in which her current condition did not forestall her, Michiko did what was expected. Now her lover, a handsome, highborn young gentleman, expected her, and she did not intend to disappoint him.

The street was quiet. The gauze veil hanging from Michiko's *boshi* covered her face so that, if anyone had been about, her identity would have been protected, likewise as discretion dictated. Mai's head and face were cowled and hidden as well, but there was no one to see them there. Everyone kept to their houses; the wall gates were all closed, and the lanterns extinguished save for the one Mai carried. Even the dogs were silent.

"Is it so very late, Mai?" Michiko asked, as she looked around.

"The people are hiding, Mistress," Mai answered. "They are afraid."

"Afraid? Of what?"

"Of what they don't understand. Of what they do understand. Of what will happen. Of what might happen." After a few moments Mai repeated what she had said before, in the same dull tone. Michiko sighed delicately. Once Mai had been a lively, mischievous girl, but she was changed now. Sometimes it was like talking to a stone buddha—responses were limited and predictable.

"Never mind," Michiko said. "I would rather think of Hiroi. He seems somewhat unwell lately. Have you noticed?"

"He is very handsome," Mai said. "My mistress is indeed fortunate."

"Yes, but he is pale—"

"He is very handsome," Mai repeated, once, and that was all.

In times like these Michiko imagined herself and Mai in some sort of play, for that is the way her world felt to her then. Only she had the better part, and poor Mai could only speak her brief bit, whatever it might be, more like a wooden *bunraku* puppet than a person. Perhaps this was what being dead meant to Mai. For Michiko's part, it was little different than before. Life went on, as did Death. But she did so miss her feet.

Mai turned off the street and through a garden path that led to Hiroi's home. He was a scholar of good family, sent to the city to study for a time under the monks at the nearby Temple of Thousand-Armed Kannon, goddess of mercy. No monk himself, it had been love at first sight when he saw Mai leading her mistress through a darkened city street. "Plum Blossom Firefly" he had called Michiko, and wrote a poem about the lantern. He never noticed her missing feet.

Michiko found herself captivated from the start, as what young woman of taste and refinement would not? Their becoming lovers had been right, and it had happened as soon as decorously possible. Now it continued. Would continue. This was right, too.

Mai stopped on the path. Michiko, in reverie, almost collided with her. She frowned. "Foolish girl! Why have you stopped?"

Mai said a new thing then, something Michiko could not remember her saying before. "I can not see the way, Mistress."

Michiko sighed. "What nonsense, Mai! Of course you can; this path leads directly to Hiroi's house."

But it was true. There was nothing in front of them now. A solid sort of nothing, like the *kuramaku* that concealed those working behind the scene in a kabuki drama. Michiko removed her hat and veil to get a better look. She put out her hand and her long fingers brushed against a wall of darkness, cold and hard, where the path to Hiroi should have been.

"This very strange, Mai."

Mai said nothing. She merely stood, with the lantern swaying back and forth on the end of its pole. A strong breeze pushed against it, and sent Michiko's long black hair flying around her like a nimbus, but the paper lantern kept the wind at bay and the light did not go out.

I shall be quite a sight to Hiroi, like this, Michiko thought. She wondered if he would laugh to see her thus, but of course she would fix her hair before he did any such thing. Yet there was no time for that just now. She peered at the *nothing* ahead of her and, as the breeze swirled past and through her, she noticed something fluttering ahead of her, like a small caged bird. Before the wind died down she leaned forward and was able to make out small rectangles of paper and, as the breeze pushed and prodded them, the *nothing* ahead also seemed to be pushed and prodded, shifting slightly, now so transparent that she could see the path, now solid again so she could see nothing.

"Someone has written something on these scraps of paper and tied them to the bushes along the path."

"Yes," Mai said, but that was all.

"If the wind was to push hard enough," Michiko said, "perhaps these impertinent scraps might be persuaded to let us pass."

The wind, which had started to die down, obediently picked up again and set the paper rectangles dancing. The barrier shimmered, and writhed, and the wind blew harder and harder. Michiko's hair flowed around her in long streams and little wavelets and curls, like the currents in a glossy black river. One of the wardings tore loose from a bush and fluttered away like a white moth, then another, then another. The black wall collapsed and blew away with them. In a moment the breeze died away.

"I will hold the lantern while you comb my hair, Mai. Do it quickly and let us be gone. Hiroi is waiting."

Someone else was waiting. They found him when they came to the small wooden bridge that arched over a stream crossing the path some little ways from Hiroi's door. He stood in front of the bridge, blocking their way: a young monk with fierce eyes and a staff of rings that jangled when he brought the staff down hard on the path in front of him.

"Stay back, demon!" he said.

Michiko just stared at him for a moment. "I am not a demon. I am Yoshitomo no Michiko and I have come to see Fujiwara no Hiroi at his own invitation. Stand aside, monk."

"Perhaps you were a girl named Michiko, once," he said. "Now you are a night demon come to steal the life from that young man. I shall not permit it. I planted wards covered in scripture from the Lotus Sutra. I don't know how you got past them, but you will not get past me."

Michiko had never been spoken to in such a manner and she was in no mood for it. "Such insolence! Are you going to claim that Fujiwara-san put you up to this?"

The monk looked a little uncomfortable. "Hiroi is not in his right mind, demon. He does not understand what you are, nor can I convince him. Yet I saw what was happening. It was my duty to prevent it."

"To keep me away from my love? How is this duty? What vow does it break, what honor uphold? Hiroi wants to see me. I can feel him calling me. Who are you to say what we should and should not do?"

"This place is for the living. You do not belong here!"

Michiko, being a well-bred young lady, covered her mouth with one dainty hand as she smiled. She stepped closer, fully into the glow of the plum blossom lantern. "Yet I *am* here, little monk. You can touch me if you doubt it."

He drew back. "Don't tempt me, demon. I am stronger than you!"

Michiko sighed. "Of course you are. I am but a frail young woman, and no match for a wise and powerful and pious monk like yourself. So let me ask you one question. If you can answer it, I will go away. I will not trouble Hiroi again, though he pines for me every day and I fear for his health."

"No tricks, demon," the monk said grimly.

"No tricks at all. No riddles, paradoxes, no great obscure pieces of knowledge known only, I am told, to demons of the Ten Hells and the Enlightened. Just a simple question. Agreed?"

The monk frowned. "Well . . . very well. What is your question?"

"First I want to be clear on your understanding. You say I do not belong here. You say I was once the girl called Michiko and am now some foul creature that stalks the night and preys upon the innocent. Is this so?"

"It is," the monk said.

"Well then, tell me: why am I here?"

"Why? To prey—"

"Please do not repeat yourself, monk. Even if I accept that what you say is true, *what* I do is not the same as *why*. Surely you understand the difference? I am here. Why? I did die; I do not dispute that. I remember a sickness that claimed half the city, and myself and my dear little Mai besides. And yet I remain. She remains, too. Sometimes I think she's here merely as a shadow of me, or of herself, but I remember for us both, and we remain. The Ten Hells did not open their gates to me, nor did Paradise, nor the River of Souls. Why?"

"Perhaps . . . perhaps the funeral rites were not properly performed."

" 'Perhaps' is not an answer, yet I am not so impatient as you think me. Pray for me now, sir monk, with all your power and piety. Open the way to where you say I should be and I promise you I will go, and with gratitude."

The monk immediately sat *zazen* on the foot of the bridge, legs crossed and eyes closed, and he began to chant. He chanted for a long time while Michiko and Mai stood in the glow of the lantern. When he opened his eyes many hours later, Michiko and Mai were waiting, and the lantern was still glowing.

"I belong here, monk," Michiko said gently. "And Hiroi chose me and he made me love him. We are fated to be together and he is waiting for me now."

"So it seems." There were tears in the monk's eyes as he stood up and moved aside. His face showed no anger, no fear, but only a great sadness. "A man's karma belongs to him alone," the monk said. "I will pray for Hiroi's soul instead."

Mai led the way over the bridge with the plum blossom lantern, and Michiko followed serenely. "I would not harm Hiroi for all the world, Mai, but I have no doubt the silly little monk meant well," she said, but Mai said nothing.

Hiroi was sleeping a restless sleep but he opened his eyes and smiled weakly when Michiko glided into the room. He did look pale, and weary, but he was so glad to see Michiko that soon they both forgot all about that. Mai found a stand for the lantern and made a discreet exit, and when the time came to leave she carried the lantern before them. There was no sign of the monk.

When Michiko went to Hiroi's home again the house was cold and dark, and Hiroi was nowhere to be found. Michiko sent Mai out to make inquiries. Later, in the empty place where they dwelled, Mai returned and told her mistress about the funeral. Hiroi's family was very sad, as was Michiko. She would never forget the beautiful young man, but she also knew that, in time, there would be another. It seemed that there was always another, sooner or later.

Michiko knew it would be soon.

One particular young man, the right young man, the correct and proper young man, would see her walking at night, her servant carrying the plum blossom lantern. He would call her his plum blossom firefly as Hiroi had done, and write poetry to her that did not seem to be about her at all, and yet always was. She would love him, for how could she not? They would be together then and would love one another and be very happy.

For a while.

"The living world was made for joy and sorrow," Michiko said to Mai. "We are part of that as well."

"Yes, Mistress," Mai said, but that was all she said. Night was coming. As she had done so many times before, Mai lit the plum blossom lantern.

• • • •

The morning after the camera came, he'd finally pulled Teresa's door shut.
That afternoon, it was open again.

Uncle
Stephen Graham Jones

It must have been just about the very last thing Teresa ordered before she died.

A handheld laser infrared thermometer.

The packaging made it look like a ray gun, complete with a red beam shooting out across the room. Even thinking about holding it, I could feel the fingers of my left hand spreading away from each other like in a Western when the camera's focused down alongside the thigh of some quick-draw artist.

I figured it was the last thing she ordered because it didn't show up until two weeks after the funeral. On some slow boat from Malaysia, probably. Meaning sending it back was going to be a headache, especially since she'd used *her* credit card.

Returning it, too—I don't know. I guess it would have felt like a betrayal, sort of. Like I was passing judgment on this one last thing that was supposed to have somehow made everything better. Like I was telling her it was going to take more than something she saw in an infomercial to fix our marriage.

Before she died, we'd been sleeping in separate rooms for three months already. Keeping our take-out on different shelves in the refrigerator. Only using the ketchup at different times, using our cells instead of the landline, all that.

Neither of us wanted to say it out loud, but it was over, me and her. Not because of any particular revelation or event, though I could name a few if pushed—her too, I'm sure—but, stupid as it sounds, it was more like we'd just started going through different drive-throughs. Our tastes had changed. I mean, you need difference, you need friction in a marriage, sure, this is talkshow gospel, but what it came down to was that I was perfectly content to let her keep on with her chicken-tacos-with-sour-cream-thing, and she felt zero need to convert over to the goodness of Caesar salads with a small bowl of chili. I didn't care what she was eating, and I don't think she felt particularly sorry for the heartburn the chili kept leaving me with.

Soon we were watching different shows in different rooms, changing our own batteries in our separate remotes, then falling asleep apart, waking up on our own.

And then, as if to complete the process, she drifted into a busy intersection under the false safety of a green light.

The police came to my office to tell me about the accident, took me to the morgue.

I identified her, I called her parents, we buried her, and now I had a handheld laser IR thermometer to show for our three-year marriage.

I unboxed it, batteried it up and held it to my forearm like a science-fiction hypodermic, pulled the trigger: 98.4 degrees.

Perfectly normal.

According to the packaging, home inspectors were big on these handheld thermometers. It made their job worlds easier. .

Supposedly you could use it to find air leaks around windows, especially in winter. The living room might be a balmy, draft-free seventy-two degrees, but run this red light around that dried-out caulk line in the sill, and you'll see where your electricity bill's really being spent.

I took it to work, checked the heat on the electric pencil sharpener, on the copy machine, on the coffee pot, on my supervisor when he was walking away. My deskmate Randall shoved it down the front of his pants before I could stop him, pulled the trigger to prove how hot he was.

The microwave was nearly the exact same temperature off or not. The only difference was probably its light bulb.

On the bus a woman across from me screamed when I pulled it from my pocket.

I got off at the next stop, my hand still on the pistol grip.

When Teresa and I had first been dating it had been winter. One of our things was to walk to the liquor store seriously bundled-up in scarves and jackets and stocking caps, so that, cutting across the parking lot, we'd joke about how we were going to stick the place up, at least that's what the clerk was going to think when we walked in.

Walking home after the bus, I stopped by a different liquor store, paid for a six-pack, the thermometer's grip warm against my stomach.

The beer was Teresa's brand. I didn't even notice until my first drink.

I drank it anyway, had two gone by the time I made it home.

Later, I settled my red pointer on the late-show host's cheek. It made me feel like a sniper.

And then I checked the living room out.

The walls were warmer behind the set, cooler by the door. The lamp that I'd had on while eating was still comparatively hot. The doorway to the kitchen was the same as the wall. My foot was the same as the wall. The late-show host was on fire. The window was the Arctic, the ceiling indifferent, the carpet the same.

I tried to write my name on the wall but wasn't fast enough.

Finally I was able to draw a heart, slash an arrow across it.

The audience on television exploded with laughter.

I nodded in acknowledgement, sighted along the top of the gun down the hall, to my bedroom, but stopped at Teresa's instead.

Everywhere else in that darkness, the temperature was hovering around seventy.

There was spot right in her doorway, though.

It registered as body heat.

I sucked the red light back into my hand.

The next morning I called in when I knew I was going to be late if I tried to make it. One more tardy and I'd have to talk to somebody about it. I was a widower now, though, right? Surely they'd give me a day or two extra.

After the sun was up and the neighbors gone to work, I strolled around the front yard to make sure I was alone and then checked the faucet under the window, followed the hose—frozen solid—around the side of the house, where I was aiming.

I peeked through Teresa's window.

Her room was just her room, her doorway her doorway.

So I aimed the gun in.

Nothing, no one.

I nodded that this made sense, this was right, thank you, and spent the day at the movies, and walking around, and buying more batteries.

We hadn't had insurance on each other, but the other driver's policy had given me a big enough check, I suppose. Not enough to buy a person, but I could buy an ATV if I wanted. Maybe two. Or all the batteries I could carry.

I would have felt guilty taking the money, as she was kind of a careless driver, even if she had been in the right this time, but we had bought that car together. I told myself it was kind of like getting my investment back. And out of the marriage to boot.

When I got home, a package was waiting for me on the stoop.

It was a little hand-held movie camera, with nightshot.

I left it in its box.

• • •

Three days later, the thermometer had lost its novelty. And I wasn't turning the light in the hall off anymore.

Sitting in my chair in the living room, I could lean over, have a clean line all the way down to my bedroom—to the one I'd claimed in the bad old days. Those days being the ones when Teresa was alive, yeah.

Now, in these good and unawkward days, I could stake out the master bedroom again.

Except I wasn't.

The morning after the camera came, I'd finally pulled Teresa's door shut, nodded to myself that this was good, that it wasn't my job to clean it out.

That afternoon, it was open again.

And her doorway was always a few degrees warmer than the hall. And the curtains over her window had shifted, so I couldn't stand in the bushes and see inside anymore.

I filed it all under Things You Never Expected to Know, and went to work, the camera in my bag.

Randall bought it from me for a hundred and fifty, half to be paid next check, half before summer.

That night he called me for a refund.

"You didn't pay me anything," I told him, still trying to watch the show I had on.

"I mean on owing you," he said.

He dropped the camera off, stood on the porch like I was supposed to invite him in, and finally looked to the street behind him like somebody was waiting, sloped off for the bus stop.

I fiddled with the camera over a second microwave dinner.

Three beers of the six-pack I'd bought were still in the refrigerator. They weren't an offering, but I couldn't seem to drink them either.

At work they'd asked if I wanted to see a grief counselor. I'd said thanks, but no. Because there was just show-grief, not real loss, real sadness.

As hard as I tried, even at the funeral with her parents and little brother there, still, it felt like more like relief than sorrow. Like I'd hit the lottery without even buying a ticket. Game over, reset, start again.

There was no way what had happened was my fault. And, as far as everybody knew, we were happily married, pretty much. As happy as anybody. Except for the debt she'd been piling up, mail-ordering stuff, we didn't even have anything to argue about, really. And the card was in her name.

Instead of throwing the camera away—the invoice said it had cost her three-fifty—I flipped through the manual, arguing with Randall in my head that it was brand new, no way could it be broke.

I fell asleep with it in my lap, woke to a distinct pop.

The kids in the street, cracking baseballs into the horizon.

I dragged my blanket to the couch, sat on it backwards, on my knees, and parted the curtains, watched them.

They were letting the new kid swing. And he could. He so could.

Without thinking, I raised the camera, zoomed in on him, and, like I hadn't been able to make the camera do all last night, the little red record-light glowed on in the eyepiece.

Because nobody had catcher pads, the kids had rigged a soccer net behind the batter.

The new kid didn't need it, though.

He lofted ball after ball into the sky, everybody craning to track it each time, run it down, his little brother—they were like different stages of the same kid—ready to collect the ball, if any of them made it over the imaginary plate.

I left them to it, trolled the refrigerator for the nothing I already knew was there then skirted Teresa's door, aiming for my own.

And it hit me, the smell.

From her room.

It was one of those thick smells that are like particles in the air, that feel like an oil on your skin.

I fell over dry-heaving, trying to hold it in because I didn't want to clean it up.

After throwing up in the toilet, I hitched my shirt up over my lower face and stood in her doorway—it didn't *feel* warm—flicked her light on, but the bulb was dead.

I came back with the flashlight, cruised its yellow beam over her magazines and pillows, her shoes and purses. Over me in her dresser mirror, standing there in my boxers. Nobody staring over my reflection's shoulder, even though my skin was crawling.

That dead-raccoon smell, though. I could feel it settling on my face.

And then, over my shoulder, the skin there sensitive in a way it hadn't been since childhood, something crashed.

At first I thought it was a hand, clamping down.

Then, rationalizing at a furious pace, I told myself it was one of the beers in the refrigerator, exploding.

Wrong, wrong.

It was our shorted-out doorbell, hanging right behind me. Pile-driving into my ear, the sound straightening my back so fast that it was going to be sore.

Somebody was at the door.

I made myself smile.

Probably the new kid, he'd fouled a ball into the backyard, wanted to walk through.

Sure, sure.

I opened the door.

It was another package.

I stood there, opened it, the white peanuts drifting down to the floor, some clinging to my legs.

Air freshener. Twenty-four cans of it.

This was all because I'd faked my way through the funeral, I knew. Or, it was all in my head, was just coincidence—she'd ordered all this weeks before—but, if it was all in my head, was just guilt, then that meant I could fix it, too.

Right?

I took the remaining three beers to the cemetery, poured them into her dirt, drinking the last drink of each like we were sharing. Like I was letting her go first. Because it hadn't all been bad. There had been a time when we—well, we weren't going to conquer the world, show them how it was done. We were going to close the front door of our house, and do whatever the hell we wanted in there. Wear pajamas all day, eating chips and playing videogames. We weren't going to play by the world's rules, we were going to make our own. Screw the rat race, all the pressure to be upstanding, start a family, leverage our way to a bigger house, better car. We could fake it for work, sure, but after we punched our timecards out, we were just us.

Because we felt the same about all that, I guess we figured that was love. Or close enough. And I'm not saying it wasn't. That it couldn't have been.

I stood at the bus stop to go home but then crossed the street, went the other way instead. Just walking.

I left the camera on the slanted-frontward brick ledge in front of a liquor store window, the manual folded back as well as I could, tucked under. The world could thank me later.

Then, when I finally made it back to the house, the baseball kids stalling their game so I could hunch-shoulder past without getting beaned in the forehead, I came back onto the porch with a screwdriver, pried the middle two numbers out of 1322, put them back as 1232.

I pulled Teresa's door shut again, and this time looped a bungee cord over the handle, tied it off on a cinderblock I dragged in from the backyard, and when I was pretty sure I'd seen a shape in the mirror I couldn't account for, I just closed my eyes.

My heart just slamming in my chest.

I went to the refrigerator to reload and stopped a couple of steps away.

The floor was tacky.

With beer. It had come from the refrigerator. No empties in there.

I laughed, rubbed my smile with my hand and turned on all the lights in the house, even the front and back porch lights, then sat there with my thermometer pistol, checking each bulb from my chair.

Teresa's door never opened. Exactly like it shouldn't have. And none of the light bulbs exploded for no reason at all.

It was just me, sitting awake all night. The kids out there playing night ball, the baseball dipped in rubbing alcohol and lit with blue flame, just like some big brother had showed them.

With nightshot, it would have looked so excellent.

I thought I was dreaming it until the two police cars rolled in, to keep the city from burning down.

Or maybe we were all dreaming.

By now I was carrying the thermometer in my pocket at all times. And calling in for the week.

Randall messaged me with warnings about how much karma I did and didn't have in the office these days, but I let it slide. I had enough cash from Teresa to ride it out for a few weeks if I needed to. If it came to that.

In a way, it was being loyal to Teresa, really. I wasn't playing the world's game, wasn't doing what it expected me to do.

Or, I was being loyal to the Teresa I'd married. Not to the one who I'd kind of started thinking was looking too closely at my sisters, maybe. At their perfect, reasonable, respectable lives. Their husbands and their nice neat families. Their living rooms that were grown-up living rooms.

We didn't want all that, though. It's not what we'd signed on for.

I sat the day out, cleaning my recorded shows off the DVR, telling myself this was a chore I had to get through. That I wasn't hiding, I was doing stuff, I was taking care of things.

Because I still didn't trust the refrigerator, I ordered a pizza.

Thirty minutes later the doorbell chugged in its diabolical way.

It wasn't the pizza delivery guy but one of those respectable dads. With a letter for me that had shown up in his box.

I nodded thanks and he reached past me, tapped the street numbers by my door.

"This is why," he said.

I turned as if just seeing them.

"Kids," he explained, and we laughed together and he asked if I needed help getting his address off my house, and the question under that was about his mail, if I'd been getting it.

I told him I'd flop the numbers, it was nothing, and thanked him, stepped inside, left him there.

Behind me, the whole house was dark. For the first time in days.

Finally the dad stepped away, walked down the sidewalk instead of crossing the grass.

I aimed my thermometer at the letter. It was just normal.

I aimed it at all the light bulbs, knowing where they were by instinct, now. They were cool, like they'd never been on.

The letter was from the city, had never touched human hands, was just machine-printed, machine-stuffed, machine-stamped, and machine-mailed.

It was a traffic ticket.

Teresa was being cited for the light she hadn't run. When the other driver had run it, it had triggered all the traffic cameras in the intersection.

The picture—black and white and grainy—was down in the corner of the ticket, supposed to be proof that she'd really done this.

I didn't look, didn't look, and then I did.

The camera had her from above, of course, and from the front.

And it was her, no doubt. That wasn't the part that made me try to step away from what I was holding.

What made me step away was what she was clutching to her chest. Over her shoulder.

A baby.

To show I could, I left all the lights off, slept curled up in my chair, the thermometer pistol-gripped in my hand, pressing into my face.

Once when I woke I'd been pushing the trigger in my sleep, the beam lasered straight down the hall. Not making it all the way to the end. Stopping at something there.

I clicked the gun off, didn't look at the temperature. Made myself close my eyes again.

She was telling me something.

I shook my head no, though. That I didn't want to know. That no way was I going to call the coroner, ask if that woman from the wreck had been pregnant.

It wouldn't mean she'd been seeing somebody else. Six weeks ago, like a game of chicken, like we were each daring the other to enjoy it less, each waiting for the other to call it off, say it wasn't worth it, call uncle, we'd had sex and ended up laughing afterwards. At ourselves.

So she *could* have been pregnant. I guess. Her parents could have been grandparents, had she not pulled into that intersection. My sisters could have been a gaggle of perfect aunts.

No.

Even if she was, it's better the way it happened. Even if she was secretly thrilled about it, it's better she pulled in front of that car. That he was late to wherever he was going.

It's wrong to say it, I know, but it's the truth.

If three people bit it in that wreck instead of two, then okay. Now her and that unborn baby, they could be together forever, I guess.

Which covers no distance at all in explaining why she's still here.

The doorbell rang again and I slammed the door open.

It was my pizza.

I took it, ate it with water from the tap. Remembered splitting pizzas with Teresa.

Our first date had been pizza, then the arcade in back.

When we were going to make it forever.

I don't know if I missed her, but I missed that, I guess.

I nodded thanks to her, stood with a mouthful of the past, went to her door and pushed it open, the bungee cord humming with tension by my leg.

The heat billowed out like a rancid breath.

I came back with the air freshener she'd thought to send, sprayed two cans' worth, until I was coughing and laughing, my hand leaving tomato-sauce stains on the wall by her door.

Somewhere in there, I cried. I tried to tell myself it was for her, for us, for what we'd had, what we'd meant, but I don't know. It just hit me, that I was here, now. Alone. That this was it. That everything was just going to keep getting worse, now, from here on out.

I cried and cried, just sitting there on my knees in the hall, holding Teresa's door open the whole time. Like telling her I was sorry and *meaning* it, now.

Like isn't this *enough*?

No.

The doorbell rang its broken ring.

I shook my head no.

I stood in the hall. The doorbell rang again. Then again.

"Wait here," I said to Teresa's open door, and let it close gently, made my way to the front door, to whatever this next punishment was going to be. From the Philippines, from China, from Kentucky.

It was from six doors down, on the other side of the street.

The new kid's little brother. He was holding a bat, shuffling his feet.

Behind him the street was empty. Just the soccer net.

He'd come out alone to practice. To get good enough to play with the big kids.

Until now.

"Let me guess," I told him, and he nodded, couldn't make eye contact, and I saw him through the camera again, from a distance, with nightshot.

The way Teresa would have.

I stepped aside, shrugged, and he leaned his bat against the porch wall, came in.

In the living room now, some of the lights were on, some off. In the whole house. Perfectly normal.

"I think it went—" he started.

"I heard it," I told him, leaving the front door open, and ushered him down the hall, pushed against Teresa's door with my fingertips.

"What's that smell?" the boy said.

Teresa's room was as scattered as it had been, just me and the boy's dim outlines in the mirror, but, in the direct center of the bed, like the bed was a nest, was a baseball, the curtains in the now-open window rustling like it could have come through the window, sure.

"If anything's broke, my dad will . . . I'm sorry," the boy said, about to cry.

"No worries," I told him, "it happens," my hand to his shoulder, and guided him in like Teresa had to be wanting, held the door open just long enough for him to get to the edge of the bed, look back to me once. And then I let the bungee cord snick the door shut, collected the bat from the front porch and settled back into my chair. There wasn't even a muted scream from down the hall. Just the sound of forever.

I aimed the gun into my mouth, pulled the trigger.

The readout said I was still alive, still human.

As far as it knew, anyway.

• • • •

Against memory one must always remain vigilant . . .

The Rag-and-Bone Men
Steve Duffy

Whispering creeps through the roofs and ridges . . . a faraway wind in tall trees, the devil in the chimney. Overhead, a cold and bony moon shines on the depopulated shtetl; as you wander these deserted streets, you may take its blankness for indifference. There are no lights in the windows of the houses, nothing but the gleam of moonlight on the snow. This must be the dark time, a black year fallen on the children of Israel. Everywhere darkness holds. In the great house of the rabbi, darkness; darkness in the villas of the tradesmen, in the shanty of the gravedigger Jew far out in potter's field. Darkness in the synagogue, and only the memory of illumination, the scent of extinguished candles, so rich and immediate on this ice-cold winter's night.

It used to be said that after midnight, the dead would come to pray in the empty synagogues. And here they come now: a band of strangers from far outside the village, tatters and bones and hollows for eyes, filing in quietly, standing at the back, self-conscious, uneasy, waiting to be noticed. What do they want here? What do they say to you? Stumbling, incoherent; they tell of a field that wells with thick dark blood, of a mountain of wedding rings, of a column of smoke by day and a column of fire by night, of an Angel all in white . . . is this Padernice? they ask, uncertainly. Have we come at last to Padernice? Listen to us, they say; listen. And then they are silent, for they cannot speak.

It snowed in the night: soft like a magic, stealthy, transformational. From my window I look out on the London suburbs silent and unmoving, over roads untracked in the unreal light of dawn. Nothing prepares one for this wizardry, the invasion of the city by the blank and gelid gods of frost. Across the capital thick with winter and baffled by drifts is laid a charm, and who may look on unchanged, unaltered? The British, of course. Depend on the British. They will queue in a huddle of stamping and breathsteam for buses that do not come, wait phlegmatically on the platforms of deserted railway stations, and all the time invoke their famous Dunkirk spirit. Perhaps it takes a foreigner to see the magic and appreciate it properly, to understand the triumph of the exceptional over the everyday. A child of snow and ice, of the Northern forests and the Northern seas: one who speaks their secret language, in secret, to himself. I grow whimsical with age and solitude, I know, perhaps overly so, but still I think there is at least a metaphoric truth in the old tales. What race does not make a legend, the better to define itself, to understand its essential character?

So presumably even the British dream. If they do, perhaps it is of Lyonesse, the sunken lands of eternal summer, the island gone down in the West. Their dream would be the memory of warmth and sun. Of course, I dream in a different language . . . For me, there is far frozen Ultima Thule, the ice realm at the top of the world; gateway to the land of Hel, to Niflheim where the dead dream of Ragnarök. All the mythologies of my birth conspire to this end, just as all magnets point North, to whiteness, to blankness, to Arktos and the Pole. Stark and unforgiving, but also a cleansing, a strength, a purity of essence. From the mystic vigor of the North sprang our nation's soul, our destiny. And at break of day on this winter solstice, I think now of those bright spring mornings in Europa, when the streets were filled with songs and banners, and a thousand years of destiny beckoned. A great cause, an entelechy; what the world was waiting for.

Last night I sat in my attic room listening to the wireless, while outside beyond the curtains fell the soft and secret snow. There was a discussion—civilized, cautious, pedantic, so British—between veterans of the late struggle, soldiers and philosophers, priests and politicians. Twenty years ago, now. But even the ones who were there, who spoke from their own knowledge, even they failed to see the absurdity. The victims, the liberators, the judges and their hangmen; what is missing? No one really understood. This is wrong. It was not enough simply to have observed, from a distance; most of all, one had to feel it, become the instrument of a Power so great, so intense . . . *Einfühlung*; perhaps it would be easier in the language of my birth. I dare not speak this language out loud any more, but sometimes I hear it—I hear it in my dreams, hollow echoes from the bottom of a well. At Christmas-time especially I remember, when I am on my own here in this dark deserted building. The radios from my youth, the flawlessness and simplicity of the *lieder*, the Valkyries singing, the great voice of the people: all now forbidden.

So my own tongue, my secret tongue, is forbidden to me, except in my dreams, and now I am Jonathan Glatzy, DP, displaced person from Lithuania, school caretaker. All the children are dismissed, and school is finished for the year, but the caretaker must stay on and discharge his duty. Today the snowfall need not be cleared away; I will check the building for leaks, attend to the boilers, and my work will soon be done. Afterwards, perhaps, I will sit at my window and watch the woods, Epping Forest in the snow, and think of those forests along the Baltic coast, where I walked so many years ago. In London no one knows of Memel by the northern seas, stronghold of the Teutonic Knights: Memel, the city of my birth, home of the family Wageknecht since generations. Through those lands the Knights once rode, forging myths for us to follow; there also lay the path of the Black Corps, and mine too. Dangerous memories, dangerous dreams; but against them there is no defense.

The city Jews, the Viennese and the Berliners, will tell you that dreams are nothing but fairytales, a droll and engaging method of relating the stories of our past, of things done and finished with. But here in the shtetl they know that some dreams belong to the future, and that in them we may see our fate, that which will come to pass and which cannot be evaded. In the shtetl, dreams are a tribunal, a court before which one dissembles in vain.

Now there are stirrings in the loosened soil; now wraiths and dybbuks hold dominion in this empty village. Now the night lies breathless, fraught with apprehension . . .

Snow all yesterday, and at intervals through the night. Today passed largely without incident, with one disturbing exception which I shall note at the appropriate place. Some children got on to the school grounds, probably through the woods, and played at snowballs in the yard; a slide makes the sloping drive down towards the main gates treacherous. I have spread it with salt. My grandmother used to leave dishes of salt on the windowsill against evil spirits, though my father laughed at her. "That's the true child of the North," he said to me, when I looked at him in surprise: "spends half her life calling on the ghosts, and when they come to her she won't even let them in."

So many memories. They come at this time of year, perhaps because there is little else to occupy my mind. As I said, in the holiday time my duties are light, and I speak with no one, except that I go for shopping, newspapers and food, a trip to the library. The high street is no more than five minutes' walk from here, due south, and beyond that London, by Central Line or bus. To the north beyond the school fence stretches Epping Forest, in summer a pleasant place to walk; I am reminded of the woods around Lake Havel, in Berlin. In the winter I go from preference into town.

There is a public house, The Woodsmen, on the roundabout near the tube station and the shops. I visit this place infrequently in the daytime, and in the evening hardly more often, but this lunchtime after shopping I felt the cold—my arthritis, the old man's curse—and stopped in for a glass of brandy, medicinal. It is small and cramped, but thankfully there were at most half-a-dozen people inside, most of them in the main bar, called the *saloon*. Here I sat, close to the frosted glass partition that divides off a smaller area to the side, called the *snug*. This serves mostly the pensioners. A few of them know me by sight, will greet me vaguely in the street; but in the saloon I am left for the most part to myself. Today when I entered the pub there was only one customer in the snug, an old man whose face is gray and much sunken. I do not know his name, but though he is largely deaf he attempts always to make a conversation with me. There is probably no harm in this, but one can never be too careful, and so I chose the saloon.

The talk was naturally of the snow: disagreements, too vague to be called arguments, about which past winter brought the heaviest falls; rumors of delays and disruption elsewhere in the country; a general agreement that the Government should do something about it. I took no part in any such discussion, and sipped my drink. The taste of brandy on a snowy day brings to mind certain memories, and had I thought more carefully I might have chosen differently.

I had finished my first glass, and been brought another, when the frosted glass to my side became briefly luminous with the leaden light of outside. Evidently, a customer had come into the snug from the snowy high street. From my position conversations in the snug may be overheard; without great interest I listened, but at first heard nothing. A shadow came level with the glass partition, waiting for service. Eventually the slow barman abandoned his game of dominoes with a sigh and tramped over to take the order. This I did not catch; however, the voice from the snug, what I heard of it, sounded oddly foreign. Always worth noting.

"Won't get rich off him, will I?" This from the barman, addressing me as he ran a glass of water from the tap. I smiled and shook my head; the barman chuckled, and slid the pint-glass along the counter, out of sight beyond the partition. Silhouetted on the screen of milky glass a shadow-figure raised it to his lips, then set it down again.

The barman returned to his table in the far corner. One of his comrades said something I could not catch, but I heard the answer: "One of them gippoes, from up in the woods there. Glass o' bleedin' water, he wanted."

"Took the pledge, has he?" This brought a ripple of laughter from the dominoes players. "It's all right, but they're all as rich as stink, aren't they? I thought?"

"They could buy and sell the likes 'o you, don't you worry." The barman is reckoned by his comrades to be an expert on all matters, and is commonly deferred to in the manner of an arbiter. "Pegs and lucky heather and rabbits' foots and suchlike . . . rag-and-boners, these ones're s'posed to be. Totters, and that. Mind you, I don't know about this one—he's a right scruffy sod. Proper bleedin' scarecrow he is; all skin an' bone, dirty clothes, worse than a tramp. Shouldn't be servin' 'im, really—lets the tone of the place down. I ask you. Glass o' water? He's like a bleedin' drink o' water himself. Foreign, too." This last in lowered voice.

"Foreign?" Here the barman, I think, indicated in my direction, or in that of the newcomer in the snug; whichever, the conversation did not continue along those lines. "No—all's I'm sayin' is, watch out. Get these lot hangin' around the place, no tellin' what they'll be up to. Lock up nights, get my drift? Keep your eyes peeled."

It amuses me, that the English consider themselves a tolerant people. They went to war for Gypsies, Poles, and Jews in faraway lands, but at home they will not have them near, and mistrust them as they mistrust all foreigners. The hypocrisy would be hard to take, was there not also protection for me in it.

The barman and his cronies resumed their game of dominoes. For a while there was peace in the saloon; and then came a voice from the snug. It was the old pensioner, who had shuffled to the counter with his empty glass of bitter. "Ernie! Ernie! When you're ready, me old son."

The barman rose wearily to his feet once more, and tramped around to the pumps. "Last of the big spenders, is it? Won't even keep me in bleedin' shoe-leather, this won't; up an' down, up an' down like a bleedin' yo-yo just to pull 'alves for the likes o' you. Have a pint and be done with it?"

"Eh? It's me bladder," said the pensioner resentfully. "You know I can't drink pints, not in my state."

"Well, that's your fourth bleedin' 'alf," said the barman. " 'Ow many was four 'alves, when you was in school?" Turning to me, he said under his breath, "Assumin' they 'ad fractions, back then."

"What?" The old man had not heard. "Speak up—I can't 'ear as well as I used to."

"Nothin', Orris; just an observation, that's all. There you go—don't drink it all at once, will you, 'cos it's gettin' very dicey with the bones over there. See if you can't give us a rest for a few minutes, there's a good 'un." Winking at me, he returned again to his game.

The old man grumbled to himself for a minute, and eventually I realized he was addressing the other man, the Gypsy who had asked for the glass of water. "It's all the same these days. No respect, no one's got the time o' day for an old man. Thinks 'e's funny, 'e does. What—I'm goin' to start drinkin' pints, in this cold? What with my bladder?"

The other man made no response. I could see him still in silhouette, unmoving, the glass of water just visible at the edge of the partition as I leaned slightly forward. I did not wish to be conspicuous: but something about that other, about the voice, unsettled me. The old man continued, "Mind you, I couldn't be drinkin' cold water neither, not on a day like today. Goes straight through you, that does. Don't you feel the cold, then? What've you got on—that's only pyjamas under your coat there, looks like. Come from the 'orspital, 'ave you? Sneaked out for a quick one?"

Still the other said nothing. The old man pursued his point, with the querulous persistence of the aged. "I say—are you from the 'orspital? You don't look well. *Are you*—" in those slow precise tones the English reserve for the foreign and feeble-witted—"*are you from the 'orspital?*"

The other man seemed about to speak, and then coughed, huskily and painfully. He reached for his water on the bar counter, where I could see it beyond the partition; a hand, smoke-gray and thin as sticks, settled around the glass. At the wrist there was the cuff of a dirty black overcoat, and beneath it some striped material. He raised the glass to his lips, gulped, and then spoke, seeming out of breath, or unused to speaking. "Padernice," he said, and though his voice was little more than a whisper I was attentive in an instant. "From Padernice." I am certain that was the word, unlikely though it seems. He set back the glass on the counter, and beneath the dirty clothes he wore I saw something on his forearm—a bluish smudge, as of ink. Once, clearly, it had been a tattoo, fresh and sharp; numbers, tattooed on his gray skin.

It speaks much for my presence of mind, for my preparedness, that I made no sound, nor betrayed myself in any other way. Instead, I drained my glass of brandy as casually as might any man, and got up from my stool, while next door in the snug the foolish old man prattled on.

"Where? Where? Foreign, is that? I been abroad once, in the war—the Great War, not the 'Itler thing, they wouldn't 'ave me, see? In the trenches, I was; trench-foot, trench-cock, gassed, you name it. Long time ago, that was; that's where me bladder first started playin' up. You sure you're not from the 'orspital? You don't look well, you don't. Like someone dug you up. Where you from, then?"

I stepped quietly towards the door, adjusting my overcoat. Still I heard the other man's answer, and this time with no shadow of a doubt. "From the woods," he said; "we come out of the woods."

"Off, are you, Mr. Glatzy?" The barman looked up from his dominoes and saw me in the doorway. "Wrap up warm, now; take care on these pavements an' that. Oh, just one more thing before you go—" he beckoned to me, and I had to step back inside to catch his confidential undertone—"watch out for these gippoes or whatever they are, in the woods. Camped up by your way they are, and they're a right dodgy lot, I'm tellin' you. There's one just come in there, now—proper Belsen 'orror, 'e is. Make sure it's all locked up round the school—you don't want that crowd 'angin' round the place, there's no tellin' what they're up to. Make off with anythin', they would. Remember, now—"

Trying not to let my voice carry, I thanked him briefly yet politely. Before he could continue I slipped outside into the freezing, already-dim afternoon, closing the door carefully so as not to make a noise. I risked one glance into the window of the snug as I walked by; there was the pensioner, and alongside him at the bar a hunched, disheveled figure with its back to me. It looked familiar—how shall I put it?—as a type rather than as an individual, and I dared not look any closer, but hurried off along the treacherous pavement. Once across the road by the roundabout I looked back towards the pub; the door to the snug was ajar, and someone, I could not tell who, was watching. Several buses came past at that moment, and when I looked back again from the shelter of a shop doorway, the snug door was once more closed, and I could see no follower. And yet I felt myself followed; all the way back.

Looking back at the incident now, I acknowledge it as nothing more than an inconvenience; an unwelcome reminder of what is past and done with. It is after all unrealistic to assume that, even if the stranger had seen me, he would be able to recognize me. One face out of thousands, millions; these are not realistic odds. Still I shall limit my visits into town for a while, and make use of my scarf and the high lapels of my overcoat. I shall also take extra care that the gates be locked, and all the doors. One forgets one's situation at one's peril; this is melodramatic, perhaps, but no less than the truth.

It is nearly ten o'clock at night now, fully dark, and it has begun snowing again. I have not turned the lights on in my attic flat; I sit and watch the snow fall, some way back from the small gabled window overlooking the playground, and the dark beyond, where lies the forest. In some ways it would have been a relief to see his face.

Joined from across the Diaspora, as if to some black malign Jerusalem . . . once before, King Herod gathered a thousand innocents together and put them to the sword, in order that one Jew-child might die. Might not another such, a second Herod, seek in the death of six million the death of one? Anonymous, unrecognized: what face in the milling transports? Which of these children at the railhead ramps?

Last night came an intruder. Around one in the morning I heard a sound from downstairs, as someone might have left ajar a door, and the wind caught it. I was not asleep, but sitting up by the window in the dark, and I took my heavy torch—unlit, I do not need it to know my way—and checked the premises. There was a back door open in the kitchens, that I had thought was shut, and there was snow blown in by the doorway, but nothing further inside. I locked the door and bolted it, and walked the empty corridors, but there was no one. Perhaps it would be best to tell the police, but this I do not wish to do—not while there are such people nearby, in the woods.

This is the first time such things have bothered me, here. Before, when I lived in East Ham, there was a synagogue and burial ground nearby, and I was obliged to be cautious. I grew a beard, and that helped, but after coming here I shaved it off. Twenty years have passed; still one never knows. I feared as much when first began my wandering. Against memory one must always remain vigilant.

The rest of the day I spent in my room up in the attic, going out only to make my customary tour of the grounds. There were footsteps in the snow on the yard; during the night someone walked all around the outside of the school, pausing at the windows where the tracks are close and crowded. In my job it is not allowed to keep a dog; and yet a dog would give me protection. I am reminded of the dogs we kept in the *Schwarze Korps*: wolfhounds, and the snow would gather on their coats, and their panting breath would fog in the winter air as they barked and leaped and plunged on their leashes. And cordite and blood and rough tobacco, and the burning of brandy in the throat on a cold day, and after the gunshots and the screaming the great stillness of the Northern forests . . . what good is it to remember?

No good; but I cannot help it. The business with the gypsy has unnerved me. Thinking back the landlord was wrong; it was a Lithuanian, surely, from the accent, and a Jew. These matters were my speciality, at the university and in the *Ahnenerbe*. Why do you study such things, said the recruiting officer with distaste. Respectfully I drew the comparison with the doctor who must study disease, the better to stamp it out. This met with approval, and so I embarked on my mission, my specialized work: first in Berlin, then in Minsk and Smolensk with Nebe, and later in the *Generalgouvernement*. Who now knows of those days? Who shall judge?

It is late on in the afternoon now, and I have just been down to the boiler-room. All is well, but I find I do not like to linger there in the dark sheds. The glow of the pilot flame through the round hole in the iron door calls forth associations, and casts odd misshapen shadows on the dirty cobwebbed brick walls. While checking the pressure gauge I heard a high whistling sound

the sound of wind in tall trees

and this too held memories. The door to the boiler-room has a habit of sticking, and as I struggled to find the knack of opening it I felt almost as if someone were pressing from the other side. Of course there was no one—I have said this already. It would be easy to slip into unwholesome patterns of speculation. I must be always on my guard.

I am back in my room now, heating some soup for the evening meal, but I have no appetite. Outside it is already dark. The trees seem very near tonight, beyond the schoolyard fence.

Into the birch woods, where the world comes to an end; a track into the forest, where lies, they say, the village of Padernice. Before he comes to the end of the journey, each sees a different village, each pictures his own shtetl or its simulacrum, comfortingly familiar. Afterwards, it is the same for each. Soul by soul, the village is populated; day by day, truckload after truckload, the pilgrims embark for Padernice, and yet still the shtetl remains empty, a dream of streets and houses on a cold dark night. Such is the paradox.

A visit this morning from the headmaster, to make sure all is well, and to bring me a present of money and some Christmas foodstuffs. We made a tour of the building together, inside and outside, and he pointed out the footsteps. I lied, and said they were my tracks, from earlier that morning. "Strange," he said; "they look almost like bare feet, see? Look, here, and here: it's for all the world like toes. I hope you had your Wellingtons on—don't want you getting frostbite, ha-ha!" So he sees it also.

Back at the main gate he shook my hand and prepared to depart in his car. "Take care over the holidays," he said; "and try not to leave the place unattended after dark if you can help it. There are some strange people about, you know. Just the other day there were some rag-and-bone men in our neighborhood, foreigners by the sound of it; I don't want to generalize or anything, but you can never be too careful." Here he blushed, remembering to whom he was talking. I promised to keep watch, and asked him for details. "Oh, they were just tinkers, I suppose," he said; "but they made my wife a little nervous—said she didn't even dare answer the door when they came knocking, bless her! If they take to loitering around here you might telephone and let me know. I'm sure the police would look in if we asked them. Do you think I ought to have a word, and get them to put you on their beat?" I assured him there was no need to trouble the police, and that I would be vigilant. Of this necessity I have no need to be reminded.

Again there had been disturbances in the night. No doors were open this time, when I looked; but still I felt someone was in the building, and many times I made my circuit of the corridors before returning to my room. How strange it is, to walk where people walk when there is only stillness and dark. Before, it used not to bother me.

The wintry spell shows no sign of abating. Now as evening sets in the snow still falls; again I sit in the darkness of my room, showing no light. A while ago I turned on the radio, as a form of company. In my youth there was a romance to the radio: at night we would listen to the songs of far-off cities up and down the dial, even distant Moscow to the east, jangling balalaikas and the groaning dirge of the Volga boatmen. "*Ach!* The ferryman on the Styx!" my father would exclaim, and make me change the station. Tonight, though, I was disappointed. Beyond Christmas carols and brash pop songs I could find no music, but at the very end of the dial there seemed to be a play for voices. The reception was poor, and I could make out nothing distinctly, but after a while I was obliged to turn it off. I thought I heard the voice from that man in the snug, the *Häftling*, the rag-and-bone man: I thought he said, Padernice, though that was of course impossible.

Padernice, the impossible village. A rumor we created for good reason: it made them feel more comfortable, thinking they were being taken to a new town, a new ghetto, whose rules they could be sure of learning before long. A place in which they might hope to shelter from the storm; somewhere the furious withering wind might pass them by. Perhaps the guards would be kind, the rations more generous, perhaps there would be stoves in the barracks, and a synagogue. Is it so cruel, to give hope where none in truth exists? At any rate, it made our task, the task of the *Einsatzgruppen*, easier. Because I spoke their language, I would say to them, in Yiddish, *Do not be afraid, nothing bad will happen to you. You are being taken to Padernice,* sonderbehandlung, *special treatment. Soon you will arrive at Padernice.* And then the short ride out into the forest, and the pits.

Padernice was our invention. In all the Eastern lands, clear out to the *chertá osédlosti,* the Russian Pale of Settlement, such a place never existed. So how could the rag-and-bone man claim that he came from Padernice? He mumbled; his voice was indistinct; but I have replayed the scenario a thousand times in my mind, and I am more and more certain that was what he said, though nothing else about him is certain any more. I must analyse the situation, and think logically. Logically. From his tattoo, he was not of those we took into the forest with *Einsatzgruppe B.* The tattoo he could only have been given on arrival at the camps. Was it Birkenau, or Belzec, or Treblinka? Kulmhof was the closest; perhaps from Kulmhof; but there they did not tattoo . . . I was at Kulmhof only a few months, so perhaps I am safe. But it is useless to conjecture. I await the night with mounting apprehension; sleep is impossible.

• • •

Chełmno, known as Kulmhof, and the castle on the banks of the Narew; Treblinka in the forest, hard by Malkinia Junction on the Bug. Upstream, Sobibor; Belzec also. South, Oświęcim of the tall birch trees in the farmlands of the Vistula. Hundreds more; but remember these, by the rivers of Poland, strung along the black spiderweb of the railway tracks. Remember these citadels of horror and despair, these ghost towns; remember these capitals of night and fog.

And the rivers of the land flowed thick and clogged with ashes; here were burnings and torments without number. Here the children were forsaken, here, the covenant broken. A black year; a darkness upon Israel.

They are coming into the building at night—whoever, or whatever, they are. I do not know how long I can hold out.

Last night, Christmas Eve, I had hoped for carol singers, but no one came near; and then, after midnight, I heard them again, as I knew I would. Footsteps, or the echoes of footsteps, and once I thought voices, and when I dared at last to go downstairs, a disturbing thing, a terrible thing.

At the rear of the building, the side that faces the woods, there is a small gymnasium and a changing-room. Here if anywhere the sounds seemed to be congregated, but when I entered there was nothing, and again I was forced to ask myself what manner of thing it is that pursues me, and then eludes me at the last. Will it come to me, or must I seek it out? The faintest glimmer of light came through the small high windows, moonlight on snowfall; in the depth of the shadows I saw a coat hanging from a peg, and for a second I thought it—why cannot I say it, even to myself?

In a corner of the changing-room is the entrance to the showers, an open portal without doors. I hesitated a second on the threshold, then went into the inky blackness and the cold. A slight skim of ice on the tiles made it slippery underfoot, and I held on to the wall as I inched around the perimeter of the room in absolute darkness; no windows in the showers, and the skylight clogged with snow. The wall at my right; one corner left, then another, then another; so I shuffled round. One more corner; but then another, and another, and now panic, that was never far from me, took me over entirely. Round and round I stumbled, faster, heedless of slipping on the treacherous tiles, and there was no way out, no way back into the changing-room. All sense of direction, of location, was gone. How could the shower-room have become so large, so echoing? A square room, ten paces on a side; where was the portal? I let go of the wall, and advanced into the center of the room, arms outstretched, clutching at thin air. My spectacles slipped from my nose—even in that cold I was sweating, my skin entirely slick with sweat—and the lenses shattered, splinters and shards of glass chittering away across the tiles. Now I could hear the sound of a thin high wind, that was perhaps nothing but the blood rushing through my body

the devil in the chimney

and hissing in my eardrums. Desperately I cast about me for escape. I came up against something; for an instant I felt flesh, and hard bone close underneath, and I screamed out loud. The shock made me open my eyes—I had not realized they were shut—and I was outside, in the changing-room, flailing at the raincoat hanging from its peg.

They said Eichmann had help, but I have no one.

We sat down by the rivers of Babylon and wept there, remembering Zion; we hung up our harps on the willow-trees, when our captors cried out for a song. We must sing at our enemies' pleasure; "A song," they call out in their mockery, "a song, from the music of Zion's house!" And shall we now sing the songs of the Lord in this stranger's land?

O Jerusalem, should I forget thee, let the skills of my right hand wither and die; let my tongue cleave to the roof of my mouth, if I cease to remember thee, if I love not Jerusalem dearer than heart's content. Babylon, thou queen without mercy, blessed be he who deals to thee the measure thou hast dealt to us; blessed be he who will catch up thy children, and dash them against the rocks!

This song we sang in Babylon, and also in Padernice.

The furnace is out, but I cannot go down to it. How many days now since it began, the incident in the bar? How long will it last? Perhaps a thousand years, or perhaps only as long as memory lasts. In any case, longer than I have left. At first light I went to the front entrance, the gates, meaning to go into town, to be among people; but they were waiting at the foot of the driveway, and at last I knew what they are, that have tracked me down. Though without spectacles one thing runs into another, and my vision is treacherously blurred, still I recognized them; I knew them in an instant. How could I not know them? I am Horst Wageknecht, Sturmbannführer SS: it is my expertise.

They stood in amongst the trees, the dull stripes of their uniforms indistinguishable from the patterns of branches against the snow, from the iron railings that afford me no defense. What did the publican call them: rag-and-bone men? Rags and bones, but he could not have seen their eyes, that watched me from out of the shadows, from out of the past. Twenty years ago, and it seemed like yesterday, as if I never escaped, never left the forests of the East with my stolen identity, my dead man's papers. Since two, three days,

I have not eaten, and I was dizzy—I almost slipped, the mouth of a pit, an abyss, a freezing wind . . .

I did not fall; I managed to turn around and stumble back to the buildings. They did not follow me inside—of course they did not need to, they must know they have me trapped here. They wait out there, where the trees begin. Were I to look out now, they would be there. I dare not try the main entrance again. At the rear there is a smaller gate, and a path through the woods that comes out near houses and the shops, but I know there will be more of them in the woods. They are creatures of the woods, I think; perhaps we all are, had we only the courage to admit it. I had the idea to telephone for a taxi, but on the line there is only static, and strange faraway voices

whispering through the roofs and ridges

and so I am trapped. Perhaps if a thaw comes . . . overwhelmingly I associate them with the snow, the forests and the snow. Last night I was forced to this conclusion: none came back, that were sent to Padernice. If these made the journey, and yet came back, then what I fear is not exposure, or a show trial in Jerusalem at the hands of the Zionist hangmen. What I now fear, I can hardly name. That which comes out of the forest does not always have a name. My grandmother knew the names of many things, but there were those of whom even she would not speak. She put salt on the window-sills as protection, and I too have done this. If I had garlic, this too would be a protection; I try to imagine the taste of garlic in my mouth, but I can taste only blood.

Towards the afternoon I seem to have slept; but when I woke there was blood on my sheets and my head ached. I may have passed out, and struck my head against the wall. For a while I could only sit on the edge of my bed, and wait for my balance to return. The room was bitterly cold; of course the heating is off—have I said this?—but also I saw the sash window was open, six or seven centimeters at the bottom. Grasping the metal frame of the bed for support I went to close it, and there I saw the saucer overturned, and the pile of salt scattered on the window-sill. There were marks in the spilled salt, that seemed to be letters traced with a finger. My head was swimming, and I could not read them, but the words were clear when I retraced them with my own finger, they said, *Komm mit uns*, that is, Come with us.

These are not men. These are not the *Untermenschen* I feared at first, not even the starved and shuffling *Mussulmänner* of my memories. My mind refuses to make the last, the obvious connection. I am very weak now; I do not know how long I can hold out.

Kaddish for Daniel Hirsch, in the lime pits at Bialystok; and for Avraham Waksszul, torn by the dogs at Majdanek. Kaddish for the cantor Samuel

Osterweil, who held the scrolls of holy Torah while the jackboots rained down on him. Kaddish for Mania Prilutzka, ten days alone in the cellar without food or water, and the villagers heaped logs on the trapdoor when she cried. Kaddish for Moshe Spiegelmann, who stole a loaf of bread; kaddish for Filip Lustig, who stepped forward in his defence, and for Yuter Springer, who cried out. Kaddish for Maurycy Naftel, left on the gallows for seven days, by way of an example. Kaddish for Lucie Berger, fifth in line on the morning Appel, and the guards counted every fifth head. Kaddish for Binyamin Handelsman, who told his eight-year-old grandson Meyer, Sei still, 's ist nur eine Dusche, hab' keine Angst, be calm, it's only a shower, don't panic. Kaddish for the column of prisoners marched out of the camp at Lieberose, April 1945, and never seen again. Kaddish for the face at the cattle-truck door, the round haunted eyes staring, pleading into the camera lens. Kaddish for Berta Fishbein, a name chalked on a suitcase, the address of an empty house in the suburbs of Berlin, where the birds cry on the dark and rippling lake. Kaddish for the ones who were not even left their names, for the ones without remembrance. Kaddish in the empty synagogue, in the darkness of a winter's night.

I cannot remember last night. At some point I went downstairs, with the idea of confronting them; I awoke in one of the classrooms, lying on the floor, aching in every bone of my body. Something was chalked on the blackboard, rough jagged lettering . . . I did not look. I had to get out; I had to come back up here, to recoup what little strength I have left. My tongue cleaves to the roof of my mouth, and I took a little snow from the window-sill, but it tastes of salt and ashes. My nose has been bleeding; certainly I have lost blood, and this also makes me dizzy. I am shivering all the time, and I am very weak. Soon I must go, while I can still walk. What else can I do? I am Horst Wageknecht . . .

It is useless to talk of justice, or to repent. I joined the SS of my own free will; willingly I went with the *Einsatzgruppen* along the Eastern front; and afterwards to the ghetto at Lodz, where I gleaned much valuable data. Then the camps: Kulmhof where we first introduced the gas-vans, then with Wirth to Treblinka, to investigate the shortfall in processing and the subsequent disruption to transport schedules. Once with Himmler to Sobibor, where they selected three hundred of the prettiest Jewesses for gassing, in honour of the *Reichsführer*'s visit. After my illness, Janovska, near Lvov. I reported to the *Ahnenerbe* in Berlin on matters of race, taking cranial measurements, securing specimens, working closely with the camp doctors and administrators. I never fired a gun till the revolt at Janovska, when the corpse-squads, the *Leichenträger*, were being liquidated out at the sands, and everyone was obliged to take part. We told them they were being taken to a safe place, a ghetto, a village in the East. You are going to Padernice, we said, as we had done at Kalisz, and Winiary, and in so many other villages; we are taking you to Padernice, and you will be safe there. And they went more easily; I do not know whether they believed it, but they wanted to believe, most of them. Mercy, deliverance; the Passover mark on the lintel, when the Angel of Death spreads his black wings. The lies we tell ourselves in the long hours of the night, to make bearable the journey into the forest.

Now I have nothing to believe, and to carry on is unbearable. I do not know what will happen to me when the darkness falls and I leave this place, and walk out into the trees where they are waiting. If I listen, I can hear their voices; sometimes a singing, as one time there was a singing in the gas chamber at Treblinka, before the whisper in the pipes, and the shrieking and the silence. And once I leave this place for the last time, what then? Is there a Padernice for me, under the branches laden with thick snow, in the mist that rises in the clearings? Or only the forest, and an end to it all? I want only an ending, and this alone seems certain.

• • • •

Tall stones and small ones, just the right size for sitting on. There were some broken stones. He knew what sort of a place this was, but it did not scare him. It was a loved place . . .

October in the Chair
Neil Gaiman

October was in the chair, so it was chilly that evening, and the leaves were red and orange and tumbled from the trees that circled the grove. The twelve of them sat around a campfire roasting huge sausages on sticks, which spat and crackled as the fat dripped onto the burning applewood, and drinking fresh apple cider, tangy and tart in their mouths.

April took a dainty bite from her sausage, which burst open as she bit into it, spilling hot juice down her chin. "Beshrew and suck-ordure on it," she said.

Squat March, sitting next to her, laughed, low and dirty, and then pulled out a huge, filthy handkerchief. "Here you go," he said.

April wiped her chin. "Thanks," she said. "The cursed bag-of-innards burned me. I'll have a blister there tomorrow."

September yawned. "You are *such* a hypochondriac," he said, across the fire. "And such *language*." He had a pencil-thin mustache, and was balding in the front, which made his forehead seem high, and wise.

"Lay off her," said May. Her dark hair was cropped short against her skull and she wore sensible boots. She smoked a small brown cigarillo, which smelled heavily of cloves. "She's sensitive."

"Oh puhlease," said September. "Spare me."

October, conscious of his position in the chair, sipped his apple cider, cleared his throat, and said, "Okay. Who wants to begin?" The chair he sat in was carved from one large block of oak wood, inlaid with ash, with cedar, and with cherrywood. The other eleven sat on tree stumps equally spaced about the small bonfire. The tree stumps had been worn smooth and comfortable by years of use.

"What about the minutes?" asked January. "We always do minutes when I'm in the chair."

"But you aren't in the chair now, are you, dear?" said September, an elegant creature of mock solicitude.

"What about the minutes?" repeated January. "You can't ignore them."

"Let the little buggers take care of themselves," said April, one hand running through her long blond hair. "And I think September should go first."

September preened and nodded. "Delighted," he said.

"Hey," said February. "Hey-hey-hey-hey-hey-hey-hey. I didn't hear the chairman ratify that. Nobody starts till October says who starts, and then nobody else talks. Can we have maybe the tiniest semblance of order here?" He peered at them; small, pale, dressed entirely in blues and grays.

"It's fine," said October. His beard was all colors, a grove of trees in autumn, deep brown and fire orange and wine red, an untrimmed tangle across the lower half of his face. His cheeks were apple red. He looked like a friend, like someone you had known all your life. "September can go first. Let's just get it rolling."

September placed the end of his sausage into his mouth, chewed daintily, and drained his cider mug. Then he stood up and bowed to the company and began to speak.

"Laurent DeLisle was the finest chef in all of Seattle; at least, Laurent DeLisle thought so, and the Michelin stars on his door confirmed him in his opinion. He was a remarkable chef, it is true—his minced lamb brioche had won se-eral awards, his smoked quail and white truffle ravioli had been described in the *Gastronome* as 'the tenth wonder of the world.' But it was his wine cellar . . . ah, his wine cellar . . . that was his source of pride and his passion.

"I understand that. The last of the white grapes are harvested in me, and the bulk of the reds: I appreciate fine wines, the aroma, the taste, the aftertaste as well.

"Laurent DeLisle bought his wines at auctions, from private wine lovers, from reputable dealers: he would insist on a pedigree for each wine, for wine frauds are, alas, too common, when the bottle is selling for perhaps five, ten, a hundred thousand dollars, or pounds, or euros.

"The treasure—the jewel—the rarest of the rare and the *ne plus ultra* of his temperature-controlled wine cellar was a bottle of 1902 Château Lafitte. It was on the wine list at $120,000, although it was, in true terms, priceless, for it was the last bottle of its kind."

"Excuse me," said August politely. He was the fattest of them all, his thin hair combed in golden wisps across his pink pate.

September glared down at his neighbor. "Yes?"

"Is this the one where some rich dude buys the wine to go with the dinner, and the chef decides that the dinner the rich dude ordered isn't good enough for the wine, so he sends out a different dinner, and the guy takes one mouthful, and he's got, like, some rare allergy and he just dies like that, and the wine never gets drunk after all?"

September said nothing. He looked a great deal.

"Because if it is, you told it before. Years ago. Dumb story then. Dumb story now." August smiled. His pink cheeks shone in the firelight.

September said, "Obviously pathos and culture are not to everyone's taste. Some people prefer their barbecues and beer, and some of us like—"

February said, "Well, I hate to say this, but he kind of does have a point. It has to be a new story."

September raised an eyebrow and pursed his lips. "I'm done," he said abruptly. He sat down on his stump.

They looked at each other across the fire, the months of the year.

June, hesitant and clean, raised her hand and said, "I have one about a guard on the X-ray machines at La Guardia Airport, who could read all about people from the outlines of their luggage on the screen, and one day she saw a luggage X-ray so beautiful that she fell in love with the person, and she had to figure out which person in the line it was, and she couldn't, and she pined for months and months. And when the person came through again she knew it this time, and it was the man, and he was a wizened old Indian man and she was pretty and black and, like twenty-five, and she knew it would never work out and she let him go, because she could also see from the shapes of his bags on the screen that he was going to die soon."

October said, "Fair enough, young June. Tell that one."

June stared at him, like a spooked animal. "I just did," she said.

October nodded. "So you did," he said, before any of the others could say anything. And then he said, "Shall we proceed to my story, then?"

February sniffed. "Out of order there, big fella. The man in the chair only tells his story when the rest of us are through. Can't go straight to the main event."

May was placing a dozen chestnuts on the grate above the fire, deploying them into patterns with her tongs. "Let him tell his story if he wants to," she said. "God knows it can't be worse than the one about the wine. And I have things to be getting back to. Flowers don't bloom by themselves. All in favor?"

"You're taking this to a formal vote?" February said. "I cannot believe this. I cannot believe this is happening." He mopped his brow with a handful of tissues, which he pulled from his sleeve.

Seven hands were raised. Four people kept their hands down—February, September, January, and July. ("I don't have anything personal on this," said July apologetically. "It's purely procedural. We shouldn't be setting precedents.")

"It's settled then," said October. "Is there anything anyone would like to say before I begin?"

"Um. Yes. Sometimes," said June, "sometimes I think somebody's watching us from the woods and then I look and there isn't anybody there. But I still think it."

April said, "That's because you're crazy."

"Mm," said September, to everybody. "She's sensitive but she's still the cruelest."

"Enough," said October. He stretched in his chair. He cracked a cobnut with his teeth, pulled out the kernel, and threw the fragments of shell into the fire, where they hissed and spat and popped, and he began.

There was a boy, October said, who was miserable at home, although they did not beat him. He did not fit well, not his family, not his town, nor even his life. He had two older brothers, who were twins, older than he was, and who hurt him or ignored him, and were popular. They played football: some games one twin would score more and be the hero, and some games the other would. Their little brother did not play football. They had a name for their brother. They called him the Runt.

They had called him the Runt since he was a baby, and at first their mother and father had chided them for it.

The twins said, "But he is the runt of the litter. Look at him. Look at us." The boys were six when they said this. Their parents thought it was cute. A name like "the Runt" can be infectious, so pretty soon the only person who called him Donald was his grandmother, when she telephoned him on his birthday, and people who did not know him.

Now, perhaps because names have power, he was a runt: skinny and small and nervous. He had been born with a runny nose, and it had not stopped running in a decade. At mealtimes, if the twins liked the food they would steal his; if they did not, they would contrive to place their food on his plate and he would find himself in trouble for leaving good food uneaten.

Their father never missed a football game, and would buy an ice cream afterward for the twin who had scored the most, and a consolation ice cream for the other twin, who hadn't. Their mother described herself as a newspaper-woman, although she mostly sold advertising space and subscriptions: she had gone back to work full-time once the twins were capable of taking care of themselves.

The other kids in the boy's class admired the twins. They had called him

Donald for several weeks in first grade, until the word trickled down that his brothers called him the Runt. His teachers rarely called him anything at all, although among themselves they could sometimes be heard to say that it was a pity the youngest Covay boy didn't have the pluck or the imagination or the life of his brothers.

The Runt could not have told you when he first decided to run away, nor when his daydreams crossed the border and became plans. By the time he admitted to himself that he was leaving he had a large Tupperware container hidden beneath a plastic sheet behind the garage, containing three Mars bars, two Milky Ways, a bag of nuts, a small bag of licorice, a flashlight, several comics, an unopened packet of beef jerky, and thirty-seven dollars, most of it in quarters. He did not like the taste of beef jerky, but he had read that explorers had survived for weeks on nothing else, and it was when he put the packet of beef jerky into the Tupperware box and pressed the lid down with a pop that he knew he was going to have to run away.

He had read books, newspapers, and magazines. He knew that if you ran away you sometimes met bad people who did bad things to you; but he had also read fairy tales, so he knew that there were kind people out there, side by side with the monsters.

The Runt was a thin ten-year-old, with a runny nose, and a blank expression. If you were to try to pick him out of a group of boys, you'd be wrong. He'd be the other one. Over at the side. The one your eye slipped over.

All through September he put off leaving. It took a really bad Friday, during the course of which both of his brothers sat on him (and the one who sat on his face broke wind, and laughed uproariously) to decide that whatever monsters were waiting out in the world would be bearable, perhaps even preferable.

Saturday, his brothers were meant to be looking after him, but soon they went into town to see a girl they liked. The Runt went around the back of the garage and took the Tupperware container out from beneath the plastic sheeting. He took it up to his bedroom. He emptied his school- bag onto his bed, filled it with his candies and comics and quarters and the beef jerky. He filled an empty soda bottle with water.

The Runt walked into the town and got on the bus. He rode west, ten-dollars-in-quarters worth of west, to a place he didn't know, which he thought was a good start, then he got off the bus and walked. There was no sidewalk now, so when cars came past he would edge over into the ditch, to safety.

The sun was high. He was hungry, so he rummaged in his bag and pulled out a Mars bar. After he ate it he found he was thirsty, and he drank almost half of the water from his soda bottle before he realized he was going to have to ration it. He had thought that once he got out of the town he would see springs of fresh water everywhere, but there were none to be found. There was a river, though, that ran beneath a wide bridge.

The Runt stopped halfway across the bridge to stare down at the brown water. He remembered something he had been told in school: that, in the end, all rivers flowed into the sea. He had never been to the seashore. He clambered down the bank and followed the river. There was a muddy path along the side of the riverbank, and an occasional beer can or plastic snack packet to show that people had been that way before, but he saw no one as he walked.

He finished his water.

He wondered if they were looking for him yet. He imagined police cars and helicopters and dogs, all trying to find him. He would evade them. He would make it to the sea.

The river ran over some rocks, and it splashed. He saw a blue heron, its wings wide, glide past him, and he saw solitary end-of-season dragonflies, and sometimes small clusters of midges, enjoying the Indian summer. The blue sky became dusk gray, and a bat swung down to snatch insects from the air. The Runt wondered where he would sleep that night.

Soon the path divided, and he took the branch that led away from the river, hoping it would lead to a house, or to a farm with an empty barn. He walked for some time, as the dusk deepened, until, at the end of the path, he found a farmhouse, half tumbled down and unpleasant-looking. The Runt walked around it, becoming increasingly certain as he walked that nothing could make him go inside, and then he climbed over a broken fence to an abandoned pasture, and settled down to sleep in the long grass with his schoolbag for his pillow.

He lay on his back, fully dressed, staring up at the sky. He was not in the slightest bit sleepy.

"They'll be missing me by now," he told himself. "They'll be worried."

He imagined himself coming home in a few years' time. The delight on his family's faces as he walked up the path to home. Their welcome. Their love.

He woke some hours later, with the bright moonlight in his face. He could see the whole world—as bright as day, like in the nursery rhyme, but pale and without colors. Above him; the moon was full, or almost, and he imagined a face looking down at him, not unkindly, in the shadows and shapes of the moon's surface.

A voice said, "Where do you come from?"

He sat up, not scared, not yet, and looked around him. Trees. Long grass. "Where are you? I don't see you."

Something he had taken for a shadow moved, beside a tree on the edge of the pasture, and he saw a boy of his own age.

"I'm running away from home," said the Runt.

"Whoa," said the boy. "That must have taken a whole lot of guts."

The Runt grinned with pride. He didn't know what to say.

"You want to walk a bit?" said the boy.

"Sure," said the Runt. He moved his schoolbag, so it was next to the fence post, so he could always find it again.

They walked down the slope, giving a wide berth to the old farmhouse.

"Does anyone live there?" asked the Runt.

"Not really," said the other boy. He had fair, fine hair that was almost white in the moonlight. "Some people tried a long time back, but they didn't like it, and they left. Then other folk moved in. But nobody lives there now. What's your name?"

"Donald," said the Runt. And then, "But they call me the Runt. What do they call you?"

The boy hesitated. "Dearly," he said.

"That's a cool name."

Dearly said, "I used to have another name, but I can't read it anymore."

They squeezed through a huge iron gateway, rusted part open, part closed into position, and they were in the little meadow at the bottom of the slope.

"This place is cool," said the Runt.

There were dozens of stones of all sizes in the small meadow. Tall stones, bigger than either of the boys, and small ones, just the right size for sitting on. There were some broken stones. The Runt knew what sort of a place this was, but it did not scare him. It was a loved place.

"Who's buried here?" he asked.

"Mostly okay people," said Dearly. "There used to be a town over there. Past those trees. Then the railroad came and they built a stop in the next town over, and our town sort of dried up and fell in and blew away. There's bushes and trees now, where the town was. You can hide in the trees and go into the old houses and jump out."

The Runt said, "Are they like that farmhouse up there? The houses?" He didn't want to go in them, if they were.

"No," said Dearly. "Nobody goes in them, except for me. And some animals, sometimes. I'm the only kid around here."

"I figured," said the Runt.

"Maybe we can go down and play in them," said Dearly.

"That would be pretty cool," said the Runt.

It was a perfect early October night: almost as warm as summer, and the harvest moon dominated the sky. You could see everything.

"Which one of these is yours?" asked the Runt.

Dearly straightened up proudly, and took the Runt by the hand. He pulled him over to an overgrown corner of the field. The two boys pushed aside the long grass. The stone was set flat into the ground, and it had dates carved into it from a hundred years before. Much of it was worn away, but beneath the dates it was possible to make out the words DEARLY DEPARTED WILL NEVER BE FORG.

"Forgotten, I'd wager," said Dearly.

"Yeah, that's what I'd say too," said the Runt.

They went out of the gate, down a gully, and into what remained of the old town. Trees grew through houses, and buildings had fallen in on themselves, but it wasn't scary. They played hide-and-seek. They explored. Dearly showed the Runt some pretty cool places, including a one-room cottage that he said was the oldest building in that whole part of the country. It was in pretty good shape, too, considering how old it was.

"I can see pretty good by moonlight," said the Runt. "Even inside. I didn't know that it was so easy."

"Yeah," said Dearly. "And after a while you get good at seeing even when there ain't any moonlight."

The Runt was envious.

"I got to go to the bathroom," said the Runt. "Is there, somewhere around here?"

Dearly thought for a moment. "I don't know," he admitted. "I don't do that stuff anymore. There are a few outhouses still standing, but they may not be safe. Best just to do it in the woods."

"Like a bear," said the Runt.

He went out the back, into the woods which pushed up against the wall of the cottage, and went behind a tree. He'd never done that before, in the open air. He felt like a wild animal. When he was done he wiped himself with fallen leaves. Then he went back out the front. Dearly was sitting in a pool of moonlight, waiting for him.

"How did you die?" asked the Runt.

"I got sick," said Dearly. "My maw cried and carried on something fierce. Then I died."

"If I stayed here with you," said the Runt, "would I have to be dead too?"

"Maybe," said Dearly. "Well, yeah. I guess."

"What's it like? Being dead."

"I don't mind it," admitted Dearly. "Worst thing is not having anyone to play with."

"But there must be lots of people up in that meadow," said the Runt. "Don't they ever play with you?"

"Nope," said Dearly. "Mostly, they sleep. And even when they walk, they can't be bothered to just go and see stuff and do things. They can't be bothered with me. You see that tree?"

It was a beech tree, its smooth gray bark cracked with age. It sat in what must once have been the town square, ninety years before.

"Yeah," said the Runt.

"You want to climb it?"

"It looks kind of high."

"It is. Real high. But it's easy to climb. I'll show you."

It was easy to climb. There were handholds in the bark, and the boys went up the big beech tree like a couple of monkeys, like pirates, like warriors. From the top of the tree one could see the whole world. The sky was starting to lighten, just a hair, in the east.

Everything waited. The night was ending. The world was holding its breath, preparing to begin again.

"This was the best day I ever had," said the Runt.

"Me too," said Dearly. "What are you going to do now?"

"I don't know," said the Runt.

He imagined himself going on, walking across the world, all the way to the sea. He imagined himself growing up and growing older, bringing himself up by his bootstraps. Somewhere in there he would become fabulously wealthy. And then he would go back to the house with the twins in it, and he would drive up to their door in his wonderful car, or perhaps he would turn up at a football game (in his imagination the twins had neither aged nor grown) and look down at them, in a kindly way. He would buy them all—the twins, his parents—a meal at the finest restaurant in the city, and they would tell him how badly they had misunderstood him and mistreated him. They would apologize and weep, and through it all he would say nothing. He would let their apologies wash over him. And then he would give each of them a gift, and afterward he would leave their lives once more, this time for good.

It was a fine dream.

In reality, he knew, he would keep walking, and be found tomorrow, or the day after that, and go home and be yelled at and everything would be the same as it ever was, and day after day, hour after hour, until the end of time he'd still be the Runt, only they'd be mad at him for leaving.

"I have to go to bed soon," said Dearly. He started to climb down the big beech tree.

Climbing down the tree was harder, the Runt found. You couldn't see where you were putting your feet, and had to feel around for somewhere to put them. Several times he slipped and slid, but Dearly went down ahead of him, and would say things like "Just a little to the right now," and they both made it down just fine.

The sky continued to lighten, and the moon was fading, and it was harder to see. They clambered back through the gully. Sometimes the Runt wasn't sure that Dearly was there at all, but when he got to the top, he saw the boy waiting for him.

They didn't say much as they walked up to the meadow filled with stones. The Runt put his arm over Dearly's shoulder, and they walked in step up the hill.

"Well," said Dearly. "Thanks for stopping by."

"I had a good time," said the Runt.

"Yeah," said Dearly. "Me too."

Down in the woods somewhere a bird began to sing.

"If I wanted to stay—?" said the Runt, all in a burst.

Then he stopped. *I might never get another chance to change it*, thought the Runt. He'd never get to the sea. They'd never let him.

Dearly didn't say anything, not for a long time. The world was gray. More birds joined the first.

"I can't do it," said Dearly eventually. "But *they* might."

"Who?"

"The ones in there." The fair boy pointed up the slope to the tumbledown farmhouse with the jagged broken windows, silhouetted against the dawn. The gray light had not changed it.

The Runt shivered. "There's people in there?" he said. "I thought you said it was empty."

"It ain't empty," said Dearly. "I said nobody lives there. Different things." He looked up at the sky. "I got to go now," he added. He squeezed the Runt's hand. And then he just wasn't there any longer.

The Runt stood in the little graveyard all on his own, listening to the birdsong on the morning air. Then he made his way up the hill. It was harder by himself.

He picked up his schoolbag from the place he had left it. He ate his last Milky Way and stared at the tumbledown building. The empty windows of the farmhouse were like eyes, watching him.

It was darker inside there. Darker than anything.

He pushed his way through the weed-choked yard. The door to the farmhouse was mostly crumbled away. He stopped at the doorway, hesitating, wondering if this was wise. He could smell damp, and rot, and something else underneath. He thought he heard something move, deep in the house, in the cellar, maybe, or the attic. A shuffle, maybe. Or a hop. It was hard to tell.

Eventually, he went inside.

• • •

Nobody said anything. October filled his wooden mug with apple cider when he was done, and drained it, and filled it again.

"It was a story," said December. "I'll say that for it." He rubbed his pale blue eyes with a fist. The fire was almost out.

"What happened next?" asked June nervously. "After he went into the house?"

May, sitting next to her, put her hand on June's arm. "Better not to think about it," she said.

"Anyone else want a turn?" asked August. There was no reply. "Then I think we're done."

"That needs to be an official motion," pointed out February.

"All in favor?" said October. There was a chorus of "Ayes." "All against?" Silence. "Then I declare this meeting adjourned."

They got up from the fireside, stretching and yawning, and walked away into the wood, in ones and twos and threes, until only October and his neighbor remained.

"Your turn in the chair next time," said October.

"I know," said November. He was pale, and thin lipped. He helped October out of the wooden chair. "I like your stories. Mine are always too dark."

"I don't think so," said October. "It's just that your nights are longer. And you aren't as warm."

"Put it like that," said November, "and I feel better. I suppose we can't help who we are."

"That's the spirit," said his brother. And they touched hands as they walked away from the fire's orange embers, taking their stories with them back into the dark.

• • • •

Did ghostly vengeance wait in the lake? Some sort of delayed retribution haunting the cold waters?

Savannah is Six
James Van Pelt

For as long as Poul could remember, he'd spent the summer at the lake where his brother drowned.

This year, as they climbed in the van, Leesa said cryptically, "Savannah is six."

Poul held his hand on the ignition key but didn't turn it. "I know."

Each year since Savannah was born, it got harder to come out. The nightmares started earlier, grew more vivid, woke him with a scream choked down, a huge hurting lump he swallowed without voicing. Poul took longer to pack the van; he delayed the day he left, and when he finally started, he drove below the speed limit.

They pulled into the long, sloping driveway down to the cottage just after noon. Leesa had slept the last hour, and Savannah colored in the back seat, surrounded by baggage and groceries. Her head was down, very serious, turning a white sky into a blue one. She always struck Poul as a somber child, for six, as if there was something sad in her life that returned to her occasionally. Not that she didn't smile or didn't act silly at times, but he'd catch her staring out the window in her bedroom before she'd go to bed, or her hand would rest on a favorite toy without picking it up, and she seemed lost. She was quick to tears if either parent scolded her, which happened seldom, but even a spilled drink at dinner filled her eyes, the tears brimming at the edge, ready to slip away.

Their cottage sat isolated by a spur of nature conservancy land on one side and on the other by a long, houseless, rocky stretch. He bought the place fourteen years earlier, the year after he married, from Dad, who didn't use it anymore.

Only a couple of hours from Terre Haute, Tribay Lake attracted a slower paced population; county covenants kept the skiers off, so the surface remained calm when the wind was low. From the air it looked like a three-leafed clover, with several miles of shoreline. An angler in a boat with a trolling motor could find plenty of isolated inlets covered with lily pads where the lunkers hung out.

By mid-June the water warmed to swimming temperature—inner tubes were stacked next to the boat house for a convenient float—and the nights cooled off for sleeping. Poul and Leesa took the front room overlooking the lake. In the first years they'd opened the big windows wide at night to listen to crickets. Lately, though, he went to bed alone while she worked crossword puzzles, or she retired early and was asleep by the time he got there.

Poul knew the lake by its smell and sounds—wet wood and fish and old barbeques, and waves lapping against the tires his dad had mounted on the pier to protect the boat, the late night birds trilling in the hills above the lake, and an echo of his mother's voice, still ringing, when Neal didn't come back. "Where's your brother?" she'd asked, her eyes already wild. "Weren't you watching Neal?" She called his name as she walked down the rocky shore looking for the younger son.

Savannah closed her book and said, "I'm going to catch a big fish this year. I'm going to see him in my raft first, then I'll hook him. But I want to visit Johnny Jacobs and his kittens first." Over Poul's objection, Leesa had bought Savannah a clear bottomed raft, just big enough to hold a child, and it was all she'd talked about for weeks.

Poul said, "They won't be kittens anymore, Speedy. That was last fall. They'll be cats by now." Gravel crunched under the wheels. Leesa didn't move, her sweater still bunched between her head and the window.

Poul wondered if she only pretended to be asleep. It was a good way to not converse, and the lean against the window kept her as far away from him as possible. "We're here, Leesa," he said, touching her hand. She didn't flinch, so maybe she actually had been sleeping.

Leesa rubbed her eyes, then pushed her short, black hair behind her ears. She'd started dyeing it last year even though Poul hadn't noticed any grey. His hair had a couple of streaks now, but his barber told him it made him distinguished. At thirty-five, he thought "distinguished" was a good look.

"I'm going to walk down to Kettle Jack's to see if he has fresh corn for the grill. I like grilled corn my first night at the lake," Leesa said. Poul wondered if she was talking to him. She'd turned her face to the side, where the oak slipped past.

Poul pulled the car under the beat-up carport next to the cottage. Scrubby brush scraped against the bumper. Leesa opened the door and was gone before he could stop the engine. Savannah said, "I don't like corn on the cob. Can we have hotdogs?"

"Sure, Speedy." On an elm next to the cottage, a frayed rope dangled, its end fifteen feet from the ground. Summers and summers ago, there'd been a knot in the end and Neal hung on while Poul pushed him. "Harder, Poul!" he'd yell, and Poul gave another shove, sending the younger boy spinning. Poul looked at the rope. He didn't remember when it had broken; it seemed like this was the first time he'd seen it in years. With the door open now, forest smells filled the car: the peculiar lake-side forest essence that was all moss and ferns and rotted logs half buried in loam, damp with Indiana summer dew. He and Neal had explored the woods from the cottage to the highway, a half-mile of deadfall and mysterious paths only the deer used. They hunted for walking sticks and giant beetles, or, with peanut butter jars in hand, trapped bulbous spiders for later examination.

Someone yelled in the distance, a child, and Poul jumped. He stood, his hands resting on the car's roof. Between the cottage and the elms beside it, a slice of lake glimmered, and a hundred feet from shore, a group of children played on a permanently anchored oil drum and wood decked diving platform, whooping in delight.

"I'd like mustard on mine, and then I'll go see the kittens," said Savannah. She had her duffel bag over her shoulder—it dragged on the ground—and was already moving toward the back door.

"Sure, Speedy," Poul said, although Savannah was already out of earshot. Poul arched, pushing his hands into his back. Sunlight cut through the leaves above in a million diamonds. He left the baggage in the car to walk to the shore. To his left, a mile away, partly around the lake's curve, Kettle Jack's long pier poked into the water. A dozen sailboats lay at anchor, their empty masts standing rock still in the windless day. Part way there, Leesa walked determinedly on the dirt path toward the lodge. Slender as the day they married. Long-legged. Satiny skin that bronzed after two days of sun. He remembered warm nights marveling at the boundaries where the dark skin became white, how she murmured encouragement, laughing deep in her throat at shared joys.

Poul unpacked the van. Most of the beach toys went around front. He stuck the yellow raft on a high, open shelf in back of the cottage where rakes and old oars were stored. Maybe she'd forget they had it.

A screen slapped shut behind him. Savannah came down the steps. "I couldn't find the hotdogs, and something smells bad in the kitchen. I'm going to count fish."

Poul said, "Let's go together. Life vest first." He found one in a pile in the storage chest against the tiny boathouse. It had a solid heft that reassured him.

She pouted as he put it on. It smelled of a winter's storage, a musty, grey odor that rose when he squeezed the belt around her. "Guess you aren't the same size as last summer? Can't have you grow up this fast. We'll have to quit feeding you."

Savannah didn't smile. "Da-ad," she said.

Minnows darted away when they stepped on the pier. To the left, weeds grew up from the mucky bottom, starting as a ten-foot wide algae belt next to the shore, and waving languidly below after that until the lake became too deep to see them. To the right, white sand began at a railroad tie border six feet from the cottage and reached into the water, a smooth, pale stretch for thirty feet. It cost two-hundred dollars every other season to have several dump truck loads of sand poured and spread to create the beach. A blunt torpedo silhouette a foot long moved toward deeper water. Probably a bass. Most perch were stockers in the lake, and a foot long blue gill would be a trophy. Only catfish and bass reached respectable size. Poul watched the fish gliding at the sand's edge, perfectly poised between the artificial beach and the lake's invisible depths. Once he'd stood at the same spot with Neal, fascinated by a three-foot long catfish, nosing its way beneath their feet. Through their reflections, through Neal's glasses and wide brown eyes and sun-blond hair, and through Poul's dark hair and blue eyes, they'd watched its broad, black back. Later they'd baited huge treble hooks with liver or soap, but the fish never returned. Dad had told them some catfish lived longer than men. That same catfish might still be prowling the lake's bottom. Would it remember a summer of two small boys? Or was it now a ghost? Did old ones die to haunt the undersides of piers? Were there places even fish were afraid to go?

Poul shivered and glanced up. Savannah was on her stomach at the pier's end. Her knees not touching wood, her weight precariously balanced. His throat seized up, and he walked quickly, almost a jog (although he didn't want to scare her) to where she looked into the water. Poul put his hand on her back, holding her there.

Savannah's hands were flat out, fingers splayed, nearly touching the surface. Without a breeze the lake was smooth as glass. "Look, Daddy. I'm underwater. Do you think she sees me?" Her reflection stared at her, its hands almost touching her own, the vision of a little girl six inches deep, looking up.

Poul's tongue felt fat in his mouth, and it was all he could do to speak without a quiver in the voice. "Yes, dear. You're lovely. Now let's go in, and I'll find the hotdogs."

Savannah held his hand as they walked toward the cottage. The boards creaked underfoot. Through the wide gaps, water undulated in a slow, fractional swell. He shook his head. She'd never been in danger. Even if she'd fallen in, the life vest would have popped her to the surface, and he was right there. He wished he'd signed her up for swimming lessons during the winter. Poul kept his head down, watching his feet next to Savannah's, her white sneakers matching his small steps. She gripped his little finger, and he smiled. After lunch, he'd break out the worms and bamboo poles (anything to avoid the clear-bottomed raft). He'd have to dig up the tall, skinny bobbers and show her again how to mount the bait on the hook.

He remembered fishing with Neal. Dad used an open bail casting reel, sending his lures to splash far away, but they had as much action tossing their bait a few feet from the boat. Poul would stare at the narrow, red and white bobber's point, held upright by the worm's weight and a couple of lead shot. The marker twitched, sending ripples away. It twitched again. "Something nibbling you, Poul," said Neal, his own pole forgotten. "Yeah," said Poul, concentrating on the bobber, which wasn't moving now. He imagined a fish eyeing it below. Could be a bass, or maybe even a pike, like the stuffed one mounted on a board above the bar at Kettle Jacks, its long mouth open and full of teeth.

Savannah cried, "Help him, Daddy."

"What?"

She pulled away, dropped to her knees and poked her head over the pier's side, trying to look under. "Help him!"

"What, Savannah? What?" Poul knelt beside her; a splinter poked his shin. "Don't fall in now!"

She sat up, her hair wet at the tips where it had dipped. "Where'd he go? Didn't you see him? He was reaching up between the boards, Daddy. You almost stepped on him."

The sun dimmed, and everything around them faded. Only Savannah was clear. Dimly children shrieked on the distant diving platform. When he spoke, it sounded to him as if they were in a bubble: his faint voice travelled no more than a yard away. "What did you see, Speedy? Who was reaching up?"

Her lip quivered. "The boy, Daddy. He was under the pier. I saw his fingers right there." She pointed. "He was stuck under the pier, but when I looked, he'd gone away. Where do you think he went to, Daddy?"

Between the boards, the lake breathed gently, the surface smooth and untroubled. A crawdad crept along the muck. Poul watched it through the gap. "I don't think there was anyone there, Speedy. Maybe your eyes played a trick on you."

Legs crossed, her hands in her lap, Savannah studied the space between the boards for a moment. Slowly, she said, "My eyes don't play tricks." She paused. "But my brain might have imagined it."

Poul released a long, slow lung full of air. He hadn't known he'd been holding it. "If you're hungry, sometimes your brain does funny things." The sun brightened. Poul shivered, and he realized sweat soaked his shirt's sides. "Let's go in and have a hotdog."

She nodded. He had to open the porch door for her; it was a high step up, and her fingers barely wrapped around the nob. Neal had been so proud his last summer when he could grip it.

Later, while Savannah put mustard on her meal, Poul said, "Why did you think it was a *boy* under the pier if all you saw was his fingers?" Savannah swallowed a bite.

"He had boy hands. Boy hands are different. I can tell." She pushed the top back on the mustard.

In the evening, Poul walked to the end of the pier. A breeze had picked up, and on the lake two sailboats glided side by side, their sails catching the sun's last yellow rays. Now all the lake was black. If he jumped in here, the water would barely come to his chest—it would be just over a six-year old's head—but within a couple strides was a steep drop-off. The wind pushed waves toward him, a series of lines that slapped against the piles as they went by. He could feel the lake in his feet. Deep in his pockets, his hands clenched. Cottages on the far shore glowed in the last light, their windows like mica specks in carved miniatures. Behind them, forest-covered hills rose to the silence of the sky.

They'd found Neal ten feet from the pier's end, his hands floating above his head, nearly on the surface, his feet firmly anchored on the bottom. Poul stood on shore, his fists jammed into his armpits, and watched them load him in the boat, wearing the face mask and snorkel, limp and small, his arms like delicate pipes, his six-year old skin as smooth and pale as milk, black boots on his feet. They were Poul's snow boots, buckled at the top and filled with sand.

Long after the sun set, and the boats disappeared and lights flickered on in cottages, music and voices drifted across the water, Poul came in to go to bed. On the porch, Savannah slept on the daybed. He checked the screens to make sure they were tight—mosquitoes were murder after dark—then locked the deadbolt, taking the key. Sometimes Savannah woke before he or Leesa did, and he didn't want her wandering outside. In the kitchen, he shook as he poured a cup of tepid coffee. A humid breeze had sucked the heat out of him. The cup warmed his hands. Moths threw themselves against the windows, pattering to get in. Leaves hushed against themselves. Years ago he'd sat at this same table, sipping hot chocolate, laughing at Neal's liquid moustache. That day they'd swam. The next they'd fish, and the summer at the lake stretched before them, a thousand holidays in a row.

Poul slipped up the stairs, keeping his weight on the side next to the wall so there would be no creaks. He left his clothes on a chair. Dock lights through the windows illuminated the room enough for him to get around without running into anything. A long lump on the bed, swaddled in shadows, was all he could see of Leesa. Except for his breathing, there was no other noise, which meant she was awake. When she slept, she whistled lightly on each exhalation. From the beginning he'd found it charming, but never mentioned it, guessing it might be embarrassing. If he spoke now, he knew she wouldn't reply.

Three years ago when they were at the cottage, she began suffering headaches at bedtime, or sore throats, or stomach cramps, or pulled muscles, or dozens of other ailments. That same summer she went from sleeping in just a pair of boxer shorts to a full, flannel nightgown. She'd start complaining about her night time illnesses before lunch, and after a while, he figured they were all a charade. The last time they'd made love had been a year ago, in this bedroom. He remembered her back to him, and he pressed against her; he could feel her muscles through the flannel, her hip's still delicate flare. She didn't move away, so he pushed against her again. It had been months since the last time, and the day had been good. She hadn't avoided him. She laughed at a joke. Maybe she's thawing, he'd thought, so he watched her, and when she went to bed, he followed. No chance for her to be sleeping before he got there. But she undressed in the bathroom, came out with the collar buttoned tightly at her neck, didn't look at him, and lay down with her back toward him. He didn't move for a while. They'd been married too long for him not to recognize all the ways she was saying, "No." Still, it *had* been months. He moved next to her, his erection painful. Outside, waves slapped upon the shore. The boat rattled in its chain.

A third time he pressed against her. Finally, without rolling, she reached back with her hand and held him. He took a sharp breath, moved into her palm, slid against her fingers. She squeezed once, not moving in any other way. When he came a few minutes later, sweat heavy on his chest, his breath quivering, Leesa slowly pulled her hand away and wiped him off on the sheets, as if she were already mostly asleep. It was the most loveless act he'd ever committed. Within moments, her whistling snore began.

That was the last time.

Why was she angry with him? Why had it gone so terribly bad? The closest they'd come to talking about it came that Christmas, after Savannah went outside to play in the snow, and he and Leesa sat wordlessly in the living room. He'd finally said, "What's wrong?" The sweater he'd given her draped across her hands; she didn't meet his eyes. "I don't like this color anymore." Later he found the gift tossed in the back of the closet.

Whatever the source of the anger, it grew worse at the lake. The distance widened, and the nightmares came more often. He lifted the covers as little as possible and lay down. Leesa didn't react. Poul looked at the ceiling. A light from a passing boat swept shadows from one side of the room to the other. It's small motor chugged faintly.

Leesa wasn't whistling. He knew she heard the same motor. If her eyes were open, she'd see the same shadows. "Savannah scared herself on the dock today," he said into the darkness, the sudden sound of his own voice startling him. Only the cooling cottage's creaks and groans answered.

Hours later, still awake, he heard a noise downstairs. A muted rasp. He propped up on his elbows. Footsteps, then another scraping sound. A bump. Nothing for a long time. His eyes ached with attention, and saliva pooled in his mouth he didn't dare swallow. After minutes, he slipped from the blankets and moved from the bed, crept down to the living room, every shadow hiding an intruder, the pulse in his ear like a throbbing announcement. He turned on a light, flicking the room into reality, then into the kitchen where moths clustered against the screens. On the porch, Savannah lay atop her covers, sleeping. Scratch marks showed where she'd pulled a chair to the door. She'd unhooked the chain, but the deadbolt defeated her. Poul tucked her in, then he grasped the door knob to check the lock again. Slick brass felt cool under his palm. Savannah had sleepwalked. When she was three, she'd done it for a few months, but she hadn't done it since. The pediatrician said it wasn't uncommon; that she'd outgrow it.

Through the porch door's window, the eastern horizon glowed, turning the lake surface purple, but the dock was black, a long, black finger with a black boat's silhouette beside it. A muskrat swam, cutting a long V in the flat water.

The knob turned under his hand. It turned again. Whoever held it on the other side was shorter than the window. Poul slapped his head against the glass. A bare stair. He ran to the kitchen, banging his shin against a stool, breath ragged in his throat, grabbed the deadbolt key from its drawer, and stumbled back to the porch. Outside, he looked up and down the shore. A quarter mile away, his closest neighbor loaded fishing gear into his boat. Poul ran around the cottage. There was no one. Mindless, he sprinted up the long dirt driveway until he stopped at the highway, bent, with his hands on his thighs, gasping. Empty road vanished into the woods on either side.

He sat on the shoulder. A deep gouge in his left foot bled freely, and he realized both feet hurt. It took ten minutes to hobble back to the cottage, and wearing only shorts, he was profoundly cold. The sun bathed the cottage's front as he walked to the door. Grass cast long shadows. His own barefooted prints showed in the dew. Poul stopped before going in. Another set of prints led to his door, rounded impressions, small, like a child wearing galoshes, coming from the lake. Then, as if the sun was an eraser passing over the yard, the dew vanished.

Leesa took Savannah into town for lunch and shopping. They needed to stock the refrigerator and freezer, and Savannah decided she couldn't live without fruit juice in the squeezable packages.

Poul sat in a lawn chair at the foot of the pier for most of the morning. The sun pressed against his forehead and eventually filled him with lazy heat. Ripples caught the light, sending it in bright, little spears at him. Waves lapped the shore. The boat, tied to the dock, thudded hollowly every once in a while like a huge aluminum drum.

If he shut his eyes, it could be thirty years earlier. The sun beat the same way, and the same ripply chorus floated in the air. On the beach he and Neal had talked about deep sea diving and fish. Poul was frustrated. He had a wonderful face mask, fins to push himself along and a snorkel, but the mask was too buoyant. He could dive underwater, but he couldn't stay near the fascinating bottom where the catfish lived. So he had a brain storm. In the boathouse he found a pair of rubber snow boots he'd left from January when he and Dad had come to the lake to fix a frozen pipe. They were supposed to fit over shoes, so his bare foot slopped around. He held the top open. "Fill them up, Neal," he said.

His brother looked at them doubtfully. "Why do you want to do that?"

"'Cause this will keep me from floating."

"Oh," Neal said with admiration. He used a yellow, plastic shovel to dump sand in. When it was full, Poul forced the bottom buckle closed. The sand squeezed his leg; he fastened the next one, and it was even tighter. Sand spilled over the top. After the last buckle, there was a strap that cinched the boot closed. It felt like his feet were in grainy cement; he couldn't even wiggle his toes.

Neal laughed when Poul tried to walk. Each foot must have weighed an extra ten pounds, and it was all he could do to shuffle forward. Poul adjusted his face mask and snorkel. "Wish me luck."

"Luck," said Neal. "Find the big catfish, okay?"

Poul nodded as he waded out. The water slapped higher on his body with each step from shore. When it reached his armpits, he put the snorkel in, then slowly squatted, his feet holding firm beneath him. He turned; underwater, the sand held ripples, a sculpture of the surface motion, while the underside of the surface undulated, meeting the beach at the shore. Then he stood, blew water from the snorkel and gave Neal a thumbs up. Neal waved back.

A few steps deeper, and the water line rose on the face mask. Another step and he was completely underwater, breathing through the snorkel. No fish, but a lot of suspended material, bits of algae. Exotic noises. A buzz that must have been a boat cruising along. A metallic clink that might be a chain under the diving platform a hundred feet away. His breath wheezing in and out of the snorkel. Other, unidentifiable sounds. Poul the adventurer, an explorer of undiscovered countries.

Then, a fish just at his vision's edge, much deeper, swam along the bottom. Poul froze, hoping it would come close, but it stayed maddeningly far. He moved toward it, sliding his foot only a few inches. It flicked away, then appeared again, still now, head on, as if it were watching him. An encounter with an alien would not have felt any more exotic. Poul leaned toward the fish, his hand out. A gesture of hello.

Water filled his mouth, straight into his throat and he was choking. It hurt! Eyes tearing, he looked up. He'd gone too deep. The top of the snorkel was below the surface. Blind panic! He flailed his arms, trying to swim up, but his feet didn't budge. He jerked, screaming through the snorkel. No air! No air! He turned toward shore, and took a step. He took another, then blew hard, clearing the water and breathed in gasps. Without pause, he continued toward shore. When he was shallow enough, he ripped the face mask off and sucked one huge breath after another. By the time he got to shore, his throat quit hurting, but he wanted to get away, to lie down and cry. He could feel it in his chest, the horrible pressure of no air, the moment when he didn't dare inhale.

"Did you see a fish?" Neal asked. He was sitting with his toes in the water, arms wrapped around his knees. "Was it totally cool?"

Poul shook his head, hiding his tears by unbuckling the boots. He scraped his feet pulling them out. Later that day Dad would smear first aid cream on them, his eyes unfocussed, his hands shaking.

Poul left the boots on the beach and went into the woods to cry. He'd never been so scared. He'd never been so scared! And when he returned an hour later, Mom was walking up the shore, calling Neal's name.

"Where's your brother?" She'd asked, her eyes already wild. "Weren't you watching Neal?"

Poul rose from the lawn chair; he could feel the nylon webbing creases in his backside. Neal was six, he thought. Savannah is six. The two facts came together with inevitable weight. For years he hadn't thought much about Neal's death. Every once in a while, a memory would flare: the two of them talking late at night, after they were supposed to be asleep, the model airplane Neal had given him for his birthday, the words carefully inscribed on the back, *For mi big brother. Luve, Neal.* Neal trusted him, looked up to him, but most of the time Neal didn't exist anymore. Then Savannah was born, and Neal came back, a little stronger each summer. Maybe that's what Leesa sensed: the younger brother, dead within him.

Savannah is six, Poul thought, and Neal has been waiting.

He went through the cottage and made sure the screens were tight. It wouldn't do for the house to be filled with mosquitoes when Leesa and Savannah returned. For a moment he held a pen over a notepad in the kitchen, but put it down without writing. A beach towel went over his shoulder, and he walked to the end of the pier. Standing with his toes wrapped over the edge, a breeze in his face, felt like leaning over an abyss. Beyond the drop-off, he saw no bottom. The big fish were there, the fishy mysteries he'd left to Neal.

He dove in, a long shallow dive that took him yards away without a stroke. Water rushed by his ears. Bubbles streamed from his nose. He came to the surface, treaded. From his shoulders to his knees, the lake was warm, a comfortable temperature perfect for swimming, but from the knees down it was cold. Neal didn't know how to swim, he thought. To even go on the pier, Dad had made him put on a life jacket, and Poul was the older brother. How many times had he been told to *protect* him, to watch out for him? And it didn't matter what he'd been told, Poul *wanted* to keep his brother safe. At the playground, he listened for Neal's voice. When someone cried, Poul stopped, afraid it was Neal. Loving his brother was like inhaling.

Neal went into the lake; he never came out. Neal must have hated him, Poul thought. At the end, he must have cried out for him, but Poul didn't come. He didn't warn him.

Poul swam deeper, put his face down, eyes open. Without a mask, his hands were blurry. Beyond them, blackness. How deep? Were there pike? He imagined a ghost catfish, its eye as broad as a swimming pool rising toward him.

But try as he might, Poul couldn't drown himself. He floated on his back, letting his feet sink until his weight drew his face under, and just when the time came to breathe, he kicked to the surface. He couldn't let the water in. Swimming parallel to the shore, he passed Kettle Jack's, swam by dozens of cottages like his own until his arms tired. Each stroke hurt, his shoulders burning with exhaustion, but they never quit working. The lake let him live, and Neal never came up to join him. Poul waited for a hand (a small hand) to wrap around his ankle, to pull him down where six-year olds never grow older. Instead, the sun moved across the sky until Poul was empty. Completely dull, drained and damaged, he turned toward shore, staggered up a stranger's beach, and walked on the lake road toward his cottage, staying in the shoulder, where the grass didn't hurt his feet.

If Neal didn't want him, who did he want?

This far above Kettle Jack's was unfamiliar to him, but the look was the same: long, dirt driveways that vanished in the trees below, or led to cottages camped along the shore. Old boats sprawled upside down on saw horses. Bamboo fishing poles leaned against weathered wood. Station wagons or vans parked behind each house. Towels drying on lines. Beyond, in the lake, sailboats cut frothy wakes; the wind had picked up, although he didn't feel it much here.

He started walking faster. Leesa and Savannah would be home by now. He wondered what they were doing. Leesa never watched Savannah like he did. Her philosophy was that kids take care of themselves, generally, and it's healthier for a child to have room to explore.

He hadn't realized how far he'd swam. Way ahead, the tip of Kettle Jack's pier poked into the lake. Maybe Savannah and Leesa would walk there to see Johnny Jacob's kittens. But it was hot, and Savannah hadn't swam yet. Yesterday she'd fished. Today she'd want to swim. He could see the scene. Leesa would pull into the driveway. Savannah would put on her swim suit to go out on the beach. She had sand toys, buckets, shovels, rakes; little molds for making sand castles. Leesa would set up a chair, lather in sun lotion and read a book. Savannah could be in the water now.

Poul broke into a jog. How idiotic it was to leave the cottage, he thought. No, not idiotic. Criminal. If vengeance waited in the lake, if some sort of delayed retribution haunted the cold waters, why would it care for him? Where would his suffering be if he drowned, like Neal, relieved of responsibility at last? He was running. Kettle Jack's passed by on his left. It was a mile to his cottage. He'd swam over a mile! And maybe that was the plan: to get him out into the lake and away. Suddenly he felt as if he'd lost his mind. What was he thinking? What sane father would dive into the water away from his daughter? Savannah is six, he thought, and she needs her daddy.

The van was parked behind the cottage. Poul ran to the front, his breath coming in great whoops. Empty lounge chair. Sand toys on the beach. A child's life vest lying next to the boathouse. No sign of her. He yelled, "Savannah!" as he went through the door onto the porch.

Leesa sat at the kitchen table, eating a sandwich. "What's wrong with you?" she said.

"Where's Savannah?"

"Puttering around in that raft I bought her. We had a heck of a time finding it."

"I didn't see her!" he said as he ran out of the kitchen.

Out front, he scanned the lake again. Boats in the distance. No yellow raft. He had a vision: Savannah paddling, looking at the bottom through the clear plastic. Sand, of course; she'd see sand and minnows. Then she'd move farther out, her head down, hoping for fish, not aware of how far from shore she was going. The water would get deeper. She'd be beyond the sand, where the depths were foggy and dark green. "What is that?" she'd think. A moving shadow, a form resolving itself, a face coming from below. The little boy from beneath the pier.

Poul pounded down the dock, scanning the water to the left and right. Leesa followed.

"She was right here a minute ago! I've only been inside a minute!"

At the dock's end, Poul stopped, within a eye blink of diving in, but the water was clear as far as he could see. Even the sailboats had retreated from sight.

"Maybe she went to see the kittens," Leesa said.

"With the raft? She wouldn't go with the raft!" Poul's voice cracked.

A bird flew by, wings barely moving. It seemed to Poul to almost have stopped. His heart beat in slow explosions. Leesa said something, but her meaning didn't reach him, the words were so far apart. Then, a round shape pushed from beneath the pier. At first he thought it was the top of a blonde head, right under his feet, and it moved a little bit further, becoming too broad to be a head, and too yellow to be blonde. It was the raft. He could feel himself saying, "No," as he bent, already knowing Savannah wouldn't be in it. He tugged on its handle. It resisted. Who is holding on? It slid out. No one held it. Six inches of water in the bottom made it heavy.

"Savannah!" Leesa screamed. Then the bird's wings beat twice and it was gone. Poul's pulse sped up. The lake had never seemed so empty. He remembered Dad, who had stood at the end of the pier, mute, when they pulled Neal out. Now he stood on the same board.

A high voice called from the lake, a child. Poul looked up, his skin suddenly cold. It called again, and Poul saw her, lying on the diving platform a hundred feet away, Savannah.

He didn't know how he got there—he didn't remember swimming, but he was up the diving platform's ladder, holding his weeping daughter instantly. She nestled her head under his chin and shook with tears. Before she stopped, Leesa arrived in the boat, and they both held her.

Finally, when Savannah's crying had settled into a sob every minute or two, Leesa said, "How did you get out here, darling? You scared us so."

Between shuddery breaths, Savannah said, "I didn't mean to go so far, and I couldn't get back. I paddled really hard, but I fell out. The wind pushed the raft away."

She looked from Poul to Leesa, her eyes red-rimmed and teary.

"I swallowed water, Daddy. I couldn't breathe."

Poul swallowed. He could feel the snorkel in his mouth, the solid, leaden ache of water in his lungs.

Leesa gasped, "Thank god you made it to the diving platform. We could have lost you," and she burst into tears herself.

Through Leesa's crying, Savannah looked at Poul solemnly. "I didn't swim, Daddy. The little boy helped me. He took my hand and put me here." Savannah rubbed her eyes with the back of her arm. "He kissed my cheek, Daddy."

Poul nodded, incapable of speech.

"He looked like the boy in your baby pictures." She sniffed, but seemed more relaxed, her fear already becoming vague. "My eyes didn't play tricks on me."

Poul spent the sunset sitting on the end of the pier, his toes dipping in the lake, surrounded by the watery symphony. Aqueous rhythms beating against the wood, lapping against the shore. And fish. He sat quietly, and the fish came: a school of bluegill, scales catching the last light in a thousand glitters swirling in front of him and then were gone. Later, when the sun had nearly disappeared, a long, black shape glided by, its eye as big as a quarter, a long row of teeth visible when it opened its mouth. Poul had finally seen a pike.

He sighed, pushed himself up and found Leesa in the kitchen. She'd already put Savannah to bed in their room upstairs.

She looked at her coffee cup dully. It was almost hard to remember what he'd loved about her when they'd first met, then she turned her head a little and brushed back her hair, and for a second, it was there, a picture of Leesa when they were young. Before Savannah. Before coming to the lake had become so reluctant. The second disappeared.

He pulled a chair out for himself and turned it around so he could lean his arms on the back. She didn't speak. Poul shut his eyes to listen to the woods behind the cottage. The air there was always so moist and living, but it didn't penetrate into the kitchen. With his eyes closed, he could swear he was alone in the room.

"I want a divorce," Poul said.

Leesa looked at him directly for maybe the first time in a year. "Why now?"

The low, slanting sun cut through the trees behind the cottage, casting a yellow light in the room. He knew that on the lake, now, it highlighted the waves, but didn't penetrate the depths. Fisherman would be out, because the big fish, the serious fish, moved in the evening. The evening was the best time to be on the lake, after a hard day of swimming, of hiking in the woods where he'd played with Neal, and just before they went to bed to tell each other stories until sleep took them, two brothers under one blanket lying head to head, and they dreamed.

Poul said, "When you realize a thing is bad, you've got to let it go or you'll drown."

• • • •

A poetic ghost from the past; the discovery of mortality; perhaps the
possibility that ghosts can be haunted as well as haunt . . .

Wonderwall
Elizabeth Hand

A long time ago, nearly thirty years now, I had a friend who was waiting to be discovered. His name was David Baldanders; we lived with two other friends in one of the most disgusting places I've ever seen, and certainly the worst that involved me signing a lease.

Our apartment was a two-bedroom third-floor walkup in Queenstown, a grim brick enclave just over the District line in Hyattsville, Maryland. Queenstown Apartments were inhabited mostly by drug dealers and bikers who met their two-hundred-dollars a-month leases by processing speed and bad acid in their basement rooms; the upper floors were given over to wasted welfare mothers from P.G. County and students from the University of Maryland, Howard, and the University of the Archangels and Saint John the Divine.

The Divine, as students called it, was where I'd come three years earlier to study acting. I wasn't actually expelled until the end of my junior year, but midway through that term my roommate, Marcella, and I were kicked out of our campus dormitory, precipitating the move to Queenstown. Even for the mid-1970s our behavior was excessive; I was only surprised the university officials waited so long before getting rid of us. Our parents were assessed for damages to our dorm room, which were extensive; among other things, I'd painted one wall floor-to-ceiling with the image from the cover of *Transformer*, surmounted by *Je suis damne par l'arc-en-ciel* scrawled in foot-high letters. Decades later, someone who'd lived in the room after I left told me that, year after year, Rimbaud's words would bleed through each successive layer of new paint. No one ever understood what they meant.

Our new apartment was at first an improvement on the dorm room, and Queenstown itself was an efficient example of a closed ecosystem. The bikers manufactured Black Beauties, which they sold to the students and welfare mothers upstairs, who would zigzag a few hundred feet across a wasteland of shattered glass and broken concrete to the Queenstown Restaurant, where I worked making pizzas that they would then cart back to their apartments. The pizza boxes piled up in the halls, drawing armies of roaches. My friend Oscar lived in the next building; whenever he visited our flat he'd push open the door, pause, then look over his shoulder dramatically.

"Listen—!" he'd whisper.

He'd stamp his foot just once, and hold up his hand to command silence. Immediately we heard what sounded like surf washing over a gravel beach. In fact it was the susurrus of hundreds of cockroaches clittering across the warped parquet floors in retreat.

There were better places to await discovery.

David Baldanders was my age, nineteen. He wasn't much taller than me, with long thick black hair and a soft-featured face: round cheeks, full red lips between a downy black beard and mustache, slightly crooked teeth much yellowed from nicotine, small well-shaped hands. He wore an earring and a bandana that he tied, pirate-style, over his bead; filthy jeans, flannel shirts, filthy black Converse high-tops that flapped when he walked. His eyes were beautiful—indigo, black-lashed, soulful. When he laughed, people stopped in their tracks—he sounded like Herman Munster, that deep, goofy, foghorn voice at odds with his fey appearance.

We met in the Divine's Drama Department, and immediately recognized each other as kindred spirits. Neither attractive nor talented enough to be in the center of the golden circle of aspring actors that included most of our friends, we made ourselves indispensable by virtue of being flamboyant, unapologetic fuckups. People laughed when they saw us coming. They laughed even louder when we left. But David and I always made a point of laughing loudest of all.

"Can you fucking believe that?" A morning, it could have been any morning: I stood in the hall and stared in disbelief at the Department's sitting area. White walls, a few plastic chairs and tables overseen by the glass windows of the secretarial office. This was where the other students chainsmoked and waited, day after day, for news: casting announcements for Department plays; cattle calls for commercials, trade shows, summer reps. Above all else, the Department prided itself on graduating Working Actors—a really successful student might get called back for a walk-on in *Days of Our Lives*. My voice rose loud enough that heads turned. "It looks like a fucking dentist's office."

"Yeah, well, Roddy just got cast in a Trident commercial," David said, and we both fell against the wall, howling.

Rejection fed our disdain, but it was more than that. Within weeks of arriving at the Divine, I felt betrayed. I wanted—hungered for, thirsted for, craved like drink or drugs—High Art. So did David. We'd come to the Divine expecting Paris in the 1920s, Swinging London, Summer of Love in the Haight.

We were misinformed.

What we got was elocution taught by the Department Head's wife; tryouts where tone-deaf students warbled numbers from *The Magic Show*; Advanced Speech classes where, week after week, the beefy Department Head would declaim Macduff's speech—All my pretty ones? Did you say all?—never failing to move himself to tears.

And there was that sitting area. Just looking at it made me want to take a sledgehammer to the walls: all those smug faces above issues of *Variety* and *Theater Arts*, all those sheets of white paper neatly taped to white cinderblock with lists of names beneath: callbacks, cast lists, passing exam results. My name was never there. Nor was David's.

We never had a chance. We had no choice.

We took the sledgehammer to our heads.

Weekends my suitemate visited her parents, and while she was gone David and I would break into her dorm room. We drank her vodka and listened to her copy of *David Live!*, playing "Diamond Dogs" over and over as we clung to each other, smoking, dancing cheek to cheek. After midnight we'd cadge a ride down to Southwest, where abandoned warehouses had been turned into gay discos—the Lost and Found, Grand Central Station, Washington Square, Half Street. A solitary neon pentacle glowed atop the old *Washington Star* printing plant; we heard gunshots, sirens, the faint bass throb from funk bands at the Washington Coliseum, ceaseless boom and echo of trains uncoupling in the railyards that extended from Union Station.

I wasn't a looker. My scalp was covered with henna-stiffened orange stubble that had been cut over three successive nights by a dozen friends. Marcella had pierced my ear with a cork and a needle and a bottle of Gordon's gin. David usually favored one long drop earring, and sometimes I'd wear its mate. Other times I'd shove a safety pin through my ear, then run a dog leash from the safety pin around my neck. I had two-inch-long black-varnished fingernails that caught fire when I lit my cigarettes from a Bic lighter. I kohled my eyes and lips, used Marcella's Chloe perfume, shoved myself into Marcella's expensive jeans even though they were too small for me.

But mostly I wore a white poet's blouse or a frayed, striped boatneck shirt, droopy black wool trousers, red sneakers, a red velvet beret my mother had given me for Christmas when I was seventeen. I chainsmoked Marlboros, three packs a day when I could afford them. For a while I smoked clay pipes and Borkum Riff tobacco. The pipes cost a dollar apiece at the tobacconist's in Georgetown. They broke easily, and club owners invariably hassled me, thinking I was getting high right under their noses. I was, but not from Borkum Riff. Occasionally I'd forgo makeup and wear Army khakis and a boiled wool Navy shirt I'd fished from a dumpster. I used a mascara wand on my upper lip and wore my bashed-up old cowboy boots to make me look taller.

This fooled no one, but that didn't matter. In Southeast I was invisible, or nearly so. I was a girl, white, neither desirable or threatening. The burly leather-clad guys who stood guard over the entrances to the L&F were always nice to me, though there was a scary dyke bouncer whom I had to bribe, sometimes with cash, sometimes with rough foreplay behind the door.

Once inside all that fell away. David and I stumbled to the bar and traded our drink tickets for vodka and orange juice. We drank fast, pushing upstairs through the crowd until we reached a vantage point above the dance floor. David would look around for someone he knew, someone he fancied, someone who might discover him. He'd give me a wet kiss, then stagger off; and I would stand, and drink, and watch.

The first time it happened David and I were tripping. We were at the L&F, or maybe Washington Square. He'd gone into the men's room. I sat slumped just outside the door, trying to bore a hole through my hand with my eyes. A few people stepped on me; no one apologized, but no one swore at me, either. After a while I stumbled to my feet, lurched a few feet down the hallway, and turned.

The door to the men's room was painted gold. A shining film covered it, glistening with smeared rainbows like oil-scummed tarmac. The door opened with difficulty because of the number of people crammed inside. I had to keep moving so they could pass in and out. I leaned against the wall and stared at the floor for a few more minutes, then looked up again

Across from me, the wall was gone. I could see men, pissing, talking, kneeling, crowding stalls, humping over urinals, cupping brown glass vials beneath their faces. I could see David in a crowd of men by the sinks. He stood with his back to me, in front of a long mirror framed with small round light bulbs. His head was bowed. He was scooping water from the faucet and drinking it, so that his beard glittered red and silver. As I watched, he slowly lifted his face, until he was staring into the mirror. His reflected image stared back at me. I could see his pupils expand like drops of black ink in a glass of water, and his mouth fall open in pure panic.

"David," I murmured.

Beside him a lanky boy with dirty-blond hair turned. He too was staring at me, but not with fear. His mouth split into a grin. He raised his hand and pointed at me, laughing.

"Poseur!"

"Shit—shit . . . " I looked up and David stood there in the hall. He fumbled for a cigarette, his hand shaking, then sank onto the floor beside me. "Shit, you, you saw—you—"

I started to laugh. In a moment David did too. We fell into each other's arms, shrieking, our faces slick with tears and dirt. I didn't even notice that his cigarette scorched a hole in my favorite shirt till later, or feel where it burned into my right palm, a penny-sized wound that got infected and took weeks to heal. I bear the scar even now, the shape of an eye, shiny white tissue with a crimson pupil that seems to wink when I crease my hand.

It was about a month after this happened that we moved to Queenstown. Me, David, Marcy, a sweet spacy girl named Bunny Flitchins, all signed the lease. Two hundred bucks a month gave us a small living room, a bathroom, two small bedrooms, a kitchen squeezed into a corner overlooking a parking lot filled with busted Buicks and shockshot Impalas. The place smelled of new paint and dry-cleaning fluid. The first time we opened the freezer, we found several plastic Ziplock bags filled with sheets of white paper. When we removed the paper and held it up to the light, we saw where rows of droplets had dried to faint gray smudges.

"Blotter acid," I said.

We discussed taking a hit. Marcy demurred. Bunny giggled, shaking her head. She didn't do drugs, and I would never have allowed her to: it would be like giving acid to your puppy.

"Give it to me," said David. He sat on the windowsill, smoking and dropping his ashes to the dirt three floors below. "I'll try it. Then we can cut them into tabs and sell them."

"That would be a lot of money," said Bunny delightedly. A tab of blotter went for a dollar back then, but you could sell them for a lot more at concerts, up to ten bucks a hit. She fanned out the sheets from one of the plastic bags. "We could make thousands and thousands of dollars!"

"Millions," said Marcy.

I shook my head. "It could be poison. Strychnine. I wouldn't do it."

"Why not?" David scowled. "You do all kinds of shit."

"I wouldn't do it 'cause it's from here."

"Good point," said Bunny.

I grabbed the rest of the sheets from her, lit one of the gas jets on the stove and held the paper above it. David cursed and yanked the bandana from his head.

"What are you doing?"

But he quickly moved aside as I lunged to the window and tossed out the flaming pages. We watched them fall, delicate spirals of red and orange like tiger lilies corroding into black ash then gray then smoke.

"All gone," cried Bunny, and clapped.

We had hardly any furniture. Marcy had a bed and a desk in her room, nice Danish modern stuff. I had a mattress on the other bedroom floor that I shared with David. Bunny slept in the living room. Every few days she'd drag a broken box spring up from the curb. After the fifth one appeared, the living room began to look like the interior of one of those pawnshops down on F Street that sold you an entire roomful of aluminum-tube furniture for fifty bucks, and we yelled at her to stop. Bunny slept on the box springs, a different one every night, but after a while she didn't stay over much. Her family lived in Northwest, but her father, a professor at the Divine, also had an apartment in Turkey Thicket, and Bunny started staying with him.

Marcy's family lived nearby as well, in Alexandria. She was a slender, Slavic beauty with a waterfall of ice-blond hair and eyes like aqua headlamps, and the only one of us with a glamorous job—she worked as a model and receptionist at the most expensive beauty salon in Georgetown. But by early spring, she had pretty much moved back in with her parents, too.

This left me and David. He was still taking classes at the Divine, getting a ride with one of the other students who lived at Queenstown, or else catching a bus in front of Giant Food on Queens Chapel Road. Early in the semester he had switched his coursework: instead of theater, he now immersed himself in French language and literature.

I gave up all pretense of studying or attending classes. I worked a few shifts behind the counter at the Queenstown Restaurant, making pizzas and ringing up beer. I got most of my meals there, and when my friends came in to buy cases of Heineken I never charged them. I made about sixty dollars a week, barely enough to pay the rent and keep me in cigarettes, but I got by. Bus fare was eighty cents to cross the District line; the newly opened subway was another fifty cents. I didn't eat much. I lived on popcorn and Reuben sandwiches from the restaurant, and there was a sympathetic waiter at the American Cafe in Georgetown who fed me ice cream sundaes when I was bumming around in the city. I saved enough for my cover at the discos and for the Atlantis, a club in the basement of a fleabag hotel at 930 F Street that had just started booking punk bands. The rest I spent on booze and Marlboros. Even if I was broke, someone would always spring me a drink and a smoke; if I had a full pack of cigarettes, I was ahead of the game. I stayed out all night, finally staggering out into some of the District's worst neighborhoods with a couple of bucks in my sneaker, if I was lucky. Usually I was broke.

Yet I really was lucky. Somehow I always managed to find my way home. At two or three or four a.m. I'd crash into my apartment, alone except for the cockroaches—David would have gone home with a pickup from the bars, and Marcy and Bunny had decamped to the suburbs. I'd be so drunk I stuck to the mattress like a fly mashed against a window. Sometimes I'd sit cross-legged with the typewriter in front of me and write, naked because of the appalling heat, my damp skin gray with cigarette ash. I read *Tropic of Cancer*, reread Dhalgren and *A Fan's Notes* and a copy of *Illuminations* held together by a rubber band. I played Pere Ubu and Wire at the wrong speed, because I was too wasted to notice, and would finally pass out only to be ripped awake by the apocalyptic scream of the firehouse siren next door—I'd be standing in the middle of the room, screaming at the top of my lungs, before I realized I was no longer asleep. I saw people in my room, a lanky boy with dark-blond hair and clogs who pointed his finger at me and shouted *Poseur!* I heard voices. My dreams were of flames, of the walls around me exploding outward so that I could see the ruined city like a freshly tilled garden extending for miles and miles, burning cranes and skeletal buildings rising from the smoke to bloom, black and gold and red, against a topaz sky. I wanted to burn too, tear through the wall that separated me from that other world, the real world, the one I glimpsed in books and music, the world I wanted to claim for myself.

But I didn't burn. I was just a fucked-up college student, and pretty soon I wasn't even that. That spring I flunked out of the Divine. All of my other friends were still in school, getting boyfriends and girlfriends, getting cast in University productions of *An Inspector Calls* and *Arturo Roi*. Even David Baldanders managed to get good grades for his paper on Verlaine. Meanwhile I leaned out my third floor window and smoked and watched the speedfreaks stagger across the parking lot below. If I jumped I could be with them: that was all it would take.

It was too beautiful for words, too terrifying to think this was what my life had shrunk to. In the mornings I made instant coffee and tried to read what I'd written the night before. Nice words but they made absolutely no sense. I cranked up Marcy's expensive stereo and played my records, compulsively transcribing song lyrics as though they might somehow bleed into something else, breed with my words and create a coherent storyline. I scrawled more words on the bedroom wall:

I HAVE BEEN DAMNED BY THE RAINBOW
I AM AN AMERICAN ARTIST,
AND I HAVE NO CHAIRS

It had all started as an experiment. I held the blunt, unarticulated belief that meaning and transcendence could be shaken from the world, like unripe fruit from a tree; then consumed.

So I'd thrown my brain into the Waring blender along with vials of cheap acid and hashish, tobacco and speed and whatever alcohol was at hand. Now I wondered: did I have the stomach to toss down the end result?

Whenever David showed up it was a huge relief.

"Come on," he said one afternoon. "Let's go to the movies."

We saw a double bill at the Biograph, *The Story of Adele H* and *Jules et Jim*. Torturously uncomfortable chairs, but only four bucks for four hours of air-conditioned bliss. David had seen *Adele H* six times already; he sat beside me, rapt, whispering the words to himself. I struggled with the French and mostly read the subtitles. Afterwards we stumbled blinking into the long ultra-violet D.C. twilight, the smell of honeysuckle and diesel, coke and lactic acid, our clothes crackling with heat like lightning and our skin electrified as the sugared air seeped into it like poison. We ran arm-in-arm up to the Café de Paris, sharing one of David's Gitanes. We had enough money for a bottle of red wine and a baguette. After a few hours the waiter kicked us out, but we gave him a dollar anyway. That left us just enough for the Metro and the bus home.

It took us hours to get back. By the time we ran up the steps to our apartment we'd sobered up again. It was not quite nine o'clock on a Friday night.

"Fuck!" said David. "What are we going to do now?"

No one was around. We got on the phone but there were no parties, no one with a car to take us somewhere else. We rifled the apartment for a forgotten stash of beer or dope or money, turned our pockets inside-out looking for stray seeds, Black Beauties, fragments of green dust.

Nada.

In Marcy's room we found about three dollars in change in one of her jean pockets. Not enough to get drunk, not enough to get us back into the city.

"Damn," I said. "Not enough for shit."

From the parking lot came the low thunder of motorcycles, a baby crying, someone shouting.

"You fucking motherfucking fucker."

"That's a lot of fuckers," said David.

Then we heard a gunshot.

"Jesus!" yelled David, and yanked me to the floor. From the neighboring apartment echoed the crack of glass shattering. "They shot out a window!"

"I said, not enough money for anything." I pushed him away and sat up. "I'm not staying here all night."

"Okay, okay, wait . . . "

He crawled to the kitchen window, pulled himself onto the sill to peer out. "They did shoot out a window," he said admiringly. "Wow."

"Did they leave us any beer?"

David looked over his shoulder at me. "No. But I have an idea."

He crept back into the living room and emptied out his pockets beside me. "I think we have enough," he said after he counted his change for the third time. "Yeah. But we have to get there now—they close at nine."

"Who does?"

I followed him back downstairs and outside.

"Peoples Drug," said David. "Come on."

We crossed Queens Chapel Road, dodging Mustangs and blasted pickups. I watched wistfully as the 80 bus passed, heading back into the city. It was almost nine o'clock. Overhead the sky had that dusty gold-violet bloom it got in late spring. Cars raced by, music blaring; I could smell charcoal burning somewhere, hamburgers on a grill and the sweet far-off scent of apple blossom.

"Wait," I said.

I stopped in the middle of the road, arms spread, staring straight up into the sky and feeling what I imagined David must have felt when he leaned against the walls of Mr. P's and Grand Central Station: I was waiting, waiting, waiting for the world to fall on me like a hunting hawk.

"What the fuck are you doing?" shouted David as a car bore down and he dragged me to the far curb. "Come on."

"What are we getting?" I yelled as he dragged me into the drugstore.

"Triaminic."

I had thought there might be a law against selling four bottles of cough syrup to two messed-up looking kids. Apparently there wasn't, though I was embarrassed enough to stand back as David shamelessly counted pennies and nickels and quarters out onto the counter.

We went back to Queenstown. I had never done cough syrup before; not unless I had a cough. I thought we would dole it out a spoonful at a time, over the course of the evening. Instead David unscrewed the first bottle and knocked it back in one long swallow. I watched in amazed disgust, then shrugged and did the same.

"Aw, fuck."

I gagged and almost threw up, somehow kept it down. When I looked up David was finishing off a second bottle, and I could see him eyeing the remaining one in front of me. I grabbed it and drank it as well, then sprawled against the box spring. Someone lit a candle. David? Me? Someone put on a record, one of those Eno albums, *Another Green World*. Someone stared at me, a boy with long black hair unbound and eyes that blinked from blue to black then shut down for the night.

"Wait," I said, trying to remember the words. "I. Want. You. To—"

Too late: David was out. My hand scrabbled across the floor, searching for the book I'd left there, a used New Directions paperback of Rimbaud's work. Even pages were in French; odd pages held their English translations.

I wanted David to read me *Le lettre du voyant*, Rimbaud's letter to his friend Paul Demeny; the letter of the seer. I knew it by heart in English and on the page but spoken French eluded me and always would. I opened the book, struggling to see through the scrim of cheap narcotic and nausea until at last I found it.

Je dis qu'il faut être voyant, se faire voyant.

Le Poète se fait voyant par un long, immense et
raisonné dérèglement de tous les sens.
Toutes les formes d'amour, de souffrance,
de folie; il cherche lui-même . . .

I say one must be a visionary,
one must become a seer.

The poet becomes a seer through a long, boundless
and systematic derangement of all the senses.
All forms of love, of suffering, of madness;
he seeks them within himself . . .

As I read I began to laugh, then suddenly doubled over. My mouth tasted sick, a second sweet skin sheathing my tongue. I retched, and a bright-red clot exploded onto the floor in front of me; I dipped my finger into it then wrote across the warped parquet:

DEAR DAV

I looked up. There was no light save the wavering flame of a candle in a jar. Many candles, I saw now; many flames. I blinked and ran my hand across my forehead. It felt damp. When I brought my finger to my lips I tasted sugar and blood. On the floor David sprawled, snoring softly, his bandana clenched in one hand. Behind him the walls reflected candles, endless candles; though as I stared I saw they were not reflected light after all but a line of flames, upright swaying like figures dancing. I rubbed my eyes, a wave cresting inside my head then breaking even as I felt something splinter in my eye. I started to cry out but could not: I was frozen, freezing. Someone had left the door open.

"Who's there?" I said thickly, and crawled across the room. My foot nudged the candle; the jar toppled and the flame went out.

But it wasn't dark. In the corridor outside our apartment door a hundred-watt bulb dangled from a wire. Beneath it, on the top step, sat the boy I'd seen in the urinal beside David. His hair was the color of dirty straw, his face sullen. He had muddy green-blue eyes, bad teeth, fingernails bitten down to the skin; skeins of dried blood covered his fingertips like webbing. A filthy bandana was knotted tightly around his throat

"Hey," I said. I couldn't stand very well so slumped against the wall, slid until I was sitting almost beside him. I fumbled in my pocket and found one of David's crumpled Gitanes, fumbled some more until I found a book of matches. I tried to light one but it was damp; tried a second time and failed again.

Beside me the blond boy swore. He grabbed the matches from me and lit one, turned to hold it cupped before my face. I brought the cigarette close and breathed in, watched the fingertip flare of crimson then blue as the match went out.

But the cigarette was lit. I took a drag, passed it to the boy. He smoked in silence, after a minute handed it back to me. The acrid smoke couldn't mask his oily smell, sweat and shit and urine; but also a faint odor of green hay and sunlight. When he turned his face to me I saw that he was older than I had first thought, his skin dark-seamed by sun and exposure.

"Here," he said. His voice was harsh and difficult to understand. He held his hand out. I opened mine expectantly, but as he spread his fingers only a stream of sand fell onto my palm, gritty and stinking of piss. I drew back, cursing. As I did he leaned forward and spat in my face.

"Poseur."

"You fuck," I yelled. I tried to get up but he was already on his feet. His hand was tearing at his neck; an instant later something lashed across my face, slicing upwards from cheek to brow. I shouted in pain and fell back, clutching my cheek. There was a red veil between me and the world; I blinked and for an instant saw through it. I glimpsed the young man running down the steps, his hoarse laughter echoing through the stairwell; heard the clang of the fire door swinging open then crashing shut; then silence.

"Shit," I groaned, and sank back to the floor. I tried to staunch the blood with my hand. My other hand rested on the floor. Something warm brushed against my fingers: I grabbed it and held it before me: a filthy bandana, twisted tight as a noose, one whip-end black and wet with blood.

I saw him one more time. It was high summer by then, the school year over. Marcy and Bunny were gone till the fall, Marcy to Europe with her parents, Bunny to a private hospital in Kentucky. David would be leaving soon, to return to his family in Philadelphia. I had found another job in the city, a real job, a GS-l position with the Smithsonian; the lowest-level job one could have in the government but it was a paycheck. I worked three twelve-hour shifts in a row, three days a week, and wore a mustard-yellow polyester uniform with a photo ID that opened doors to all the museums on the Mall. Nights I sweated away with David at the bars or the Atlantis; days I spent at the newly-opened East Wing of the National Gallery of Art, its vast open white-marble space an air-conditioned vivarium where I wandered stoned, struck senseless by huge moving shapes like sharks spun of metal and canvas: Calder's great mobile, Miro's tapestry, a line of somber Rothkos darkly shimmering waterfalls in an upstairs gallery. Breakfast was a Black Beauty and a Snickers bar, dinner whatever I could find to drink.

We were at the Lost and Found, late night early August. David as usual had gone off on his own. I was, for once, relatively sober: I was in the middle of my three-day work week, normally I wouldn't have gone out but David was leaving the next morning. I was on the club's upper level, an area like the deck of an ocean liner where you could lean on the rails and look down onto the dance floor below. The club was crowded, the music deafening. I was watching the men dance with each other, hundreds of them, maybe thousands, strobelit beneath mirrorballs and shifting layers of blue and gray smoke that would ignite suddenly with white blades of laser-light, strafing the writhing forms below so they let out a sudden single-voiced shriek, punching the air with their fists and blasting at whistles. I rested my arms on the rounded metal rail and smoked, thinking how beautiful it all was, how strange, how alive. It was like watching the sea.

And as I gazed slowly it changed, slowly something changed. One song bled into another, arms waved like tendrils; a shadow moved through the air above them. I looked up, startled, glanced aside and saw the blond young man standing there a few feet from me. His fingers grasped the railing; he stared at the dance floor with an expression at once hungry and disdainful and disbelieving. After a moment he slowly lifted his head, turned and stared at me.

I said nothing. I touched my hand to my throat, where his bandana was knotted there, loosely. It was stiff as rope beneath my fingers: I hadn't washed it. I stared back at him, his green-blue eyes hard and somehow dull; not stupid, but with the obdurate matte gleam of unpolished agate. I wanted to say something but I was afraid of him; and before I could speak he turned his head to stare hack down at the floor below us.

"*Cela s'est passé*," he said, and shook his head.

I looked to where he was gazing. I saw that the dance floor was endless, eternal: the cinderblock warehouse walls had disappeared. Instead the moving waves of bodies extended for miles and miles until they melted into the horizon. They were no longer bodies but flames, countless flickering lights like the candles I had seen in my apartment, flames like men dancing; and then they were not even flames but bodies consumed by flame, flesh and cloth burned away until only the bones remained and then not even bone but only the memory of motion, a shimmer of wind on the water then the water gone and only a vast and empty room, littered with refuse: glass vials, broken plastic whistles, plastic cups, dog collars, ash.

I blinked. A siren wailed. I began to scream, standing in the middle of my room, alone, clutching at a bandana tied loosely around my neck. On the mattress on the floor David turned, groaning, and stared up at me with one bright blue eye.

"It's just the firehouse," he said, and reached to pull me back beside him. It was five a.m. He was still wearing the clothes he'd worn to the Lost and Found. So was I; I touched the bandana at my throat and thought of the young man at the railing beside me. "C'mon, you've hardly slept yet," urged David. "You have to get a little sleep."

He left the next day. I never saw him again.

A few weeks later my mother came, ostensibly to visit her cousin in Chevy Chase but really to check on me. She found me spreadeagled on my bare mattress, screenless windows open to let the summer's furnace heat pour like molten iron into the room. Around me were the posters I'd shredded and torn from the walls; on the walls were meaningless phrases, crushed remains of cockroaches and waterbugs, countless rust-colored handprints, bullet-shaped gouges where I'd dug my fingernails into the drywall.

"I think you should come home," my mother said gently. She stared at my hands, fingertips netted with dried blood, my knuckles raw and seeping red. "I don't think you really want to stay here. Do you? I think you should come home."

I was too exhausted to argue. I threw what remained of my belongings into a few cardboard boxes, gave notice at the Smithsonian, and went home.

• • •

It's thought that Rimbaud completed his entire body of work before his nineteenth birthday; the last prose poems, *Illuminations*, indicate he may have been profoundly affected by the time he spent in London in 1874. After that came journey and exile, years spent as an arms trader in Abyssinia until he came home to France to die, slowly and painfully, losing his right leg to syphilis, electrodes fastened to his nerveless arm in an attempt to regenerate life and motion. He died on the morning of November 10, 1891, at ten o'clock. In his delirium he believed that he was back in Abyssinia, readying himself to depart upon a ship called "Aphinar." He was thirty-seven years old.

I didn't live at home for long—about ten months. I got a job at a bookstore; my mother drove me there each day on her way to work and picked me up on her way home. Evenings I ate dinner with her and my two younger sisters. Weekends I went out with friends I'd gone to high school with. I picked up the threads of a few relationships begun and abandoned years earlier. I drank too much but not as much as before. I quit smoking.

I was nineteen. When Rimbaud was my age, he had already finished his life work. I hadn't even started yet. He had changed the world; I could barely change my socks. He had walked through the wall, but I had only smashed my head against it, fruitlessly, in anguish and despair. It had defeated me, and I hadn't even left a mark.

Eventually I returned to D.C. I got my old job back at the Smithsonian, squatted for a while with friends in Northeast, got an apartment, a boyfriend, a promotion. By the time I returned to the city David had graduated from the Divine. We spoke on the phone a few times: he had a steady boyfriend now, an older man, a businessman from France. David was going to Paris with him to live. Marcy married well and moved to Aspen. Bunny got out of the hospital and was doing much better; over the next few decades, she would be my only real contact with that other life, the only one of us who kept in touch with everyone.

Slowly, slowly, I began to see things differently. Slowly I began to see that there were other ways to bring down a wall: that you could dismantle it, brick by brick, stone by stone, over years and years and years. The wall would always be there—at least for me it is—but sometimes I can see where I've made a mark in it, a chink where I can put my eye and look through to the other side. Only for a moment; but I know better now than to expect more than that.

I talked to David only a few times over the years, and finally not at all. When we last spoke, maybe fifteen years ago, he told me that he was HIV positive. A few years after that Bunny told me that the virus had gone into full-blown AIDS, and that he had gone home to live with his father in Pennsylvania. Then a few years after that she told me no, he was living in France again, she had heard from him and he seemed to be better.

Cela s'est passé, the young man had told me as we watched the men dancing in the L&F twenty-six years ago. That is over.

Yesterday I was at Waterloo Station, hurrying to catch the train to Basingstoke. I walked past the Eurostar terminal, the sleek Paris-bound bullet trains like marine animals waiting to churn their way back through the Chunnel to the sea. Curved glass walls separated me from them; armed security patrols and British soldiers strode along the platform, checking passenger IDs and waving people towards the trains.

I was just turning towards the old station when I saw them. They were standing in front of a glass wall like an aquarium's: a middle-aged man in an expensive-looking dark blue overcoat, his black hair still thick though graying at the temples, his hand resting on the shoulder of his companion. A slightly younger man, very thin, his face gaunt and ravaged, burned the color of new brick by the sun, his fair hair gone to gray. He was leaning on a cane; when the older man gestured he turned and began to walk, slowly, painstakingly down the platform. I stopped and watched: I wanted to call out, to see if they would turn and answer, but the blue-washed glass barrier would have muted any sound I made.

I turned, blinking in the light of midday, touched the bandana at my throat and the notebook in my pocket; and hurried on. They would not have seen me anyway. They were already boarding the train. They were on their way to Paris.

• • • •

He waited in silence, afraid to speak, afraid to give voice to his questions,
afraid that they would be answered . . .

Between the Cold Moon and the Earth
Peter Atkins

They only brushed his cheek for a second or two, but her lips were fucking *freezing*.

"Christ, Carol," he said. "Do you want my coat?"

She laughed. "What for?" she asked.

"Because it's one in the morning," he said. "And you're cold."

"It's summer," she pointed out, which was undeniably true but wasn't really the issue. "Are you going to walk me home, then?"

Michael had left the others about forty minutes earlier. Kirk had apparently copped off with the girl from Woolworth's that they'd met inside the pub so Michael and Terry had tactfully peeled away before the bus stop and started walking the long way home around Sefton Park. He could've split a taxi-fare with Terry but, given that they were still in the middle of their ongoing argument about the relative merits of T.Rex and Pink Floyd and that it was still a good six months before they'd find Roxy Music to agree on, they'd parted by unspoken consent and Michael had opted to cut across the park alone.

Carol had been standing on the path beside the huge park's large boating lake. He'd shit himself for a moment when he first saw the shadowed figure there, assuming the worst—a midnight skinhead parked on watch ready to whistle his mates out of hiding to give this handy glam-rock faggot a good kicking—but Carol had been doing nothing more threatening than staring out at the center of the lake and the motionless full moon reflected there.

"Alright, Michael," she'd said, before he'd quite recognized her in the moonlight, and had kissed his cheek lightly in further greeting before he'd spoken her name. Now, he fell into step beside her and they began to walk the long slow curve around the lake.

"God, Carol. Where've you been?" he asked. "Nobody's seen you for months."

It was true. Her mum had re-married just before last Christmas and they'd moved. Not far away, still in the same city, but far enough for sixteen-year-olds to lose touch.

"I went to America," Carol said.

Michael turned his head to see if she was kidding. "You went to *America*?" he said. "What d'you mean, you went to America? When? Who with?"

Her eyes narrowed for a moment as if she were re-checking her facts or her memory. "I think it was America," she said.

"You *think* it was America?"

"It might have been an imaginary America," she said, her voice a little impatient. "Do you want to hear the fucking story or not?"

Oh. Michael didn't smile or attempt to kiss her, but he felt like doing both. Telling stories—real, imagined, or some happy collision of the two—had been one of the bonds between them, one of the things he'd loved about her. Not the only thing of course. It's not like he hadn't shared Kirk and Terry's enthusiastic affection for her astonishingly perfect breasts and for the teasingly challenging way she had about her that managed to suggest two things simultaneously: That, were circumstances to somehow become magically right, she might . . . you know . . . actually *do it* with you; and that you were probably and permanently incapable of ever conjuring such circumstance. But her stories, and her delight in telling them, were what he'd loved most and what, he now realized, he'd most missed. So yes, he said, he wanted to hear the story.

There was some quick confusion about whether she'd got there by plane or by ship—Carol had never been a big fan of preamble—but apparently what mattered was that, after a few days, she found herself in a roadside diner with a bunch of people she hardly knew.

They were on a road trip and had stopped for lunch in this back-of-beyond and unpretentious diner—a place which, while perfectly clean and respectable, looked like it hadn't been painted or refurbished since about 1952. They were in a booth, eating pie and drinking coffee. Her companions were about her age—but could, you know, *drive* and everything. Turned out boys in America could be just as fucking rude as in Liverpool. One of them—Tommy, she thought his name was—was giving shit to the waitress. Hoisting his empty coffee mug, he was leaning out of the booth and looking pointedly down the length of the room.

"Yo! Still need a refill here!" he shouted to the counter.

Carol stood up and, announcing she was going to the ladies' room, slid her way out of the booth. Halfway down the room, she crossed paths with the waitress, who was hurrying toward their booth with a coffee pot. The woman's name-tag said *Cindi*, a spelling Carol had never seen before and hoped could possibly be short for Cinderella because that'd be, you know, great. Carol spoke softly to her, nodding back towards Tommy, who was impatiently shaking his empty coffee mug in the air.

"Don't mind him, love," Carol said. "He's a bit of a prick, but I'll make sure he leaves a nice tip."

Cindi, who looked to be at least thirty and harried-looking, gave her a quick smile of gratitude. "Little girls' room's out back, sweetheart," she said.

Carol exited the main building of the diner and saw that a separate structure, little more than a shack really, housed the bathrooms. She started across the graveled parking lot, surrounded by scrub-grass that was discolored and overgrown, looking down the all-but-deserted country road—the type of road, she'd been informed by her new friends, which was known as a two-lane blacktop. The diner and its shithouse annex were the only buildings for as far as her eye could see, apart from a hulking grain silo a hundred yards or so down the road. As Carol looked in that desolate direction, a cloud drifted over the sun, dimming the summer daylight and shifting the atmosphere into a kind of pre-storm dreariness. Carol shivered and wondered, not without a certain pleasure in the mystery, just where the hell she was.

Done peeing and alone in the bathroom, Carol washed her hands and splashed her face at the pretty crappy single sink that was all the place had to offer. The sound of the ancient cistern laboriously and noisily refilling after her flush played in the background. Carol turned off the tap and looked for a moment at her reflection in the pitted and stained mirror above the sink. As the cistern finally creaked and whistled to a halt, the mirror suddenly cracked noisily across its width as if it was just too tired to keep trying.

"Fuckin' 'ell!" said Carol, because it had made her jump and because she didn't like the newly mismatched halves of her reflected face. She turned around, ready to walk out of the bathroom, and discovered she was no longer alone.

A little girl—what, six, seven years old?—was standing, silent and perfectly still, outside one of the stall doors, looking up at her. Oddly, the little girl was holding the palm of one hand over her right eye.

"Oh shit," said Carol, remembering that she'd just said *fucking hell* in front of a kid. "I didn't know you were . . . " She paused, smiled, started over. "Hello, pet. D'you live around here?"

The little girl just kept looking at her.

"What's your name?" Carol asked her, still smiling but still getting no response. Registering the hand-over-the-eye thing, she tried a new tack. "Oh," she said, "are we playing a game and nobody told me the rules? All right then, here we go."

Raising her hand, Carol covered her own right eye with her palm. The little girl remained still and silent. Carol lowered her hand from her face. "Peek-a-boo," she said.

Finally, the little girl smiled shyly and lowered her own hand. She had no right eye at all, just a smooth indented bank of flesh.

Carol was really good. She hardly jumped at all and her gasp was as short-lived as could reasonably be expected.

The little girl's voice was very matter-of-fact. "Momma lost my eye patch," she said.

"Oh. That's a shame," said Carol, trying to keep her own voice as equally everyday.

"She's gonna get me another one. When she goes to town."

"Oh, well, that's good. Will she get a nice color? Do you have a favorite color?"

The little girl shrugged. "What are you, retarded?" she said. "It's an eye patch. Who cares what color it is?"

Carol didn't know whether to laugh or slap her.

"You can go now, if you like," said the little girl. "I have to make water."

"Oh. All right. Sure. Well, look after yourself," Carol said and, raising her hand in a slightly awkward wave of farewell, headed for the exit door. The little girl called after her.

"You take care in those woods now, Carol," she said.

"I hadn't told her my name," said Carol.

"Well, that was weird," Michael said.

Carol smiled, pleased. "*That* wasn't weird," she said. "It *got* weird. Later. After I got lost in the woods."

"You got lost in the woods?"

Carol nodded.

"Why'd they let you go wandering off on your own?"

"Who?"

"Your new American friends. The people you were in the café with."

"Ha. Café. *Diner*, stupid. We were in America."

"Whatever. How could they let you get lost?"

"Oh, yeah." She thought for a second, looking out to their side at the boating lake and its ghost moon. "Well, p'raps they weren't there to begin with. Doesn't matter. Listen."

Turned out Carol *did* get lost in the woods. Quite deep in the woods, actually. Heart of the forest, Hansel and Gretel shit, where the sunlight, through the thickening trees, was dappled and spotty and where the reassuring blue sky of what was left of the afternoon could be glimpsed only occasionally through the increasingly oppressive canopy of high leafy branches.

Carol was tramping her way among the trees and the undergrowth on the mossy and leaf strewn ground when she heard the sound for the first time. Faint and plaintive and too distant to be truly identifiable, it was nevertheless suggestive of something, something that Carol couldn't quite put her finger on yet. Only when it came again, a few moments later, did she place it. It was the sound of a lonely ship's horn in a midnight ocean, melancholy and eerie. Not quite as eerie, though, as the fact that once the horn had sounded this second time, all the other sounds stopped, all the other sounds that Carol hadn't even been consciously aware of until they disappeared; birdsong, the footsteps of unseen animals moving through the woods, the sigh of the breeze as it whistled through the branches.

The only sounds now were those she made herself; the rustle and sway of the living branches she was pushing her way through and the crackle and snap of the dead ones she was breaking beneath her. Carol began to wonder if moving on in the same direction she'd been going was that great of an idea. She turned around and started heading back and, within a few yards, stepping out from between two particularly close trees, she found herself in a small grove-like clearing that she didn't remember passing through earlier.

There was a downed and decaying tree trunk lying in the leafy undergrowth that momentarily and ridiculously put Carol in mind of a park bench. But she really wasn't in the mood to sit and relax and it wasn't like there was, you know, a boating lake to look at the moon in or anything. So she kept moving, across the clearing, past the downed trunk, and stopped only when the voice spoke from behind her.

"What's your rush, sweetheart?"

Carol turned back. Sitting perched on the bench-like trunk was a sailor. He was dressed in a square-neck deck shirt and bell-bottomed pants and Carol might have taken a moment to wonder if sailors still dressed like that these days if she hadn't been too busy being surprised just to see him at all. He was sitting in profile to her, one leg on the ground, the other arched up on the trunk and he didn't turn to face her fully, perhaps because he was concentrating on rolling a cigarette.

"Ready-mades are easier," the sailor said. "But I like the ritual—opening the paper, laying in the tobacco, rolling it up. Know what I mean?"

"I don't smoke," said Carol, which wasn't strictly true, but who the fuck was he to deserve the truth.

"You chew?" he asked.

"Chew what?"

"Tobacco."

"Eugh. No."

The sailor chanted something rhythmic in response, like he was singing her a song but knew his limitations when it came to carrying a tune:

"Down in Nagasaki,
Where the fellas chew tobaccy
And the women wicky-wacky-woo."

Carol stared at him. Confused. Not necessarily nervous. Not yet. She gestured out at the woods. "Where'd you come from?" she said.

"Dahlonega, Georgia. Little town Northeast of Atlanta. Foot of the Appalachians."

That wasn't what she'd meant and she started to tell him so, but he interrupted.

"Ever been to Nagasaki, honeybun?"

"No."

"How about Shanghai?"

The sailor was still sitting in profile to her. Talking to her, but staring straight ahead into the woods and beyond. He didn't wait for a reply. "Docked there once," he said. "Didn't get shore-leave. Fellas who did told me I missed something, boy. Said there were whores there could practically tie themselves in knots. Real limber. Mmm. A man likes that. Likes 'em limber."

Carol was very careful not to say anything at all. Not to move. Not to breathe.

"Clean, too," said the sailor. "That's important to me. Well, who knows? Maybe I'll get back there one of these days. Course, once they get a good look at me, I might have to pay extra." He turned finally to face her. "Whaddaya think?"

Half of his face was bone-pale and bloated, as if it had drowned years ago and been underwater ever since. His hair hung dank like seaweed and something pearl-like glinted in the moist dripping blackness of what used to be an eye socket.

"Jesus Christ!" Carol said, frozen in shock, watching helplessly as the sailor put his cigarette in his half-ruined mouth, lit it, and inhaled.

"Calling on the Lord for salvation," he said. "Good for you. Might help." Smoke oozed out from the pulpy white flesh that barely clung to the bone beneath his dead face. "Might not."

He rose to his feet and grinned at her. "Useta chase pigs through the Georgia pines, sweet thing," he said, flinging his cigarette aside. "Let's see if you're faster than them little squealers."

And then he came for her.

• • •

"I was a lot faster, though," said Carol. "But it still took me ten minutes to lose him."

"Fuck, Carol," said Michael. "That wasn't funny."

"I didn't say it was funny. I said it was weird. Remember?"

Michael turned to look at her and she tilted her face to look up at his, dark eyes glinting, adorably proud of herself. They'd walked nearly a full circuit of the lake now, neither of them even thinking to branch off in the direction of the park's northern gate and the way home.

"Well, it was weird all right," Michael said. "Creepy ghost sailor. Pretty good."

"Yeah," she said. "Turns out there was a ship went down there in the second World War. All hands lost."

"Went down in the woods. That was a good trick."

"It wasn't the *woods*. Didn't I tell you that? It was the beach. That's where it all happened."

"Was it Redondo?"

"The fuck's *Redondo*?" she said, genuinely puzzled.

"It's a beach. In America. I've heard of it. It's on that Patti Smith album."

"Oh, yeah. No. This wasn't in America. It was in Cornwall." She thought about it for a moment. "Yeah. Had to be Cornwall because of the rock pool."

"You didn't say anything about a rock pool."

"I haven't *told* you yet," she said, exasperated. "God, you're rubbish."

Michael laughed, even though something else had just hit him. He was walking on a moonlit night alone with a beautiful girl and it apparently wasn't occurring to him to try anything. He hadn't even put his arm around her, for Christ's sake. Terry and Kirk would give him such shit for this when he told them. He wondered for the first time if that was something Carol knew, if that was what had always been behind her stories, why she found them, why she told them, like some instinctive Scheherazade keeping would-be lovers at bay with narrative strategies. He felt something forming in him, a kind of sadness that he couldn't name and didn't understand.

"Is everything all right, Carol?" he asked, though he couldn't say why.

"Well, it is *now*," she said, deaf to the half-born subtext in his question. "I got away. I escaped. But that spoils the story, dickhead. You've got to hear what *happened* first."

The park was silver-gray in the light from the moon. He wondered what time it was. "The rock pool," he said.

"Exactly," she said, pleased that he was paying attention.

She hadn't seen it at first. Had kept moving along the deserted beach until the sandy shore gave way to rocky cave-strewn outcrops from the cliffs above the coastline. It was only when she clambered over an algae and seaweed coated rock wall that she found it. Orphaned from the sea and held within a natural basin formation, the pool was placid and still and ringed by several large boulders about its rim. It was about twenty feet across and looked to be fairly deep.

On one of the boulders, laid out as if waiting for their owner, were some items of clothing. A dress, a pair of stockings, some underwear. Carol looked from them out to the cool inviting water of the pool. A head broke surface as she looked, and a woman started swimming toward the rock where her clothes were. Catching sight of Carol, she stopped and trod water, looking at her suspiciously. "What are you doing?" she said. "Are you spying?" She was older than Carol, about her mum's age maybe, a good-looking thirty-five.

"No, I'm not," Carol said. "Why would I be spying?"

"You might be one of them," the woman said.

"One of who?"

The woman narrowed her eyes and looked at Carol appraisingly. "You know who," she said.

"No, I don't," Carol said. "And I'm not one of anybody. I was with some friends. We went to France. Just got back. The boat's down there on the beach."

"They've all got stories," the woman said. "That's how they get you."

"Who?! Stop talking shit, willya? I . . ." Carol bit her tongue.

For the first time, the woman smiled. "Are you moderating your language for me?" she said. "That's adorable."

Carol felt strangely flustered. Was this woman *flirting* with her?

"I understand," the woman said, still smiling, still staring straight into Carol's eyes. "I'm an older lady and you want to be polite. But, you know, I'm not really *that* much older." She stepped out of the pool and stood there right in front of Carol, glistening wet and naked. "See what I mean?" she said.

Carol felt funny. She swallowed. The woman kept her eyes fixed on Carol as she stepped very close to her. "I'm going to tell you a secret," she said, and leaned forward to whisper the secret in Carol's ear. "I'm real limber for my age."

Carol jumped back as the woman's voice began a familiar rhythmic chant.

"Down in Nagasaki,
Where the fellas chew tobaccy,
And the women wicky-wacky-woo."

Carol tried to run but the woman had already grabbed her by the throat. "What's your rush, sweetheart?" she said, and her voice was different now, guttural and amused. "Party's just getting started."

Carol was struggling in the choking grip. She tried to swing a fist at the woman's head but her punch was effortlessly blocked by the woman's other arm.

"Your eyes are so pretty," the woman said. "I'm going to have them for earrings."

Her mouth opened inhumanly wide. Her tongue flicked out with reptile speed. It was long and black and forked.

"But like I said," said Carol, "I escaped."

"How?" said Michael, expecting another previously unmentioned element to be brought into play, like a knife or a gun or a really sharp stick or a last-minute rescue from her Francophile friends from the recently invented boat. But Carol had a different ending in mind.

"I walked into the Moon," she said.

Michael looked up to the night sky.

"No," said Carol. "Not that Moon. This one."

She was pointing out towards the center of the utterly calm lake and the perfect Moon reflected there. Looking at it with her, neither of them walking now, Michael felt the cold of the night as if for the first time. He waited in silence, afraid to speak, afraid to give voice to his questions, afraid that they would be answered.

She told another story then, the last, he knew, that his sweet lost friend would ever tell him, the tale of how the other Moon had many ways into and out of this world: Through placid lakes on summer evenings; through city streets on rain-slicked nights; from out the ocean depths for the eyes of lonely night-watch sailors.

And when she was done, when Michael could no longer pretend not to know in whose company he truly was, she turned to him and smiled a heartbreaking smile of farewell.

She looked beautiful in monochrome, in the subtle tones of the Moon that had claimed her for its own. Not drained of color, but richly re-imagined, painted in shades of silver, gray, and black, and delicate lunar blue. She looked almost liquid, as if, were Michael to reach out a hand and even try to touch her, she might ripple into strange expansions of herself.

"Thanks, Michael," she said. "I can make it home from here."

Michael didn't say anything. Didn't know what he could possibly find to say that the tears in his young eyes weren't already saying. The beautiful dead girl pointed a silver finger beyond him, in the direction of his life. "Go on," she said kindly. "Don't look back."

And he didn't look back, not even when he heard the impossible footsteps on the water, not even when he heard the shadow Moon sigh in welcome, and the quiet lapping of the lake water as if something had slipped effortlessly beneath it.

He'd later hear the alternative versions of course—the stories of how, one moonlit night, Carol had walked out of the third-floor window of her step-father's house and the vile rumors as to why—but he would prefer, for all his days, to believe the story that the lost girl herself had chosen to tell him.

He continued home through the park, not even breaking step as his fingers sought and found the numb spot on his cheek, the frozen place where her cold lips had blessed him, waiting for her frostbite kiss to bloom in tomorrow's mirror.

• • • •

We stood, right in the spot where the mirror should have reflected us.
Right where Grandpa died.

The Muldoon
Glen Hirshberg

"He found that he could not even concentrate for more than an instant on Skeffington's death, for Skeffington, alive, in multiple guises, kept getting in the way."

— John O'Hara

That night, like every night we spent in our grandfather's house, my older brother Martin and I stayed up late to listen. Sometimes, we heard murmuring in the white, circular vent high up the cracking plaster wall over our heads. The voices were our parents', we assumed, their conversation captured but also muffled by the pipes in the downstairs guest room ceiling. In summer, when the wind went still between thunderstorms, we could almost make out words. Sometimes, especially in August, when the Baltimore heat strangled even the thunderclouds, we heard cicadas bowing wildly in the grass out our window and twenty feet down.

On the dead-still September night after my grandfather's *shiva*, though, when all of the more than two thousand well-wishers we'd hosted that week had finally filed through the house and told their stories and left, all Martin and I heard was the clock. *Tuk, tuk, tuk,* like a prison guard's footsteps. I could almost see it out there, hulking over the foyer below, nine feet of carved oak and that bizarre, glassed-in face, brass hands on black velvet with brass fittings. Even though the carvings all the way up the casing were just wiggles and flourishes, and even though the velvet never resembled anything but a blank, square space, the whole thing had always reminded me more of a totem pole than a clock, and it scared me, some.

"Miriam," my brother whispered. "Awake?"

I hesitated until after the next *tuk*. It had always seemed bad luck to start a sentence in rhythm with that clock. "Think they're asleep?"

He sat up. Instinctively, my glance slipped out our open door to the far hallway wall. My grandfather had died right out there, felled at last by the heart attack his physician had warned him for decades was coming if he refused to drop fifty pounds. It seemed impossible that his enormous body had left not the slightest trace in the threadbare hallway carpet, but there was none. What had he even been doing up here? In the past four years or so, I'd never once seen him more than two steps off the ground floor.

The only thing I could see in the hallway now was the mirror. Like every other mirror in the house, it had been soaped for the *shiva*, and so, instead of the half-reassuring, half-terrifying blur of movement I usually glimpsed there, I saw only darkness, barely penetrated by the single butterfly nightlight plugged in beneath it.

Reaching over the edge of the bed, I found my sweatpants and pulled them on under my nightgown. Then I sat up, too.

"Why do they soap the mirrors?"

"Because the Angel of Death might still be lurking. You don't want him catching sight of you." Martin turned his head my way, and a tiny ray of light glinted off his thick owl-glasses.

"That isn't why," I whispered.

"You make the ball?"

"Duh."

With a quick smile that trapped moonlight in his braces, my brother slid out of bed. I flipped my own covers back but waited until he reached the door, poked his head out, and peered downstairs. Overhead, the vent pushed a useless puff of cold air into the heat that had pooled around us. In the foyer, the clock *tuk*-ed.

"Voices," I hissed, and Martin scampered fast back to bed. His glasses tilted toward the vent. I grinned. "Ha. We're even."

Now I could see his eyes, dark brown and huge in their irises, as though bulging with all the amazing things he knew. One day, I thought, if Martin kept reading like he did, badgered my parents into taking him to enough museums, just stood there and *watched* the way he could sometimes, he'd literally pop himself like an over-inflated balloon.

"For what?" he snapped.

"Angel of Death."

"That's what Roz told me."

"She would."

He grinned back. "You're right."

From under my pillow, I drew out the sock-ball I'd made and flipped it to him. He turned it in his hands as though completing an inspection. Part of the ritual. Once or twice, he'd even torn balls apart and made me redo them. The DayGlo-yellow stripes my mother hoped looked just a little athletic on his spindle-legs had to curve just so, like stitching on a baseball. And the weight had to be right. Three, maybe four socks, depending on how worn they were and what brand mom had bought. Five, and the thing just wouldn't arc properly.

"You really think we should play tonight?"

Martin glanced up, as though he hadn't even considered that. Then he shrugged. "Grandpa would've."

I knew that he'd considered it plenty. And that gave me my first conscious inkling of just how much our grandfather had meant to my brother.

This time, I followed right behind Martin to the door, and we edged together onto the balcony. Below us, the grandfather clock and the double-doored glass case where our Roz, the tall, orange-skinned, sour-faced woman grandpa had married right after I was born, kept her prized porcelain poodle collection and her milky blue oriental vases with the swans gliding around the sides lay hooded in shadow. Beyond the foyer, I could just see the straightened rows of chairs we'd set up for the week's last mourner's Kaddish, the final chanting of words that seemed to have channeled a permanent groove on my tongue. The older you get, my mother had told me, the more familiar they become. *Yit-barah, v'yish-tabah, v'yit-pa-ar, v'yit-roman, v'yit-na-sey . . .*

"You can throw first," my brother said, as though granting me a favor.

"Don't you want to?" I teased. "To honor him?" Very quietly, I began to make chicken clucks.

"Cut it out," Martin mumbled, but made no move toward the stairs. I clucked some more, and he shot out his hand so fast I thought he was trying to hit me. But he was only flapping in that nervous, spastic wave my parents had been waiting for him to outgrow since he was three. "Shush. Look."

"I am look . . . " I started, then realized he wasn't peering over the balcony at the downstairs hall from which Roz would emerge to scream at us if she heard movement. He was looking over his shoulder toward the mirror. "Not funny," I said.

"Weird," said Martin. Not until he took a step across the landing did I realize what he meant.

The doors to the hags' rooms were open. Not much. I couldn't see anything of either room. But both had been pushed just slightly back from their usual positions. Clamminess flowed from my fingertips up the peach fuzz on my arms.

Naturally, halfway across the landing, Martin stopped. If I didn't take the lead, he'd never move another step. The clammy sensation spread to my shoulders, down my back. I went to my brother anyway. We stood, right in the spot where the mirror should have reflected us. Right where Grandpa died. In the butterfly-light, Martin's face looked wet and waxy, the way it did when he had a fever.

"You really want to go through those doors?" I whispered.

"Just trying to remember."

I nodded first toward Mrs. Gold's room, then Sophie's. "Pink. Blue." The shiver I'd been fighting for the past half-minute snaked across my ribs.

Martin shook his head. "I mean the last time we saw them open. Either one."

But he already knew that. So did I. We'd last glimpsed those rooms the week before the hags had died. Four years—almost half my life—ago.

"Let's not," I said, and Martin shuffled to the right, toward Mrs. Gold's. "Martin, come on, let's play. I'm going downstairs."

But I stayed put, amazed, as he scuttled forward with his eyes darting everywhere, like a little ghost-shrimp racing across an exposed patch of sea bottom. *He'll never do it,* I thought, *not without me.* I tried chicken-clucking again, but my tongue had dried out. Martin stretched out his hand and shoved.

The door made no sound as it glided back, revealing more shadows, the dark humps of four-poster bed and dresser, a square of moonlight through almost-drawn curtains. A split second before, if someone had asked me to draw Mrs. Gold's room, I would have made a big, pink smear with a crayon. But now, even from across the hall, I recognized that everything was just the way I'd last seen it.

"Coming?" Martin asked.

More than anything else, it was the plea in his voice that pulled me forward. I didn't bother stopping, because I knew I'd be the one going in first anyway. But I did glance at my brother's face as I passed. His skin looked even waxier than before, as though it might melt right off.

Stopping on the threshold, I reached into Mrs. Gold's room with my arm, then jerked it back.

"*What?*" my brother snapped.

I stared at the goose bumps dimpling the skin above my wrist like bubbles in boiling water. But the air in Mrs. Gold's room wasn't boiling. It was freezing cold. "I think we found this house's only unclogged vent," I said.

"Just flick on the lights."

I reached in again. It really was freezing. My hand danced along the wall. I was imagining fat, pink spiders lurking right above my fingers, waiting while I stretched just that last bit closer . . .

"Oh, *fudder,*" I mumbled, stepped straight into the room, and switched on the dresser lamp. The furniture leapt from its shadows into familiar formation, *surprise*! But there was nothing surprising. How was it that I remembered this so perfectly, having spent a maximum of twenty hours in here in my entire life, none of them after the age of six?

There it all was, where it had always been: The bed with its crinoline curtain and beige sheets that always looked too heavy and scratchy to me, something to make drapes out of, not sleep in; the pink wallpaper; the row of perfect pink powder puffs laid atop closed pink clam-lids full of powder or God-knows-what, next to dark pink bottles of lotion; the silver picture frame with the side-by-side posed portraits of two men in old army uniforms. Brothers? Husbands? Sons? I'd been too young to ask. Mrs. Gold was Roz's mother, but neither of them had ever explained about the photographs, at least not in my hearing. I'm not sure even my mother knew.

As Martin came in behind me, the circular vent over the bed gushed frigid air. I clutched my arms tight against myself and closed my eyes and was surprised to find tears between my lashes. Just a few. Every visit to Baltimore for the first six years of my life, for one hour per day, my parents would drag chairs in here and plop us down by this bed to "*chat*" with Mrs. Gold. That was my mother's word for it. Mostly, what we did was sit in the chairs or—when I was a baby—crawl over the carpet—and make silent faces at each other while Mrs. Gold prattled endlessly, senselessly, about horses or people we didn't know with names like Ruby and Selma, gobbling the Berger cookies we brought her and scattering crumbs all over those scratchy sheets. My mother would nod and smile and wipe the crumbs away. Mrs. Gold would nod and smile, and strands of her poofy white hair would blow in the wind from the vent. As far as I could tell, Mrs. Gold had no idea who any of us were. All those hours in here, and really, we'd never even met her.

Martin had slipped past me, and now he touched the fold of the sheet at the head of the bed. I was amazed again. He'd done the same thing at the funeral home, stunning my mother by sticking his hand into the coffin during the visitation and gently, with one extended finger, touching my grandfather's lapel. Not typical timid Martin behavior.

"Remember her hands?" he said.

Like shed snakeskin. So dry no lotion on Earth, no matter how pink, would soften them

"She seemed nice," I said, feeling sad again. For Grandpa, mostly, not Mrs. Gold. After all, we'd never known her when she was . . . whoever she was. "I bet she was nice."

Martin took his finger off the bed and glanced at me. "Unlike the one we were actually related to." And he walked straight past me into the hall.

"Martin, no." I paused only to switch out the dresser lamp. As I did, the clock in the foyer *tuk*-ed, and the dark seemed to pounce on the bed, the powder puffs, and the pathetic picture frame. I hurried into the hall, conscious of my clumping steps. Was I *trying* to wake Roz?

Martin stood before Sophie's door, hand out, but he hadn't touched it. When he turned to me, he had a grin on his face I'd never seen before. "*Mamzer*," he drawled.

My mouth dropped open. He sounded exactly like her. "Stop it."

"*Come to Gehenna. Suffer with me.*"

"Martin, *shut up*!"

He flinched, bumped Sophie's door with his shoulder and then stumbled back in my direction. The door swung open, and we both held still and stared.

Balding carpet, yellow-white where the butterfly light barely touched it. Everything else stayed shadowed. The curtains in there had been drawn completely. When was the last time light had touched this room?

"Why did you say that?" I asked

"It's what she said. To Grandpa, every time he dragged himself up here. Remember?"

"What's *mamzer*?"

Martin shook his head. "Aunt Paulina slapped me once for saying it."

"What's *henna*?"

"*Gehenna*. One sixtieth of Eden."

Prying my eyes from Sophie's doorway, I glared at my brother. "What does that mean?"

"It's like hell. Jew hell."

"Jews don't believe in hell. Do we?"

"Somewhere wicked people go. They can get out, though. After they suffer enough."

"Can we play our game now?" I made a flipping motion with my hand, cupping it as though around a sock-ball.

"Let's . . . take one look. Pay our respects."

"Why?"

Martin looked at the floor, and his arms gave one of their half-flaps. "Grandpa did. Every day, no matter what she called him. If we don't, no one ever will again."

He strode forward, pushed the door all the way back, and actually stepped partway over the threshold. The shadows leaned toward him, and I made myself move, half-thinking I might snatch him back. With a flick of his wrist, Martin switched on the lights.

For a second, I thought the bulbs had blown, because the shadows glowed rather than dissipated, and the plain, boxy bed in there seemed to take slow shape, as though reassembling itself. Then I remembered. Sophie's room wasn't blue because of wallpaper or bed coverings or curtain fabric. She'd liked dark blue light, barely enough to see by, just enough to read if you were right under the lamp. She'd lain in that light all day, curled beneath her covers with just her thin, knife-shaped head sticking out like a moray eel's.

Martin's hand had found mine, and after a few seconds, his touch distracted me enough to glance away, momentarily, from the bed, the bare dresser, the otherwise utterly empty room. I stared down at our palms. *"Your brother's only going to love a few people,"* my mother had told me once, after he'd slammed the door to his room in my face for the thousandth time so he could work on his chemistry set or read Ovid aloud to himself without me bothering him. *"You'll be one of them."*

"How'd they die?" I asked.

Martin seemed transfixed by the room, or his memories of it, which had to be more defined than mine. Our parents had never made us come in here. But Martin had accompanied grandpa, at least some of the time. When Sophie wasn't screaming, or calling everyone names. He took a long time answering. "They were old."

"Yeah. But didn't they like die on the same day or something?"

"Same week, I think. Dad says that happens a lot to old people. They're barely still in their bodies, you know? Then someone they love goes, and it's like unbuckling the last straps holding them in. They just slip out."

"But Sophie and Mrs. Gold hated each other."

Martin shook his head. "Mrs. Gold didn't even know who Sophie was, I bet. And Sophie hated everything. You know, Mom says she was a really good grandma, until she got sick. Super smart, too. She used to give lectures at the synagogue."

"Lectures about what?"

"Hey," said Martin, let go of my hand, and took two shuffling steps into Sophie's room. Blue light washed across his shoulders, darkening him. On the far wall, something twitched. Then it rose off the plaster. I gasped, lunged forward to grab Martin, and a second something joined the first, and I understood.

"No one's been in here," I whispered. The air was not cold, although the circular vent I could just make out over the bed coughed right as I said that. Another thought wriggled behind my eyes, but I shook it away. "Martin, the mirror."

Glancing up, he saw what I meant. The glass on Sophie's wall—aimed toward the hall, not the bed, she'd never wanted to see herself—stood unsoaped, pulling the dimness in rather than reflecting it, like a black hole. In that light, we were just shapes, our faces featureless. Even for grandpa's *shiva*, no one had bothered to prepare this room.

Martin turned from our reflections to me, his pointy nose and glasses familiar and reassuring, but only until he spoke.

"Miriam, look at this."

Along the left-hand wall ran a long closet with sliding wooden doors. The farthest door had been pulled almost all the way open and tipped off its runners, so that it hung half-sideways like a dangling tooth.

"Remember the dresses?"

I had no idea what he was talking about now. I also couldn't resist another glance in the mirror, but then quickly pulled my eyes away. There were no pictures on Sophie's bureau, just a heavy, wooden gavel. My grandfather's, of course. He must have given it to her when he retired.

"This whole closet used to be stuffed with them. Fifty, sixty, maybe more, in plastic cleaners bags. I don't think she ever wore them after she moved here. I can't even remember her getting dressed."

"She never left the room," I muttered.

"Except to sneak into Mrs. Gold's."

I closed my eyes as the clock *tuk*-ed and the vent rasped.

It had only happened once while we were in the house. But Grandpa said she did it all the time. Whenever Sophie got bored of accusing her son of kidnapping her from her own house and penning her up here, or whenever her ravaged, rotting lungs allowed her enough breath, she'd rouse herself from this bed, inch out the door in her bare feet with the blue veins popping out of the tops like rooster crests, and sneak into Mrs. Gold's room. There she'd sit, murmuring God knew what, until Mrs. Gold started screaming.

"It always creeped me out," Martin said. "I never liked looking over at this closet. But the dresses blocked *that*."

"Blocked wh—" I started, and my breath caught in my teeth. Waist-high on the back inside closet wall, all but covered by a rough square of wood that had been leaned against it rather than fitted over it, there was an opening. A door. "Martin, if Roz catches us in here—"

Hostility flared in his voice like a lick of flame. "Roz hardly ever catches us playing the balcony ball game right outside her room. Anyway, in case you haven't noticed, she *never* comes in here."

"What's with you?" I snapped. Nothing about my brother made sense tonight.

"What? Nothing. It's just . . . Grandpa brings Roz's mother here, even though she needs constant care, can't even feed herself unless she's eating

Berger cookies, probably has no idea where she is. Grandpa takes care of her, like he took care of everyone. But when it comes to *his* mother, Roz won't even bring food in here. She makes him do everything. And after they die, Roz leaves her own mother's room exactly like it was, but she cleans out every trace of Sophie, right down to the closet."

"Sophie was mean."

"She was sick. And ninety-two."

"And mean."

"I'm going in there," Martin said, gesturing or flapping, I couldn't tell which. "I want to see Grandpa's stuff. Don't you? I bet it's all stored in there."

"I'm going to bed. Goodnight, Martin."

In an instant, the hostility left him, and his expression turned small, almost panicked.

"I'm going to bed," I said again.

"You don't want to see Grandpa?"

This time, the violence in my own voice surprised me. "Not in there." I was thinking of the way he'd looked in his coffin. His dead face had barely even resembled his real one. His living one. His whole head had been transformed into a waxy, vaguely grandpa-shaped *bulge* balanced atop his bulgy, overweight body, like the top of a snowman.

"Please," Martin said, and something moved downstairs.

"Shit," I mouthed, going completely still.

Clock tick. Clock tick. Footsteps. *Had I left the lights on in Mrs. Gold's room?* I couldn't remember. If Roz wasn't looking, she might not see Sophie's blue light from downstairs. Somehow, I knew she didn't want us in here.

I couldn't help glancing behind me, and then my shoulders clenched. The door had swung almost all the way shut.

Which wasn't so strange, was it? How far had we even opened it?

Footsteps. Clock tick. Clock tick. Clock tick. Clock tick. When I turned back to Martin, he was on his hands and knees, scuttling for the closet.

"Martin, *no*," I hissed. Then I was on my knees too, hurrying after him. When I drew up alongside him, our heads just inside the closet, he looked my way and grinned, tentatively.

"Sssh," he whispered.

"What do you think you'll find in there?"

The grin slid from his face. "Him." With a nod, he pulled the square of wood off the opening. Then he swore and dropped it. His right hand rose to his mouth, and I saw the sliver sticking out of the bottom of his thumb like a porcupine quill.

Taking his wrist, I leaned over, trying to see. In that murky, useless light, the wood seemed to have stabbed straight through the webbing into his palm. It almost looked like a new ridge forming along his lifeline. "Hold still," I murmured, grabbed the splinter as low down as I could, and yanked.

Martin sucked in breath, staring at his hand. "Did you get it all?"

"Come where it's light and I'll see."

"No." He pulled his hand from me, and without another word crawled through the opening. For one moment, as his butt hovered in front of me and his torso disappeared, I had to stifle another urge to drag him out, splinters be damned. Then he was through. For a few seconds, I heard only his breathing, saw only his bare feet through the hole. The rest of him was in shadow.

"Miriam, get in here," he said.

In I went. I had to shove Martin forward to get through, and I did so harder than I had to. He made no protest. I tried lifting my knees instead of sliding them to keep the splinters off. When I straightened, I was surprised to find most of the space in front of us bathed in moonlight.

"What window is that?" I whispered.

"Must be on the side."

"I've never seen it."

"How much time have you spent on the side?"

None, in truth. No one did. The space between my grandfather's house and the ancient gray wooden fence that bordered his property had been overrun by spiders even when our mom was young. I'd glimpsed an old bike back there once, completely draped in webs like furniture in a dead man's room.

"Probably a billion spiders in here, too, you know," I said.

But Martin wasn't paying attention, and neither was I, really. We were too busy staring. All around us, stacked from floor to four-foot ceiling all the way down the length of the half-finished space, cardboard boxes had been stacked, sometimes atop each other, sometimes atop old white suitcases or trunks with their key-coverings dangling like the tongues on strangled things. With his shoulder, Martin nudged one of the nearest stacks, which tipped dangerously but slid back a bit. Reaching underneath a lid flap, Martin stuck his hand in the bottom-most box. I bit my cheek and held still and marveled, for the hundredth time in the last fifteen minutes, at my brother's behavior. When he pulled out a *Playboy*, I started to laugh, and stopped because of the look on Martin's face.

He held the magazine open and flat across both hands, looking terrified to drop it, almost in awe of it, as though it were a Torah scroll. It would be a long time, I thought, before Martin started dating.

"You said you wanted to see grandpa's stuff," I couldn't resist teasing.

"This wasn't his."

Now I did laugh. "Maybe it was Mrs. Gold's."

I slid the magazine off his hands, and that seemed to relieve him, some. The page to which it had fallen open showed a long, brown-haired woman with strangely pointed feet poised naked atop a stone backyard well, as though she'd just climbed out of it. The woman wasn't smiling, and I didn't like the picture at all. I closed the magazine and laid it face down on the floor.

Edging forward, Martin began to reach randomly into other boxes. I did the same. Mostly, though, I watched my brother. The moonlight seemed to pour over him in layers, coating him, so that with each passing moment he grew paler. Other than Martin's scuttling as he moved down the row on his knees, I heard nothing, not even the clock. That should have been a comfort. But the silence in that not-quite-room was worse.

To distract myself, I began to run my fingers over the boxes on my right. Their cardboard skin had sticky damp patches, bulged outward in places but sank into itself in others. From one box, I drew an unpleasantly damp, battered, black rectangular case I thought might be for pens, but when I opened it, I found four pearls strung on a broken chain, pressed deep into their own impressions in the velvet lining like little eyes in sockets. My real grandmother's, I realized. Roz liked showier jewelry. I'd never met my mother's mother. She'd died three months before Martin was born. Dad had liked her a lot. I was still gazing at the pearls when air gushed across me, pouring over my skin like ice.

Martin grunted, and I caught his wrist. We crouched and waited for the torrent to sigh itself out. Eventually, it did. Martin started to speak, and I tightened my grasp and shut him up.

Just at the end, as the gush had died . . .

"Martin," I whispered.

"It's the air-conditioning, Miriam. See?"

"Martin, did you hear it?"

"Duh. Look at—"

"Martin. The vents."

He wasn't listening, didn't understand. Dazed, I let him disengage, watched him crab-walk to the next stack of boxes and begin digging. I almost started screaming at him. If I did, I now knew, the sound would pour out of the walls above our bed, and from the circular space above Mrs. Gold's window, and from Sophie's closet. Because these vents didn't connect to the guest room where our parents were, like we'd always thought. They connected the upstairs rooms and this room. And so the murmuring we'd always heard—

that we'd heard as recently as twenty minutes ago—hadn't come from our parents at all. It had come from right—

"Jackpot," Martin muttered.

Ahead, wedged between the last boxes and the wall, something stirred. Flapped. Plastic. Maybe.

"Martin . . . "

"Hi, Grandpa."

I spun so fast I almost knocked him over, banging my arms instead on the plaque he was wiping free of mold and dust with the sleeve of his pajamas. Frozen air roared over us again, as though I'd rattled a cage and woken the house itself. Up ahead, whatever it was flapped some more.

"Watch *out*," Martin snapped. He wasn't worried about me, of course. He didn't want anything happening to the plaque.

"We have to get out of here," I said.

Wordlessly, he held up his treasure. Black granite, with words engraved in it, clearly legible despite the fuzzy smear of grime across the surface. *To the Big Judge, who takes care of his own. A muldoon, and no mistake. From his friends, the Knights of Labor.*

"The Knights of Labor?"

"He knew everyone," Martin said. "They all loved him. The whole city."

This was who my grandfather was to my brother, I realized. Someone as smart and weird and defiant and solitary as he was, except that our grandfather had somehow figured out people enough to wind up a judge, a civil rights activist, a bloated and beloved public figure. Slowly, like a snake stirring, another shudder slipped down my back.

"What's a *muldoon*?"

"Says right here, stupid." Martin nodded at the plaque. "He took care of his own."

"We should go, Martin. Now."

"What are you talking about?"

As the house unleashed another frigid breath, he tucked the plaque lovingly against his chest and moved deeper into the attic. The plastic at the end of the row was rippling now, flattening itself. It reminded me of an octopus I'd seen in the Baltimore Aquarium once, completely changing shape to slip between two rocks.

"There," I barked suddenly, as the air expired. "Hear it?"

But Martin was busy wedging open box lids, prying out cufflinks in little boxes, a ceremonial silver shovel marking some sort of groundbreaking, a photograph of grandpa with Earl Weaver and two grinning grounds crew guys in the Orioles dugout. The last thing he pulled out before I moved was a book. Old, blue binding, stiff and jacketless. Martin flipped through it once, mumbled, "Hebrew," and dumped it behind him. Embossed on the cover, staring straight up at the ceiling over my brother's head, I saw a single, lidless eye.

Martin kept going, almost to the end now. The plastic had gone still, the air-conditioning and the murmurs that rode it temporarily silent. I almost left him there. If I'd been sure he'd follow—as, on almost any other occasion, he would have—that's exactly what I'd have done. Instead, I edged forward myself, my hand stretching for the book. As much to get that eye hidden again as from any curiosity, I picked the thing up and opened it. Something in the binding snapped, and a single page slipped free and fluttered away like a dried butterfly I'd let loose.

"Ayin Harah," I read slowly, sounding out the Hebrew letters on the title page. But it wasn't the words that set me shuddering again, if only because I wasn't positive what they implied; I knew they meant "Evil Eye." But our Aunt Pauline had told us that was a protective thing, mostly. Instead, my gaze locked on my great-grandmother's signature, lurking like a blue spider in the top left-hand corner of the inside cover. Then my head lifted, and I was staring at the box from which the book had come.

Not my grandfather's stuff in there. Not my grandmother's, or Roz's, either. That box—and maybe that one alone—was hers.

I have no explanation for what happened next. I knew better. That is, I knew, already. Thought I did. I didn't want to be in the attic even one second longer, and I was scared, not curious. I crept forward and stuck my hand between the flaps anyway.

For a moment, I thought the box was empty. My hand kept sliding deeper, all the way to my elbow before I touched fabric and closed my fist over it. Beneath whatever I'd grabbed was plastic, wrapped around some kind of heavy fabric. The plastic rustled and stuck slightly to my hand like an anemone's tentacles, though everything in that box was completely dry. I pulled, and the boxes balanced atop the one I'd reached into tipped back and bumped against the wall of the attic, and my hands came out, holding the thing I'd grasped, which fell open as it touched the air.

"Grandpa with two presidents, look," Martin said from down the row, waving a picture frame without lifting his head from whatever box he was looting.

Cradled in my palms lay what could have been a *matzoh* covering, maybe for holding the *afikomen* at a *seder*. When I spread out the folds, though, I found dark, rust-colored circular stains in the white fabric. Again I thought of the seder, the ritual of dipping a finger in wine and then touching it to a plate or napkin as everyone chanted plagues God had inflicted upon the Egyptians. In modern Hagadahs, the ritual is explained as a symbol of Jewish regret that the Egyptian people had to bear the brunt of their ruler's refusal to free the slaves. But none of the actual ceremonial instructions say that. They just order us to chant the words. *Dam. Tzfar de'ah. Kinim. Arbeh.*

Inside the fold where matzoh might have been tucked, I found only a gritty, black residue. It could have been dust from the attic, or split spider sacs, or tiny dead things. But it smelled, faintly, on my fingers. An old and rotten smell, with just a hint of something else. Something worse.

Not worse. *Familiar*. I had no idea what it was. But Sophie had smelled like this.

"Martin, please," I heard myself say. But he wasn't listening. Instead, he was leaning almost *into* the last box in the row. The plastic jammed against the wall had gone utterly still. At any moment, I expected it to hump up like a wave and crash down on my brother's back. I didn't even realize my hands had slipped back inside Sophie's box until I touched wrapping again.

Gasping, I dragged my hands away, but my fingers had curled, and the plastic and the heavy fabric it swaddled came up clutched between them.

A dress, I thought, panicking, shoving backward. *From her closet*. I stared at the lump of fabric, draped now half out of the box, the plastic covering rising slightly in the stirring air.

Except it wasn't a dress. It was two dresses, plainly visible now through the plastic. One was gauzy and pink, barely there, with wispy flowers stitched up the sleeves. The other, white and heavy, had folded itself inside the pink one, the long sleeves encircling the waist. Long, black smears spread across the back of the white dress, like finger-marks, from fingers dipped in Sophie's residue . . .

I don't think I had any idea, at first, that I'd started shouting. I was too busy scuttling backwards on my hands, banging against boxes on either side as I scrambled for the opening behind us. The air-conditioning triggered, blasting me with its breath, which didn't stink, just froze the hairs to the skin of my arms and legs. Martin had leapt to his feet, banging his head against the attic ceiling, and now he was waving his hands, trying to quiet me. But the sight of him panicked me more. The dresses on the ground between us shivered, almost rolled over, and the plastic behind him rippled madly, popping and straining against the weight that held it, all but free. My hand touched down on the *Playboy*, and I imagined the well-woman climbing out of the magazine on her pointy feet and finally fell hard half out of the attic opening, screaming now, banging my spine on the wood and bruising it badly.

Then there were hands on my shoulder, hard and horny and orange-ish, yanking me out of the hole and dragging me across the floor. Yellow eyes flashing fury, Roz leaned past me and ducked her head through the hole, screeching at Martin to get out. Then she stalked away, snarling *"Out"* and *"Come on."*

Never had I known her to be this angry. I'd also never been happier to see her pinched, glaring, unhappy face, the color of an overripe orange thanks to the liquid tan she poured all over herself before her daily mah-jongg games at the club where she sometimes took us swimming. Flipping over and standing, I hurried after her, the rattle of the ridiculous twin rows of bracelets that ran halfway up her arms sweet and welcome in my ears as the tolling of a dinner bell. I waited at the lip of the closet until Martin's head appeared, then fled Sophie's room.

A few seconds later, my brother emerged, the *Knights of Labor* plaque clutched against his chest, glaring bloody murder at me. But Roz took him by the shoulders, guided him back to his bed in my mother's old room, and sat him down. I followed, and fell onto my own bed. For a minute, maybe more, she stood above us and glowed even more than usual, as though she might burst into flame. Then, for the first time in all my experience of her, she crossed her legs and sat down between our beds on the filthy floor.

"Oh, kids," she sighed. "What were you doing in there?"

"Where are Mom and Dad?" Martin demanded. The shrillness in his tone made me cringe even farther back against the white wall behind me. Pushing with me feet, I dug myself under the covers and lay my head on my pillow.

"Out," Roz said, in the same weary voice. "They're on a walk. They've been cooped up here, same as the rest of us, for an entire week."

"Cooped up?" Martin's voice rose still more, and even Roz's leathery face registered surprise. "As in, sitting *shiva*? Paying tribute to Grandpa?"

After a long pause, she nodded. "Exactly that, Martin."

From the other room, I swore I could hear the sound of plastic sliding over threadbare carpet. My eyes darted to the doorway, the lit landing, the streaks of soap in the mirror, the floor.

"How'd they die?" I blurted.

Roz's lizard eyes darted back and forth between Martin and me. "What's with you two tonight?"

"Mrs. Gold and Sophie. Please, please, please. Grandma." I didn't often call her that. She scowled even harder.

"What are you babbling about?" Martin said to me. "Roz, Miriam's been really—"

"Badly, Miriam," Roz said, and Martin went quiet. "They died badly."

Despite what she'd said, her words had a surprising, almost comforting effect on me. "Please tell me."

"Your parents wouldn't want me to."

"Please."

Settling back, Roz eyed me, then the vent overhead. I kept glancing into the hall. But I didn't hear anything now. And after a while, I only watched her. She crossed her arms over her knees, and her bracelets clanked.

"It was an accident. A horrible accident. It really was. You have to understand . . . you have no idea how awful those days were. May you never have such days."

"What was so awful?" Martin asked. There was still a trace of petulance in his tone. But Roz's attitude appeared to be having the same weirdly soothing effect on him as on me.

She shrugged. "In the pink room, you've got my mother. Only she's not my mother anymore. She's this sweet, stupid, chattering houseplant."

I gaped. Martin did, too, and Roz laughed, kind of, without humor or joy.

"Every single day, usually more than once, she shit all over the bed. The rest of the time, she sat there and babbled mostly nice things about cookies or owls or whatever. Places she'd never been. People she may have known, but I didn't. She never mentioned me, or my father, or my brother, or anything about our lives. It was like she'd led some completely different life, without me in it."

Roz held her knees a while. Finally, she went on. "And in the blue room, there was Sophie, who remembered everything. How it had felt to walk to the market, or lecture a roomful of professors about the Kabbalah or whatever other weird stuff she knew. How it had been to live completely by herself, with her books, in her own world, the way she had for twenty-two years after your great-grandfather died. Best years of her life, I think. And then, just like that, her bones gave out on her. She couldn't move well. Couldn't drive. She couldn't really see. She broke her hip twice. When your grandpa brought her here, she was so angry, kids. So angry. She didn't want to die. She didn't want to be dependent. It made her mean. That's pretty much your choices, I think. Getting old—getting *that* old, anyway—makes you mean, or sick, or stupid, or lonely. Take your pick. Only you don't get to pick. And sometimes, you get all four."

Rustling, from the vent. The faintest hint. Or had it come from the hallway?

"Grandma, what happened?"

"An accident, Miriam. Like I said. Your goddamn grandfather . . . "

"You can't—" Martin started, and Roz rode him down.

"Your goddamn grandfather wouldn't put them in homes. Either one. *'Your mother's your mother.'* " When she said that, she rumbled, and sounded just like grandpa. " *'She's no trouble. And as for my mother . . . it'd kill her.'*

"But having them here, kids . . . it was killing us. Poisoning every single day. Wrecking every relationship we had, even with each other."

Grandma looked up from her knees and straight at us. "Anyway," she said. "We had a home care service. A private nurse. Mrs. Gertzen. She came one night a week, and a couple weekends a year when we just couldn't take it and had to get away. When we wanted to go, we called Mrs. Gertzen, left the dates, and she came and took care of both our mothers while we were gone. Well, the last time . . . when they died . . . your grandfather called her, same as always. Sophie liked Mrs. Gertzen, was probably nicer to her than anyone else, most of the time. Grandpa left instructions, and we headed off to the Delaware shore for five days. But Mrs. Gertzen had a heart attack that first afternoon, and never even made it to the house. And no one else on Earth had any idea that my mother and Sophie were up here."

"Oh my God," I heard myself whisper, as the vent above me rasped pathetically. For the first time in what seemed hours, I became aware of the clock, *tuk*-ing away. I was imagining being trapped in this bed, hearing that sound. The metered pulse of the living world, just downstairs, plainly audible. And—for my great-grandmother and Mrs. Gold—utterly out of reach.

When I looked at my grandmother again, I was amazed to find tears leaking out of her eyes. She made no move to wipe them. "It must have been worse for Sophie," she half-whispered.

My mouth fell open. Martin had gone completely still as well as silent.

"I mean, I doubt my mother even knew what was happening. She probably prattled all the way to the end. If there is an Angel of Death, I bet she offered him a Berger cookie."

"You're . . . " *nicer than I thought,* I was going to say, but that wasn't quite right. *Different than I thought.*

"But Sophie. Can you imagine how horrible? How infuriating? To realize—she must have known by dinner time—that no one was coming? She couldn't make it downstairs. We'd had to carry her to the bathroom, the last few weeks. All she'd done that past month was light candles and read her Zohar and mutter to herself. I'm sure she knew she'd never make it to the kitchen. I'm sure that's why she didn't try. But I think she came back to herself at the end, you know? Turned back into the person she must have been. The woman who raised your grandfather, made him who he was or at least let him be. Because somehow she dragged herself into my mother's room one last time. They died with their arms around each other."

The dresses, I thought. *Had they been arranged like that on purpose? Tucked together, as a memory or a monument?* Then I was shivering, sobbing, and my brother was, too. Roz sat silently between us, staring at the floor.

"I shouldn't have told you," she mumbled. "Your parents will be furious."

Seconds later, the front door opened, and our mom and dad came hurtling up the stairs, filling our doorway with their flushed, exhausted, everyday faces.

"What are you doing up?" my mother asked, moving forward fast and stretching one arm toward each of us, though we were too far apart to be gathered that way.

"I'm afraid I—" Roz started.

"Grandpa," I said, and felt Roz look at me. "We were feeling bad about Grandpa."

My mother's mouth twisted, and her eyes closed. "I know," she said. "Me, too."

I crawled over to Martin's bed. My mother held us a long time, while my father stood above her, his hands sliding from her back to our shoulders to our heads. At some point, Roz slipped silently from the room. I didn't see her go.

For half an hour, maybe more, our parents stayed. Martin showed them the plaque he'd found, and my mother seemed startled mostly by the realization of where we'd been.

"You know I forgot that room was there?" she said. "Your cousins and I used to hide in it all the time. Before the hags came."

"You shouldn't call them that," Martin said, and my mother straightened, eyes narrowed. Eventually, she nodded, and her shoulders sagged.

"You're right. And I don't think of them that way, it's just, at the end . . . Goodnight, kids."

After they'd gone, switching out all the lights except the butterfly in the hall, I thought I might sleep. But every time I closed my eyes, I swore I felt something pawing at the covers, as though trying to draw them back, so that whatever it was could crawl in with me. Opening my eyes, I found the dark room, the moon outside, the spider shadows in the corners. Several times, I glanced toward my brother's bed. He was lying on his back with the plaque he'd rescued on his chest and his head turned toward the wall, so that I couldn't see whether his eyes were open. I listened to the clock ticking and the vents rasping and muttering. *A muldoon, and no mistake,* I found myself mouthing. *Who takes care of his own.* When I tried again to close my eyes, it seemed the vent was chanting with me. *No mistake. No mistake.* My heart seemed to twist in its socket, and its beating bounced on the rhythm of the clock's tick like a skipped stone. I think I moaned, and Martin rolled over.

"Now let's play," he said.

Immediately, I was up, grabbing the sock-ball off the table where I'd left it. I wasn't anywhere near sleep, and I wasn't scared of Roz anymore. I wanted to be moving, doing anything. And my brother still wanted me with him.

I didn't wait for Martin this time, just marched straight out to the landing, casting a single, held-breath glance at Sophie's door. Someone had pulled it almost closed again, and I wondered if the wooden covering over the opening to the attic had also been replaced. Mrs. Gold's door, I noticed, had been left open. *Pushed open?*

Squelching that thought with a shake of my head, I started down the stairs. But Martin galloped up beside me, pushed me against the wall, took the sock-ball out of my hands, and hurried ahead.

"My ups," he said.

"Your funeral," I answered, and he stopped three steps down and turned and grinned. A flicker of butterfly light danced in his glasses, which made it look as though something reflective and transparent had moved behind me, but I didn't turn around, didn't turn around, turned and found the landing empty.

"She's asleep," Martin said, and for one awful moment, I didn't know whom he meant.

Then I did, and grinned weakly back. "If you say so." Retreating upstairs, I circled around the balcony into position.

The rules of Martin-Miriam Balcony Ball were simple. The person in the foyer below tried to lob the sock-ball over the railing and have it hit the carpet anywhere on the L-shaped landing. The person on the landing tried to catch the sock and slam it to the tile down in the foyer, triggering an innings change in which both players tried to bump each other off balance as they passed on the steps, thereby gaining an advantage for the first throw of the next round. Play ended when someone had landed ten throws on the balcony, or when Roz came and roared us back to bed, or when any small porcelain animal or *tuk*-ing grandfather clock or crystal chandelier got smashed. In the five year history of the game, that latter ending had only occurred once. The casualty had been a poodle left out atop the cabinet. This night's game lasted exactly one throw.

In retrospect, I think the hour or so between the moment our parents left and his invitation to play were no more restful for Martin than they had been for me. He'd lain more still, but that had just compressed the energy the evening had given him, and now he was fizzing like a shaken pop bottle. I watched him glance toward Roz's hallway, crouch into himself as though expecting a hail of gunfire, and scurry into the center of the foyer. He looked skeletal and small, like some kind of armored beetle, and the ache that prickled up under my skin was at least partially defensive of him. He would never fill space the way our grandfather had. No one would. That ability—*was that the right word?*—to love people in general more than the people closest to you, was a rare and only partly desirable thing. Martin, I already knew, didn't have it.

He must have been kneading the sock-ball all the way down the stairs, because as soon as he reared back and threw, one of the socks slipped free of the knot I'd made and dangled like the tail of a comet. Worse, Martin had somehow aimed straight up, so that instead of arching over the balcony, the sock-comet shot between the arms of the chandelier, knocked crystals together as it reached its apex, and then draped itself, almost casually, over the arm nearest the steps. After that, it just hung.

The chandelier leaned gently left, then right. The clock *tuk*-ed like a clucking tongue.

"Shit," Martin said, and something rustled.

"*Sssh.*" I resisted yet another urge to jerk my head around. I turned slowly instead, saw Sophie's almost closed door, Mrs. Gold's wide-open one. Butterfly light. Our room. Nothing else. If the sound I'd just heard had come from downstairs, then Roz was awake. "Get up here," I said, and Martin came, fast.

By the time he reached me, all that fizzing energy seemed to have evaporated. His shoulders had rounded, and his glasses had clouded over with his exertion. He looked at me through his own fog.

"Mir, what are we going to do?"

"What do you think we're going to do, we're going to go get it. *You're* going to go get it."

Martin wiped his glasses on his shirt, eyeing the distance between the landing where we stood and the gently swinging chandelier. "We need a broom." His eyes flicked hopefully to mine. He was Martin again, all right.

I glanced downstairs to the hallway I'd have to cross to get to the broom closet. "Feel free," I said.

"Come on, Miriam."

"You threw it."

"You're braver."

Abruptly, the naked woman from the well in the magazine flashed in front of my eyes. I could almost see—almost *hear*—her stepping out of the photograph, balancing on those pointed feet. Tiptoeing over the splinter-riddled floor toward those wrapped-together dresses, slipping them over her shoulders.

"What?" Martin said.

"I can't."

For the second time that night, Martin took my hand. Before the last couple hours, Martin had last held my hand when I was six years old, and my mother had made him do it whenever we crossed a street, for his protection more than mine, since he was usually thinking about something random instead of paying attention.

"I have a better idea," he whispered, and pulled me toward the top of the staircase.

As soon as he laid himself flat on the top step, I knew what he was going to do. "You can't," I whispered, but what I really meant was that I didn't believe he'd dare. There he was, though, tilting onto his side, wriggling his head through the railings. His shoulders followed. Within seconds he was resting one elbow in the dust atop the grandfather clock.

Kneeling, I watched his shirt pulse with each *tuk*, as though a second, stronger heart had taken root inside him. *Too* strong, I thought, *it could pop him to pieces.*

"Grab me," he said. "Don't let go."

Even at age ten, my fingers could touch when wrapped around the tops of his ankles. He slid out farther, and the clock came off its back legs and leaned with him. *"Fuck!"* he blurted, wiggling back as I gripped tight. The clock tipped back the other way and banged its top against the railings and rang them.

Letting go of Martin, I scrambled to my feet, ready to sprint for our beds as I awaited the tell-tale bloom of lights in Roz's hallway. Martin lay flat, breath heaving, either resigned to his fate or too freaked out to care. It seemed impossible that Roz hadn't heard what we'd just done, and anyway, she had a sort of lateral line for this kind of thing, sensing movement in her foyer the way Martin said sharks discerned twitching fish.

But somehow, miraculously, no one came. Nothing moved. And after a minute or so, without even waiting for me to hold his legs, Martin slithered forward once more. I dropped down next to him, held tighter. This time, he kept his spine straight, dropping as little of his weight as possible atop the clock. I watched his waist wedge briefly in the railings, then slip through as his arms stretched out. It was like feeding him to something. Worse than the clock's *tuk* was the groan from its base as it started to lean again. My hands went sweaty, and my teeth clamped down on my tongue, almost startling me into letting go. I had no idea whether the tears in my ears were fear or exhaustion or sadness for my grandfather or the first acknowledgement that I'd just heard rustling, right behind me.

"Ow," Martin said as my nails dug into his skin. But he kept sliding forward. My eyes had jammed themselves shut, so I felt rather than saw him grab the chandelier, felt it swing slightly away from, felt his ribs hit the top of the clock and the clock start to tip.

I opened my eyes, not looking back, not behind, it was only the vents, had to be, and then Roz stepped out of her hallway.

Incredibly, insanely, she didn't see us at first. She had her head down, bracelets jangling, hands jammed in the pockets of her shiny silver robe, and she didn't even look up until she was dead center under the chandelier, under my brother stretched full-length in mid-air twenty feet over her head with a sock in his hands. Then the clock's legs groaned under Martin's suspended weight, and the chandelier swung out, and Roz froze. For that one split second, none of us so much as breathed. And that's how I knew, even before she finally did lift her eyes. This time, I really had heard it.

"Get back," my grandmother said, and burst into tears.

It made no sense. I started babbling, overwhelmed by guilt I wasn't even sure was mine. "Grandma, I'm sorry. Sorry, sorry—"

"BACK!" Roz screamed. "Get away! Get away from them." With startling speed, she spun and darted up the steps, still shouting.

Them. Meaning us. Which meant she wasn't talking to us.

The rest happened all in one motion. As I turned, my hands came off Martin's legs. Instantly, he was gone, tipping, the clock rocking forward and over. He didn't scream, maybe didn't have time, but his body flew face-first and smacked into the floor below just as Roz hurtled past and my parents emerged shouting from the guest bedroom and saw their son and the clock smashing and splintering around and atop him and I got my single glimpse of the thing on the landing.

Its feet weren't pointed, but bare and pale and swollen with veins. It wore some kind of pink, ruffled something, and its hair was white and flying. I couldn't see its face. But its movements . . . The arms all out of rhythm with the feet, out of order, as if they were being jerked from somewhere else on invisible strings. And the legs, the way they moved . . . not Mrs. Gold's mindless, surprisingly energetic glide . . . more of a tilting, trembling lurch. Like Sophie's.

Rooted in place, mouth open, I watched it stagger past the blacked-out mirror, headed from the pink room to the blue one.

"Takes care of his own," I found myself chanting, helpless to stop. "Takes care of his own. And no mistake. No mistake." There had been no mistake.

My grandmother was waving her hands in front of her, snarling, stomping her feet as though scolding a dog. Had she already known it was here? Or just understood, immediately? In seconds, she and the lurching thing were in the blue room, and Sophie's door slammed shut.

"No mistake," I murmured, tears pouring down my face.

The door flew open again, and out Roz came. My voice wavered, sank into silence as my eyes met hers and locked. Downstairs, my father was shouting frantically into the phone for an ambulance. Roz walked, jangling, to the step above me, sat down hard, put her head on her knees and one of her hands in my hair. Then she started to weep.

Martin had fractured his spine, broken one cheekbone, his collarbone, and both legs, and he has never completely forgiven me. Sometimes I think my parents haven't, either. Certainly, they drew away from me for a long time after that, forming themselves into a sort of protective cocoon around my brother. My family traded phone calls with Roz for years. But we never went back to Baltimore, and she never came to see us.

So many times, I've lunged awake, still seeing the Sophie-Mrs. Gold creature lurching at random into my dreams. If I'd ever had the chance, I would have asked Roz only one thing: how much danger had Martin and I really been in? Would it really have hurt us? Was it inherently malevolent, a monster devouring everything it could reach? Or was it just a peculiarly Jewish sort of ghost, clinging to every last vestige of life, no matter how painful or beset by betrayal, because only in life—*this* life—is there any possibility of pleasure or fulfillment or even release?

I can't ask anyone else, because Roz is the only one other than me who knows. I have never talked about it, certainly not to Martin, who keeps the plaque he lifted from the attic that night nailed to his bedroom wall.

But I know. And sometimes, I just want to scream at all of them, make them see what's staring them right in the face, has been obvious from the moment it happened. My grandfather, the *muldoon* who took care of his own, during the whole weekend he was away with Roz, never once called his mother? Never called home? Never checked in with Mrs. Gertzen, just to see how everyone was? And Mrs. Gertzen had no family, had left no indication to the service that employed her of what jobs she might have been engaged in?

My grandfather had called Mrs. Gertzen's house before leaving for Delaware, all right. He'd learned about Mrs. Gertzen's heart attack. Then he'd weighed his shattering second marriage, his straining relationships with his children, his scant remaining healthy days, maybe even his own mother's misery.

And then he'd made his decision. Taken care of his own, and no mistake. And in the end—the way they always do, whether you take care of them or no—his own had come back for him.

• • • •

Haunted by his fame as "America's Hamlet" even before his infamous brother became an assassin, Edwin Booth also had another ghost or two . . .

Booth's Ghost
Karen Joy Fowler

One:

I have that within which passeth show.

On November 25, 1864, Edwin Booth gave a benefit performance of *Julius Caesar*. One night only, in the Winter Garden Theater in New York City, all profits to fund the raising of a statue of Shakespeare in Central Park. Edwin played the role of Brutus; his older brother, Junius, was Cassius; his younger, John Wilkes, was Mark Antony. The best seats went for as much as five dollars, and their mother and sister Asia were in the audience, flushed with pride.

Act 2, scene I. Brutus' orchard. Fire engines could be heard outside the theater, and four firemen came into the lobby. The audience began to buzz and shift in their seats. Brutus stepped forward into the footlights. "Everything is all right," he told them. "Please stay as you are."

The play continued.

People used to say that Edwin owned the East Coast, Junius the West, and John Wilkes the South, but on this occasion, the applause was mostly for John. Asia overheard a Southerner in the audience. *Our* Booth is like a young god, the man said.

From the newspaper the next morning, they learned that the fires near the theater had been set by Southern rebels. Had they been in California, Junius said, the arsonists would have been strung up without a trial. He was for that. Edwin was for the Union. He told them that a few days earlier, he'd voted for the first time. He'd voted for Lincoln's reelection. John dissolved in rage. Edwin would see Lincoln become a king, John shouted, and have no one to blame but himself. Their mother intervened. No more talk of politics.

• • •

The next night the Winter Garden Theater saw the debut of *Hamlet* with Edwin in the title role. The play ran for two weeks, three, eight, ten, until Edwin felt the exhaustion of playing the same part, night after night. He begged for a change, but the play was still selling out. This run, which would last one hundred nights, was the making of Edwin's name. Ever after, he would be America's Hamlet. It was more than a calling, almost a cult. Edwin referred to this as "my terrible success."

It was a shame Shakespeare couldn't see him, the critics wrote, he was so exactly what Hamlet ought to be, so exactly what Shakespeare had envisioned. One morning his little daughter, Edwina, was offered an omelet. "That's my daddy," she said.

There came a night when, deadened from the long run, Edwin began to miss his cues. He had the curtain brought down, retired to his dressing room to gather himself. "O God! O God!" he said to himself. "How weary, stale, flat, and unprofitable/ Seem to me all the uses of this world."

When the ghost appeared, Edwin was not surprised. He'd been born with a caul, which meant protection, but also the ability to see spirits. Almost a year earlier, his beloved young wife had died of tuberculosis. She'd been in Boston, he in New York. He was Hamlet then, too, a week's worth of performances and often drunk when onstage. "Fatigued," one of the critics said, but others were not so kind.

The night she died, he'd felt her kiss him. "I am half frozen," she'd said. He'd stopped drinking and begun to spend his money on séances instead.

Initially he'd gotten good value; his wife sent many messages of love and encouragement. Her words were general, though, impersonal, and lately he'd been having doubts. He'd begun to host séances himself, with no professional medium in attendance. A friend described one such evening. He was seized, this friend said, by a powerful electricity and his hands began to shake faster and harder than mortal man could move. He was given pen and paper, which he soon covered in ink. But when he came back to his senses, he'd written no words, only scrawl. It had all been Edwin, he decided then, doing what Edwin did best. Night after night on the stage, Edwin made people believe.

The ghost visiting Edwin now was about the height of a tall woman or else a short man. It wore a helmet, but unlike the ghost in Hamlet, its visor was lowered so its face could not be seen. Its armor was torn and insubstantial, half chain mail, half cobweb. It stood wrapped in a blue-green light, shaking its arms. There was an icy wind. A sound like the dragging of chains. Edwin knew who it was. His father's acting had always been the full-throated sort.

"Why are you here?" Edwin asked.

"Why are you here?" his father's ghost asked back. His tone reverberated with ghostly disappointment. It was a tone Edwin knew well. "You have an audience in their seats. The papers will put it down to drink." More arm shaking, more dragging of chains.

Edwin pulled himself together and returned to the stage.

Two:

The serpent that did sting thy father's life
Now wears his crown.

Drink and the theater ran heavy in Edwin's blood. His father, Junius Brutus Booth, was famous for both. Born in England, Junius had come to America in 1821 on a ship named *The Two Brothers*. He brought with him his mistress and child. He left a wife and child behind.

Junius Brutus Booth leased a property in northern Baltimore, a remote acreage of farmland and forest. When he wasn't touring, he and his family lived in isolation in a small cabin. He refused to own slaves, forbid his family to eat meat or fish, or to kill any animal. When he inadvertently injured a copperhead with the plow, he brought it home, kept it on the hearth in a box padded with a blanket until it recovered.

Edwin's earliest memory was of returning to the farm after dark on the back of a horse. As they passed through the forest toward home, his night terror grew. There were branches that grabbed for him, the screaming of owls. The horses came to a halt. His father dismounted, swung Edwin down and across the fence. "Your foot is on your native heath, boy," his father said, and Edwin never forgot the overwhelming sense of belonging, of safety, of home that washed through him.

He was not his father's favorite child nor his mother's, either. The favorite was Henry, until he died, and then it was John Wilkes. Four of the Booth children passed before adulthood. They were all older than Edwin or would have been had they lived. These deaths drove their father into an intermittent raving madness. In later years, Junius Booth was much admired for his King Lear.

Surviving from the older set were Rosalie and Junius Jr. Edwin was the eldest of the younger set, followed by Asia, John Wilkes, and Joseph. The youngest three in particular were very close.

All but Edwin were well educated. At the age of thirteen, Edwin had been taken permanently out of school to go on the road with his father. His job was to see that Junius showed up for performances and to keep him out of taverns. It was a job no one could do with complete success. The most difficult time was after the curtain.

This seems to have been the rule: that Junius would not drink if Edwin was watching. Some nights Edwin managed to lock his father in his room. On one of these occasions, Junius bribed the innkeeper and drank mint juleps with a straw through the keyhole.

More often Junius would insist on going out, Edwin trailing silently close enough to watch his father, but far enough behind to escape invective. He was a child with enormous beauty and dark, anxious eyes.

His father's goal on these evenings was to give him the slip. Then Edwin would be forced to search through a midnight landscape of deserted streets for the one tavern his father was in. He received little affection and no gratitude for this. When found, Junius would curse at Edwin, shout, threaten to see him shanghaied into the navy if he didn't go away.

One afternoon his father woke up from a nap and refused to go to the theater. He was scheduled to play Richard III. "You do it," he told Edwin. "I'm sick of it."

Lacking an alternative, the manager sent Edwin onstage in his father's hump, his father's outsized costume. No warning had been given the audience, whose applause fell away into a puzzled silence. Edwin began tentatively. He tried to imitate his father's inflections, his gestures. The actors nearest him provided every possible support while those offstage crowded the wings, watching in friendly, nervous sympathy. The audience, too, found themselves filled with pity for the young boy, so obviously out of his depth, drowning in his own sleeves. He had them on the edge of their seats, wondering if he'd get through his next line, his next scene. The play ended with Edwin's first ovation. He had won it merely by surviving.

Junius Jr., Edwin's oldest brother, relocated to San Francisco, where he ran a theater company. In 1852, he talked his father into coming west on tour. No one imagined Junius Sr. could make the trip alone. Junius Jr. traveled east to pick his father up. Edwin, now eighteen years old, was to be, at long last, left at home.

The party had tickets on a steamer leaving from New York and traveling around the cape. As soon as he arrived in the city, Junius the elder and an actor friend, George Spear, shook Junius the younger loose and went off on a toot. The boat sailed without them. Clearly Junius Jr. was not up to the task. While they waited for the next boat, Edwin was fetched from Baltimore.

After the long voyage, the Booths landed finally in San Francisco. They did several engagements at Junius Jr.'s theater, Both sons took minor supporting roles, and they all made money, but lost it again in Sacramento, where the playhouses were empty. Junius the elder went home, tired and discouraged, after only two months. Edwin remained in California with Junius the younger.

Edwin turned nineteen, and celebrated his freedom from responsibility by, in his own words, drinking and whoring, often in the very taverns his father had frequented, until his older brother had had enough. Edwin then joined a company touring the mining camps. He played in Nevada City, Yuba City, Grass Valley. In Downieville, the company was caught in a tremendous blizzard. They made their slow way back over snowy roads to Nevada City.

It was night. Edwin was wandering drunk and alone along the main street in the bright moonlit snow when he saw his father coming toward him. He wore no costume, but was dressed as himself in a stained coat and shabby hat. Edwin stopped to wait for him. "Cut off even in the blossoms of my sin," his father said. A bobbing lantern shone through his body. "I'm sick to the heart of it. You do it now." The light grew brighter as his father dimmed until he finally vanished completely. The man holding the lantern was George Spear. "I've come to fetch you, boy," said George.

A letter following behind them had finally caught up. On the last leg of his voyage back, Junius Brutus Booth had drunk a glass of water from the Mississippi River that made him so ill he died within days. He'd never reached home, and his final hours had been filled with torment. In spite of the raving and drunkenness, the Booth children had adored their father. Edwin believed Junius had secretly come to watch on that night he'd stood in as Richard III, although there was no evidence to support this. Edwin believed he'd caused his father's death by choosing not to see him safely home.

He'd promised his father to someday play Hamlet. On April 25, 1853, he talked Junius Jr. into giving him the role for the first time. Junius found him inadequate and wouldn't let him repeat it. But a young critic, Ferdinand Cartwright Ewer, thought otherwise. Ewer left the San Francisco theater in great excitement and went to the newspaper offices to write a long review. Edwin Booth, he wrote, had made Hamlet "the easy, undulating, flexible thing" Shakespeare intended.

Tastes were changing. Edwin's Hamlet, as it developed over the years, was subtle where his father had been theatrical and natural where his father had declaimed. Junius Jr. may not have liked it, but Ferdinand Cartwright Ewer wrote, in that very first review of Edwin's very first Hamlet, that, in concept if not in polish, Edwin had already surpassed his father.

• • •

Three:

O horrible, O horrible, most horrible!

In February of 1865, Junius Jr. traveled to Washington, D.C., to see John Wilkes. Junius had always admired his younger brother, but now found him hysterical and unhinged on the subject of the Richmond campaign.

Their mother wrote to John that she was miserable and lonely visiting Edwin in his Boston house. "I always gave you praise," she wrote, "for being the fondest of all my boys, but since you leave me to grief I must doubt it. I am no Roman mother. I love my dear ones before country or anything else." She went back to her home in New York, where she lived with Rosalie, her oldest daughter.

In March, John Wilkes attended Lincoln's second inauguration, standing on the platform, close to the president. After that, he came to Boston briefly, charmed his little niece Edwina with stories of his childhood. These stories were remarkable in part for how little a role her father, Edwin, had in them. Edwin and John had lived completely different lives.

Then John quarreled again with Edwin about the war, and again he left the house in anger. Back in Washington he joined thousands of others on the White House lawn when Lincoln spoke from the balcony about extending voting rights to the Negroes. John retired to a bar to drink his way through his fury. A quart of brandy in, another drinker told him he'd never be the actor his father was.

"I'll be the most famous man in America," John Wilkes answered.

On the night of April 14, 1865, Edwin Booth was in Boston, playing the villain in a melodrama called *The Iron Chest* to a sold-out house. The Civil War had just ended; the city was celebrating. Edwin Booth was thirty-one years old and engaged to be married again.

Some of his audience, on the way home from the theater, heard that the president had been shot, and some of those dismissed this as idle rumor. Edwin knew nothing until the newspaper arrived the next morning. When he saw his brother's name in print, Edwin wrote later to a friend, he felt he'd been struck on the head with a hammer. Soon a message arrived from the manager of the Boston Theater, Although he prayed, the note said, that what everyone was saying about Wilkes would yet prove untrue, he thought it best and right to cancel all further performances.

Edwin's daughter, Edwina, was visiting her aunt Asia in Philadelphia. Asia read the news in the paper and collapsed. While her husband was trying to calm her, a U.S. marshal arrived, forbid them to leave the house, and put a guard at every door.

Junius Jr. was on tour in Cincinnati. When he entered his hotel lobby for breakfast, the clerk immediately sent him back upstairs. Moments later, a mob of some five hundred people arrived. They had stripped the lampposts of Junius' playbills and come to hang him. His life was saved by the hotel clerk, who convinced the mob that Junius had gone in the night, and the staff, who hid him in an attic room until the danger passed.

Mrs. Booth and Rosalie were at home in New York. A letter from John arrived that afternoon, written the day before. "I only drop you these few lines to let you know I am well." It was signed, "I am your affectionate son." His mother wrote to Edwin that her dearest hope now was that John would shoot himself. "Please don't let him live to be hanged," she wrote.

Junius Jr. was arrested, charged with conspiracy, taken to Washington and imprisoned there. A letter had been found from him to John that referenced the "oil business," the phrase so oblique it was obviously code. Asia's husband, John Sleeper Clarke, was also imprisoned. There was an irony in this: Clarke was a comic actor of great ambition. John Wilkes had warned Asia before she married him that Clarke didn't love her. All he'd wanted was the magic of the Booth name, John had said.

In Clarke's case there wasn't even a vague, incriminating phrase, only the partiality of his wife to her little brother. Asia would surely have been imprisoned herself, if she hadn't been pregnant. Instead she was put under house arrest.

It's not clear how Edwin escaped the conspiracy charges. He'd once saved Lincoln's son from a train accident. He was known as a Union man. He had powerful friends who exerted themselves. He'd been born with a caul. Somehow he stayed out of jail. Still, he couldn't leave his house; the streets were too dangerous. His daughter returned from her aunt's under police escort. His fiancée broke off their engagement by letter.

More letters arrived, hundreds of them, to all members of the Booth family. They came for months; they came for years. "I am carrying for you." "Your life is forfeit." "We hate the very name Booth." "Your next performance will be a tragedy."

John Wilkes was exposed as a debaucher as well as a murderer. Junius Sr.'s bigamy was suddenly remembered; the whole Booth clan was bastard-born. Plus there was Jewish blood. What a Shylock Junius Brutus Booth had once played! Asia's husband was furious to be in jail while Edwin was out. They were a nest of vipers, he told the press, a family of Iagos. His honor demanded he divorce his pregnant wife as soon as he regained his freedom.

Before dawn on April 26, John Wilkes Booth was discovered in a barn in the Maryland swamps. A torch was thrown inside. The straw caught immediately, illuminating the scene as clearly as if he were onstage. "I saw him standing upright," one Colonel Conger said later, "leaning on a crutch. He looked so like his brother Edwin I believed for a moment the whole pursuit to have been a mistake."

Four:

If it be now, 'tis not to come; if it be not to come, it will be now . . .

In the months that followed, Edwin could only leave the house at night. He walked for miles through the dark Boston streets, his hat pulled over his face. During the day, he hid in his house, writing letters of his own. He'd worked so hard to make the name of Booth respectable, he wrote. He repeated often the story of how he had once saved the life of Robert Lincoln on a train. At a friend's suggestion, to distract himself, he wrote an autobiography of his early childhood for his daughter to read, but then destroyed it before she could. He made several unsuccessful efforts, on his mother's behalf, to recover his brother's body. "I had such beautiful plans for the future," he said. "All is ruin and ever will be."

He was forced to Washington during the trial of the co-conspirators. The defense had planned to call him to attest to John Wilkes' insanity, and also to the charismatic power he held over the minds of others. The lawyers interviewed Edwin for several hours and then decided not to put him on the stand. While he was in the capital, he visited his brother and brother-in-law, still in jail. His brother-in-law repeated his plan to divorce Asia. He wondered aloud at Edwin's freedom.

"Those who have passed through such an ordeal," Asia wrote, "if there are any such . . . never relearn to trust in human nature, they never resume their old place in the world, and they forget only in death."

Edwin thought he might go mad. He had a chronic piercing headache, frequent nightmares. His friends worried that he'd return to drink, and Tom Aldritch, one of the closest, moved into the house to keep him company. Edwin swore that he would never act again. It would be grotesque for any Booth to perform anywhere. The rest must be silence.

Nine months passed. Lewis Paine, George Atzerodt, David Herold, and Mary Surratt were hanged as co-conspirators in the prison yard before a large, enthusiastic crowd. Junius Booth and John Sleeper Clarke were released. Though he never forgave her, Asia's husband did not ask for a divorce. Instead they retreated to England, where they lived for the rest of their lives. Edwin's continued requests for his brother's body continued to go unanswered. Within a very few months, the entire Booth family, none of whom were working, was deeply in debt.

The bills mounted. The creditors pressed. "I don't know what will become of us," his mother wrote to Edwin. "I don't see how we'll survive." His mother, like his father, did not believe in subtlety.

In January, 1866, the Winter Garden Theater in New York announced Edwin's return to the stage. "Will it be *Julius Caesar*?" an outraged newspaper asked, "Will he perhaps, as would be fitting, play the assassin?"

He would be playing Hamlet.

Long before the performance, every ticket had sold. There would be such a crush as the Winter Garden had never seen before.

On the night of the performance, some without tickets forced their way in as far as the lobby. The play began. From his dressing room, Edwin Booth knew when the ghost had made his entrance. Marcellus: *Peace, break thee off, look, where it comes again.* And then Bernardo: *In the same figure, like the king that's dead.* Edwin couldn't actually hear the words. He recognized the lines from their stress and inflections. He knew the moment of them. He knew exactly how much time remained until he took his place for the second scene.

Edwin leaned into the mirror to stare past his own painted face into the space behind him. On the wall to the right of the small dressing-table mirror was a coat rack, so overwhelmed with hats and capes that it loomed over the room, casting the shadow of a very large man. Swords of all sorts lay on the table tops, boots on the floor, doublets and waistbands on the chairs.

A knock at the door. His father's old friend, George Spear, had come to beg Edwin to reconsider. What is out there, he said, what is waiting for you is not an audience so much as a mob. Yet Edwin couldn't hear them at all. It seemed they sat in a complete, uncanny silence.

"I am carrying a bullet for you." "Your life is forfeit."

No one in his family had dared to come. His daughter, Edwina, was at his mother's house. He imagined her descending the stairs in her nightgown to give her grandmother a kiss. He imagined her ascending again. He imagined her safe in her bed. He was called to take his place onstage for the second scene, but could not make his legs move.

"We hate the very name Booth." "Your next performance will be a tragedy."

Now he could hear the audience, stamping their feet, impatient at the delay. He waited for his father's ghost to arrive, ask why he kept an audience waiting in their seats. But there was only the stage manager, knocking a second time, calling with some agitation. "Mr. Booth? Mr. Booth?" What did it mean that his father had not come?

I'm ready, Edwin said, and having said so, he could rise. He left the dressing room and took his place on the stage. The actors around him were stiff with tension.

One of the hallmarks of Edwin's Hamlet was that he made no entrance. As the curtain opened on the second scene, it often took the audience time to locate him among the busy Danish court. He sat unobtrusively off to one side, under the standard of the great Raven of Denmark, his head bowed. "Among a gaudy court," a critic had written of an earlier performance, " 'he alone with them, alone,' easily prince, and nullifying their effect by the intensity and color of his gloom." On this particular night he seemed a frail figure, slight and dark and unremarkable save for the intensity and color of his gloom. The audience found him in his chair. There sat their American Hamlet.

Someone began to clap and then someone else. The audience came to their feet. The next day's review in *The Spirit of the Times* reported nine cheers, then six, then three, then nine more. The play could not continue, and as they clapped, many of them, men and women both, began to weep.

Edwin stood and came forward into the footlights. He bowed very low, and then he couldn't straighten, but continued to sink. Someone caught him from behind, just before he fell. "There, boy," his father said, unseen, a whisper in Edwin's ear as he was lifted to his feet.

When he stood again upright, the audience saw that Edwin, too, was weeping. It made them cheer him again. And again.

His fellow actors gathered tightly in, clapping their hands. His father's arms were wrapped around him. Edwin smelled his father's pipe and beyond it, the forest, the fireplace of his childhood home. "There, boy. There, boy," his father said. "Your foot is on your native heath."

• • • •

The thing raised its head and fixed her with eyes like pearls and mercury,
quicksilver fire, and then she couldn't have moved for all
the angels in Heaven . . .

Apokatastasis
Caitlín R. Kiernan

"Well, it was there," Terry says, pointing, pointing again in case he wasn't paying attention before, and Aaron sighs and makes a show of looking at the alarm clock. He tells her what time it is, 3:38 a.m., like she might care, like that makes any difference at all. She's sitting at the foot of their bed, watching the dark hallway beyond the open door; third night in a row and she knows better than to hope that maybe this time he'll believe her, maybe this time it'll come back and he'll have to see it, too.

"Well, was it a dog or not?"

"I don't *know*," she says again, sounding more annoyed than the first time he asked. "It was like a dog."

"I don't know what that's supposed to mean."

"It was an animal," Terry says, not taking her eyes off the hall, the night driven back a few grudging feet by the glow from her reading lamp. "It was an animal like a dog."

"It was a dream," he says. "Now go back to sleep," and lies down again, turning his back to her and the lamp and the bedroom door. Terry looks away from the hall long enough to glance at him over her shoulder.

"I know the difference," she says, trying not to sound angry or irrational, trying to sound calm and not at all afraid, her heart still beating just a little too fast and her mouth gone dry as dust, but he doesn't have to know that. "I wasn't asleep."

"Then where the hell is it now? And how's it getting in and out of the apartment?" He's talking to her without opening his eyes, without turning over to look at her. "Jesus, Terry. Go back to sleep, please."

So she watches the hallway alone, the straight, white walls, plaster washed the delicate color of eggshells, and an oil painting in a walnut frame that her grandmother did when she was only seventeen. A field with wildflowers and a line of trees in the distance, but the shadows hide everything and the canvas is only an indistinct outline in the gloom.

"I know the difference," she says again, even though Aaron's probably already asleep and she's talking to no one but herself. Maybe if she hadn't been so frightened when it woke her, the eager, snuffling sounds it made nosing about in the hall, maybe if she'd awakened Aaron immediately he would have seen it too and somehow it would have been something that was easier for two people to understand. The answer not half so strange, not so difficult, if *two* people have to think about it together. But instead she lay perfectly still, waiting for it to see her, waiting for it not to be there anymore, until, finally, the thing raised its head and fixed her with those eyes like pearls and mercury, quicksilver fire, and then she couldn't have moved for all the angels in Heaven. It might have smiled, she thinks, but it was only an animal and dogs don't smile.

"Go to sleep, Terry," Aaron says. "We'll talk about it in the morning."

"I don't want to sleep anymore," she tells him and he doesn't reply. A few minutes more and Aaron's snoring softly, gentle-rough sound that she's always found so comforting, and now it's nothing but a reminder that he doesn't believe her, that whatever waits for her between this moment and the next and dawn is there for her and her alone. Terry thinks about her legs dangling carelessly over the edge of the bed, her bare feet and the blackness between the floor and the box springs, blackness that might hide more than old photo albums and lost socks. She pulls her legs up, feet tucked safely beneath her thighs, protective lotus, and she watches the hallway and waits for morning.

Meeting Cyn for lunch at the little coffee shop and deli down the street from the shoe store where she works, expensive hipster shoes for hipster yuppies and suburban punker kids, Doc Martens and Birkenstocks, London Underground and Fluevogs, and they sit at one of the outside tables despite the August heat because there's no smoking inside. A faded green-and-white canvas umbrella for shade and hardly any breeze at all; Cyn orders the curried chicken salad plate and Terry only orders iced coffee, black, and sips it while Cyn picks indifferently at slices of tomato and avocado.

"Have you thought about trying to take a picture of it'?" Cyn asks, brushing her lavender bangs from her eyes. "If it worked and you had a photograph, well, he'd have to believe you then, wouldn't he?" She stabs a slice of tomato with her fork and then shakes it loose again.

Terry shrugs and takes another sip of coffee, doesn't want to admit that she's afraid what might happen if she did try to take a picture of the animal.

Maybe it wouldn't much like having its picture taken. Or maybe it isn't anything that can be photographed and where would she be then? No proof one way or another, and "There's something wrong with our camera," she lies. "It's been acting up and I haven't had time to have it fixed."

"I could loan you mine," Cyn offers unhelpfully, pushing, cornering her, and Terry knows better than to think this means that Cyn believes she's really seeing anything at all.

"I don't even believe in ghosts," Terry says and shakes her head, hoping Cyn will shut up about the camera. "If it wasn't happening to me, if it was happening to you instead, and you were trying to convince me, I wouldn't believe you."

"Gee, thanks, kiddo."

"I just don't believe in ghosts, that's all. I don't even think I believe in souls, so how can I believe in ghosts'? And if l did, I don't think I'd believe that animals have them."

"Souls or ghosts?"

"What?"

Cyn frowns at her and chews a forkful of avocado and chicken, washes it down with ginger ale before she answers. "*Which* wouldn't you believe that animals have, souls or ghosts?"

"Well, either. If I don't believe animals have souls, I can't very well believe they have ghosts."

"I thought you were Catholic?"

"My mother was Catholic. I'm not anything."

"Hell, I always thought being Catholic was practically genetic. I didn't know you had a choice."

Cyn stares at her plate for a moment, then pushes it away and takes a pack of cigarettes from her purse. She lights one and the smoke hangs in the stagnant air above the table.

"I fucking hate dogs," she says. "When I was five, I was bitten by a dog. I still have a scar on my ass from where the damned thing took a plug out of me. I thought sure it was gonna eat me, just like the wolf in 'Little Red Riding Hood.' "

"It might not be a dog. I only said it looked like a dog."

Cyn takes another drag off her cigarette, glances up at the simmering, Wedgwood sky while smoke leaks slow from her nostrils. "Scared the holy shit out of me. I had to have eight fucking stitches," she says. "Jesus, if I woke up and there was a big, black dog in my bedroom, I'd probably have a heart attack."

"It wasn't in the bedroom. It was in the hall."

"Pete keeps saying he wants a Doberman and I told him no fucking way, mister, not if he wants me around."

Terry sips her bitter, icy coffee, watches Cyn and her purple hair, and she wishes that she hadn't stopped smoking, wishes she'd taken her lunch break alone today. "I'm not afraid of dogs," she says when Cyn finally stops talking. "But I'm not sure this is a dog."

Cyn looks at her watch and sighs, stubs her cigarette out in her plate. "Damn. I gotta get back to work, kiddo. Listen, if you change your mind about the camera, give me a ring."

"Thanks."

"Hey, anytime at all. That's what I'm here for," and she leaves a ten-dollar bill on the table, leaves Terry alone in the heat and the summer sun as bright as the eyes of God.

Home an hour before Aaron, almost always home before Aaron, and she stands in the hall, the bathroom at her back, bedroom to her left, dining room to her right. Listening and hearing only the traffic sounds from the street, the windy whup-whup-whup of the ceiling fan from the living room, all the small and inconsequential daytime noises that the building makes. Faint smell of garbage from the kitchen because she forgot to take it down before work, coffee grounds and last night's spaghetti, soap and potpourri from the bathroom—everything in its place, nothing that shouldn't be there.

"Here, doggy," she whispers. "Here, boy."

No reply but a car alarm going off somewhere, and Terry feels more foolish than she can remember ever having felt before. What if someone heard her, what if Mr. Dugan next door heard her? He might think she and Aaron had gotten a dog, and all pets are strictly forbidden by their lease. No dogs, no cats, no birds, not even fish because someone on the second floor once had a huge salt-water aquarium that broke and soaked straight through the floor.

Terry chews at a nubby thumbnail and stares at her grandmother's oil painting, the field, the careful dabs of orange and blue and red, a thousand shades of green beneath a wide and perfect sky. No signature, but there's a date—1931—in the lower righthand corner, and for a moment she's only thinking about how long it's been since she's taken flowers to the old woman's grave instead of thinking about the black animal watching her while she slept. A whole house full of antiques when her grandmother died, but her sisters claiming most of them, and Terry not really wanting anything but the painting, anyway. A long ago day in June, maybe, a June afternoon seventy years ago and Terry leans closer, examining the trees at the far edge of the field; never really daylight beneath those trees, between those crooked trunks, the sagging limbs, and then Terry notices the tiny figure standing where the trees begin. Her whole life and all the time spent staring at this painting and that's something she somehow hasn't seen before.

"Who are you?" Terry asks the canvas. touching it gently with her ring finger, wedding-ring finger, and she squints because she isn't wearing her reading glasses; trying to make out the features, the cherub-round face, golden hair, dress the color of butter, and she realizes that the canvas feels cold, damp, and pulls her hand quickly away. She curses under her breath and takes a step back from the wall, and now she can clearly see the damp spot, no larger than a dime, but completely surrounding, enclosing, the girl in the yellow dress standing at the edge of the forest. She lifts the painting off its hook and there's a slightly larger stain hiding on the wall behind it. Something that glistens like a slug trail, and Terry sets the canvas down on the floor.

"Goddamn it," she mutters and thinks it's probably the plumbing, the ancient pipes that should have been replaced decades ago, and just the other day Aaron was complaining about the way they clank and wheeze, the way water sometimes comes out of the tap brown after a particularly heavy rain. Terry imagines the leak behind the wall, corroding iron or copper, the patient trickle to seep through the plaster and ruin her grandmother's painting. She touches the wall and it feels slick, sticky, colder than the spot on the canvas. When she sniffs her fingertip the smell isn't anything that she'd expected, not the moldy, dank scent of wet rot, but something meaty, more like a piece of steak that's gone over, or a dead animal at the side of a road.

A dead dog, she thinks, wiping her fingers on her pants leg, and there's a sound behind her, then, the sharp, staccato click of long nails against the hardwood floor. Don't look, don't see it, just wait for it to go away again, but she's already turning, worse not to know, worse to have to lay awake wondering and wishing she'd had the nerve . . .

And there's only the empty hallway, a shaft of late afternoon sunlight spilling through the bathroom window, dust motes drifting from shadow into light and back into shadow again. Terry stands very still for a minute, five minutes, and then she goes to the sink to wash the rotting-meat smell off her hand.

"You've just never noticed it, that's all," he said, not looking at her, reading his novel in bed and only half listening while she talked about the girl in the painting, the blond girl in the yellow dress who hadn't ever been there before, the sticky spot behind the stained canvas. She'd shown him both as soon as he'd come home and Aaron had only shrugged his shoulders, shaken his head and "Maybe it's a mouse," he suggested. "Maybe a mouse died back there somewhere," and then he'd asked if she thought they should order Thai or Chinese take-out for dinner.

"It wasn't there before," she said and he turned a page, scowled at the book instead of scowling at her.

"Of course it's always been there. Don't be silly."

"But Aaron, the wall—"

"I'll call Mrs. White to get a plumber up here to look at the wall," he said. "I'll call her first thing tomorrow."

And now, hours and hours later, she lies wide awake, alone with the night and the contented sound of his snoring, all the restless, old building noises, the muffled murmur of the city outside that never quite goes to sleep, never completely. Like me, she thinks, wishing now that she'd shut the bedroom door so she couldn't see the hallway or her grandmother's painting propped there against the wall beneath the stain. But Aaron doesn't like to sleep with the door shut, so she left it standing open. Terry forces herself to close her eyes.

Of course it's always been there, he said. *Don't be silly*, but she knows better, because she has a photograph, a Polaroid of herself sitting beneath the painting when it was still hanging in the dining room, before Aaron asked her to move it to the hall to make room for a Rothko print he'd ordered from a catalog. The Polaroid is very clear and there's no girl standing where the trees meet the edge of the field. She showed it to him after dinner, but he only frowned and told her that the girl was too small to see, that there wasn't enough detail in the picture to make her out.

Click, click, click, click, claws on wood, and when she opens her eyes it's standing in the hall, sniffing at the painting.

Wake him up. Wake him up now, but then it turns its head, sleek skull, skin stretched too tight, those shining, silver eyes and she doesn't say a word, doesn't move a muscle. Would stop breathing, would stop her heart from beating if she knew how, and the black thing sits back on velvet haunches and watches her from the doorway. It holds its head cocked to one side, curious dog expression on its not-quite-dog face, and the dim light through the bedroom window plays tricks in its eyes.

Like rain, the sudden, soft patter of something falling against the roof, and *Let me shut my eyes*, she thinks. *Please God let me shut my eyes*. In the doorway, ebony lips pull back to show teeth like antique ivory, and there's that smile for her again, that smile for her fear, her silent prayers, and now the rain against the roof is so much louder, the loudest raindrops she's ever heard and how the hell could Aaron sleep through that?

The animal opens its jaws wide and its howl is the thunder waiting behind the rain, the brittle crackling of the sky, and Terry thinks that there are words in there, too. A small voice sewn up taut, held fast in the rumbling cacophony, lost little girl at the edge of a wood that runs on and on forever.

Let me not see, not hear, please not ever again I won't have to see this, ready to give up eternity for an instant, begging to a god she doesn't believe in as the black thing steps, finally, across the threshold into the room, stands at the foot of the bed, and the air smells like wildflowers and oil paints, turpentine and warm sunshine on grass.

And then the rain stops falling (if it was rain) and the summer and brush-stroke smells are gone (if they were ever there at all), and where the black thing stood there's only a view of the hallway and the stained wall and the painting leaned against it.

Sleepwalking though the sun-drowned morning, waking disoriented and more exhausted than when she went to bed. Terry called the shoe store and told them she was sick and wouldn't be in today, not so sure it was a lie, nausea and the dull beginnings of a headache, sweating even though the air conditioning was turned down to sixty-five. Not bothering to get dressed, no point if she wasn't going to work, just the gaudy Six Flags T-shirt she'd slept in, panties, bare legs, bare feet. "You don't look so good," Aaron said on his way out the door and then she was alone. Another cup of coffee, too much milk and not enough sugar, and she's watching sparrows at the bird feeder outside the kitchen window, tiny, nervous beaks snatching greedy mouthfuls of millet and canaryseed until a big blue jay comes along to frighten them away.

A heavy, tumbling sound from the hall, like falling books or rocks, and then surprise that it doesn't startle her or the hungry bird at the windowsill. She turns to see, the perfect, unobstructed view through the dining room to show her nothing at all, and Terry sets her coffee cup down on the table. The jay watches cautiously as she gets up, slides her chair back, and goes to the drawer where Aaron keeps the few tools they own; she takes out the hammer, a pair of needle-nosed pliers, a sharp linoleum knife, and carries them with her to the hall.

There are no fallen books, or anything else, but she's sure the stain is much larger than it was the day before, that it's grown in the night, almost as big as a grapefruit now. The smell much stronger, too, and Terry lays the tools on the floor, presses the fingertips of her right hand against the damp place and discovers that it's grown soft, as well. It gives a little when she pushes and then slowly springs back again when she takes her hand away. She wipes her sticky fingers on the front of her shirt and moves the painting into the bedroom, leans it carefully against the foot of the bed. The girl in the yellow dress is still waiting at the edge of the forest, though Terry thinks that maybe the sky isn't quite as bright as it was, gray-blue hint of storm clouds that she doesn't recall, and then the phone rings.

She sits on Aaron's side of the bed and talks to Cyn, but doesn't look away from the wall.

"I was worried, kiddo. You never get sick."

"It's probably something I picked up from a customer. I hate having to handle money. It's probably just a virus."

"Lots of clear fluids and vitamin C," Cyn says.

"Right."

"So, how's the ghost dog? Have you seen it again?"

"No," she says, answering too quickly and wishing she were a better liar. "No, I haven't. I think Aaron was right. I think it was only a bad dream."

A moment's silence from Cyn's end, and Terry doesn't have to see her to know her expression, that practiced skepticism, the doubtful frown, and "No kidding," Cyn says. "That's really too bad. I was starting to look forward to the séance."

"I was being silly. But I never said it was a ghost, did I?"

"No, you didn't. You never said it was a dog, either."

"It might have been a dog," Terry says, staring at the wall, the soft, wet spot, and trying hard to think of a way to end the conversation without making Cyn more suspicious. "It might have been a dream about a dog."

"You know what, kiddo? I get off at two-thirty today. Maybe I should stop by on my way home, just to see how you're doing. See if you need some chicken soup or anything—"

"But I'm not even on your way home, Cyn. I'll be fine, really. I'm feeling much better already. Listen, I left the kettle on the stove. I was making tea when you called."

"I'll call you later," Cyn says, sounding confused, sounding almost angry, and she makes Terry promise to call her if she needs anything before then, if she needs anything at all.

"Sure thing," Terry tells her, and they say good-bye, Cyn drawing it out as long as she can. Like she's afraid she's never going to talk to me again, like she's afraid I'll disappear the second she hangs up. "Just take it easy, you hear me? I mean it," and a moment later there's only the dial-tone drone and the work that's waiting for her in the hall.

Maybe I won't need the hammer after all, she thinks, picking up the linoleum knife instead, and that's when Terry notices the single, dark drop of blood on the floor at her feet. And she stands there, wondering what it means, this new wrinkle, how it fits or doesn't fit, until she finds the smear running down the inside of her left thigh, the red bloom at her crotch. Only that, nothing ghostly, nothing strange, and the relief makes her smile; she briefly considers going to the bathroom to deal with it, but that would take time and the damage is already done, the stain on her panties, so she sets the curved blade against the wall and drives it in all the way to the wooden handle. It requires hardly any effort at all, the plaster gone soft as cheese, and a stream of something clear leaks from the wound she's made.

"You think it's ever as simple as that?" the black dog (if it is a dog, which she doubts) asks from somewhere directly behind her. "Having cut it out, you can cut it right back in again?"

"I never cut anything," Terry says, no longer smiling and she draws the blade down the length of the soft, wet spot. The edges of the slit fold back like the petals of a flower, sticky, sweating orchid flesh, and now she can see that the wall isn't white inside.

The black dog laughs and its claws click, click, click like rosary beads. "Of course you didn't," it chuckles. "Are you sure you have the stomach for this?"

"Go away," Terry growls. "I'm done with you now. I don't have to see you anymore."

"He'll see this, you know," it says. "When he comes home, he'll see this and know what you've done."

"Go away!" and she yanks the blade free of the wall and turns quickly around, slashing the empty air where the taunting black dog might have been standing an instant before. Stringy droplets fly from the tip of the linoleum knife and spatter the walls.

"I'm not hiding anything from him," she says. "I've never tried to hide anything from him," and Terry thinks that she can still hear it laughing at her from somewhere very, very far away. Laughter like bad memories and wasted time, laughter black as its skin, and she turns back to the hole she's made in the wall. At least twice as big as only the moment before, tearing itself wider as she watches, and the linoleum knife slips from her fingers and clatters to the floor.

The laughter fades like thunder, rumbling, rolling away.

When she reaches into the wall, it's warm and soft and Terry breathes in the clinging odor that is as much being born as it is dying, as much conception as decay. She removes the small, hard thing from the quivering center and holds it cupped in one palm, the tiny porcelain doll grown so old the glaze has cracked and some of the paint has flaked away to show bone white underneath.

"You did the right thing," she whispers to the doll. "Never go into those woods alone," and Terry sits down on the floor, dabs the porcelain clean with the hem of her shirt. In a few more minutes, the hole in the wall has closed completely, no sign that it was ever there at all. She glances through the doorway to the bedroom and there's the canvas still leaned against the footboard, paint dried seventy years ago, whole long lifetimes ago, and now there's no one standing at the shadowy place where the wildflowers end and the dark trees start.

• • • •

There are some things you can't take back. Shake hands with an ineffable enigma and it knows you. It has you, if it wants . . .

The *Lagerstätte*
Laird Barron

October 2004

Virgil acquired the cute little blue-and-white pinstriped Cessna at an auction; this over Danni's strenuous objections. There were financial issues; Virgil's salary as department head at his software development company wasn't scheduled to increase for another eighteen months and they'd recently enrolled their son Keith in an exclusive grammar school. Thirty-grand a year was a serious hit on their rainy-day fund. Also, Danni didn't like planes, especially small ones, which she asserted were scarcely more than tin, plastic, and balsawood. She even avoided traveling by commercial airliner if it was possible to drive or take a train. But she couldn't compete with love at first sight. Virgil took one look at the four-seater and practically swooned, and Danni knew she'd had it before the argument even started. Keith begged to fly and Virgil promised to teach him, teased that he might be the only kid to get his pilot's license before he learned to drive.

Because Danni detested flying so much, when their assiduously planned week-long vacation rolled around, she decided to boycott the flight and meet her husband and son at the in-laws' place on Cape Cod a day late, after wrapping up business in the city. The drive was only a couple of hours—she'd be at the house in time for Friday supper. She saw them off from a small airport in the suburbs, and returned home to pack and go over last minute adjustments to her evening lecture at the museum.

How many times did the plane crash between waking and sleeping? There was no way to measure that; during the first weeks, the accident cycled through a continuous playback loop, cheap and grainy and soundless like a closed circuit security feed. They'd recovered pieces of fuselage from the water, bobbing like cork—she caught a few moments of news footage before someone, probably Dad, killed the television.

They threw the most beautiful double funeral courtesy of Virgil's parents, followed by a reception in his family's summer home. She recalled wavering shadowbox lights and the muted hum of voices, men in black hats clasping cocktails to the breasts of their black suits, and severe women gathered near the sharper, astral glow of the kitchen, faces gaunt and cold as porcelain, their dresses black, their children underfoot and dressed as adults in miniature; and afterward, a smooth descent into darkness like a bullet reversing its trajectory and dropping into the barrel of a gun.

Later, in the hospital, she chuckled when she read the police report. It claimed she'd eaten a bottle of pills she'd found in her mother-in-law's dresser and curled up to die in her husband's closet among his little league uniforms and boxes of trophies. That was simply hilarious because anyone who knew her would know the notion was just too goddamned melodramatic for words.

March 2005

About four months after she lost her husband and son, Danni transplanted to the West Coast, taken in by a childhood friend named Merrill Thurman, and cut all ties with extended family, peers, and associates from before the accident. She eventually lost interest in grieving just as she lost interest in her former career as an entomologist; both were exercises of excruciating tediousness and ultimately pointless in the face of her brand new, freewheeling course. All those years of college and marriage were abruptly and irrevocably reduced to the fond memories of another life, a chapter in a closed book.

Danni was satisfied with the status quo of patchwork memory and aching numbness. At her best, there were no highs, no lows, just a seamless thrum as one day rolled into the next. She took to perusing self-help pamphlets and treatises on Eastern philosophy, and trendy art magazines; she piled them in her room until they wedged the door open. She studied Tai Chi during an eight week course in the decrepit gym of the cross-town YMCA. She toyed with an easel and paints, attended a class at the community college. She'd taken some drafting as an undergrad. This was helpful for the technical aspects, the geometry of line and space; the actual artistic part proved more difficult. Maybe she needed to steep herself in the bohemian culture—a coldwater flat in Paris, or an artist commune, or a sea shanty on the coast of Barbados.

Oh, but she'd never live alone, would she?

Amidst this reevaluation and reordering, came the fugue, a lunatic element that found genesis in the void between melancholy and nightmare. The fugue made familiar places strange; it wiped away friendly faces and replaced them with beekeeper masks and reduced English to the low growl of the swarm. It was a disorder of trauma and shock, a hybrid of temporary dementia and selective amnesia. It battened to her with the mindless tenacity of a leech.

She tried not to think about its origins, because when she did she was carried back to the twilight land of her subconscious; to Keith's fifth birthday party; her wedding day with the thousand dollar cake, and the honeymoon in Niagara Falls; the Cessna spinning against the sun, streaking downward to slam into the Atlantic; and the lush corruption of a green-black jungle and its hidden cairns—the bones of giants slowly sinking into the always hungry earth.

The palace of cries where the doors are opened with blood and sorrow. The secret graveyard of the elephants. The bones of elephants made a forest of ribcages and tusks, dry riverbeds of skulls. Red ants crawled in trains along the petrified spines of behemoths and trailed into the black caverns of empty sockets. Oh, what the lost expeditions might've told the world!

She'd dreamt of the Elephants' Graveyard off and on since the funeral and wasn't certain why she had grown so morbidly preoccupied with the legend. Bleak mythology had interested her when she was young and vital and untouched by the twin melanomas of wisdom and grief. Now, such morose contemplation invoked a primordial dread and answered nothing. The central mystery of her was impenetrable to casual methods. Delving beneath the surface smacked of finality, of doom.

Danni chose to endure the fugue, to welcome it as a reliable adversary. The state seldom lasted more than a few minutes, and admittedly it was frightening, certainly dangerous; nonetheless, she was never one to live in a cage. In many ways the dementia and its umbra of pure terror, its visceral chaos, provided the masochistic rush she craved these days—a badge of courage, the martyr's brand. The fugue hid her in its shadow, like a sheltering wing.

May 6, 2006
(D.L. Session 33)

Danni stared at the table while Dr. Green pressed a button and the wheels of the recorder began to turn. His chair creaked as he leaned back. He stated his name, Danni's name, the date and location.

—How are things this week? he said.

Danni set a slim metal tin on the table and flicked it open with her left hand. She removed a cigarette and lighted it. She used matches because she'd lost the fancy lighter Merrill got her as a birthday gift. She exhaled, shook the match dead.

—For a while, I thought I was getting better, she said in a raw voice.

—You don't think you're improving? Dr. Green said.

—Sometimes I wake up and nothing seems real; it's all a movie set, a humdrum version of *This is Your Life!* I stare at the ceiling and can't shake this sense I'm an imposter.

—Everybody feels that way, Dr. Green said. His dark hands rested on a clipboard. His hands were creased and notched with the onset of middle age; the cuffs of his starched lab coat had gone yellow at the seams. He was married; he wore a simple ring and he never stared at her breasts. Happily married, or a consummate professional, or she was nothing special. A frosted window rose high and narrow over his shoulder like the painted window of a monastery. Pallid light shone at the corners of his angular glasses, the shiny edges of the clipboard, a piece of the bare plastic table, the sunken tiles of the floor. The tiles were dented and scratched and bumpy. Fine cracks spread like tendrils. Against the far walls were cabinets and shelves and several rickety beds with thin rails and large, black wheels.

The hospital was an ancient place and smelled of mold and sickness beneath the buckets of bleach she knew the custodians poured forth every evening. This had been a sanitarium. People with tuberculosis had gathered here to die in the long, shabby wards. Workers loaded the bodies into furnaces and burned them. There were chutes for the corpses on all the upper floors. The doors of the chutes were made of dull, gray metal with big handles that reminded her of the handles on the flour and sugar bins in her mother's pantry.

Danni smoked and stared at the ceramic ashtray centered exactly between them, inches from a box of tissues. The ashtray was black. Cinders smoldered in its belly. The hospital was "no smoking," but that never came up during their weekly conversations. After the first session of him watching her drop the ashes into her coat pocket, the ashtray had appeared. Occasionally she tapped her cigarette against the rim of the ashtray and watched the smoke coil tighter and tighter until it imploded the way a demolished building collapses into itself after the charges go off.

Dr. Green said, —Did you take the bus or did you walk?

—Today? I walked.

Dr. Green wrote something on the clipboard with a heavy golden pen. —Good. You stopped to visit your friend at the market, I see.

Danni glanced at her cigarette where it fumed between her second and third fingers.

—Did I mention that? My Friday rounds?

—Yes. When we first met. He tapped a thick, manila folder bound in a heavy duty rubber band. The folder contained Danni's records and transfer papers from the original admitting institute on the East Coast. Additionally, there was a collection of nearly unrecognizable photos of her in hospital gowns and bathrobes. In several shots an anonymous attendant pushed her in a wheelchair against a blurry backdrop of trees and concrete walls.

—Oh.

—You mentioned going back to work. Any progress?

—No. Merrill wants me to. She thinks I need to reintegrate professionally, that it might fix my problem, Danni said, smiling slightly as she pictured her friend's well-meaning harangues. Merrill spoke quickly, in the cadence of a native Bostonian who would always be a Bostonian no matter where she might find herself. A lit major, she'd also gone through an art-junkie phase during grad school which had wrecked her first marriage and introduced her to many a disreputable character as could be found haunting the finer galleries and museums. One of said characters became ex-husband the second and engendered a profound and abiding disillusionment with the fine arts scene entirely. Currently, she made an exemplary copy editor at a rather important monthly journal.

—What do you think?

—I liked being a scientist. I liked to study insects, liked tracking their brief, frenetic little lives. I know how important they are, how integral, essential to the ecosystem. Hell, they outnumber humans trillions to one. But, oh my, it's so damned easy to feel like a god when you've got an ant twitching in your forceps. You think that's how God feels when He's got one of us under His thumb?

—I couldn't say.

—Me neither. Danni dragged heavily and squinted. —Maybe I'll sell Bibles door to door. My uncle sold encyclopedias when I was a little girl.

Dr. Green picked up the clipboard. —Well. Any episodes—fainting, dizziness, disorientation? Anything of that nature?

She smoked in silence for nearly half a minute. —I got confused about where I was the other day. She closed her eyes. The recollection of those bad moments threatened her equilibrium. —I was walking to Yang's Grocery. It's about three blocks from the apartments. I got lost for a few minutes.

—A few minutes.

—Yeah. I wasn't timing it, sorry.

—No, that's fine. Go on.

—It was like before. I didn't recognize any of the buildings. I was in a foreign city and couldn't remember what I was doing there. Someone tried to talk to me, to help me—an old lady. But, I ran from her instead. Danni swallowed the faint bitterness, the dumb memory of nausea and terror.

—Why? Why did you run?

—Because when the fugue comes, when I get confused and forget where I am, people frighten me. Their faces don't seem real. Their faces are rubbery and inhuman. I thought the old lady was wearing a mask, that she was hiding something. So I ran. By the time I regained my senses, I was near the park. Kids were staring at me.

—Then?

—Then what? I yelled at them for staring. They took off.

—What did you want at Yang's?

—What?

—You said you were shopping. For what?

—I don't recall. Beets. Grapes. A giant zucchini. I don't know.

—You've been taking your medication, I presume. Drugs, alcohol?

—No drugs. Okay, a joint occasionally. A few shots here and there. Merrill wants to unwind on the weekends. She drinks me under the table—Johnny Walkers and Manhattans. Tequila if she's seducing one of the rugged types. Depends where we are. She'd known Merrill since forever. Historically, Danni was the strong one, the one who saw Merrill through two bad marriages, a career collapse and bouts of deep clinical depression. Funny how life tended to put the shoe on the other foot when one least expected.

—Do you visit many different places?

Danni shrugged.

—I don't—oh, the Candy Apple. Harpos. That hole in the wall on Decker and Gedding, the Red Jack. All sorts of places. Merrill picks; says it's therapy.

—Sex?

Danni shook her head.

—That doesn't mean I'm loyal.

—Loyal to whom?

—I've been noticing men and . . . I feel like I'm betraying Virgil. Soiling our memories. It's stupid, sure. Merrill thinks I'm crazy.

—What do *you* think?

—I try not to, Doc.

—Yet, the past is with you. You carry it everywhere. Like a millstone, if you'll pardon the cliché.

Danni frowned.

—I'm not sure what you mean—

—Yes, you are.

She smoked and looked away from his eyes. She'd arranged a mini gallery of snapshots of Virgil and Keith on the bureau in her bedroom, stuffed more photos in her wallet and fixed one of Keith as a baby on a keychain. She'd built a modest shrine of baseball ticket stubs, Virgil's moldy fishing hat, his car keys, though the car was long gone, business cards, cancelled checks, and torn up Christmas wrapping. It was sick.

—Memories have their place, of course, Dr. Green said. —But, you've got to be careful. Live in the past too long and it consumes you. You can't use fidelity as a crutch. Not forever.

—I'm not planning on forever, Danni said.

August 2, 2006

Color and symmetry were among Danni's current preoccupations. Yellow squash, orange baby carrots, an axis of green peas on a china plate; the alignment of complementary elements surgically precise upon the starched white table cloth—cloth white and neat as the hard white fabric of a hospital sheet.

Their apartment was a narrow box stacked high in a cylinder of similar boxes. The window sashes were blue. All of them a filmy, ephemeral blue like the dust on the wings of a blue emperor butterfly; blue over every window in every cramped room. Blue as dead salmon, blue as ice. Blue shadows darkened the edge of the table, rippled over Danni's untouched meal, its meticulously arrayed components. The vegetables glowed with subdued radioactivity. Her fingers curled around the fork; the veins in her hand ran like blue-black tributaries to her fingertips, ran like cold iron wires. Balanced on a window sill was her ant farm, its inhabitants scurrying about the business of industry in microcosm of the looming cityscape. Merrill hated the ants and Danni expected her friend to poison them in a fit of revulsion and pique. Merrill wasn't naturally maternal and her scant reservoir of kindly nurture was readily exhausted on her housemate.

Danni set the fork upon a napkin, red gone black as sackcloth in the beautiful gloom, and moved to the terrace door, reaching automatically for her cigarettes as she went. She kept them in the left breast pocket of her jacket alongside a pack of matches from the Candy Apple.

The light that came through the glass and blue gauze was muted and heavy. Outside the sliding door was a terrace and a rail; beyond the rail, a gulf. Damp breaths of air were coarse with smog, tar and pigeon shit. Eight stories yawned below the wobbly terrace to the dark brick square. Ninety-six feet to the fountain, the flagpole, two rusty benches and Piccolo Street where winos with homemade drums, harmonicas, and flutes composed their symphonies and dirges.

Danni smoked on the terrace to keep the peace with Merrill, straight-edge Merrill, whose poison of choice was Zinfandel and fast men in nice suits, rather than tobacco. Danni smoked Turkish cigarettes that came in a tin she bought at the wharf market from a Nepalese ex pat named Mahan. Mahan sold coffee too, in shiny black packages; and decorative knives with tassels depending from brass handles.

Danni leaned on the swaying rail and lighted the next to the last cigarette in her tin and smoked as the sky clotted between the gaps of rooftops, the copses of wires and antennas, the static snarl of uprooted birds like black bits of paper ash turning in the Pacific breeze. A man stopped in the middle of the crosswalk. He craned his neck to seek her out from amidst the jigsaw of fire escapes and balconies. He waved and then turned away and crossed the street with an unmistakably familiar stride, and was gone.

When her cigarette was done, she flicked the butt into the empty planter, one of several terra cotta pots piled around the corroding barbeque. She lighted her remaining cigarette and smoked it slowly, made it last until the sky went opaque and the city lights began to float here and there in the murk, bubbles of iridescent gas rising against the leaden tide of night. Then she went inside and sat very still while her colony of ants scrabbled in the dark.

May 6, 2006
(D.L. Session 33)

Danni's cigarette was out; the tin empty. She began to fidget. —Do you believe in ghosts, doctor?

—Absolutely. Dr. Green knocked his ring on the table and gestured at the hoary walls. —Look around. Haunted, I'd say.

—Really?

Dr. Green seemed quite serious. He set aside the clipboard, distancing himself from the record. —Why not. My grandfather was a missionary. He lived in the Congo for several years, set up a clinic out there. Everybody believed in ghosts—including my grandfather. There was no choice.

Danni laughed. —Well, it's settled. I'm a faithless bitch. And I'm being haunted as just desserts.

—Why do you say that?

—I went home with this guy a few weeks ago. Nice guy, a graphic designer. I was pretty drunk and he was pretty persuasive.

Dr. Green plucked a pack of cigarettes from the inside pocket of his white coat, shook one loose and handed it to her. They leaned toward one another, across the table, and he lighted her cigarette with a silvery Zippo.

—Nothing happened, she said. —It was very innocent, actually.

But that was a lie by omission, was it not? What would the good doctor think of her if she confessed her impulses to grasp a man, any man, as a point of fact, and throw him down and fuck him senseless, and refrained only because she was too frightened of the possibilities? Her cheeks stung and she exhaled fiercely to conceal her shame.

—We had some drinks and called it a night. I still felt bad, dirty, somehow. Riding the bus home, I saw Virgil. It wasn't him; he had Virgil's build and kind of slouched, holding onto one of those straps. Didn't even come close once I got a decent look at him. But for a second, my heart froze. Danni lifted her gaze from the ashtray. —Time for more pills, huh?

—Well, a case of mistaken identity doesn't qualify as a delusion.

Danni smiled darkly.

—You didn't get on the plane and you lived. Simple. Dr. Green spoke with supreme confidence.

—Is it? Simple, I mean.

—Have you experienced more of these episodes—mistaking strangers for Virgil? Or your son?

—Yeah. The man on the bus, that tepid phantom of her husband, had been the fifth incident of mistaken identity during the previous three weeks. The incidents were growing frequent; each apparition more convincing than the last. Then there were the items she'd occasionally found around the apartment—Virgil's lost wedding ring gleaming at the bottom of a pitcher of water; a trail of dried rose petals leading from the bathroom to her bed; one of Keith's crayon masterpieces fixed by magnet on the refrigerator; each of these artifacts ephemeral as dew, transitory as drifting spider thread; they dissolved and left no traces of their existence. That very morning she'd glimpsed Virgil's bomber jacket slung over the back of a chair. A sunbeam illuminated it momentarily, dispersed it amongst the moving shadows of clouds and undulating curtains.

—Why didn't you mention this sooner?

—It didn't scare me before.

—There are many possibilities. I hazard what we're dealing with is survivor's guilt, Dr. Green said. —This guilt is a perfectly normal aspect of the grieving process.

Dr. Green had never brought up the guilt association before, but she always knew it lurked in the wings, waiting to be sprung in the third act. The books all talked about it. Danni made a noise of disgust and rolled her eyes to hide the sudden urge to cry.

—Go on, Dr. Green said.

Danni pretended to rub smoke from her eye. —There isn't any more.

—Certainly there is. There's always another rock to look beneath. Why don't you tell me about the vineyards. Does this have anything to do with the *Lagerstätte*?

She opened her mouth and closed it. She stared, her fear and anger tightening screws within the pit of her stomach. —You've spoken to Merrill? Goddamn her.

—She hoped you'd get around to it, eventually. But you haven't and it seems important. Don't worry—she volunteered the information. Of course I would never reveal the nature of our conversations. Trust in that.

—It's not a good thing to talk about, Danni said. —I stopped thinking about it.

—Why?

She regarded her cigarette. Norma, poor departed Norma whispered in her ear, *Do you want to press your eye against the keyhole of a secret room? Do you want to see where the elephants have gone to die?*

—Because there are some things you can't take back. Shake hands with an ineffable enigma and it knows you. It has you, if it wants.

Dr. Green waited, his hand poised over a brown folder she hadn't noticed before. The folder was stamped in red block letters she couldn't quite read, although she suspected *asylum* was at least a portion.

—I wish to understand, he said. —We're not going anywhere.

—Fuck it, she said. A sense of terrible satisfaction and relief caused her to smile again. —Confession is good for the soul, right?

August 9, 2006

In the middle of dressing to meet Merrill at the market by the wharf when she got off work, Danni opened the closet and inhaled a whiff of damp, moldering air and then screamed into her fist. Several withered corpses hung from the rack amid her cheery blouses and conservative suit jackets. They were scarcely more than yellowed sacks of skin. None of the desiccated, sagging faces were recognizable; the shade and texture of cured squash, each was further distorted by warps and wrinkles of dry cleaning bags. She recoiled and sat on the bed and chewed her fingers until a passing cloud blocked the sun and the closet went dark.

Eventually she washed her hands and face in the bathroom sink, staring into the mirror at her pale, maniacal simulacrum. She skipped makeup and stumbled from the apartment to the cramped lift that dropped her into a foyer with its rows of tarnished mailbox slots checkering the walls, its low, grubby light fixtures, a stained carpet and the sweet and sour odor of sweat and stagnant air. She stumbled through the security doors into the brighter world.

And the fugue descended.

Danni was walking from somewhere to somewhere else; she'd closed her eyes against the glare and her insides turned upside down. Her eyes flew open and she reeled, utterly lost. Shadow people moved around her, bumped her with their hard elbows and swinging hips; an angry man in brown tweed lectured his daughter and the girl protested. They buzzed like flies. Their miserable faces blurred together, lit by some internal phosphorous. Danni swallowed, crushed into herself with a force akin to claustrophobia, and focused on her watch, a cheap windup model that glowed in the dark. Its numerals meant nothing, but she tracked the needle as it swept a perfect circle while the world spun around her. The passage, an indoor-outdoor avenue of sorts. Market stalls flanked the causeway, shelves and timber beams twined with streamers and beads, hemp rope and tie-dye shirts and pennants. Light fell through cracks in the overhead pavilion. The enclosure reeked of fresh salmon, salt water, sawdust, and the compacted scent of perfumed flesh.

—*Danni*. Here was an intelligible voice amid the squeal and squelch. Danni lifted her head and tried to focus.

—*We miss you*, Virgil said. He balanced a pomegranate in his palm. The fruit had been split, exposing the red pulp and the seeds.

—What? Danni said, accepting the fruit without thinking because she was thinking his face was the only face not changing shape like the flowery crystals in a kaleidoscope. —What did you say?

The man beside the stall gleamed like a piece of ivory. He grinned at the shopkeeper, a thick, swarthy fellow who watched them warily. —*Eat*, the stranger said.

It was apparent this man wasn't Virgil, although in this particular light the eyes were similar, and he drawled. Virgil spent his adult life trying to bury that drawl and eventually it only emerged when he was exhausted or angry.

Red pomegranate juice dripped on her wrist and trickled along her arm to the elbow joint. She squinted at the shop sign.

—How much? She said to the shopkeeper.

—On the house. The shopkeeper wiped his knife on his apron and smiled unhappily. He began loading his apples and nectarines and honeydews into charming wicker baskets, utterly dismissive of her presence.

The stranger winked at her and continued along the boardwalk. Beneath an Egyptian cotton shirt, his back was almost as muscular as Virgil's. But, no.

Danni turned away into the bright, jostling throng. Someone took her elbow. She yelped and wrenched away and nearly fell.

—Honey, you okay? The jumble of insectoid eyes, lips, and bouffant hair coalesced into Merrill's stern face. Merrill wore white-rimmed sunglasses that complemented her vanilla dress with its wide shoulders and brass buttons, and her elegant vanilla gloves. Her thin nose peeled with sunburn. —Danni, are you all right?

—Yeah. Danni wiped her mouth.

—The hell you are. C'mon. Merrill led her away from the moving press to a small open square and seated her in a wooden chair in the shadow of a parasol. The square hosted a half dozen vendors and several tables of squawking children, overheated parents with flushed cheeks, and senior citizens in pastel running suits. Merrill bought soft ice cream in tiny plastic dishes and they sat in the shade and ate the ice cream while the sun dipped below the rooflines. The vendors began taking down the signs and packing it in for the day.

—Okay, okay. I feel better. Danni's hands had stopped shaking.

—You do look a little better. Know where you are?

—The market. Danni wanted a cigarette. —Oh, damn it, she said.

—Here, sweetie. Merrill drew two containers of Mahan's foreign cigarettes from her purse and slid them across the table, mimicking a spy in one of those '70s thrillers.'

—Thanks, Danni said as she got a cigarette burning. She dragged frantically, left hand cupped to her mouth so the escaping smoke boiled and foamed between her fingers like dry ice vapors. Nobody said anything despite the No Smoking signs posted on the gate.

—Hey, what kind of bug is that? Merrill intently regarded a beetle hugging the warmth of a wooden plank near their feet.

—It's a beetle.

—How observant. But what kind?

—I don't know.

—What? You don't know?

—I don't know. I don't really care, either.

—Oh, please.

—Fine. Danni leaned forward until her eyeballs were scant inches above the motionless insect. —Hmm. I'd say a *Spurious exoticus, minor*, closely related to, but not to be confused with, the *Spurious eroticus, major*. Yep.

Merrill stared at the beetle, then Danni. She took Danni's hand and gently squeezed. —You fucking fraud. Let's go get liquored up, hey?

—Hey-hey.

• • •

May 6, 2006
(D.L. Session 33)

Dr. Green's glasses were opaque as quartz.

—The *Lagerstätte*. Elucidate, if you will.

—A naturalist's wet dream. Ask Norma Fitzwater and Leslie Runyon, Danni said and chuckled wryly. —When Merrill originally brought me here to Cali, she made me join a support group. That was about, what? A year ago, give or take. Kind of a twelve-step program for wannabe suicides. I quit after a few visits. Group therapy isn't my style and the counselor was a royal prick. Before I left, I became friends with Norma, a drug addict and perennial house guest of the state penitentiary before she snagged a wealthy husband. Marrying rich wasn't a cure for everything, though. She claimed to have tried to off herself five or six times, made it sound like an extreme sport.

A fascinating woman. She was pals with Leslie, a widow like me. Leslie's husband and brother fell off a glacier in Alaska. I didn't like her much. Too creepy for polite company. Unfortunately, Norma had a mother hen complex, so there was no getting rid of her. Anyway, it wasn't much to write home about. We went to lunch once a week, watched a couple of films, commiserated about our shitty luck. Summer camp stuff.

—You speak of Norma in the past tense. I gather she eventually ended her life, Dr. Green said.

—Oh, yes. She made good on that. Jumped off a hotel roof in the Tenderloin. Left a note to the effect that she and Leslie couldn't face the music anymore. The cops, brilliant as they are, concluded Norma made a suicide pact with Leslie. Leslie's corpse hasn't surfaced yet. The cops figure she's at the bottom of the bay, or moldering in a wooded gully. I doubt that's what happened though.

—You suspect she's alive.

—No, Leslie's dead under mysterious and messy circumstances. It got leaked to the press that the cops found evidence of foul play at her home. There was blood or something on her sheets. They say it dried in the shape of a person curled in the fetal position. Somebody compared it to the flash shadows of victims in Hiroshima. This was deeper, as if the body had been pressed hard into the mattress. The only remains were her watch, her diaphragm, her *fillings*, for Christ's sake, stuck to the coagulate that got left behind like afterbirth. Sure, it's bullshit, urban legend fodder. There were some photos in *The Gazette*, some speculation amongst our sorry little circle of neurotics and manic depressives.

—Very unpleasant, but, fortunately, equally improbable.

Danni shrugged. —Here's the thing, though. Norma predicted everything. A month before she killed herself, she let me in on a secret. Her friend Leslie, the creepy lady, had been seeing Bobby. He visited her nightly, begged her to come away with him. And Leslie planned to.

—Her husband, Dr. Green said. —The one who died in Alaska.

—The same. Trust me, I laughed, a little nervously, at this news. I wasn't sure whether to humor Norma or get the hell away from her. We were sitting in a classy restaurant, surrounded by execs in silk ties and Armani suits. Like I said, Norma was loaded. She married into a nice Sicilian family; her husband was in the import-export business, if you get my drift. Beat the hell out of her, though; definitely contributed to her low self-esteem. Right in the middle of our luncheon, between the lobster tails and the éclairs, she leaned over and confided this thing with Leslie and her deceased husband. The ghostly lover.

Dr. Green passed Danni another cigarette. He lighted one of his own and studied her through the blue exhaust. Danni wondered if he wanted a drink as badly as she did.

—How did you react to this information? Dr. Green said.

—I stayed cool, feigned indifference. It wasn't difficult; I was doped to the eyeballs most of the time. Norma claimed there exists a certain quality of grief, so utterly profound, so tragically pure, it resounds and resonates above and below. A living, bleeding echo. It's the key to a kind of limbo.

—The *Lagerstätte*. Dr. licked his thumb and sorted through the papers in the brown folder. —As in the Burgess Shale, the La Brea Tar Pits. Were your friends amateur paleontologists?

—*Lagerstätten* are *resting places* in the Deutsch, and I think that's what the women meant.

—Fascinating choice of mythos.

—People do whatever it takes to cope. Drugs, kamikaze sex, religion, anything. In naming, we seek to order the incomprehensible, yes?

—True.

—Norma pulled this weird piece of jagged, gray rock from her purse. Not rock—a petrified bone shard. A fang or a long, wicked rib splinter. Supposedly human. I could tell it was *old*; it reminded me of all those fossils of trilobites I used to play with; it radiated an aura of antiquity, like it had survived a shift of deep geological time. Norma got it from Leslie and Leslie had gotten it from someone else; Norma claimed to have no idea who, although I suspect she was lying; there was definitely a certain slyness in her eyes. For all I know, it's osmosis. She pricked her finger on the shard and gestured at the blood that oozed on her plate. Danni shivered and clenched her left hand. —The scene was surreal. Norma said: *Grief is blood, Danni. Blood is the living path to everywhere. Blood opens the way.* She said if I offered myself to the *Lagerstätte*, Virgil would come to me and take me into the house of dreams. But I wanted to know whether it would really be him and not . . . an imitation. She said, *Does it matter?* My skin crawled as if I were waking from a long sleep to something awful, something my primal self recognized and feared. Like fire.

—You believe the bone was human.

—I don't know. Norma insisted I accept it as a gift from her and Leslie. I really didn't want to, but the look on her face, it was intense.

—Where did it come from? The bone.

—The *Lagerstätte*.

—Of course. What did you do?

Danni looked down at her hands, the left with its jagged white scar in the meat and muscle of her palm, and deeper into the darkness of the earth. —The same as Leslie. I called them.

—You called them. Virgil and Keith.

—Yes. I didn't plan to go through with it. I got drunk, and when I'm like that, my thoughts get kind of screwy. I don't act in character.

—Oh. Dr. Green thought that over. —When you say called, what exactly do you mean?

She shrugged and flicked ashes into the ashtray. Even though Dr. Green had been there the morning they stitched the wound, she guarded the secret of its origin with a zeal bordering on pathological.

Danni had brought the weird bone to the apartment. Once alone, she drank the better half of a bottle of Makers Mark and then sliced her palm with the sharp edge of the bone and made a doorway in blood. She slathered a vertical seam, a demarcation between her existence and the abyss, in the plaster wall at the foot of her bed. She smeared Virgil and Keith's initials and sent a little prayer into the night. She shredded her identification, her (mostly defunct) credit cards, her social security card, a lock of her hair, and burned the works with the tallow of a lamb in a small clay pot she'd bought at market. Then, in the smoke and shadows, she finished getting drunk off her ass and promptly blacked out.

Merrill wasn't happy; Danni had bled like the proverbial stuck pig, soaked through the sheets into the mattress. Merrill decided her friend had horribly botched another run for the Pearly Gates. She had brought Danni to the hospital for a bunch of stitches and introduced her to Dr. Green. Of course Danni didn't admit another suicide attempt. She doubted her conducting a black magic ritual would help matters either. She said nothing, simply agreed to return for sessions with the good doctor. He was blandly pleasant, eminently non-threatening. She didn't think he could help, but that wasn't the point. The point was to please Merrill and Merrill insisted on the visits.

Back home, Merrill confiscated the bone, the ritual fetish, and threw it in the trash. Later, she tried like hell to scrub the stain. In the end she gave up and painted the whole room blue.

A couple days after that particular bit of excitement, Danni found the bone at the bottom of her sock drawer. It glistened with a cruel, lusterless intensity. Like the monkey's paw it had returned and that didn't surprise her. She folded it into a kerchief and locked it in a jewelry box she'd kept since first grade.

All these months gone by, Danni remained silent on the subject.

Finally, Dr. Green sighed. —Is that when you began seeing Virgil in the faces of strangers? These doppelgangers? He smoked his cigarette with the joyless concentration of a prisoner facing a firing squad. It was obvious from his expression that the meter had rolled back to zero.

—No, not right away. Nothing happened, Danni said. —Nothing ever does, at first.

—No, I suppose not. Tell me about the vineyard. What happened there?

—I . . . I got lost.

—That's where all this really begins, isn't it? The fugue, perhaps other things.

Danni gritted her teeth. She thought of elephants and graveyards. Dr. Green was right, in his own smug way. Six weeks after Danni sliced her hand, Merrill took her for a daytrip to the beach. Merrill rented a convertible and made a picnic. It was nice; possibly the first time Danni felt human since the accident; the first time she'd wanted to do anything besides mope in the apartment and play depressing music.

After some discussion, they chose Bolton Park, a lovely stretch of coastline way out past Kingwood. The area was foreign to Danni, so she bought a road map pamphlet at a gas station. The brochure listed a bunch of touristy places. Windsurfers and birdwatchers favored the area, but the guide warned of riptides. The women had no intention of swimming; they stayed near a cluster of great big rocks at the north end of the beach—below the cliff with the steps that led up to the posh houses; the summer homes of movie stars and advertising executives; the beautiful people.

On the way home, Danni asked if they might stop at Kirkston Vineyards. It was a hole in the wall, only briefly listed in the guide book. There were no pictures. They drove in circles for an hour tracking the place down—Kirkston was off the beaten path; a village of sorts. There was a gift shop and an inn, and a few antique houses. The winery was fairly large and charming in a rustic fashion, and that essentially summed up the entire place.

Danni thought it was a cute setup; Merrill was bored stiff and did what she always did when she'd grown weary of a situation—she flirted like mad with one of the tour guides. Pretty soon, she disappeared with the guy on a private tour.

There were twenty or thirty people in the tour group—a bunch of elderly folks who'd arrived on a bus and a few couples pretending they were in Europe. After Danni lost Merrill in the crowd, she went outside to explore until her friend surfaced again.

Perhaps fifty yards from the winery steps, Virgil waited in the lengthening shadows of a cedar grove. That was the first the phantoms. Too far away for positive identification, his face was a white smudge. He hesitated and regarded her over his shoulder before he ducked into the undergrowth. She knew it was impossible, knew that it was madness, or worse, and went after him, anyway.

Deeper into the grounds she encountered crumbled walls of a ruined garden hidden under a bower of willow trees and honeysuckle vines. She passed through a massive marble archway, so thick with sap it had blackened like a smoke stack. Inside was a sunken area and a clogged fountain decorated with cherubs and gargoyles. There were scattered benches made of stone slabs, and piles of rubble overrun by creepers and moss. Water pooled throughout the garden, mostly covered by algae and scum; mosquito larvae squirmed beneath drowned leaves. Ridges of broken stone and mortar petrified in the slop and slime of that boggy soil and made waist-high calculi amongst the freestanding masonry.

Her hand throbbed with a sudden, magnificent stab of pain. She hissed through her teeth. The freshly knitted, pink slash, her Freudian scar, had split and blood seeped so copiously her head swam. She ripped the sleeve off her blouse and made hasty a tourniquet. A grim, sullen quiet drifted in; a blizzard of silence. The bees weren't buzzing and the shadows in the trees waxed red and gold as the light decayed.

Virgil stepped from behind stalagmites of fallen stone, maybe thirty feet away. She knew with every fiber of her being that this was a fake, a body double, and yet she wanted nothing more than to hurl herself into his arms. Up until that moment, she didn't realize how much she'd missed him, how achingly final her loneliness had become.

Her glance fell upon a gleaming wedge of stone where it thrust from the water like a dinosaur's tooth, and as shapes within shapes became apparent, she understood this wasn't a garden. It was a graveyard.

Virgil opened his arms—

—I'm not comfortable talking about this, Danni said. —Let's move on.

• • •

August 9, 2006

Friday was karaoke night at the Candy Apple.

In the golden days of her previous life, Danni had a battalion of friends and colleagues with whom to attend the various academic functions and cocktail socials as required by her professional affiliation with a famous East Coast university. Barhopping had seldom been the excursion of choice.

Tonight, a continent and several light-years removed from such circumstances, she nursed an overly strong margarita while up on the stage, a couple of drunken women with big hair and smeared makeup stumbled through that old Kenny Rogers standby, "Ruby, Don't Take Your Love to Town." The fake redhead was a receptionist named Sheila, and her blond partner, Delores, a vice president of human resources. Both of them worked at Merrill's literary magazine and they were partying off their second and third divorces respectively.

Danni wasn't drunk, although mixing her medication with alcohol wasn't helping matters; her nose had begun to tingle and her sensibilities were definitely sliding toward the nihilistic side. Also, she seemed to be hallucinating again. She'd spotted two Virgil look-alikes between walking through the door and her third margarita; that was a record, so far. She hadn't noticed either of the men enter the lounge, they simply appeared.

One of the mystery men sat amongst a group of happily chattering yuppie kids; he'd worn a sweater and parted his hair exactly like her husband used to before an important interview or presentation. The brow was wrong though, and the smile way off. He established eye contact and his gaze made her prickle all over because this simulacrum was so very authentic; if not for the plastic sheen and the unwholesome smile, he was the man she'd looked at across the breakfast table for a dozen years. Eventually he stood and wandered away from his friends and disappeared through the front door into the night. None of the kids seemed to miss him.

The second guy sat alone at the far end of the bar; he was much closer to the authentic thing; he had the nose, the jaw, even the loose way of draping his hands over his knees. However, this one was a bit too raw-boned to pass as *her* Virgil; his teeth too large, his arms too long. He stared across the room, too-dark eyes fastened on her face and she looked away and by the time she glanced up again he was gone.

She checked to see if Merrill noticed the Virgil impersonators. Merrill blithely sipped her Corona and flirted with a couple lawyer types at the adjoining table. The suits kept company with a voluptuous woman who was growing long in the tooth and had piled on enough compensatory eye shadow and lipstick to host her own talk show. The woman sulked and shot dangerous glares at Merrill. Merrill smirked coyly and touched the closest suit on the arm.

Danni lighted a cigarette and tried to keep her expression neutral while her pulse fluttered and she scanned the room with the corners of her eyes like a trapped bird. Should she call Dr. Green in the morning? Was he even in the office on weekends? What color would the new pills be?

Presently, the late dinner and theatre crowd arrived en masse and the lounge became packed. The temperature immediately shot up ten degrees and the resultant din of several dozen competing conversations drowned all but shouts. Merrill had recruited the lawyers (who turned out to be an insurance claims investigator and a CPA) Ned & Thomas, and their miffed associate Glenna, (a court clerk) to join the group and migrate to another, hopefully more peaceful watering hole.

They shambled through neon-washed night, a noisy herd of quasi-strangers, arms locked for purchase against the mist-slick sidewalks. Danni found herself squashed between Glenna and Ned the Investigator. Ned grasped her waist in a slack, yet vaguely proprietary fashion; his hand was soft with sweat, his paunchy face made more uncomely with livid blotches and the avaricious expression of a drowsy predator. His shirt reeked so powerfully of whiskey it might've been doused in the stuff.

Merrill pulled them to a succession of bars and nightclubs and all-night bistros. Somebody handed Danni a beer as they milled in the vaulted entrance of an Irish pub and she drank it like tap water, not really tasting it, and her ears hurt and the evening rapidly devolved into a tangle of raucous music and smoke that reflected the fluorescent lights like coke-blacked miners lamps, and at last a cool, humid darkness shattered by headlights and the sulfurous orange glow of angry clouds.

By her haphazard count, she glimpsed in excess of fifty incarnations of Virgil. Several at the tavern; solitary men mostly submerged in the recessed booths, observing her with stony diffidence through beer steins and shot glasses; a dozen more scattered along the boulevard; listless nomads whose eyes slid around, not quite touching anything. When a city bus grumbled past, every passenger's head swiveled in unison beneath the repeating flare of dome lights. Every face pressed against the dirty windows belonged to him. Their lifelike masks bulged and contorted with inconsolable longing.

Ned escorted her to his place, a warehouse apartment in a row of identical warehouses between the harbor and the railroad tracks. The building was converted to a munitions factory during the Second World War, then housing in the latter '60s. It stood black and gritty; its greasy windows sucked in the feeble illumination of the lonely beacons of passing boats and the occasional car.

They took a clanking cargo elevator to the top, the penthouse as Ned laughingly referred to his apartment. The elevator was a box encased in grates that exposed the inner organs of the shaft and the dark tunnels of passing floors. It could've easily hoisted a baby grand piano. Danni pressed her cheek to vibrating metal and shut her eyes tight against vertigo and the canteen-like slosh of too-many beers in her stomach.

Ned's apartment was sparsely furnished and remained mostly in gloom even after he turned on the floor lamp and went to fix nightcaps. Danni collapsed onto the corner of a couch abridging the shallow nimbus of light and stared raptly at her bone-white hand curled into the black leather. Neil Diamond crooned from velvet speakers. Ned said something about his record collection and faintly, ice cracked from its tray and clinked in glass with the resonance of a tuning fork.

Danni's hand shivered as if it might double and divide. She was cold now, in the sticky hot apartment, and her thighs trembled. Ned slipped a drink into her hand and placed his own hand on her shoulder, splayed his soft fingers on her collar, traced her collar bone with his moist fingertip. Danni flinched and poured gin down her throat until Ned took the glass and began to nuzzle her ear, his teeth clicking against the pearl stud, his overheated breath like smoldering creosote and kerosene, and as he tugged at her blouse strap, she began to cry. Ned lurched above her and his hands were busy with his belt and pants, and these fell around his ankles and his loafers. He made a fist in a mass of her hair and yanked her face against his groin; his linen shirttails fell across Danni's shoulders and he bulled himself into her gasping mouth. She gagged, overwhelmed by the ripeness of sweat and whiskey and urine, the rank humidity, the bruising insistence of him, and she convulsed, arms flailing in epileptic spasms, and vomited. Ned's hips pumped for several seconds and then his brain caught up with current events and he cried out in dismay and disgust and nearly capsized the couch as he scrambled away from her and a caramel gush of half-digested cocktail shrimp and alcohol.

Danni dragged herself from the couch and groped for the door. The door was locked with a bolt and chain and she battered at these, sobbing and choking. Ned's curses were muffled by a thin partition and the low thunder of water sluicing through corroded pipes. She flung open the door and was instantly lost in a cavernous hall that telescoped madly. The door behind her was a cave mouth, the windows were holes, were burrows. She toppled down a flight of stairs.

Danni lay crumpled, damp concrete wedged against the small of her back and pinching the back of her legs. Ghostly radiance cast shadows upon the piebald walls of the narrow staircase and rendered the scrawls of graffiti into fragmented hieroglyphics. Copper and salt filled her mouth. Her head was thick and spongy and when she moved it, little comets shot through her vision. A moth jerked in zigzags near her face, jittering upward at frantic angles toward a naked bulb. The bulb was brown and black with dust and cigarette smoke. A solid shadow detached from the gloom of the landing; a slight, pitchy silhouette that wavered at the edges like gasoline fumes.

Mommy? A small voice echoed, familiar and strange, the voice of a child or a castrato and it plucked at her insides, sent tremors through her.

—Oh, God, she said and vomited again, spilling herself against the rough surface of the wall. The figure became two, then four and a pack of childlike shapes assembled on the landing. The pallid corona of the brown bulb dimmed. She rolled away, onto her belly, and began to crawl . . .

August 10, 2006

The police located Danni semiconscious in the alley behind the warehouse apartments. She didn't understand much of what they said and she couldn't muster the resolve to volunteer the details of her evening's escapades. Merrill rode with her in the ambulance to the emergency room where, following a two-hour wait, a haggard surgeon determined Danni suffered from a number of nasty contusions, minor lacerations and a punctured tongue. No concussion, however. He punched ten staples into her scalp, handed over a prescription for painkillers and sent her home with an admonishment to return in twelve hours for observation.

After they'd settled safe and sound at the apartment, Merrill wrapped Danni in a blanket and boiled a pot of green tea. Lately, Merrill was into feng shui and Chinese herbal remedies. It wasn't quite dawn and so they sat in the shadows in the living room. There were no recriminations, although Merrill lapsed into a palpable funk; hers was the grim expression of guilt and helplessness attendant to her perceived breach of guardianship. Danni patted her hand and drifted off to sleep.

When Danni came to again, it was early afternoon and Merrill was in the kitchen banging pots. Over bowls of hot noodle soup Merrill explained she'd called in sick for a couple days. She thought they should get Danni's skull checked for dents and rent some movies and lie around with a bowl of popcorn and do essentially nothing. Tomorrow might be a good day to go window shopping for an Asian print to mount in their pitifully barren entryway.

Merrill summoned a cab. The rain came in sheets against the windows of the moving car and Danni dozed to the thud of the wipers, trying to ignore the driver's eyes upon her from the rearview. He looked unlike the fuzzy headshot on his license fixed to the visor. In the photo his features were burnt teak and warped by the deformation of aging plastic.

They arrived at the hospital and signed in and went into the bowels of the grand old beast to radiology. A woman in a white jacket injected dye into Danni's leg and loaded her into a shiny, cold machine the girth of a bread truck and ordered her to keep her head still. The technician's voice buzzed through a hidden transmitter, repulsively intimate as if a fly had crawled into her ear canal. When the rubber jackhammers started in on the steel shell, she closed her eyes and saw Virgil and Keith waving to her from the convex windows of the plane. The propeller spun so slowly she could track its revolutions.

—The doctor says they're negative. The technician held photographic plates of Danni's brain against a softly flickering pane of light. See? No problems at all.

The crimson seam dried black on the bedroom wall. The band of black acid eating plaster until the wall swung open on smooth, silent hinges. Red darkness pulsed in the rift. White leaves crumbled and sank, each one a lost face. A shadow slowly shaped itself into human form. The shadow man regarded her, his hand extended, approaching her without moving his shadow legs.

Merrill thanked the woman in the clipped manner she reserved for those who provoked her distaste, and put a protective arm over Danni's shoulders. Danni had taken an extra dose of tranquilizers to sand the rough edges. Reality was a taffy pull.

Pour out your blood and they'll come back to you, Norma said and stuck her bleeding finger into her mouth. Her eyes were cold and dark as the eyes of a carrion bird. Bobby and Leslie coupled on a squeaking bed. Their frantic rhythm gradually slowed and they began to melt and merge until their flesh rendered to a sticky puddle of oil and fat and patches of hair. The forensics photographers came, clicking and whirring, eyes deader than the lenses of their cameras. They smoked cigarettes in the hallway and chatted with the plainclothes about baseball and who was getting pussy and who wasn't; everybody had sashimi for lunch, noodles for supper, and took work home and drank too much. Leslie curdled in the sheets and her parents were long gone, so she was already most of the way to being reduced to a serial number and forgotten in a cardboard box in a storeroom. Except, Leslie stood in a doorway in the grimy bulk of a nameless building. She stood, hip-shot and half-silhouetted, naked and lovely as a Botticelli nude. Disembodied arms circled her from behind, and large, muscular hands cupped her breasts. She nodded, expressionless as a wax death masque, and stepped back into the black. The iron door closed.

Danni's brain was fine. No problems at all.

Merrill took her home and made her supper. Fried chicken; Danni's favorite from a research stint studying the migration habits of three species of arachnids at a southern institute where grits did double duty as breakfast and lunch.

Danni dozed intermittently, lulled by the staccato flashes of the television. She stirred and wiped drool from her lips, thankfully too dopey to suffer much embarrassment. Merrill helped her to bed and tucked her in and kissed her goodnight on the mouth. Danni was surprised by the warmth of her breath, her tenderness; then she was heavily asleep, floating facedown in the red darkness, the amniotic wastes of a secret world.

August 11, 2006

Merrill cooked waffles for breakfast; she claimed to have been a "champeen" hash-slinger as an undergrad, albeit Danni couldn't recall that particular detail of their shared history. Although food crumbled like cardboard on her tongue, Danni smiled gamely and cleared her plate. The fresh orange juice in the frosted glass was a mouthful of lye. Merrill had apparently jogged over to Yang's and picked up a carton the exact instant the poor fellow rolled back the metal curtains from his shop front, and Danni swallowed it and hoped she didn't drop the glass because her hand was shaking so much. The pleasant euphoria of painkillers and sedatives had drained away, usurped by a gnawing, allusive dread, a swell of self disgust and revulsion.

The night terrors tittered and scuffled in the cracks and crannies of the tiny kitchen, whistled at her in a pitch only she and dogs could hear. Any second now, the broom closet would creak open and a ghastly figure shamble forth, licking lips riven by worms. At any moment the building would shudder and topple in an avalanche of dust and glass and shearing girders. She slumped in her chair, fixated on the chipped vase, its cargo of wilted geraniums drooping over the rim. Merrill bustled around her, tidying up with what she dryly attributed as her latent German efficiency, although her mannerisms suggested a sense of profound anxiety. When the phone chirped and it was Sheila reporting some minor emergency at the office, her agitation multiplied as she scoured her little address book for someone to watch over Danni for a few hours.

Danni told her to go, she'd be okay—maybe watch a soap and take a nap. She promised to sit tight in the apartment, come what may. Appearing only slightly mollified, Merrill agreed to leave, vowing a speedy return.

Late afternoon slipped over the city, lackluster and overcast. Came the desultory honk and growl of traffic, the occasional shout, the off-tempo drumbeat from the square. Reflections of the skyline patterned a blank span of wall. Water gurgled, and the disjointed mumble of radio or television commentary came muffled from the neighboring apartments. Her eyes leaked and the shakes traveled from her hands into the large muscles of her shoulders. Her left hand ached.

A child murmured in the hallway, followed by scratching at the door. The bolt rattled. She stood and looked across the living area at the open door of the bedroom. The bedroom dilated. Piles of jagged rocks twined with coarse brown seaweed instead of the bed, the dresser, her unseemly stacks of magazines. A figure stirred amid the weird rocks and unfolded at the hips with the horrible alacrity of a tarantula. *You filthy whore.* She crossed the room and hooked the door with her ankle and kicked it shut.

Danni went to the kitchen and slid a carving knife from its wooden block. She walked to the bathroom and turned on the shower. Everything seemed too shiny, except the knife. The knife hung loosely in her fingers; its blade was dark and pitted. She stripped her robe and stepped into the shower and drew the curtain. Steam began to fill the room. Hot water beat against the back of her neck, her spine and buttocks as she rested her forehead against the tiles.

What have you done? You filthy bitch. She couldn't discern whether that accusing whisper had bubbled from her brain, or trickled in with the swirling steam. *What have you done?* It hardly mattered now that nothing was of any substance, of any importance besides the knife. Her hand throbbed as the scar in her palm separated along its seam. Blood and water swirled down the drain.

Danni. The floorboards settled and a tepid draft brushed her calves. She raised her head and a silhouette filled the narrow door; an incomprehensible blur through the shower curtain. Danni dropped the knife. She slid down the wall into a fetal position. Her teeth chattered, and her animal self took possession. She remembered the ocean, acres of driftwood littering a beach, Virgil's grin as he paid out the tether of a dragonhead kite they'd bought in Chinatown. She remembered the corpses hanging in her closet, and whimpered.

A hand pressed against the translucent fabric, dimpled it inward, fingers spread. The hand squelched on the curtain. Blood ran from its palm and slithered in descending ladders.

—Oh, Danni said. Blearily, through a haze of tears and steam, she reached up and pressed her bloody left hand against the curtain, locked palms with the apparition, giddily cognizant this was a gruesome parody of the star-crossed lovers who kiss through glass. —Virgil, she said, chest hitching with sobs.

—You don't have to go, Merrill said and dragged the curtain aside. She too wept, and nearly fell into the tub as she embraced Danni and the water soaked her clothes, and quantities of blood spilled between them, and Danni saw her friend had found the fetish bone, because there it was, in a black slick on the floor, trailing a spray of droplets like a nosebleed. —You can stay with me. Please stay, Merrill said. She stroked Danni's hair, hugged her as if to keep her from floating away with the steam as it condensed on the mirror, the small window, and slowly evaporated.

May 6, 2006
(D.L. Session 33)

—Danni, do you read the newspapers? Watch the news? Dr. Green said this carefully, giving weight to the question.

—Sure, sometimes.

—The police recovered her body months ago. He removed a newspaper clipping from the folder and pushed it toward her.

—Who? Danni did not look at the clipping.

—Leslie Runyon. An anonymous tip led the police to a landfill. She'd been wrapped in a tarp and buried in a heap of trash. Death by suffocation, according to the coroner. You really don't remember.

Danni shook her head. —No. I haven't heard anything like that.

—Do you think I'm lying?

—Do you think I'm a paranoid delusional?

—Keep talking and I'll get back to you on that, he said, and smiled. —What happened at the vineyard, Danni? When they found you, you were quite a mess, according to the reports.

—Yeah. Quite a mess, Danni said. She closed her eyes and fell back into herself, fell down the black mineshaft into the memory of the garden, the *Lagerstätte*.

Virgil waited to embrace her.

Only a graveyard, an open charnel, contained so much death. The rubble and masonry were actually layers of bones; a reef of calcified skeletons locked in heaps; and mummified corpses; enough withered faces to fill the backs of a thousand milk cartons, frozen twigs of arms and legs wrapped about their eternal partners. These masses of ossified humanity were cloaked in skeins of moss and hair and rotted leaves.

Norma beckoned from the territory of waking dreams. She stood upon the precipice of a rooftop. She said, Welcome to the Lagerstätte. *Welcome to the secret graveyard of the despairing and the damned. She spread her arms and pitched backwards.*

Danni moaned and hugged her fist wrapped in its sopping rags. She had come unwitting, although utterly complicit in her devotion, and now stood before a terrible mystery of the world. Her knees trembled and folded.

Virgil shuttered rapidly and shifted within arm's reach. He smelled of aftershave and clove; the old, poignantly familiar scents. He also smelled of earthiness and mold, and his face began to destabilize, to buckle as packed dirt buckles under a deluge and becomes mud.

Come and sleep, he said in the rasp of leaves and dripping water. His hands bit into her shoulders and slowly, inexorably drew her against him. His chest was icy as the void, his hands and arms iron as they tightened around her and laid her down in the muck and the slime. His lips closed over hers. His tongue was pliant and fibrous and she thought of the stinking, brown rot that carpeted the deep forests. Other hands plucked at her clothes, her hair; other mouths suckled her neck, her breasts, and she thought of misshapen fungi and scurrying centipedes, the ever scrabbling ants, and how all things that squirmed in the sunless interstices crept and patiently fed.

Danni went blind, but images streamed through the snarling wires of her consciousness. *Virgil and Keith rocked in the swing on the porch of their New England home. They'd just finished playing catch in the backyard; Keith still wore his Red Sox jersey, and Virgil rolled a baseball in his fingers. The stars brightened in the lowering sky and the street lights fizzed on, one by one. Her mother stood knee deep in the surf, apron strings flapping in a rising wind. She held out her hands. Keith, pink and wrinkled, screamed in Danni's arms, his umbilical cord still wet. Virgil pressed his hand to a wall of glass. He mouthed, I love you, honey.*

I love you, Mommy, Keith said, his wizened infant's face tilted toward her own. Her father carefully laid out his clothes, his police uniform of twenty-six years, and climbed into the bathtub. We love you, girlie, Dad said and stuck the barrel of his service revolver into his mouth. Oh, quitting had run in the family, was a genetic certainty given the proper set of circumstances. Mom had drowned herself in the sea, such was her grief. Her brother, he'd managed to kill himself in a police action in some foreign desert. This gravitation to self destruction was ineluctable as her blood.

Danni thrashed upright. Dank mud sucked at her, plastered her hair and drooled from her mouth and nose. She choked for breath, hands clawing at an assailant who had vanished into the mist creeping upon the surface of the marsh. Her fingernails raked and broke against the glaciated cheek of a vaguely female corpse; a stranger made wholly inhuman by the slow, steady vise of gravity and time. Danni groaned. Somewhere, a whippoorwill began to sing.

Voices called for her through the trees; shrill and hoarse. Their shouts echoed weakly, as if from the depths of a well. These were unmistakably the voices of the living. Danni's heart thudded, galvanized by the adrenal response to her near-death experience, and, more subtly, an inchoate sense of guilt, as if she'd done something unutterably foul. She scrambled to her feet and fled.

Oily night flooded the forest. A boy cried, *Mommy, Mommy*! amid the plaintive notes of the whippoorwill. Danni floundered from the garden, scourged by terror and no small regret. By the time she found her way in the dark, came stumbling into the circle of rescue searchers and their flashlights, Danni had mostly forgotten where she'd come from or what she'd been doing there.

Danni opened her eyes to the hospital, the dour room, Dr. Green's implacable curiosity.

She said, —Can we leave it for now? Just for now. I'm tired. You have no idea.

Dr. Green removed his glasses. His eyes were bloodshot and hard, but human after all. —Danni, you're going to be fine, he said.

—Am I?

—Miles to go before we sleep, and all that jazz. But yes, I believe so. You want to open up, and that's very good. It's progress.

Danni smoked.

—Next week we can discuss further treatment options. There are several medicines we haven't looked at; maybe we can get you a dog. I know you live in an apartment, but service animals have been known to work miracles. Go home and get some rest. That's the best therapy I can recommend.

Danni inhaled the last of her cigarette and held the remnants of fire close to her heart. She ground the butt into the ashtray. She exhaled a stream of smoke and wondered if her soul, the souls of her beloved, looked anything like that. Uncertain of what to say, she said nothing. The wheels of the recorder stopped.

• • • •

We all know talking on a cell phone while driving can be dangerous.
But you may not be aware just how *dangerous . . .*

Cell Call
Marc Laidlaw

He wasn't used to the cell phone yet, and when it rang in the car there was a moment of uncomfortable juggling and panic as he dug down one-handed into the pocket of his jacket, which he'd thrown onto the passenger seat. He nipped the end of the antenna in his teeth and pulled, fumbling for the "on" button in the dark, hoping she wouldn't hang up before he figured this out. Then he had to squeeze the phone between ear and shoulder because he needed both hands to finish the turn he'd been slowing to make when the phone rang. He realized then that for a moment he'd had his eyes off the road. He was not someone who could drive safely while conducting a conversation, and she ought to know that. Still, she'd insisted he get a cell phone. So here he was.

"Hello?" he said, knowing he sounded frantic.

"Hi." It was her. "Where are you?"

"I'm in the car."

"Where?"

"Does it matter that much?"

"I only meant, are you on your way home? Because if you are I wanted to see if you could pick up a pack of cigarettes. If you have money."

"I'm on my way home, yes." He squinted through the window for a familiar landmark, but considering the turn he'd just taken, he knew he was on a stretch of older suburban road where the streetlights were infrequent. There was parkland here, somewhere, and no houses visible. "But I don't think there's a store between here and home."

"You'll pass one on the way."

"How do you know which way I went?"

"There's only one way to go.

"No there isn't."

"If you have any sense, there is."

"I have to get off. I can't drive and talk at the same time. I'm driving the stickshift, remember?"

"If you don't want to then forget it."

"No, I don't mind. I'll take a detour."

"Just forget it. Come home. I'll go out later."

"No, really. I'll get them."

"Whatever. Goodbye."

He took the phone out of the vise he'd made with jaw and shoulder. His neck was already starting to cramp, and he didn't feel safe driving with his head at such an angle, everything leaning on its side. He had to hold the phone out in front of him a bit to be sure the light had gone out. It had. The readout still glowed faintly, but the connection was broken. He dropped the phone onto the seat beside him, onto the jacket.

The parkland continued for another few blocks. The headlights caught in a tangle of winter-bared hedges and stripped branches thrusting out into the street so far that they hid the sidewalk. It would be nice to find a house this close to woods, a bit of greenbelt held in perpetuity for when everything else had been bought up and converted into luxury townhouses. If all went well then in the next year, maybe less, they'd be shopping for a house in the area. Something close to his office, but surrounded by trees, a view of mountains, maybe a stream running behind the house. It was heaven here but still strange, and even after six months most of it remained unfamiliar to him. She drove much more than he did, keeping busy while he was at work; she knew all the back roads already. He had learned one or two fairly rigid routes between home and office and the various shopping strips. Now with winter here, and night falling so early, he could lose himself completely the moment he wandered from a familiar route.

That seemed to be the case now. In the dark, without any sort of landmark visible except for endless bare limbs, he couldn't recognize his surroundings. The houses that should have been lining the streets by now were nowhere to be seen, and the road itself was devoid of markings: No center line, no clean curb or gutter. Had he turned into the parkland, off the main road? He tried to think back, but part of his memory was a blank—and for good reason. When the phone rang he'd lost track of everything else. There had been a moment when he was fumbling around in the dark, looking at the seat next to him, making a turn at a traffic light without making sure it was the right light. He could have taken the wrong turn completely.

But he hadn't turned since then. It still wasn't too late to backtrack.

He slowed the car, then waited to make sure no headlights were coming up behind him. Nothing moved in either direction. The road was narrow—

definitely not a paved suburban street. Branches scraped the hood as he pulled far to the right, readying the car for a tight turn, his headlights raking the brittle shadows. He paused for a moment and rolled the window down, and then turned back the key in the ignition to shut off the motor. Outside, with the car quieted, it was hushed. He listened for the barking of dogs, the sigh of distant traffic, but heard nothing. A watery sound, as if the parkland around him were swamp or marsh, lapping at the roots of the trees that hemmed him in. He wasn't sure that he had room to actually turn around; the road was narrower than he'd thought. He had better just back up until it widened.

He twisted the key and heard nothing. Not even a solenoid click. He put his foot on the gas and the pedal went straight to the floor, offering no resistance. The brake was the same. He stamped on the clutch, worked the gearshift through its stations—but the stick merely swiveled then lolled to the side when he released it. The car had never felt so useless.

He sat for a moment, not breathing, the thought of the repair bills surmounting the sudden heap of new anxieties. A walk in the dark, to a gas station? First, the difficulty of simply getting back to the road. Did he have a flashlight in the glove box? Was he out of gas? Would he need a jump-start or a tow? In a way, it was a relief that he was alone, because his own fears were bad enough without hers overwhelming him.

He started again, checking everything twice. Ignition, pedals, gears. All useless. At least the headlights and the dashboard were still shining. He rolled up the window and locked the door. How long should he sit here? Who was going to come along and . . .

The phone.

Jesus, the cell phone. How he had put off buying one, in spite of her insistence. He didn't care for the feeling that someone might always have tabs on him, that he could never be truly alone. What was it people were so afraid of, how could their lives be so empty, and their solitude of so little value, that they had to have a phone with them at every minute, had to keep in constant chattering contact with someone, anyone? Ah, how he had railed at every driver he saw with the phone in one hand and the other lying idly on the steering wheel. And now, for the first time, he turned to the damned thing with something like hope and relief. He wasn't alone in this after all.

The cell phone had some memory but he'd never programmed it because he relied on his own. He dialed his home number and waited through the rings, wondering if she was going to leave the answering machine to answer, as she sometimes did—especially if they had been fighting and she expected him to call back. But she answered after three rings.

"It's me," he said.

"And?" Cold. He was surprised she hadn't left the machine on after all.

"And my car broke down."

"It what?"

"Right after you called me, I got . . . " He hesitated to say lost; he could anticipate what sort of response that would get out of her. "I got off the regular track and I was looking to turn around and the engine died. Now it won't start."

"The regular track? What's that supposed to mean?"

"Just that I, uh—"

"You got lost." The scorn, the condescension. "Where are you?"

"I'm not sure."

"Can you look at a street sign? Do you think you could manage that much or am I supposed to figure out everything myself?"

"I don't see any," he said. "I'm just wondering if something happened to the engine, maybe I could take a look."

"Oh, right. Don't be ridiculous. What do you know about cars?"

He popped the hood and got out of the car. It was an excuse to move, to pace. He couldn't sit still when she was like this. It was as if he thought he'd be harder to hit if he made a moving target of himself. Now he raised the hood and leaned over it, saying, "Ah," as if he'd discovered something. But all he could see beneath the hood was darkness, as if something had eaten away the workings of the car. The headlights streamed on either side of his legs, losing themselves in the hedges, but their glare failed to illuminate whatever was directly before his eyes.

"Uh . . . "

"You don't know what you're looking at."

"It's too dark," he said. "There aren't any streetlights here."

"Where the hell are you?"

"Maybe I got into a park or something. Just a minute." He slammed the hood, wiped his gritty feeling fingers on his legs, and went back to the door. "There are lots of roads around here with no lights . . . it's practically . . . " He pressed the door handle. " . . . wild . . . "

At his lengthy silence, she said, "What is it?"

"Uh . . . just a sec."

The door was locked. He peered into the car, and could see the keys dangling in the ignition. He tried the other doors, but they were also locked. They were power doors, power windows, power locks. Some kind of general electrical failure, probably a very small thing, had rendered the car completely useless. Except for the headlights?

"What is it?" she said again.

"The keys . . . are in . . . the car." He squeezed hard on the door handle, wrenching at it, no luck.

"Do you mean you're locked out?"

"I, uh, do you have the insurance card? The one with the emergency service number on it?"

"I have one somewhere. Where's yours?"

"In the glove box."

"And you're locked out."

"It looks that way."

Her silence was recrimination enough. And here came the condescension: "All right, stay where you are. I'll come get you. We can call the truck when I'm there, or wait until morning. I was just about to get in bed, but I'll come and bring you home. Otherwise you'll just get soaked."

Soaked, he thought, tipping his head to the black sky. He had no sense of clouds or stars, no view of either one. It was just about the time she'd have been lying in bed watching the news; there must have been rain in the forecast. And here he was, locked out, with no coat.

"How are you going to find me?" he asked.

"There are only so many possible wrong turns you could have taken."

"I don't even remember any woods along this road."

"That's because you never pay attention."

"It was right past the intersection with the big traffic light."

"I know exactly where you are."

"I got confused when you called me," he said. "I wasn't looking at the road. Anyway, you'll see my headlights."

"I have to throw on some clothes. I'll be there in a few minutes."

"Okay."

"Bye."

It was an unusually protracted farewell for such a casual conversation. He realized that he was holding the phone very tightly in the dark, cradling it against his cheek and ear as if he were holding her hand to his face, feeling her skin cool and warm at the same time. And now there was no further word from her. Connection broken.

He had to fight the impulse to dial her again, instantly, just to reassure himself that the phone still worked—that she was still there. He could imagine her ridicule; he was slowing her down, she was trying to get dressed, he was causing yet another inconvenience on top of so many others.

With the conversation ended, he was forced to return his full attention to his surroundings. He listened, heard again the wind, the distant sound of still water. Still water made sounds only when it lapped against something, or when something waded through it. He couldn't tell one from the other right now. He wished he were still inside the car, with at least that much protection.

She was going to find him. He'd been only a few minutes, probably less than a mile, from home. She would be here any time.

He waited, expecting raindrops. The storm would come, it would short out his phone. There was absolutely no shelter on the empty road, now that he had locked himself out of it. He considered digging for a rock, something big enough to smash the window, so he could pull the lock and let himself in. But his mistake was already proving costly enough; he couldn't bring himself to compound the problem. Anyway, it wasn't raining yet. And she would be here any minute now.

It was about time to check in with her, he thought. She had to be in her car by now. Did he need a better excuse for calling her?

Well, here was one: the headlights were failing.

Just like that, as if they were on a dimmer switch. Both at once, darkening, taken down in less than a minute to a dull stubborn glow. It was a minute of total helpless panic; he was saved from complete horror only by the faint trace of light that remained. Why didn't they go out all the way? By the time he'd asked himself this, he realized that his wife had now lost her beacon. That was news. It was important to call her now.

He punched the redial number. That much was easy. The phone rang four times and the machine answered, and then he had to suppress himself from smashing the phone on the roof of the car. She wouldn't be at home, would she? She'd be on the road by now, looking for him, cruising past dark lanes and driveways, the entrance to some wooded lot, hoping to see his stalled headlights—and there would be none.

What made all this worse was that he couldn't remember the number of her cell phone. He refused to call her on it, arguing that she might be driving if he called her, and he didn't want to cause an accident.

Should he . . . head away from the car? Blunder back along the dark road without a flashlight until he came in sight of the street? Wouldn't she be likely to spot him coming down the road, a pale figure stumbling through the trees, so out of place?

But he couldn't bring himself to move away. The car was the only familiar thing in his world right now.

There was no point breaking the window. The horn wouldn't sound if the battery had died. No point in doing much of anything now. Except wait for her to find him.

Please call, he thought. Please please please call. I have something to tell—

The phone chirped in his hand. He stabbed the on button.

"I'm coming," she said.

"The headlights just died," he said. "You're going to have to look closely. For a . . . a dark road, a park entrance maybe . . . "

"I know," she said, her voice tense. He pictured her leaning forward, driving slowly, squinting out the windshield at the streetsides. "The rain's making it hard to see a damn thing."

"Rain," he said. "It's raining where you are?"

"Pouring."

"Then . . . where are you? It's dry as a bone here." Except for the sound of water, the stale exhalation of the damp earth around him.

"I'm about three blocks from the light."

"Where I was turning?"

"Where you got turned around. It's all houses here. I thought there was a park. There is some park, just ahead . . . that's what I was thinking of. But . . . "

He listened, waiting. And now he could hear her wipers going, sluicing the windshield; he could hear the sizzle of rain under her car's tires. A storm. He stared at the sky even harder than before. Nothing up there. Nothing coming down.

"But what?" he said finally.

"There's a gate across the road. You couldn't have gone through there."

"Check it," he said. "Maybe it closed behind me."

"I'm going on," she said. "I'll go to the light and start back, see if I missed anything."

"Check the gate."

"It's just a park, it's nothing. You're in woods, you said?"

"Woods, marsh, parkland, something. I'm on a dirt road. There are . . . bushes all around, and I can hear water."

"Ah . . . "

What was that in her voice?

"I can . . . wait a minute . . . I thought I could see you, but . . . "

"What?" He peered into the darkness. She might be looking at him even now, somehow seeing him while he couldn't see her.

"It isn't you," she said. "It's, a car, like yours, but . . . it's not yours. That's not you, that's not your . . . "

"What's going on?" The headlights died all the way down.

"Please, can you keep on talking to me?" she said. "Can you please just keep talking to me and don't stop for a minute?"

"What's the matter? Tell me what's going on?"

"I need to hear you keep talking, please, please, please," and whatever it was in her voice that was wrenching her, it wrenched at him too, it was tearing at both of them in identical ways, and he knew he just had to keep talking. He had to keep her on the phone.

"Don't be afraid," he said. "Whatever it is. I won't make you stop and tell me now, if you don't want to talk, if you just want to listen," he said. "I love you," he said, because surely she needed to hear that. "Everything's going to be fine. I'm just, I wish you could talk to me but—"

"No, you talk," she said. "I have to know you're all right, because this isn't, that's not, it can't be—"

"Sh. Shhh. I'm talking now."

"Tell me where you are again."

"I'm standing by my car," he said. "I'm in a dark wooded place, there's some water nearby, a pond or marsh judging from the sound, and it's not raining, it's kind of warm and damp, but it's not raining. It's quiet. It's dark. I'm not . . . I'm not afraid," and that seemed the thing to tell her, too. "I'm just waiting, I'm fine, I'm just waiting here for you to get to me, and I know you will. Everything will be . . .fine."

"It's raining where I am," she said. "And I'm . . . " She swallowed. "And I'm looking at your car."

Static, then, a cold blanket of it washing out her voice. The noise swelled, peaked, subsided, and the phone went quiet. He pushed the redial button, then remembered that she had called him and not the other way round. It didn't matter, though. The phone was dead. He wouldn't be calling anyone, and no one would be calling him.

I'll walk back to that road now, he thought. While there's still a chance she can find me.

He hefted the cell phone, on the verge of tossing it overhand out into the unseen marshes. But there was always a chance that some faint spark remained inside it; that he'd get a small blurt of a ring, a wisp of her voice, something. He put it in a pocket so he wouldn't lose it in the night.

He tipped his face to the sky and put out his hand before he started walking.

Not a drop.

It's raining where I am, and I'm looking at your car.

• • • •

I know you mama, miss me since I'm gone;
I know you mama, miss me since I'm gone;
One more thing before I journey on.

Cruel Sistah
Nisi Shawl

"You and Neville goin out again?"

"I think so. He asked could he call me Thursday after class."

Calliope looked down at her sister's long, straight, silky hair. It fanned out over Calliope's knees and fell almost to the floor, a black river drying up just short of its destined end. "Why don't you let me wash this for you?"

"It takes too long to dry. Just braid it up like you said, okay?"

"Your head all fulla dandruff," Calliope lied. "And ain't you ever heard of a hair dryer? Mary Lockett lent me her portable."

"Mama says those things bad for your hair." Dory shifted uncomfortably on the sofa cushion laid on the hardwood floor where she sat. Dory (short for Dorcas) was the darker-skinned of the two girls, darker by far than their mama or their daddy. "Some kinda throwback," the aunts called her.

Mama doted on Dory's hair, though, acting sometimes as if it was her own. Not too surprising, seeing how good it was. Also, a nervous breakdown eight years back had made Mama completely bald. Alopecia was the doctor's word for it, and there was no cure. So Mama made sure both her daughters took care of their crowning glories. But especially Dory.

"All right, no dryer," Calliope conceded. "We can go out in the back garden and let the sun help dry it. 'Cause in fact, I was gonna rinse it with rainwater. Save us haulin it inside."

Daddy had installed a flexible hose on the kitchen sink. Calliope wet her sister's hair down with warm jets of water, then massaged in sweet-smelling shampoo. White suds covered the gleaming black masses, gathering out of nowhere like clouds.

Dory stretched her neck and sighed. "That feels nice."

"Nice as when Neville kisses you back there?"

"Ow!"

"Or over here?"

"OW! Callie, what you doin?"

"Sorry. My fingers slipped. Need to trim my nails, hunh? Let's go rinse off."

Blood from the cuts on her neck and ear streaked the shampoo clouds with pink stains. Unaware of this, Dory let her sister lead her across the red and white linoleum to the back porch and the creaky wooden steps down to the garden. She sat on the curved cement bench by the cistern, gingerly at first. It was surprisingly warm for spring. The sun shone, standing well clear of the box elders crowding against the retaining wall at the back of the lot. A silver jet flew high overhead, bound for Seatac. The low grumble of its engines lagged behind it, obscuring Calliope's words.

"What?"

"I said 'Quit sittin pretty and help me move this lid.'"

The cistern's cover came off with a hollow, grating sound. A slice of water, a crescent like the waning moon, reflected the sun's brightness. Ripples of light ran up the damp stone walls. Most of the water lay in darkness, though. Cold smells seeped up from it: mud, moss. Mystery.

As children, Dory, Calliope and their cousins had been fascinated by the cistern. Daddy and Mama had forbidden them to play there, of course, which only increased their interest. When their parents opened it to haul up water for the garden, the girls hovered close by, snatching glimpses inside.

"Goddam if that no good Byron ain't lost the bucket!" Calliope cursed the empty end of the rope she'd retrieved from her side of the cistern. It was still curled where it had been tied to the handle of the beige plastic bucket.

Byron, their fourteen year old cousin, liked to soak sticks and strips of wood in water to use in his craft projects. He only lived a block away, so he was always in and out of the basement workshop. "You think he took it home again?" Dory asked.

"No, I remember now I saw it downstairs, fulla some trash a his, tree branches or somethin."

"Yeah? Well, that's all right, we don't wanna—"

"I'll go get it and wipe it out good. Wait for me behind the garage."

"Oh, but he's always so upset when you mess with his stuff!"

"It ain't his anyhow, is it?" Calliope took the porch steps two at a time. She was a heavy girl, but light on her feet. Never grew out of her baby fat. Still, she could hold her own in a fight.

The basement stairs, narrow and uneven, slowed her down a bit. Daddy had run a string from the bare-bulb fixture at their bottom, looping it along the wooden wall of the stairwell. She pulled, and the chain at its other end slithered obediently against porcelain, clicked and snapped back. Brightness flooded the lowering floor joists.

Calliope ignored the beige bucket full of soaking willow wands. Daddy's tool bench, that's where she'd find what she wanted. Nothing too heavy, though. She had to be able to lift it. And not too sharp. She didn't want to have to clean up a whole lot of blood.

Hammer? Pipe wrench? What if Mama got home early and found Calliope carrying one of those out of the house? What would she think?

It came to her with the same sort of slide and snap that had turned the light on. Daddy was about to tear out the railroad ties in the retaining wall. They were rotten; they needed replacing. It was this week's project. The new ones were piled up at the end of the driveway.

Smiling, Calliope selected a medium-sized mallet, its handle as long as her forearm. And added a crowbar for show.

Outside, Dory wondered what was taking her sister so long. A clump of shampoo slipped down her forehead and along one eyebrow. She wiped it off, annoyed. She stood up from the weeds where she'd been waiting, then quickly knelt down again at the sound of footsteps on the paving bricks.

"Bend forward." Calliope's voice cracked. Dory began twisting her head to see why. The mallet came down hard on her right temple. It left a black dent in the suds, a hollow. She made a mewing sound, fell forward. Eyes open, but blind. Another blow, well-centered, this time, drove her face into the soft soil. One more. Then Calliope took control of herself.

"You dead," she murmured, satisfied.

A towel over her sister's head disguised the damage. Hoisting her up into a sitting position and leaning her against the garage, Calliope hunkered back to look at her and think. No one was due home within the next couple of hours. For that long, her secret would be safe. Even then she'd be all right as long as they didn't look out the kitchen windows. The retaining wall was visible from there, but if she had one of the new ties tamped in place, and the dirt filled back in . . .

A moment more she pondered. Fast-moving clouds flickered across the sun, and her skin bumped up. There was no real reason to hang back. Waiting wouldn't change what she'd done.

The first tie came down easily. Giant splinters sprung off as Calliope kicked it to one side. The second one, she had to dig the ends out, and the third was cemented in place its full length by dried clay. Ants boiled out of the hundreds of holes that had been hidden behind it, and the phone rang.

She wasn't going to answer it. But it stopped, and started again, and she knew she'd better.

Sweat had made mud of the dirt on her hands. She cradled the pale blue princess phone against one shoulder, trying to rub the mess clean on her shirt as she listened to Mama asking what was in the refrigerator. The cord barely stretched that far. Were they out of eggs? Butter? Lunch meat? Did Calliope think there was enough cornmeal to make hush puppies? Even with Byron coming over? And what were she and Dory up to that it took them so long to answer the phone?

"Dory ain't come home yet. No, I don't know why; she ain't tole me. I was out in back, tearin down the retaining wall."

Her mother's disapproving silence lasted two full seconds. "Why you always wanna act so mannish, Calliope?"

There wasn't any answer to that. She promised to change her clothes for supper.

Outside again, ants crawled on her dead sister's skin.

Dory didn't feel them. She saw them, though, from far off. Far up? What was going on didn't make regular sense. Why couldn't she hear the shovel digging? Whoever was lying there on the ground in Dory's culottes with a towel over her head, it was someone else. Not her.

She headed for the house. She should be hungry. It must be supper time by now. The kitchen windows were suddenly shining through the dusk. And sure enough, Calliope was inside already, cooking.

In the downstairs bathroom, Daddy washed his hands with his sleeves rolled up. She kissed him. She did; on his cheek, she couldn't have missed it.

The food look good, good enough to eat. Fried chicken, the crisp ridges and golden valleys of its skin glowing under the ceiling light. Why didn't she want it? Her plate was empty.

Nobody talked much. Nobody talked to her at all. There were a lot of leftovers. Cousin Byron helped Calliope clear the table. Daddy made phone calls, with Mama listening in on the extension. She could see them both at the same time, in the kitchen and in their bedroom upstairs. She couldn't hear anything.

Then the moon came out. It was bedtime, a school night. Everyone stayed up though, and the police sat in the living room and moved their mouths till she got tired of watching them. She went in the backyard again, where all this weird stuff had started happening.

The lid was still off the cistern. She looked down inside. The moon's reflection shone up at her, a full circle, uninterrupted by shadow. Not smooth, though. Waves ran through it, long, like swirls actually. Closer, she saw them clearly: hairs. Her hairs, supple and fine.

Suddenly, the world was in daylight again. Instead of the moon's circle, a face covered the water's surface. Her sister's face. Calliope's. Different, and at first Dory couldn't understand why. Then she realized it was her hair, *her* hair, Dory's own. A thin fringe of it hung around her big sister's face as if it belonged there. But it didn't. Several loose strands fell drifting towards Dory. And again, it was night.

And day. And night. Time didn't stay still. Mostly, it seemed to move in one direction. Mama kept crying; Daddy too. Dory decided she must be dead. But what about heaven? What about the funeral?

Byron moved into Dory's old room. It wasn't spooky; it was better than his mom's house. There, he could never tell who was going to show up for drinks. Or breakfast. He never knew who was going to start yelling and throwing things in the middle of the night: his mom, or some man she had invited over, or someone else she hadn't.

Even before he brought his clothes, Byron had kept his instruments and other projects here. Uncle Marv's workshop was wonderful, and he let him use all his tools.

His thing now was gimbris, elegant North African ancestors of the cigar-box banjos he'd built two years ago when he was just beginning, just a kid. He sat on the retaining wall in the last, lingering light of the autumn afternoon, considering the face, neck, and frame of his latest effort, a variant like a violin, meant to be bowed. He'd pieced it together from the thin trunk of an elder tree blown down in an August storm, sister to the leafless ones still upright behind him.

The basic structure looked good, but it was kind of plain. It needed some sort of decoration. An inlay, ivory or mother of pearl or something. The hide backing was important, obviously, but that could wait; it'd be easier to take care of the inlay first.

Of course, real ivory would be too expensive. Herb David, who let him work in his guitar shop, said people used bone as a substitute. And he knew where some was. Small bits, probably from some dead dog or rabbit. They'd been entangled in the tree roots. He planned to make tuning pegs out of them. There'd be plenty, though.

He stood up, and the world whited out. It had been doing that a lot since he moved here. The school nurse said he had low blood pressure. He just had to stand still a minute and he'd be okay. The singing in his ears, that would stop, too. But it was still going when he got to the stairs.

Stubbornly, he climbed, hanging onto the handrail. Dory's—his—bedroom was at the back of the house, overlooking the garden. His mom kept her dope in an orange juice can hung under the heat vent. He used the same system for his bones. No one knew he had them; so why was he afraid they'd take them away?

He held them in his cupped palms. They were warm, and light. The shimmering whiteness had condensed down to one corner of his vision. Sometimes that meant he was going to get a headache. He hoped not. He wanted to work on this now, while he was alone.

When he left his room, though, he crossed the hall into Calliope's instead of heading downstairs to Uncle Marv's workshop. Without knowing why, he gazed around him. The walls were turquoise, the throw rugs and bedspread pale pink. Nothing in here interested him, except—that poster of Wilt Chamberlain her new boyfriend, Neville, had given her . . .

It was signed, worth maybe one hundred dollars. He stepped closer. He could never get Calliope to let him anywhere near the thing when she was around, but she took terrible care of it. It was taped to the wall all crooked, sort of sagging in the middle.

He touched the slick surface—slick, but not smooth—something soft and lumpy lay between the poster and the wall. What? White light pulsed up around the edges of his vision as he lifted one creased corner.

Something black slithered to the floor. He knelt. With the whiteness, his vision had narrowed, but he could still see it was nothing alive. He picked it up.

A wig! Or at least part of one. Byron tried to laugh. It was funny, wasn't it? Calliope wearing a wig like some old bald lady? Only . . . only it was so weird. The bones. This—hair. The way Dory had disappeared.

He had to think. This was not the place. He smoothed down the poster's tape, taking the wig with him to the basement.

He put the smallest bone in a clamp. It was about as big around as his middle finger. He sawed it into oblong disks.

The wig hair was long and straight. Like Dory's. It was held together by shriveled-up skin, the way he imagined an Indian's scalp would be.

What if Calliope had killed her little sister? It was crazy, but what if she had? Did that mean she'd kill him if he told on her? Or if she thought he knew?

And if he was wrong, he'd be causing trouble for her, and Uncle Marv, and Aunt Cookie, and he might have to go live at home again.

Gradually, his work absorbed him, as it always did. When Calliope came in, he had a pile of bone disks on the bench, ready for polishing. Beside them, in a sultry heap, lay the wig, which he'd forgotten to put back.

Byron looked up at his cousin, unable to say anything. The musty basement was suddenly too small. She was three years older than him, and at least thirty pounds heavier. And she saw it, she had to see it. After a moment, he managed a sickly smirk, but his mouth stayed shut.

"Whatchoodoon?" She didn't smile back. "You been in my room?"

"I—I didn't—"

She picked it up. "Pretty, ain't it?" She stroked the straight hair, smoothing it out. "You want it?"

No clue in Calliope's bland expression as to what she meant. He tried to formulate an answer just to her words, to what she'd actually said. Did he want the wig. "For the bow I'm makin, yeah, sure, thanks."

"Awright then."

He wished she'd go away. "Neville be here tonight?"

She beamed. It was the right question to ask. "I guess. Don't know what he sees in me, but the boy can't keep away."

Byron didn't know what Neville saw in her either. "Neville's smart," he said diplomatically. It was true.

So was he.

There was more hair than he needed, even if he saved a bunch for restringing. He coiled it up and left it in his juice can. There was no way he could prove it was Dory's. If he dug up the backyard where the tree fell, where he found the bones, would the rest of the skeleton be there?

The police. He should call the police, but he'd seen *Dragnet*, and *Perry Mason*. When he accepted the wig, the hair, he'd become an accessory after the fact. Maybe he was one even before that, because of the bones.

It was odd, but really the only time he wasn't worried about all this was when he worked on the gimbri. By Thanksgiving, it was ready to play.

He brought it out to show to Neville after dinner. "That is a seriously fine piece of work," said Neville, cradling the gimbri's round leather back. "Smaller than the other one, isn't it?" His big hands could practically cover a basketball. With one long thumb he caressed the strings. They whispered dryly.

"You play it with this." Byron handed him the bow.

He held it awkwardly. Keyboards, reeds, guitar, drums, flute, even accordion: he'd fooled around with plenty of instruments, but nothing resembling a violin. "You sure you want me to?"

It was half-time on the TV, and dark outside already. Through the living room window, yellow light from a street lamp coated the grainy, gray sidewalk, dissolving at its edges like a pointillist's reverie. A night just like this, he'd first seen how pretty Dory was: the little drops of rain in her hair shining, and it stayed nice as a white girl's.

Not like Calliope's. Hers was as naturally nappy as his, worse between her legs. He sneaked a look at her while Byron was showing him how to position the gimbri upright. She was looking straight back at him, her eyes hot and still. Not as pretty as Dory, no, but she let him do things he would never have dreamed of asking of her little sister.

Mr. Moore stood up from the sofa and called to his wife. "Mama, you wanna come see our resident genius's latest invention in action?"

The gimbri screamed, choked, and sighed. "What on earth?" said Mrs. Moore from the kitchen doorway. She shut her eyes and clamped her lips together as if the awful noise was trying to get in through other ways besides her ears.

Neville hung his head and bit his lower lip. He wasn't sure whether he was trying to keep from laughing or crying.

"It spozed to sound like that, Byron?" asked Calliope.

"No," Neville told her. "My fault." He picked up the bow from his lap, frowning. His older brother had taken him to a Charles Mingus concert once. He searched his memory for an image of the man embracing his big bass, and mimicked it the best he could.

A sweeter sound emerged. Sweeter, and so much sadder. One singing note, which he raised and lowered slowly. High and yearning. Soft and questioning. With its voice.

With its words.

"I know you mama, miss me since I'm gone;
I know you mama, miss me since I'm gone;
One more thing before I journey on."

Neville turned his head to see if anyone else heard what he was hearing. His hand slipped, and the gimbri sobbed. He turned back to it.

"Lover man, why won't you be true?
Lover man, why won't you ever be true?
She murdered me, and she just might murder you."

He wanted to stop now, but his hands kept moving. He recognized that voice, that tricky hesitance, the tone smooth as smoke. He'd never expected to hear it again.

"I know you daddy, miss me since I'm gone;
I know you daddy, miss me since I'm gone;
One more thing before I journey on.

"I know you cousin, miss me since I'm gone;
I know you cousin, miss me since I'm gone;
It's cause of you I come to sing this song.

"Cruel, cruel sistah, black and white and red;
Cruel, cruel sistah, black and white and red;
You hated me, you had to see me dead.

"Cruel, cruel sistah, red and white and black;
Cruel, cruel sistah, red and white and black;
You killed me and you buried me out back.

"Cruel, cruel sistah, red and black and white;
Cruel, cruel sistah, red and black and white;
You'll be dead yourself before tomorrow night."

Finally, the song was finished. The bow slithered off the gimbri's strings with a sound like a snake leaving. They all looked at one another warily.

Calliope was the first to speak. "It ain't true," she said. Which meant admitting that something had actually happened.

But they didn't have to believe what the song had said.

Calliope's suicide early the next morning, that they had to believe: her body floating front down in the cistern, her short, rough hair soft as a wet burlap bag. That, and the skeleton the police found behind the retaining wall, with its smashed skull.

It was a double funeral. There was no music.

· · · ·

Far from being haunted, the Box was a kind of tabula rasa.
It had no history, and it held no ghosts . . .

The Box
Stephen Gallagher

It was a woman who picked up the phone and I said, "Can I speak to Mr. Lavery, please?"

"May I ask what it concerns?" she said.

I gave her my name and said, "I'm calling from Wainfleet Maritime College. I'm his instructor on the helicopter safety course."

"I thought that was all done with last week."

"He didn't complete it."

"Oh." I'd surprised her. "Excuse me for one moment. Can you hold on?"

I heard her lay down the phone and move away. Then, after a few moments, there came the indistinct sounds of a far-off conversation. There was her voice and there was a man's, the two of them faint enough to be in another room. I couldn't make out anything of what was being said.

After a while, I could hear someone returning.

I was expecting to hear Lavery's voice, but it was the woman again.

She said, "I'm terribly sorry, I can't get him to speak to you." There was a note of exasperation in her tone.

"Can you give me any indication why?"

"He was quite emphatic about it," she said. The implication was that no, he'd not only given her no reason, but he also hadn't appreciated being asked. Then she lowered her voice and added, "I wasn't aware that he hadn't finished the course. He told me in so many words that he was done with it."

Which could be taken more than one way. I said, "He does know that without a safety certificate he can't take up the job?"

"He's never said anything about that." She was still keeping her voice down, making it so that Lavery—her husband, I imagined, although the woman hadn't actually identified herself—wouldn't overhear. She went on, "He's been in a bit of a funny mood all week. Did something happen?"

"That's what I was hoping he might tell me. Just ask him once more for me, will you?"

She did, and this time I heard Lavery shouting.

When she came back to the phone she said, "This is very embarrassing."

"Thank you for trying," I said. "I won't trouble you any further, Mrs. Lavery."

"It's *Miss* Lavery," she said. "James is my brother."

In 1950 the first scheduled helicopter service started up in the UK, carrying passengers between Liverpool and Cardiff. Within a few short years helicopter travel had become an expensive, noisy, and exciting part of our lives. No vision of a future city was complete without its heliport. Children would run and dance and wave if they heard one passing over.

The aviation industry had geared up for this new era in freight and passenger transportation, and the need for various kinds of training had brought new life to many a small airfield and flight school. Wainfleet was a maritime college, but it offered new aircrew one facility that the flight schools could not.

At Wainfleet we had the dunker, also known as The Box.

We'd been running the sea rescue and safety course for almost three years, and I'd been on the staff for most of that time. Our completion record was good. I mean, you expect a few people to drop out of any training program, especially the dreamers, but our intake were experienced men with some living under their belts. Most were ex-navy or air force, and any romantic notions had been knocked out of them in a much harder theatre than ours. Our scenarios were as nothing, compared to the situations through which some of them had lived.

And yet, I was thinking as I looked at the various records spread across the desk in my little office, our drop-outs were gradually increasing in their numbers. Could the fault lie with us? There was nothing in any of their personal histories to indicate a common cause.

I went down the corridor to Peter Taylor's office. Peter Taylor was my boss. He was sitting at his desk signing course certificates.

I said, "Don't bother signing Lavery's."

He looked up at me with eyebrows raised, and I shrugged.

"I'm no closer to explaining it," I said.

"Couldn't just be plain old funk, could it?"

"Most of these men are war heroes," I said. "Funk doesn't come into it."

He went back to his signing, but he carried on talking.

"Easy enough to be a hero when you're a boy without a serious thought in your head," he said. "Ten years of peacetime and a few responsibilities, and perhaps you get a little bit wiser."

Then he finished the last one and capped the fountain pen and looked at me. I didn't quite know what to say. Peter Taylor had a background in the merchant marine but he'd sat out the war right here, in a reserved occupation.

"I'd better be getting on," I said.

I left the teaching block and went over to the building that housed our sea tank. It was a short walk and the sun was shining, but the wind from the ocean always cut through the gap between the structures. The wind smelled and tasted of sand and salt, and of something unpleasant that the new factories up the coast had started to dump into the estuary.

Back in its early days, Wainfleet had been a sanatorium for TB cases. Staffed by nuns, as I understood it; there were some old photographs in the mess hall. Then it had become a convalescent home for mine workers and then, finally, the maritime college it now was. We had two hundred boarding cadets for whom we had dormitories, a parade ground, and a rugby field that had a pronounced downward slope toward the cliffs. But I wasn't part of the cadet teaching staff. I was concerned only with the commercial training arm.

Our team of four safety divers was clearing up after the day's session. The tank had once been an ordinary swimming pool, added during the convalescent-home era but then deepened and re-equipped for our purposes. The seawater was filtered, and in the winter it was heated by a boiler. Although if you'd been splashing around in there in December, you'd never have guessed it.

Their head diver was George "Buster" Brown. A compact and powerful-looking man, he'd lost most of his hair and had all but shaved off the rest, American GI-style. With his barrel chest and his bullet head, he looked like a human missile in his dive suit. In fact, he'd actually trained on those two-man torpedoes toward the end of the war.

I said to him, "Cast your mind back to last week. Remember a trainee name of Lavery?"

"What did he look like?"

I described him, and added, "Something went wrong and he didn't complete."

"I think I know the one," Buster said. "Had a panic during the exercise and we had to extract him. He was almost throwing a fit down there. Caught Jacky Jackson a right boff on the nose."

"What was he like after you got him out?"

"Embarrassed, I think. Wouldn't explain his problem. Stamped off and we didn't see him again."

Buster couldn't think of any reason why Lavery might have reacted as he did. As far as he and his team were concerned, the exercise had gone normally in every way.

I left him to finish stowing the training gear, and went over to inspect the Box.

The Box was a stripped-down facsimile of a helicopter cabin, made of riveted aluminium panels and suspended by cable from a lifeboat davit. The davit swung the Box out and over the water before lowering it. The cabin seated four. Once immersed, an ingenious chain-belt system rotated the entire cabin until it was upside down. It was as realistic a ditching as we could make it, while retaining complete control of the situation. The safety course consisted of a morning in the classroom, followed by the afternoon spent practising escape drill from underwater.

The Box was in its rest position at the side of the pool. It hung with its floor about six inches clear of the tiles. I climbed aboard, and grabbed at something to keep my balance as the cabin swung around under my weight.

There had been no attempt to dress up the interior to look like the real thing; upside-down and six feet under, only the internal geography needed to be accurate. The bucket seats and harnesses were genuine, but that was as far as it went. The rest was just the bare metal, braced with aluminium struts and with open holes cut for the windows. In appearance it was like a tin Wendy House, suspended from a crane.

I'm not sure what I thought I was looking for. I put my hand on one of the seats and tugged, but the bolts were firm. I lifted part of the harness and let the webbing slide through my fingers. It was wet and heavy. Steadying myself, I used both hands to close the buckle and then tested the snap-release one-handed.

"I check those myself," Buster Brown said through the window. "Every session."

"No criticism intended, Buster," I said.

"I should hope not," he said, and then he was gone.

It happened again the very next session, only three days later.

I'd taken the files home and I'd studied all the past cases, but I'd reached no firm conclusions. If we were doing something wrong, I couldn't see what it was.

These were not inexperienced men. Most were in their thirties and, as I'd pointed out to Peter Taylor, had seen service under wartime conditions. Some had been ground crew, but many had been flyers who'd made the switch to peacetime commercial aviation. Occasionally we'd get students whose notes came marked with a particular code, and whose records had blank spaces where personal details should have been; these individuals, it was acknowledged but never said, were sent to us as part of a wider MI5 training.

In short, no sissies. Some of them were as tough as you could ask, but it wasn't meant to be a tough course. It wasn't a trial, it wasn't a test. The war was long over.

As I've said, we began every training day in the classroom. Inevitably, some of it involved telling them things they already knew. But you can't skip safety, even though some of them would have loved to; no grown man ever looks comfortable in a classroom situation.

First I talked them through the forms they had to complete. Then I collected the forms in.

And then, when they were all settled again, I started the talk.

I said, "We're not here to punish anybody. We're here to take you through a scenario so that hopefully, if you ever *do* need to ditch, you'll have a much greater chance of survival. Most fatalities don't take place when the helicopter comes down. They happen afterwards, in the water."

I asked if anyone in the room had been sent to us for re-breather training, and a couple of hands were raised. This gave me a chance to note their faces.

"Right," I said. "I'm going to go over a few points and then after the break we'll head for the pool."

I ran through the routine about the various designs of flight suits and harnesses and life vests. Then the last-moment checks; glasses if you wore them, false teeth if you had them, loose objects in the cabin. Hold onto some part of the structure for orientation. Brace for impact.

One or two had questions. Two men couldn't swim. That was nothing unusual.

After tea break in the college canteen, we all went over together. Buster Brown and his men were already in the water, setting up a dinghy for the lifeboat drill that would follow the ditch. The students each found themselves a suit from the rail before disappearing into the changing room, and I went over to ready the Box.

When they came out, they lined up along the poolside. One of the divers steadied the Box and I stayed by the controls and called out, "Numbers one to four, step forward."

The Box jiggled around on its cable as the first four men climbed aboard and strapped themselves into the bucket seats. Buster Brown checked everyone's harness from the doorway, and then signalled to me before climbing in with them and securing the door from the inside. I sounded the warning klaxon and then eased back the lever to raise the Box into the air.

In the confines of the sea tank building, the noise of the crane's motor could be deafening. Once I'd raised the payload about twelve feet in the air, I swung the crane around on its turntable to place the Box directly over the pool. It swung there, turning on its cable, and I could see the men inside through the raw holes that represented aircraft windows.

Two divers with masks and air bottles were already under the water, standing by to collect the escapees and guide them up to the surface. Buster would stay inside. This was routine for him. He'd hold his breath for the minute or so that each exercise took, and then he'd ride the Box back to the poolside to pick up the next four.

Right now he was giving everyone a quick recap of what I'd told them in the classroom. Then it was, *Brace, brace, brace for impact!* and I released the Box to drop into the water.

It was a controlled drop, not a sudden plummet, although to a first-timer it was always an adrenalin moment. The Box hit the water and then started to settle, and I could hear Buster giving out a few final reminders in the rapidly filling cabin.

Then it went under, and everything took on a kind of slow-motion tranquility as the action transferred to below the surface. Shapes flitted from the submerged Box in all directions, like wraiths fleeing a haunted castle. They were out in seconds. As each broke the surface, a number was shouted. When all four were out, I raised the Box.

It was as fast and as straightforward as that.

The exercise was repeated until every student had been through a straightforward dunk. Then the line reformed and we did it all again, this time with the added refinement of a cabin rotation as the Box went under. It made for a more realistic simulation, as a real helicopter was liable to invert with the weight of its engine. To take some of the anxiety out of it, I'd tell the students that I considered escape from the inverted cabin to be easier—you came out through the window opening facing the surface, which made it a lot easier to strike out for.

Again, we had no problems. The safety divers were aware of the non-swimmers and gave them some extra assistance. The Box functioned with no problems. No one panicked, no one got stuck. Within the hour, everyone was done.

At that point, we divided the party. The two men on rebreather training stayed with Buster Brown, and everyone else went to the other end of the pool for lifeboat practice. I ran the Box through its paces empty yet again, as Buster stood at the poolside with them and ran through his piece on the use of the rebreather unit.

The rebreather does pretty much what its name suggests. Consisting of an airbag incorporated into the flotation jacket with a mouthpiece and a valve, it allows you to conserve and re-use your own air. There's more unused oxygen in an expelled breath than you'd think. It's never going to replace the aqualung, but the device can extend your underwater survival time by a vital minute or two.

Both men looked as if they might be old hands at this. Their names were Charnley and Briggs. Even in the borrowed flight suit, Charnley had that sleek, officer-material look. He had an Errol Flynn moustache and hair so heavily brilliantined that two dunks in the tank had barely disturbed it. Briggs, on the other hand, looked the non-commissioned man to his fingertips. His accent was broad and his hair looked as if his wife had cut it for him, probably not when in the best of moods.

Buster left them practicing with the mouthpieces and came over to pick up his mask and air bottle. I was guiding the empty Box, water cascading from every seam, back to the poolside.

"Just a thought, Buster," I said, raising my voice to be heard as I lowered the cabin to the side. "Wasn't Lavery on the rebreather when he had his little episode?"

"Now that you mention it, yes he was."

"How many were in the Box with him?"

"Two others. Neither of them had any problem."

I didn't take it any further than that. None of our other non-finishers had been on the rebreather when they chose to opt out, so this was hardly a pattern in the making.

The rebreather exercise was always conducted in three stages. Firstly, the Box was lowered to sit in the water so that the level inside the cabin was around chest-height. The student would practice by leaning forward into the water, knowing that in the event of difficulty he need do no more than sit back. This confidence-building exercise would then be followed by a total immersion, spending a full minute under the water and breathing on the apparatus. Assuming all went well, the exercise would end with a complete dunk, rotate and escape.

All went well. Until that final stage.

The others had all completed the lifeboat drill and left the pool by then. The Box hit the water and rolled over with the spectacular grinding noise that the chain belt always made. It sounded like a drawbridge coming down, and worked on a similar principle.

Then the boomy silence of the pool as the water lapped and the Box stayed under.

The minute passed, and then came the escape. One fleeting figure could be seen under the water. But only one. He broke surface and his number was called. It was Briggs. I looked toward the Box and saw Buster going in through one of the window openings. My hand was on the lever, but I waited; some injury might result if I hauled the Box out in the middle of an extraction. But then Buster came up and made an urgent signal and so I brought the cabin up out of the water, rotating it back upright as it came. Tank water came out of the window openings in gushers.

Buster came out of the pool and we reached the Box together. Charnley was still in his harness, the rebreather mouthpiece still pushing his cheeks out. He was making weak-looking gestures with his hands. I reached in to relieve him of the mouthpiece, but he swatted me aside and then spat it out.

Fending his hands away, Buster got in with him and released his harness. By then, Charnley was starting to recognize his surroundings and to act a little more rationally. He didn't calm down, though. He shoved both of us aside and clambered out.

He stood at the poolside, spitting water and tearing himself out of the flotation jacket.

"What was the problem?" I asked him.

"You want to get that bloody thing looked at," Charnley gasped.

Buster, who had a surprisingly puritan streak, said in a warning tone, "Language," and I shot him a not-now look.

"Looked at for what?" I said, but Charnley just hurled all his gear onto the deck as if it had been wrestling him and he'd finally just beaten it.

"Don't talk to me," he said, "I feel foul." And he stalked off to the changing room.

The two of us got the Box secure, and while we were doing it I asked Buster what happened. Buster could only shrug.

"I tapped his arm to tell him it was time to come out, but he didn't move," Buster said. "Just stayed there. I thought he might have passed out, but when I went in he started to thrash around and push me away."

So, what was Charnley's problem? I went to find him in the changing room. Briggs had dressed in a hurry in order to be sure of getting out in time for his bus. As he passed me in the doorway he said, "Your man's been wasting a good shepherd's pie in there."

Shepherd's pie or whatever, I could smell vomit hanging in the air around the cubicles at the back of the changing room. Charnley was out. He was standing in front of the mirror, pale as watered milk, knotting his tie. An RAF tie, I noted.

"Captain Charnley?" I said.

"What about it?"

"I just wondered if you were ready to talk about what happened."

"Nothing happened," he said.

I waited.

After a good thirty seconds or more he said, "I'm telling you nothing happened. Must have got a bad egg for breakfast. Serves me right for trusting your canteen."

I said, "I'll put you back on the list for tomorrow. You can skip the classroom session."

"Don't bother," he said, reaching for his blazer.

"Captain Charnley . . ."

He turned to me then, and fixed me with a look so stern and so urgent that it was almost threatening.

"I didn't see anything in there," he said. "Nothing. Do you understand me? I don't want you telling anyone I did."

Even though I hadn't suggested any such thing.

There was a bus stop outside the gates, but Captain Charnley had his own transport. It was a low, noisy, open-topped sports car with a Racing Green paint job, all dash and Castrol fumes. Off he went, scaring the birds out of the trees, swinging out onto the road and roaring away.

I went back to my office and reviewed his form. According to his record, he'd flown Hurricanes with 249 Squadron in Yorkshire. After the war he'd entered the glass business, but he'd planned a return to flying with BEA.

Hadn't seen anything? What exactly did that mean? What was there to see anyway?

I have to admit that in a fanciful moment, when we'd first started to suspect that there might be some kind of a problem on the course, I'd investigated the Box's history. But it had none. Far from being the salvaged cabin of a wrecked machine, haunted by the ghosts of those who'd died in it, the Box had been purpose-built as an exercise by apprentices at the local aircraft factory.

It was no older than its three-and-a-half years, and there was nothing more to it than met the eye. The bucket seats were from scrap, but they'd been salvaged from training aircraft that had been decommissioned without ever having seen combat or disaster.

When I went back to the sea tank, Buster Brown was out of his diving gear and dressed in a jacket and tie, collecting the men's clocking-off cards prior to locking up the building. The other divers had cleared away the last of their equipment and gone.

I said, "Can I ask a favor?"

He said, "As long as it doesn't involve borrowing my motor bike, my missus, or my money, ask away."

I think he knew what I was going to say. "Stay on a few minutes and operate the dunker for me? I want to sit in and see if I can work out what all the fuss is about."

"I can tell you what the fuss is about," he said. "Some can take it and some can't."

"That doesn't add up, Buster," I said. "These have all been men of proven courage."

Suddenly it was as if we were back in the Forces and he was the experienced NCO politely setting the greenhorn officer straight.

"With respect, sir," he said, "You're missing the point. Being tested doesn't diminish a man's regard for danger. I think you'll find it's rather the opposite."

We proceeded with the trial. I found a suit that fit me and changed into it. I put on a flotation jacket and rebreather gear. No safety divers, just me and Buster. Like the tattooed boys who ride the backs of dodgems at the fairground, you feel entitled to get a little cavalier with the rules you're supposed to enforce.

I strapped myself in, and signaled my readiness to Buster. Then I tensed involuntarily as the cable started moving with a jerk. As the Box rose into the air and swung out over the pool, I looked all around the interior for anything untoward. I saw nothing.

Buster followed the normal routine, lowering me straight into the water. The box landed with a slap, and immediately began to rock from side to side as it filled up and sank. It was cold and noisy when the seawater flooded into the cabin, but once you got over that first moment's shock it was bearable. I've swum in colder seas on Welsh holidays.

Just as it reached my chin, I took a deep breath and ducked under the surface. Fully submerged, I looked and felt all around me as far as I could reach, checking for anything unusual. There was nothing. I wasn't using the rebreather at this point. I touched the belt release, lifting the lever plate, and it opened easily. There was the usual slight awkwardness as I wriggled free of the harness, but it wasn't anything to worry about. I took a few more moments to explore the cabin, again finding nothing, and then I went out through a window opening without touching the sides.

I popped up no more than a couple of seconds later. When Buster saw that I was out in open water, he lifted the dunker. As I swam to the side it passed over me, streaming like a raincloud onto the heaving surface of the pool.

By the time I'd climbed up the ladder, the Box was back in its start position and ready for reboarding. I said to Buster, "So which seat was Charnley in? Wasn't it the left rear?"

"Aft seat on the port side," he said.

So that was the one I took, this second time. Might as well try to recreate the experience as closely as possible, I thought. Not that any of this seemed to be telling me anything useful. I strapped myself in and gave Buster the wave, and we were off again.

I had to run through the whole routine, just so that I could say to Peter Taylor that the check had been complete. It was second nature. In all walks of life, the survivors are the people who never assume. This time I inflated the rebreather bag while the cabin was in midair, and had the mouthpiece in by the time I hit the water. Again it came flooding in as the cabin settled, but this time there was a difference. Almost instantly the chain belt jerked into action and the cabin began to turn.

It feels strange to invert and submerge at the same time. You're falling, you're floating . . . . of course people get disoriented, especially if they've never done it before. This time I determined to give myself the full minute under. Without a diver on hand to tap me when the time was up, I'd have to estimate it. But that was no big problem.

The cabin completed its turn, and stopped. All sound ended as well, apart from boomy echoes from the building above, pushing their way through several tons of water. I hung there in the harness, not breathing yet. I felt all but weightless in the straps. The seawater was beginning to make my eyes sting.

I'd forgotten how dark the cabin went when it was upside down. The tank was gloomy at this depth anyway. I'd heard that the American military went a stage further than we did, and conducted a final exercise with everyone wearing blacked-out goggles to simulate a night-time ditching. That seemed a little extreme to me; as I'd indicated to the men in the classroom, the Box was never intended as a test of endurance. It was more a foretaste of something we hoped they'd never have to deal with.

I found myself wondering if Buster had meant anything by that remark. The one about men who'd been tested. As if he was suggesting that I wouldn't know.

I'd been too young to fight at the very beginning of the war, but I joined up when I could and in the summer of 1940 I was selected for Bomber Command. In training I'd shown aptitude as a navigator. I flew twelve missions over heavily defended Channel ports, bombing the German invasion barges being readied along the so-called 'Blackpool Front.'

Then Headquarters took me out and made me an instructor. My crew was peeved. It wasn't just a matter of losing their navigator; most crews were superstitious, and mine felt that their luck was being messed with. But you could understand Bomber Command's thinking. Our planes were ill equipped for night navigation, and there was a knack to dead reckoning in a blackout. I seemed to have it, and I suppose they thought I'd be of more value passing it on to others.

My replacement was a boy of no more than my own age, also straight out of training. His name was Terriss. He, the plane, and its entire crew were lost on the next mission. I fretted out the rest of the war in one classroom or another.

And was still doing that, I supposed.

How long now? Thirty seconds, perhaps. I breathed out, and then drew warm air back in from the bag.

It tasted of rubber and canvas. A stale taste. The rebreather air was oddly unsatisfying, but its recirculation relieved the aching pressure that had been building up in my lungs.

I looked across at one of the empty seats, and the shadows in the harness looked back.

That's how it was. I'm not saying I saw an actual shape there. But the shadows fell as if playing over one. I turned my head to look at the other empty seat on that side of the cabin, and the figure in it raised its head to return my gaze.

The blood was pounding in my ears. I was forgetting the drill with the rebreather. Light glinted on the figure's flying goggles. On the edge of my vision, which was beginning to close in as the oxygen ran down, I was aware of someone in the third and last seat in the cabin right alongside me.

That was enough. I didn't stop to think. I admit it, I just panicked. All procedure was gone from my head. I just wanted to get out of there and back up to the surface. I was not in control of the situation. I wondered if I was hallucinating, much as you can know when you're in a nightmare and not have it help.

Now I was gripping the sides of the bucket seat and trying to heave myself out of it but, of course, the harness held me in. My reaction was a stupid one. It was to try harder, over and over, slamming against resistance until the webbing cut into my shoulders and thighs. I was like a small child, angrily trying to pound a wooden peg through the wrong shape of hole.

Panic was burning up my oxygen. Lack of oxygen was making my panic worse. Somewhere in all of this I managed the one clear thought that I was never going to get out of the Box if I didn't unbuckle my harness first.

It was at this point that the non-existent figure in the seat opposite leaned forward. In a smooth, slow move, it reached out and placed its hand over my harness release. The goggled face looked into my own. Between the flat glass lenses and the mask, no part of its flesh could be seen. For a moment I believed that it had reached over to help me out. But it kept its hand there, covering the buckle. Far from helping me, it seemed intent on preventing my escape.

I felt its touch. It wore no gloves. I'd thought that my own hand might pass through it as through a shadow, but it was as solid as yours or mine. When I tried to push it aside, it moved beneath my own as if all the bones in it had been broken. They shifted and grated like gravel inside a gelid bag.

When I tried to grab it and wrench it away, I felt its fingers dig in. I was trying with both hands now, but there was no breaking that grip. I somehow lost the rebreather mouthpiece as I blew out, and saw my precious breath go boiling away in a gout of bubbles. I wondered if Buster would see them break the surface but of course they wouldn't, they'd just collect and slide around inside the floorpan of the Box until it was righted again.

I had a fight not to suck water back into my emptied lungs. Some dead hand was on my elbow. It had to be one of the others. It felt like a solicitous touch, but it was meant to hamper me. Something else took a firm grip on my ankle. Darkness was overwhelming me now. I was being drawn downward into an unknown place.

And then, without sign or warning, it was over. The Box was revolving up into the light, and all the water was emptying out through every space and opening. As the level fell, I could see all around me. I could see the other seats, and they were as empty as when the session had begun.

I was still deaf and disoriented for a few seconds, and it lasted until I tilted my head and shook the water out of my ears. I had to blow some of it out of my nose as well, and it left me with a sensation like an ice cream headache.

My harness opened easily, but once I'd undone it I didn't try to rise. I wasn't sure I'd have the strength. I gripped the seat arms and hung on as the Box was lowered.

I was still holding on when Buster Brown looked in though one of the window holes and said, "What happened?"

"Nothing," I said.

He was not impressed. "Oh, yes?"

"Had a bit of a problem releasing the buckle. Something seemed to get in the way."

"Like what?"

"I don't know."

He looked at the unsecured harness and said, "Well, it seems to be working well enough now."

I'd thought I could brazen it through, but my patience went all at once. "Just leave it, will you?" I exploded, and shoved him aside as I climbed out.

I never did tell Buster what I'd seen. That lost me his friendship, such as it was. I went on sick leave for three weeks, and during that time I applied for a transfer to another department. My application was successful, and they moved me onto the firefighting course. If they hadn't, I would have resigned altogether. There was no force or duty on earth that could compel me into the tank or anywhere near the Box again.

The reason, which I gave to no one, was simple enough. I knew that if I ever went back, they would be waiting. Terriss, and all the others in my crew. Though the choice had not been mine, I had taken away their luck. Now they kept a place for me amongst them, there below the sea.

Wherever the sea might be found. Far from being haunted, the Box was a kind of tabula rasa. It had no history, and it held no ghosts. Each man brought his own.

My days are not so different now. As before they begin in the classroom, with forms and briefings and breathing apparatus drill. Then we go out into the grounds, first to where a soot-stained, mocked-up tube of metal stands in for a burning aircraft, and then on to a maze of connected rooms which we pump full of smoke before sending our students in to grope and stumble their way to the far exit.

They call these rooms the Rat Trap, and they are a fair approximation of the hazard they portray. Some of the men emerge looking frightened and subdued. When pressed, they speak of presences in the smoke, of unseen hands that catch at their sleeves and seem to entreat them to remain.

I listen to their stories. I tell them that this is common.

And then I sign their certificates and let them go.

• • • •

She had been dead for over seventy years, and she would be dead forever and forever.

Ancestor Money
Maureen F. McHugh

In the afterlife, Rachel lived alone. She had a clapboard cabin and a yard full of gray geese which she could feed or not and they would do fine. Purple morning glories grew by the kitchen door. It was always an early summer morning and had been since her death. At first, she had wondered if this were some sort of Catholic afterlife. She neither felt the presence of God nor missed his absence. But in the stasis of this summer morning, it was difficult to wonder or worry, year after year.

The honking geese told her someone was coming. Geese were better than dogs, and maybe meaner. It was Speed. "Rachel?" he called from the fence.

She had barely known Speed in life—he was her husband's uncle and not a person she had liked or approved of. But she had come to enjoy his company when she no longer had to fear sin or bad companions.

"Rachel," he said, "you've got mail. From China."

She came and stood in the doorway, shading her eyes from the day. "What?" she said.

"You've got mail from China," Speed said. He held up an envelope. It was big, made of some stiff red paper, and sealed with a darker red bit of wax.

She had never received mail before. "Where did you get it?" she asked.

"It was in the mailbox at the end of the hollow," Speed said. He said "holler" for "hollow." Speed had a thick brush of wiry black hair that never combed flat without hair grease.

"There's no mailbox there," she said.

"Is now."

"Heavens, Speed. Who put you up to this?" she said.

"It's worse 'n that. No one did. Open it up."

She came down and took it from him. There were Chinese letters going up and down on the left side of the envelope. The stamp was as big as the palm of her hand. It was a white crane flying against a gilt background. Her name was right there in the middle in beautiful black ink.

Rachel Ball
b. 1892 d. 1927
Swan Pond Hollow, Kentucky
United States

Speed was about to have apoplexy, so Rachel put off opening it, turning the envelope over a couple of times. The red paper had a watermark in it of twisting Chinese dragons, barely visible. It was an altogether beautiful object.

She opened it with reluctance.

Inside it read: Honorable Ancestress of Amelia Shaugnessy: an offering of death money and goods has been made to you at Tin Hau Temple in Yau Ma Tei, in Hong Kong. If you would like to claim it, please contact us either by letter or phone. HK8-555-4444.

There were more Chinese letters, probably saying the same thing.

"What is it?" Speed asked.

She showed it to him.

"Ah," he said.

"You know about this?" she asked.

"No," he said, "except that the Chinese do that ancestor worship. Are you going to call?"

She went back inside and he followed her. His boots clumped on the floor. She was barefoot and so made no noise. "You want some coffee?" she asked.

"No," he said. "Are you going to write back?"

"I'm going to call," she said. Alexander Graham Bell had thought that the phone would eventually allow communication with the spirits of the dead, and so the link between the dead and phones had been established. Rachel had a cell phone she had never used. She dialed it now, standing in the middle of her clean kitchen, the hem of her skirt damp from the yard and clinging cool around her calves.

The phone rang four times, and then a voice said, "Wei."

"Hello?" she said.

"Wei," said the voice again. "Wei?"

"Hello, do you speak English?" she said.

There was the empty sound of ether in the airwaves. Rachel frowned at Speed.

Then a voice said, "Hello? Yes?"

Rachel thought it was the same voice, accented but clear. It did not sound human, but had a reedy, hollow quality.

"This is Rachel Ball. I got an envelope that said I should call this number about, um," she checked the letter, "death money." Rachel had not been able to read very well in life, but it was one of those things that had solved itself in the afterlife.

"Ah. Rachel Ball. A moment . . . "

"Yes," she said.

"Yes. It is a substantial amount of goods and money. Would you like to claim it?"

"Yes," she said.

"Hold on," said the voice. She couldn't tell if it was male or female.

"What's going on?" Speed asked.

Rachel waved her hand to shush him.

"Honorable Ancestress, your claim has been recorded. You may come at any time within the next ninety days to claim it," said the strange, reedy voice.

"Go there?" she asked.

"Yes," said the voice.

"Can you send it?"

"Alas," said the voice, "we cannot." And the connection was closed.

"Wait," she said. But when she pushed redial, she went directly to voicemail. It was in Chinese.

Speed was watching her, thoughtful. She looked at her bare feet and curled her toes.

"Are you going to go?" Speed asked her.

"I guess," she said. "Do you want to come?"

"I traveled too much in life," he said, and that was all. Rachel had never gone more than twenty-five miles from Swan Pond in life and had done less in death. But Speed had been a hobo in the Depression, leaving his wife and kids without a word and traveling the south and the west. Rachel did not understand why Speed was in heaven, or why some people were here and some people weren't, or where the other people were. She had figured her absence of concern was part of being dead.

Rachel had died, probably of complications from meningitis, in 1927, in Swan Pond, Kentucky. She had expected that Robert, her husband, would eventually be reunited with her. But in life, Robert had remarried badly and had seven more children, two of whom died young. She saw Robert now and again and felt nothing but distant affection for him. He had moved on in life, and even in death he was not her Robert anymore.

But now something flickered in her that was a little like discontent. Amelia Shaugnessy was . . . her granddaughter. Child of her third child and second daughter, Evelyn. Amelia had sent her an offering. Rachel touched her fingers to her lips, thinking. She touched her hair.

What was it she had talked to on the phone? Some kind of Chinese spirit? Not an angel.

"I'll tell you about it when I get back," she said.

She did not take anything. She did not even close the door.

"Rachel," Speed said from her door. She stopped with her hand on the gate. "Are you going to wear shoes?" he asked.

"Do you think I need them?" she asked.

He shrugged.

The geese were gathered in a soft gray cluster by the garden at the side of the little clapboard cabin where they had been picking among the tomato plants. All their heads were turned towards her.

She went out the gate. The road was full of pale dust like talcum powder, already warmed by the sun. It felt so good, she was glad that she hadn't worn shoes.

As she walked, she seemed to walk forward in time. She came down and out the hollow, past a white farmhouse with a barn and silo and a radio in the windowsill playing a Red's baseball game against the Padres. A black Rambler was parked in the driveway and laundry hung drying in the breeze, white sheets belling out.

Where the road met the highway was a neat brick ranch house with a paved driveway and a patient German shepherd lying in the shade under a tree. There was a television antenna like a lightning rod. The German shepherd watched her but did not bark.

She waited at the highway and after a few minutes saw a Greyhound bus coming through the valley, following the Laurel River. She watched it through the curves, listening to the grinding down and back up of its gears. The sign on the front of the bus said LEXINGTON, so that was where she supposed she would go next.

The bus stopped in front of her, sighing, and the door opened.

By the time she got to Lexington, the bus had modernized. It had a bathroom and the windows were tinted smoky colored. Highway 25 had become Interstate 75, and outside the window they were passing horse farms with white board fence rising and falling across bluegreen fields. High-headed horses with manes like women's hair that shone in the sun.

"Airport, first," the driver called. "Then bus terminal with connections to Cincinnati, New York City, and Sausalito, California." She thought he sounded northern.

Rachel stepped down from the bus in front of the terminal. The tarmac was pleasantly warm. As the bus pulled out, the breeze from its passing belled her skirt and tickled the back of her neck. She wondered if perhaps she should have worn a hat.

She wasn't afraid—what could happen to her here? She was dead. The bus had left her off in front of glass doors that opened to some invisible prompt. Across a cool and airy space was a counter for Hong Kong Air, and behind it, a diminutive Chinese woman in a green suit and a tiny green pillbox cap trimmed with gold. Her name tag said "Jade Girl," but her skin was as white as porcelain teeth.

Rachel hesitated for the first time since she had walked away from her own gate. This grandchild of hers who had sent her money, what obligation had she placed on Rachel? For more than seventy years, far longer than she had lived, Rachel had been at peace in her little clapboard house on the creek, up in the hollow. She missed the companionable sound of the geese, and the longing was painful in a way she had forgotten. She was so startled by the emotion that she lifted her hand to her silent heart.

"May I help you?" the woman asked.

Wordlessly, Rachel showed her the envelope.

"Mrs. Ball?" the woman behind the counter said. "Your flight is not leaving for a couple of hours. But I have your ticket."

She held out the ticket, a gaudy red plastic thing with golden dragons and black. Rachel took it because it was held out to her. The Chinese woman had beautiful hands, but Rachel had the hands of a woman who gardened—clean but not manicured or soft.

The ticket made something lurch within her and she was afraid. Afraid. She had not been afraid for more than seventy years. And she was barefoot and hadn't brought a hat.

"If you would like to shop while you are waiting," the woman behind the counter said, and gestured with her hand. There were signs above them that said "Terminal A/Gates 1-24A" with an arrow, and "Terminal B/Gates 1-15B."

"There are shops along the concourse," the Chinese woman said.

Rachel looked at her ticket. Amidst the Chinese letters, it said, "Gate 4A." She looked back up at the sign. "Thank you," she said.

The feeling of fear had drained from her like water in sand and she felt like herself again. What had that been about, she wondered. She followed the arrows to a brightly lit area full of shops. There was a book shop and a flower shop, a shop with postcards and salt and pepper shakers and stuffed animals. It also had sandals, plastic things in bright colors. Rachel's skirt was pale blue, so she picked a pair of blue ones. They weren't regular sandals. The sign said *flip-flops*, and they had a strap sort of business that went between the big toe and second toe that felt odd. But she decided if they bothered her too much, she could always carry them.

She picked a postcard of a beautiful horse and found a pen on the counter. There was no shop girl. She wrote, "Dear Simon, The bus trip was pleasant." That was Speed's actual name. She paused, not sure what else to say. She thought about telling him about the odd sensations she had had at the ticket counter but didn't know how to explain it. So she just wrote, "I will leave for Hong Kong in a few hours. Sincerely, Rachel."

She addressed it to Simon Philpot, Swan Pond Hollow. At the door to the shop there was a mailbox on a post. She put the card in and raised the flag. She thought of him getting the card out of the new mailbox at the end of the hollow and a ghost of the heartsickness stirred in her chest. So she walked away, as she had from her own gate that morning, her new flip-flops snapping a little as she went. Partway down the concourse she thought of something she wanted to add and turned and went back to the mailbox. She was going to write, "I am not sure about this." But the flag was down, and when she opened the mailbox, the card was already gone.

There were other people at Gate 4A. One of them was Chinese with a blue face and black around his eyes. His eyes were wide, the whites visible all the way around the very black pupils. He wore strange shoes with upturned toes, red leggings, elaborate red armor, and a strange red hat. He was reading a Chinese newspaper.

Rachel sat a couple of rows away from the demon. She fanned herself with the beautiful red envelope, although she wasn't warm. There was a TV, and on it a balding man was telling people what they should and should not do. He was some sort of doctor, Dr. Phil. He said oddly rude things, and the people sat, hands folded like children, and nodded.

"Collecting ancestor money?" a man asked. He wore a dark suit, white shirt and tie, and a fedora. "My son married a Chinese girl and every year I have to make this trip." He smiled.

"You've done this before?" Rachel asked. "Is it safe?"

The man shrugged. "It's different," he said. "I get a new suit. They're great tailors. It's a different afterlife, though. Buddhist and all."

Buddhism, detachment. And for a moment, it felt as if everything swirled around her, a moment of vertigo. Rachel found herself unwilling to think about Buddhism.

The man was still talking. "You know, I can still feel how strongly my son wants things. The pull of the living and their way of obliging us," he said, and chuckled.

Rachel had not felt much obligation to the living for years. Of her children, all but two were dead. There was almost no one still alive who remembered her. "What about—" she pointed at the demon.

"Don't look at him," the man said quietly.

Rachel looked down at her lap, at the envelope and the plastic ticket. "I'm not sure I should have come," she said.

"Most people don't," the man said. "What's your seat number?"

Rachel looked at her ticket. Now, in addition to saying "Gate 4A," it also said, "Seat 7A."

"I was hoping we were together," said the man. But I'm afraid I'm 12D. Aisle seat. I prefer the aisle; 7A—that's a window seat. You'll be able to see the stars."

She could see the stars at home.

"There's the plane," he said.

She could hear the whine of it, shrill, like metal on metal. It was a big passenger 747, red on top and silver underneath, with a long, swirling gold dragon running the length of the plane. She didn't like it.

She stayed with the man with the fedora through boarding. A young man in a golden suit, narrow and perfectly fitted, took their tickets. The young man's name tag said "Golden Boy." His face was as pale as platinum. At the door of the plane, there were two women in those beautiful green suits and little pillbox stewardess hats, both identical to the girl at the counter. Standing, Rachel could see that their skirts fell to their ankles but were slit up one side almost to the knee. Their nametags both said "Jade Girl." On the plane, the man with the fedora pointed out to Rachel where her seat was.

She sat down and looked out the window. In the time they had been waiting for the plane, it had started to get dark, although she could not yet see the first star.

They landed in Hong Kong at dawn, coming in low across the harbor which was smooth and shined like pewter. They came closer and closer to the water until it seemed they were skimming it, and then suddenly there was land and runway and the chirp of their wheels touching down.

Rachel's heart gave a painful thump, and she said, "Oh," quite involuntarily and put her hand to her chest. Under her hand she felt her heart lurch again, and she gasped, air filling her quiet lungs until they creaked a bit and found elasticity. Her heart beat and filled her with—she did not know at first with what, and then she realized it was excitement. Rising excitement and pleasure and fear in an intoxicating mix. Colors were sharp and when one of the Jade Girls cracked the door to the plane, the air had an uncertain tang—sweet and underneath that, a many-people odor like old socks.

"Welcome to the Fragrant Harbor," the Jade Girls chorused, their voices so similar that they sounded like a single voice. The man with the Fedora passed her and looked back over his shoulder and smiled. She followed him down the aisle, realizing only after she stood that the demon was now behind her. The demon smelled like wet charcoal and she could feel the heat of his body as if he were a furnace. She did not look around. Outside, there were steps down to the tarmac and the heat took her breath away, but a fresh wind blew off the water. Rachel skimmed off her flip-flops so they wouldn't trip her up and went down the stairs to China.

A Golden Boy was waiting for her, as a Jade Girl had been waiting for the man with the fedora. "Welcome to San-qing, the Heaven of Highest Purity," he said.

"I am supposed to be in Hong Kong," Rachel said. She dropped her flip-flops and stepped into them.

"This is the afterlife of Hong Kong," he said. "Are you here to stay?"

"No," she said. "I got a letter." She showed him the Chinese envelope.

"Ah," he said. "Tin Hau Temple. Excellent. And congratulations. Would you like a taxi or would you prefer to take a bus? The fares will be charged against the monies you collect."

"Which would you recommend?" she asked.

"On the bus, people may not speak English," he said. "So you won't know where to get off. And you would have to change to get to Yau Ma Tei. I recommend a taxi."

"All right," she said. People wouldn't speak English? Somehow it had never occurred to her. Maybe she should have seen if someone would come with her. This granddaughter, maybe she had burned ancestor money for Robert as well. Why not? Robert was her grandfather. She didn't know any of them, so why would she favor Rachel? That had been foolish, not checking to see if Robert had wanted to come. He hadn't been on the plane, but maybe he wouldn't come by himself. Maybe he'd gone to find Rachel and she'd already been gone.

She hadn't been lonely before she came here.

The Golden Boy led her through the airport. It was a cavernous space, full of people, all of whom seemed to be shouting. Small women with bowed legs carried string bags full of oranges, and men squatted along the wall, smoking cigarettes and grinning at her as she passed with the Golden Boy. There were monkeys everywhere, dressed in Chinese gowns and little caps, speaking the same language as the people. Monkeys were behind the counters and monkeys were pushing carts and monkeys were hawking Chinese newspapers. Some of the monkeys were tiny black things with wizened white faces and narrow hands and feet that were as shiny as black patent leather. Some were bigger and waddled, walking on their legs like men. They had stained yellow teeth and fingernails the same color as their hands. They were businesslike. One of the little ones shouted something in Chinese as she passed in a curiously human voice, and then shrieked like an animal, baring its teeth at another monkey. She started.

The Golden Boy smiled, unperturbed.

Out front, he flagged a taxi. The car that pulled up was yellow with a white top and said TOYOTA and CROWN COMFORT on the back—it had pulled past them and the Golden Boy grabbed her elbow and hustled her to it. Rachel expected the driver to be a monkey, but he was a human. The Golden Boy leaned into the front seat and shouted at the driver in Chinese. The driver shouted back.

Rachel felt exhausted. She should never have come here. Her poor heart! She would go back home.

The Golden Boy opened the back door and bowed to her and walked away.

"Wait!" she called.

But he was already inside the airport.

The driver said something gruff to her and she jumped into the taxi. It had red velour seats and smelled strongly of cigarette smoke. The driver swung the car out into traffic so sharply that her door banged shut. A big gold plastic bangle with long red tassels swayed below his mirror. He pointed to it and said, "Hong Kong in-sur-ance pol-i-cy," and smiled at her, friendly and pleased at his joke, if it was a joke.

"I've changed my mind," she said. "I want to go home."

But apparently, "Hong Kong insurance policy" was most, if not all, of his English. He smiled up into his rearview mirror. His teeth were brown and some were missing.

This was not what Rachel thought of as death.

The street was full of cars, bicycles, single-piston two-cycle tractors, and palanquins. Her driver swung through and around them. They stopped at an intersection to wait for the light to change. Two men were putting down one of the palanquins. In it was a woman sitting in a chair. The woman put a hand on one of the men's shoulders and stood up carefully. Her gown was a swirl of greenish blues and silvers and golds. Her face was turned away, but she was wearing a hat like a fox's head. There was something about her feet that were odd—they looked no bigger than the palm of a human hand. Rachel thought, "She's walking on her toes." The woman looked over towards the taxi, and Rachel saw that it wasn't a hat, that the woman had marvelous golden fox eyes and that the tip of her tongue protruded from her muzzle, dog-like. The light changed and the taxi accelerated up a hill, pushing Rachel back into her seat, queasy.

Narrow streets strung overhead with banners. The smells—dried fish and worse—made Rachel feel more and more sick. Nausea brought with it visceral memories of three years of illness before she died, of confusion and fear and pee in the bed. She had not forgotten before, but she hadn't felt it. Now she felt the memories.

The streets were so narrow that the driver's mirror clipped the shoulder of a pedestrian as they passed. The mirror folded in a bit and then snapped out, and the angry startled cry dopplered behind them. Rachel kept expecting the face of the driver to change, maybe into a pig, or worse, the demon from the plane.

The taxi lurched to a stop. "Okay," the driver said and grinned into the mirror. His face was the same human face as when they had started. The red letters on the meter said $72.40. And then they blinked three times and said $00.00. When Rachel didn't move, the driver said, "Okay" again and said something in Chinese.

She didn't know how to open the car door.

He got out and came around and opened the door. She got out.

"Okay!" he said cheerfully and jumped back in and took off, leaving the smell of exhaust.

She was standing in an alley barely wider than the taxi. Both sides of the alley were long red walls, punctuated by wide doors, all closed. A man jogged past her with a long stick over his shoulders, baskets hanging from both ends. The stick was bowed with the weight and flexed with each step. Directly in front of her was a red door set with studs. If she tilted her head back, above the wall she could see a building with curved eaves, rising tier upon tier like some exotic wedding cake.

The door opened easily when she pushed on it.

Inside was the temple, and in front of it, a slate stone paved courtyard. A huge bronze cauldron filled with sand had incense sticks smoking in it, and she smelled sandalwood. After the relative quiet of the alley, the temple was loud with people. A Chinese band was playing a cacophony of drums and gongs, chong, chong, chang-chong, while a woman stood nodding and smiling. The band was clearly playing for her. Rachel didn't think the music sounded very musical.

There were red pillars holding up the eaves of the temple, and the whole front of the building was open, so that the courtyard simply became the temple. Inside was dim and smelled even more strongly of sandalwood. A huge curl of the incense hung down in a cone from the ceiling. The inside of the temple was full of birds; not the pleasant, comforting, and domestic animals her geese were. They had long sweeping tails and sharply pointed wings and they flickered from ground to eaves and watched with bright, black, reptilian eyes. People ignored them.

A man in a narrow white suit came up to her, talking to the air in Chinese. He was wearing sunglasses. It took her a moment to realize that he was not talking to some unseen spirit but was wearing a headset for a cell phone, most of which was invisible in his jet-black hair. He pushed the mic down away from his face a little and addressed her in Chinese.

"Do you speak English?" she asked. She had not gotten accustomed to this hammering heart of hers.

"No English," he said and said some more in Chinese.

The envelope and letter had Chinese letters on it. She handed it to him. After she had handed it to him, it occurred to her that she didn't know if he had anything to do with the temple or if he was, perhaps, some sort of confidence man.

He pulled the sunglasses down his nose and looked over them to read the letter. His lips moved slightly as he read. He pulled the mic back up and said something into it, then pulled a thin cell phone no bigger than a business card and tapped some numbers out with his thumb.

"Wei!" he shouted into the phone.

He handed her back the letter and beckoned for her to follow, then crossed the temple, walking fast and weaving between people without seeming to have had to adjust. Rachel had to trot to keep up with him, nearly stepping out of her foolish flip-flops.

In an alcove off to one side, the wall was painted with a mural of a Hong Kong street with cars and buses and red and white taxis, traffic lights and crosswalks. But no jade girls or fox-headed women, no palanquins or tractors. Everything in it looked very contemporary; the light reflecting off the plate-glass windows, the briefcases and fur coats. As contemporary as the white-suited man. The man held up his hand that she was to wait here. He disappeared back into the crowd.

She thought about going back out and getting in a taxi and going back to the airport. Would she need money? She hadn't needed money to get here, although they had told her that the amount of the taxi had been subtracted from her money. Did she have enough to get back? What if she had to stay here? What would she do?

An old woman in a gray tunic and black pants said, "Rachel Ball?"

"Yes?"

"I am Miss Lily. I speak English. I can help you," the woman said. "May I see your notification?"

Rachel did not know what a "notification" was. "All I have is this letter," she said. The letter had marks from handling, as if her hands had been moist. What place was this where the dead perspired?

"Ah," said Miss Lily. "That is it. Very good. Would you like your money in bills or in a debit card?"

"Is it enough to get me home?" Rachel asked.

"Oh, yes," Miss Lily said. "Much more than that."

"Bills," Rachel said. She did not care about debit cards.

"Very good," said Miss Lily. "And would you like to make arrangements to sell your goods, or will you be shipping them?"

"What do people do with money?" Rachel asked.

"They use it to buy things, to buy food and goods, just as they do in life. You are a Christian, aren't you?"

"Baptist," Rachel said. "But is this all there is for Chinese people after they die? The same as being alive? What happens to people who have no money?"

"People who have no money have nothing," said Miss Lily. "So they have to work. But this is the first of the seven heavens. People who are good here progress up through the heavens. And if they continue, they will eventually reach a state of what you would call transcendence, what we call the three realms, when they are beyond this illusion of matter."

"Can they die here?"

Miss Lily inclined her head. "Not die, but if they do not progress, they can go into the seven hells."

"But I have enough money to get back home," Rachel said. "And if I left you the rest of it, the money and the goods, could you give it to someone here who needs it?

"At home you will not progress," Miss Lily said gently.

That stopped Rachel. She would go back to her little clapboard cabin and her geese and everything would become as timeless as it had been before. Here she would progress.

Progress for what? She was dead. So the dead here progressed, and eventually they stopped progressing. Death is eternity.

She had been dead for over seventy years, and she would be dead forever and forever. Dead longer than those buried in the tombs of Egypt, where the dead had been prepared for an afterlife as elaborate as this one. In her mind, forever spread back and forward through the epochs of dinosaurs, her time of seventy years getting smaller and smaller in proportion. Through the four billion years of the earth.

And still farther back and forward, through the time it took the pinwheel galaxy to turn, the huge span of a galactic day, and a galactic year, in which everything recognizable grew dwarfed.

And she would be dead.

Progress meant nothing.

It made no difference what she chose.

And she was back at her gate in Swan Pond standing in the talcum dust and it was no difference if this was 1927 or 2003 or 10,358. Hong Kong left behind in the blink of an eye. She wasn't surprised. In front of her was the empty clapboard cabin, no longer white-painted and tidy but satiny gray with age. The windows were empty of glass and curtains, and under a lowering evening sky a wind rhythmically slapped a shutter against the abandoned house. The tomatoes were gone to weeds, and there were no geese to greet her.

And it did not matter.

A great calm settled over her, and her unruly heart quieted in her chest.

Everything was still.

• • • •

There was no point in arguing cosmology with a three-year-old who
couldn't possibly conceptualize that an accepted pre-requisite
for being a ghost was being dead . . .

Dhost
Melanie Tem

The disembodied little voice on the phone made Gail's breath catch, so sweet it was, so complete and so vulnerable. "Guess what, Grandma?"

"What, Corry?" *Corazon. Heart. My heart.*

"Guess what I'm gonna be for Halloween?"

"What, Corry?"

"I'm gonna be a DHOST!" Corry shrieked with the utter delight of it, and Gail joined in the cascade of giggles that spun out then like the shimmering tail of a kite. Quite literally, she could not believe how much she loved this child.

How much she loved Corry's father was, by reason of familiarity and cost, entirely believable. She loved him steadfastly and, despite everything, with a brilliant core of joy. The pain he brought into the lives of everyone who cared about him and some who didn't—and, yes, the fear—were constants, but most of the time they no longer caused her real suffering. Loving detachment, the Buddhists called it. *I love you, Bryce. I keep myself open to loving you, and I protect myself from you. Both.*

"A dhost, Corry? Really?" This was entirely ingenuous, for one of the best things about being a grandparent instead of a parent was that you weren't required to correct these wonderful mispronunciations.

"Yes!" said Corry.

"Will you say 'Boo!' and scare people?"

"Yes!" said Corry.

"Say it to me."

"BOO!" screamed the child, and Gail gave a little cry, and they both laughed.

"Will you be all covered up in a white sheet with holes cut in it so you can see out?"

There was a pause. Corry's ghost costume was probably a white plastic cape with a separate plastic mask. Amused by her own snobbery, Gail reminded herself that this was a perfectly respectable way to be a ghost for Halloween; indeed, all her kids had, to her considerable distress at the time, pointedly eschewed her repeated offers of homemade costumes. Bryce had been a rubber-fanged vampire three years in a row. Or was that Matthew?

Evidently giving up any attempt to make sense of her grandmother's silly question about a sheet, Corry repeated smugly, "I'm gonna be a dhost."

"Will Grandpa and I get to see you when you're a dhost?"

Corry's "yes" was a bit less emphatic this time. Gail and Dennis weren't exactly friends with Corry's mother, having even less in common with her than with their son, absent the sparse shared history of pets, houses, vacations, the few memories that could honestly be called happy. But they were definitely family. Anna made sure they were part of Corry's life, even though Bryce had left her before he'd gone to prison this time—precisely when Gail would have thought you'd want somebody waiting on the outside, and Anna would have waited. If Anna had been her daughter, Gail would have strongly advised against waiting for a man like Bryce, her beloved son.

"A dhost," Corry repeated, maybe savoring the feel of the word or maybe having more to say on the subject. Or maybe it was just a placeholder, keeping the conversation going, making sure her grandmother didn't say good-bye. Gail waited. "A dhost," said Corry. "Like my daddy."

"Corry, your daddy isn't a ghost." Gail was almost angry.

"Yes," Corry insisted, and Gail could well imagine her stubborn expression, little brow furrowed, lower lip protruding. So like her daddy. "He is."

There was no point in arguing cosmology—questionable at best—with a three-year-old who couldn't possibly conceptualize that an accepted prerequisite for being a ghost was being dead. Her daddy wasn't dead. Bryce wasn't dead.

As far as we know, Gail thought against her will. *How would we know?* She couldn't quite stop herself from entertaining the possibility that Corry might know something, by virtue of her youth and canny innocence and adoration of her absent father; that she could be in touch with forces the rest of them couldn't or didn't dare access. Didn't she cry for him by name when she was hurt or scared, never mind that he'd been away for most of her life? Didn't she still announce, beaming, "My daddy's at work. He's coming home tomorrow," though she understood the concept of "tomorrow"? Given her relationship with this father she surely could remember in only the dimmest, most mythical way, was it such a leap to think she might have a mystical connection to him as well?

Leap or not, Gail knew better than to indulge thoughts like that. Bryce was hard enough without adding a supernatural twist.

There was always noise in the background at Corry's house, usually just the TV or VCR, sometimes argument or laughter. Now it spiked into gleeful shrieks. Corry squealed into the phone, "We're carving punkins, Grandma! Bye!" and was gone without hanging up. Gail held on for a few seconds, hoping Corry would think to mention to her mom that Grandma Gail was on the phone. No such luck.

While she waited, *I hope he is dead* came into her mind. *It would be better for everybody if he were dead.* Both the thought itself and the horror of it were weakened by repetition, and it was easy enough to let them go.

Eventually she replaced the receiver on the hook and went off to do something else. Whenever this happened, she tried not to imagine and certainly not to ascribe meaning to the wasted possibility for connection dangling on the other end of the line.

Halloween was cold, of course; no matter how bright and balmy the autumn, Trick-or-Treat night was invariably rainy, snowy, blustery, so coats obscured costumes and neither kids nor parents could stay out long enough for treat bags to get full. Every year Gail was reminded of the time one of the kids had come home after less than an hour out, shivering and miserable, and Dennis had hustled him into a long warm bath. A sweet, sad, poignant memory, especially if it had been Bryce.

Anna did bring Corry by at the end of the evening. When Gail opened the door, Corry yelled, "Boo!" from behind the plastic mask and under the hood of her jacket.

Gail and Dennis both jumped back and gasped. Anna and Corry came in, and Gail noted the younger woman's harried look and tightly controlled tone. "Could Corry stay with you for a few minutes while I run to the store? I think we need a break from each other." Anna tried a smile.

"Of course."

Corry had shrugged off her bundling outer garments and was spinning in the middle of the kitchen, making her ghost costume billow and scattering the occasional piece of candy out of her plastic pumpkin. Gail hooted, "Look! It's a spinning dhost"

The moment her mother left, Corry sang out, "I saw my daddy!"

Gail and Dennis exchanged a look, and Dennis asked with studied lightness, "You saw your daddy tonight? Where?"

"I saw my daddy! I saw my daddy!"

Careful to be gentle, Gail tried to stop the little girl in mid-spin. "Corry, listen to me. Where did you see your daddy?"

"He's a dhost, too, just like me!"

Dennis said, "What?" but Corry, still twirling, wouldn't repeat it. None of them knew what else to say.

Well past Thanksgiving, Corry insisted on wearing her ghost costume, to day care and to the grocery store and when she came to spend the night at Grandma and Grandpa's. Anna complained but couldn't see enough real harm in it to confiscate the thing, and Gail couldn't, either, though it made her uneasy. Sometimes you could hear the little girl singing and talking to herself about dhosts and daddies. But when Gail or Dennis tried to engage her in a conversation about her dad, she would employ every deflective technique known to a stubborn and inventive three-year-old, from chattering instead about her new shoes to sticking her thumb in her mouth and staring silently at them with wide eyes.

There was no word from Bryce. His letters from prison, always unreliable in every conceivable way—frequency, veracity, intent—seemed to have stopped altogether. His collect phone calls, always unpredictable because of his own or the prison system's vagaries, weren't happening at all; Gail checked every time she came home, and found no stern message informing them that an inmate was calling and the call would be recorded and press 1 to accept the charges.

"I miss my daddy," Corry sobbed. "My daddy's a dhost," she chortled. "I saw my daddy last night," she remarked.

Gail didn't mention any of this in her weekly letters to Bryce, though she was tempted if for no other reason than that, having nothing from him to respond to, she ran out of things to say. She sent him family news, not knowing whether he was or dared to let himself be interested. She wrote about Corry's intelligence and creativity and cuteness, and how Corry talked about him all the time—then worried that that might make him feel worse. She didn't, of course, know that he felt bad in the first place. Sometimes, when she was with him or talking with him on the phone or reading a letter from him, they seemed actually to connect, two such vastly different people. But now, in his protracted silence, she couldn't guess anything about him. He might just as well be a ghost.

Dennis didn't like to talk about this perpetually troubled son, and Matthew and Samantha, each after one or countless betrayals too many, claimed to have no use for their older brother. Gail broached the subject with Anna, with whom broaching any subject felt risky: "Corry seems to be talking a lot about her dad lately."

Guarded as always, Anna said, "Does she?"

"She keeps saying she sees him."

"He's still in jail, isn't he?" Gail supposed it was alarm that turned Anna's voice hard.

"I haven't heard otherwise. His sentence runs another three years."

"Yeah," said Anna. "Well."

A few days before Christmas, there arrived a card for "Mom. Dad, Sis, and Bro"—no note, just that salutation which without too much of a stretch could be called personal, and "love, Bryce"—and a couple of toys and a T-shirt with flowers on it, unwrapped, for Corry. Anticipating ebullience or upset—in any event, distraction—Gail waited until the last batch of star- and snowflake-shaped cookies was cooling on the racks before she said, trying not to make it a grand proclamation, "Your daddy sent you some Christmas presents."

Corry's flour-smudged face lit up. "He did? Presents? For me?"

Gail brought out the small bag, trusting Corry wouldn't notice that the wrapping paper was the same as on her gifts from Grandpa and Grandma. "Do you want to open them now?"

"Yes!"

She pulled the child onto her lap and set the packages one, two, three on the couch. Corry didn't reach for them or squirm, just sat up straight and stared at them, one hand absently on her grandmother's arm, the other thumb in her mouth. When Gail asked again if she wanted to open them, there was no response. When Gail tried to pull her close, she didn't resist, but she just allowed herself to be held. When Gail asked if she was all right, she gave a single tiny nod.

The T-shirt was too small, but Corry wore it as often as her mother would let her, sometimes several days in a row, according to Anna's exasperated report. Both toys were, Gail would have thought, bland and uninteresting, and in fact Corry didn't really play with them, just carried them around in her backpack. Anna said she slept with the pack.

A new ritual developed: "I like your shirt," Gail would say, and Corry would crow, "My daddy gave it to me" and Gail would answer, "Yes! He did!" And they'd hug each other.

It was just after the new year that Corry started disappearing. She was with Dennis the first time it happened. At his knee waiting for the popcorn, holding his hand until he needed both hands to pay, then she simply wasn't there. He bent to give her her Kids' Pack and she simply wasn't there. He called her name in the crowd. He searched the lobby, the video arcade, the men's and even the women's restrooms. No sign of her. Then he went back to the place at the counter where he'd bought the snacks, and there she was, right where she'd been, thumb in her mouth, eyes very big. When she saw him she raced to him and flung her arms around his thigh. "Where'd you go, Grandpa? Did you get lost?"

Squatting among the legs of the other moviegoers, Dennis held her tight. "Corry, Corry, don't ever run away from me like that!"

"Did not run away."

"You have to stay right by me all the time. You're too little to go off by yourself."

"Was not by myself, Grandpa." Her voice against his shoulder was firm.

"Who were you with? You know not to go off with strangers—"

"My daddy," she said into his neck.

Dennis held her away from him to look into her tear-streaked, somehow luminous little face. "Corry, stop it now. Your daddy isn't here."

"He is, too! He said to go with him, just for a minute, and he's my daddy so it's okay."

"Your daddy's not here. He's in jail."

She shook her head vehemently and burrowed against him. Unsure of the best way to respond, Dennis opted not to. He carried Corry who carried the snacks, and they managed to miss only a few minutes of the previews. She seemed to enjoy the movie, and he loved cartoons as much as she did.

In the car on the way home, he carefully brought it up again. "Where did you really go when you got lost from me, honey? I won't be mad. I just need to know the truth." Very softly she said something about her daddy. Dennis couldn't hear the rest. He decided to try, "Where did your daddy take you?"

"Somewhere."

Telling Gail about it later, Dennis confessed, "I guess I panicked a little. I said, 'Where? What did it look like? What did your daddy say about it?' But you know how she is. When she doesn't want to talk about something, you don't talk about it."

Before she thought, Gail observed, almost fondly, "Just like her dad."

Not for the first time he snapped, "Corry is not Bryce."

Gail had not meant it as a hex. "No," she said. "She's not."

"Then she started singing about the cars and trucks on the road—"

"Red truck, blue car, white car, blue truck," they chanted together, and laughed, in uneasy delight.

"—and she wouldn't say any more."

In that sweet little patch of sunlight through their kitchen window, Gail put her arms around him, and they held each other, swaying slightly as if to gentle music. Each knew the other was thinking of Corry and Corry's father and whether this would be the moment upon which they looked back as the beginning of Corry's trouble. There were several such moments with Bryce.

But the value of hindsight was minimal and imperfect; even if you saw the future, you still wouldn't know what to do. "Three-year-olds wander off all the time," they assured each other. "Three-year-olds have vivid imaginations. Should we tell Anna? I guess we have to tell Anna," both of them feeling allied with Corry. "Of course we do."

Anna's response was grim. They never knew how she handled it with Corry, but Corry stopped talking about her daddy and she didn't run off again. The disappearances, however, continued, in altered form.

"Look at her hair!" Anna's usual impatience with Corry had hardened into disgust. She all but jerked the child forward, and her tug on the furry little hood was nearly a violent act. The curly dark hair, Anna's pride and joy more than her daughter's, was six inches shorter on one side than on the other, and ragged.

When Gail's hand went to the ravaged place, her granddaughter flinched. "Oh, my," Gail said mildly. "Did you cut your hair?"

Corry shook her head and started to put her thumb in her mouth, but her mother slapped it down. "Now I've got to spend money I don't have on a haircut."

"Would it be okay if I did it?"

"Do you know how to cut hair?"

Gail almost said she used to cut Bryce's. "I've cut a lot of little heads of hair in my time."

"Fine, sure, whatever. I'm late." Anna dropped a brusque kiss onto her daughter's forehead and strode out the door.

Corry didn't object to having her hair cut. She let Gail lift her onto the high kitchen stool, drape a towel around her neck, spray her head with water, comb out the poor chopped locks and the rest of the tangled mass. She cried out once or twice when the comb caught especially hard, but otherwise she was silent.

Getting no response to her "We'll make it look nice" and "You'll look cute in short hair" and "The thing about hair is, it grows again," she finally ventured, "I remember when your daddy cut his own hair and I had to cut it really, really short."

This elicited a tiny, tentative giggle. Encouraged, Gail went on as she made the first terrible cut on the undamaged side and ringlets fell glossy and stomach-wrenching to the floor.

"He looked almost bald."

"He did?"

"I have a picture of him. I'll show you."

"My daddy cutted my hair."

Surely the child could feel her stiffen and try to hide it. "Your daddy?"

"He wanted my hair. He likes it."

"Your daddy cut your hair and took it with him?"

Corry's nod pulled the hair stretched in the comb and made the scissor-snip crooked.

"Oh," Gail said helplessly. "Corry."

Gingerly she talked to Corry's mother about grief counseling, a subject far more intimate than they were used to. Anna reacted with seething incredulity, and the only change Gail and Dennis saw, which might not even be a result of the conversation, was that now Corry wouldn't talk about her father at all.

"As you can see from this picture," Gail wrote to Bryce, "she looks adorable with short hair. But this incident shows how much she misses you, how important you are to her. I'm enclosing a money order so you can buy stamps. Please write to her, honey." No doubt many things competed with stamps for that ten dollars—cigarettes; drugs, she supposed; outstanding bills to the prison system for dental work, haircuts, medical care, shoes; arcane debts to other prisoners. He didn't write.

Next it was the birthmark on the back of Corry's neck. Over the course of her lifetime, they'd tenderly called it a butterfly, a flower; tiny, pale pink and slightly raised, asymmetrically winged, not noticeable to anyone who didn't know it was there, it had been a sweet little family secret. Somewhat surprisingly, Anna had never seemed put off by it. Bryce used to kiss it, an image Gail treasured even as it broke her heart.

Now the birthmark was gone. Dennis noticed it when he was toweling Corry off after a bath. Using the excuse of a hair trim, Gail confirmed for herself what he'd told her. The little neck was smooth and unmarked.

"Maybe it just faded naturally," they said to each other. This time, though they knew it was wrong, they didn't mention it to her mother, and Gail couldn't think how to tell Bryce.

Gail invited Corry to plant pansies with her one afternoon in early April, taking a chance on both the weather and the child. She always bought the ones with faces, black on yellow, yellow on purple, and took great delight in pointing them out to whichever child over the years had been with her. Corry didn't quite seem to see faces but took delight anyway. The sun was high and bright in the southern sky, warm on the boards of the deck. When they dug in the wet dirt it smelled like spring. Gail's shadow was long, low, fat. Corry had no shadow.

Could that be true? Gail brushed the dirt off her gardening gloves and, under cover of an embrace, moved the child into another and another and another angle in relation to the sun. Corry had no shadow. This time, Gail couldn't think how to tell anyone. She wrote to Bryce about planting pansies and watched for proof of a trick of the light, an optical or meteorological illusion. But the little shadow didn't reappear.

Within the week Corry had lost her voice. "One minute she could talk and the next minute she couldn't," Anna complained on the phone.

"Any other symptoms?" Gail wouldn't have been able to explain the horror that prickled her skin and forced her to sit down. "Fever? Nausea? Stiff neck or headache?"

"Nothing," Anna said flatly. "She's faking."

Days later Corry was still silently mouthing words, and now in frustration howling, also with no sound. Anna wouldn't look at her when she did that, Gail could hardly stand to watch, Dennis stared appraisingly and played intent one-sided word games. Dutifully, furiously, Anna took her to the doctor, who could find no physical cause and referred her to a child psychologist, at which Anna bitterly scoffed.

To Bryce, Gail wrote, "Corry hasn't been able to talk for almost two weeks. She doesn't seem sick, and the doctor can't find anything wrong with her. Any ideas?"

Of Corry, Gail inquired gently while they were coloring together one evening, "Sweetheart, can you tell me why you can't talk?"

Corry put her thumb in her mouth and shook her head.

"Can you draw me a picture about it?"

Corry started to shake her head again, then stopped, took the proffered orange crayon, and made careful lines on the paper. A lopsided circle with squiggles on top, a straight line and four slanted ones.

Watching the human stick figure take shape, Gail felt her heart race and her throat close. Her own voice sounded hollow in her ears as she asked, because she had to, "Who is that?"

But Corry wasn't finished drawing. Laboriously she made a vertical line below the figure, and then to its left, imperfectly attached, a curve like an opening parenthesis. A backwards D.

"Daddy," Gail breathed. She turned the child around on her lap to face her. "Corry, is that Daddy?"

A small, fearful nod.

"Did Daddy steal your voice?" She could scarcely believe what she was saying, or how plausible it seemed.

Tears in the brown eyes, thumb in the mouth, and an emphatic series of nods.

By Corry's fourth birthday in mid-May, Anna, worried now, but still not willing to concede that this wasn't just another way to make her life difficult, had had her seen by a second pediatrician and had made an appointment with a child psychologist. At the party, the three small guests made plenty of noise, but the birthday girl, running in the sprinklers and riding her new bike and playing with the clown, squealed and giggled eerily without a sound. When Anna stood her up against the bedroom doorframe to make a pencil mark for her height, they all saw that she had shrunk about half an inch since last year; no one said anything about it. There was no present or card from her father; no one said anything about that, either.

Gail wrote a short, furious, disjointed, not quite forthcoming letter to her son. "What are you doing, Bryce? What are you doing to your daughter? Today was her birthday. Did you forget? She can't talk. She's shrinking. Her birthmark and her shadow have disappeared." Tempted to delete that last bizarre sentence, she repeated hastily, "What are you doing?" then saved, printed, signed with love, and mailed the letter before she could change her mind.

Throughout the spring, more of Corry vanished or faded away. She lost weight. She forgot how to do things—count, write her name, button. At certain moments Gail thought she could almost see through her. Anna was frightened now, which made her angry, rough and sharp with Corry, sullen with Dennis and Gail, so they didn't hear much about what the psychologist and pediatrician and various specialists said, only that nobody knew what was wrong.

Then, on the Saturday before Father's Day, a letter from Bryce arrived. Dennis brought it in from the mailbox and they sat together to read it. But he had sent no message for them, and Gail wept. The letter was for Corry. Obviously they were supposed to read it to her, and of course they had to know what was in it before they did, so Dennis read it aloud.

"Baby girl," it began. Dennis's voice broke, and Gail was crying freely. "This is the hardest thing I ever had to do. I'm saying good-bye. I have to stay away from you. I'm bad for you. All I do is hurt you, even when I try not to. I love you so much. You won't ever hear from me again. I'm letting you go. Corazon. My heart. Daddy."

Telling Anna about the letter was a betrayal, but not telling her would have been more so. Predictably, she exploded in vile and not unjustified sentiments about Bryce that they'd never heard from her before though she must have thought them many times, must have said them to somebody not his parents, maybe—though they fervently hoped not, it seemed likely—his daughter. "Sure! Read it to her! She needs to know the truth about her father! Go ahead!" She didn't exactly hang up on them, but she might as well have.

They sat together, too, to read the letter to Corry, between them on the couch. Dennis read it first, and, when Corry didn't react, Gail read it again.

Both of them were crying. Corry was not. After a silence very long for a four-year-old, she removed her thumb from her mouth, took the letter from her grandmother's hand, studied it, pointed, and asked in a clear voice, "What's that word?"

That summer Corry learned to read, gained two inches and six pounds, grew her hair long enough that Anna could wind braids on top of her head. In the heat of the sun her birthmark returned, a butterfly, a flower, and her shadow skipped on the sidewalk ahead of or behind her or off to the side like a wing.

"My daddy's a ghost," she sang to her dolls, the "g" sound unmistakable, heartbreaking and wonderful. "A ghost! A ghost! My daddy is a ghost!" she chanted to the jump rope beat. Sometimes when she spent the night, Gail or Dennis would hear her crying, and would go in and lie down beside her and hold her close while she whispered, "My daddy's a ghost. He went far, far away. I miss my daddy."

More than ever, she said, "My daddy's a ghost," playfully, dreamily, in sorrow or in rage, as she grew accustomed to the knowledge that she really had lost him. But she did not again say, "Just like me."

• • • •

Some old things are best left buried and unrevived. Just because
it's old doesn't mean it's good; quite the opposite sometimes.

Mrs. Midnight
Reggie Oliver

What's the worst thing about being a celebrity? The intrusive press coverage? Forget it! I do. No. It's being roped into these charity projects, because nowadays you've got to be hands on, or they mark you down as a complete toe-rag. Oh, look at Lenny Henry, they say, look at Julie Walters: they weren't prepared just to swan around like celebs, they got their hands dirty, their feet wet: they endangered some extremity or other. And if you present a program like *I Can Make You a Star*, you're generally assumed to be someone who got where they are by being lucky, or sleeping with the right people, so you have to prove yourself all the more. Well, I got to be the presenter of *I Can Make You a Star* by sheer hard graft, and it tops the ratings because I am bloody good at my job. My qualifications: a first class honors degree in the University of Life, having passed my entrance exam from the School of Hard Knocks with straight A's in all subjects. That's the sort of bloke I am, as if anyone gives a flying fuck. Pardon my French. Anyway, that was why I was recruited to head up the Save the Old Essex Music Hall project.

The Old Essex: what can I say about the Old Essex? It's a glorious relic of those magical bygone days of Music Hall? No, it isn't. It's a filthy, rat-infested, dry-rotten, draughty, crumbling, mildewed dump that hasn't had anything to do with show business for well over a hundred years. Most recently it has been a hangout for winos and junkies; before that it was a warehouse and a motorcycle repair shop. Before that, God knows. The only reason it's survived is that some nutter slapped a preservation order on it. A few of its original features have remained intact, not that they're much to write home about. But I can't say all this, can I? I have to say something like: "It's an amazing piece of living history which must be revived to serve the needs of the modern community." Call me a cynic, if you like. I prefer the word *realist*.

The Old Essex fronts onto Alie Street, Whitechapel, and it was in some godforsaken courtyard round the back of it that Jack the Ripper did for one of his victims. Which one? Look it up for yourself. I have never understood why people should take the remotest interest in that squalid old monster, whoever he or she was. Eh? Well, why shouldn't it have been a *she*? I'm no sexist; I'm an equal opportunities sort of guy, me. I merely mention the fact, just to give you an impression of the kind of glorious, heritage-packed part of London we're talking about. As a matter of fact it was shortly after the Ripper murder that there had been a fire at the Old Essex, after which it stopped being a theatre, and embarked on its checkered history as a hangout for bikers and junkies. God knows how or why it escaped the Blitz: the Devil told Hitler to give it a miss, I reckon.

It was a mad March day when I first saw the Old Essex and the rain was blowing in great icy gusts across the East End. Even though it was eleven in the morning the sky was nearly black, and streetlights were reflected fitfully in the water-lashed pavements. There were three of us who got out of the minicab outside the Old Essex, all kitted-out with yellow hard hats, Day-Glo jackets, and torches. There was Jill, a bloke with the stupid name of Crispin de Hartong, and me, Danny Sheen, as if you didn't know. There was also supposed to be a camera crew, to film the whole thing for posterity, but their van had got lost—a likely story!—and they didn't show up till a lot later.

Jill was the reason I was in on the project, as a matter of fact. Her name is Jill Warburton and she has some sort of cultural adviser job in the Mayor's Office and had adopted this project as her baby. I hadn't much taken to her when she first rang me up because she had a posh accent, but at least she wasn't pushy so I invited her to come round to see me at my house in Primrose Hill. After a few minutes in her company I felt easier about her. I'm not saying she's a raving beauty or anything, but she looks nice. She's tall and quiet. She laughed at the jokes I made, and she wasn't faking it. That counts a lot with me. I know it sounds weird of me to say this, but she seemed to me like a good person. So I agreed to help the project, before almost instantly regretting it, and that was why I was here, about to inspect a derelict building in the pouring rain.

The other bloke tagging along, Crispin de Hartong, was there because he was an architectural expert. He was also a minor celeb who pronounces on that TV property makeover show, *Premises, Premises* . . . you remember: he's the poncy type who goes in for shoulder length blond hair, bow ties. and plumcolored velvet jackets. I got the impression that he had his eye on Jill, and maybe that didn't exactly endear him to me.

The frontage of the Old Essex is mostly boarded up now to stop the druggies getting in. Jill undid a number of padlocks and we entered. At least we're out of the rain, I thought.

We shine our torches around and immediately Crispin starts raving about pilasters and spandrels and architraves. I don't want to hear all this rubbish, especially as I know he is just showing off to Jill. I only want to look.

We are in what I suppose was once the foyer. It is quite a narrow space and everything has been covered at some stage with a thick mud-colored paint. The floor is covered in rubble and bits of plasterwork that have fallen from the ceiling, some of them quite recently, so I am glad we are wearing our hard hats.

Our feet crackle and crunch on the floor. The most powerful thing in this area is the smell: it's a mixture of damp, decay, dust, and death. You know when your cat has brought a dead rat or something into the house and has left its remains somewhere.

Then you get that awful sweetish smell that seems to stick in your nostrils and as you haven't the nose of a dog and your cat can't tell you, you drive yourself mad trying to find out where it is coming from.

The other thing that I don't like is that there's a draft that feels like it's come straight from the Arctic, but, like the smell, I can't locate its source. I wet my finger and put it up to gauge the direction, but it's no use. Now I have a numb finger.

"Let's go into the auditorium, shall we?" says Jill. She opens another temporarily padlocked door and we enter the Hall proper.

This is something of a shock. After the reeking claustrophobia of the foyer, it seems vast. The roof looks as high as a cathedral's and we can see a little without our torches because gray shafts of light come down at crazy angles from holes in the roof and from broken windows on either side high up. Through these shafts of light little sprinkles of rain fall down from outside like silver dust. We have come in under a gallery which curves in a great horseshoe around the auditorium supported by thin wrought iron columns. Facing us is the desert of an auditorium stripped of its original seating, and strewn about with all sorts of debris from its motorcycle and junkie days.

"Watch out for the odd used needle," said Jill. "As you can see we haven't even begun the clearing up operation."

Beyond the auditorium is an oblong black hole which I assume to be the orchestra pit and then the remains of a raised stage, its floorboards cracked and rotten, with a dirty great hole in the middle. Part of the stage is thrust forward into the pit beyond a great rounded proscenium arch behind which hang a few tattered threadbare remnants of curtains and stage cloths. Close to the stage, at either side under the wings of the gallery I can just detect the remnants of two long bars where customers once drank as they watched the entertainment. I feel as if I am breathing an eternity of dust and decay. I don't think I would have liked the place even when it was alive. It would have been too much like a giant version of those Northern clubs where I once had a brief inglorious career as a comic.

"Get off! We want the bingo, not you, yer boring boogger!" That voice from the past echoed in my head almost audibly. I look round at the others, half expecting them to have heard something, but they were just staring at it all. I was left to my own thoughts. The night I "got the bird" in that club all those years ago was the night I quit the show business for tabloid journalism. It was the best move of my life. And now I'm presenting *I Can Make You a Star*, and the man behind the "Get off . . . yer boring boogger?" Cancer, heart failure maybe: he had been a fat bloke with a face like a potato. I can see him now through a haze of booze fumes and cigarette smoke, and his voice still echoes. No, revenge is not sweet.

Meanwhile Crispin had said the thing that people always seem obliged to say when they enter some great cultural edifice: "What an incredible space!"

I was happy to be spared the necessity of saying this stupid, meaningless phrase myself. Anyway, Jill was paying no attention; she was on her mobile to the camera crew.

"Look, where the hell are you . . . ? Hold on, you're breaking up. . . . Look, just come now. . . . The doors are unlocked. . . . We'll be here for another . . . fifteen minutes—"

I shivered and said: "Wouldn't it be better to cancel them and come back some other time when the weather's a bit better?"

"No, I'm sorry, Danny," said Jill. "I just can't afford to waste them. We're on this incredibly tight budget."

I thought of offering to pay for the camera crew to come back later, much later, but something prevented me. I thought it might lower me in Jill's estimation, but why should I care about that?

"You know," said Crispin, pausing after this introduction in that way people do when they feel they have something incredibly important to announce, "I have a theory that this could be a very early Frank Matcham." He looked at me. "Matcham, you know, was the great theatre architect of the late nineteenth, early twentieth centuries and—"

"I know who Frank Matcham was," I said. I caught Jill's eye and she smiled, but even this little victory didn't make me any happier. I was cold, I needed a drink; I was beginning to hate the Old Essex with a passion. The idea of waiting around here for another quarter of an hour for a poxy television crew made me livid. I strode away from the other two towards the bar on the left side of the auditorium.

"Careful how you go," said Jill. "The floor can be a bit treacherous."

As I crunched over to the bar, I heard her and Crispin having an earnest discussion about Matcham and architecture: "The Old Essex was thoroughly renovated in 1877 by the firm of Jethro T. Robinson who was Matcham's father-in-law, and so it could be. . . . " I didn't want to leave those two together. After all, Crispin may have been a ponce but at least he was her age and her class; he wasn't a twice-divorced forty-year-old father of three, as I was. But I felt so angry.

What was I doing here? I shone my torch. The bar was in surprisingly good condition with a fine marble top, cracked in two places and thickly overlaid with dust, but otherwise intact. I began to shift a lot of debris to get behind the bar. I had this vague idea, you see, that I might find some ancient bottle of Scotch or Brandy, or something. A likely scenario! Even a bottle of Bass would have done.

I managed to squeeze behind the bar by shifting several wooden joists and a broken chair or two. It probably wasn't at all safe, but I didn't care. There were some shelves behind the bar into which I shone my torch. Their contents consisted mainly of rubble, the odd dead rat and, as Jill had predicted, a used needle or two, but at the back of one I thought I saw a wad of paper. I reached in a gloved hand and tentatively drew it out.

It was a sheaf of handbills from the Old Essex days. They were singed at the corners and buckled with damp but still legible. I was excited almost in spite of myself. The date on the top sheet was 1888, the year of the fire at the Old Essex, the year it closed down. The acts were listed and some of the names were familiar:

GUS ELEN
ALBERT CHEVALIER
MARIE LLOYD
DAN LENO
LITTLE TICH

Then there were others who were not known to me.

LITTLE Miss ELLEN TOZER
The Juvenile Prodigy

THE GREAT 'HERCULE'
Astonishing Feats of Strength

And then, this:

Mrs. MIDNIGHT
And her Animal Comedians

I don't know why, but that name Mrs. Midnight struck a chord somewhere. Was her name really Midnight? It sounded too good to be true. And what, for God's sake were "animal comedians"?

I looked up from the bar where I had laid out the papers and across to the stage. I was not shining my torch in that direction, but I thought I caught sight of someone sitting just behind the proscenium arch in what legits call the "prompt corner." It looked like a great bulky old woman with a shawl over her head and shoulders, wearing a floorlength dress, but I could barely see more than an outline in the gloom. The figure was leaning forward slightly and quite motionless. The face was completely obscured by the cowl of the shawl, but I had the impression that it was staring in my direction.

I flashed my torch towards the figure and saw at once that it had been an illusion. It was no more than a pile of furniture and junk covered by a tarpaulin. All the same it had been uncannily lifelike. I switched the torch off to recreate the effect, but the magic had gone. It just looked like a pile of junk covered with a tarpaulin.

"Are you okay, Danny?" said Jill.

As a matter of fact I was shaking all over, but I said: "Come over here! Look what I've found."

Jill was very excited by the old music hall bills; even Crispin was reluctantly impressed. I don't know why—to please Jill I suppose—but I said I would do some research into the playbills and the history of the theatre. Then Crispin started offering me advice about how and where to research. I let him go on a bit; then I quietly reminded him that I had been quite a successful journalist for over a dozen years, so I did know a little about the techniques of research. Crispin shut up, and again I thought I saw Jill smile.

Finally the camera crew arrived and we did some fake shots of us arriving at the Old Essex and being amazed. Crispin repeated his line about it being an incredible space and his Matcham theory. He wanted me to ask him who Matcham was on camera, but I wasn't playing ball. We were about to film my "discovery" of the playbills when the crew started to get technical glitches: jams in the camera, gremlins in the sound system, erratic variations in the light levels. The sound technician was particularly jumpy. At one point he said he had got the noise of some animal crying out in pain, perhaps a cat, on his cans; but the rest of us had heard nothing.

I know camera crews: they can be very touchy and difficult when they want to be. Perhaps it's because they think they are doing all the work and us guys in front of the camera are taking all the credit. I could see they were getting into a state, so I tried to calm them down, but it was no good. The sound man said straight out that the place was giving him "the willies." At this Crispin started to be very sarcastic until I told him to shut the fuck up. It was all beginning to get a bit hairy so I made a cutthroat gesture at Jill to let her know that I thought we should wrap. She understood immediately, gave the word and we cleared out. I wasn't sorry to go.

For about a week or so I put the Old Essex out of my mind. I was heavily into meetings with some producers about hosting a new Reality TV show called *Celebrity Dog Kennel.* Apparently they were finding it hard to sign up even the B and C listers who were asking silly money anyway. In the end it was Jill who spurred me. She rang me up and asked me how the research was going. I was vague but invited her to have dinner with me in a couple of day's time when I would tell her all about it. The following morning I took myself off to the newspaper library at Colindale.

I had already got the bare facts about the Old Essex from Mander and Mitchenson, that the theatre had suffered a very damaging fire on Saturday, December 1st, 1888, from which its fortunes had never recovered and it had been abandoned as a place of entertainment very soon after. So I began my researches by looking in the newspapers of that period for reports of the fire at the Old Essex.

Most of the national dailies contained little more than a few lines stating that the fire had been started shortly after the Saturday night performance and that there were no "human fatalities," but that one man, a Mr. Graham, had been severely injured. I did, however, come across a passing reference to it in a letter to *The Times* on December 5th, stating that: "the recent riot and conflagration at the Old Essex provides further evidence of the extreme unrest among the denizens of Whitechapel following the appalling murders recently perpetrated in that district." I presumed that the writer meant the Ripper murders, the last of which had been committed in November 1888. Rather fatuously the letter ended by urging the Metropolitan Police to "redouble their efforts in hunting down the person responsible for these unspeakable atrocities."

Eventually I tracked down a more detailed account of the fire in a local paper called *The East London Gazette.* Monday December 3rd 1888. In it I read as follows:

" . . . the evening's entertainment at the Old Essex was proceeding as normal when, towards the end of the bill, there was introduced an act known as *Mrs. Midnight and her Animal Comedians*. In it a lady by the name of 'Mrs. Midnight,' dressed as a gypsy vagrant (but in reality personated by a Mr. Simpson Graham) appears on stage with a number of animals, including a cat, a Learned Pig, a miniature bulldog, a cockerel and a Barbary ape. These creatures under instructions from Mrs. Midnight performed a number of astonishing mental and physical feats. Especially notable we are told was the 'Learned Pig' Belphagor who was capable of solving elementary mathematical conundrums with the aid of numbered cards. On this particular evening, however, parts of the audience, especially those who had been drinking at the bars, became restive and took against Mrs. Midnight. These vulgar objections reached their height while the Barbary ape, called Bertram, was performing the act of rescuing the miniature bulldog, Mary, from the top of a miniature tower of wood and canvas, designed to look like a castle keep. Coins and other small hard objects were thrown onto the stage, one of which hit Bertram, the ape. The animal was so provoked by this act that he became visibly agitated and having reached the top of the tower, instead of rescuing the bulldog, Mary, he bit her head off.

"That disgusting incident, needless to say, only incensed the troublemakers further and a full scale riot ensued. The local constabulary was summoned and the theatre was cleared. The artists appearing on the bill, which included Mr. Dan Leno, were led to safety, but Mr. Graham remained behind because he was fearful of being set upon by the mob who were indeed calling for him. It was at this point that smoke was seen to be coming from one of the dressing room windows at the back of the theatre, though precisely when and how the fire was started has been disputed. Our reporter who arrived on the scene with the fire brigade was told by one member of the crowd that the reason for the animus surrounding 'Mrs. Midnight' was that her impersonator Mr. Graham (formerly, we understand, a medical practitioner) was suspected by many to have some connection with the Whitechapel Murders, though quite why he should have fallen under suspicion we have been unable to ascertain. The gallant members of the Fire Service, under their leader Captain Shaw, soon had the fire under control and were able to spirit Mr. Graham away unseen by the crowd. However Mr. Graham is understood to have sustained severe injuries from the blaze and his entire menagerie of 'animal comedians' has perished in the conflagration."

As I was coming out of Colindale with my photocopy of the article I had a brain wave. My last job before TV celebrity took me to its silicone-enhanced bosom was as Showbiz Editor of the *Daily Magnet*. There I got to know Bill Beasely, the head of crime news. We had worked together on the Spice Girl Shootings and rubbed along fairly well. He wasn't a bad bloke if you could put up with his smoker's cough, and the fact that he smelt of gin and peppermints at nine in the morning. One of his fads was his fascination with the Ripper murders: he'd even come up with a theory of his own about it and done yet another Ripper book. I think his idea was that it was Gladstone and Queen Victoria in collaboration, which is loony of course, but not as loony as that daft American bint who thinks it was Sickert the painter. (I happen to own a Sickert. I'm not a complete muppet.) I thought Bill might know about this Graham bloke if he was a suspect.

I gave him a ring and he asks me over. I suggest meeting in a pub, but he insists I come to his flat. I don't want to go because Bill is a bachelor—well so am I at the moment, but you know what I mean—and a bit of a slob and lives at the wrong end of Islington.

My worst fears are confirmed. There is even some old gypsy tramp woman with a filthy plaid shawl over her head crouching on his doorstep. She holds out her hand, palm upwards for cash. Luckily Bill buzzes me up fairly quickly when I ring the doorbell. His flat is on the top floor and is everything I had been dreading, and more. It is all ashtrays, booze bottles and books, plus a sofa and a couple of armchairs that, like Bill, were bulging in all the wrong directions. The books are everywhere. They look as if they'd spread out from the ceiling-high shelves like some sort of self-perpetuating fungus. It is ten in the morning and Bill offers me a Gin and Tonic. He's barely changed in five years: a bit more flab maybe, a more phlegm-filled cough. I ask if I could have a tea or coffee.

He looks at me as if I'd demanded quail sandwiches and an avocado pear, but wanders into the kitchen to light the gas for the kettle.

"Does that gypsy woman regularly camp out on your doorstep?" I asked.
"Who?"

I went to the window to point her out to him but she'd gone.

Bill managed to make some proper coffee in one of those percolator things, but it was still filthy. When I mentioned what I was here about, Graham and the Ripper connection, he became all excited. What is it about Jack the Ripper and some people? He started pacing round the room, talking enthusiastically and pulling books out of the shelves.

"Ah, yes. Well of course Dr. Graham is known to ripperologists, but he comes fairly low down on the list of possible suspects, mainly because we don't know much about him. But this new stuff you've dug up is fascinating. Perhaps you and I could collaborate on a new Ripper book about it?"

Not wanting to put him off at this early stage, I merely shrugged. "You called him 'Doctor' Graham?" I said.

"Yes. He was a doctor. Struck off, if I remember rightly. Of course being a doctor is always a plus when it comes to Ripper suspects. Anatomical expertise, you see. Knowing how to cut up bodies." He is leafing through a rather squalid looking giant paperback entitled *The A to Z of Ripperology*. "Where are we? Ah, here we are! 'Graham, Dr. Simpson S. Date of birth unknown.' That ought to be easy enough to find out. 'Medical practitioner with eccentric theories. Devised a treatment known as *zoophagy* in which patients were treated by being fed organs from still living animals, by means of vivisection.' Bloody hell, that's absolutely disgusting!" Bill, the ripperologist, seemed genuinely shocked. "'Wrote a book on the subject: *A Treatise on Brain Food, Or the Benefits of Zoophagy Explained* . . .' Etcetera, etcetera. 'Struck off the register for misconduct towards a female patient. Thought to have been suffering from the early stages of tertiary syphilis . . .' Ah! Listen to this! 'Became an entertainer known as "Mrs. Midnight" who performed with a troupe of trained animals. The times and locations of his appearance at various East London music halls were said to have coincided with some of the Ripper murders, but this has not been confirmed. It is believed that he died in 1889 or 1890 in an institution for the insane, having been injured by fire in an accident.' He gets two bleeding daggers out of five on the Suspect Rating. Wait a minute, there's a book referred to here in the bibliography: *Quacks and Charlatans, Alternative Medicine in late Nineteenth Century England* by Harrison Bews. Might be worth a look."

He then asked me why I was so keen on the Old Essex project. I tried to sound genuinely enthusiastic, but I think he saw through it.

After a pause he said: "The thing these restoration nuts don't get is that some old things are best left buried and unrevived. Just because it's old doesn't mean it's good; quite the opposite sometimes. I come from down that way myself, and my old Dad wouldn't go near the Old Essex. He never really told me why, but he did say that just after the war they tried to turn it back into a theatre or something. I don't know what happened exactly, but he said it was a disaster."

That afternoon I rang Jill and proposed that we should meet for dinner in the evening at my local gastro-pub, The Engineer in Primrose Hill. I thought dinner at my house might seem a bit forward for her. She accepted.

Sometimes I'm a good judge, though that's not what people say about me in *I Can Make You a Star,* but I thought Jill would like The Engineer and she did. The food's well cooked and imaginative, all organic of course and that sort of rubbish; but it's classy and modern without being pretentious and overpriced. She seemed in her element there.

You know how when you meet someone and you go away and start fantasizing about them; then when you meet them again it's a terrible letdown? With Jill, it was the opposite. She was even better. I don't want to go on about it but everything about her was somehow clear: clear skin, clear eyes, clear laugh. She dressed nicely but obviously didn't worry much about her appearance. Her hair was mousy colored, not dyed.

Immediately I wanted to start talking about her and me, but I knew this would be fatal, so I told her about my researches. She gave me her full attention and seemed thrilled by the information I gave.

I said: "You don't think it's all a bit sordid and sinister?"

"Good grief no! Fascinating stuff. It all helps to raise the profile. There's no such thing as bad publicity. You of all people should know that."

I could tell she was teasing me, which I liked, but it was in the way you tease a favourite uncle, not a friend, or a lover.

Still, I had done well, so I told her grandly that there were a couple of books I thought I would look out at the British Library which might help. She stretched out her hand and touched mine.

"You know, when somebody suggested you to help raise money for the Old Essex, I didn't like the idea. I thought you would be, well . . . I mean, your reputation, the kind of programs you do . . . "

"I know. A case of Pride and Prejudice on your part."

"Well, sort of. Not that I'd exactly describe you as Mr. Darcy."

"You wound me, Jill."

We both laughed, but she had wounded without knowing.

Then we discussed the practicalities of fund-raising events, television air time, recruiting other "names" to support the cause and all the rest of it. I realized that by now it was far too late for me to bow out of the Old Essex project, even if I wanted to, but I couldn't because it would mean losing her. Then at the coffee stage, she said something, though I can't remember how it came up. Mature people are supposed to take these things better than the young, but I don't think that's true.

She said: "By the way, you may as well know, I'm engaged to Crispin."

"Crispin de Hartong?"

"That's right."

"But you can't!" The words were out before I could stop myself. She seemed amused rather than shocked by my reaction.

"Why not?"

"Because he's a pretentious pillock."

"Actually, he's really rather sweet when you get to know him."

There was something very steely about the way she said that.

I had offended her, so I apologized. Then I told her gently that in my very humble opinion I thought she deserved better.

"Thank you for your fatherly concern," she said coolly.

"I hope I'm more than a father to you."

"What do you mean by that?"

Quickly I said: "And what does *your* father think about it all?"

"My father is dead; my mother lives in Leamington Spa," she added, as if that explained the situation.

"I see."

She giggled. I laughed. The rest of that evening would have been pleasant in a trivial sort of way if I hadn't felt this great weight on my chest, brought on by her announcement. It was only then, I think, that I admitted to myself how much I felt about Jill. It often happens that when you confess to yourself, your feelings come to be like a physical pain. Call it heart ache if you like; I won't. Since I stopped working for the tabloids I've tried to avoid clichés like the plague.

Shortly after eleven I put Jill into a taxi outside The Engineer, and kissed her chastely on the cheek. This was not like me at all. Then I walked slowly back to my house. I took a long way round so that I could think, but I didn't really think at all. My mind was too full of Jill, and what a pillock Crispin was. I have a little Georgian terraced house in Princess Road. It was one of those ones with railings along the front and steps going up to the front door. I was quite some way off when I noticed that someone was sitting on my steps. It was no more than a squat black shadow in a long dress from this distance. A ridiculous hope that it might be Jill vanished almost as soon as it came. The figure was motionless. Perhaps someone had just dumped some black bin bags on my doorstep, but no; the form was too precise. It must be a tramp and I would have to give her or him something before they cleared off. The thought enraged me. Hadn't I enough problems already?

As I approached I could see more clearly what it was. It was dark of course but there was enough light from the street lamps for me to tell. It was a tramp of some kind, a bag lady, except that she had no bags. She was a big bulky old woman in a rusty black dress. Over her head and shoulders was a plaid shawl, greenish in color I thought, but so dirty I could barely make out the pattern. It was only when I had come right up to her that I could see the face under the shawl and even then half of it was in shadow.

It was an old face, jowled and wrinkled with pale pendulous cheeks and a puckered, lipless, dog's bottom of a mouth. I could not see the eyes clearly as they were shadowed by the thick overhanging brow, but I sensed that they were looking at me fixedly. Something about the heaviness of the chin and the thickness of the nose was making me suspect that the figure in the dress was not a woman at all but a man. This was confirmed when it thrust out a hand, palm upwards, from the folds of the plaid shawl. It was a big, heavy, dirty man's hand and there were great scars on it like old burn marks.

He wanted money. Well, that was simple enough. I fished for pound coins in my pocket. Even so, the idea of coming close enough to this thing to give them filled me with loathing. I stretched out my hand to be able to drop the coins into his while remaining as far as possible from him, but just as I was about to let the money go he gripped my wrist.

It felt like a handcuff of ice. I screamed like a girl. I felt dizzy; I suppose I must have passed out; drink I suppose, but it had not been my imagination because when I came to I looked for the coins. They and the bloke in the dress had gone.

From that moment I became a driven man. The following morning I went to the British Library and ordered up *Quacks and Charlatans*, as well as *A Treatise on Brain Food*. In the B. L. catalogues, I noticed that Simpson Graham M.D. was also credited with another book entitled *Mother Midnight's Catechism*, so I ordered that as well.

Research is like fitting together the pieces of a jigsaw puzzle. *Quacks and Charlatans* had only a few pages about Graham, and was completely ignorant about his Music Hall Career, but it gave me this:

> He had been a brilliant if erratic medical student and early showed an almost insatiable desire to make his mark in the world. . . . Dr. Graham developed the idea that ingesting organs, in particular the brain, from a living animal was extraordinarily beneficial to human health. Several times he gave a demonstration before an interested and alarmed public in which he trepanned a fully conscious dog or cat, an operation which can, if skilfully done, be executed without much pain to the subject. He would then proceed to dip a spoon into the brain pan and devour the contents until the wretched animal finally lost consciousness. Many colleagues poured scorn on his unorthodox methods, but very few of them objected from an animal welfare point of view. . . . After his disgrace, he continued to give lectures and demonstrations on what he called *zoophagy* (the eating of a still living being), often doing so in female dress for no apparent reason. Doubts as to his sanity naturally grew and he was finally consigned to an asylum.

I only skimmed though *A Treatise on Brain Food, Or the Benefits of Zoophagy Explained* by Simpson Graham M.D. Something about the very act of reading it, even in the antiseptic surroundings of the B. L. seemed poisonous. I did gather from a cursory glance that Dr. Graham was no stylist and did a lot of boasting. All the same, I couldn't help noting down one passage which comes towards the end of this tedious little book.

If we could only overcome the contemptible prejudice against using our fellow human beings in such experiments I am convinced that the benefits would be extraordinary. At present criminals, condemned by law and society, are either executed or left to languish in unhygienic conditions, an unconscionably wasteful practice. How much better for us, and indeed them, if their living, palpitating organs and brain cells were to be used to refresh and rejuvenate a select few. With the skills that I have perfected, the suffering of the reprobates in question could be kept to a minimum; or indeed prolonged and exacerbated, if required, to point a necessary moral lesson. By ingesting these living substances and fluids the health and sanity of our finest men (and women) of genius would not only be enhanced but also greatly prolonged. Through this use of 'living brain food' as I term it, human lives of two or three hundred years might in the future, I sincerely believe, become a commonplace.

The third book, *Mother Midnight's Catechism* was subtitled *Zoophagy Explained to the Young*. Graham did not claim authorship on the title page, and I am not surprised. It is printed on cheap paper and decorated with crude, muddy woodcuts. Nearly all of it is in verse. It begins:

> How can you be big and strong?
> Hear then Mother Midnight's song . . .

Then there were a number of stories or anecdotes told in verse.

> Edward ate a living mouse
> And he learned to build a house;
> David downed a wriggling rat,
> And so he grew big and fat . . .
> Concluding with the moral:
> Make your meal off breathing things
> And become as great as kings.

The final set of verses tells the story of a boy called Alfred who catches his sister out in the act of cheating him at cards. Thereupon he ties her to a chair and proceeds to cut her open with his "trusty knife." It was all told in a light-hearted almost humorous way that was very difficult to gauge. How serious was the man being?

> Then he cut a slice of liver
> While she still did quake and quiver . . .

I wanted to be sick, so I started to skip this stuff, but I know it finished:

> When he'd eaten all his sister,
> Do you think that Alfred missed her?
> No, for all her wit and vigour
> Had been used to make him bigger.
> All his wants she could provide him
> By being safely there inside him.

I'd had enough, and I left the British Library in a hurry, nearly tripping over an old bag lady in the courtyard outside.

Then my mobile started to ring. It was Bill Beaseley. He seemed far away and his voice kept breaking up.

"Danny, I think I've found something which may . . . I'll send you a . . . " The phone went dead. I tried calling him but the line was engaged. On an impulse I rang Jill and asked if she would like to come to the recording of the final of *I Can Make You a Star* the following night.

"Great!" She said. "Can I bring Crispin too? I'm sure he'd be fascinated."

I bit my lip and told her I would have two tickets biked round to her that afternoon. I could have sold them on eBay for silly money.

The following morning a rather grubby envelope arrived for me by first class post. It could only be from Bill Beaseley. Sure enough, inside was a photocopy. (Bill was one of those Luddites who refuse to use PCs and e-mails.) On the back of it he had scrawled:

> "Page from a book called *The Complete Ripper Letters*, containing all the letters that were sent to the Police about the Whitechapel murders in both facsimile and transcript. This just may be the clue that clinches it!!! But don't forget, we go 50/50 on any book deal. All right, mate? Bill."

The facsimile showed a few lines written in a big scrawly handwriting on a scrap of paper. I got the feeling that the writer was trying to make his handwriting look rather more primitive and uneducated than it actually was. The legend above the facsimile read:

Note addressed to "Inspector Frederick Abberline at Scotland Yard," which arrived 3rd October 1888, three days after the double murder of Stride and Eddowes. It was dismissed as a hoax at the time as, though the message had been written in blood, it was found to be the blood of a cat.

Here was the message:

I have eaten some of the lights out of them girlies as you will see. I'd send you a morsel, Mr. Abbaline [sic], only it'd be long dead and won't be no use. Still we may meat, some time, but you won't know me from midnight as I'm not wot I seam.

That night was the Big One. Well, you all saw the final of *I Can Make You a Star*, this year, didn't you? The tenor in the wheelchair won it because of the viewers' phone-in votes, even though the judges and I thought it should have been the blind juggler. Anyway the audience ratings went through the roof. Jill and Crispin came round afterwards for the champagne do with all the celebs. Jill was excited by it all and just thought it was a hoot, but Crispin was being very snotty and stand-offish, I'm glad to say. I kept my eye on them and, when I noticed that they seemed to be having a little argument, I came over. He was bored and wanted to go home apparently, but she wanted to stay. So I touched her bare arm and took her to meet some of my famous friends, purely because they might help out on the Save the Old Essex campaign, you understand. She loved that.

I was feeling pretty good the next morning, even when the doorbell rang shortly after seven thirty. Those bloody tabloids, I thought, they'll be asking me to confirm some stupid rumor, or they want a picture of me looking rough in the altogether. I took care to dress carefully before I opened the door, but it wasn't the press, it was the police.

"Good morning, sir. Could we step inside for a moment . . . ? Do you know a Mr. Bill Beasely of Flat C. 31 Congreve Street . . . ? Well, the thing is, sir, Mr. Beaseley was found dead last night . . . murdered, sir. . . . There was a notebook on the desk and it was open at a page on which your name and address had been written. . . . I wonder if you could possibly account for your movements last night. . . . "

They actually asked me where I had been that night! I told them that my alibi was pretty impeccable as I had about twenty million witnesses to my whereabouts. Oh, says, the Inspector, all sophisticated, we thought those programs like *I Can Make You a Star* were pre-recorded. No, I said, you can check, it was all live, every fizzing second of it. I believe in live. If it isn't live it hasn't got that something.

I asked for details about poor Bill and they seemed happy to oblige. His skull had been split open with something like a meat cleaver and it looked as if part of his brain had been removed. That scared me, I must say, but I said nothing. They asked me if Bill had had enemies. No, I could not think of any enemies, but Bill had been a crime reporter, you know.

The next day I let the press have it, and by the time the late editions of the *Evening Standard* were on the streets, there was a nice little spread on the inside pages:

I CAN MAKE YOU A STAR MAN CLAIMS:
"I HAVE SOLVED RIPPER MYSTERY"

Well, not exactly, but near enough by press standards. I had given them a pretty coherent run-down of the evidence, and they got most of it right. The one thing I'm afraid I hadn't told them about was old Bill's part in my discovery, but I thought what with his murder and everything, it would just make things too complicated. I did feel bad about that for a while.

I had rung Jill naturally, and she seemed delighted by the news coverage.

"I'm beginning to think you're a bit of a star too," she said.

"You are too kind, Miss Bennett."

"By no means, Mr. Darcy." That was progress.

I discussed with her the television feature on the Old Essex and the Ripper suspect that I was arranging for the Local London TV News and the possibility of a full-length documentary.

Three days later Jill, Crispin, and I were down at the Old Essex with a camera crew. I had specially asked Crispin to come along as our "architectural expert," which pleased Jill.

Once again it was raining, but not as heavily as the last time. We decided to film indoors first and wait for it to clear to do the establishing shots outside in the street. I did my stuff to camera about this wonderful old building and how it was steeped in the rich history of the East End, and then Crispin did his architecture bit. I wasn't going to tell him that his material was bound to end up on the cutting room floor. He wasn't bad, but he was too fond of his own voice.

Then there was a lightening in the rain so Jill and the crew went out to do the establishing shots. Crispin and I voted to stay indoors and drink the skinny lattes the P.A. had got us from the nearest Starbucks.

So there we were, the two of us, alone in the auditorium of that great dirty old Cathedral of Sin. It was so quiet; you could almost hear the dust falling through the shafts of gray light. Somewhere in the deep distance traffic rumbled in a twenty-first century street, but it was miles and ages away. Crispin started to look at me very intently, so I looked back at him. He was not bad looking, I suppose, in a rather girly way, with his shoulder length blond hair and his pretty mouth. The looks won't last, though, I thought. I'm dark with good cheekbones. I may be forty, but I'm built to last. I go to the gym.

"You really are a little shit," he said. I was astonished, but I said nothing. Crispin went on. "You may as well know; you haven't a chance with Jill. She is, as you would say, 'out of your league.' You do realize that, don't you?"

He was expecting me to react, to say something, but I didn't. I just went on staring at him. He reckoned without the fact that I didn't get where I am today without being a bit of a psychologist. After a pause, he started up again, but not quite as confident as before.

"I know all about your efforts to impress her. Visits to the British Library; dinners at gastro-pubs, tickets to that truly ghastly show of yours. It won't do you any good, you know. She isn't remotely interested in you, never will be, and shall I tell you why—? Good God, what's that?"

"What?"

"Didn't you see it? Some sort of flicker of light, there on stage, just behind the pros arch."

No. Nothing. Then, yes, there *was* something. By the proscenium arch, I saw a yellow light flicker, like a candle flame.

Someone was holding a lighted candle on the stage. Then it began to move and we saw the outline of the thing that carried it. It was a big old woman with a long dress and a shawl over her head. Her back was to us. She looked like a huge huddled heap of old clothes. Slowly she began to shuffle away from us upstage.

"Excuse me!" said Crispin, in his best public school prefect voice. He was talking loud and slow as if to an idiot child.

"Excuse me, I don't know who you are, but I don't think you're supposed to be here. This is a listed building, you know! Excuse me!"

Then he started to move towards the stage.

"Christ, where are you going?" I said.

"I want to know what the hell's going on," he said. "Come on!" I couldn't stop him, so I just followed.

He climbed up onto the stage and I warned him about the floorboards. Dammit, there was a great hole in the middle of the stage; but he ignored me and I climbed up after him.

It was a funny thing. That great shambling lump of an old woman kept ahead of us the whole time as we threaded our way over piles of junk and rubble. We weren't able to catch up with her, but she was always in our sight. It was almost as if she were leading us somewhere. Crispin called out to her several times, but she simply did not react. She shambled on with her flickering candle.

When she got to the back of the stage she turned right and went through a narrow brick archway. There was now no light apart from the candle and our torches. Once through the archway we were in a backstage corridor. It was all brick, black with age or fire. To our right was a stone staircase up which we could see a flicker of candle and hear the heavy footsteps of the old woman ascending, accompanied by long groaning breaths.

Surely now we could catch up with her, so we plunged up the dirty, lightless stair, barely considering now what we were doing or why.

At the top of the steps we found ourselves in another dim, black brick corridor. And we were amazed to see that the old woman, now practically bent double and so headless to us, was halfway along it, about twenty yards ahead, hobbling away. We shouted at her, but on she went regardless.

The corridor smelt of something oily and old, and when I touched the wall by accident a black tarry substance stuck to my hand.

At last we were beginning to catch up with the woman when she suddenly stopped in a viscous looking puddle, turned and then started to climb yet another staircase to her right. When we arrived at the bottom of this flight we heard her steps cease and saw that she had halted ten steps up, her back to us. The groaning breaths were beginning to sound like some dreadful kind of singing. I thought I could recognize some words of the old Music Hall song:

> *Why am I always the bridesmaid,*
> *Never the blushing bride?*
> *Ding dong, wedding bells,*
> *Only ring for other gells . . .*

With little shuffles she was turning slowly round to face us, and I knew now that my worst fears would be confirmed. As she moved she let the plaid shawl slip from her head to reveal a greasy white cranium planted with wild tufts of white hair, sprouting like winter trees in frost on a barren landscape. Half of her face I had seen before. There was the heavy brow, the wild gray eye, the great blob nose, the thick mannish chin, but the other half was a mangled mess, an angry chaos of fiery scar tissue, utterly unrecognizable as a face at all. Mrs. Midnight lifted the candle to his head so that we could see it all.

> *Why am I always the bridesmaid,*
> *Never the blushing bride . . . ?*

Then he hurled the candle down the stairs towards us. I thought it would extinguish itself in the oily pool at the bottom of the steps. But it did not. It guttered for a moment, then a great tongue of flame leapt up from the pool and began to lick at Crispin's jeans. There was a roar and the next minute he was engulfed in flame. I took off my jacket and tried to smother the fire, but he was screaming and fighting me off. The only thing to do was to hurry him back down the corridor which was now spitting little gobs of flame from every tarry crevice. Before we had reached the stairs leading down to the stage, Crispin collapsed. First I beat out the fire on his body with my jacket, then picking him up in a fireman's lift I carried him downstairs. Behind me the flames were roaring like an angry ghost.

I had got down onto the stage level with Crispin on my back. I thought we were home safe so I began to run across the stage, but I had forgotten how rotten the boards were. There was a crack and suddenly we were falling into a pit. Crispin broke my fall a little, but I felt a sharp pain in my shoulder and one leg appeared to be useless. We were in the dark. I could see nothing, but there was a reek of corpses all around us.

I had a mobile in my pocket and was able to summon help. They told me later that Crispin and I had tumbled into a cellar where they had also found a large number of dead cats in various stages of decomposition. What was odd, they told me, was that so many of the cats had suffered injuries to the head. Some of them looked as if the tops of their skulls had been surgically removed. I did not want to know.

I had broken several bones in my body and needed a couple of operations, so I wasn't going to be pushed out of the hospital in a hurry as usually happens. I'm afraid Crispin was rather worse off. As well as other injuries, the fire had burned the beauty out of half his face. I genuinely feel bad about that.

I have a private room at the hospital, of course. In the evenings Jill, my angel, comes to see me with grapes or something else I don't really want, but I feel better for her coming. I want to say something to her so much, but I can't because I'm frightened of being turned down, rejected.

Get off! We want the bingo, not you, yer boring boogger!

And then, just recently, I have woken up in the early hours of the morning to find the great bulk of Mrs. Midnight crouched by my bed. From the folds of the plaid shawl Mrs. Midnight will take a kitten, still alive and mewing, and out of its trepanned head Mrs. Midnight will scoop a quiver of gray jelly with a teaspoon. "This is your brain food," says Mrs. Midnight. "Eat up!"

• • • •

He walked the hallways, thinking of everything that happened in the house,
so he wasn't all that surprised or shocked when he first saw the naked girl . . .

Tin Cans
Ekaterina Sedia

I am an old man—too old to really care. My wife died on the day the Moscow
Olympics opened, and my dick had not done anything interesting since the too
optimistic Chechen independence. I shock people when I tell them how young I
was when the battleship *Aurora* gave its fateful blast announcing the Revolution.
And yet, life feels so short, and this is why I'm telling you this story.

My grand-nephew Danila—smug and slippery, like all young people
nowadays, convinced they know the score even though they don't know shit,
and I always get an urge to take off my belt and wail some humility on their
asses—called and asked if I needed a job. Tunisian Embassy, he said, easy
enough. Night watchman duty only, since for business hours they had their
own guards, tall and square-chested, shining and black like well-polished
boots, their teeth like piano keys. You get to guard at night, old man, old
husk, when no one would see you.

Now, I needed a job; of course I did, who didn't? After the horrible
and hungry 1990, even years later, I was just one blind drunken stagger of
the inflation away from picking empty bottles in the streets or playing my
accordion by the subway station. So of course I said yes, even though Danila's
combination of ignorance and smarm irritated me deeply, just like many
things did—and it wasn't my age, it was these stupid times.

The Embassy was located in Malaya Nikitskaya, in a large mansion
surrounded by a park with nice shady trees and flowerbeds, all tucked away
behind a thirty-foot brick fence. I saw it often enough. The fence, I mean.
I had never been inside before the day of my interview. All I knew about
Tunisia was that they used to be Carthage at some point, very long ago, and
that they used to have Hannibal and his elephants—I thought of elephants in
the zoo when I paused by the flowerbeds to straighten my jacket and adjust
the bar ribbons on my lapel. There used to be a time when war was good and
sensible, or at the very least there were elephants involved.

There were no lines snaking around the building, like you would see at the American embassy—not surprising really, because no one wanted to immigrate to Tunisia and everyone was gagging for Brooklyn. I've been, I traveled—and I don't know why anyone would voluntarily live in Brighton Beach, that sad and gray throwback to the provincial towns of the USSR in the seventies, fringed by the dirty hem of a particularly desperate ocean. The irony is of course that every time you're running from something, it follows you around, like a tin can tied to dog's shaggy tail. Those Brooklyn inhabitants, they brought everything they hated with them.

That was the only reason I stayed here, in this cursed country, in this cursed house, and now stood at the threshold, staring at the blue uniforms and shining buttons of two strapping Tunisians—guards or attachés, I wasn't sure—and I wasn't running anywhere, not to Brooklyn, nor to distant and bright Tunisia with its ochre sands and suffocating nights. Instead, I said, "I heard you're hiring night watchmen."

They showed me in and let me fill out the application. There were no pens, and I filled it out with the stubby pencil I usually carried with me, wetting its blunt soapy tip on my tongue every few letters—this way, my words came out bright and convincing. As much as it chafed me, I put Danila's name as a reference.

They called me the next day to offer me the job, and told me to come by after hours two days later.

It was May then. May with its late sunsets and long inky shadows, pooling darkness underneath the blooming lilac bushes, and clanging of trams reaching into the courtyard of the house in Malaya Nikitskaya from the cruel and dirty world beyond its walls. I entered in a shuffling slow walk—not the walk of old age, but of experience.

And yet, soon enough there I was. As soon as the wrought iron gates slammed shut behind my back, I felt cut off from everything, as if I had really escaped into glorious Carthage squeezed into a five-storied mansion and the small garden surrounding it. A tall diplomat and his wife, her head wrapped in a colorful scarf, strolled arm in arm, as out of place in Moscow as I would be in Tunisia. They did not notice me, of course—after you reach a certain age, people's eyes slide right off of you, afraid that the sight of you will corrupt and age their vision, and who wants that?

So I started at the embassy—guarding empty corridors, strolling with my flashlight along the short but convoluted paths in the garden, ascending and descending stairs in no particular order. Sometimes I saw one diplomat or another walking down the hall to the bathroom, their eyes half-closed and filled with sleep. They moved right past me, and I knew better than to say anything—because who wants to be acknowledged while hurrying to the john in the middle of the night. So I pretended that I was invisible, until the day I saw the naked girl.

Of course I knew whose house it was—whose house it used to be. I remembered Lavrentiy Beria's arrest, back in the fifties, his fat sausage fingers on the buttonless fly, holding up his pants. Khrushchev was so afraid of him, he instructed Marshal Zhukov and his men who made the arrest to cut off the buttons so that his terrible hands would be occupied. It should've been comical, but it was terrible instead, those small ridiculous motions of the man whose name no one said aloud, for fear of summoning him. Worse than Stalin, they said, and after Stalin was dead they dared to arrest Beria, his right hand, citing some ridiculous excuses like British espionage and imaginary plots. The man who murdered Russians, Georgians, Polacks with equal and indiscriminating efficiency when he was the head of NKVD, before it softened up into the KGB. And there he was then, being led out of the Presidium session, unclean and repulsive like a carrion fly.

He was shot soon after, they said, but it was still murder; at least, I thought so, seeking to if not justify, then comprehend, thinking around and around and hastening my step involuntarily.

Sometimes the attachés, while rushing for the bathrooms, left their doors ajar, illuminated by the brass sconces on the walls, their semicircles of light snatching the buttery gloss of mahogany furniture and the slightly indecent spillage of stiff linen, the burden of excess. But mostly I walked the hallways, thinking of everything that happened in this house, so I wasn't all that surprised or shocked when I first saw the naked girl.

She must've been barely thirteen—her breasts uncomfortable little hillocks, her hips narrow and long. She ran down the hall, and I guessed that she did not belong—she did not seem Tunisian, or alive, for that matter. She just ran, her mouth a black distorted silent hole in her face, her eyes bruised. Her hair, shoulder-length, wheat-colored, streamed behind her, and I remember the hollow on the side of her smooth lean hip, the way it reflected light from my flashlight, the working of ropy muscles under her smooth skin. Oh, she really ran, her heels digging into the hardwood floors as if they were soft dirt, her fists pumping.

I followed her with the beam of my flashlight. I stopped dead in my tracks, did not dare to think about it yet, just watched and felt my breathing grow lighter. She reached the end of the hallway and I expected her to disappear or take off up or down the stairs, or turn around; instead, she stopped just before the stairwell, and started striking the air in front of her with both fists, as if there was a door.

She turned once, her face half-melting in the deluge of ghost tears, her fists still pummeling against the invisible door, but without conviction, her heart ready to give out. Then an invisible but rough hand jerked her away from the door—I could not see who was doing it, but I saw her feet leave the ground, and then she was dragged along the hardwood floors through the nearest closed door.

I stood in the hallway for a while, letting it all sink in. Of course I knew who she was—not her name or anything, but what happened to her. I stared at the locked door; I knew that behind it the consul and his wife slept in a four-postered bed. And yet, in the very same bed, there was that ghost girl, hairs on her thin arms standing on end and her mouth still torn by a scream, invisible hands pressing her face into a pillow, her legs jerking and kicking at the invisible assailant . . . I was almost relieved that I could not see him, even though the moment I turned and started down the hallway again, his bespectacled face slowly materialized, like a photo being developed, on the inside of my eyelids, and I could not shake the sense of his presence until the sun rose.

I soon found a routine with my new job: all night I walked through the stairwells and the corridors, sometimes dodging the ghosts of girls—there were so many, so many, all of them between twelve and eighteen, all of them terrible in their nudity—and living diplomats who stayed at the Embassy stumbling past the soft shine of their gold-plated fixtures on their way to the bathrooms. In the mornings, I went to a small coffee house to have a cup of very hot and sweet and black coffee with a thick layer of sludge in the bottom. I drank it in deliberate sips and thought of the heavy doors with iron bolts and the basement with too many chambers and lopsided cement walls no one dared to disturb because of what they were afraid to find buried under and inside of them. And then I hurried home, in case my son decided to call from his time zone eight hours behind, before he went to bed.

You know that you're old when your children are old, when they have heart trouble and sciatica, when their hearing is going too so that both of you yell into the shell of the phone receiver. But most often, he doesn't call—and I do not blame him, I wouldn't call me either. He hadn't forgiven and he never fully will, except maybe on his deathbed—and it saddens me to think that he might be arriving there before me, like it saddens me that my grandchildren cannot read Cyrillic.

I come home and wait for the phone to speak to me in its low sentimental treble, and then I go to bed. I close my eyes and I watch the images from the previous night. I watch seven girls, none of whom can be older than fourteen, all on their hands and knees in a circle, their heads pressed together, their naked bottoms raised high, I watch them flinch away from the invisible presence that circles and circles them, endlessly. I think that I can feel the gust of Beria's stroll on my face, but that too passes.

I only turn away when one of them jerks as her leg rises high in the air— and from the depressions on the ghostly flesh I know that there's a hand seizing her by the ankle. He drags her away from the circle as she tries to kick with her free foot, grabbing at the long nap of the rug, as her elbows and breasts leave troughs in it, as her fingers tangle in the Persian luxury and then let go with the breaking of already short nails. I turn away because I know what happens next, and even though I cannot see him, I cannot watch.

Morning comes eventually, and always at the time when I lose hope that the sun will ever rise again. I swear to myself that I will not come back here, Never again, I whisper—the same oath I gave to myself back before the war, and just like back then I know that I will break it over and over, every night.

On my way out of the light blue embassy house, I occasionally run into the cook, a Pakistani who has been working there for a few years. We sometimes stop for a smoke and he tells me about a bag of bones he found in the wall behind the stove some years back. He offers to show it to me but I refuse politely, scared of the stupid urban legend about a man who buys a hotdog and inside finds his wife's finger bone with her wedding ring still on. The ghosts are bad enough.

During this time, my son only called once. He complained at length, speaking hastily, as if trying to prevent me from talking back. I waited. I did not really expect him to talk about things we did not talk about—why he left or why he never told his wife where I was working. In turn, I made sympathetic noises and never mentioned how angry I was that his emigration back in the '70s fucked me over. What was the point? I did not blame him for his mother's death, and he didn't blame me for anything. He just complained that his grandkids don't understand Russian. I don't even remember what they, or their parents, my own grandchildren, look like.

When he was done talking, I went to bed and even slept until the voices of children outside woke me in the early afternoon. They always carried so far in this weather, those first warm days of not-quite summer, and I lay awake on my back listening to the high-pitched squealing outside, too warm in my long underwear. And if your life is like mine—if it's as long as mine, that is— then you find yourself thinking about a lot of shit. You start remembering the terrible sludge of life at the bottom of your memory, and if you stir it by too much thinking, too much listening to the shouts and bicycle bells outside, then woe is you, and the ghosts of teenage girls will keep you up all night and all day.

•••

The cars NKVD drove were called *black ravens,* named for both color and the ominous nature of their arrival in one's neighborhood. Narodniy Komissariat Vnutrennih Del—it's a habit, to sound out the entire name in my head. Abbreviations just don't terrify me. The modern yellow canaries of the police seemed harmless in comparison, quaint even. But those black ravens . . . I remembered the sinister yellow beams of the headlights like I remembered the squeaking of leather against leather, uniform against the seats, like I remembered the roundness of the hard wheel under my gloved hands.

Being a chauffer was never a prestigious job, but driving him—driving Beria—filled one with quiet dread. I remember the blue dusk and the snowdrifts of late February, the bright pinpricks of the streetlamps as they lit up ahead of my car, one by one, as if running from us—from him, I think. I have never done anything wrong, but my neck prickles with freshly cut hairs, and my head sweats under my leather cap. I can feel his gaze on me, like a touch of greasy fingers. Funny, that: one can live ninety years, such a long life, and still shiver in the warm May afternoon just thinking about that one February night.

It started to snow soon after the streetlights all flickered on, lining along the facades of the houses—all old mansions, being in the center of the city and all, painted pale blues and yellows and greens. The flight of the lights reminded me of a poem I read some years ago; only I could not remember it but tried nonetheless—anything to avoid the sensation of the sticky unclean stare on the back of my head, at the base of my skull, and I felt cold, as if a gun barrel rested there.

"Slow down," he tells me in a soft voice. There's no one but him in the car, and I am grateful for small mercies, I am grateful that except for directions he does not talk to me.

I slow down. The wind is kicking up the snow and it writhes, serpentine, close to the ground, barely reaching up high enough to get snagged in the lights of the car beams.

"Turn off the lights."

I do, and then I see her—bundled up in an old, moth-eaten fur coat, her head swaddled in a thick kerchief. I recognize her—Ninochka, a neighbor who is rumored to be a bit addled in the head, but she always says hello to me and she is always friendly. The coat and kerchief disfigure and bloat her as she trundles through the snow, her walk waddling in her thick felt boots that look like they used to belong to her grandfather. I hope that this misshapen, ugly disguise would be enough to save her.

I pick up the speed slightly, to save her, to drive past her and perhaps find another girl walking home from work late, find another one—someone I do not know, and it is unfair that I am so willing to trade one for another but here we are—just God please, let us pass her. In my head, I make deals with God, promises I would never be able to keep. I do not know why it's so important, but it feels that if I could just save her, just this one, then things would be all right again, the world would be revealed as a little bit just and at least somewhat sensible. Just this one, please god.

"Slow down," he says again, and I feel the leather on the back of my seat shift as he grips the top of it. "Stop right there." He points just ahead, at the pool of darkness between two cones of light, where the snow changes color from white to blue. The wind is swirling around his shoes as he steps out, and the girl, Ninochka, looks up for the first time. She does not recognize him—not at first, not later when she is sobbing quietly in the back seat of the car, her arms twisted behind her so that she cannot even wipe her face and her tears drip off the reddened tip off her nose, like a melting icicle. I still cannot remember the poem—something about the running streetlights, and I concentrate on the elusive rhythm and stare straight ahead, until I stop by the wrought iron gates of his house and let him and Ninochka out. I am not allowed beyond that point, being just a chauffer and not an NKVD man. I am grateful.

So I thought that my presence in the sky-blue house was not coincidental, and the fact that I kept seeing the dead naked girls everywhere I looked meant something. I tried to not look into their faces, not when they were clumped, heads together, in a circle. I did not need to see their faces to know that Ninochka was somewhere among them, a transparent long-limbed apparition being hauled off into some secret dungeon to undergo things best not thought about—and I squeezed my eyes shut and shook my head, just not to think about that, not to think.

My son was a dissident, and to him there was no poison more bitter than the knowledge that his father used to work for NKVD, used to turn people in, used to sit on people's tribunals that condemned enemies of the state. His shame for my sins forced his pointless flight into the place that offered none of the freedoms it had previously promised, the illusory comforts of the familiar language and the same conversations, of the slowly corrupting English words and the joys of capitalism as small and trivial as the cockroaches in a Brighton Beach kitchen. He still does not see the irony in that.

But he does manage to feel superior to me; he feels like he is better because he's not the one with naked dead girls chasing him through dreams and working hours, crowding in his head during the precious few minutes of leisure. The bar ribbons of all my medals and orders are of no consequence, as if there had been no war after the slow stealthy drives through the streets. Seasons changed but not the girls, forever trapped in the precarious land between adolescence and maturity, and if there were no victories and marching through mud all the way to Germany and back, as if there was nothing else after these girls. Time stopped in 1938, I suspect, and now it just keeps replaying in the house in Malaya Nikitskaya. And I cannot look away and I cannot quit the job in the embassy—not until I either figure out why this is happening or decide that I do not care enough to find out.

I remember the last week I worked in the Tunisian Embassy. The dead girls infected everything, and even the diplomats and the security saw them out of the corners of their eyes—I saw them tossing up their heads on the way to the bathroom, their eyes wide and awake like those of spooked horses. The girls—long-limbed, bruised-pale—ran down every hallway, their faces looming up from every stairwell, every corner, every glass of sweet dark tea the Pakistani cook brewed for me in the mornings.

The diplomats whispered in their strange tongue, the tongue, I imagined, that remained unchanged since Hannibal and his elephants. I guessed that the girls were getting to them too, and for a brief while I was relating to these foreign dignitaries. Then they decided to deal with the problem, something I had not really considered, content in my unrelenting terror. They decided to take apart the fake partitions in the basement.

I was told to not come to work for a few days, and that damn near killed me. I could not sleep at night, thinking of the pale wraiths streaming in the dark paneled hallways of the sky-blue house. But the heart, the heart of it were all these dead girls, and I worried about them—I feared that they would exorcise them, would chase them away, leaving me no reason to ever go back, no reason to wake up every day, shave, leave the house. I could not know whether the semblance of life granted to them was torturous, and yet I hoped that they would survive.

They did not. When I came back, I found the basement devoid of its fake cement partitions, and the bricks in the basement walls were held together with fresh mortar. The corridors and the rooms were empty too—I often turned, having imagined a flick of movement on the periphery of my vision. I looked into the empty rooms, hoping to catch a glimpse of long legs shredding the air into long, sickle-shaped slivers.

I found them after morning came and the cook offered me the usual glass of tea, dark and sweet and fragrant.

"They found all these bones," he told me, his voice regretful. "Even more than my bag, the one I told you about before."

"Where did they take them?"

He shrugged and shook his head, opening his arms palms-out in a pantomime of sincere puzzlement. I already knew that they were not in the house, because of course I already looked everywhere I could look without disturbing any of the diplomats' sleep.

Before I left for the day, I looked in the yard. It was so quiet there, so separate from the world outside. So peaceful. I found the skulls lined under the trees behind the building, where the graveled path traveled between the house and the wall.

I looked at the row of skulls, all of them with one hole through the base, and I regretted that I had never seen Ninochka's face among the silent wraiths. I did not know which one of these skulls was hers; all of them looked at me with black holes of their sockets, and I thought I heard the faint rattling of the bullets inside them, the cluttering that grew louder like that of the tin cans dragging behind a running dog.

I turned away and walked toward the gates, trying to keep my steps slow and calm, trying to ignore the rattling of the skulls that had been dragging behind me for the last sixty years.

• • • •

*An old memory resurfaces. That often happens on a night when someone
in the vicinity dies—death seems to awaken something . . .*

Mr. Aickman's Air Rifle
Peter Straub

1

On the twenty-first, or "Concierge," floor of New York's Governor General
Hospital, located just south of midtown on Seventh Avenue, a glow of
recessed lighting and a rank of framed, eye-level graphics (Twombley,
Shapiro, Marden, Warhol) escort visitors from a brace of express elevators
to the reassuring spectacle of a graceful cherry wood desk occupied by a red-
jacketed gatekeeper named Mr. Singh. Like a hand cupped beneath a waiting
elbow, this gentleman's enquiring yet deferential appraisal and his stupendous
display of fresh flowers nudge the visitor over hushed beige carpeting and
into the wood-paneled realm of Floor 21 itself.

First to appear is the nursing station, where in a flattering chiaroscuro
efficient women occupy themselves with charts, telephones, and the ever-
changing patterns traversing their computer monitors; directly ahead lies the
first of the great, half-open doors of the residents' rooms or suites, each with
its brass numeral and discreet nameplate. The great hallway extends some
sixty yards, passing seven named and numbered doors on its way to a bright
window with an uptown view. To the left, the hallway passes the front of the
nurses' station and the four doors directly opposite, then divides. The shorter
portion continues on to a large, south-facing window with a good prospect
of the Hudson River, the longer defines the southern boundary of the station.
Hung with an Elizabeth Murray lithograph and a Robert Mapplethorpe calla
lily, an ochre wall then rises up to guide the hallway over another carpeted
fifty feet to a long, narrow room. The small brass sign beside its wide, pebble-
glass doors reads SALON.

The Salon is not a salon but a lounge, and a rather makeshift lounge at
that. At one end sits a good-sized television set; at the other, a green fabric
sofa with two matching chairs. Midpoint in the room, which was intended

for the comfort of stricken relatives and other visitors but has always been patronized chiefly by Floor 21's more ambulatory patients, stands a white-draped table equipped with coffee dispensers, stacks of cups and saucers, and cut-glass containers for sugar and artificial sweeteners. In the hours from four to six in the afternoon, platters laden with pastries and chocolates from the neighborhood's gourmet specialty shops appear, as if delivered by unseen hands, upon the table.

On an afternoon early in April, when during the hours in question the long window behind the table of goodies registered swift, unpredictable alternations of light and dark, the male patients who constituted four-fifths of the residents of Floor 21, all of them recent victims of atrial fibrillation or atrial flutter, which is to say sufferers from that dire annoyance in the life of a busy American male, non-fatal heart failure, the youngest a man of fifty-eight and the most senior twenty-two years older, found themselves once again partaking of the cream cakes and petit fours and reminding themselves that they had not, after all, undergone heart attacks. Their recent adventures had aroused in them an indulgent fatalism. After all, should the worst happen, which of course it would not, they were already at the epicenter of a swarm of cardiologists!

To varying degrees, these were men of accomplishment and achievement in their common profession, that of letters.

In descending order of age, the four men enjoying the amenities of the Salon were Max Baccarat, the much respected former president of Gladstone Books, the acquisition of which by a German conglomerate had lately precipitated his retirement; Anthony Flax, a self-described "critic" who had spent the past twenty years as a full-time book reviewer for a variety of periodicals and journals, a leisurely occupation he could afford due to his having been the husband, now for three years the widower, of a sugar-substitute heiress; William Messinger, a writer whose lengthy backlist of horror/mystery/ suspense novels had been kept continuously in print for twenty-five years by the bi-annual appearance of yet another new astonishment; and Charles Chipp Traynor, child of a wealthy New England family, Harvard graduate, self-declared veteran of the Vietnam conflict, and author of four non-fiction books, also (alas) a notorious plagiarist.

The connections between these four men, no less complex and multi-layered than one would gather from their professional circumstances, had inspired some initial awkwardness on their first few encounters in the Salon, but a shared desire for the treats on offer had encouraged these gentlemen to reach the accommodation displayed on the afternoon in question. By silent agreement, Max Baccarat arrived first, a few minutes after opening, to avail himself of the greatest possible range of selection and the most comfortable seating position, which was on that end side of the sofa nearest the pebble-glass doors, where the cushion was a touch more yielding than its mate. Once the great publisher had installed himself to his satisfaction, Bill Messinger and Tony Flax happened in to browse over the day's bounty before seating themselves at a comfortable distance from each other. Invariably the last to arrive, Traynor edged around the door sometime around 4:15, his manner suggesting that he had wandered in by accident, probably in search of another room altogether. The loose, patterned hospital gown he wore fastened at neck and backside added to his air of inoffensiveness, and his round glasses and stooped shoulders gave him a generic resemblance to a creature from *The Wind in the Willows*.

Of the four, the plagiarist alone had surrendered to the hospital's tacit wishes concerning patients' in-house mode of dress. Over silk pajamas of a glaring, Greek-village white, Max Baccarat wore a dark, dashing navy blue dressing gown, reputedly a Christmas present from Graham Greene, which fell nearly to the tops of his velvet fox-head slippers. Over his own pajamas, of fine-combed baby-blue cotton instead of white silk, Tony Flax had buttoned a lightweight tan trench coat, complete with epaulettes and grenade rings. Wth his extra chins and florid complexion, it made him look like a correspondent from a war conducted well within striking distance of hotel bars. Bill Messinger had taken one look at the flimsy shift offered him by the hospital staff and decided to stick, for as long as he could get away with it, to the pin-striped Armani suit and black loafers he had worn into the ER. His favorite men's stores delivered fresh shirts, socks and underwear.

When Messinger's early, less successful books had been published by Max's firm, Tony Flax had given him consistently positive reviews; after Bill's defection to a better house and larger advances for more ambitious books, Tony's increasingly bored and dismissive reviews accused him of hubris, then ceased altogether. Messinger's last three novels had not been reviewed anywhere in the *Times*, an insult he attributed to Tony's malign influence over its current editors. Likewise, Max had published Chippie Traynor's first two anecdotal histories of World War I, the second of which had been considered for a Pulitzer Prize, then lost him to a more prominent publisher whose shrewd publicists had placed him on NPR, the *Today* show, and—after the film deal for his third book—*Charlie Rose*. Bill had given blurbs to Traynor's first two books, and Tony Flax had hailed him as a great vernacular historian. Then, two decades later, a stunned graduate student in Texas discovered lengthy, painstakingly altered parallels between Traynor's books and the contents of several Ph.D. dissertations containing oral histories taken in the 1930s.

Beyond that, the student found that perhaps a third of the personal histories had been invented, simply made up, like fiction.

Within days, the graduate student had detonated Chippie's reputation. One week after the detonation, his university placed him "on leave," a status assumed to be permanent. He had vanished into his family's Lincoln Log compound in Maine, not to be seen or heard from until the moment when Bill Messinger and Tony Flax, who had left open the Salon's doors the better to avoid conversation, had witnessed his sorry, supine figure being wheeled past. Max Baccarat was immediately informed of the scoundrel's arrival, and before the end of the day the legendary dressing gown, the trench coat, and the pin-striped suit had overcome their mutual resentments to form an alliance against the disgraced newcomer. There was nothing, they found, like a common enemy to smooth over complicated, even difficult relationships.

Chippie Traynor had not found his way to the lounge until the following day, and he had been accompanied by a tremulous elderly woman who with equal plausibility could have passed for either his mother or his wife. Sidling around the door at 4:15, he had taken in the trio watching him from the green sofa and chairs, blinked in disbelief and recognition, ducked his head even closer to his chest, and permitted his companion to lead him to a chair located a few feet from the television set. It was clear that he was struggling with the impulse to scuttle out of the room, never to reappear. Once deposited in the chair, he tilted his head upward and whispered a few words into the woman's ear. She moved toward the pastries, and at last he eyed his former compatriots.

"Well, well," he said. "Max, Tony, and Bill. What are you in for, anyway? Me, I passed out on the street in Boothbay Harbor and had to be air-lifted in. Medevaced, like back in the day."

"These days, a lot of things must remind you of Vietnam, Chippie," Max said. "We're heart failure. You?"

"Atrial fib. Shortness of breath. Weaker than a baby. Fell down right in the street, boom. As soon as I get regulated, I'm supposed to have some sort of echo scan."

"Heart failure, all right," Max said. "Go ahead, have a cream cake. You're among friends."

"Somehow, I doubt that," Traynor said. He was breathing hard, and he gulped air as he waved the old woman further down the table, toward the chocolate slabs and puffs. He watched carefully as she selected a number of the little cakes. "Don't forget the decaf, will you, sweetie?"

The others waited for him to introduce his companion, but he sat in silence as she placed a plate of cakes and a cup of coffee on a stand next to the television set, then faded backward into a chair that seemed to have materialized, just for her, from the ether. Traynor lifted a forkful of shiny brown goo to his mouth, sucked it off the fork, and gulped coffee. Because of his long, thick nose and recessed chin, first the fork, then the cup seemed to disappear into the lower half of his face. He twisted his head in the general direction of his companion and said, "Health food, yum yum."

She smiled vaguely at the ceiling. Traynor turned back to face the other three men, who were staring open-eyed, as if at a performance of some kind.

"Thanks for all the cards and letters, guys. I loved getting your phone calls, too. Really meant a lot to me. Oh, sorry, I'm not being very polite, am I?"

"There's no need to be sarcastic," Max said.

"I suppose not. We were never friends, were we?"

"You were looking for a publisher, not a friend," Max said. "And we did quite well together, or so I thought, before you decided you needed greener pastures. Bill did the same thing to me, come to think of it. Of course, Bill actually wrote the books that came out under his name. For a publisher, that's quite a significant difference." (Several descendants of the Ph.D.s from whom Traynor had stolen material had initiated suits against his publishing houses, Gladstone House among them.)

"Do we have to talk about this?' asked Tony Flax. He rammed his hands in the pockets of his trench coat and glanced from side to side. "Ancient history, hmmm?"

"You're just embarrassed by the reviews you gave him," Bill said. "But everybody did the same thing, including me. What did I say about *The Middle of the Trenches*? 'The . . . ' The what? 'The most truthful, in a way the most visionary book ever written about trench warfare.'"

"Jesus, you remember your blurbs?" Tony asked. He laughed and tried to draw the others in.

"I remember everything," said Bill Messinger. "Curse of being a novelist— great memory, lousy sense of direction."

"You always remembered how to get to the bank," Tony said.

"Lucky me, I didn't have to marry it," Bill said.

"Are you accusing me of marrying for money?" Tony said, defending himself by the usual tactic of pretending that what was commonly accepted was altogether unthinkable. "Not that I have any reason to defend myself against you, Messinger. As that famous memory of yours should recall, I was one of the first people to support your work."

From nowhere, a reedy English female voice said, "I did enjoy reading your reviews of Mr. Messinger's early novels, Mr. Flax. I'm sure that's why I went round to our little book shop and purchased them. They weren't at all my usual sort of thing, you know, but you made them sound . . . I think the word would be imperative."

Max, Tony, and Bill peered past Charles Chipp Traynor to get a good look at his companion. For the first time, they took in that she was wearing a long, loose collection of elements that suggested feminine literary garb of the 1920s: a hazy, rather shimmery woolen cardigan over a white, high-buttoned blouse, pearls, an ankle-length heather skirt, and low-heeled black shoes with laces. Her long, sensitive nose pointed up, exposing the clean line of her jaw; her lips twitched in what might have been amusement. Two things struck the men staring at her: that this woman looked a bit familiar, and that in spite of her age and general oddness, she would have to be described as beautiful.

"Well, yes," Tony said. "Thank you. I believe I was trying to express something of the sort. They were books . . . well. Bill, you never understood this, I think, but I felt they were books that deserved to be read. For their workmanship, their modesty, what I thought was their actual decency."

"You mean they did what you expected them to do," Bill said.

"Decency is an uncommon literary virtue," said Traynor's companion.

"Thank you, yes," Tony said.

"But not a very interesting one, really," Bill said. "Which probably explains why it isn't all that common."

"I think you are correct, Mr. Messinger, to imply that decency is more valuable in the realm of personal relations. And for the record, I do feel your work since then has undergone a general improvement. Perhaps Mr. Flax's limitations do not permit him to appreciate your progress." She paused. There was a dangerous smile on her face. "Of course you can hardly be said to have improved to the extent claimed in your latest round of interviews."

In the moment of silence that followed, Max Baccarat looked from one of his new allies to the other and found them in a state too reflective for commentary. He cleared his throat. "Might we have the honor of an introduction, Madame? Chippie seems to have forgotten his manners."

"My name is of no importance," she said, only barely favoring him with the flicker of a glance. "And Mr. Traynor has a thorough knowledge of my feelings on the matter."

"There's two sides to every story," Chippie said. "It may not be grammar, but it's the truth."

"Oh, there are many more than that," said his companion, smiling again.

"Darling, would you help me return to my room?"

Chippie extended an arm, and the Englishwoman floated to her feet, cradled his root-like fist against the side of her chest, nodded to the gaping men, and gracefully conducted her charge from the room.

"So who the fuck was that?" said Max Baccarat.

2

Certain rituals structured the night-time hours on Floor 21. At 8:30 p.m., blood pressure was taken and evening medications administered by Tess Corrigan, an Irish softie with a saggy gut, an alcoholic, angina-ridden husband, and an understandable tolerance for misbehavior. Tess herself sometimes appeared to be mildly intoxicated. Class resentment caused her to treat Max a touch brusquely, but Tony's trench coat amused her to wheezy laughter. After Bill Messinger had signed two books for her niece, a devoted fan, Tess had allowed him to do anything he cared to, including taking illicit journeys downstairs to the gift shop. "Oh, Mr. Messinger," she had said, "a fella with your gifts, the books you could write about this place." Three hours after Tess's departure, a big, heavily-dreadlocked nurse with an islands accent surged into the patients' rooms to awaken them for the purpose of distributing tranquilizers and knockout pills. Because she resembled a greatly inflated, ever-simmering Whoopi Goldberg, Max, Tony, and Bill referred to this terrifying and implacable figure as "Molly." (Molly's real name, printed on the ID card attached to a sash used as a waistband, was permanently concealed behind beaded swags and little hanging pouches.) At six in the morning, Molly swept in again, wielding the blood-pressure mechanism like an angry deity maintaining a good grip on a sinner. At the end of her shift, she came wrapped in a strong, dark scent, suggestive of forest fires in underground crypts. The three literary gentlemen found this aroma disturbingly erotic.

On the morning after the appearance within the Salon of Charles Chipp Traynor and his disconcerting muse, Molly raked Bill with a look of pity and scorn as she trussed his upper arm and strangled it by pumping a rubber bulb. Her crypt-fire odor seemed particularly smoky.

"What?" he asked.

Molly shook her massive head. "Toddle, toddle, toddle, you must believe you're the new postman in this beautiful neighborhood of ours."

Terror seized his gut. "I don't think I know what you're talking about."

Molly chuckled and gave the bulb a final squeeze, causing his arm to go numb from bicep to his fingertips. "Of course not. But you do know that we have no limitations on visiting hours up here in our paradise, don't you?"

"Um," he said.

"Then let me tell you something you do not know, Mr. Postman. Miz LaValley in 21R-12 passed away last night. I do not imagine you ever took it upon yourself to pay the poor woman a social call. And *that*, Mr. Postman, means that you, Mr. Baccarat, Mr. Flax, and our new addition, Mr. Traynor, are now the only patients on Floor 21."

"Ah," he said.

As soon as she left his room, he showered and dressed in the previous day's clothing, eager to get out into the corridor and check on the conditions in 21R-14, Chippie Traynor's room, for it was what he had seen there in the hours between Tess Corrigan's florid departure and Molly Goldberg's first drive-by shooting that had led to his becoming the floor's postman.

It had been just before nine in the evening, and something had urged him to take a final turn around the floor before surrendering himself to the hateful "gown" and turning off his lights. His route took him past the command center, where the Night Visitor, scowling over a desk too small for her, made grim notations on a chart, and down the corridor toward the window looking out toward the Hudson River and the great harbor. Along the way he passed 21R-14, where muffled noises had caused him to look in. From the corridor, he could see the bottom third of the plagiarist's bed, on which the sheets and blanket appeared to be writhing, or at least shifting about in a conspicuous manner. Messinger noticed a pair of black, lace-up women's shoes on the floor near the bottom of the bed. An untidy heap of clothing lay beside the in-turned shoes. For a few seconds ripe with shock and envy, he had listened to the soft noises coming from the room. Then he whirled around and rushed toward his allies' chambers.

"Who *is* that dame?" Max Baccarat had asked, essentially repeating the question he had asked earlier that day. "*What* is she? That miserable Traynor, God damn him to hell, may he have a heart attack and die. A woman like that, who cares how old she is?"

Tony Flax had groaned in disbelief and said, "I swear, that woman is either the ghost of Virginia Woolf or her direct descendant. All my life, I had the hots for Virginia Woolf, and now she turns up with that ugly crook, Chippie Traynor? Get out of here, Bill, I have to strategize."

3

At 4:15, the three conspirators pretended not to notice the plagiarist's furtive, animal-like entrance to the Salon. Max Baccarat's silvery hair, cleansed, stroked, clipped, buffed, and shaped during an emergency session with a hair therapist named Mr. Keith, seemed to glow with a virile inner light as he settled into the comfortable part of the sofa and organized his decaf cup and plate of chocolates and little cakes as if preparing soldiers for battle. Tony Flax's rubber chins shone a twice-shaved red, and his glasses sparkled. Beneath the hem of the trench coat, which appeared to have been ironed, colorful argyle socks descended from just below his lumpy knees to what seemed to be a pair of nifty two-tone shoes. Beneath the jacket of his pin-striped suit, Bill Messinger sported a brand-new, high-collared black silk T-shirt delivered by courier that morning from 65th and Madison. Thus attired, the longer-term residents of Floor 21 seemed lost as much in self-admiration as in the political discussion under way when at last they allowed themselves to acknowledge Chippie's presence. Max's eye skipped over Traynor and wandered toward the door.

"Will your lady friend be joining us?" he asked. "I thought she made some really very valid points yesterday, and I'd enjoy hearing what she has to say about our situation in Iraq. My two friends here are simple-minded liberals, you can never get anything sensible out of them."

"You wouldn't like what she'd have to say about Iraq," Traynor said. "And neither would they."

"Know her well, do you?" Tony asked.

"You could say that." Traynor's gown slipped as he bent over the table to pump coffee into his cup from the dispenser, and the three other men hastily turned their glances elsewhere.

"Tie that up, Chippie, would you?" Bill asked. "It's like a view of the Euganean Hills."

"Then look somewhere else. I'm getting some coffee, and then I have to pick out a couple of these yum-yums."

"You're alone today, then?" Tony asked.

"Looks like it."

"By the way," Bill said, "you were entirely right to point out that nothing is really as simple as it seems. There are more than two sides to every issue. I mean, wasn't that the point of what we were saying about Iraq?"

"To you, maybe," Max said. "You'd accept two sides as long as they were both printed in *The Nation*."

"Anyhow," Bill said, "please tell your friend that the next time she cares to visit this hospital, we'll try to remember what she said about decency."

"What makes you think she's going to come here again?"

"She seemed very fond of you," Tony said.

"The lady mentioned your limitations." Chippie finished assembling his assortment of treats and at last refastened his gaping robe. "I'm surprised you have any interest in seeing her again."

Tony's cheeks turned a deeper red. "All of us have limitations, I'm sure. In fact, I was just remembering . . ."

"Oh?' Chippie lifted his snout and peered through his little lenses. "Were you? What, specifically?"

"Nothing," said Tony. "I shouldn't have said anything. Sorry."

"Did any of you know Mrs. LaValley, the lady in 21R-12?" Bill asked. "She died last night. Apart from us, she was the only other person on the floor."

"I knew Edie LaValley," Chippie said. "In fact, my friend and I dropped in and had a nice little chat with her just before dinner-time last night. I'm glad I had a chance to say goodbye to the old girl."

"Edie LaValley?" Max said. "Hold on. I seem to remember . . ."

"Wait, I do, too," Bill said. "Only . . . "

"I know, she was that girl who worked for Nick Wheadle over at Viking, thirty years ago, back when Wheadle was everybody's golden boy," Tony said. "Stupendous girl. She got married to him and was Edith Wheadle for a while, but after the divorce she went back to her old name. We went out for a couple of months in 1983, '84. What happened to her after that?"

"She spent six years doing research for me," Traynor said. "She wasn't my *only* researcher, because I generally had three of them on the payroll, not to mention a couple of graduate students. Edie was very good at the job, though. Extremely conscientious."

"And knockout, drop-dead gorgeous," Tony said. "At least before she fell into Nick Wheadle's clutches."

"I didn't know you used so many researchers," Max said. "Could that be how you wound up quoting all those . . . ?"

"Deliberately misquoting, I suppose you mean," Chippie said. "But the answer is no." A fat, sugar-coated square of sponge cake disappeared beneath his nose.

"But Edie Wheadle," Max said in a reflective voice. "By God, I think I . . ."

"Think nothing of it," Traynor said. "That's what she did."

"Edie must have looked very different toward the end," said Tony. He sounded almost hopeful. "Twenty years, illness, all of that."

"My friend and I thought she looked much the same." Chippie's mild, creaturely face swung toward Tony Flax. "Weren't you about to tell us something?"

Tony flushed again. "No, not really."

"Perhaps an old memory resurfaced. That often happens on a night when someone in the vicinity dies—the death seems to awaken something."

"Edie's death certainly seemed to have awakened you," Bill said. "Didn't you ever hear of closing your door?"

"The nurses waltz right in anyhow, and there are no locks," Traynor said. "Better to be frank about matters, especially on Floor 21. It looks as though Max has something on his mind."

"Yes," Max said. "If Tony doesn't feel like talking, I will. Last night, an old memory of mine resurfaced, as Chippie puts it, and I'd like to get it off my chest, if that's the appropriate term."

"Good man," Traynor said. "Have another of those delicious little yummies and tell us all about it."

"This happened back when I was a little boy," Max said, wiping his lips with a crisp linen handkerchief.

Bill Messinger and Tony Flax seemed to go very still.

"I was raised in Pennsylvania, up in the Susquehanna Valley area. It's strange country, a little wilder and more backward than you'd expect, a little hillbillyish, especially once you get back in the Endless Mountains. My folks had a little store that sold everything under the sun, it seemed to me, and we lived in the building next door, close to the edge of town. Our town was called Manship, not that you can find it on any map. We had a one-room schoolhouse, an Episcopalian church and a Unitarian church, a feed and grain store, a place called The Lunch Counter, a tract house, and a tavern called the Rusty Dusty, where, I'm sad to say, my father spent far too much of his time.

"When he came home loaded, as happened just about every other night, he was in a foul mood. It was mainly guilt, d'you see, because my mother had been slaving away in the store for hours, plus making dinner, and she was in a rage, which only made him feel worse. All he really wanted to do was to beat himself up, but I was an easy target, so he beat me up instead. Nowadays, we'd call it child abuse, but back then, in a place like Manship, it was just normal parenting, at least for a drunk. I wish I could tell you fellows that everything turned out well, and that my father sobered up, and we reconciled, and I forgave him, but none of that happened. Instead, he got meaner and meaner, and we got poorer and poorer. I learned to hate the old bastard, and I still hated him when a traveling junk wagon ran over him, right there in front of the Rusty Dusty, when I was eleven years old. 1935, the height of the Great Depression. He was lying passed out in the street, and the junkman never saw him.

"Now, I was determined to get out of that god-forsaken little town, and out of the Susquehanna Valley and the Endless Mountains, and obviously I did, because here I am today, with an excellent place in the world, if I might pat myself on the back a little bit. What I did was, I managed to keep the store going even while I went to the high school in the next town, and then I got a scholarship to U. Penn., where I waited on tables and tended bar and sent money back to my mother. Two days after I graduated, she died of a heart attack. That was her reward.

"I bought a bus ticket to New York. Even though I was never a great reader, I liked the idea of getting into the book business. Everything that happened after that you could read about in old copies of *Publisher's Weekly*. Maybe one day I'll write a book about it all.

"If I do, I'll never put in what I'm about to tell you now. It slipped my mind completely—the whole thing. You'll realize how bizarre that is after I'm done. I forgot all about it! Until about three this morning, that is, when I woke up too scared to breathe, my heart going *bump bump*, and the sweat pouring out of me. Every little bit of this business just came *back* to me, I mean everything, ever god-damned little tiny detail . . ."

He looked at Bill and Tony. "What? You two guys look like you should be back in the ER."

"Every detail?" Tony said. "It's . . ."

"You woke up then, too?" Bill asked him.

"Are you two knotheads going to let me talk, or do you intend to keep interrupting?"

"I just wanted to ask this one thing, but I changed my mind," Tony said. "Sorry, Max. I shouldn't have said anything. It was a crazy idea. Sorry."

"Was your dad an alcoholic, too?" Bill asked Tony Flax.

Tony squeezed up his face, said, "Aaaah," and waggled one hand in the air. "I don't like the word 'alcoholic.' "

"Yeah," Bill said. "All right."

"I guess the answer is, you're going to keep interrupting."

"No, please, Max, go on," Bill said.

Max frowned at both of them, then gave a dubious glance to Chippie Traynor, who stuffed another tiny cream cake into his maw and smiled around it.

"Fine. I don't know why I want to tell you about this anyhow. It's not like I actually *understand* it, as you'll see, and it's kind of ugly and kind of scary—I guess what amazes me is that I just remembered it all, or that I managed to put it out of my mind for nearly seventy years, one or the other. But you know? It's like, it's real even if it never happened, or even if I dreamed the whole thing."

"This story wouldn't happen to involve a house, would it?" Tony asked.

"Most goddamned stories involve houses," Max said. "Even a lousy book critic ought to know that."

"Tony knows that," Chippie said. "See his ridiculous coat? That's a house. Isn't it, Tony?"

"You know what this is," Tony said. "It's a *trench coat*, a real one. Only from World War II, not World War I. It used to belong to my father. He was a hero in the war."

"As I was about to say," Max said, looking around and continuing only when the other three were paying attention, "when I woke up in the middle of the night I could remember the feel of the old blanket on my bed, the feel of pebbles and earth on my bare feet when I ran to the outhouse, I could remember the way my mother's scrambled eggs tasted. The whole anxious thing I had going on inside me while my mother was making breakfast.

"I was going to go off by myself in the woods. That was all right with my mother. At least it got rid of me for the day. But she didn't know that I had decided to steal one of the guns in the case at the back of the store.

"And you know what? She didn't pay any attention to the guns. About half of them belonged to people who swapped them for food because guns were all they had left to barter with. My mother hated the whole idea. And my father was in a fog until he could get to the tavern. After that he couldn't think straight enough to remember how many guns were supposed to be back in that case. Anyhow, for the past few days, I'd had my eye on an over-under shotgun that used to belong to a farmer called Hakewell, and while my mother wasn't watching I nipped in back and took it out of the case. Then I stuffed my pockets with shells, ten of them. There was something going on way back in the woods, and while I wanted to keep my eye on it, I wanted to be able to protect myself, too, in case anything got out of hand."

Bill Messinger jumped to his feet and for a moment seemed preoccupied with brushing what might have been pastry crumbs off the bottom of his suit jacket. Max Baccarat frowned at him, then glanced down at the skirts of his dressing gown in a brief inspection. Bill continued to brush off imaginary particles of food, slowly turning in a circle as he did so.

"There is something you wish to communicate," Max said. "The odd thing, you know, is that for the moment, you see, I thought communication was in my hands."

Bill stopped fiddling with his jacket and regarded the old publisher with his eyebrows tugged toward the bridge of his nose and his mouth a thin, downturned line. He placed his hands on his hips. "I don't know what you're doing, Max, and I don't know where you're getting this. But I certainly wish you'd stop."

"What are you talking about?"

"He's right, Max," said Tony Flax.

"You jumped-up little fop," Max said, ignoring Tony. "You damned little show pony. What's your problem? You haven't told a good story in the past ten years, so listen to mine, you might learn something."

"You know what you are?" Bill asked him. "Twenty years ago, you used to be a decent second-rate publisher. Unfortunately, it's been all downhill from there. Now you're not even a third-rate publisher, you're a sellout. You took the money and went on the lam. Morally, you don't exist at all. You're a fancy dressing gown. And by the way, Graham Greene didn't give it to you, because Graham Greene wouldn't have given you a glass of water on a hot day."

Both of them were panting a bit and trying not to show it. Like a dog trying to choose between masters, Tony Flax swung his head from one to the other. In the end, he settled on Max Baccarat. "I don't really get it either, you know, but I think you should stop, too."

"Nobody cares what you think," Max told him. "Your brain dropped dead the day you swapped your integrity for a mountain of coffee sweetener."

"You did marry for money, Flax," Bill Messinger said. "Let's try being honest, all right? You sure as hell didn't fall in love with her beautiful face."

"And how about you, Traynor?" Max shouted. "I suppose you think I should stop, too."

"Nobody cares what I think," Chippie said. "I'm the lowest of the low. People despise me."

"First of all," Bill said, "if you want to talk about details, Max, you ought to get them *right*. It wasn't an 'over-under shotgun,' whatever the hell that is, it was a—"

"His name wasn't Hakewell," Tony said. "It was Hackman, like the actor."

"It wasn't Hakewell or Hackman," Bill said. "It started with an A."

"But there was a *house*," Tony said. "You know, I think my father probably was an alcoholic. His personality never changed, though. He was always a mean son of a bitch, drunk or sober."

"Mine, too," said Bill. "Where are you from, anyhow, Tony?"

"A little town in Oregon, called Milton. How about you?"

"Rhinelander, Wisconsin. My dad was the chief of police. I suppose there were lots of woods around Milton."

"We might as well have been in a forest. You?"

"The same."

"I'm from Boston, but we spent the summers in Maine," Chippie said. "You know what Maine is? Eighty percent woods. There are places in Maine, the roads don't even have names."

"There was a *house*," Tony Flax insisted. "Back in the woods, and it didn't belong there. Nobody builds houses in the middle of the woods, miles away from everything, without even a road to use, not even a road without a name."

"This can't be real," Bill said. "I had a house, you had a house, and I bet Max had a house, even though he's so long-winded he hasn't gotten to it yet. I had an air rifle, Max had a shotgun, what did you have?"

"My Dad's .22," Tony said. "Just a little thing—around us, nobody took a .22 all that seriously."

Max was looking seriously disgruntled. "What, we all had the same *dream?*"

"You said it wasn't a dream," said Chippie Traynor. "You said it was a memory."

"It felt like a memory, all right," Tony said. "Just the way Max described it— the way the ground felt under my feet, the smell of my mother's cooking."

"I wish your lady friend was here now, Traynor," Max said. "She'd be able to explain what's going on, wouldn't she?"

"I have a number of lady friends," Chippie said, calmly stuffing a little glazed cake into his mouth.

"All right, Max," Bill said. "Let's explore this. You come across this big house, right? And there's someone in it?"

"Eventually, there is," Max said, and Tony Flax nodded.

"Right. And you can't even tell what age he is—or even if it *is* a he, right?"

"It was hiding in the back of a room," Tony says. "When I thought it was a girl, it really scared me. I didn't want it to be a girl."

"I didn't, either," Max said. "Oh—imagine how that would feel, a girl hiding in the shadows at the back of a room."

"Only this never happened," Bill said. "If we all seem to remember this bizarre story, then none of us is really remembering it."

"Okay, but it was a boy," Tony said. "And he got older."

"Right there in that house," said Max. "I thought it was like watching my damnable father grow up right in front of my eyes. In what, six weeks?"

"About that," Tony said.

"And him in there all alone," said Bill. "Without so much as a stick of furniture. I thought that was one of the things that made it so frightening."

"Scared the shit out of me," Tony said. "When my Dad came back from the war, sometimes he put on his uniform and tied us to the chairs. Tied us to the chairs!"

"I didn't think it was really going to injure him," Bill said.

"I didn't even think I'd hit him," Tony said.

"I knew damn well I'd hit him," Max said. "I wanted to blow his head off. But my Dad lived another three years, and then the junkman finally ran him over."

"Max," Tony said, "you mentioned there was a tract house in Manship. What's a tract house?"

"It was where they printed the religious tracts, you ignoramus. You could go in there and pick them up for free. All of this was like child abuse, I'm telling you. Spare-the-rod stuff."

"It was like his eye exploded," Bill said. Absentmindedly, he took one of the untouched pastries from Max's plate and bit into it.

Max stared at him.

"They didn't change the goodies this morning, " Bill said. "This thing is a little stale."

"I prefer my pastries stale," said Chippie Traynor.

"I prefer to keep mine for myself, and not have them lifted off my plate," said Max, sounding as though something were caught in his throat.

"The bullet went straight through the left lens of his glasses and right into his head," said Toby. "And when he raised his head, his eye was full of blood."

"Would you look out that window?" Max said in a loud voice.

Bill Messinger and Tony Flax turned to the window, saw nothing special— perhaps a bit more haze in the air than they expected—and looked back at the old publisher.

"Sorry," Max said. He passed a trembling hand over his face. "I think I'll go back to my room."

4

"Nobody visits me," Bill Messinger said to Tess Corrigan. She was taking his blood pressure, and appeared to be having a little trouble getting accurate numbers. "I don't even really remember how long I've been here, but I haven't had a single visitor."

"Haven't you now?" Tess squinted at the blood pressure tube, sighed, and once again pumped the ball and tightened the band around his arm. Her breath contained a pure, razor-sharp whiff of alcohol.

"It makes me wonder, do I have any friends?"

Tess grunted with satisfaction and scribbled numbers on his chart. "Writers lead lonely lives," she told him. "Most of them aren't fit for human company, anyhow." She patted his wrist. "You're a lovely specimen, though."

"Tess, how long have I been here?"

"Oh, it was only a little while ago," she said. "And I believe it was raining at the time."

After she left, Bill watched television for a little while, but television, a frequent and dependable companion in his earlier life, seemed to have become intolerably stupid. He turned it off and for a time flipped through the pages of the latest book by a highly regarded contemporary novelist several decades younger than himself. He had bought the book before going into the hospital, thinking that during his stay he would have enough uninterrupted time to dig into the experience so many others had described as rich, complex, and marvelously nuanced, but he was having problems getting through it. The book bored him. The people were loathsome and the style was gelid. He kept wishing he had brought along some uncomplicated and professional trash he could use as a palate cleanser. By 10:00, he was asleep.

At 11:30, a figure wrapped in cold air appeared in his room, and he woke up as she approached. The woman coming nearer in the darkness must have been Molly, the Jamaican nurse who always charged in at this hour, but she did not give off Molly's arousing scent of fires in underground crypts. She smelled of damp weeds and muddy riverbanks. Bob did not want this version of Molly to get any closer to him than the end of his bed, and with his heart beating so violently that he could feel the limping rhythm of his heart, he commanded her to stop. She instantly obeyed.

He pushed the button to raise the head of his bed and tried to make her out as his body folded upright,. The river-smell had intensified, and cold air streamed toward him. He had no desire at all to turn on any of the three lights at his disposal. Dimly, he could make out a thin, tallish figure with dead hair plastered to her face, wearing what seemed to be a long cardigan sweater, soaked through and (he thought) dripping onto the floor. In this figure's hands was a fat, unjacketed book stained dark by her wet fingers.

"I don't want you here," he said. "And I don't want to read that book, either. I've already read everything you ever wrote, but that was a long time ago."

The drenched figure glided forward and deposited the book between his feet. Terrified that he might recognize her face, Bill clamped his eyes shut and kept them shut until the odors of river-water and mud had vanished from the air.

When Molly burst into the room to gather the new day's information the next morning, Bill Messinger realized that his night's visitation could have occurred only in a dream. Here was the well-known, predictable world around him, and every inch of it was a profound relief to him. Bill took in his bed, the little nest of monitors ready to be called upon should an emergency take place, his television and its remote control device, the door to his spacious bathroom, the door to the hallway, as ever half-open. On the other side of his bed lay the long window, now curtained for the sake of the night's sleep. And here, above all, was Molly, a one-woman Reality Principle, exuding the rich odor of burning graves as she tried to cut off his circulation with a blood-pressure machine. The bulk and massivity of her upper arms suggested that Molly's own blood pressure would have to be read by means of some other technology, perhaps steam gauge. The whites of her eyes shone with a faint trace of pink, leading Bill to speculate for a moment of wild improbability if the ferocious night nurse indulged in marijuana.

"You're doing well, Mr. Postman," she said. "Making good progress."

"I'm glad to hear it," he said. "When do you think I'll be able to go home?"

"That is for the doctors to decide, not me. You'll have to bring it up with them." From a pocket hidden beneath her swags and pouches, she produced a white paper cup half-filled with pills and capsules of varying sizes and colors. She thrust it at him. "Morning meds. Gulp them down like a good boy, now." Her other hand held out a small plastic bottle of Poland Spring water, the provenance of which reminded Messinger of what Chippie Traynor had said about Maine. Deep woods, roads without names . . .

He upended the cup over his mouth, opened the bottle of water, and managed to get all his pills down at the first try.

Molly whirled around to leave with her usual sense of having had more than enough of her time wasted by the likes of him, and was half way to the door before he remembered something that had been on his mind for the past few days.

"I haven't seen the *Times* since I don't remember when," he said. "Could you please get me a copy? I wouldn't even mind one that's a couple of days old."

Molly gave him a long, measuring look, then nodded her head. "Because many of our people find them so upsetting, we tend not to get the newspapers up here. But I'll see if I can locate one for you." She moved ponderously to the door and paused to look back at him again just before she walked out. "By the way, from now on you and your friends will have to get along without Mr. Traynor's company."

"Why?" Bill asked. "What happened to him?"

"Mr. Traynor is . . . gone, sir."

"Chippie died, you mean? When did that happen?" With a shudder, he remembered the figure from his dream. The smell of rotting weeds and wet riverbank awakened within him, and he felt as if she were once again standing before him.

"Did I say he was dead? What I said was, he is . . . *gone*."

For reasons he could not identify, Bill Messinger did not go through the morning's rituals with his usual impatience. He felt slow-moving, reluctant to engage the day. In the shower, he seemed barely able to raise his arms. The water seemed brackish, and his soap all but refused to lather. The towels were stiff and thin, like the cheap towels he remembered from his youth. After he had succeeded in drying off at least most of the easily reachable parts of his body, he sat on his bed and listened to the breath laboring in and out of his body. Without him noticing, the handsome pin-striped suit had become as wrinkled and tired as he felt himself to be, and besides that he seemed to be out of clean shirts. He pulled a dirty one from the closet. His swollen feet took some time to ram into his black loafers.

Armored at last in the costume of a great worldly success, Bill stepped out into the great corridor with a good measure of his old dispatch. He wished Max Baccarat had not called him a "jumped-up little fop" and a "damned little show pony" the other day, for he genuinely enjoyed good clothing, and it hurt him to think that others might take this simple pleasure, which after all did contain a moral element, as a sign of vanity. On the other hand, he should have thought twice before telling Max that he was a third-rate publisher and a sellout. Everybody knew that robe hadn't been a gift from Graham Greene, though. That myth represented nothing more than Max Baccarat's habit of portraying and presenting himself as an old-line publishing grandee, like Alfred Knopf.

The nursing station—what he liked to think of as "the command center"—was oddly understaffed this morning. In a landscape of empty desks and unattended computer monitors, Molly sat on a pair of stools she had placed side by side, frowning as ever down at some form she was obliged to work through. Bill nodded at her and received the non-response he had anticipated. Instead of turning left toward the Salon as he usually did, Bill decided to stroll over to the elevators and the cherry wood desk where diplomatic, red-jacketed Mr. Singh guided newcomers past his display of Casablanca lilies, tea roses, and lupines. On his perambulations through the halls, he often passed through Mr. Singh's tiny realm, and he found the man a kindly, reassuring presence.

Today, though, Mr. Singh seemed not to be on duty, and the great glass vase had been removed from his desk. OUT OF ORDER signs had been taped to the elevators.

Feeling a vague sense of disquiet, Bill retraced his steps and walked past the side of the nursing station to embark upon the long corridor that led to the north-facing window. Max Baccarat's room lay down this corridor, and

Bill thought he might pay a call on the old gent. He could apologize for the insults he had given him, and perhaps receive an apology in return. Twice, Baccarat had thrown the word "little" at him, and Bill's cheeks stung as if he had been slapped. About the story, or the memory, or whatever it had been, however, Bill intended to say nothing. He did not believe that he, Max, and Tony Flax had dreamed of the same bizarre set of events, nor that they had experienced these decidedly dream-like events in youth. The illusion that they had done so had been inspired by proximity and daily contact. The world of Floor 21 was as hermetic as a prison.

He came to Max's room and knocked at the half-open door. There was no reply. "Max?" he called out. "Feel like having a visitor?"

In the absence of a reply, he thought that Max might be asleep. It would do no harm to check on his old acquaintance. How odd, it occurred to him, to think that he and Max had both had relations with little Edie Wheadle. And Tony Flax, too. And that she should have died on this floor, unknown to them! *There* was someone to whom he rightly could have apologized—at the end, he had treated her quite badly. She had been the sort of girl, he thought, who almost expected to be treated badly. But far from being an excuse, that was the opposite, an indictment.

Putting inconvenient Edie Wheadle out of his mind, Bill moved past the bathroom and the "reception" area into the room proper, there to find Max Baccarat not in bed as he had expected, but beyond it and seated in one of the low, slightly cantilevered chairs, which he had turned to face the window.

"Max?"

The old man did not acknowledge his presence in any way. Bill noticed that he was not wearing the splendid blue robe, only his white pajamas, and his feet were bare. Unless he had fallen asleep, he was staring at the window and appeared to have been doing so for some time. His silvery hair was mussed and stringy. As Bill approached, he took in the rigidity of Max's head and neck, the stiff tension in his shoulders. He came around the foot of the bed and at last saw the whole of the old man's body, stationed sideways to him as it faced the window. Max was gripping the arms of the chair and leaning forward. His mouth hung open, and his lips had been drawn back. His eyes, too, were open, hugely, as they stared straight ahead.

With a little thrill of anticipatory fear, Bill glanced at the window. What he saw, haze shot through with streaks of light, could hardly have brought Max Baccarat to this pitch. His face seemed rigid with terror. Then Bill realized that this had nothing to do with terror, and Max had suffered a great, paralyzing stroke. That was the explanation for the pathetic scene before him. He jumped to the side of the bed and pushed the call button for the nurse.

When he did not get an immediate response, he pushed it again, twice, and held the button down for several seconds. Still no soft footsteps came from the corridor.

A folded copy of the *Times* lay on Max's bed, and with a sharp, almost painful sense of hunger for the million vast and minuscule dramas taking place outside Governor General, he realized that what he had said to Molly was no more than the literal truth: it seemed weeks since he had seen a newspaper. With the justification that Max would have no use for it, Bill snatched up the paper and felt, deep in the core of his being, a real greed for its contents—devouring the columns of print would be akin to gobbling up great bits of the world. He tucked the neat, folded package of the *Times* under his arm and left the room.

"Nurse," he called. It came to him that he had never learned the real name of the woman they called Molly Goldberg. "Hello? There's a man in trouble down here!"

He walked quickly down the hallway in what he perceived as a deep, unsettling silence. "Hello, nurse!" he called, at least in part to hear at least the sound of his own voice.

When Bill reached the deserted nurses' station, he rejected the impulse to say, "Where is everybody?" The Night Visitor no longer occupied her pair of stools, and the usual chiaroscuro had deepened into a murky darkness. It was as though they had pulled the plugs and stolen away.

"I don't get this," Bill said. "*Doctors* might bail, but nurses don't."

He looked up and down the corridor and saw only a gray carpet and a row of half-open doors. Behind one of those doors sat Max Baccarat, who had once been something of a friend. Max was destroyed, Bill thought; damage so severe could not be repaired. Like a film of greasy dust, the sense descended upon him that he was wasting his time. If the doctors and nurses were elsewhere, as seemed the case, nothing could be done for Max until their return. Even after that, in all likelihood very little could be done for poor old Max. His heart failure had been a symptom of a wider systemic problem.

But still. He could not just walk away and ignore Max's plight. Messinger turned around and paced down the corridor to the door where the nameplate read Anthony Flax. "Tony," he said. "Are you in there? I think Max had a stroke."

He rapped on the door and pushed it all the way open. Dreading what he might find, he walked into the room. "Tony?" He already knew the room was empty, and when he was able to see the bed, all was as he had expected: an empty bed, an empty chair, a blank television screen, and blinds pulled down to keep the day from entering.

Bill left Tony's room, turned left, then took the hallway that led past the Salon. A man in an unclean janitor's uniform, his back to Bill, was removing the Mapplethorpe photographs from the wall and loading them face-down onto a wheeled cart.

"What are you doing?" he asked.

The man in the janitor uniform looked over his shoulder and said, "I'm doing my job, that's what I'm doing." He had greasy hair, a low forehead, and an acne-scarred face with deep furrows in the cheeks.

"But why are you taking down those pictures?"

The man turned around to face him. He was strikingly ugly, and his ugliness seemed part of his intention, as if he had chosen it. "Gee, buddy, why do you suppose I'd do something like that? To upset *you*? Well, I'm sorry if you're upset, but you had nothing to do with this. They tell me to do stuff like this, I do it. End of story." He pushed his face forward, ready for the next step.

"Sorry," Bill said. "I understand completely. Have you seen a doctor or a nurse up here in the past few minutes? A man on the other side of the floor just had a stroke. He needs medical attention."

"Too bad, but I don't have anything to do with doctors. The man I deal with is my supervisor, and supervisors don't wear white coats, and they don't carry stethoscopes. Now if you'll excuse me, I'll be on my way."

"But I need a doctor!"

"You look okay to me," the man said, turning away. He took the last photograph from the wall and pushed his cart through the metal doors that marked the boundary of the realm ruled by Tess Corrigan, Molly Goldberg, and their colleagues. Bill followed him through, and instantly found himself in a functional, green-painted corridor lit by fluorescent lighting and lined with locked doors. The janitor pushed his trolley around a corner and disappeared.

"Is anybody here?" Bill's voice carried through the empty hallways. "A man here needs a doctor!"

The corridor he was in led to another, which led to another, which went past a small, deserted nurses' station and ended at a huge, flat door with a sign that said MEDICAL PERSONNEL ONLY. Bill pushed at the door, but it was locked. He had the feeling that he could wander through these corridors for hours and find nothing but blank walls and locked doors. When he returned to the metal doors and pushed through to the private wing, relief flooded through him, making him feel light-headed.

The Salon invited him in—he wanted to sit down, he wanted to catch his breath and see if any of the little cakes had been set out yet. He had forgotten to order breakfast, and hunger was making him weak. Bill put his hand on one of the pebble-glass doors and saw an indistinct figure seated near the table. For a moment, his heart felt cold, and he hesitated before he opened the door.

Tony Flax was bent over in his chair, and what Bill Messinger noticed first was that the critic was wearing one of the thin hospital gowns that tied at the neck and the back. His trench coat lay puddled on the floor. Then he saw that Flax appeared to be weeping. His hands were clasped to his face, and his back rose and fell with jerky, uncontrolled movements.

"Tony?" he said. "What happened to you?"

Flax continued to weep silently, with the concentration and selfishness of a small child.

"Can I help you, Tony?" Bill asked.

When Flax did not respond, Bill looked around the room for the source of his distress. Half-filled coffee cups stood on the little tables, and petits fours lay jumbled and scattered over the plates and the white table. As he watched, a cockroach nearly two inches long burrowed out of a little square of white chocolate and disappeared around the back of a Battenburg cake. The cockroach looked as shiny and polished as a new pair of black shoes.

Something was moving on the other side of the window, but Bill Messinger wanted nothing to do with it. "Tony," he said, "I'll be in my room."

Down the corridor he went, the tails of his suit jacket flapping behind him. A heavy, liquid pressure built up in his chest, and the lights seemed to darken, then grow brighter again. He remembered Max, his mind gone, staring open-mouthed at his window: what had he seen?

Bill thought of Chippie Traynor, one of his mole-like eyes bloodied behind the shattered lens of his glasses.

At the entrance to his room, he hesitated once again as he had outside the Salon, fearing that if he went in, he might not be alone. But of course he would be alone, for apart from the janitor no one else on Floor 21 was capable of movement. Slowly, making as little noise as possible, he slipped around his door and entered his room. It looked exactly as it had when he had awakened that morning. The younger author's book lay discarded on his bed, the monitors awaited an emergency, the blinds covered the long window. Bill thought the wildly alternating pattern of light and dark that moved across the blinds proved nothing. Freaky New York weather, you never knew what it was going to do. He did not hear odd noises, like half-remembered voices, calling to him from the other side of the glass.

As he moved nearer to the foot of the bed, he saw on the floor the bright jacket of the book he had decided not to read, and knew that in the night it had fallen from his moveable tray. The book on his bed had no jacket, and at first he had no idea where it came from. When he remembered the circumstances under which he had seen this book—or one a great deal like it—he felt revulsion, as though it were a great slug.

Bill turned his back on the bed, swung his chair around, and plucked the newspaper from under his arm. After he had scanned the headlines without making much effort to take them in, habit led him to the obituaries on the last two pages of the financial section. As soon as he had folded the pages back, a photograph of a sly, mild face with a recessed chin and tiny spectacles lurking above an overgrown nose levitated up from the columns of newsprint. The header announced CHARLES CHIPP TRAYNOR, POPULAR WAR HISTORIAN TARRED BY SCANDAL.

Helplessly, Bill read the first paragraph of Chippie's obituary. Four days past, this once-renowned historian whose career had been destroyed by charges of plagiarism and fraud had committed suicide by leaping from the window of his fifteenth-story apartment on the Upper West Side.

Four days ago? Bill thought. It seemed to him that was when Chippie Traynor had first appeared in the Salon. He dropped the paper, with the effect that Traynor's fleshy nose and mild eyes peered up at him from the floor. The terrible little man seemed to be everywhere, despite having *gone*. He could sense Chippie Traynor floating outside his window like a small, inoffensive balloon from Macy's Thanksgiving Day Parade. Children would say, "Who's that?" and their parents would look up, shield their eyes, shrug, and say, "I don't know, hon. Wasn't he in a Disney cartoon?" Only he was not in a Disney cartoon, and the children and their parents could not see him, and he wasn't at all cute. One of his eyes had been injured. This Chippie Traynor, not the one that had given them a view of his backside in the Salon, hovered outside Bill Messinger's window, whispering the wretched and insinuating secrets of the despised, the contemptible, the rejected and fallen from grace.

Bill turned from the window and took a single step into the nowhere that awaited him. He had nowhere to go, he knew, so nowhere had to be where he was going. It was probably going to be a lot like this place, only less comfortable. Much, *much* less comfortable. With nowhere to go, he reached out his hand and picked up the dull brown book lying at the foot of his bed. Bringing it toward his body felt like reeling in some monstrous fish that struggled against the line. There were faint watermarks on the front cover, and it bore a faint, familiar smell. When he had it within reading distance, Bill turned the spine up and read the title and author's name: *In the Middle of the Trenches* by Charles Chipp Traynor. It was the book he had blurbed. Max Baccarat had published it, and Tony Flax had rhapsodized over it in the

Sunday *Times* book review section. About a hundred pages from the end, a bookmark in the shape of a thin silver cord with a hook at one end protruded from the top of the book.

Bill opened the book at the place indicated, and the slender bookmark slithered downwards like a living thing. Then the hook caught the top of the pages, and its length hung shining and swaying over the bottom edge. No longer able to resist, Bill read some random sentences, then two long paragraphs. This section undoubtedly had been lifted from the oral histories, and it recounted an odd event in the life of a young man who, years before his induction into the Armed Forces, had come upon a strange house deep in the piney woods of East Texas and been so unsettled by what he had seen through its windows that he brought a rifle with him on his next visit. Bill realized that he had never read this part of the book. In fact, he had written his blurb after merely skimming through the first two chapters. He thought Max had read even less of the book than he had. In a hurry to meet his deadline, Tony Flax had probably read the first half.

At the end of his account, the former soldier said, "In the many times over the years when I thought about this incident, it always seemed to me that the man I shot was myself. It seemed my own eye I had destroyed, my own socket that bled."

• • • •

*She'd lived a long time and never seen anything to make her believe
that any part of us could survive after death . . .*

The Score
Alaya Dawn Johnson

*Don't matter what we sing
Every window we open, they jam another door
They gladhand, pander, lie for the king
It's our song, but their score*

—Jake Pray, "What We Sing"
(First documented performance:
February 15, 2003 at the pre-invasion
anti-Iraq War marches in New York City)

•

Gmail—Inbox—jimmy.sullivan@gmail.com—chat

me: violet, i'm so sorry. if you need someone to come over . . .
Sent at 3:16 PM on Sunday

Violet: he never liked you, you know
Sent at 4:43 PM on Sunday

Violet's new status message:
*Two bleeding hearts drank ginger beer / and mocked and stung their
gingered fears / to know the future, and still die here. Rahimahullah, Jake.*

•

NEW YORK CITY MEDICAL EXAMINER

NAME: Jacob Nasser	AUTOPSY-NO. 43-6679
SEX: Male	DATE OF AUTOPSY: 3/21/2007
RACE: White (Arab)	TIME OF AUTOPSY: 3:36 p.m.
DOB: 2/1/81	DATE OF REPORT: 4/1/2007
DATE OF DEATH: 3/17/07–3/18/07	

FINAL PATHOLOGICAL DIAGNOSES:

I.   25 MICRON TEAR IN CORONARY ARTERY, POSSIBLE
     INDICATION OF SPONTANEOUS CORONARY ARTERY
     DISSECTION

II. MINIMAL DRUG INTOXICATION
     A. Probable non-contributory drugs present:
          1. Acetaminophen (2 mg/L)
          2. Cannabis (30.0 ng/mL)

OPINION:

Jacob Nasser was a 26-year-old male of Arab descent who died of undetermined causes. The presence of a 25 micron tear in his coronary artery might indicate SCAD (Spontaneous Coronary Artery Dissection), however it was deemed too small to lead to a definitive finding. The presence of cannabis was small and non-contributing.

The manner of death is determined to be: COULD NOT BE DETERMINED.

> M. Andy Pilitokis
> M.D., LL.B, M.Sc.
> Chief Medical Examiner
>
> Andrea Varens, MD
> Associate Medical Examiner

Jake Pray (Jacob Nasser) prelim autopsy notes **[Recovered]**
Last saved with AutoRecover
4:33 AM Thursday, March 22, 2007

Andrea Varens
3/21/07

The subject was first discovered dead in his holding cell the morning of March 18 in the "Tombs" Manhattan Detention Center. The subject was discovered with a rope in his hand, and so police at first surmised it had contributed in some manner to his death, but there are no consistent contusions on the neck or, indeed, anywhere else on the body.

A preliminary physical examination reveals what looks to be a normal, healthy twenty-six year old man with no signs of ill-health or infirmity (beyond the obvious).

Drug interactions? Probably SCAD, poor fucker.

I saw him. I went to the hallway to get a coke from the machine and I saw him. Leaning against the wall looking out the window. Oh fuck. Fuck fuck fuck. I've been staring at his sorry face for the last two days, I oughta know. Maybe he has a long lost twin brother?

Mom was right, I should have gone into

•

The New York Post
Anti-War Songster "Scored" Dope, Autopsy Says
April 2, 2007

Bad news for the anti-Bush peaceniks who've turned Jake Pray into a martyr: turns out he was stoned on dope (the equivalent of "one joint of strong chronic," according to a well-placed source) when police took him into custody. And he died of a "spontaneous" heart attack. Not police abuse.

Of course, you didn't hear any of that damning data at the packed memorial service in the ultra-liberal Riverside Church this Sunday. In fact, Pray's memorial service sounded more like an anti-war rally.

Violet Omura, a Columbia grad student who spoke at the memorial, had nothing but contempt for the city's Medical Examiner. "It's ridiculous," she said. "It's like if you shot me in the head and the autopsy said I had died due to 'spontaneous brain leakage.' "

Pray's fellow protesters were convinced police abuse was responsible. "[The police] really picked on him at the rally," said Billy Davis, a close friend who had been present at the protest. "Guess they saw his skin and hair, you know, and drew their conclusions," Davis said, referring to Pray's Palestinian heritage. "They called him a terrorist. Said ragheads like him were responsible for bringing down the Twin Towers." Davis also accused the officers of using tasers on the unruly protestors. Conspiracy theories abounded at the memorial of how the non-lethal crowd-control devices could have contributed to his death.

In a statement issued today, the Police Commissioner denied all accusations of wrongdoing by the officers on the scene, and restated the findings of yesterday's autopsy report. "Should any new evidence surface regarding this case, rest assured that we will pursue it with all due diligence."

•

Rock & Rap Confidential
"What We Still Sing"
Issue 4, Volume 78; May, 2007

Jake Pray may never have had a hit song, but to the latest crop of anti-war protestors, "What We Sing" has the same iconic resonance that "Bring the Boys Home" or "Masters of War" had for their parents. And over three hundred youngbloods turned out for the memorial of this iconoclastic musician, held this past March in Riverside Church.

Jake Pray was born as Jacob Nasser to Palestinian immigrants who settled in suburban New Jersey when he was just three years old. His father was a professor of Linguistics and Cultural Anthropology at a university in the Gaza strip who was forced to emigrate after he received death threats for his political positions.

Not surprisingly, Pray became a lightning rod for activists across the world when his life ended in Manhattan's "Tombs" detention facility. He was arrested after an incident with police during the anti-war protests this March. The autopsy report declared its findings inconclusive. The police commissioner, in a written statement, called Pray's death a "tragic incident." The arresting officer taunted the twenty-six year old man with racial slurs like "raghead." He shot 50,000 excruciating volts of electricity into his body, and then detained him in unspeakable conditions for endless hours. A *tragic incident*? The mind would boggle, if it wasn't so painfully predictable.

The larger meaning of Jake's life was best captured by Violet Omura, a twenty-five year-old graduate student in the Physics department at Columbia.

"Perhaps the experiences of his parents in the occupied territories influenced his decision to turn to political activism and the thankless efforts of those who argue from right, not expedience. But I think, perhaps, that he mostly just wanted to tell, he just wanted to sing, he just wanted others to know they had a voice. Our parents were optimists. They gave us 'Imagine,' and 'Blowin' in the Wind.' We're not pessimists. God knows Jake wasn't a pessimist. But he wasn't so sure that singing could change anything. Some people complain that 'What We Sing' is bleak. I disagree. It's furious, it's strident, and it's real. Jake wanted to change the world, but he couldn't hide from the fact that it might never change."

•

Billboard Pop 100
Top Ten
Issue Date: 2007-5-19
#1: Beyonce & Shakira: Beautiful Liar
#2: Gwen Stefani featuring Akon: The Sweet Escape
#3: Fergie featuring Ludacris: Glamorous
#4: Avril Lavigne: Girlfriend
#5: Diddy featuring Keyshia Cole: Last Night
#6: Tim McGraw: Last Dollar
#7: Mims: This Is Why I'm Hot
#8: Jake Pray: What We Sing
#9: Gym Class Heroes: Cupid's Chokehold
#10: Fall Out Boy: This Ain't A Scene, It's An Arms Race

•

MSNBC TRANSCRIPT
"TUCKER" with Tucker Carlson
Original Air Date: 5/20/07

TUCKER CARLSON: Jake Pray has been in the news a lot lately. After all, the blame-America-firster's mysterious death in police custody, his illicit marijuana use and his surprise hit song, "What We Sing," have made him the perfect martyr for self-defeating liberal elitists.

But now, one of Pray's own radicals has come out against him. In a damning exposé published in the online fringe-left newsletter *Counterpunch*, James Sullivan has laid bare the despicable anti-Semitic and vitriolic anti-American hate that underlies the rabid far-left.

Welcome to the show, Mr. Sullivan.

JAMES SULLIVAN: Thank you very much for having me.

TC: We know you were detained with Jake Pray at the Chelsea Piers before he was taken to the Manhattan Detention Facility. How well did you know him?

JS: Well, when you're as heavily involved in the peace movement as I was, you kind of get to know everyone. Jake was, you know, dedicated. A bit too dedicated. He was a musician, but you could tell it wasn't really about the music for him. It was about the fame. People loved him. I did too, for a while.

TC: But eventually you realized—

JS: Yeah, you know, he was just full of—sorry, yeah, full of it. A bit of a megalomaniac.

TC: I understand that you're also a musician? Did he ever support you, or . . .
JS: Never. Jake really resented the presence of another musician in the, well, what he would have called the "inner circle."

TC: Now, I'm going to read a passage from your *Counterpunch* article. It's pretty damning, detailing what happened the afternoon you were both detained by the police. You write: "Pray was furious after the arrest. On the ride down to the pier he just sat in the police truck shaking and clenching his fists. His girlfriend, Violet Omura, tried to calm him down, but he just lashed out at her, called her an 'ignorant bitch' and a few other expressions I'll choose not to print here. He was always like that, in fact, willing—and sometimes eager—to take out his own personal frustrations and failings on others. Billy Davis and Violet and his other cronies are trying to claim that the police officers called him a 'raghead' that day. If they did I never heard it." And then, further on, you write: "Around the police, Pray was like a rabid dog. At Pier 57 it was like something had popped. He wasn't quiet anymore. We all heard him: Violet and Billy and the rest who are trying to pretend that it didn't happen."

You go on to list some of the epithets Pray hurled at our men in blue, some of which are not, um, fit for television. Could you share some of the milder ones?

JS: [Laughter] Yeah. They're—sure. "Filthy murdering bigots," that was one. He said they were all "closet fags," and accused them of ah—"practicing on Abner Louima." He just wouldn't stop. Finally, one of the officers tried to get him to calm down. He had dark curly hair, a big nose—you know, obviously Jewish, and Jake nearly tackled him. Said "his kind" was supporting genocide and maybe "they deserved what they got."

TC: "Deserved what they got." What do you think he meant by that?

JS: I think it's obvious. He was saying the Jewish people deserved the Holocaust.

TC: Wow. Now, I hear you're starting to distance yourself from all this and the so-called "peace" movement.

JS: Yeah. Actually, I'm [Laughter] yeah, I'm halfway through *Atlas Shrugged*.

TC: [Laughter] How do you like it so far?

JS: Really good. It's giving me a new perspective.

•

JakePrayTruth.org
Action Statement

Jake Pray, the radical anti-war protestor and singer, died as a result of police abuse on the night of March 17, 2007. This fact, supported by activists present during his arrest and reports from within the holding facility itself, has been systematically covered up by the New York City Police Department and coroner's office. This is just a part of an overall, covert strategy to undermine the vocal anti-war movement with acts of state-sponsored terror. Jake Pray, whose anti-war songs had energized a new generation of protestors, was first on their list because of his growing influence. COINTELPRO had thousands and thousands of pages about John Lennon in their files, because he posed a similar threat. In this age of increasing government control and ongoing illegal wars (one million dead and counting!), Jake Pray's powerful voice and even more powerful message posed an unacceptable threat.

But guess what? So do we. And we resolve to uncover the TRUTH about Jake Pray's murder and bring his message to the world.

—Billy Davis
Founder, JakePrayTruth.org
December 15, 2007

[UPDATE 1/3/08: For our official statement on the allegations made by James Sullivan, please visit our FAQ.]

•

Just Another (Libertarian) Weblog: Ron Paul 2008!
Rockin' For the Fatherland
Posted January 4, 2008 5:45 pm by BigFish

Well, Billy Davis over at JakePrayTruth has <u>finally responded</u> to the accusations James Sullivan made <u>such a big splash with</u> a few months ago.

Short version: Ole Jimmy is an opportunistic lying asshole.

Still, we have to thank him. "Practicing on Abner Louima" is an expression now enshrined in my soul. Hey Jake, wherever you are, I never look at a toilet plunger without thinking of you. (Unfortunately none of the <u>inexplicably frequent ghost-sightings of Pray</u> these last few months have involved home plumbing equipment. Though I hear he was spotted outside The Pink PussyCat last Thursday).

In other news, the redoubtable Jimmy Sullivan has <u>made himself a webpage</u>! Check out the "latest music" section. And here I had thought right-wing volks-rock had gone out of fashion in the Third Reich.

Oh. Never mind.

Sieg Heil!

•

To: Professor Violet Omura <vomura12@nyu.edu>
New York University
Department of Applied Physics

From: Zacharias Tibbs <zachknowsthelord@cheese.org>
15 East Rock Way
Topeka, Kansas

March 16, 2015

Dear PROFESSOR Omura:

I hope you are prepared & have sat down to read this letter for I have here enclosed the most ASTONISHING and SECRET mathematical formula whereby all events heretofore UNEXPLAINED by the greatest scientists of the world are rendered clear by a simple proof. If you do not believe this, don't trust me, but read on for yourself!

I see from reading your very fascinating articles and biography that you once had the privilege of knowing the great Jake Pray, whose every album I own. Would you believe me if I said that this GREAT MATHEMATICAL PROOF would even make clear the mystery of the rumors of his ghostly resurrection and spectral warnings of future wars & conflicts? Have I intrigued you? Yes, of course, for you have a keen intellect and open heart and would surely not want to deny your colleagues the benefit of the knowledge I have so HUMBLY stumbled upon.

Merely scroll down to see the world's greatest secret revealed . . .

$$p(R) = (As * (t(d)/Gw)) * B/V$$

Thus, the probability of any INDIVIDUAL, upon their DEATH & DEPARTURE from this world, becoming a REVENANT is revealed . . .

Where As = Astrological Sign, with the following values assigned:

Aries = .2
Taurus =.5
Gemini = 1
Cancer = 5
Leo = 1
Virgo = 3
Libra = .7
Scorpio = -1
Sagittarius = 2
Capricorn = 0
Aquarius = 1
Pisces = 2

As determined through intensive STUDY of GOD'S HOLY WORD & observations & deductions of a PERSONAL nature.

t(d) = the time spent in the process of dying

Gw = the number of GOOD WORKS performed in their lives, with the average being 500 for a CHRISTIAN and less than 100 for ALL OTHERS (& in particular those of the apostate MORMON faith)

B = that which belongs to BEELZEBUB, otherwise known as SATAN or the DEVIL. The values are assigned thusly:

If the subject is a Mormon, B = 1000, for all MORMONS shall surely walk the EARTH for ETERNITY
For ATHEISTS, B = 500
For CHRISTIANS of pure and godly EVANGELICAL faith, B = 0.1
For ALL OTHERS, B = 1

V = the number of verses in our HOLY BIBLE the departed knew & memorized in life

But perhaps you, in your SECULAR University and GODLESS education, do not understand the true significance of explaining the

REVENANTS among us. For do not mistake me, the revenants are responsible for all manner of WEIRD & UNEXPLAINED events. Not merely ghosts (like that of your (sadly GODLESS) REVENANT & FRIEND Jake Pray), but also such sundry as possession by DEMONS, ALIEN ABDUCTIONS and sightings of UFO'S!

Even the INEXPLICABLE behavior of SUBATOMIC particles through the EXTRA DIMENSIONS is caused by these revenants & of course not to mention the riddle of GRAVITY.

I am sure you can see the potential of this astonishing EQUATION and I will be happy to travel to the GODLESS city of New York to discuss it with you further. Though you are only an Assistant Professor, I feel you are the perfect VESSEL of this KNOWLEDGE.

Yours in RESPECT & ANTICIPATION,

Zacharias Tibbs

•

From: Violet Omura [vomura12@nyu.physics.edu]
To: zachknowsthelord@cheese.org
Date: March 18, 2015, 4:13 am, EST

Dear Zacharias:

you can bet that I have no aspirations to be the perfect VESSEL for your KNOWLEDGE, or even the person who has to open your crackpotty emails (what, you didn't think I got the first three?)

but I'm drunk and bored and this is definitely the worst day of my year, so I'll bite. taking it as a given that you wouldn't know a quantum theory of gravity from a hemorrhoid, why don't all these horrible sinners and atheists and (!) mormons just go to, you know, hell? seems easier than having billions of revenants wandering the earth like thetans or something. you're not a scientologist, are you?

I don't know what you might have read or whatever about jake and me but you honestly can't believe that a godless intellectual like yours truly believes the woowoo crackpots who say he still shows up at their rallies?

god i wish he did.

(I mean 'god' in a purely rhetorical, godless way, of course).

violet, future revenant

•

From: zachknowsthelord@cheese.org
To: vomura12@nyu.physics.edu
Date: March 18, 2015, 6:21 pm, CMT

PROFESSOR Omura:

Disregarding your DRUNKEN (and, indeed, Godless) aspersions on my theory & character, you have indeed hit upon the crux of the matter.

For through other EQUATIONS & RESEARCH, I have hit upon the fundamental truth: these revenants do not go to HELL, for we are ALREADY LIVING THERE.

Yes, I say. The present EARTH merged with BEELZEBUB'S kingdom on the night of MARCH 20, 2003.

I trust you recognize the date? Yes, for your friend Jake Pray was present at every RALLY and PEACE MARCH in protest of this war, which I of course included in his calculation for GOOD WORKS.

Contemplate our SINFUL world and tell me that you do not agree? We have been DENIZENS of hell for the last twelve years!

And as a side note, I am of course entirely OPPOSED to all false gods, including the ABSURD teachings of SCIENTOLOGISTS. I must thank you for reminding me of them, for both they AND Mormons should receive a Beelzebub score of 1000 . . .

When would you like to meet?

Zacharias Tibbs

●

Warp & Weft: An Inclusive Community for Alternative Paradigms and Progressive Politics

Virtual Town Meeting (Excerpt)
Transcript and Audio archived on the community bulletin board
Original event April 1, 2017

[Rose_Granny] Thank you all for inviting me here today. I'm Rose, and as my husband used to say, I don't look much like my avatar. [Laughter] I've never really believed in ghosts. Oh, I've heard stories and some were eerie enough to make me shiver, but I've lived a long time and I had never seen anything to make me believe that any part of us could survive after death.

When my husband died last year, after a long and painful fight with liver cancer, I was devastated. I decided that it was my duty to make Harold's life count as much as it could, by taking his ideals and courage and using that to further work he would have approved of. So I became, at age 75, a political activist. I attended rallies. I spoke up at virtual town meetings like this one for our local congress members. I made signs, I wrote letters, I organized petitions . . . and I discovered Jake Pray. I'd heard "What We Sing" on the radio years ago, of course, but at the time I hadn't paid any attention to the man or the story behind the song. When I learned of how he died, I was shocked. How could such a young man, with such promise of the future, die so suddenly? He had no serious drugs in his body. There were no signs of violence, self-inflicted or otherwise. He was found dead on the floor of his holding cell, with a bit of rope in his hand.

And then I saw him. Perhaps it will not surprise most of you to learn that I mean this literally. I saw Jake Pray, sitting beside me in the dark early-morning during a sit-in protest in front of the White House. A rope was wrapped around his left hand. He looked very young—the exact image of the twenty-five year old I'd seen in all the pictures. Still, I tried to rationalize it as an uncanny coincidence, a kid who happened to look just like him.

"Aren't you cold?" I asked, when I saw his short-sleeved T-shirt. He smiled and shook his head. The cold obviously didn't bother him. That's when I knew he was a ghost: it was at least twenty degrees that morning.

All these questions bubbled inside of me, but I was so nervous I didn't know if I could get them out. "Do you think we'll be able to stop this escalation with China?" I finally asked.

He looked very sad. Just then, a friend tapped me on my shoulder. I glanced away for just a second, but when I turned back, he was gone.

Would it surprise you to learn that I attended that sit-in on March 15? And yes, India sent the first cruise missiles into Nanjing two days later.

•

Warp & Weft Message Boards

Topic: Jake Pray was MURDERED and gov't is COVERING it up!
Username: FightAllPwr4
Date: April 2, 2017 – 3:34 EST

Rose_Granny is a government dupe. She says "there were no signs of violence," but how can we trust the coroners report when it was commissioned by the same government that first marked Pray for assassination?! That's like trusting the tobacco industry to give an accurate autopsy to the Marlboro man! Billy Davis, who was THERE, said the arresting officer called him a 'fucking raghead' and 'commie' and that he was a 'mass murderer' who 'flew the planes into the Twin Towers.' This jerk couldn't wait to get his hands on Jake. Just consider a few things:

Why is the coroner report dated APRIL 1?! A subtle hint, maybe, that all is not what it seems? APRIL 1, 2007 was a SUNDAY. Who publishes a coroner report on a SUNDAY? This is a fucking ten-year-old April Fools' joke, people!

He had a "spontaneous cardiac artery dissection" but he only had a 25 micron tear? How was that enough to kill him? Do you know how big 25 microns is? Half the width of a STRAND OF HAIR!

Where did this famous rope come from? Violet Omura, a respected physicist, was his lover at the time. She visited him a few hours before he was discovered dead. She says he seemed distressed by the racist cop's treatment, but showed no signs of chest pain or anything that could lead to his "spontaneous" death! Significantly, *she saw no rope anywhere in the cell!* Where did it come from? The forgotten remains of a top-secret government 'alternative interrogation' technique, imported from our gulags in Guantanamo, Stare Kjekuty and Iraq?

Jake Pray was tortured to death by our own government. Maybe the reason he's haunting us, Rose_Granny, is because he wants the truth to come out!

JakePrayTruth.org

•

Warp & Weft Message Boards

Topic: Re: Jake Pray was MURDERED and gov't is COVERING it up!
Username: SweetGreenOnions
Date: April 2, 2017 – 3:45 EST

omura did it. evidence from "not a factor", the last song he ever wrote:

The invisible hand blasts the cradle
Spreading peace by throwing bombs
We feast beneath the master's table
Sating growls with salvaged crumbs
Save the world? It's just a song

she told jake to provoke a fight with those officers. the NSA <i>paid</i her to be the yoko ono of the antiwar left.

•

Excerpt from *Real Ghosts: The Warp & Weft Guide to Specters and Revenants of the 21st Century* by Dede Star Flower (HarperPenguin, New York, 2018)

The accuracy of his revenant predictions is quite remarkable. Two days after the New York Medical Examiner saw Pray's ghost in her office building, the Iranians kidnapped 15 UK soldiers. In 2009, a cocktail waitress sighted Pray in an alley, and that very night the US dropped the first round of tactical nuclear weapons on Iran. In 2011, Amina Okrafour was marking the anniversary of John Lennon's death in Central Park when she saw Pray's ghost. The next day the Chinese government shipped 1000 support troops to the Iranian front. The list goes on: 13 activists see Pray at an anti-globalization rally in Sweden; the next day India tests a nuclear bomb and the cease-fire ends in Kashmir. When San Francisco representative Linda Xiaobo reported seeing Pray during a ceremony in the Mojave desert, we all knew that the talks to bring India into NATO were a certainty. Sure enough, a few days later, the US honored its obligations under the treaty and declared itself officially at war with China and Pakistan.

As a revenant, Jake cannot stop these horrors from occurring, but he can stand witness to them. He can accuse us, like Hamlet's father, of not doing enough.

•

Written Communication from Zacharias Tibbs; Topeka, Kansas
To: Violet Omura, NYU, Department of Applied Physics
Date: November 18, 2020 – 10:44 pm, EST

[**Sender:** Verified]

Professor Omura:

Perhaps you have wondered why I have not yet responded to your Communication which you sent to me this past April. In fact it is because I have UNDERTAKEN to follow your kind & SAGE ADVICE and read those very ERUDITE & SCHOLARLY works by the great Einstein, Feynman & Chatterjee. I found the latter's work on M-THEORY and the QUANTUM GRAVITY SYNTHESIS most Fascinating, though I must confess that I found a great deal of it Difficult, and indeed, sometimes quite IMPOSSIBLE to understand. GOD, it is clear, has GIFTED her with a great mind. As did HE to YOU.

It's strange, I thought upon my completion of these works, how very CLEAR my errors in the past are to me now. Though I maintain my belief in REVENANTS & the HOLY SPIRIT, it is clear that my EQUATIONS & THEORIES, which I had thought could explain the WORLD, were not worth a Greasy Rag. I see the DEPTH of THOUGHT of those PHYSICISTS exploring the universe, and I feel a small INCHWORM in comparison. I must thank you for your most UNUSUAL & FAITHFUL correspondence over the years. Without it I fear I would never have understood my Gross Errors.

I have also Considered your Strange words to me regarding your SAD & PAINFUL feelings of guilt & regret over some mysterious Life Event. I say to you that your grief GRIEVES ME, for I know that you, too, could find solace in the LORD, if only you would open your heart to HIM. You say you Cannot, because "a scientist does not work from faith, but evidence." This is a Worthy Philosophy, but I say that because I KNOW GOD EXISTS, the EVIDENCE for him will someday be FOUND. Cannot you SEE His HAND in Chatterjee's Equations?

Can you not SEE that the reason your friend Jake still WALKS AMONG US is because he is a Revenant on Earth?

I await your Response with great Eagerness & Anticipation.

Zach Tibbs

•

Excerpt from "Changing the Score: My Life with Jake Pray"
By Violet Omura
Vanity Fair, May 2025

Before I say anything else, before I tell my story, or what little I'm privileged to know of Jake's, let me make this perfectly clear:

I loved Jake Pray. For a certain period of time he, and the anti-war movement, were my entire life. When he died, that life fell apart so completely that for the first and only time I considered suicide. In some ways, on some nights, that pain has never left me. I could never have harmed Jake. Those who suggest otherwise reveal a lack of understanding about our relationship so profound I can only pity them. To those whose critical faculties have not been addled by baseless conspiracy-mongering, I offer my story.

• • •

I first saw him at The West End, in December of 2003. I was a senior at Columbia, a physics major so obsessed with quantum mechanical particle interactions and Feynman diagrams that I had only dimly registered our country's illegal invasion of a sovereign state. (Such ignorance was possible, then; over a certain income level, foreign wars didn't touch your daily life). I gleaned my news from articles my sister sent me, or my suitemates' overheard conversations. I felt the appropriate outrage, and promptly forgot about it. What, after all, does outrage look like at the Planck scale?

Later, while drunk, I would amend that rhetorical question: what does it *sound* like? The bar was packed that night. Some were the typical Friday-night crowd of loud freshmen and bored frat brothers, but others had heard Jake at the big rally in February and were excited to see him again. He didn't even perform "What We Sing," the song that was already turning into an anthem. It didn't matter. Jake had a voice that stuck you to your chair and forced you to listen. Almost gentle, with an ironic bite. "Like fresh ginger," a simile-inclined local reviewer once called it (and Jake and I laughed until we had to stop to breathe. We ate in Chinatown that night; he bought me ginger beer). His falsetto was eerie; his bass rough. Sometimes his vibrato wavered so wildly you thought he might lose the note, but he never did. His lyrics were passionate and only sometimes political. He had thick, wavy brown hair; a high forehead; wide eyes with camel's lashes; and a chin that dimpled when he smiled. He was young, talented, and beautiful. I was twenty-two and I felt as though I'd just crawled from Plato's cave.

I introduced myself after the set. He bought me a drink. We talked, I don't remember about what. For all I know I babbled about brane-theory and quantum gravity all night. I had never been very good at talking to people. But he didn't seem to mind me. He told me a little about himself. He had graduated from NYU that year as a film major, but he didn't want to make movies. And the usual: he was appalled by the Iraq war, President Bush, our foreign policies. He quoted Chomsky, which was familiar, and Said, which surprised me. He said he had met Edward Said as a child, when his parents had first moved to the States from Palestine. I asked him if he was Muslim; he said he was a "closet atheist." He asked me if I was religious; I said I was a physicist.

He took me back to my dorm that night; my philosophy of alcohol consumption at the time did not include moderation. He kissed me as he pressed the call button for the elevator, as though I might not notice if he were doing something else.

"Do I get your number?" he asked.

What odd syntax, I thought, many years later. Like it was a game show and my number was the all-expense-paid trip to the Bahamas.

• • •

My good friend Billy Davis, who died last year, spent his life advocating for a full inquiry into Jake's death. I find it ironic that even now, in the midst of our global war with China and Iran, the relatively insignificant Iraq War has so much cultural relevance. Perhaps because it is the first moment when our generation, collectively, began to realize that something had gone terribly wrong in our political and social system. Jake's death symbolized too much of that moment for us to ever let it go.

• • •

They took us to Pier 57, that detention center turned toxic waste dump where they liked to herd activists during overcrowded demonstrations. Jake was furious that day, on a manic high. He was no stranger to racism—was any Arab living in New York City after 9-11?—but the arresting officer that day reveled in a particularly nasty brand of invective. "Raghead" was the least of it (and if Jimmy Sullivan can even tell the difference between his mouth and his lower orifice, I've yet to see the evidence). After they arrested us, Jake could hardly sit still. The floor was covered in an unidentifiable sludge that slid beneath our shoes and smelled like decomposing tires. We were all chilly and desperate to get out. Jake went to ask the officers when they would release us. I never heard what they said to him, and I never got to ask. Jake started yelling and shouting. His hands trembled as he gesticulated, like a junkie coming off a high, though I knew that he hadn't had any more than half a joint. I remember being terrified, afraid that they would shoot him. When they set off the Taser, he dropped to the floor like a marionette loosed of its strings. He groaned, but he couldn't even seem to speak. The police officers laughed, I remember.

What did he yell? "Pigs," certainly. But Jake hated few things more than he hated the ongoing Palestinian/Israeli conflict, and he would have *never* used the despicable anti-Semitic tripe certain opportunistic faux-rock musicians attribute to him. We had been unlawfully detained and verbally abused. Did Jake's behavior represent a failure to turn the other cheek? Of course. But he never meant to be a martyr.

• • •

I went to the Tombs late that night, after they released us from the Pier and arrested him. His lawyer said the police insisted on detaining him for questioning and were charging him with "disorderly conduct." Jake was happy to see me. The police had confiscated his guitar and one of the officers conducting the interrogation was a real (to put it more genteelly than Jake) ignorant racist. I asked Jake if he was okay. He said he was, but he couldn't wait to get out of there. There was no rope in the cell that I can recall.

He was acting a little more restless than normal. Tapping his fingers against the bars and rocking back on his heels like a smoker with the DTs. It didn't seem remarkable at the time, and it might be that I am merely creating false positives, searching for a clue where none exists.

He held my hand before I left and kissed my palm. He liked romantic gestures.

"There's something happening here," he sang softly. Buffalo Springfield.

I kissed him. "I'll get Neil Young and the gang down here tomorrow."

"I'll see you, Angel."

It was the last thing he ever said to me.

But he had never called me "Angel" before.

•

Written Communication from Violet Omura,
NYU, Department of Applied Physics
To: Zacharias Tibbs; Topeka, Kansas
Date: December 25, 2025 – 1:05 am, EST

[**Sender:** Verified]

I woke up twenty minutes ago and couldn't fall asleep. Chaterjee has posted a new paper on the public archives. Did you see it?

It's been a while. Hope you're doing okay.

Merry (godless) Christmas, Zach.

•

Written Communication from Zacharias Tibbs; Topeka, Kansas
To: Violet Omura, General Communications Inbox,
Columbia University Physics Department
Date: March 18, 2027 – 6:01 pm, EST

[Hi! This message has been approved by your filters, but contains some questionable material. Would you like to proceed?]

[Okay! Message below.]

Professor Omura:

Though I know you have not heard from me these past two years, I hope you do remember our long correspondence and will still read my messages despite your new Tenured Position at the venerable Columbia University.

I have not Written due to increased Problems with my Health and also, perhaps more importantly, a crisis with my Faith. You might think that facing Death & the Great Beyond, as I am (a persistent Cancer, which no medicine can treat) would drive one in to the Bosom of their Lord, but I find myself instead Contemplating the letters you have sent me over the twelve years of our correspondence.

You have presented to me a mind steeped in rationality, who does not even let deep grief over personal loss sway her to the side of a comfort that she does not feel has a basis in reason. Is Faith a Good Thing, I ask myself? As a child, I loved mathematics. At the library, I read books about Pythagoras and Newton and Einstein. But in the end I preferred Money to Knowledge, as any Ignorant eighteen-year-old might. I passed over my chance at College. My Father got me a good job as an auto mechanic in his Cousin's shop. Last year, I retired. I had worked there for Sixty Five Years. I had kept my Faith and raised children. I had read the Bible and tried to use Math to Prove the Beauty of it.

I have wondered why I still Wrote to you, Professor, when you so Clearly held my Views in Disdain. I think now that I Respected the Knowledge you held. The Mathematics that I had loved in Childhood are your Life's Work. I thought if I could Convince you of the Truth of my Faith then it would not be Faith any longer but Reason.

And now, I think I have failed. I face death without the solace of Christ and I think it is not as Hard as I imagined in my youth, but hard enough.

With My Thanks and Respect,

Zacharias Tibbs

•

Written Communication from Violet Omura; Brooklyn, New York
To: Zacharias Tibbs; Topeka, Kansas
Date: March 19, 2027 – 3:20 am, EST

Zach,

Call me Violet. Would you like to meet for lunch sometime soon? I know of a great fondue place on Flatbush Avenue (that's in Brooklyn, where I live).

Violet

•

AUDIO-VISUAL TRANSCRIPT OF U.S. INTERNAL INVESTIGATIONS FILES
Originally archived on the diffuse-network, proprietary GlobalNet, intercepted and transcribed by Chinese Intelligence
Subject: Omura, Violet; U.S. Scientific Authority and Academic;
Status: Dissident
Date: September 12, 2027 – 2:22 am, EST

The subject's apartment is dark. She walks to the window overlooking the street. She removes her shoes and stockings (a run in the back: 4.2 cm). The subject's hair is styled in an elaborate bun. She removes several bobby pins and tosses them to the floor. The subject empties a small, gold purse onto her coffee table.

Contents:
One (1) funeral program. The cover reads: *Zacharias Tibbs: He was Right with Our Lord*
One (1) small rolled marijuana cigarette.

The subject lights the cigarette with a match. Upon completing half the joint, she extinguishes it on the windowsill.

OMURA: [Soft laughter]

OMURA: [Inaudible]

The subject turns from the window. She abruptly ceases almost all movement. Her breathing resumes after 2.4 seconds. It is at this point that the subject begins to behave very erratically. Her eyes are fixed at a point in the room, as though she is interacting with a person, though motion sensors and audio bots indicate she is alone. The subject has no known history of mental illness. [NOTE: However, our own psychiatrist has stated that her behavior here strongly indicates a psychotic break possibly triggered by the marijuana usage. Hearing voices is common in such incidences.]

OMURA: What . . . Jesus Christ. Jesus Fucking Christ, what's going on?

The subject pauses. Her body relaxes and her head movements are consistent with someone listening to someone else in conversation.

OMURA: Jake? Holy fuck, what was in that pot?

The subject takes two steps forward. [NOTE: The consulting psychiatrist has determined that the person to whom she believes she is addressing herself is standing between the coffee table and her couch.]

OMURA: What do ghosts look like at the Planck scale . . .

[20 second pause.]

OMURA: Zack did this?

[3 second pause. She shakes her head.]

OMURA: Maybe. Yes. In a strange way. He could have changed the world. But he fixed other people's cars.

[The subject begins to cry. Her hands have a pronounced tremble.]

OMURA: Jake, oh fuck. Fucking God, why are you . . . why now? I never believed, not once, and fuck do you know how much I wanted to? I could kill you! Christ Jake, 30 nanograms of *pot* and not a fucking drop of lithium!

[12 second pause. A siren is heard in the background.]

OMURA: I knew that. You think it makes me feel better? I should have known! The DTs, I said. Like you were manic. I saw it all then. I've known it all for years. 30 nanograms of pot, 2 milligrams of Tylenol. 0 nanograms of your fucking life.

[The subject steps closer.]

OMURA: Then why did you? Oh, you came back from the grave for me? God, my maudlin subconscious.

[11 second pause.]

OMURA: Like Hamlet's father? Did the ghost love?

[2 second pause.]

OMURA: Like me. Jake . . . if you're real and not my own degenerating brain . . . I'm sorry I asked you— No, listen, I should have known what you were going through. I shouldn't have put you in that position. Not with those trigger-happy assholes. Engineer a conflict? Get it on the news? What a fucking cunt I was.

[The subject is silent for nearly one minute and thirty (1:30) seconds. Halfway through this period, she closes her eyes and shudders. NOTE: From the heat patterns in her body, it appears as though she is having a sexual reaction.]

OMURA: The last thing you said to me, what did it mean? Why did you call me Angel?

[The subject opens her eyes and looks around. Apparently, the room now appears empty to her. She staggers backwards and sits on the couch. After a minute (1:00) she begins to cry with audible sobs.]

OMURA: I don't know either.

•

Associated Press
War Desk: For Immediate Release

September 14, 2027 (SEOUL): Accounts of Chinese warships equipped with long-range nuclear warheads heading into the Hawaiian archipelago have been confirmed, and evacuations of major targets on the United States West coast will begin within the hour.

• • • •

No doubt about it, death changes people.

The Ex
Steve Rasnic Tem

The old guy started taking his meals at the restaurant again, but his wife wasn't with him. Janet figured she must have died; surely people that age didn't divorce, did they? Later one of the other waitresses said the wife had passed away from a stroke. She figured the old man was at least sixty. Too bad—she thought they were pretty cute, the way they passed butter and salt to each other, and stuff like that, like they were just two normal people out on a date. She always tried to get them into her section—they left good tips.

But now she was wondering if the old guy should be out by himself. He just stared across the table all the time, chewing at his food and making these faces, little smiles, little frowns, widening his eyes, sometimes pressing his lips together like he was irritated. It was weird. She'd call somebody about him but it really wasn't any of her business.

Lately she'd noticed his face changed color sometimes. A little redder, or a little paler. She knew what that meant—her sister had a brand new baby. How *gross* was that! Right there in public! She never smelled anything, but maybe he wore one of those big diapers? If she ever got that old she'd just stay at home.

You shouldn't slump, Fred. It makes a poor first impression.

Fred sighed at his dead wife's Sunday-school-teacher posture, so uncomfortably erect, as if an invisible hand were dragging her up by the hair. It was her I'm-so-good-I'm-sacrificing-my-own-needs-for-you pose. *Bette, you don't approve of this—now you're pretending to be my romantic counselor?*

Oh, I don't think we're likely to see any romance here tonight. I think the best you can hope for right now is a pitying civility, given that jacket you're wearing.

What's wrong with it? I wore it to my brother's wedding. Everyone was very complimentary.

That was forty years ago. It looks like you shot and killed an old couch, and now you're wearing it.

So it's a classic. Why are you here, Bette?

I'm your wife.

Ex-wife, honey. Ex-wife.

We never divorced.

You died!

Oh, so that's it, is it? And you've resented it all this time. I shouldn't have to remind you that 'til death do us part' wasn't in our vows.

We were young—we thought it was too morbid. Besides, I thought that part would just go without saying.

Your problem as a husband, Fred, was that you thought pretty much everything would 'just go without saying'!

"Now that's out of order!"

The young waitress appeared suddenly at his shoulder, dressed in white like some kind of apparition. "I'm sorry, sir. You say you're ready to order?"

Fred looked up, embarrassed, smiling wanly. She seemed very tall, or else he was very short today. "Erm, just some tea for now. I'm still expecting someone."

She smiled and put her hand on his shoulder. "She's probably just so busy making herself pretty for you she's lost track of the time. We ladies are all the same you know. I'll be right back with that tea." She left.

Silly bitch.

Bette! When did you start cursing?

Death changes you, Fred. Politeness doesn't get you very far on the spiritual plane. You have to assert yourself. Do you know just how many dead people there are? It's worse than that vacation we took to Miami Beach.

Fred shuddered involuntarily. *She was just trying to be nice.*

She had her hands all over you! Is this what you were always waiting for? Get me out of the way just so you can play 'old man and the waitress' with that piece of trash?

She opened her mouth then, much wider than Fred could have expected, and out of a rising hiss and hush of wind beginning somewhere so deep you'd hate to lose your keys there, developed a long and mournful howl that filled the restaurant. Fred looked around, expecting at least a few complaints or tossed condiments, but people went about their meals as if nothing had happened. Except here and there the glasses resting on tables vibrated, the water stirring in concentric ripples.

Fred stared at her, his thoughts on vacation. *What in the world?*

Banshee. My death counselor says it sometimes happens.

You have a counselor?

Dying is VERY stressful, Fred! Especially when your surviving spouse is making a fool out of himself.

I'm sorry. Anything I can do?

She stood up then, closed her eyes, and spun around like a shattered merry-go-round, threads of skin floating away from bony arms, bits of her dress disintegrating. She finally stopped and looked at him. *Don't mention the dangling eyeball*, he cautioned himself.

Be honest. Does death make me look fat?

No, he said automatically. *No, in fact I think your translucency is very flattering.*

How about the blurriness? Help or hurt?

Oh, help, definitely. Very becoming.

"I'm so sorry I'm late!" A slightly plump, pleasant-looking woman plopped into the chair opposite, the one his dead wife had been sitting in moments before. Fred was startled, and so relieved (but not without considerable metaphysical confusion) that the two hadn't attempted to occupy the same space that he yelped like a goosed Disney princess.

Both women, the living and the dead, stared at him. "Sorry," he said. "Gas."

He stood up to greet her. She looked up at him from the chair, confused, then started to get up as well. "Oh no," he said, reddening, "don't get up." He sat down again.

Can I just say that a lady doesn't plop at a strange man's table? She waits, permits him to stand and invite her, and only then does she sit down.

You know, I don't recall your being so concerned with manners before. "Hi. I'm Fred." He reached across the table and gently took the woman's hand. *Don't you have other things you should be doing?*

You mean like mouldering?

"I'm, Mary. So pleased . . . "

Is that what you think I do all day?

" . . . to meet you, Fred."

Lie around and moulder?

Scattered jigsaw puzzle pieces of Bette's flesh dropped onto the table, including several into his tea: a nostril, what might have been a portion of earlobe, that little mole she worried was cancerous but he used to love.

Fred stalled with his hand holding Mary's, grin frozen awkwardly, an electrocuted hyena. Mary looked at him nervously. "Something wrong?"

"Umm." Bette was slowly picking up the random pieces of herself, actually managing to look embarrassed beneath her pallor, attempting to push the putty-like bits into more-or-less their correct position. "Could I have a moment, perhaps? Excuse me." He headed for the men's washroom, more quickly than he'd considered himself capable.

He grabbed both sides of the reassuringly solid sink and stared at himself appraisingly. He looked surprisingly normal, except for a certain wildness of hair and eyebrow. And the beginnings of a twitch at the left corner of his mouth, as if a moth were trapped beneath the skin. And his wife's forefinger jammed into his right ear like a Bluetooth headset.

A bloodied hand came around from behind his head and retrieved the finger. *Sorry*, Bette said, as she stood beside him replanting the finger. *I was afraid I might lose it when things began to, well, fall apart.*

I have to move on, he said. *I think we both do.* Bette was staring at the floor. *Bette?*

This bathroom is disgusting! she said, shaking her head. Fearing another collapse, he watched nervously as her features slid about her skull. When they settled she locked eyes with him in the mirror. *Do you men even bother to aim anymore, or is it just this shotgun approach?*

Bette, are you crying?

I can't tell. Am I?

I'm not sure. There's something moving down your face, but it's so transparent I can't be sure what it is.

She straightened up a bit, patted her hair. *I should have dyed it when I had the chance, remember? That lady was going to do it for no extra charge.*

That was the mortician's make-up artist, sweetheart. I told her no. I wanted you to be exactly the way I remembered you.

At least you bought me a new dress. The color was awful, but the thought was nice.

You're welcome.

No one in the restaurant appeared to be paying any attention as he made his way back toward his table. His glass of tea was still there, but his date was gone.

I guess I ruined things with your new friend.

That's okay. Maybe she just wasn't the sticking around kind. And I need something a little more permanent . . . sorry . . . I guess "committed" would be a better word.

Either one's okay. That's just not my neighborhood anymore.

If there's ever anything . . .

The problem with you men, dear, is that you imagine an older woman has no options. I'll have you know I've had my eye on someone for a few months now. He seems to be missing a few things, a few dozen vertebrae, about half his pelvis, but he never walks away when I'm speaking to him. And he's right next door to my new place.

Like the Cheshire, her grin was the last thing to fade.

When Janet went back to check on the old guy, she was bothered that both he and his date were gone. Maybe things had really started clicking—but thankfully she stopped herself before imagining further.

At least he had thought to leave a tip, then she discovered that instead of his usual thirty-plus percent he'd left her a buck and a quarter. Old bastard. She didn't care that he only had a glass of tea—she had bills to pay.

Chalk it up as another life lesson. No doubt about it, death changes people.

• • • •

He sees things in the swirling dust. Minute dancing ballerinas and crystalline cogs. And the faces appearing in the wall. Appearing, and vanishing . . .

Faces in Walls
John Shirley

I wake up in room 230, Wemberly Sanitarium, a fifteen by twenty-three foot room with peeling green walls. A dream of freedom and intimacy vanishes and the truth comes thudding back like a door slamming. I'm strapped loosely to a narrow bed, where I've lain, unmoving, for six years. I lie on my back, sharply aware that the overhead light has just switched on for the morning. It's only later that the sunlight comes through the high window, to my right. I lay there waiting for the faces in the walls. And the one face that talks to me.

Mostly, nothing happens in this room, except waking, and waiting, and watching the light change; the nurse coming and going, thoughts coming and going. Enduring the pain of bedsores. The paralysis.

I can move my eyes to look around, and blink—and thank God I can close my eyes. I'm able to breathe without help. I'm unable to speak. I can move my tongue very slightly. There's a little movement in the thumb of my right hand. That's it, that's all of it.

I mentioned being strapped in. The only reason they strap me down at all is just because maybe I might have a seizure, and that could make me fall off the bed. But I haven't had a seizure in years. Some kind of virus got into my brain, years ago, and gave me some really ferocious seizures. The paralysis came after the last seizure, like the jaws of a bear trap closing on me. Anyway, despite the restraints, this is not a mental hospital, this is the Wemberly Geriatric Sanitarium. Geriatric home or not, I'm not old, I'm one of the fairly young patients, for all the good it does me. Thirty-two, by my count, now. Does it sound bad? It's worse. Maybe the distinct feeling of my life burning away, second by second, like a very, very slow fuse that's burning down to a dud firecracker—maybe that's the worst part . . . that and Sam Sack.

I imagine a guy in a band saying, "Fellas, let's play 'Paralyzed'—and play it with feeling." I can *feel*. I feel more than someone with a snapped spine could. Sometimes I'm glad I can feel things—and sometimes I wish I couldn't. I can feel the straps over my chest, though they're not on tightly. I can feel a new bedsore developing on my right shoulder blade. I can feel the thin blanket over my lower half. I can feel the warm air from the vent as the furnace comes on; it blows, left to right, across on my face. I hear the fan that drives the air from the vent; I hear sleety rain hit the window. I can taste a sourness in my mouth—the staff rarely cleans my teeth—and I can taste food, when they bring it, but they give me very little, mostly soups, and not enough. And the way they make the soup there's nothing much to taste.

Now I hear voices. People talking. They take talking for granted and so did I. We waste so much of it . . .

There is something, lately, that gives me some murky sort of hope. *Bethany*. Though I'm not sure what exactly I'm hoping for . . .

Before Beth, I had my sad little ways of coping. Daydreaming of course. And writing in my mind—I tell stories, only I tell them in my mind. I think them out and try to memorize them, word for word, and tell them over again, to myself. Sometimes I make the stories up. Sometimes they're things that really happened.

The story I'm telling now, and trying to etch into a little corner of my brain, is a true one. I know it's true because I'm telling it even as it unfolds. I have an irrational belief that somehow, someone will hear this story. Maybe I'll be able to transmit it to them with my mind. Because in a certain way, my mind has become the strongest part of me. I'll transmit the story all in one piece, out into the ether, and it'll bounce around like a radio signal. A random writer will just pick it up out of the air, maybe years from now, and write it down—and he'll suppose it's all his idea.

My mother abandoned me here, but I guess it's not like abandoning a child. I was an adult, after all, in my mid-twenties, when it happened. I'd been staying with her while I was recovering from a drug relapse.

My mother and I were never close. That's an understatement—we had a simmering mutual aversion, muffled by a truce. It got worse after I grew up and went to college. You're supposed to understand your parents better when you're grown up.

I did understand her—I just couldn't respect her. And she knew it.

I won't say she was a whore, because she didn't take money from her lovers. (I could almost respect her if she'd done it for money.) No, not a whore—but I do think she drove my dad away with her casual adultery, when I was a teenager, and I know she discouraged him from being in touch with me later. And I know she is an alcoholic and a woman who sleeps with the random men she meets in bars. Or that's how she was—I don't even know if she's still alive.

I don't know why Mom invited me to stay with her, after I got fired, and lost my apartment. Maybe she wanted me there to take revenge on me—she didn't have my dad to take revenge on, so she took it out on me. It felt like she wanted me to always be saying, "I'm sorry, I'm sorry." Sorry for something I didn't do.

"You're just like him, Douglas, that's the awful thing," she'd say. Not that my dad was ever a drug addict. And not that I was always one either.

I got into speedballs in the early '70s, when a lot of us went from Summer of Love thinking, to the whole '70s glam decadence thing. I would get off work and go right out and score. Always a speedball—heroin and cocaine; heroin and methedrine. I got sick and tired of being sick and tired—so I got clean. I had five years clean, and a good job—before I relapsed. I started using again—and it got me fired. That was another wake-up call. I needed a place to get clean. Spoke to my mom, in a fit of familial yearning, she said, "You may as well come here."

Six months with my mom. Staying clean, partly because she was staying drunk. She inspired me to sobriety in a backward kind of way. I was just about to move out into a clean-and-sober hostel—anywhere, to get away from her—when the virus hit me. The seizures, the paralysis. The doctors said it was incubating in me, all that time—that I'd gotten it from a needle, fixing drugs, maybe a year or two before.

My mom said it was my comeuppance, it was God's way to say, "No more, Douglas!" She took care of me for a month—when she was sober enough. Thought I'd get over the virus, in time. But finally she put me here. And here I am still. Six years later.

Because I'm going to talk about Bethany, I should say that this place wasn't always a Geriatric Sanitarium. It was, for years, a TB Sanitarium. Tuberculosis, consumption. The White Death. In the mid-sixties, when they had TB mostly licked in this country, Mr. Wemberly, the owner, changed it over to a Geriatrics Sanitarium—only, from what I hear, listening to the nurses, it's only about seventy percent old-age dementia cases. The rest are just odds and ends of damaged people, all ages, who end up here because it's cheap. Very cheap indeed.

Mom left me here, in 1976. So here it is, 1982.

Punishment. Punishment, punishment. Here I am. I'm sorry. Does that help, to say I'm sorry? If I say it again, does it help? I'm sorry. I'm sorry. Now can I get up and walk out of here?

No. The tired gray sunlight coming through the windows says no.

• • •

Not much happened to me, for almost six years.

I ingest, I eliminate waste, I breathe. A few minutes of physical therapy, once a month; some electrical therapy; Sister Maria for a brief time. The day nurse and the visits of Sam Sack. That's all. Anything really new that happens is profoundly exciting—makes my breath come faster, my heart pound. Anything new that has nothing to do with Sam Sack, I mean. I get some stimulation from Sack, sure, but that's not excitement; that's nausea in the shape of a man . . .

About four years ago, for almost seven months, I was visited once a week by a nun, a chubby little Hispanic lady named Sister Maria. She used to sit with me for almost an hour. She'd bring one of those cheap one-speaker cassette tape recorders along, play canticles and the like for me, and read to me. Not always from the Bible. She read from *Quo Vadis?* That was pretty exciting. She had a soft Mexican accent and she used to smile at me and wag her finger and say, "Are you laughing at my accent, Douglas? I think you are!"

It was almost ecstasy, when she talked to me like that—because I did think her accent was amusing. So that was almost like communicating. And when she played music for me, it felt excruciatingly good. It hurt that I couldn't tell her thank you, and please come back.

She even touched my arm, a soft warm slightly moist touch, when she was ready to leave.

Then she stopped coming. I heard someone in the hall talking about a convent being closed. I think that's what they said, I couldn't hear it clearly. I wanted to believe that's what it was—something out of her control. Sister Maria . . .

No more music, since then. Except what's in my mind. The old songs from the sixties that replay, over and over in my mind. The whirling dust motes. The sounds from the hall; sometimes a patient crying.

But something important *has* happened—it happened, for the first time, three weeks ago. One of the faces in the walls has started talking to me . . .

Seeing faces in the wall was one of the ways I kept my mind busy.

It's funny how the people who take care of me feel like ghosts—and Beth feels like a living person to me. That's because she talks to me.

Beth spoke to me, in my mind and I replied to her—in my mind. And she heard me!

I wish I could talk out loud—to Beth, to anyone. It's enough that I can't move—but if I could at least talk . . . If I could berate the nurses, flirt with the woman who comes in to mop the floor, ask for things, demand to see an attorney, sing to myself—and tell a story to a nurse . . . that'd be worth something.

I can make just one little sound—a high-pitched *immmm* sound produced way deep in my throat—but it's hard to make, and it's such an embarrassingly piteous, subhuman noise I hate to do it. I only do it when I'm trying to ease the pressure, trying to avoid the inner hysteria, that's like a funhouse in a very bad earthquake. If I feel that coming, then I might *immmm*.

I have to be sure the nurses and attendants are nowhere around when I make the noise. If they hear it, they get irritated, asking, "Well? What's the point if you know you can't tell us what you want?" Figuring I'm trying to get attention. They find ways to show they're angry with me. They "forget" to change the diaper.

There—I hear the sound of the little metal cabinet on wheels that they roll around to feed those who can't feed themselves. It clinks with dishes and rattles and its wheels squeak. I'm the first one in this corridor. So that means the morning nurse is coming in, just a few minutes late. I think of her as Mrs. White because she's an old white woman with puffy white hair and a dirty white uniform. She smells old and talks old, when she mutters to herself, and she's barely aware of what she's doing, as she goes through the motions of cleaning me with her twisty old fingers, feeding me breakfast porridge, giving me a shot, brushing my teeth, putting antiseptic—a bandage if she feels like it—on my bedsores. She turns me, props me up back there with special little pillow to give the bedsore a chance to heal. I sort of enjoy that, since I can feel it. She's supposed to change the sheet, but that's a complicated process involving moving me a lot, hard work, so she doesn't do it today. I am aware that her Polydent isn't quite working and her false teeth are coming loose from her gums. I can hear the sound of them sucking loose as she mumbles to herself.

Sometimes Mrs. White says something to me. Always a kind of complaint. "You're getting fat and hard to move. They're going to want to put those electric things on your arms again to keep them muscles up. But don't think they'll keep on with it, they're cutting back on treatment again, laying people off. Well, see there, you don't poop much, I'll give you that. But you still smell. That sore of yours, that smells. I don't know why I got to do this. I should have some real retirement. You can't live on what I'd have. Some of it got stolen. My husband died and left me nothing but debts. So here I am with you . . . "

I like her visits, though—I can see parts of the room I can't normally see, when she moves me about. I can think about the things she says and try to imagine her life. It's better than hearing nothing from anyone. It's better than Sam Sack.

After she's gone, I listen to people talking in the hallway. They come, and they go. Now I pass the time with my worn out old fantasy that someday my dad will come looking for me and take me out of here. I imagine the whole scene, where he wheels me out, and tells me he's going to find a cure for me. That doesn't last long.

Sometimes I have other fantasies—I try to avoid the sexual sort. They're particularly torturous. And I can still get a hard-on. Which makes the aides laugh.

There are darker daydreams, that come to me, at times. Furious, bone-deep violence against Sack; against certain orderlies; against the people who run this place . . .

I push all that down, deep down, because it only hurts me, not them. And I think about what I'll say to Beth, instead. It's not time for her to come yet. She won't come till after it starts to get dark outside. I have to wait . . .

I watch the slanting sun make warped squares on the wall to my left. I start watching the dust whirling in the sunbeams. I try to count them. I select pieces of dust to study individually. To imagine as something else. Sometimes at night before the light goes out, I can watch moths. I've watched spiders cross the ceiling, watched them very closely. My eyes hurt with all this staring, but it's all I've got.

Once in a while they bring in a machine that makes my muscles jump with mild electrical jolts. It hurts a little, but I like it, because it's some movement, and I guess it keeps my muscles from atrophying. It's experimental. Someone donated it. But Mrs. White says the muscle therapy is going to end.

No one comes today. No electricity, nothing but waiting for lunch. Patiently waiting. The hours are like blocks of ice in a room just two degrees above freezing. Ever so slowly melting. It's a mystery, why I don't go completely insane. But how would I know if I was insane?

I've tried really hard to go totally mad, cuckoo, out of my mind, lost in space. *Definitively* insane, in a mad hatter way. The important phrase is, *out of my mind*. That'd be a kind of escape. I've never quite gotten there. The most I've gotten to is some vicious fantasies and some hallucinations, now and then. The hallucinations are some kind of sensory deprivation effect maybe. Those faces. Except one.

I've seen things in the swirling dust. Minute dancing ballerinas and crystalline cogs. And the faces appearing in the wall. Appearing, and vanishing. The faces frighten me, but at least it's some kind of stimulation. They sometimes seem amused—sometimes hostile. I used to be afraid they'd come out of the wall somehow and bite me. But they never do. They look at me as if they're threatening me, but they're as powerless, as stuck within walls, as I am stuck on the bed in room 230. They move their lips sometimes. I never heard any of the faces speak, though, till Beth showed up.

I'm waiting for her now, my eyes turned to watch the wall to my right, under the window. I can feel she's near. Maybe she's a hallucination, maybe that's how I know she's coming—because she's from my own mind. But I want to believe she's real. I do believe it. She must be. She knows things that I never knew.

I wait for Bethany. She's never the first to come. It starts with the other faces . . .

Now I see a face in the dull-green wall, turning to look at me. The face is made partly of places where the paint on the concrete is wrinkly, and partly from a wall crack and partly from shadow and partly from my mind connecting all these things. I can tell this one's a hallucination. It's a jowly man, balding, looking sullen, almost angry, put-upon, circles under his little eyes. His lips move but I can't hear what he's saying. I think I might know who he is. That happens sometimes—the faces are people from memory. I think this man might be Mr. Wemberly. I saw his face six years ago when Mom brought me in here. He looked me over and wasn't too pleased. Talked about how the necessary staff time made it hardly worthwhile. "Put him in room 230." That was the last I saw of him.

Now his face recedes into the wall. I see another—it's a pretty girl, one I sometimes dream about. She looks a little like Jayne Mansfield. She makes a kissy puckering with her lips at me. I'm sorry when she fades away. Another face takes her place—my mother. Her lips sneer, her eyes are heavy with disappointment. Sorry, Mother, I say to her, in my mind. Okay? As if that satisfies her for now, she melts away, and I'm glad. Now comes a face I don't know—it's a frightened looking man. He opens his mouth. He screams. Is that my face? It's too old to be my face. But I haven't seen my own face in six years.

That face collapses into another face, a little boy with colorless hair and very dark eyes. He seems to be praying. I don't know him, do I? There's something about him that makes me deeply afraid, but I don't know what. He slips back into the wall, and along comes another face—a black woman, looking amused, curious. A pleasant middle-aged face.

She seems to be singing to herself, judging by the movement of her head, from side to side, the way her lips move, but I can't hear her. I like her. But . . .

I want to see the one I can hear. The one who can step out of the wall. I'm impatient to see her today.

I try to call her with my mind.

I think, *Beth . . . Bethany . . . Beth!*

I can feel her responding almost immediately. I hear her voice, phasing in and out of audibility: "Was . . . coming . . . anyway . . . don't . . . so . . . imp . . . "

Don't so imp? *Don't be so impatient.*

Then the singing black lady melts away, and I see Beth.

I wish I could smile to greet her. All I can do is lift my right thumb a little. She's just a face in the wall, but then she thrusts her hand from it and wiggles her thumb at me. It's a little mocking when she does that but honestly it's just her sense of humor. She's in a better mood than last time, it seems to me. That's good. But I know that can change. Her sorrow's never far away. She's anchored in Wemberly Sanitarium by sorrow.

Bethany steps out of the wall, into the room. Beth is a slim, barefoot girl in a short hospital gown—her legs are quite skinny, knees knobby. She has a mousy sort of face, but kind of cute the way a mouse's face is, and long dull-brown hair, a bit lank, and brown freckles on her cheeks and brown eyes. Her coloration comes and goes—sometimes she seems to be made of a cream colored mist. She's a little foggy below the neck but her arms come into focus when she uses them to gesture, or point. Her lips don't move when she talks except that they smile or frown or purse themselves.

Her voice seems to echo around, and the last echo comes clearest into my mind. Now and then a word drops out. "Douglas. I've come to see you again . . ."

I reply in my mind. "Hello, Beth. Thank you for coming. I love it when you come here."

"Has he . . . back?"

"Sack? Not for eleven nights now."

"He'll come tonight. I've seen him, he's been looking at that pillowcase with the holes . . ."

I try to sound brave, and blithe, to impress her with my courage. "It makes a change. But he gets worse every time. I don't know how the worst kind of guy can get worse." I tried to make a laughing sound in my mind.

"Don't do that," she says, frowning.

"Don't do what?"

" . . . make that fake laughing. It sounds like one of . . . gag laughing toys. My father used to sell gags. He was . . . traveling salesman . . . "

She's already told me about her eccentric father, but I let her tell me about it again.

After a while that story runs down. "Are you talking to someone else?" she asks.

I'm surprised. "I'm sort of filing everything that happens in another part of my mind, as we talk. In the form of a narrative. You can hear it?"

"Not exactly," she says. "It's okay. Your mind . . . a strong one. Some people here . . . very feeble. Almost not there at all."

"I've got nothing to do but make my mind work, in different ways. I'd forgotten algebra but I worked it out again to keep my mind busy, about a year ago. Are you ready to tell me, now, how you got here? You said you would, last time."

Her frown deepens. "I guess so. I should." She seems to look around the room, as if trying to remember something. I yearn to ask her to touch me, anywhere at all, but I'm afraid I won't be able to feel her touch since she isn't precisely alive. "One reason I came to this room," she says, "is because I used to live in here. Right in this room." I am hearing her voice more clearly now. That happens when we've been talking for a while. It's like we hone in on each other's frequency. "It really started in 1943. I was a nurse's aide, for soldiers coming back from the war. Volunteering. I thought I might meet a husband that way. I wasn't very pretty and I was almost thirty and wasn't married. I was taking care of a soldier who was coughing all the time, he'd been in North Africa, and he caught something there. I thought it was just a bad cold. But then after a while I started coughing too, and then I was coughing up yellow and red stuff, like mustard and catsup. But it was bloody sputum. And I got feverish and started waking up in the middle of the night with the sheets soaked, all covered with sweat. So I went to the doctor and they said I had consumption—the tuberculosis—and they took me to the sanitarium. This sanitarium. This same room. The owner was Randall Wemberly and there was a young fat man who was his son, Charles. This boy Charles worked as an orderly, but he was going to inherit the place. He was learning the job and said we'd all better be good to him because he was going to take over the whole place someday. He'd laugh and wink like that was a joke but it was what was in his mind. Charles Wemberly. He would take us for our treatments. People thought, back then, that cold fresh air would kill the bacillus, so they took us to open windows and made us sit there, and breathe the cold air in the winter. And snow would come in, sometimes, and cover us. I saw two people die right there, in that room. The worst was the balloon, though. They'd put a balloon in your lung, and they'd inflate it. They said it would help the lung heal. I don't know why they thought that. And it was a very awful feeling when they put it in but the worst was when they expanded it and that was the very worst pain I'd ever felt. Up till then. Blood would squirt out my nose, the first spurt shooting in an arc all the way down to my thighs. And they'd cut away people's ribs, so the lungs could expand. All those people died, the ones who lost part of their ribcage. They didn't do that surgery on me. But I thought I was going to die soon anyway. They had a tunnel they used for taking the dead people out—it's still down there, I'll show it to you sometime, Douglas—it goes out back, to a little building. That's so the patients and their families wouldn't see all the dead people going out of the hospital—it happened so often. Because most patients died. Almost all of them." She hesitates. She looks at me with her head tilted. She seems to be trying to remember how it was. "I lingered on for a long time and I kept wanting to run away and find some peaceful place to die alone, without anyone watching. But then the streptomycin came in. And it worked!" She gives an ironic little smile. "That was in 1946. People were getting better from it. So they gave it to me for a while, and I improved—a lot! I wasn't even infectious anymore, and I wasn't coughing. I thought I would be leaving soon. I was planning what I would do when I was released." She makes a gesture in the air, like she wants to push something away that isn't there. "And then Charles came to me, alone. He was supposed to give me my medicine, but he said I couldn't have it unless I let him play with my body. 'It has to be however I want to touch you, any way at all,' he said. 'Or you will die.' He pushed up against me and I remember his breath smelled like rotten eggs. I said, 'Why did you choose me?' I was just stalling. He said it was my legs, they were like the legs of a little girl. I shouted that I'd tell his father on him. Then he hit me with a bedpan, and that knocked me senseless for a while, and when I came to, we were on the floor and he was holding onto me, and humping my hips talking about how my legs were the legs of a little girl—he was not even inside me, but humping me more like a dog would hump on a person's legs—and he saw I was awake so he started whispering that he would kill me, he would simply kill me if I didn't do what he wanted and I shouldn't imagine that he wouldn't . . . " She breaks off and looks at me. "Does this story offend you?"

"No," I reply, in my mind. "Well yes: I'm offended that you were hurt. But I want to know what happened."

She smiles. She nods and looks at the overhead light. "I can see the electricity in the wires, if I squint," she says.

"Did he kill you?" I prompt her.

She sticks out her lower lip as she thinks it over. "No. Not exactly. He said his father was away on a trip, and now *he* was in charge and he would see I spoke to no one but him, and I would get no more medicine . . . unless . . . "

She looks at the door. I hear people passing outside, in the hall, talking. A woman weepily talking about her aunt, saying she's all the family she has. The nurse saying, "We can only do so much."

Then they've moved on. I don't know why Beth waited, since they can't hear us talking. Maybe she is afraid someone might come in to check on me, and see her. Maybe she doesn't realize how rarely anyone comes in here.

If she's worried about that, does that mean that I'm not the only one who can see her?

"So," Beth goes on, "I said, 'Charles, do what you have to, but don't hit me again.' My head hurt so badly. And then he raped me. I laid still for it, like he wanted, and didn't fight him, but it was raping. It hurt a lot . . . I was afraid I'd throw up and choke on the vomit while he was doing it . . . "

We are silent for a while. I felt like making the *immmm* sound but I didn't. Not doing that now is the only way I have of being strong for her.

She turns like she is going to melt back into the wall.

"Don't go, Beth!" I call to her, in my mind.

She looks back at me, and I can see she wants to cry but, like me, she can't. "I have to go. I have to rest in the wall. But I'll just tell you this much more. Charles gave me something he said was streptomycin, but it wasn't. It was just placebo. The symptoms started to come back. And he started coming to me wearing a surgical mask. Forced me to open my legs for him. Holding a hand over my mouth to keep me quiet. Then I guessed what was going on. I said, 'You want me to die, so I don't talk about what you've been doing to me. You're not giving me the medicine at all now.' He wouldn't say anything and then I didn't see him for a couple of days. I tried to talk to a nurse but I was locked in here and they wouldn't respond, wouldn't come to the door. I was shouting and shouting and then when I screamed really loud something broke in my lungs and I spit up blood, so much blood came up I choked. And then there was a lot of pain and then it was dark . . . " She shrugs. "And then I was in the walls. Just in the walls. But sometimes I can come out and look at things. Mostly they can't see me but sometimes they do." She smiles at that. "I don't like them to see me, I'm afraid they'll bring Charles but . . . I like to see them afraid of me, too."

"He's still here?"

The color is going out of her. She seems to flatten, like she's a cut-out, or something drawn on paper. "I'm tired . . . yes. Yes he's here. Charles is Mr. Wemberly now. He's in charge, like he said he'd be. He's the one who put you in here, this room. Goodbye, Douglas, for now. Try to pretend you're someone else when Sack comes in. That's what I always did when Charles . . . and the nurses would pretend . . . can't . . . "

That's all I can hear. She is slipping into the wall—almost as if something in it is pulling her slowly in, against her will. The wall is drinking her in the way water sinks out of sight into deep sand. Then she's gone.

I feel like I've fallen into a wall, too. I close my eyes. I don't try to call to her, though. Bethany needs to rest.

A nurse comes, looks at my sore, mutters that it's not so bad. Goes away. An orderly comes, checks my lower parts, shrugs, and goes away. I hear the sound of a mop in a bucket in the hallway. Some kind of broth is brought to me, and I'm fed with something like a turkey baster. They have to crank the bed up a bit so I don't choke. They get irritated when I choke.

The bedsore is tormenting me. It hurts and it itches. The itching always makes me imagine insects are crawling into the bedsore. They're getting into it and laying eggs that will become hungry little grubs that will eat their way out of my brain. Sometimes I think I can feel them beginning to chew through the soft tissue inside my skull.

I must not think about that because if I do it just gets more and more vivid, worse and worse and I have to *immmm*. One of the ways I change the direction of my thoughts is to try to remember a song, note for note. There's one by The Turtles.

So happy together . . .

They're crawling into the wound . . .

So happy to-geth-errrrrr . . .

I think of songs and I watch dust motes. I watch the color of the sunlight deepen, and the crooked squares of light from the window travel down the left hand wall and vanish entirely, and the dread of Sam Sack comes on me, much later, when the light is switched off. I try to sleep, hoping for a good dream. But I can't sleep.

Sack.

He comes into the dark room, I know it's him from the smells—rancid sweat and Top tobacco. I can just barely see his silhouette. I hear the rustle of his homemade mask. He puts it over his head in the darkness. He switches on the little lantern he's brought, dialed down low, and raises it up to see me, and so I can see him. There's the sack on his head with holes cut in it—actually it's a small pillowcase, but for a long time I thought it was a sack. So I think of it that way and I call him Sam Sack.

"Glad to see me?" he asks, his head cocked, his voice hoarse. It's always hoarse. He adjusts the pillowcase with his free hand to let him see out the crudely cut holes better. I can't see his face, only the eyes. Around his covered mouth, the cloth gets damp and dark with his breath. Why does he even bother with the mask? Maybe he's got the "sack" on in case anyone turns on the light. Maybe he's hoping he can run before they identify him. Or maybe he doesn't want me to see his face. Because even though I couldn't tell anybody who he is, he feels more powerful, stronger, if I don't know. Maybe his face is one a man would laugh at.

But I think I know who he might be—kind of. No, he's not Charles Wemberly. I can tell from smells on him—and the dirt under his yellow fingernails, his calluses, his oily overalls—that he's probably on the maintenance staff. I think he's the night janitor. He's a white man, gangly, but with a pot belly. He has cigarette stains on two fingers of his right hand. Once I heard an aide walking by in the hall, saying, "Maybe Sam can clean it up tonight, I'm not going to do it, I'm going off shift." I figured maybe he was that Sam. Sick Sam Sack.

He climbs up on the narrow bed, and straddles me, and I close my eyes. He starts pressing my eyes with my thumbs. "I could cram 'em back into your brain," he says, "and you couldn't do nothin' about it.'"

He pushes hard, and it hurts, but he's careful not to break anything there. He broke a couple of my toes once, and the nurses never seemed to notice. But they'd notice if he poked out my eyes.

He says, "I was thinking of the sewing needles today, how maybe I could do you with the pins again, they don't leave much mark, and the aides just think it's another sore or such." He slaps me, once, hard. Stinging the left side of my face. It makes a loud noise in the room. The mark will fade before the nurses see it. And would they do anything if they did see it? I don't think so.

He slaps me again, and twice more. "Maybe this'll wake you up. Wake up in there, dummy! Wake up!" He laughs softly.

His eyes in the pillowcase holes are bright.

Sometimes he'll pull hair from my head, my pubes, my armpits, one hair at a time. Once he started pulling out a fingernail, but blood came, and he decided that might draw too much attention, so he left it partly pulled. No one noticed. They clipped it like they always do, without a comment.

Sack puts his weight on my chest, presses down with his knees. I can't breathe. He waits. Spots appear over my eyes. I'm close to dying. I wouldn't mind if he'd finish it but I know he won't. He won't let me off the hook. I make the *immmm* sound and he gives out a soft laugh of pleasure. Then he lets up, easing off, letting me breathe. Then he does it again, almost smothering me, two times more.

Maybe I'm starting to turn blue, because he quits, and climbs off the table. "I've got something else for you." As I lay there, breath rasping, he reaches into his pocket, takes out something brassy. He fiddles with it and holds it up so I can see it better. Lipstick. "I'm gonna pretty you up a little. I got a lady's brassiere, and this. I'm gonna put this on your lips and rub it on your cheeks. I'll clean it off before I go. And this time, I'm gonna have your ass. The girl I use—she died. She killed herself. So it's you, now. We got to make you a little more like a girl. I'm gonna call you Sissy Thing . . . "

He starts drawing on my lips with the lipstick, whistling a song. "Camptown Ladies."

I feel something I haven't felt for a while. I try not to feel it, because if I do, it's like I'm on fire and can't put the fire out.

It's pure rage. And there's nothing I can do to express it, but breathe harder. I can sort of snort out my nose at him. That's all. This only makes him laugh, and he hits my testicles hard with his knee. The pain brings the rage up like a siren blasting full volume in my mind.

I fight the rage. Rage hurts me. I have to keep it down. Pretend to be someone else, like Beth says. *Beth . . .*

She's there, suddenly. Standing to my right. Sack doesn't seem to see her.

"Douglas," she says, in my mind, "let yourself rage at him. If you do, then you'll go into the rage, and you'll be gone enough into it, and that'll open a door for me, so I can help you . . . "

And I stop fighting it. The rage was like a pot of water boiling over, making the lid rattle and fall away . . . I was uncovered by it . . .

I feel an unspeakable, glutinous intimacy. Is this being raped? But he hasn't started that yet. This is up higher, coming from somewhere else—*something* is pushing into my gut, right under my rib cage. It's passing through the skin without breaking it. But I feel it force its way into whatever it is, inside my body, and brain, that I think of as me. It's doing it insistently, not brutally. I realize it's Beth.

Then I feel something strange in the muscles of my face. Like I have a muscle twitch. But it's a muscle twitch that makes my mouth move. My tongue. A jabbery sound croaks out of me. Then some control comes and I say a word *right out loud.*

"Sack," I say. Not in my mind—I say it with my mouth.

He turns to look at me, his head cocked to one side again. Staring. "You can't talk . . . "

"Sam Sack," I say. "You're Sam."

Only it's not me saying it. She's saying it for me. She's joined me. She's with me in here. *Beth!* I can feel her there, a warm presence, twined about my spine, swirling at the back of my head, and stretching into my arms . . .

My arms are twitching. Jumping. They're wriggling. The straps are loose. My hand is fumbling at a buckle on the restraints.

Sack raises a fist, slowly, over his head. I can see him flexing his arm muscle. I realize he's going to hit me. Beat me to death, to keep me quiet.

My right arm comes free. I watch my own arm as it rises up like a cobra— some creature I have no control over. Sack stares at it, hesitating—and then my left hand gets free. It jumps up and grabs him by the back of the neck. Holds him. His surprisingly skinny neck. My left hand makes a kind of claw, with the index finger, and thumb, and it stabs out, and jabs him in the eyes. As we do it, I remember all the times he dug his thumbs into my eyes. My own will, set free, joins Beth's, and I push my thumb and finger *hard*, into his eyes. Popping through his eyeballs, digging into the eye socket.

He gives out with a long, bubbling squeal, and blood splashes into the pillowcase and changes the color of the cloth.

He quivers and shakes in my hands—and then he wrenches free and falls flailing back, blind.

"Okay now," Beth says, in my mind. "That's enough. We stopped him." Her voice is crystal clear. I can see her face in my mind, looking worried and almost pretty. "Let's just get out of here, together. I can leave here with you. I can't make it out of here alone . . . We can go out through that old tunnel . . . " It takes some time to get better control of my limbs. But I get the straps off completely, and I stand. I'm dizzy, once I almost fall over, but I manage to stay upright. I feel firmer with every passing second. "I'm standing! Beth! I can move! You're helping me do this?"

"I'm connecting something that was broken in your brain, just by being here, inside you," she says. "Let's go . . . "

"Wait," I say, my voice shaking.

I feel waves of emotion go through me, rage and joy all mixed together, driving me along. I step over to the writhing man on the floor, and I kneel down to press my knee on his neck, and I put all my weight on it. I crush his throat, hard and slow.

"Let's *go,*" Beth says, sounding worried. "They've heard him scream! They'll lock you up. We have to go."

"You're doing this too," I tell her, gasping the words out, breathing hard as I feel him struggling under my crushing knee. The blood is coming from his mouth now as well as his eyes. I'm feeling pain with all this movement, as if my joints are all rusty. *Oil can,* squeaks the Tin Man. "You're doing it, Beth, as much as me."

"No. I didn't even put out his eyes. I was just trying to push him back. Knock him down. Not that. You did that. No, I'm just *here,* but I'm not . . . doing that."

I can barely hear her through the roaring. The roaring that is coming out of me. Then I realize that Sam Sack has stopped moving. He's dead.

I pull the sack off his head—the bloody child's pillowcase—and I throw it in the corner and I look at him in the light from his own lantern.

He's a monkey-faced man with a big red nose. Old, his face deeply lined. His eyes are gone, blood running like red tears from the sockets. My hands are slick with the remains of his eye matter.

I stand up, feeling sick, and wracked with pain, but seething with a fierce delight. Roaring to myself with exhilaration!

I pick up his lantern and open the door, ripples of disorientation going through me as I step into the hallway. An orderly, a thick-bodied black man with a shaved head, is coming toward me, frowning, investigating the noise—he stops, staring at me. Seeing the blood on me and the lantern and the diaper—and the lipstick. He backs away. I roar at him. He turns and runs, and I laugh.

"We have to go downstairs," Beth says, in my mind. "The tunnel . . . "

"No tunnel yet," I say. Because it's coming clear to me, now.

I stumble along, managing to walk, spastic and hurting but loving every step. I hum to myself, sing bits of songs, just to hear my creaky voice. I find some stairs and go down—but only one floor. I step into the ground floor hallway, find the front door out into the grounds. It's late, there's no one watching it. It unlocks easily enough and I step out into the cold night. I'm almost naked, but I like the cold wind on me, the cold wet ground under my feet. I even like shivering. The stars, seen through the broken, racing clouds, are blue-white points of sheer intensity. I see the house in the corner of the grounds, near the front gate, close to the mossy concrete wall. I stumble across the wet lawn, through a pool of darkness. I make my way to the house, a white cottage trimmed in pale blue, in the corner of the grounds. I see there's a light on at the small back porch.

"We should just keep going out the front gate," Beth says.

I keep on to the little house. Beth comes with me, she has to. She has no choice.

I've heard the orderlies refer to the cottage. *You want the time off, go see Wemberly in that house out front, and ask. He lives out there . . . "*

I find the backdoor unlocked, and step into the kitchen, still carrying the lantern. The kitchen is painted a sunny yellow.

There is Charles Wemberly at the kitchen table, a fat balding elderly man in yellow pajamas. He's eating a big piece of yellow cheese, which he's cut up on a carving board, with a large knife. A bottle of Riesling is uncorked beside him. A wine glass brims in his age-spotted hand.

He looks up; he stares; his jowly mouth hangs open, showing half-chewed cheese. His hand shakes; the wine spills.

I stalk toward him and he gibbers something and flails, dropping the wine glass. I smash him in the face with the lantern. He rocks back. I drop the lantern and pick up the half empty wine bottle, and hit him in the face with it, over and over. The skin splits over the bones of his face, and I can see them showing through, till they're covered with blood. He howls for help and thrashes at me and I keep smashing into him, knocking him off his chair, till the bottle shatters.

I discard the neck of the bottle and take the knife he was using—and I straddle him, like Sack did to me, and I start sawing at the back of Wemberly's neck. Cutting here, cutting there. Sawing through neck muscles, tissue I can't even identify. I'm smelling blood; feeling its wet hot thick warmth on my hands, my wrists.

"Oh no," Beth is saying. Her voice in my head is a sustained high note on a violin. "Oh, no Douglas. We have to go . . . "

"It's Charles," I tell her, quite reasonably, saying it right out loud, as I saw at his back. He thrashes under me. I saw away, hacking down further, digging a trench in him around the spine, all the way from neck to tailbone.

"Yes. But . . . "

"He's the one who raped you and let you die. And he hired Sam Sack. He left me in a moronically cruel state of neglect for six years."

"Yes, but Douglas, listen please . . . We have to go."

"Wait!" I shout. "Almost done!" I keep sawing, working hard to separate the vertebrae from the body. I feel the strength of years of rage coming out in my hands, and he's thrashing and squeaking and I drop the knife and I get a grip on the spine, I pull and wrench . . .

It comes loose from his body, his entire spine comes out rather nicely, with his head attached. I have to cut through a few more connective threads around his neck, some cartilage, and then . . .

I'm standing over the rest of his body holding his spine in my two hands. His head, his mind, is still alive in it, attached to the spine; his face is twitching convulsively, eyes going back and forth, back and forth.

I swing his head on his spine, like swinging a polo mallet; it's cumbersome, and I think of Alice in the Lewis Carroll book, trying to play croquet with a flamingo. But this one drips blood, and sputters.

"This is to you, from me," I tell Beth. "I am your man, Beth, and my strong arm has done this for you."

A shout comes from the back door and I turn to see the big black orderly and a white man in a uniform; he's a security guard with longish hair and a cigarette in his lips and a gun in his hand.

"Oh my fucking stars," the security guard says. He's staring at Wemberly's wet-red spine, the attached head coated in blood.

I swing the head on the spine and roar at them—and the guard's gun roars back.

"Beth!" I'm staggering back with the shot, which has struck me in the lower left side. Blood spurts out of me.

And something else is leaving me—Beth.

She's draining out of me, with the blood flow. I see her floating away from me—she's drifting away, turning around in the air to face me so she can see me as she goes. She's getting smaller, going into a vast distance that shouldn't be there, in a kitchen.

"I'm out," she says, speaking to my mind. "I'm free, Douglas. But I wish we . . ."

Her voice trails off. She vanishes. She's gone. The guard is staring at me, uncertain what to do.

But I realize—

I can still stand. I can move! Beth's presence in me, the movement since then—it seems to have permanently bound up the broken connections in my brain. I no longer need Beth to move.

I swing Wemberly's head and spine, release it at the guard like an Olympics hammer throw—it trails blood through the air, falls short; the head, breaking from the spine, thunks and rolls, trailing blood. The guard makes a yelping sound and steps back. As he does, I switch the knife to my left hand, use my right to cover the wound, slow the bleeding. This wound will not kill me. It is shallow.

The guard and the orderly are coming cautiously back into the kitchen. The guard's hand, pointing the gun, is wavering. The gun is shaking.

I start toward them. The orderly tells him, "Shoot him again, you damn fool!"

I roar—and the gun roars back, once more. Then again.

I feel a cold, punching impact in my neck. I fall, fall slowly back through space. The room around me is suddenly a different color. It's painted red, and the red paint swirls and thickens and carries me somewhere . . . into dreams . . .

The hard part is waking up.

I'm lying on my back. I don't want to open my eyes. I can feel the warmth of the light bulb over me. I can smell the room. Must *not* open my eyes.

But I do. I see where I am. I try to get up. I can't. I try to lift my arm. Can't.

I can't feel anything, below my neck. I'm aware of a bandage, taut around my throat. A hose going into my mouth helping me breathe.

I see a doctor, in his white coat—a red-faced man with a mustache—talking to a frightened looking black-haired wisp of a nurse, near the door. He's saying, "Oh he can't hurt you." He glances at me. "He's paralyzed . . . The bullet destroyed his spine. And this time the restraints are quite tight. As tight as we can make them. So even if he could move . . ."

I had my chance. I didn't listen to Beth. Now I'm being punished. But this place was always my punishment.

So I had to come back here. To room 230. Does it do any good to say I'm sorry? I'm sorry. I'm sorry . . .

. . . .

There are certainly horrors that exist in broad daylight, but the bulk of the supernormal seems to prefer nightfall, if not particularly the witching hour.

The Case of the Lighthouse Shambler
Joe R. Lansdale

I guess you could say it's a kind of organization, but we think of it as a club. It's not just a men's club. Women come too. Or at least a couple do. And then, of course, there's Dana Roberts. She was our guest.

The club is simple. We meet once a month to chat and have drinks, eat a little bit of food. Sometimes we invite a guest. We always make an effort to have someone interesting, and not just someone to fill the slot. We'd rather not have a guest than have someone come in and tell us how to dry lumber or make strawberry jam.

Fact is, we vote on who our speaker is. When Dana Roberts came up, I didn't actually plan to vote for her. I didn't want a supernatural investigator there, as I find that kind of stuff silly and unbelievable, and mostly just annoying.

There are all the shows on TV about ghost hunters, and psychic kids, and so on, and they make me want to kick the set in. I guess it's good business, making shows where it's all shadow and innuendo. People saying they hear this, or they hear that, they see this, or they see that, and you don't actually see or hear jack. You've just got to take their word for it.

Another thing, when they do have something, it's a blurry camera image, or a weird sound on their recordings that they say is the ghost telling them to get out of the house, or some such. I don't become more of a believer when they do that, I become less of one. The sounds just sound like one of the investigators getting cute, and the images look a lot like my bad vacation photos.

But the rest of the members pushed Dana on me, and I was outvoted. So on Thursday night, right after we had a general meeting, talking about a few things that had to do with the club, Dana showed up.

She was a tall woman in her forties, and though she wasn't what you'd call a model, there was certainly something about her. Her face was shaped nice and sharp by her cheekbones. She had a wide full mouth and eyes that looked right through you. She had shoulder-length blond hair. She looked to be in good shape, and, in fact, looked more like a physical trainer than someone who chased spooks and such.

She went around and shook hands with everyone, and said thanks for inviting her. While she's doing this, all I could think about was that our club dues were paying for this. We always give a stipend for speakers, and sometimes it's pretty sizeable if the guest has some fame. I didn't know how much the treasurer had agreed to pay her, but whatever it was, I thought it was too much.

Dana Roberts is famous for her books, her now and again interviews on television. I will give her this, she didn't do TV interviews much, and she wasn't someone that was always popping up in the news or predicting this or that, or saying a body would be found near water or that the murderer has a name that has a *J* in it.

When it was time for drinks, we went into the big room, which is part of Kevin Dell's house and library, and where we always retire to. There's no smoking at our club, and it's usually right about halfway into our two- to three-hour talk or discussion that we let the smokers go outside and suck some burning tobacco.

That was a bad rule, I thought, as it could break up a good presentation. But it was the way we maintained three of our members, and though I would just as soon see them go, Kevin, who was also our treasurer, liked their dues as much as anyone else's, because it paid for our food and drinks and occasional guests.

Anyway, we're in the big room, and we're about to start, and Dana says something that sort of endears me to her right off.

She said, "Now, if you watch all those ghost shows, and those people who predict the future, or find dead bodies, or missing people, then you'll be disappointed. I should also say I can't stand those fakers. What I do is real, and the truth is, I don't care if you believe me or not. I'm just going to tell you about my most recent case, and you can take it or leave it.

There were some nods around the room, and Kevin said, "Certainly. Of course."

Then we settled into the chairs and the couch, a few seated themselves on cushions on the floor, and Dana took the guest chair, the most comfortable chair in the room. She leaned back and sipped her drink and looked at the ceiling.

"I'm going to tell this how it went, as best I can. Keep in mind, I don't think of myself as a ghost hunter per se, nor do I claim to be psychic. I'm a detective. A detective of the supernormal. Most of what I encounter isn't real. It's a mouse in the attic, or some kids wanting attention by throwing plates or some such thing when people aren't looking, scratching themselves and saying the devil did it.

"Let me say this too: I'm not religious. I don't believe in God. I'm an atheist. But I do believe there are things we don't understand, and that's what I look into. I believe that religious symbols are often just symbols of power as far as the supernormal is concerned. It's not religion, or an exorcism, anything like that that effects the supernormal. It's the power those things possess when they are used by those who believe in magic or religion, that is what makes them work. The idea of religion has thought and purpose and substance, even if the religion itself is no more real than a three-year-straight win streak by the Red Sox.

"I like to give my cases a name when I write about them, and I gave this one a name too. It's a little exaggerated, I admit. I'm not entirely immune to the melodramatic. I call it, the Case of the Lighthouse Shambler. Cute, huh?"

With that, she took a sip of her drink and Kevin dimmed the lights. There was a glow from the fire, but it was a small light, and flickered just enough so you could see who was who in the room. Shadows jumped along the side of Dana's face as she spoke.

Due to the bit of celebrity that I have as an author and investigator, the popularity of my books, I am often offered jobs that deal with the supernatural, or as I prefer, when it's real, the supernormal. As I said before, the bulk of these turn out to be something silly or a hoax, and because of that I always send out my assistants Nora Sweep and Gary Martin to check it out. I don't even do that if what's being suggested to me sounds uninteresting, or old hat, or deeply suspicious, but every now and then I come across something that might be genuine. More often than not, it isn't.

But if a request hits my desk that sounds like it might be of some curiosity, I send them first to check it out. One of the queries was from a Reggie, whose last name I will not reveal. Reggie had a lighthouse he claimed was infected. Those were his words. In his e-mail to my web site, which is how we obtain most of our queries, he said that the haunting, if it could be called that, had occurred as of late, and that he felt it more resembled the sort of things I dealt with than so-called ghost hunters. He added that he wasn't one who believed in life after death, or hadn't before all this, but was certain that whatever was going on was beyond his explanations and that the lighthouse, which he had been converting into a kind of home, had only recently been subject to the events that were causing him to write for my assistance. It was intriguing, and I've always been prone to an interest in lighthouses. I find them an odd kind of structure, and by their nature, perched as they are on the edge of the sea, mysterious.

Anyway, I sent Nora and Gary over for a look and then forgot about it, as I was involved in a small case that took me out of the country for a few days and was easy to solve. It turned out to be a nest of birds inside an air vent, and nothing supernormal at all. I collected my fee, which was sizeable, and disappointing to the couple who had hired me. They felt certain the wife's old uncle was responsible and was trying to speak to her from beyond the grave in a fluttering kind of way because he had died without teeth. The flutter, of course, was the beating of the bird's wings.

I won't give you the location of the lighthouse, as that is a private matter between myself and the client, but I will say it was located along the Gulf Coast, and had once been important for ships, but had long since been abandoned. For a time it was a tourist site, but it drew few tourists, and then it was sold to my client, Reggie, who had begun to remodel it to make a home for himself and his soon-to-be wife. However, after a few days working alone in the place, breaking up the ground, and repairing an old stairway, he began to have the sensation that he was being watched, and that the watcher was, in his words, malignant. He didn't feel as if it were looking over his shoulder, but was instead at the bottom of the winding metal stairs and was looking up, as if it could see through the top floor and spy on him at work.

He had no reason to think this, other than a sensation, but he felt that as the day wound on, as the night came closer, the watcher became more bold, present, if you will. When it was just dark, Reggie heard a creaking on the metal stairs, which was startling to him, as he had locked the door at the bottom of the lighthouse. Next he heard a slow sort of thudding on the stairs. So certain was he that someone was there, he went out on the landing and looked down. He could see nothing, but he could hear a kind of labored, or angry breathing, and he noticed that the metal steps leading up would take turns bending with pressure, as if someone heavy were climbing up, but there was nothing there. It frightened him, so he locked the door at the upper entrance, for he had built a wall and placed a door there for a bedroom and backed away from it, waiting. Then there came a sound at the door like someone breathing heavily. This was followed by a light tapping, a delay, and then a scratching not too unlike a dog wanting in. And then the door began to bulge around the hinges, as if it were being pushed, and he felt for certain it was about to blow, and whatever was on the other side, whatever was pushing and breathing and scratching, would soon enter the room in a rush.

Well, there was a trap hole as well, in the middle of the room. He had built it and attached an old fire pole there for fun. He dropped through the opening and slid down the pole as way of exit, and looked back up. He couldn't see the landing completely, but he could see it partly, and there was nothing there. Nothing. When he got to the bottom of the pole, he was brave enough to go to the base of the stairs and look up. That was when he heard a kind of screech and an exhaust of wind, and the stairs began to quiver; and something, most assuredly, even though he could not see it, was hastening down after him.

He broke and ran, feeling certain the thing was behind him. Once, he glanced back and saw what he said was an unidentifiable shadowy shape, and then he came to a point where all of a sudden his fear was gone, and he slowed down and turned around and looked. And there was nothing there. It was as if there had been a line of demarcation between fear and sanity, and he had crossed it.

This was what Reggie told me in his e-mail, and as I said, it was intriguing enough that I sent Nora and Gary for a look, and I went about my other business.

When I was back from Europe, I asked my assistants about the lighthouse. They had been enthusiastically waiting for me, and told me quite firmly this was the real deal, and that I would be interested, and Reggie seemed willing to let go of the proper fee to find out the cause, and if at all possible, banish it.

They had gone there during the day and placed talcum powder on the stairs that wound up to the top, to the light, which was still workable, and they had come back the next morning to find someone, or something, had gone up the steps and left prints in the talc; though neither thought the prints were foot or shoe prints. They couldn't quite explain what they thought they were. They had photographs, and my first thought was that in some of these, they looked a little bit like the hooves of a goat. In other photos, the prints were quite different, and less comparable to anything I could think of.

The following night they replaced the talc and locked the upper door and stayed at the top. What followed for them was an event like what Reggie had experienced, only they had seen the shadow of something through the crack under the door, pacing in front of it like an anxious parent waiting for a child to come home.

"It was a feeling like I have never experienced," Nora said. "And working for you, I've experienced a lot. But I felt, quite surely, that beyond that door was something purely evil. I know that's silly, and not particularly scientific, but that's how it was, and I was frightened to the bone."

Gary agreed. He said the door began to heave, as before when Reggie was there, and the two of them took to the fire pole and slid down. No sooner had they reached bottom, then whatever was at the top of the stairs shifted loudly, and came charging down the steps with a wild sound somewhere between a burst of breath and a screech, the stairs vibrating as it came, the steps seeming in danger of coming loose of their bolts.

"I think that whatever is there is building its reserve," Gary said. "That a night will come when that thing will burst through that door, and going through the hole in the floor, sliding down that pole Reggie installed, will just not be enough. Whatever is there, wants whoever is inside that lighthouse to be somewhere else. And my feeling is, once it builds its presence to a crescendo, something horrible will happen."

My assistants often experience incredible things, which is their job, but the way they talked, it was clear to me that they had been thoroughly impressed with the thing in the lighthouse. So we packed our bags, and on Reggie's dime, we flew out there, rented a car and drove the rest of the way to our destination.

In the daylight, the lighthouse was interesting, but it seemed far less than sinister. Of course, that is often the situation with these kinds of cases. You can't judge them quite as well in the day. There are certainly horrors that exist in broad daylight, but the bulk of the supernormal seems to prefer nightfall, if not particularly the witching hour.

Reggie met us at the base of the lighthouse, shook hands, exchanged a few pleasantries. He gave me the keys to the place, shook my hand again, as if he thought it might be the last time, wished us luck, and went on his way.

Since my assistants had already convinced themselves there was something in the tower, I didn't bother with the talc, or other measures of that sort, but instead sent them to town with a lunch order, and went to the top and looked around. The summit of the lighthouse, at least that part that was livable, had been remodeled as a bedroom, and the glass that wound its way about did nothing more now than provide a view completely around the circumference of the lighthouse. It was a lovely view, and I could see why Reggie would want to make this the master bedroom, turning other areas of the tower, eventually, into other living spaces. It would indeed make a unique home.

There was a bathroom slightly to the side, built into a kind of cubicle, so as not to he pressed against the glass and diminish the view. I went there and washed my face and then examined the "fire hole" in the floor, and the pole that went straight to the bottom of the tower. I slid down it, and when

I reached the floor, I looked back, noted that I could see through gaps in the stairs the upper landing, which was purposely pocked with holes so as to provide for the drip of water should it ever invade the upper quarters. A problem perhaps, if this was to be turned into a home, but not my concern. I'm a seeker of the supernormal, not an architect.

Climbing back up the stairs, I was suddenly accosted—that's the word that comes to me—by a feeling of anxiety. This is not new in my business, but as Nora and Gary explained, it was different here: stronger and more absorbing. I felt for a moment as if I might turn and bolt to the bottom and race out the door. Again, not all that unusual, but what was different was how hard I had to work to make myself climb to the top of the stairs. Usually, I can shake off those kinds of feelings with less effort than this took. I also felt an odd sensation as I climbed. That of air that at first seemed cool, and then gave me a feeling akin to dry ice, which is so cold it can burn. My arm was freckled with goose bumps until I had gone up at least six feet from the floor.

In the top room, the sensation of fear did not go away, but it did subside considerably. Enough for me to once again move comfortably about the room. Looking out the window, I saw that the light on the water was bright, and night was some time off, and it calmed me.

It seemed to me that whatever was here was not only dangerous, but somehow the stairs were its main area of strength. This didn't mean that it was weak away from the stairs, but the stairs were its prime location, and the area where its supernormal connection was most profound.

I decided not to spend the night in the lighthouse the first night, but instead sent Nora and Gary to the library, and any other source of information they could locate, to find out about the history of the lighthouse. I left the lighthouse several times during the day, and went back as it neared nightfall, and each time, I felt the presence in the building was growing more observant of my actions.

That night, I watched the lighthouse from a distance, observing the upper windows.

As the night fell, my vantage point from a nearby hill, where I sat with a cool drink in a lawn chair looking through binoculars, revealed to me a flash inside the upper darkness. I leaned forward. I saw it again. The flash moved before the window in a bobbing fashion, and then it was gone.

I had an idea that it had raced down the stairwell. I also determined from prior experience, that the light I saw would not be visible up close, and would in fact be the manifestation of the thing if viewed from a distance. Up close and personal, it would be the presence itself that one would have to confront, lit or unlit.

That night, I retired to the hotel and read the information that Nora and Gary had provided for me, while they shared a room next door. They thought because they each had a bed in their room, that I believed there weren't any shenanigans going on. Actually, I suspected they had been intimate for some time, and for reasons known only to them, didn't want me to know. I decided not to question their reasoning, or reveal my suspicions which were founded on evidence, and I'll add to that statement that they are now married, so anything I'm telling you here does not matter; not that I cared in the first place.

In the notes they provided, there was nothing particularly interesting about the lighthouse. I read from a book on local history, to see if anything else might stand out as a catalyst for the thing on the stairs. Nothing jumped out at me. There had been a number of shipwrecks, in spite of the lighthouse, including a famous one before its existence in the early seventeen hundreds.

That offered a note of interest. The problem was, there wasn't anything of detail on the wreck, other than that an unnamed ship had collided with the rocky shoreline, and that on examination of the wrecked vessel, a man named Greenberg was located alive. All others on the ship were found dead, and due to their condition, it was assumed they had been killed and cannibalized as the ship had been becalmed for weeks at sea, and all food had been exhausted.

The article said Greenberg had committed the murders with an axe. When they took him off the ship, he said it had not been him who had committed the crime and the cannibalism—but that there was something else on the ship. A demon that he said lived in a brass jug—his words and it was there now, and that it had been assigned to protect him after he did a good deed for an Arab trader. He thought nothing of it at the time, and merely thought the jug given him was a nice item that he would sell when he arrived on the mainland. But the demon in the bottle seemed jealous and upset and chose to protect him, even when he felt he did not need protecting; the mere presence of anyone near him drove the thing in the bottle into a frenzy. Its main purpose was to dispatch anyone nearby, so that it might return to the tranquility inside the jug. That was his story, and as you might judge, it wasn't taken seriously.

The ship was in terrible shape. It was searched, but no demon was found, nor was a brass jug located. Most of what could be salvaged was salvaged.

Nora and Gary's research showed that the ship dealt in antiquities, and that the crew was well experienced, and becalmed or not, there should have been enough food on board. The survivor was duly tried and hung, and that was the end of him. If he had a protecting demon in a jug, neither jug nor demon presented itself during his last moments as he stood on the gallows.

I think you might see where I'm going here, as I have discovered in my investigations, that old trinkets, or odd items, like a brass jug, might in fact have some connection to the supernormal. But, since it was not recovered, and there wasn't any evidence of Greenberg being protected from even so much as a rope burn, there was little to go on.

I looked over maps and documentation to locate the exact site of the ship wreck, but there was nothing that could be fully determined. On a hunch, I went to the butcher shop and bought some soup bones, and some animal skin, and a pint of calf's blood, and went to the lighthouse and began to search around the concrete floor near the stairwell.

I didn't necessarily expect to find anything, but I did satisfy myself with a thermometer that the air on the left side near the floor was quite cold and it wasn't my imagination. Still, the cool air there presented a sensation different from that of the garden variety presence one sometimes encounters in these sort of spots: the kind of presence that is commonly called a ghost or spook.

I climbed the stairs with an uncomfortable consciousness of being observed, and made my way to the top room and closed the door. There, I sat the plastic bag containing the soup bone and skin, removed my shoulder bag, and took out my tools, and went to work.

I first placed the bone on the floor, and placed the stretch of hairless animal skin beside it. I set up a camera in a shelf in the room, the sort sometimes referred to as a nanny cam—a hidden device parents use to make sure their nannies are acting appropriately with their children. I then placed a mirror on the floor beside the bone and the skin, moved back, and drew a circle with blessed chalk. Now, the blessing isn't necessarily a Christian one. In this case, the chalk had been blessed by an African wizard who chanted over it with words of juju; to simplify, juju is an African term for magic and spells. I drew a large circle about ten feet in circumference with white chalk, and inside it I drew around its edge symbols of power in other colors of chalk, each blessed by different priests, wizards, rabbis, and so on. These symbols do not belong to any one theology, but are universal in the supernormal. I covered the inside of the circle with flour, not blessed, just plain flour, and then placed another soup bone and piece of skin in its center. I sprinkled more flour all around the circle so that it was next to the first soup bone and skin I had laid out. I then poured the flour on the floor as I backed toward the door and the stairway. I sprinkled it on the landing, stopped and looked down the stairs. It was not yet night, so I hadn't been followed up the stairway and forced to exit by means of the fire pole, but I certainly felt the thing's attendance in the lighthouse.

It could see what I was doing, I was sure. But if this thing was what I thought it might be, its nature and design would consign it to certain decisions. I went down the stairs, and I will tell you quite frankly, it was hard to do. I found near the bottom that I was leaning away from the side where it was cold. But as a last test, I stuck my hand out in that direction, and felt the air hit me as briskly as if I had poked my arm into a meat freezer. I kept it there, and the cold turned so cold it felt hot. My arm began to feel singed, as if I were too close to a fire. I pulled it back before the heat became too intense.

I went out into the daylight, and I was grateful for the heat of the sun.

As I was, in a sense, gaining artillery range on my specter, I didn't stay in the lighthouse that night either. I felt I needed another night of information before I made an attempt to remove the thing. I knew too, that if I was right, what was in the lighthouse would make a deadly enemy. I didn't take this lightly.

Next morning, I took Nora and Gary with me, for they had been lying quite low in their bedroom, doing what you might expect. They were not altogether eager to go, which had nothing to do with facing danger, but had a considerable amount to do with their libidos.

Inside the lighthouse, I showed them the cold-hot spot, and then we went upstairs. The flour on the landing was disturbed. There were marks in it that looked hoof-like in spots, dog-like in others, and there were those other marks I had seen in the photographs that reminded me of nothing I could describe.

In the room, the flour was bothered as well, and in fact, it looked as if something had rolled in it. The bone and skin were there, but they had changed. The bone had grown meat on it, and the skin had grown fur. The mirror was cracked. When I picked it up, the image of the intruder—as I expected—was still frozen in the glass.

I showed it to Nora and Gary, and I would try here to describe what we saw, but it was indescribable. I will come back to that later.

The circle was only slightly disturbed, and I could see where the chalk had been pushed at, but not actually broken. Inside the circle the symbols were as visible as when I wrote them, and the bone and skin there had not changed at all, except to putrefy a little. I had them removed, and refreshed the circle where it showed some minor contact, and then I examined the nanny cam.

There was nothing present in the film but the flour being disturbed and the mirror cracking. Whatever had caused this was invisible to film. I knew that in person it would not be invisible, but would have a very visible and menacing presence.

We went away and had lunch and waited until it was close to an hour before dark.

We went up the stairs, and this time the air was very cold and uncomfortable, in that dry ice manner.

At the top, I had Nora and Gary get inside the circle and sit down cross-legged. I sat with them. They had actually brought a sack lunch with them, with bottled Cokes, and though I started to admonish them for it, they had brought enough for me as well, so we all sat their eating fried chicken from a bag, drinking Cokes.

As we ate, I said, "It hasn't been deadly before, but tonight will be different. We have caught its image in the mirror. It can't tolerate that."

"You call that an image?" Gary said.

"What we are dealing with is a jinn, or something like one. A demonic presence that resides in another dimension, and enters into this one by way of a device to which it has been confined. Like a brass jug."

"The Greenberg story," Nora said.

"Bingo," I said.

"The demonic figure I'm talking about has the power to regenerate meat on bone, hair on flesh," I said. "But do not let that fool you. This is not a positive power in the universe, or the dimension from where it came. It hates being in the jug, or bottle, or container, but it's cursed to be drawn to just that. It can come out if called, or if the container is destroyed, but it must return to a container if one is presented to it."

"You mean if the jug were found, it would have to go back inside?"

"Exactly," I said. "There is an ancient line by an anonymous Arab wizard that reads something like, 'And when the mouth of the container is presented, and a request is made, then to its prison it must return.'"

"But we don't have the jug," Nora said.

"No, we don't. And that presents a problem. All I have are protection spells, and one juju spell that has proved powerful in other situations; I hope it will serve us as soundly this time out."

"Hope?" Gary said.

"Well," I said, "having not tried it on a jinni, having never dealt with one before, I must consign the idea to that area labeled: Speculation."

Long shadows had begun to crawl across the floor.

"How did you know it was a jinni?" Gary asked.

"I was clued by the air at the bottom of the stair. Supernormal manifestations often present themselves by a chilling of the air, even in the hottest of places. But this spirit, its air is so cold it burns. That is the trait of a jinni; they are often credited with the hot winds that blow across the deserts of the Middle East. That face you saw in the mirror. That is only a momentary presentation. It can shift its features, its shape. It is powerful. At some point, a commanding wizard, someone who understood dimensional spells, trapped this creature in a brass jug, and then, he consigned it to the protection of someone he felt he owed a favor. Someone, who unfortunately, thought the idea of a jinni in a jug was all talk."

"That would be Greenberg again," Gary said.

"Absolutely," I said. "For whatever reason, the protector of Greenberg, this jinni, felt that it had to protect its master from, well, everyone. It didn't judge if they did anything to Greenberg or not. Its nature is ferocious, and it's a nasty sort of creature. It's possible it did what it did just because it could. So it ran rampant on the ship, and my guess is somehow, after all the slaughter, Greenberg—its master—was able to have it go back in the jug, where it was stopped up tight."

"Like a fly in a Coke bottle," Nora said.

"Exactly," I said. "I'm surmising a bit, but after it was contained in the jug, the ship ran aground, having no one to sail it, and the damage the jinni did looked like ax murders and cannibalism. It wasn't. Greenberg told them the truth. But no one believed his story, and he was hanged for the crime. I don't think even he understood what he had. He popped the cork, the jinni came out, and started to 'protect him.' It was so full of passion and hunger and anger, it tore the crew apart. Greenberg most likely had been given a spell by the Arabic trader, and though he had thought nothing of it at the time, he remembered it, and by speaking it, he caused the jinni to return to the confines of the jug. But too late for the crew."

"Where's the jug?"

"Ah, and here I speculate again, though quite well, I venture to say. It was lost in the shipwreck, buried in the sand, and in time sand was packed over it. The jug was sealed, and so was the jinni. The lighthouse was built on top of the jug, and where Reggie reinforced the stair rail, near the bottom, he broke the concrete and the jug was underneath. He didn't see it, but it was there, and as he worked—"

"The stopper was popped free," Gary said.

"Yes, but it had been confined for some time, and it no longer had its master, so it had been learning on its own how to be free, how to use its own will. That's why it had only been a sensation, a sound, a glance, up until now. After I saw it had the ability to grow flesh on a bone, hair on skin, I felt it had come back to itself, so to speak. And with one of its many images trapped in a mirror, it will be angry; a jinni does not like to show any part of its true self in a reflection."

"Being back to itself is not good, is it?" Nora said.

"No, it's not," I said. "There is little in the supernormal universe nastier than a jinni on the loose."

I looked outside.

"We should have evidence of that shortly, so I suggest you do not get outside the circle. Not a finger. Not a nose. Not a toe."

"Can it break through?" Nora asked.

"We will soon find out," I said, and removed a couple of thick incense candles from my bag, and lit them. The incense was supposed to contain powerful properties to combat evil. I hoped they did. I had never before had the opportunity to use them.

It was then that we heard the footsteps on the stairs.

I could feel Nora close to me, shivering, or maybe it was me shivering, or the both of us. Behind and to my left, I could hear Gary. He was breathing like a horse about to make the grade.

Outside the door, we heard the jinni stop. We saw its shadow move along the floor, and slide under like an oil spill. The shadow quivered in the candlelight. The jinni paused. Then the door started to buckle, and there was a sound like a wind blowing through a canyon, followed by a brisk scratching noise. From the vigor of the scratching, it was obvious that it had gained tremendous strength in just the few days we had been there. The room filled with a stench like carrion. It turned warm in the room. But my guess was that outside the circle it was even warmer. I saw the paint on the walls beading.

Then the door sagged in the middle, creaked at the hinges, and blew across the room. It smacked into the field around our protective circle and bounced to the side and skidded across the floor, hitting the runner at the base of the tall window glass. The circle, if it held, would keep out anything that was brought about my supernormal means. I tried to let that reassure me.

"You two," I said, "get behind me."

They didn't hesitate.

It came into the room in a whirl of shadows. The whirl made dust rise up and twist about, and the dust hit the field around our circle as if we were behind glass. The jinni leaped right at us, so fast it made me jump. It hit the force field, bounced back, whirled in a tight spin of darkness, and came again.

This time the field wobbled and the chalk circle dented slightly. I reached into my bag and brought out the blessed chalk. I reached out to tighten the circle, and felt it touch me.

I don't know how to describe its It was a horrid touch. I know that sounds very . . . Lovecraftian, or Poe-like. What is a horrid touch? What does that actually mean? But I have no other words to describe it. I can only say it was like black electricity leaping through my bones, topping out at my skull to the degree that I thought the summit of my head might blow off.

And it had only been a touch. My finger was smoking and blistered from the burn.

Around and around it went, marking the circle I had drawn. Out of the whirl, long fingers, spiked with nails like daggers, touched the field, and the field ripped. I pulled a paper from my bag and started to quote the spells the juju man had given me; they were written across the page in chicken blood and were easy to read even by candle light. My reading them made the jinni howl all the louder. I don't know if it was in anger or pain, or both.

It bounced again and again against the chalk wall, causing the chalk to dust slightly, and move. The circle was not holding. I had not only foolishly put myself in this bad position, but I had put my friends in the same position as well.

I kept reciting the juju spell, but it didn't seem to be working. I finally realized that I was showing fear, that my recital of it didn't have the African tone for the words; they sounded exactly like what they were words read off paper and pronounced poorly.

I admit all this reluctantly, for I've faced many horrors, but this one was strong well beyond my expectations. I had never seen the chalk line break so easily. I closed my eyes, started to quote the words again, this time not by rote, but with feeling.

When I opened my eyes, my heart sank. It hadn't mattered. The field was starting to fade, and the long fingers of the thing took hold of the tip of my shoe, jerked it off my foot, and snapped into the spinning vortex. The room became dark. The light of the candles flickered; a sure sign that the jinni was breaking through. The air stank and it grew warm, like a campfire had been built all around us.

As it was tearing its way in, I attempted to draw the line with the chalk again, but each time I reached, it reached too, and finally it caught me by the tip of my finger. I tried to pull it back, but it had me in a snug grip, and in a moment I felt a burning, tearing pain that nearly made me faint. It pulled the tip of my finger off like it was snapping loose a damp piece of taffy. Blood dotted the floor with hot red splashes.

The chalk was buckling. The rip was widening. The field was about to break completely.

On instinct, for a weapon, I grabbed up one of the Coke bottles by the neck, just as this thing, this shape-shifting thing, plunged through the barrier. I swatted at it with the bottle, and in a rush, the jinni turned thin and smoky, and was sucked directly into the bottle: all of it.

I quickly put the open bottle top against the floor, gently, and told Nora to roll up the paper with the juju spell on it, and she did. I took it, and with one quick move, lifted the bottle and jammed the paper inside. Then I grabbed up the candle, and ignoring what the hot wax was doing to my fingers, I packed the mouth of the bottle with it. The wax had another effect; it sealed off my finger wound.

The jinni roiled around inside the bottle like a lava lamp, but it didn't come out.

Nora said, "What happened?"

"I have to admit to an accident," I said. "It wouldn't have occurred to me. But remember the quote I told you that was anonymous, about the jinn. 'And when the mouth of the container is presented, and a request is made—' "

"Then to its prison it must return," Nora said, finishing off the line.

"I misunderstood. I thought it had to be the container it was placed in originally. But it's clear now. Once it was subject to a spell, if a container was put before it, it had to enter it. It didn't have to return to its original confinement, it just had to imprison itself. It was merely responding to its initial commands, given to it those long years ago."

"So, our jinni wasn't so bad after all," Nora said.

"Bad enough," Gary said.

I remembered I had considered scolding them for bringing a lunch and Cokes into a power circle. I decided not to mention that.

Not much more to tell. We put the bottle in a metal ice chest and covered the bottle in four or five inches of dry concrete, and put water in it, and let it dry for a couple of days on the landing of our hotel room. The day after it was solid dry, we rented a boat and motored it out into the Gulf where it was deep, and dropped the chest full of concrete and the trapped jinni into the depths of the water.

Dana leaned back, and said, "Well, that's it."

We all sat silent for a while. The smokers had forgotten to call time and go smoke. They had listened without interruption from start to finish.

Finally, I said, "It's a good story, but how are we to know it's nothing more than a story?"

"Oh," she said, holding her glass while Kevin refilled it and someone turned on the lights, "you don't. Remember? I said it didn't matter to me . . . But . . . "

She reached inside her coat pocket and brought out something small and round.

"This is the mirror in which the jinn's image was trapped, and considering

I thought you might ask something like that, just for grins, I brought it with me."

"It's easy to fake things," I said, but then my mouth fell open.

She held the mirror toward us, and all I can tell you is what Dana said before. There's no way to truly describe the image that had been trapped inside that broken mirror. It sent chills down my back, and in fact, the whole room for a moment seemed as if it were made of ice. None of us questioned its validity.

Another thing. As Dana held the mirror out, I noted that the tip of her index finger on her right hand was missing; where the tip should have been there was a glistening wink of bone.

She smiled, put the mirror away, then without another word, downed her drink, rose from her chair, and departed leaving us speechless.

• • • •

About the Authors

Peter Atkins was born in Liverpool, England and now lives in Los Angeles. He is the author of the novels *Morningstar*, *Big Thunder*, and *Moontown* and the screenplays *Hellraiser II*, *Hellraiser III*, *Hellraiser IV*, *Wishmaster*, and *Prisoners of the Sun*. His short fiction has appeared in such bestselling anthologies as *The Museum of Horrors*, *Dark Delicacies II*, and *Hellbound Hearts*. He is the co-founder, with Dennis Etchison and Glen Hirshberg, of The Rolling Darkness Revue, who tour the west coast annually bringing ghost stories and live music to any venue that'll put up with them. A new collection of his short fiction, *Rumours of the Marvellous*, was recently shortlisted for the British Fantasy Award. He blogs at www.peteratkins.blogspot.com.

Richard Bowes has won major and minor awards, published seven books and many, many stories. His Lambda-winning novel *Minions of the Moon* will be reprinted by Lethe Press in late 2012. Other recent and forthcoming appearances include *The Magazine of Fantasy & Science Fiction*, *Icarus*, *Apex*, *Jenny*, and anthologies *The Million Writers Award: The Best Online SF & Fantasy*, *After*, *Wilde Stories 2012*, *Bloody Fabulous*, and *Hauntings*.

Laird Barron's first novel, *The Croning*, was published earlier this year. His most recent story collection, *Occultation*, and novella *Mysterium Tremendum* both received Shirley Jackson Awards in 2011. An earlier collection, *The Imago Sequence*, was also a Jackson award winner. His fiction has appeared in *SciFiction*, *The Magazine of Fantasy & Science Fiction*, and numerous anthologies and is frequently reprinted in various "year's best" anthologies.

Steve Duffy's third collection of short supernatural fiction, *Tragic Life Stories*, was published in 2010. A fourth collection, *The Moment of Panic*, is due out soon, and will include the International Horror Guild award-winning short story included here, "The Rag-and-Bone Men." Duffy lives in North Wales.

Jeffrey Ford is the author of the novels, *The Physiognomy*, *Memoranda*, *The Beyond*, *The Portrait of Mrs. Charbuque*, *The Girl in the Glass*, *The Cosmology* *of the Wider World*, and *The Shadow Year*. His story collections are *The Fantasy Writer's Assistant*, *The Empire of Ice Cream*, and *The Drowned Life*. His new collection, *Crackpot Palace*, was published recently. Ford is the recipient of the Edgar Allan Poe Award, the Shirley Jackson Award, the Nebula, the World Fantasy Award, and the *Grand Prix de l'imaginaire*.

Karen Joy Fowler is the author of six novels and five short story collections. Her novel *The Jane Austen Book Club* spent thirteen weeks on the *New York Times* bestseller list and was a *New York Times* Notable Book. *Sister Noon* was a finalist for the PEN/Faulkner Award for fiction. Both *Sarah Canary* and *The Sweetheart Season* were *New York Times* Notable Books as well. In addition, *Sarah Canary* won the Commonwealth medal for best first novel by a Californian, and was short-listed for the *Irish Times* International Fiction Prize and the Bay Area Book Reviewers Prize. Fowler's short story collection *Black Glass* won the World Fantasy Award in 1999; her collection *What I Didn't See* also won the 2011 World Fantasy Award.

Neil Gaiman is the *New York Times* bestselling author of novels *Neverwhere*, *Stardust*, *American Gods*, *Coraline*, *Anansi Boys*, *The Graveyard Book*, and (with Terry Pratchett) *Good Omens*; the Sandman series of graphic novels; and the story collections *Smoke and Mirrors* and *Fragile Things*. He has won numerous literary awards including the Hugo, the Nebula, the World Fantasy, and the Stoker Awards, as well as the Newbery medal.

Winner of British Fantasy and International Horror Guild awards, **Stephen Gallagher** is a novelist, screenwriter, and director specializing in contemporary suspense. His television work began with the BBC's *Doctor Who* series and includes miniseries adaptations of his novels *Chimera* and *Oktober*. He was lead writer on NBC's *Crusoe* and wrote for Jerry Bruckheimer's U.S. version of *Eleventh Hour*, the series he created for British TV in 2006. *The Bedlam Detective* was published in 2012 and he's now working on a third Sebastian Becker novel. The author's website is www.stephengallagher.com.

Elizabeth Hand (www.elizabethhand.com) is the multiple-award-winning author of twelve novels and three collections of short fiction. Her most recent novel for adults, *Available Dark*, was named as one of the Top Ten Best Mystery/ Thrillers of the year by *Publishers Weekly*. *Radiant Days*, a young adult novel, was published earlier this year as well. A *New York Times* and *Washington Post* Notable Author, Hand is also a longtime book critic and essayist who frequently contributes to the *Washington Post*, *Salon*, *Village Voice*, and *DownEast Magazine*, among many others. She has two children and divides her time between Maine and North London.

Glen Hirshberg's awards include the 2008 Shirley Jackson Award (for his novelette, "The Janus Tree") and three International Horror Guild Awards, including two for Best Collection (for *American Morons* in 2006 and *The Two Sams* in 2003). He is also the author of two novels, *The Snowman's Children* and *The Book of Bunk*. A third, *Motherless Child,* will be published fall 2012. His latest collection is *The Janus Tree and Other Stories* (Subterranean Press). With Dennis Etchison and Peter Atkins, he co-founded the Rolling Darkness Revue, a traveling ghost story performance troupe that tours the west coast of the United States and elsewhere each October. His fiction has been published in numerous magazines and anthologies.

Alaya Dawn Johnson is the author of *Moonshine* and *Wicked City*, urban fantasy novels set in the Lower East Side of 1920s New York City. She has also written *Racing the Dark* and *The Burning City*, the first two books of a fantasy trilogy called The Spirit Binders. Her YA debut, *The Summer Prince*, will be published in spring 2013. Her short stories have appeared in the anthologies *Welcome to Bordertown* and *Zombies Vs. Unicorns*. She can be contacted via her website, www.alayadawnjohnson.com.

Stephen Graham Jones is the author of ten novels and two collections. Most recent are *Zombie Bake-Off* and *Growing Up Dead in Texas*. Next are *The Last Final Girl* and *Flushboy*. Stephen's been a Stoker finalist, a Shirley Jackson Award finalist, a Black Quill finalist, and has been an NEA fellow and won the Texas Institute of Letters Award for fiction. He teaches in the MFA program at University of Colorado Boulder and in the low-res MFA at UCR Palm Desert.

Caitlín R. Kiernan is the author of several novels, including the award-winning *Threshold, Daughter of Hounds, The Red Tree*, and, most recently, *The Drowning Girl*. Her short fiction has been collected in *Tales of Pain and Wonder; From Weird and Distant Shores; To Charles Fort, with Love; Alabaster; A Is for Alien;* and *The Ammonite Violin & Others*. Her erotica has been collected in two volumes, *Frog Toes and Tentacles* and *Tales from the Woeful Platypus*. Subterranean Press published a retrospective of her early writing, *Two Worlds and In Between: The Best of Caitlín R. Kiernan (Volume One)* last year. She lives in Providence, Rhode Island with her partner, Kathryn.

Marc Laidlaw is the author of six novels, including the International Horror Guild Award winner, *The 37th Mandala*. His short stories have appeared in numerous magazines and anthologies since the 1970s. In 1997, he joined Valve Software as a writer and creator of *Half-Life*, which has become one of the most popular videogame series of all time. He lives in Washington State with his wife and two daughters, and continues to writes occasional short fiction between playing too many videogames.

Margo Lanagan writes novels and short stories. Her collection *Black Juice* was a Michael L. Printz Honor Book, won two World Fantasy Awards, two Aurealis Awards, two Ditmar Awards and a Victorian Premier's Prize, and was shortlisted for several other awards including a Hugo and a Nebula. The collection *Red Spikes* was the CBCA Book of the Year for Older Readers, a *Publishers Weekly* Best Book of the Year, a Horn Book Fanfare title, was shortlisted for the Commonwealth Writer's Prize, and longlisted for the Frank O'Connor International Short Story Award. Margo's novel *Tender Morsels* won the World Fantasy Award for Best Novel and was a Michael L. Printz Honor Book. Her latest novel is *The Brides of Rollrock Island* (*Sea Hearts* in Australia), and her fourth collection will be *Yellowcake*. She lives in Sydney.

John Langan is the author of a novel, *House of Windows*, and a collection of stories, *Mr. Gaunt and Other Uneasy Encounters*. He recently co-edited *Creatures: Thirty Years of Monsters* with Paul Tremblay. Langan lives in upstate New York with his wife, son, dog, and a trio of mutually suspicious cats.

Joe R. Lansdale is the author of over thirty novels and numerous short stories. His novella, *Bubba Ho-tep*, was made into an award-winning film of the same name, as was *Incident On and Off a Mountain Road*. Both were directed by Don Coscarelli. His works have received numerous recognitions, including the Edgar, eight Bram Stoker awards, the Grinzane Cavour Prize for Literature, American Mystery Award, the International Horror Award, British Fantasy Award, and many others. *All the Earth, Thrown to the Sky*, his first novel for young adults, was published last year. His most recent novel for adults is *Edge of Dark Water*.

Maureen F. McHugh has published four novels and two collections of short stories. She's won a Hugo and a Tiptree award. Her most recent collection, *After the Apocalypse*, was named a *Publishers Weekly* Top Ten Best Book of 2011, was a Philip K. Dick Award finalist, a Story Prize Notable Book, and named to the io9 Best SF&F Books of 2011 List as well as the Tiptree Award Honor List. McHugh lives in Los Angeles, where she is attempting to sell her soul to the entertainment industry.

Sarah Monette lives in a 106-year-old house in the Upper Midwest with a great many books, two cats, and one husband. Her first four novels were published by Ace Books. Her short stories have appeared in *Strange Horizons*, *Weird Tales*, and *Lady Churchill's Rosebud Wristlet*, among other venues, and have been reprinted in several Year's Best anthologies. *The Bone Key*, a 2007 collection of interrelated short stories, was re-issued last year in a new edition. A non-themed collection, *Somewhere Beneath Those Waves*, was published in 2011. Sarah has written two novels (*A Companion to Wolves* and *The Tempering of Men)* and three short stories with Elizabeth Bear. Her next novel, *The Goblin Emperor*, will come out from Tor under the name Katherine Addison. Visit her online at www.sarahmonette.com.

Reggie Oliver has been a professional playwright, actor, and theatre director since 1975. Besides plays, his publications include the authorized biography of Stella Gibbons, *Out of the Woodshed,* published by Bloomsbury in 1998, and five collections of stories of supernatural terror, of which the latest is *Mrs Midnight* (Tartarus, 2011). His novel, *The Dracula Papers I: The Scholar's Tale* (Chomu, 2011), is the first of a projected four and he is now working on the second volume, *The Monk's Tale*. An omnibus edition of his stories entitled *Dramas from the Depths* is published by Centipede, as part of its *Masters of the Weird Tale* series. His stories have appeared in over thirty anthologies.

Richard Parks has been writing and publishing science fiction and fantasy longer than he cares to remember . . . or probably can remember. His work has appeared in (among many others) *Asimov's, Realms of Fantasy, Lady Churchill's Rosebud Wristlet*, and several "year's best" anthologies. His second print novel, *To Break the Demon Gate*, is due out in late 2012 or early 2013 from PS Publishing. He blogs at "Den of Ego and Iniquity Annex #3" (www.richard-parks.com).

James Van Pelt teaches high school and college English in western Colorado. His fiction has made numerous appearances in most of the major science fiction and fantasy magazines. His first collection of stories, *Strangers and Beggars*, was recognized as a Best Book for Young Adults by the American Library Association. His second collection, *The Last of the O-Forms and Other Stories,* includes the Nebula-finalist title story, and was a finalist for the Colorado Blue Spruce Young Adult Book Award. His novel *Summer of the Apocalypse* was released November 2006. The recently released *The Radio Magician and Other Stories* received the Colorado Book Award. James blogs at jimvanpelt.livejournal.com.

Tim Powers is the author of twelve novels, including *The Anubis Gates*, *Declare*, *Hide Me Among the Graves*, and *On Stranger Tides*, which was adapted for the fourth Pirates of the Caribbean movie of the same title. His novels have twice won the Philip K. Dick Memorial Award, twice won the World Fantasy Award, and four times won the Locus Poll Award. Powers has taught fiction writing classes at the University of Redlands, Chapman University, and the Orange County High School of the Arts. He has been an instructor at the Writers of the Future program and the Clarion Science Fiction Workshop at Michigan State University. Powers lives with his wife, Serena, in San Bernardino, California.

Barbara Roden is a World Fantasy Award-winning editor and publisher, and a World Fantasy Award-nominated writer whose first collection, *Northwest Passages*, was published in 2009. She was born in Vancouver, B.C., and spent several years in the hotel industry in that city in the 1980s. She worked the graveyard shift for eighteen months, and drew on that experience when writing "The Palace." In a letter to August Derleth, ghost story writer H.R. Wakefield said, "Night-working life is a thing apart & those who live it souls apart," and that sense of being caught up in "a thing apart" is very much what the author had in mind with the story. She also drew on two notorious cases of real-life murder: the Yorkshire Ripper murders in England in the 1970s, and the serial killings in what's now known as Vancouver's Downtown Eastside—the setting for "The Palace"—between the 1980s and the early twenty-first century. Several of the characters in the story are based on real people, none more so than Sylvia, the Poe-reading desk clerk; readers can make the obvious conclusion from the fact that the Penguin edition of Poe that Sylvia reads still forms part of the author's collection (and the keen-eyed might spot, in the story's structure, a homage to Poe's poem "The Haunted Palace").

Ekaterina Sedia resides in the Pinelands of New Jersey. Her critically acclaimed novels, *The Secret History of Moscow*, *The Alchemy of Stone*, *The House of Discarded Dreams*, and *Heart of Iron* were published by Prime Books. Her short stories have sold to *Analog*, *Baen's Universe*, *Subterranean* and *Clarkesworld*, as well as numerous anthologies, including *Haunted Legends* and *Magic in the Mirrorstone*. She is also the editor of *Paper Cities* (World Fantasy Award winner), *Running with the Pack,* and *Bewere the Night*, as well as forthcoming *Bloody Fabulous* and *Wilful Impropriety*. Visit her at www. ekaterinasedia.com.

Nisi Shawl's story collection *Filter House* won the James Tiptree, Jr. Award. *Something More and More*, a collection of stories and essays, celebrates her WisCon 35 Guest of Honor status. Shawl is the co-author (with Cynthia Ward) of *Writing the Other: A Practical Approach*; a founder of the Carl Brandon Society; and a member of Clarion West's Board of Directors. With Dr. Rebecca Holden, Shawl co-edited *Strange Matings: Octavia E. Butler, Science Fiction, Feminism, and African American Voices*, forthcoming in 2013 from Aqueduct Press. She edits reviews for the *Cascadia Subduction Zone*, a literary quarterly. Recently published online fiction includes "Black Betty" at *Crossed Genres*, and "Honorary Earthling" at *Expanded Horizons*.

John Shirley is the author of more than thirty novels. The latest, *Everything Is Broken*, was published earlier this year. His numerous short stories have been compiled into eight collections including *Black Butterflies: A Flock on the Darkside*, winner of the Bram Stoker Award, International Horror Guild Award, and named as one of the best one hundred books of the year by *Publishers Weekly* and, most recently, *In Extremis: The Most Extreme Short Stories of John Shirley*. He has written scripts for television and film, and is best known as co-writer of *The Crow*. As a musician, Shirley has fronted several bands over the years and written lyrics for Blue Öyster Cult and others. To learn more about John Shirley and his work, please visit his website at john-shirley.com.

Peter Straub is the author of seventeen novels, which have been translated into more than twenty languages. They include *Ghost Story, Koko, Mr. X, In the Night Room, A Dark Matter*, and two collaborations with Stephen King, *The Talisman* and *Black House*. He has written two volumes of poetry and two collections of short fiction. Straub edited the Library of America's edition of *H.P. Lovecraft's Tales* as well as the Library of America's two-volume anthology *American Fantastic Tales*. He has won the British Fantasy Award, thirteen Bram Stoker Awards, two International Horror Guild Awards, and two World Fantasy Awards. In 1998, he was named Grand Master at the World Horror Convention. In 2006, he was given the HWA's Life Achievement Award and, in 2008, both the International Horror Guild's Living Legend Award and the Barnes & Noble Writers for Writers Award by Poets & Writers.

Melanie Tem is the author of twelve novels and many short stories. She received a Bram Stoker Award for her debut novel, *Prodigal*, and the Icarus Award from the British Fantasy Society. Crossroad Press recently released the ebook version of *In Concert*, collecting all her collaborations with husband Steve Rasnic Tem. Their co-written novella *The Man on the Ceiling* won the Bram Stoker, World Fantasy, and International Horror Guild Awards.

Steve Rasnic Tem is the author of over three hundred published works. His latest novel is *Deadfall Hotel* (Solaris Books). Fall 2012 will see publication of *Ugly Behavior* collecting the best of his noir fiction, from New Pulp Press. In 2013 ChiZine will publish *Celestial Inventories*, collecting the best of his recent contemporary fantasy and slipstream fiction.

• • • •

About the Editor

Paula Guran serves as senior editor for Prime Books. This is her fifteenth anthology; two more will be published before the end of 2012. Her Year's Best Dark Fantasy and Horror series appears annually. She edited the Juno fantasy imprint for six years from its small press inception through its incarnation as an imprint of Simon & Schuster's Pocket Books. When Guran began this book she did not believe in ghosts; she now prays that they exist.

• • • •

Acknowledgments

Special thanks to all the editors who first published many of these stories.

"Between the Cold Moon and the Earth" by Peter Atkins © 2007 Peter Atkins. First publication: *Postscripts*, Spring 2007, eds. Nick Gevers, Peter Crowther (PS Publishing).

"There's a Hole in the City" by Richard Bowes © 2005 Richard Bowes. First publication: *SciFiction*, 6 June 2005.

"The *Lagerstätte*" by Laird Barron © 2008 Laird Barron. First publication: *The Del Rey Book of Science Fiction and Fantasy: Sixteen Original Works by Speculative Fiction's Finest Voices*, ed. Ellen Datlow (Del Rey/Ballantine).

"The Rag-and-Bone Men" by Steve Duffy © 2000 Steve Duffy. First publication: *Shadows and Silence*, eds. Barbara Roden & Christopher Roden (Ash-Tree Press).

"The Trentino Kid" by Jeffrey Ford © 2003 Jeffrey Ford. First publication: *The Dark: New Ghost Stories*, ed. Ellen Datlow (Tor).

"Booth's Ghost" by Karen Joy Fowler © 2010 Karen Joy Fowler. First publication: *What I Didn't See and Other Stories* (Small Beer Press).

"October in the Chair" by Neil Gaiman © 2002 Neil Gaiman. First publication: *Conjunctions: 39, The New Wave Fabulists*, ed. Peter Straub (Bard College).

"The Box" by Stephen Gallagher © 2006 Stephen Gallagher. First publication: *Retro Pulp Tales*, ed. Joe R, Lansdale (Subterranean Press).

"Wonderwall" by Elizabeth Hand © 2004 Elizabeth Hand. First publication: *Flights: Extreme Visions of Fantasy*, ed. Al Sarrantonio (Roc).

"The Muldoon" by Glen Hirshberg © 2006 Glen Hirshberg. First publication: *American Morons* (Earthling Publications).

"The Score" by Alaya Dawn Johnson © 2009. First publication: *Interfictions 2: An Anthology of Interstitial Writing*, eds. Delia Sherman & Christopher Barzak (Small Beer Press).

"Uncle" by Stephen Graham Jones © 2012 Stephen Graham Jones. First publication. Original to this volume.

"Apokatastasis" by Caitlín R. Kiernan © 2002 Caitlín R. Kiernan, First publication: *The Spook*, January 2002.

"Cell Call" by Marc Laidlaw © 2003 Marc Laidlaw. First publication: *By Moonlight Only*, ed. Stephen Jones (PS Publishing).

"The Proving of Smollett Standforth" by Margo Lanagan © 2011 Margo Lanagan. First publication: *Ghosts by Gaslight: Stories of Steampunk and Supernatural Suspense*, eds. Jack Dann & Nick Gevers (HarperVoyager).

"The Third Always Beside You" by John Langan © 2011 John Langan. First Publication: *Blood and Other Cravings*, ed. Ellen Datlow (Tor).

"The Case of the Lighthouse Shambler" by Joe R. Lansdale © 2011 Joe R. Lansdale. First publication: *The Cases of Dana Roberts* (Subterranean Press).

"Ancestor Money" by Maureen F. McHugh © 2003 Maureen F. McHugh. First publication: *SciFiction*, 1 October 2003.

"The Watcher in the Corners" by Sarah Monette © 2007 Sarah Monette. First publication: *Notes From the Labyrinth* (author's blog), 23 April 2007.

"Mrs. Midnight" by Reggie Oliver © 2009 Reggie Oliver. First publication: *The Fifth Black Book of Horror* (Mortbury Press).

"The Plum Blossom Lantern" by Richard Parks © 2003 Richard Parks. First publication: *Lady Churchill's Rosebud Wristlet, #12*, June 2003.

"Savannah is Six" by James Van Pelt. © 2000 James Van Pelt. First publication: *Dark Terrors 5: The Gollancz Book of Horror*, ed. Stephen Jones, David Sutton (Gollancz/Orion).

"A Soul in a Bottle" by Tim Powers © 2006 Tim Powers. First publication: *A Soul in a Bottle* (Subterranean Press).

"The Palace" by Barbara Roden © 2007 Barbara Roden. First publication: *At Ease With the Dead*, eds. Christopher Roden & Barbara Roden (Ash-Tree Press).

"Tin Cans" by Ekaterina Sedia © 2010 Ekaterina Sedia. First publication: *Haunted Legends*, eds. Ellen Datlow & Nick Mamatas (Tor).

"Cruel Sistah" by Nisi Shawl © 2005 Nisi Shawl. First publication: *Asimov's*, October/November 2005.

"Faces in Walls" by John Shirley © 2010 John Shirley. First Publication: *Black Static*, June-July 2010.

"Mr. Aickman's Air Rifle" by Peter Straub © 2004 Peter Straub. First publication: *McSweeney's Enchanted Chamber of Astonishing Stories*, ed. Michael Chabon (Vintage).

"Dhost" by Melanie Tem © 2007 Melanie Tem. First publication: *At Ease With the Dead*, eds. Christopher Roden & Barbara Roden (Ash-Tree Press).

"The Ex" by Steve Rasnic Tem © 2011 Steve Rasnic Tem. First publication: *Box of Delights*, ed. John Kenny (Aeon Press).

• • • •